VOODOO TALES

VOODOO TALES

The Ghost Stories of

Henry S. Whitehead

with an Introduction by
David Stuart Davies

WORDSWORTH EDITIONS

For my husband
Anthony John Ranson
with love from your wife, the publisher
Eternally grateful for your unconditional
love, not just for me but for our children
Simon, Andrew and Nichola Trayler

I

Customers interested in other titles from
Wordsworth Editions are invited to visit our
website at www.wordsworth-editions.com

For our latest list and a full mail order service contact
Bibliophile Books, Unit 5 Datapoint,
South Crescent, London E16 4TL
Tel: +44 020 74 74 24 74
Fax: +44 020 74 74 85 89
orders@bibliophilebooks.com

This edition published 2012 by Wordsworth Editions Limited
8B East Street, Ware, Hertfordshire SG12 9HJ

ISBN 978 1 84022 690 4

Typeset in Great Britain by Roperford Editorial
Printed and bound by Clays Ltd, St Ives plc

CONTENTS

INTRODUCTION

The advice often given to those who wish to turn their hand to storytelling is to write about what they know. This has always seemed to me to be rather a restricting approach to fiction. It makes no allowance for the writer's flights of fancy or the creative elements that his unfettered imagination can bring to the narrative. Certainly those who work in the genres of science and supernatural fiction would be greatly hampered if they followed this advice. In fact they write about what they do not know!

However, ironically, Henry St. Clair Whitehead (1882–1932) was to a large extent able to combine the facilities of both a vivid imagination with factual knowledge of his subject, which he acquired during time spent in the West Indies. He developed a strong interest in black Caribbean folklore and Voodoo practices through the years of living on the island of Santa Cruz. He met with practitioners of black magic and high priests of the Voodoo cult and became familiar with their ways and ceremonies. He learned that their power was rooted in the unswerving belief of their flock. As a result of Whitehead's experiences, he was able to infuse his narratives with a chilling verisimilitude. He seems to believe and accept the fantastic nature of the events that take place in his tales and thus his persuasive voice plays very nicely on the reader's initial scepticism and undermines it.

In reviewing one of Whitehead's collections, the critic of the *New York Times* observed:

> With deceptive gentleness and clerical decorum, Dr Whitehead wrote of voodoo spells, fiendish manikins and other terrors to be found in the tropic nights of the Virgin Islands. So quietly did he edge up on horrors that his stories seem quite like the truthful reminiscences they purport to be, which means they are pretty good.

That paragraph effectively sums up the essence of Whitehead's craft and why he has, over the years, built up a strong appreciative following amongst fans of supernatural fiction.

Henry S. Whitehead was born in Elizabeth, New Jersey and spent most of his life in New England, except for that interesting and creatively stimulating period when he lived in the West Indies. He was possessed of two differing natures: the serious academic and the gregarious sportsman. He led an active early life, playing football at Harvard and serving as commissioner of athletics of the AAU. He resigned this post to enter the ministry and in 1912 he was ordained deacon of the Episcopal Church. After serving his 'deacon's year' as curate of Trinity Church Torrington, Connecticut he went out to other pastorates, including the Virgin Islands where he gathered the content and colour which later went into his Voodoo tales. As a Christian, the Reverend Whitehead seemed to have no compunction in presenting this pagan material in the form of convincing fiction. It was as though when he was writing he was exercising another part of his brain which had nothing to do with his own religious convictions and duties. But then he was a man who was constantly surprising. His friend, the writer Robert Barlow, commented: 'In later life he could be prevailed upon . . . to startle social gatherings by tearing a pack of cards in two and then quartering them.' A habit which clearly shows that Whitehead took pleasure in shocking people. Barlow added: 'His friends ranged from ship's surgeons to safe-crackers.' One of these friends was the notable horror story writer H. P. Lovecraft who said of Whitehead: 'He has nothing of the musty cleric about him, but dresses in sports clothes, swears like a he-man on occasion, & is an utter stranger to bigotry or priggishness of any sort.' Lovecraft was also a great admirer of his friend's dark stories. He commented on 'the charm and erudition of the writing – a pleasing relief from the dominant crudeness and illiterateness of popular magazine stuff.'

Whitehead spent his last years in the Gulf Coast town of Dunedin, Florida where he was rector of the Episcopal Church. He died on 23 November 1932, of a chronic gastric ailment, just as he was hitting his stride as a writer. In the opinion of some, this was the reason he was not as well known as his pulp-era contemporaries, especially since his stories were not collected until well after his death. The first such collection was *Jumbee and Other Uncanny Tales*, published by Arkham House in 1944 and this was followed by *West India Lights* in 1946, also by Arkham House.

His strange tales first began appearing in the American pulp fiction magazine *Weird Tales* and other similar publications in 1924. However his first short story was 'Williamson', written in 1910 but not published until 1946 in the posthumous collection *West India Lights*. This is a remarkable piece of work with a stunning climax, containing many of the elements that the author wove effectively into the canvas of all his tales: suspense, mystery, a cool delivery of events and yet told with an insidious sense of impending horror. It was in this story that he introduced the narrator who featured in most of his tales: Gerald Canevin, who E. F. Bleiler, one of the world's greatest authorities on supernatural fiction, believed was 'a mask for the author, whose ancestral name was Caernavon.' Whitehead took great pleasure in pointing out that the name was made up of 'cane' and 'vin', which is cane wine, in other words rum, the typical product of the West Indies.

At first glance Whitehead's realistic treatment of Voodoo and its spells may seem to sit oddly with a minister of the Christian church, but in many instances the fearsome spells he writes about are able to be overcome by the power of Christianity: the force of good over evil. In 'Black Terror', for example, where a young black man has been condemned to death by a curse, a 'sweat ouanga', the narrator hits upon an idea how to beat the curse.

> Perhaps I could prevail upon the English Church Clergy to help. It was, when one came down the brass tacks of the situation, a question of belief. A similar ouanga 'buried against' me would have no effect whatever, because to me, such means of getting rid of a person was merely the height of absurdity . . .

Later in the story, an English priest, Father Richardson tells the afflicted boy:

> God is intervening for you, my child, and God's power is supreme over all things, visible *and invisible*. He holds all in the hollow of His hand. He will now put away your fear, and take this weight from your soul, *and you shall live*.

The point is that power of the Voodoo lies in the belief and imagination of the victim rather than in some dark satanic being. Whitehead implies that it is a power that can be destroyed by Christian beliefs and prayers. The author was at pains to show that supernatural forces are real, but are also susceptible to the powers of goodness.

To the modern reader, some of Whitehead's themes may sound racist, but his treatment of the West Indian blacks and 'coloured' people (i.e. natives of mixed ancestry) is presented cordially and with relatively little condescension. He perceived them as God's children after all.

It may be thought that as a representative of the Episcopal Church, Whitehead might have been hesitant in demonstrating the powers and efficacy of a primitive and alternative culture of belief, but he did not. He relayed in his stories the facts of the matter as he had learned them and it was this approach that gives his narratives their chilling effectiveness.

This collection contains all the stories from Whitehead's three collections, *West India Lights*, *Jumbee*, and *The Black Beast*, rare volumes all, but in addition there are five other stories which have never been collected together in a popular edition before: 'No Eye-Witnesses', (1932), is an unusual take on the werewolf tale, set in New York; 'Across the Gulf' (1926) concerns a dead mother who appears in a dream to warn her son of danger; 'The Tabernacle' (1930) is a departure in style and content for the author, retelling in a modern setting an ancient tale concerning a mysterious hive of bees; 'The Door' (1924), a spookily adroit tale with a surprise ending; 'The Moon Dial' (1931), an elegiac and atmospheric piece set in India; and 'The Sea Tiger' (1932), a dreamlike tale, featuring an hallucinatory premonition and a sea battle with a barracuda, the sea-tiger of the title.

In Whitehead's stories you encounter supernatural or evil beings which are unique to this kind of fiction. There is, for example the jumbee from the story of the same name; this is a corpse-like spirit that hovers in the air, and there is also a sheen who is an old woman who turns into a were-bitch. There is a kind of bizarre and unpleasant humour inherent in some of the tales, such as the unusual creature that appears in 'Cassius'. It is a beast that looks like a gigantic frog which terrorizes a neighbourhood, and it turns out to be a partly absorbed Siamese twin which had taken on a life of its own after being surgically removed. This kind of grotesquery is found in a few other stories also. A fine example of this graphic, nightmare-type horror can be found in 'The Lips' in which the captain of a slave ship is bitten on the neck by an Ibo woman who whispers the word '*l'kindu*' in his ear. This incident eventually causes his insanity and he commits suicide on the voyage home when it is revealed that where the wound had been there is now a mouth – complete with full lips, and a long pink tongue – which talks to him.

Many of the stories in the collection deal with hauntings by spirits of people killed long ago. The ghost in 'The Shadows' is of a man who was murdered while seeking eternal life. In 'Black Tancrède', the hand of an executed slave looks for revenge. The soul of a man is trapped in a bull during a Voodoo ceremony in 'The Black Beast'. A pirate is imprisoned in a painting in 'Seven Turns in a Hangman's Rope' when a former lover paints his soul into the picture in an act of revenge. The spirit of a vicious gambler possesses 'Mrs Lorriquer', turning a kind, courteous woman hostile and unpleasant when she plays cards. A witch's curse figures in 'Sweet Grass', which is considered one of Whitehead's best stories. In 'Passing of a God' a Voodoo god enters and animates a man's tumour, causing the natives to worship him.

Scattered about the collection, however, are stories which, while strange and ghoulish, are set away from Voodoo territory. For example there is 'The Fireplace', which concerns the ghost of a murdered man who appears in a hotel in Mississippi and persuades someone to relate the circumstances of his death. 'The Shut Room' is about the haunting of an old English coaching inn; and 'The Napier Limousine' also takes place in England.

Both the long tale 'Bothon' and 'Scar Tissue' involve the lost city of Atlantis. 'Bothon' is particularly accomplished, beginning in modern New York with the central character at first experiencing strange noises of catastrophe and battle which only he can hear. It is a unnerving case of 'clairaudience'.

One of Whitehead's more ghoulish tales is 'The Chadbourne Incident' and it is heavily influenced by the work of Lovecraft. This story is set in the New England village of Chadbourne, which is Whitehead's version of Lovecraft's blighted Arkham, and tells of ghouls who eat little children.

The combination of Whitehead's early death and the fact that his stories had only appeared in pulp magazines, is the main reason that his name and his work is not more well known. His fascinating tales are certainly as effective and meritorious as those of Lovecraft and Algernon Blackwood, for example. It was over a decade after he died before his short stories were collected into book form and they now have been long out of print. Therefore this Wordsworth Edition is a treasure trove for those lovers of these strange and unsettling tales penned by a master craftsman of the genre. We hope that this will not only please those who already admire Henry S. Whitehead, but attract a whole new legion of fans.

DAVID STUART DAVIES

WEST INDIA LIGHTS

Black Terror

I woke up in the great mahogany bed of my house in Christiansted with an acute sense of something horribly wrong, something frightful, tearing at my mind. I pulled myself together, shook my head to get the sleep out of my eyes, pulled aside the mosquito-netting. That was better! The strange sense of horror which had pursued me out of sleep was fading now.

I groped vaguely, back into the dream, or whatever it had been – it did not seem to have been a dream; it was something else. I could now, somehow, localize it. I found now that I was listening, painfully, to a sustained, aching sound, like a steam calliope fastened onto one high, piercing, raucous note. I knew it could not be a steam calliope. There had been no such thing on the Island of Santa Cruz since Columbus discovered it on his Second Voyage in 1493. I got up and into my slippers and muslin bathrobe, still puzzled.

Then abruptly the note ended, cut off clean like the ceasing of the drums when the Black people are having one of their *ratas* back of the town in the hills.

Then, and only then, I knew what it was that had disturbed me. It had been a woman, screaming.

I ran out to the semi-enclosed gallery which runs along the front of my house on the Copagnie Gade, the street of hard-pounded earth below, and looked down.

A group of early risen Blacks in nondescript garb was assembled down there, and the number was increasing every instant. Men, women, small Black children were gathered in a rapidly tightening knot directly in front of the house, their guttural mumbles of excitement forming a contrapuntal background to the solo of that sustained scream; for the woman, there in the center, was at it again now, with fresh breath, uttering her blood-curdling, hopeless, screeching wail, a thing to make the listener wince.

Not one of the throng of Blacks touched the woman in their midst. I listened to their guttural Creole, trying to catch some clue to what this disturbance was about. I would catch a word of the broad *patois* here and there, but nothing my mind could lay hold upon. At last it came, the clue; in a childish, piping treble; the clear-cut word, *Jumbee*.

I had it now. The screaming woman believed, and the crowd about her believed, that some evil witchery was afoot. Some enemy had enlisted the services of the dreaded witch-doctor – the *papaloi* – and something fearful, some curse or charm, had been 'put on' her or someone belonging to her family. All that the word 'Jumbee' had told me clearly.

I watched now for whatever was going to happen. Meanwhile I wondered why a policeman did not come along and break up this public gathering. Of course the policeman, being a Black man himself, would be as much intrigued as any of the others, but he would do his duty nevertheless. 'Put a Black to drive a Black!' The old adage was as true nowadays as in the remote days of West Indian slavery.

The woman, now convulsed, rocking backward and forward, seemed as though possessed. Her screams had now an undertone or cadence of pure horror. It was ghastly.

A policeman, at last! Two policemen, in fact, one of them Old Kraft, once a Danish top-sergeant of garrison troops. Kraft was nearly pure Caucasian, but, despite his touch of African, he would tolerate no nonsense. He advanced, waving his truncheon threateningly, barking hoarse reproaches, commands to disperse. The group of Black people began to melt away in the general direction of the Sunday Market, herded along by Sergeant Kraft's dark brown patrolman.

Now only Old Kraft and the Black woman who had screamed remained, facing each other in the street below. I saw the old man's face change out of its harsh, professional, man-handling frown to something distinctly more humane. He spoke to the woman in low tones. She answered him in mutters, not unwillingly, but as though to avoid being overheard.

I spoke from the gallery.

'What is it, Herr Kraft? Can I be of assistance?'

Old Kraft looked, recognized me, touched his cap.

'Stoopide-ness!' exploded Old Kraft, explanatorily. 'The woo-man, she haf had – ' Old Kraft paused and made a sudden, stiff, dramatic gesture and looked at me meaningly. His eyes said: 'I could tell you all about it, but not from here.'

'A chair on the gallery for the poor woman?' I suggested, nodding to him.

'Come!' said he to the woman, and she followed him obediently up the outside gallery steps while I walked across to unfasten the door at the gallery's end.

We placed the woman, who seemed dazed now and kept a hand on her head, in one of my chairs, where she rocked slowly back and forth whispering to herself, and Kraft and I went inside the house, where I led him through to the dining-room.

There, at the sideboard, I did the honors for my friend Sergeant Kraft of the Christiansted Police.

'The woman's screaming awakened me, half an hour early,' I began, invitingly, as soon as the sergeant had been duly refreshed and had said his final 'skoal', his eyes on mine in the Danish manner.

'Yah, yah,' returned Kraft, nodding a wise old head. 'She tell me de Obiman fix her right, dis time!'

This sounded promising. I waited for more.

'But joost what it iss, I can not tell at all,' continued Kraft, disappointingly, as though aware of the secretiveness which should animate a police sergeant.

'Will you have – another, Herr Kraft?' I suggested.

The sergeant obliged, ending the ceremony with another 'skoal'. This libation, as I had hoped, had the desired effect. I will spare Kraft's accent, which could be cut with a knife. What he told me was that this woman, Elizabeth Aagaard, living in a village estate-cabin near the Central Factory, a few miles outside of Christiansted, had a son, one Cornelis McBean. The young fellow was what is locally known as a 'gallows-bird,' in short a gambler, thief, and general bad-egg. He had been in the police court several times for petty offenses, and in jail in the Christiansfort more than once.

But, as Kraft expressed it, 'it ain' de thievin' dat make de present difficoolty.' No! it was that young Cornelis McBean had presumed beyond his station, and had committed the crime of falling in love with Estrella Collins, the daughter of a prosperous Black store-keeper in one of Christiansted's side streets. Old Collins, utterly disapproving, and his words to McBean having had no effect whatever upon that stubborn lover, had, in short, employed the services of a *papaloi* to get rid of McBean.

'But,' I protested, 'I know Old Collins. I understand, of course, how he might object to the attentions of such a young ne'er-do-well, but – a storekeeper like him, a comparatively rich man, to call in a *papaloi* – it seems – '

'Him Black!' replied Sergeant Kraft with a little, significant gesture which made everything plain.

'What,' said I, after thinking a little, 'what particular kind of *ouanga* has Collins had "put on" him?'

The old sergeant gave me a quick glance at that word. It is a meaningful word. In Haiti it is very common. It means both talisman and amulet; something, that is, to attract, or something to repel, to defend the wearer. But here in Santa Cruz the magic of our Blacks is neither so clear-cut nor (as some imagine) quite so deadly as the magickings of the *papalois* and the *hougans* in Haiti's infested hills with their thousands of *vodu* altars to Ougoun Badagaris, to Damballa, to the Snake of far, dreadful Guinea. Over even so much as the manu-facture of *ouangas* I may not linger. One can not. The details –

'It is, I think, a "sweat-ouanga", ' whispered Old Kraft, and went a shade lighter than his accustomed sunburned ivory. 'De wooman allege,' he continued, 'that the boy sicken an' die at noon – today. For that reason she is walk into de town early, because there is no help. She desire to bewail-like, dis trouble restin' 'pon her head.'

Kraft had given me all the information he possessed. He rated a reward. I approached the sideboard a third time.

'You will excuse me again, Sergeant. It is a little early in the day for me. Still, "a man can't walk on one leg!" '

The sergeant grinned at this Santa Crucian proverb which means that a final stirrup-cup is always justified, and remarked: 'He should walk goot – on three!' After this reference to the number of his early-morning refreshments, he accepted the last of these, boomed his 'skoal', and became a police sergeant once more.

'Shall I take de wooman along, sir?' he inquired as we reached the gallery where Elizabeth Aagaard still rocked and moaned and whis-pered to herself in her trouble.

'Leave her here, please,' I replied, 'and I will see that Esmerelda finds her something to eat.' The sergeant saluted and departed.

'Gahd bless yo', sar,' murmured the poor soul. I left her there and went to the kitchen to drop a word in the sympathetic ear of my old cook. Then I started toward my belated shower-bath. It was nearly seven by now.

After breakfast I inquired for Elizabeth Aagaard. She had had food and had delivered herself at length upon her sorrows to Esmerelda and the other house-servants. Esmerelda's account established the belief that young McBean had been marked for death by one of the oldest and deadliest devices known to primitive barbarism; one which, as all Caucasians who know of it will assure you, derives its sole efficacy from the psychology of fear, that fear of the occult which has stultified the African's mind through countless generations of warfare against the jungle and the dominance of his fetish-men and *vodu* priests.

As is well known to all students of African 'magic', portions of the human body, such as hair, the clippings of nails, or even some garment long worn in contact with the body, is regarded as having a magical connection with the body itself and a corresponding influence upon it. A portion of the shirt which has been worn next the body and which has absorbed perspiration is especially highly regarded as material for the making of a protective charm or amulet, as well as for its opposite, planted against a person for the purpose of doing him harm. Blood, etc., could be included in this weird category.

In the case of young Cornelis McBean, this is what had been done. The *papaloi* had managed to get hold of one of Cornelis' shirts. In this he had dressed the recently buried body of an aged negro who had died a few days before, of senility. This shirt, after it had been in the coffin for three days and nights, had been cunningly put back for Cornelis to find and wear again. It had been, supposedly, mislaid. Young McBean, finding it in his mother's cabin, *had worn it again*.

And, as if this, in itself enough to cause his death from sheer terror as soon as he knew of it, was not sufficient, it had just come to the knowledge of the mother and son by the curious African method known as the Grapevine Route, that a small *ouanga*, made up of some of Cornelis' nail-parings, stubble of a week's beard collected from discarded lather after shaving, various other portions of his exterior personality, had been 'fixed' by the Christiansted *papaloi*, and 'buried against him'.

This meant that unless the *ouanga* could be discovered and dug up and burned, he would die at noon. As he had learned of the 'burying' of the *ouanga* only the evening before, and as the Island of Santa Cruz has an area of more than eighty square miles, there was, perhaps, one chance in some hundred trillion that he could find the *ouanga*, disinter it, and render it harmless by burning. Taking into consideration that his ancestors for countless eons had given their full and firm belief to this method of murder by mental process, it looked as though young Cornelis McBean, ne'er-do-well, Black island gallow's-bird, aspiring admirer of a young negress somewhat beyond his station in life according to African West Indian caste systems, was doomed to pass out on the stroke of twelve that day.

That, with an infinitude of detail, was the substance of the story of Elizabeth Aagaard.

I sat and looked at her, quiet and humble now, no longer the screaming fury she had appeared to be at that morning's crack of dawn. And as I looked at the poor soul, with the dumb, distressed motherhood in her dim eyes from which the unchecked tears ran down her coal-black face, it came to me that I wanted to help; that this thing was outrageous; wicked with a wickedness far surpassing the ordinary sinfulness of ordinary people. I did not want to sit by, as it were, and allow the unknown McBean to pass out at the behest of a paid rascal of a *papaloi* merely because unctuous Old Collins had decided on that method for his exit from this life – a matter involving, perhaps fifteen dollars' fee to the witch-doctor; the collection and burial of some bits of offal somewhere on Santa Cruz.

I could imagine the young Black fellow, livid with a nameless fear, a complex of ancient, inherited, unreasonable dreads, shivering, cowering, sickened to his dim soul by what lay ahead of him, three hours away when twelve should strike from the Christiansfort clock in the old tower by the harbor; writhing helplessly in his mind before the approach of the ghastly doom which he had brought upon himself because he had happened to fall in love with brown Estrella Collins, whose sleek brown father carried a collection-plate every Sunday up and down the aisle of his place of worship!

There was an element of absurdity in it all, now that I was actually sitting here looking at McBean's mother. She had given up now, it appeared, was resigned to the fate of her only son. 'Him Black!' Old Kraft had remarked.

That thought of the collection-plate in Old Collins' pudgy, store-keeper's hands, reminded me of something.

'What is your church, Elizabeth?' I inquired suddenly.

'Me English Choorch, sar – de boy also. Him make great *shandramadan*, sar, him gamble an' perhaps a tief, but him one-time communicant, sar.'

An inspiration came to me then. Perhaps I could prevail upon one of the English Church clergy to help. It was, when one came down to the brass tacks of the situation, a question of *belief*. A similar *ouanga*, 'buried against' me, would have no effect whatever, because to me, such a means of getting rid of a person was merely the height of absurdity, like the charm-killing of the Polynesians by making them look at their reflection in a gourd of water and then shaking the gourd and so destroying the image! Perhaps, if Elizabeth and her son could be persuaded to do their parts . . . I spoke long and earnestly to Elizabeth.

At the end of my speech, which had emphasized the superior power of Divinity when compared to even the most powerful of the African fetishes, even the dreaded snake himself, Elizabeth, her hopes somewhat aroused, I imagined, took her departure, and I jumped into my car and ran up the hill toward the English Church rectory.

Father Richardson, the pastor, himself a West Indian born, was at home. To him I explained the case. When I had ended –

'I am obliged to you, Mr Canevin,' said the clergyman. 'If only they would realize – er – precisely what you told the woman; that Divinity is infinitely more powerful than their beliefs! I will accompany you, at once. It is, really, the release, perhaps, of a human soul. And they come to us clergy over such things as the theft of a couple of coconuts!'

Father Richardson left me, came back in two minutes with a black bag, and we started for Elizabeth Aagaard's village along a lovely shore road by the gleaming, placid, blue Caribbean.

The negro estate-village was surprisingly quiet when we arrived. The clergyman got out at Elizabeth's cabin, and I drove the car out of the way, off the road into rank guinea-grass. I saw Father Richardson, a commanding, tall figure, austere in his long, black cassock, striding in at the cabin door. I followed, and got inside just in time to witness a strange performance.

The Black boy, livid and seeming shrunken with terror, cowered under a thin blanket on a small iron bedstead. Over him towered the clergyman, and just as I came in, he stooped and with a small, sharp pocket-knife cut something loose from the boy's neck and flung it contemptuously on the hard-earth floor of the cabin. It landed just at my feet and I looked at it curiously. It was a small black bag, of some kind of cotton material, with a tuft of black cock's feathers at its top which was bound around with many windings of bright red thread. The whole thing was about the size of an egg. I recognized it as a protective amulet.

His teeth chattering, the cold fear of death upon him, the Black boy protested in the guttural *Creole*. The clergyman answered him gravely.

'There can be no half-way measures, Cornelis. When a person asks God for His help, he must put away everything else.' A mutter of assent came from the woman, who was arranging a small table with a candle in the corner of the cabin.

From his black bag Father Richardson now took a small bottle with a sprinkler arrangement at its top, and from this he cast a shower of drops upon the *ouanga* charm lying on the floor. Then he proceeded to sprinkle the whole cabin with this holy water, ending with Elizabeth, myself, and finally, the boy on the bed. As the water touched his face the boy winced visibly and shuddered; and suddenly it came over me that here was a strange matter; again, I dare say, a matter of belief. The change from the supposed protection of the charm which the priest had cut away from his neck and contemptuously tossed away, to the prescribed method of the Church must have been, somehow, and in some obscure mental fashion, a very striking one to the young fellow.

The bottle went back into the bag and now Father Richardson was speaking to the boy on the bed.

'God is intervening for you, my child, and – God's power is supreme over all things, visible *and invisible*. He holds all in the hollow of His hand. He will now put away your fear, and take this weight from your soul, *and you shall live*. You must now do your part, if you would be fortified by the Sacrament. You just purify your soul. Penance first. Then – '

The boy, now appreciably calmer, nodded his head, and the priest motioned me out, including the woman in his gesture. I opened the cabin door and stepped out, closely followed by Elizabeth Aagaard. I left her, twenty paces from her cabin, wringing her hands, her lips murmuring in prayer, while I went and sat in my car.

Ten minutes later the cabin door opened and the priest beckoned us within. The boy lay quiet now, and Father Richardson was engaged in repacking his black bag. He turned to me: 'Good-bye, and – thank you. It was very good of you to bring me.'

'But – aren't you coming?'

'No' – this reflectively. 'No – I must see him through.' He glanced at his wrist-watch. 'It is eleven-fifteen now. It was at noon you said – '

'I'm staying with you, then,' said I, and sat down on a chair in the far corner of the little cabin room.

The priest stood by the bedside, looking down at the Black boy, his back to me. The woman was, apparently, praying earnestly to herself in another corner, out of the way. The priest stooped and took the limp hand and wrist in his large, firm white hands, and counted the pulse, glancing at his watch. Then he came and sat beside me.

'Half an hour!' he murmured.

The Black woman, Elizabeth, prayed without a sound in her corner on the hard, earth floor, where she knelt, rigidly. We sat, without conversation, for a long twenty minutes during which the sense of strain in the cabin became more and more apparent to me.

Abruptly the boy's mouth fell open. The priest sprang toward him, seized and chafed the dull-black hands. The boy's head turned on the pillow and his jaws came together again, his eyelids fluttering. Then a slight spasm, perceptible through the light covering, ran through him, and, breathing a few times deeply, he resumed his coma-like sleep. The priest now remained beside him. I counted off the minutes to noon. Nine – eight – seven – at least, three minutes before noon. When I had got that far I heard the priest's deep, monotonous voice reciting in a low tone. Listening, I caught his words here and there. He held the boy's hand while the words rolled out low and impressively.

' . . . to withstand and overcome all assaults of thine adversary . . . unto thee ghostly strength . . . and that he nowise prevail against thee.' Then, dropping a note, to my surprise, the clerical voice of this most Anglican of clergymen began to declaim the words of an older liturgical language: ' . . . *et effugiat atque discedat omnis phantasia et nequitia . . . vel versutia diabolicae fraudis omnisque spiritus immundis adjuratis . . .* '

The words, gaining in volume with the priest's earnestness, rolled out now. I saw that we were on the very verge of noon, and, looking back to the bed from my glance at my watch, I saw convulsion after convulsion shake the thin body on the bed. Then the cabin itself began to tremble in a sudden wind that had sprung up from nowhere. The dry palm fronds lashed back and forth outside and the whistle of the wind blew under the crazily hung door. The muslin curtain of the small window suddenly billowed like a sail. Then, suddenly, the harsh voice of the Black boy.

'Damballa!' it said, clearly, and moaned.

Damballa is one of the Greater Mysteries of the *vodu* worship. I shuddered in spite of myself.

But now higher, more commanding, came the voice of Father Richardson, positively intoning now – great sentences of Power, formulas interposed, as he himself stood, interposed, between the feeble Black boy and the Powers of Evil which seemed to seek him out for their own fell ends. The priest seemed to stretch a mantle of mystic protection over the grovelling, writhing body.

The mother lay prone on the dirt floor, now, her arms stretched out crosslike – the last, most abject gesture of supplication of which humanity is physically capable. As I glanced down at her I saw, in the extreme corner of the little room, something oddly shaped projecting from a pile of discarded garments.

It was now exactly noon. As I looked carefully at my watch, the distant stroke of the Angelus came resoundingly from the heavy bell of St John's Church. Father Richardson ceased his recitation, laid back the boys hand on the coverlid, and began the Angelus. I stood up at this, and, as he finished, I plucked his sleeve. The wind, curiously enough, was gone, utterly. Only the noon sun beat down suffocatingly on the iron roof of the frail cabin. Father Richardson looked at me inquiringly. I pointed to that corner, under the pile of clothes. He walked to the corner, stooped, and drew out a crude wooden image of a snake. He glanced accusingly at Elizabeth, who grovelled afresh.

'Take it up, Elizabeth,' commanded Father Richardson, 'break it in two, and throw it out of the doorway.'

The woman crawled to the corner, lifted the thing, snapped it in two, and then, rising, her face gray with fear, opened the cabin door and threw out the pieces. We went back to the bedside, where the boy breathed quietly now. The priest shook him. He opened swimming eyes, eyes like a drunken man's. He goggled stupidly at us.

'You are alive – by the mercy of God,' said the priest, severely. 'Come now, get up! It is well past noon. Here! Mr Canevin will show you his watch. You are not dead. Let this be a lesson to you to leave alone what God has put outside your knowledge.'

The boy sat up, still stupidly, the thin blanket drawn about him, on the side of the bed.

'We may as well drive back now,' said Father Richardson, picking up his black bag in a business-like manner.

As I turned my car to the right just outside the estate-village stone gateway, I glanced back toward the village. It swarmed with Blacks, all crowding about the cabin of Elizabeth Aagaard. Beside me, I heard the rather monotonous voice of Father Richardson. He seemed to be talking to himself; thinking aloud, perhaps.

'Creator – of all things – visible *and invisible*.'

I drove slowly to avoid the ducks, fowls, small pigs, pickaninnies and burro-carts between the edge of town and the rectory.

'It was,' said I, as I held his hand at parting, 'an experience – that.'

'Oh – that! Yes, yes, quite! I was thinking – you'll excuse me, Mr Canevin – of my afternon sick-calls. My curate isn't quite over that last attack of dengue fever. I have a full afternoon. Come in and have tea with us – any afternoon, about five.'

I drove home slowly. A West Indian priest! That sudden wind – the little wooden snake – the abject fear in the eyes of the Black boy! All that had been merely in the day's work for Father Richardson, in those rather awkward, large, square hands, the hands which held the Sacrament every morning. Sometimes I would get up early and go to church myself on a weekday morning, along the soft roads through the pre-dawn dusk along with scores of soft-stepping, barefooted Blacks, plodding to church in the early dawn, going to get strength, power, to fight the age-long battle between God and Satan – the Snake – here where the sons of Ham tremble beneath the lingering fears of that primeval curse which came upon their ancestor because he dared to laugh at his father Noah.

West India Lights

I had engaged Melbourne House, a fine old mansion on the hill back of Fredericksted on the West India Island of Santa Cruz, for the winter. And I found when I arrived one November day that I was to have one more room at my disposal than I had bargained for. This was, really, an end of the second-floor passageway, which had been made into a room by a slat-partition.

My landlady, Old Mistress James Desmond, had had moved out certain articles of decrepit furniture for the housing of which I had agreed to give up the use of that 'room', which looked like an old-fashioned wine-closet.

I bestowed my trunks and packing cases on its floor and had Esmerelda, my coal-black servant, clear off the shelves for hand-luggage and odds and ends.

In order to do so Esmerelda had to move several discarded belongings which had been left there, and among these was a large, old-fashioned picture in a heavy wooden frame which had escaped the ravages of wood-worms for countless decades. I noticed the old picture when I was bestowing some of my own odds and ends near where it stood, and carried it into my workroom to have a look at it.

At first I had thought it was a chromo. But this was no chromo, olio, nor anything mechanically produced. It was paint.

I looked at it closely, with interest. The composition was amateurish. The coloring was too faded with the dimness of years for me to make much of it.

I carried the painting into the bathroom, made a lather and, after taking the ancient and brittle canvas out of its frame, began to clean it with soap and water. I dried it, and then used a little typewriter oil on it.

The colors began to jump out at me. The artist had been, plainly, a lover of color. My restoration accentuated the amateurishness of the thing, but I forgave the artist much because of the subject he – or she – had chosen.

My imaginary young lady in her flowered muslin dress of a century ago had chosen to depict the execution of a pirate, and – the pirate could have been none other than Fawcett.

There could be no doubt about it whatever. That bloody villain was the only pirate that had been executed at St Thomas – except his own two mates who had paid the penalty of their murderous rascality at the same time – and this was a picture of St Thomas, painted photographically, apparently from the deck of some vessel conveniently anchored offshore.

The costumes, too, were of Fawcett's period. His execution had taken place in September, 1824, and that, too, fixed the period of the painting.

High as the colors were pitched, stilted as were the many characters, there was something convincingly lifelike about the thing. Apparently this picture had been painted from actual observation.

The colors too, on reflection, were not so much exaggerated. Did not one do well here to wear smoked glasses in the middle of the day? Was not the glowing indigo of the Caribbean incredible – the scarlet of the hibiscus painful to the unaccustomed eye?

I fastened up the canvas with carpet tacks on the wall of my workroom where it would catch the north light. I began at its upper corners, pressing tacks along its upper edge, and then, pulling it down flat, inserted others along the lower edge and up the sides.

The last tack went through the arm of one of Fawcett's lieutenants, just where he had hurtled through the air at the end of his rope over at the extreme lefthand of the picture. A little, trailing 'C. L.' was the signature.

That afternoon at Estate Montparnasse, where I had been invited hospitably for tea, I told my kind hosts, the Maclanes, about my find. And I made it an excuse – though none was needed – to ask them to drive in for tea with me the following afternoon.

When they saw it I think it made the same impression on them that it had upon me, at first. I imagine that only their impeccable courtesy prevented their telling me that I had been gloating over something very like a chromo!

It was Miss Gertrude Maclane who first began to get the real charm of it. I noticed her leaning close and examining it very carefully.

Suddenly, as I talked with Mr and Mrs Maclane, there came from Miss Gertrude a little, smothered cry – an exclamation almost like a sigh – but so poignant, though subdued, that her mother turned quickly toward her on hearing it. We both stepped toward her.

'What is it, Miss Gertrude?' I inquired.

'What is it, my dear?' echoed her mother.

'It's this poor creature,' replied Miss Gertrude Maclane, indicating the fellow whose arm I had transfixed.

'Why – he's in agony! It's dreadful, I think! It's wonderfully done. It quite startled me, in fact. The little figures are wonderfully done, if you look at them closely. I think they must – some of them, anyhow – be portraits, just as you said yesterday, Mr Canevin. This one, certainly, is almost uncanny.'

We all looked at the dangling fellow. I had not seen him since yesterday. Curious! He was not, as I had supposed, *dangling*. He was hurtling through the air; had not quite reached the end of that fatal fall from the drop where stood the hangman, a terrible, fierce fellow.

No – the rope was not yet wholly taut. That knot of seven turns had not broken the poor devil's neck. He was as alive as any of the spectators.

But it was not this new interpretation of the artist's skill, not the look of tortured horror, which had so moved Miss Gertrude. No!

What caused me to close my eyes in a spasmodic, futile effort to shut out a deeper horror, caused me to lean heavily against the table, fighting to retain some measure of my composure, was the fact that the man's expression had *changed since yesterday*. Now out of his horror-shot, protruding, agonized eyes came straight at me a look of strange reproachfulness.

And down his little, painted arm, from the place where I had driven the carpet tack through it, were running little drops of bright red blood . . .

I opened my eyes and turned to my guests. I had pulled myself together with an effort which was like a wrench. I bowed to Mrs Maclane.

'Shall we go down for tea?' I inquired.

Miss Gertrude lingered behind after the rest had passed out of the room. She took my arm and I could feel her slim white hand trembling.

'I think it is very dreadful, somehow, that picture,' she whispered confidingly, 'but oh, Mr Canevin, it's fascinating. I wonder if "C. L." really was a girl. Perhaps we can find out!'

'We'll see what can be done,' I replied with an attempt at lightness, and she smiled up at me most charmingly in a way she has. A lively young girl is Miss Gertrude Maclane, daughter of Old Scottish Gentry-Planters, people who had come to the island in the old days.

When the Maclanes had gone after tea, I went upstairs and pulled out that tack. I will admit that I almost expected to see fresh blood flow from the wound. Nothing of the sort happened, of course.

I looked closely at the place. Red paint, put on a hundred years ago. The reproachful expression I had imagined was, too, wholly absent from the man's face. I was looking at the picture now by electric light.

The marked differences in light-effects that we get in the West Indies might well be expected to play queer optical tricks. They are a land of imagination, the islands. Some of the original crudity, too, seemed, somehow, to have got back into the picture.

After breakfast the next morning I went straight in to the picture. In this clear, raw, morning light there remained only that look of apprehension which the artist had painted in.

No agony. Certainly no reproach. Queer tricks, strange illusions, those begotten of our tropical sun!

I examined the tiny hole left by the carpet tack under a magnifying glass. The 'bloodstains' of my aroused imagination of yesterday were stains of century-old, brittle paint – probably a slip of the brush just after touching-in those flamboyant trees or a scarlet head-turban or so – mere little meaningless, incidental dabs they were, and nothing more that I was able to discover.

That afternoon I called upon old Mrs Desmond, who owns Melbourne House. She is a little, faded lady of the Old Irish Gentry; of a family which has been in the West Indies since early in the eighteenth century.

She was dressed, as usual, in hot-looking black silk, with a little lace around the edges. There is about her a penumbra of veils and a suggestion of quaint, leather reticules. She has, too, that dead-white, colorless complexion of the West Indian Caucasian lady who has spent the bulk of a long lifetime avoiding the direct rays of the sun.

I told Mrs Desmond about finding the picture, and our curiosity about the identity of the artist. She smiled at me kindly, rocking herself back and forth in an enormous Copenhagen mahogany rocking-chair the while, and fanning herself with a regularity which suggested doom.

'It was painted by my aunt, Mr Canevin,' said Mrs Desmond, 'who was Camilla Lanigan, my mother's elder sister. She died before I was born, about 1841 – I'll not be positive. 'Tis said she was a remarkable woman in her day, and if you'll wait till I'm dead and gone, I'll tell you what's known about her.'

'With pleasure, Mistress Desmond, and may that day be a long way off; as long as you care to have it yourself!'

'What I can tell you is indeed no credit to the Lanigans and their gentry, you'll understand,' continued Mrs Desmond. 'She was of a very inquiring disposition and I dare say she learned much that she would have done better to leave alone – about the doings of the blacks and all! My grandfather, Cornelius Lanigan that was, and her father, was a gentleman-merchant there in St Thomas.

'It was from St Thomas that James Desmond took me when we were married to live here on Santa Cruz, and I no more than a child of eighteen, Mr Canevin. It was in 'sixty-four I was married, and all I know of my Aunt Camilla Lanigan I learned from the sayings of my mother before that year when I was a girl at home.

'There was little she did not know about the Obeah of the black people, so 'tis said – nor, indeed, of the voodoo as well, belike! Their mother being long dead and my own mother the younger of the two sisters, there was no one to stop my Aunt Camilla from doing much as she liked. The black people held her in great respect, so 'twas said.

'As to the picture itself, I can tell you but little about it. It was in the house when I was born, in 'forty-six that was, and my mother had a great dislike for it. 'Twas I who would be taking it out of an old dust-box where it was kept, now and again, and frightening myself, as a child would, with the queer little figures and the hanging!

'When I was married I begged for it, and I think my mother was glad to be rid of it, for the memory of my Aunt Camilla was still in the house there in St Thomas.

'James Desmond, my husband, would never allow it to be hung on the wall, saying that it was indelicate of a lady to have painted such a scene. And I believe he was in the right of it, Mr Canevin, with all respect to my Aunt Camilla!'

I thanked the dear old lady for her information as I bowed over her withered hand at parting. Her last remark was cryptic and somewhat startling: ' 'Twas more than paint, belike, went into the composition of that picture, Mr Canevin!'

I called up Miss Gertrude as soon as I was back at Melbourne House.

'I have some information about the picture and the artist,' said I.

'Come as early as you can manage it,' said Miss Gertrude, and after dinner I started.

'Oh, Mr Canevin,' said she eagerly, when I had recounted what Mrs Desmond had told me. 'How I wish I might see it again now at once!'

'I had anticipated that,' said I. 'It lies on the table in the entryway.'

We laid it out on the mahogany centre-table and looked down at it together in silence. At last Miss Gertrude spoke.

'What do you see now in his expression, Mr Canevin?'

I did not need inquire in whose expression.

A baffling, elusive change appeared to have taken place now that we were looking down at him under the electric light.

'Expectation,' said I slowly.

I hesitated. It was not quite expectation. Interest? Not quite that, either. I pondered the matter, the bizarre whimsicality of it making its natural appeal to my mind the while.

'Hope!' I cried at last. 'And, coming through the hope, a wish!'

'Yes, yes!' cried Miss Gertrude, clasping her hands excitedly. 'It – it seemed to me almost as though there were something – something he wanted to tell us!'

She hurried over these hesitating words and, now that they were spoken, there was a look of relief on her lovely face.

'Your moral courage is better than mine, Miss Gertrude,' said I. 'For that is what was really in the back of my mind. It seemed to me too – well, too preposterous to put into words.'

Her eyes glowed with an enthusiasm almost childish. She placed her hand upon my arm.

'Do you suppose we could find out what it is?'

Her voice was very low.

'We could try,' said I.

The whimsicality of the proposal had intrigued me.

'But how?' cried Miss Gertrude.

'That's what I'm puzzling my poor brains about,' I answered. 'One cannot converse with a little figure two and one-half inches high and made of paint!

'No! We cannot just talk to him – and expect him to answer. He hasn't the – the apparatus. He's only a brittle little manikin fastened down flat on some very tender old canvas. He can't speak and he can't write. But, somehow, he does seem able to change his expression.

'If there really is something in him – something besides paint, as old Mrs Desmond hinted – at least we're not meddling with *that* for any wicked purpose, whatever Mrs Desmond's Aunt Camilla Lanigan may have had in mind.'

'Do you remember that paralyzed old man in *Monte Cristo*?' inquired Miss Gertrude eagerly. 'Noirtier, de Villefort's father; you remember?'

'He was one of the friends of my childhood,' said I. 'What about him?'

'He could move only his eyes, and yet his granddaughter "talked" with him. She asked him questions that could be answered by "yes" or "no", and he closed the right eye for one and the left for the other!'

'Yes?' said I dubiously.

'Well!' said she, looking down at the picture, 'shall we try him?'

I stepped over and looked at the manikin closely.

'I'm looking to see if Mrs Desmond's Aunt Camilla gave him ears,' said I lightly. 'Apparently she put "blood" in him.'

And I proceeded to tell Miss Gertrude the incident of the carpet tack.

'We'll have to work out the questions very carefully,' said she.

I looked at her in amazement.

'Can you seriously mean it?' I asked.

'Look at him!' cried Miss Gertrude and put her hands over her eyes and sank down upon the sofa.

I stepped quickly toward her, alarmed.

'No, no!' she cried. 'I'm all right – only startled a little. Look for yourself, if you please, Mr Canevin.'

I looked, and for the life of me I could not escape the conviction that there was a wry smile on the manikin's face.

'My God!' said I, and did not apologize.

I almost hesitate to proceed.

Well, we sat down together after that and worked the thing out. The evening was before us. The rest of the family were dining with friends and would not be home before eleven.

It was plain to us that 'he' could move, although he had not done so while anyone was actually looking at him. The fact that this last 'change' had come upon his countenance in the briefest of intervals would indicate, somehow, that he could also 'hear'.

For it seemed plain to us in our eerie mood of that strange evening that the smile was one of satisfaction, induced by our conversation. He wanted us to try to talk to him!

We decided to formulate certain questions, ask them, then turn away and, after a short interval, look at the manikin again. The method of communication we derived from 'Noirtier', as the simplest possible.

Miss Gertrude asked the first question.

'We think you wish to communicate with us,' said she, in a still small voice. 'We shall ask you questions, and you are to close your right eye if the answer is "yes", and your left if it is "no". Will you answer?'

Then we sat, side by side, on the sofa, watching the great clock in the corner of the drawing-room ticking off the seconds of that minute which we had decided to allow to pass before looking at him again.

It was a long, long minute, that one! At first I felt like a fool, but that feeling dissipated itself as soon as we had, together, bent over the picture at the expiration of that first minute.

The right eye had drooped in a kind of leering half-wink – precisely as though Miss Camilla Lanigan had painted it so one hundred years ago.

After several long minutes of silence between us there on the sofa. I said: 'I'm going to ask the next question, if you don't mind.'

She nodded.

I walked over to the table. The eyes were alike again!

'Have you more than one thing to communicate?' I inquired.

I came back to the sofa again and sat down, my eyes once more on the clock.

Again we bent over the picture.

'There's a slight droop in the right eye,' said Miss Gertrude.

The manikin had answered 'yes' again.

After that, somehow, we felt freer. Two questions – the real ordeal of the thing – were over and past.

There was little feeling of strangeness from then on. It was precisely as though we were talking with some person of flesh and blood like ourselves, with someone not immediately present – as though we were talking over the telephone. It was something like that.

He had two things to communicate. We took thought now how to proceed. The eyes, alike, were always open and staring straight ahead whenever we approached with a new question. And so it continued through to the end.

I thought of a necessary question.

'Have you more than two things to communicate?' I asked.

'No,' came the answer.

'Does the first thing concern you?' I ventured.

'Yes.'

'And the second thing? Does that also concern you?'

This time, when we looked for the answer, the eyes had not moved at all so far as we could tell.

I glanced up at the electric light. Our lights not infrequently change their density, go up and down, without warning. We have only the little, local electrical plants, one in each of the towns. The light appeared even enough.

We were a little nonplused, for, although I had been telling myself subconsciously all along that the whole thing was a farce, a bit of childish play, I had come by now to expect an answer!

'Perhaps it's because we asked him an unanswerable question,' I suggested. 'I'll try to clear it up.'

'He's helping,' said Miss Gertrude. 'He's only showing us that it was asked wrong!'

I looked down at her and smiled, and she smiled back at me.

'Does the second thing concern more than you – that is, someone else?' I asked the pirate.

'Yes,' came the answer.

'Is Mr Canevin the other person?' asked Miss Gertrude.

I smiled again at this. If there was anything that could be construed as an answer, I certainly expected that it would be 'no'.

The answer was 'yes'.

I began to feel the beginnings of a cold consternation, but I found Miss Gertrude smiling happily.

'I thought so,' said she simply.

Women, most of them certainly, are beyond me! It was a woman who had painted this picture!

Miss Gertrude hastened to ask another question.

'Do you want to tell Mr Canevin what he can do for you first, and then what you're going to do for him in return?'

'Yes.'

'Do you wish to be released from something?'

'Yes, he does,' reported Miss Gertrude, who was now asking the questions, I being seated for the time being alone on the sofa.

'Do you wish to pass out of existence?'

She nodded over to me to show that he did.

'Can we accomplish that for you?'

'He says we can.'

We were making progress, it appeared! She clapped her hands gaily. All her gravity had disappeared. It *was* merely a game to her, then. I had almost begun to suspect that she had been taking the thing seriously.

'I thought it would come out more or less like that!' she announced. Then: 'The poor, poor man!' said she softly, and I wondered once more.

She returned to the picture and looked down at it for a long time.

'Is there anything else that can be done for you?' she inquired.

There wasn't, it seemed.

I will summarize, for brevity's sake, the series of questions which followed and the 'replies'.

We were to find out how to obtain the 'reward'. Then we were to ask no further questions. I was to take the picture home, put it back on the wall, and destroy it the next morning – tomorrow.

All this seemed to me, on the sofa, grotesque, unintelligible. I was almost becoming bored with this seemingly foolish play, but nothing would stop Gertrude Maclane.

'Is it a material reward for Mr Canevin?'

'Yes,' came the answer to this one. And, going over and looking down at the manikin, such is human nature – or our somewhat unstable lighting system on Santa Cruz – that it seemed even to me in that mood, that I could discern the merest ghost of a twisted grin on that strange little face beneath the looming, cruelly twisted knot of hangman's rope.

I will bring what seemed to me an increasingly absurd performance to its conclusion. I left, with definite instructions to dig in the northeast corner of the cellar under Melbourne House – that cellar once devoted to the housing of materials for planter's punches and sangaree, and now fallen to a low estate of habitation for spiders and perhaps an occasional scorpion thriving in its ancient dust.

My brain, I will confess it, was in a kind of whirl as I drove home that night from Montparnasse House. When I had obediently hung the picture back in its place on my workroom wall, I took a good, long, searching look at it. It seemed as wooden, as laboriously limned, as amateurish, as on that day when I had rescued it from the dustroom.

There were the strutting St Thomas gentry and merchants, a lordly group of aristocrats, who had come out to see Captain Fawcett die. There, too, were their silken and be-muslined ladyfolk; the Danish soldiers in their boxlike, Frederick-the-Great uniforms; the swarming, pop-eyed negroes; the hangman, Fawcett and his two mates . . .

I went to bed. That had been a strange, weird evening.

To dig under my own house. It was too much. And I had promised Gertrude Maclane to do so!

Promised, too, to destroy this picture the next morning. Awkward, that! Gentlemen do not build bonfires in their back yards in the West Indies.

Our very cooking is done on charcoal-pots, or on an occasional oilstove. We have no gas, and coal we know only as a commodity for fueling ships. It would have to be a coal-pot.

That is the idea I carried with me into sleep, the last thing I remembered until the sun, the bright, morning sun, saluted me awake.

'Keep a fire in the coal-pot, Esmerelda, if you please,' I called through the bathroom door. 'I want to use it myself a little later.'

I stepped into the workroom to take down the picture. I had promised to destroy it, I would keep my word.

I looked at it, for the last time, under that clear, pitiless, blazing morning sunlight.

Probably the nervous strain had been heavier than I had imagined. I managed to control myself. I made no *shandramadan* – which is the black's term for foolishness or rascality! I avoided, too, by holding on tight to the table's edge, a *caffoon*, which means a fall.

For 'he' was not, it seemed now, and could never indeed have been, if paint is paint, hurtling through the air in his last instant of life, so to express it. The rope as I looked at it was unmistakably taut.

That deadly knot of seven turns of good, new manila rope must already have struck home under one of those strange little ears into which, last night, Gertrude Maclane and I had . . .

I set my face down for a moment in my shaking hands. The eyes of the figure which we had watched last night – his eyes were, unmistakably, closed like those of his two companions in wicked-ness. He had joined Captain Fawcett of the fine, plum-colored, laced coat and Hessian boots.

Our pirate really *swung* now. He was dead – delivered, it came through my shuddering mind, from those uncanny sorceries of Camilla Lanigan, she who had been so strangely respected by the black people of St Thomas; she who knew their Obeah and their voodoo.

I pulled down the picture a moment later with a firm hand and laid it out flat on my work table. I cut it into convenient strips for burning in a coal-pot. Some of the old, brittle paint flaked off in this process, and this I gathered up to the final crumb on a sheet of paper.

But for the most part my penknife went cleanly through the old canvas.

Downstairs I found that Esmerelda had gone after the morning's supply of ice for the drinking water with the large thermos bottle. But a glowing coal-pot stood on the floor of the little stone gallery outside the kitchen door.

Into this I poured the fragments of the chipped paint and watched them bubble and hiss. I thrust in the strips, one after another. They curled, caught, and were swiftly consumed.

Then I stirred the charcoal and a few sparks came out. Not a vestige of Camilla Lanigan's picture remained.

I should have to wait until Esmerelda was gone for the afternoon, and dig in that cellar in the hottest part of the day among the ghosts of wine-barrels and demijohns. I stepped out into the yard to investigate.

In a shed I found an ancient spade and, best of all, a thing like a mattock which might have been dug up on the site of Persepolis. These I carried down into the dim, cool cellar. With the spade I knocked loose the hooks of a hurricane shutter. That would dissipate the slight, musty smell and also provide a better light for me that afternoon.

Esmerelda was still bargaining among the bebustled vendors in the market when I returned upstairs to wash by hands.

After lunch I waited until I heard Esmerelda leave. I watched the good soul as she walked down the hill, through slanted jalousies. And when she passed out of sight around the corner by St Paul's Church, I locked the front door and descended into the cellar. It was fairly cool and hardly musty at all. I hung my coat on an ancient, hand-wrought nail and set to work.

The hard-pounded earth came away reluctantly as I picked at it. loosening the surface for a hole about six feet square. Alternately with this I shoveled out the loose dirt, placing it well to one side, so that it would not run back.

It was two when I began. The fort clock had chimed three-thirty a few minutes before I struck something metallic. It took me at least fifteen minutes more before I had uncovered a small iron trunk in the corner of the large square I had opened.

I broke the rusty lock with the edge of the spade, raised it, and there before me – and such is human nature that I must say I was more surprised than amazed, at the very first – lay, neatly stacked in rouleaus from which the ancient cotton cloth fell away in shreds and flakes, row after row of gold coin – all the coinage of romance: doubloons, of course; ancient American eagles; Louis d'Or; even a few East Indian Mohurs!

In a side compartment by themselves lay, carefully packed in, an assortment of jeweled implements, jeweled chalices and patens from the loot, doubtless, of those rich Spanish Churches of Central and South American seaside cities, perhaps even from Porto Rico and Santo Domingo; jewelry, much of it monogrammed; gold plate such as had graced the hospitable boards of many a fabulously rich sugar baron of the islands of the seventeenth and eighteenth centuries.

At the very bottom of this separate compartment, which was of the capacity of about one-third the trunk's cubical contents, lay, flattened and stiff, a sack of oiled silk. I picked it up and had to untie the leather pouch-strings, so well was it preserved.

I looked in and then thrust in my right hand, and even in the comparatively dim light of the old cellar there leaped out at me the myriad coruscations of cut jewels, throwing back the light they had not known for fully a century. My hand was full of jewels, and I had hardly taken off the edge – the very topmost.

Diamonds, rubies, sapphires, blazing emeralds. A king's, an emperor's ransom here, in the cellar of Melbourne House.

The pirate! He had not misled us. What, in God's name, did it mean!

Well, I had other things to think of besides mooning over *that* problem there in the cellar, with a fair-sized fortune held in my hand and God knows how much else there in the iron trunk – gold, vessels, jewels.

I spent the next half-hour carrying the trunk's contents up to my bedroom in the wholly unromantic iron pail in which Esmerelda boils the drinking water. I deposited them all, in a kind of order – gold coin all together, vessels and jewels separate – in two bureau drawers, turning out shirts and collars for this accommodation.

I locked the drawers, stuffed the shirts into the mahogany wardrobe, placed the bureau key in my pocket and returned to the cellar. There, by leaving open the old trunk's lid, I was able in another half-hour of feverish work, which left me literally dripping and soaking, to get back and roughly to pound down all the dry earth I had taken out.

When I had tossed the spade and mattock behind some ancient lumber, closed and hooked the hurricane shutter and returned to my bedroom to strip off my soaking clothes, before the most refreshing bath I can remember, it was precisely nine minutes before five. And Esmerelda would not be back until five precisely.

I remember sitting, about six-thirty, fresh and cool now, in white drill, waiting for Esmerelda to announce dinner, with the necklace of emeralds which I had taken out from the rest as soon as I saw it, to give to Miss Gertrude Maclane.

I had telephoned to Montparnasse House, and explained to her that I must see her as soon as possible. She had arranged that I was to call that evening after dinner.

Among other matters, I had been considering my duty with respect to this find. It involved certain responsibilities, I began to see. I resolved to return anything that might prove identifiable.

Apparently this was the hoard of some master pirate, possibly even that of Fawcett himself. Its disappearance, or rather the fact that it had never been discovered, was one of the standard mysteries of the islands. How, if that were the case, it had got itself under Melbourne House was apparently an insoluble mystery.

I may as well mention here that the restoration has proved an actuality in one or two cases. A dozen gold spoons, monogrammed, have gone back to the representatives of the Despard family in Christiansted. And a lovely old 'tulip' chalice, filigreed, with its attendant paten, all the way to Valparaiso.

I dined that evening with the necklace loose in the pocket of my drill jacket. I fear I made only a sketchy meal.

Esmerelda seemed disturbed. She thought, good soul, as she told me the next morning, that the *crustadas* of shell-fish had not been up to standard! I had not, really, been certain what I was eating.

On my arrival at Montparnasse House I felt a note of constraint. It is very hard to describe what I mean. I can only say I *felt* it. Santa Crucian moods and similar delicacies of feeling are most difficult to describe!

I remembered that I had called three times in the past four days! I was not unwelcome. It was not that. Otherwise Robert Maclane, Esq., would have waited perhaps fifteen minutes, instead of five, before having a swizzel served.

But – it was conveyed to me so subtly that I despair of making the matter clear, that Mr and Mrs Maclane, while recognizing me as an equal and a friend, were not quite clear as to what I was up to!

They were not, precisely, objecting to my coming so often. They wanted me to know they thought it unusual. That is the best I can do by way of saying how I felt.

Mr Maclane and I conversed about new kinds of canes which were being tried out; about the labor situation; about the pink boll-worm and how certain Montserrat cotton planters were meeting its ravages; about the newly inaugurated onion crop; about the perennial subject of the rainfall.

The ladies, of course, joined in from time to time as Victorian ladies did, and as Crucian ladies do to this day. But the burden of that evening's conversation lay upon Mr Maclane and myself.

Not so much as the overt flicker of an eyelash served to indicate the natural curiosity of my hosts as to why I was paying their hospitable estate house so many visits. But – I could *feel* it, all the time, circulating in my blood!

It was half-past nine when Miss Gertrude took her courage in her hands, looked straight at me, and said: 'May I speak with you aside for a few moments, Mr Canevin? Father and mother will excuse us.'

I rose and followed her out onto the great gallery which runs all along the front of Montparnasse House. And I knew, in my blood and bones, that Mr and Mrs Maclane did not so much as glance at one another when we had left the drawing-room. I could hear their voices as they conversed quietly together, all the time we were on the gallery.

Miss Gertrude led me to its extreme end and there, in the mellow light of a full moon and to the intoxicating accompaniment of jessamine and night-tuberose odors, faced me.

'I have something for you,' said I, and laid the necklace across her hands. 'This is for you, Miss Gertrude, with all my gratitude and all my admiration.'

'But – I cannot accept this,' she said, looking at the emeralds as they glowed in the moonlight.

'You will wear it, I was hoping, on your wedding day.'

'But, Mr Canevin, I am not considering being married. I am only nineteen.'

'But you will be married some day – God send, happily. Keep the necklace and bring it out when that delightful young gentleman who may be half-way worthy of you comes along. Let it be a portion of your trousseau.'

'But – I am not interested in "delightful young gentlemen", Mr Canevin.'

This conversation, it seemed to me, had got rather far away from what Miss Gertrude had summoned me out there on the gallery to talk about.

She was speaking again.

'I do not see why you should suggest such a thing to me, Mr Canevin.'

Women! I should never understand them! This, at that moment, I felt instinctively, hopelessly. I remembered, sharply, that almost telepathic feeling I have mentioned on my arrival.

'I am sure I ask your pardon if I have offended you,' I said lamely and stood aside, waiting for her to precede me back into the drawing-room.

I bowed slightly to indicate that I was waiting for her to pass. I think I even may have made a slight, indicative motion of the hand.

But she did not move, and I looked down at her, troubled, vaguely puzzled. Was this the simple, sweet Miss Gertrude who had entered into the comedy of that picture with an almost childish enthusiasm?

That picture! I think I shuddered slightly. She reached out the necklace toward me, but I did not take it back. With the strangest, most poignant look on her face, she was speaking again.

Like 'Annie Laurie's', her voice is low and sweet. All the phrases of that ballad of sentimental nonsense, as I was suddenly reminded, looking down at her, fit her like a glove.

'I think you have failed to understand me, and that is why you are vexed, Mr Canevin. You see – I cannot accept your gift. I am no longer a child, you will remember, and such a gift could come only from a near relative, or – or . . . '

She looked down. Her courage had given out. I saw her face, red as a red rose in the faint whiteness of that pouring moonlight.

The delicate, moaning coo of a disturbed wood dove came through the silent mahogany trees, and a little, faint puff of the evening trade wind came wandering across from the sea, across acres of sweet grass.

Light came to me then and blinded me.

' – or one who is to be your husband,' I finished for her, bending my head toward her. She did not move, and I reached out and took both her dear hands in mine, where they lay like lilies. The necklace hung across her wrists between us.

It was, suddenly, as though 'Annie Laurie', played very softly and sweetly and yet, somehow, madly, played by many well-tuned violins and fairy horns, surged all about me, and it went to my head like strong wine.

'And will you let me be that one?' I asked her quietly.

She left her hands where they were, and raised her lovely face and looked at me, all her shame gone now, and I took her into my arms . . .

A little after we went back into the drawing-room. Mr and Mrs Maclane were chatting quietly, precisely as we had left them. I bowed to both of them.

'I must not delay the happiness I have in informing you,' said I, and the words seemed to come to me with a clarity almost uncanny – the right words, for such an announcement – 'that I expect to have the honor of becoming your son-in-law.'

But, I assure you, no one, not even a Canevin, can get ahead of a real Crucian of the Old Scottish Gentry when it comes to these matters of courtesy.

'We are happy to welcome you into the family, Gerald,' said Mrs Maclane, without the flicker of an eyelash.

She rose and made me a quaint, Old World courtesy, and I bowed in return as she resumed her chair.

Mr Maclane took his wife's hand in his and said: 'My wife has spoken for both of us, Mr Canevin.'

'Gerald has given me this,' said Gertrude, and laid the necklace, blazing now under the electric chandelier, in her mother's lap.

Mrs Maclane examined it with interest, polite interest. Its value would easily have purchased Estate Montparnasse – yes, and several other contiguous estates thrown in.

'It is very kind of him,' said she, and handed the necklace back to her daughter.

Gertrude gave it to her father to examine. He looked at it with much the same type of merely courteous interest, and then clasped the lovely thing about his daughter's neck, which is 'like the swan', as 'Annie Laurie' has it. He kissed her gravely on her white forehead.

'We must have in a bottle of champagne to drink your health,' said he, and paused to bow to me again as he left the room to get it.

Of course I told Mrs Desmond about everything.

But no information could I derive from her that would throw any light on anything. She would only say: 'After I am dead, Mr Canevin!'

But on the matter of the picture's destruction she waxed eloquent.

'God be praised,' said she, 'that the fearful thing is no more! 'Twas my poor mother, God rest her soul, that was always wishful of having it destroyed and never daring; and as for me, Mr Canevin, as I've told you, there was more than paint went into it.

'But I believe every word. 'Tis enough of my Aunt Camilla's capabilities that I've heard about to leave no doubt in my mind. After I'm dead, Mr Canevin – after I'm dead, and not before!'

And that was all we were able to learn.

We had been married less than two months; the restoration of my estate was only just beginning to be under way, when Mrs Desmond departed this life at the age of seventy-six.

The English Church was full – St Paul's – and so, too, was the churchyard itself, for virtually the entire island turned out to pay its last respects to one of its most notable old inhabitants, a member of the Old Island Gentry who pass, these days, one by one.

Gertrude and I had come back on foot from the funeral – it is only a step to Melbourne House, where we were living until the estate-house should be ready – to be met by a young colored fellow, a clerk in Lawyer Esperson's employ. He handed me a long envelope and asked for a receipt, which I gave him.

The envelope, addressed to me, was one of Lawyer Esperson's. I tore it open, and within was a brief document, also addressed to me, and in the fine, beautifully formed, almost continental handwriting of Mistress Desmond herself.

I called Gertrude and we sat down together and I read it out.

Dear Mr Canevin

I have left instructions with Esperson that this is to be handed to you after my burial. I told you that I would clear up certain matters for you after I was gone.

There are two mysteries connected. One is why I would not touch a penny's value of what you discovered under Melbourne House. The other is how the evil takings of a 'Freetrader' could come there, to the residence of a respectable family.

I shall hope to clear up both of these. As to how it was done, God – and Satan – know. I cannot tell you that.

But this much I can, and will, tell you.

Even before my time, we of the gentry have been constrained to marry among ourselves. It's new blood, like your own, these islands are needing. I hope you will remain, now that you are to be married, and to one of a blood as good as your own.

For the reason I mention, we are mostly related like royalty!

I was courted by my cousin, James Desmond, whom I married. It was the uncle of my husband, Saul Macartney, who sought to marry my Aunt Camilla Lanigan in the generation before mine. This Saul was the only living child of his father, Thomas Macartney, who lived here on Santa Cruz, and was a merchant and shipowner in the island trade.

It is because James Desmond was his nephew that Melbourne House came to us by inheritance. It belonged to Saul Macartney.

This young gentleman was accustomed to go about the islands in charge of his father's vessel, the *Hope*. And in the intervals of these voyages he would be courting my Aunt Camilla Lanigan in St Thomas. A young man he was, so it is said, with but little of the fear of God, and none of the love, in his heart.

When his father died, leaving him Melbourne House, the ships, three sugar estates and a grand store here in Fredericksted, he was not content to marry my Aunt Camilla and settle down.

Off he went in the *Hope* again before his father was well settled in his grave. And on that very voyage, from which my Aunt Camilla had sought to disuade him, the *Hope* was captured off Caracas by Fawcett himself.

Saul Macartney, willing as always to turn to his own advantage what might betide, 'joined' Fawcett and rose to be second in command to the bloodiest villain that ever scourged the Caribbean.

Now, I am thinking, you begin to see light. The connection with the picture. What depended on that bitter fact?

It had not been known to me before you dug it up that treasure had been placed under Melbourne House. But consider, Mr Canevin, where better? It was Saul Macartney's property and only came, indeed, into the hands of my husband, James Desmond, his nephew, on Macartney's disgraceful death on the gallows in St Thomas.

Nothing could have been easier than for him to come ashore here, and Captain Fawcett with him belike, and do as he pleased on his own property. The people would bow to the ground before a 'Freetrader' in those days, and the fat of the land was not too good for them. Many had their fine houses ashore. Was not Henry Morgan himself knighted and made Leftenant Governor of Jamaica?

Saul Macartney went and came as he wished, and even sought to continue his courtship with my Aunt Camilla Lanigan. It was that which roused the bitter hatred of her against him, Mr

Canevin, and – woe betide the man that roused my Aunt Camilla Lanigan to hate!

For she knew how to hate, and how to make her hatred count, and may God our Heavenly Father have mercy on her soul.

Ann Jane Desmond

That was all. Granting it was true – and it was plausible enough, to be sure – it cleared up much that had been obscure; the identity of the pirate mate, for example.

But, as Mrs Desmond herself had said, it could not clear up how the thing had been brought about. Granted that Camilla Lanigan had acquired skill in black magic, and that is a great deal to grant in any such case, or any case at all, the rest fitted together like the halves of a trysting ring. I saw it all, from that point of view, and I shuddered internally.

I raised my head and looked at my dear wife. Her eyes were shining, and there was in them rather more than a suspicion of tears.

'What a vengeance!' she said, in her low, sweet voice. 'Saul Macartney choosing the life of a Freetrader as against that of a decent merchant! Reduced to what appeared on that canvas!

'Well – he is released now, Gerald. *We* released him. And he has rewarded us. I think we should pray for the repose of his soul. He is a century behind the others in Purgatory!'

'You believe – ' said I.

'If I were not certain you would call me "Victorian", ' my dear wife smiled through that suspicion of tears, 'I should say: "There are more things in heaven and earth, Horatio!" '

'We shall have to let it go at that, I imagine,' said I, 'but I am going to give St Paul's Church a complete new set of altar hangings in brocades, with some such idea as you have suggested.'

'Which idea?' inquired my wife.

'For the repose of his soul,' I answered.

'Williamson'

The death of Mrs Williamson Morley occurred in the early part of October, in San Francisco, only a couple of weeks before I was due to sail from New York for St Thomas, Virgin Islands, my usual winter habitat. It was too far to get to the funeral, although, being an old friend and school mate of Morley's, I should have attended under any ordinary circumstances. I do not happen to know what the Morleys were doing in San Francisco. They lived in New York, and had a summer place on Long Island and I never knew Morley to move about very much. I wrote him at once, of course, a long and intimate letter. In it I suggested his coming down to stay with me in St Thomas. I was there when I received his reply. He accepted, and said that he would be arriving about the middle of November and would cable me accordingly.

When he arrived he made quite a flutter among my negro house-servants; an impression, it seemed to me, that went much deeper, for some strange reason, than his five huge trunks of clothes would cause among such local dandies as my house-man, Stephen Penn. I am anything but 'psychic', despite some experience with various out-of-the-way matters among the Caribbean Islands and in various parts of the globe. Indeed, one of my chief aversions is the use of this word by anyone as applying to one's own character. But, 'psychic' or not, I could not help but feel that flutter, as I have called it. Mr Williamson Morley made a very striking impression indeed. I mention it because it recalled to me something I had entirely dropped out of my mind in the year or more since I had seen Sylvia, Morley's late wife. My servants, very obviously, showed an immediate, and inexplicable dread of him. I cannot, honestly, use a less emphatic word. When you notice your cook making the sign of the cross upon herself when she lays rolling, anxious eyes upon your house-guest, observe an unmistakable grayish tinge replacing the shining brown of your house-man's 'Zambo' cheeks as he furtively watches that guest at his morning setting-up exercises which Morley performed with vigor and gusto – when you notice things like this, you can hardly help wondering what it is all about, especially when you remember that the late wife of that house-guest was as unmistakably afraid of her genial husband!

I had never known Sylvia very well, but I had known her well enough to realize that during Williamson Morley's courtship there was no such element of fear in her reception of his advances preliminary to a marriage. I tried, when I did notice this thing, beginning not long after the wedding, not so much to explain it – I regarded it as inexplicable that anyone should have such feelings toward Morley whom I had known since we were small boys together in the same form at Berkeley School in New York City – as to classify it. I found that I could give it several names – dread, repulsion, even loathing.

It was too much for me. Williamson Morley inspiring any of these feelings, especially in the wife of his bosom! The thing, you see, was quite utterly ridiculous. There never was, there could not possibly be, a more kindly, normal, open-hearted and reasonable fellow than Morley himself. He was, and always had been, good-natured to the degree of a fault. He was the kind who would let anyone smack him in the face, and laugh at it, without even the thought of hitting back. He had always had a keen sense of humor. He was generous, and rich. He had inherited good-sized fortunes both from his father and mother, and had made a good deal more in his Wall Street office. Williamson Morley was what some people call 'a catch', for any woman.

Knowing him as well as I did it seemed rather tough that his wife, whom he plainly loved, should take things the way she did. Morley never said anything about it, even to me. But I could see what certain novelists name 'the look of pain in his eyes' more than once.

Morley's good-nature, more like that of a friendly big dog than anything else I could compare it to, was proverbial. His treatment of his wife, in the six or seven years of their married life, a good deal of which I saw with my own eyes, was precisely what anyone who knew him very well would expect of him. Sylvia had been a comparatively poor girl. Married to Morley, she had everything a very rich man's petted darling could possibly desire, Morley indulged her, lavished upon her innumerable possessions, kindnesses, privileges –

And yet, through it all there ran that unmistakable note of a strange unease, of a certain suggestion of dread in his presence on Sylvia's part.

I put it down to perverseness pure and simple after seeing it for the first year or so. I wasn't doing any guessing, you see, about Morley's 'inside' treatment of his wife. There was no bluff about the fellow, nothing whatever in the way of deceit or double-mindedness. I have seen him look at her with an expression which almost brought the tears into my eyes – a compound expression mingled out of respect and devotion, and puzzlement and a kind of dogged undertone as though he were saying, mentally, 'All right, my dear, I've done all I know how to make things go right and have you happy and contented, and I'm keeping it up indefinitely, hoping you'll see that I love you honestly, and would do anything in the world for you; and that I may find out what's wrong so that I can make it right.'

That invincible good-nature I have spoken of, that easy-going way of slipping along through life letting people smack you and not smacking them back which was always characteristic of Williamson Morley, was, I should hasten to make clear, not in the slightest degree due to any lack of ability on Morley's part to take care of himself, physically or otherwise. Quite the contrary! Morley had been, by far, our best athlete in school days. He held the interscholastic record for the twelve-pound shot and the twelve-pound hammer, records which, I believe, still stand. He was slow and a trifle awkward on his feet, it is true, but as a boxer and wrestler he was simply invincible. Our school trainer, Ernie Hjertberg, told me that he was the best junior athlete he had ever handled, and Ernie had a long and reputable record.

Morley went on with this in college. In fact, he became a celebrity, what with his succession of record-breaking puts of the sixteen-pound shot, and his tremendous heaves of the hammer of the same weight. Those two events were firsts for Haverford whenever their star heavyweight competed during his four years at that institution. He quit boxing after he had nearly killed the Yale man who was heavyweight champ in Morley's Freshman year, in the first round. He was intercollegiate champion wrestler of all weights for three and one-half years. Watching him handle the best of them was like watching a mother put her baby to bed! Morley simply brushed aside all attempts to hammerlock or half-nelson him, took hold of his opponent, and put him on his back and held him there long enough to record the fall; and then got up with one of those deprecating smiles on his face as much as to say: 'I hated to do that to you, old man – hope I didn't hurt you too much.'

All through his athletic career at school, for the four years we were together there, he showed only one queer trait. That, under the circumstances, was a very striking one. Morley would never get under the showers. No. A dry-rub for him, every time. He was a hairy fellow, as many very powerfully-built men are, and I have seen him many a time, after some competition event or a strenuous workout at our athletic field or winter days in the gymnasium shining with honest sweat so that he might have been lacquered! Nevertheless, no shower for Morley! Never anything but four or five dry towels, then the usual muscle-kneading and alcohol rub afterwards – invariably with his track or gym shoes on. That, in its way, was another, and the last, of Morley's peculiarities. From first to last, he never, to my knowledge, took off even for muscle-kneadings at the capable hands of Black Joe, our rubber, the shoes he had been wearing, nor, of course, the heavy woolen stockings he always wore under them.

When quizzed about his dry-rubs, Morley always answered with his unfailing good-nature, that it was a principle with him. He believed in the dry-rub. He avoided difficulty and criticism in this strange idea of his, as it seemed to the rest of us, because Ernie Hjertberg, whose word was law and whose opinions were gold and jewels to us boys, backed him up in it. Many of the older athletes, said Ernie, preferred the dry-rub, and a generation ago nobody would have thought of taking a shower after competition or a workout. So it became a settled affair that Williamson Morley should dry-rub himself while the rest of us revelled under our cascades of alternate hot and cold water and were cool and comfortable while Morley at least looked half-cooked, red, and uncomfortable after his plain towellings!

It was, too, entirely clear to the rest of us that Morley's dry-rubs were taken on principle. That he was a bather – at home – was entirely evident. He was, besides being by long odds the best-dressed fellow in a very dressy, rather 'fashionable' New York City school, the very pink and perfection of cleanliness. Indeed, if it had not been for Morley's admirable disposition, self-restraint, and magnificent muscular development and his outstanding athletic preëminence among us – our football teams with Morley in were simply invincible, and his inordinately long arms made him un-beatable at tennis – the school would very likely have considered him a 'dude'. A shot-putter, if it had been anybody else than Morley, who, however modestly, displays a fresh manicure twice a week at the group-critical age of fifteen or sixteen is – well, it was Morley, and whatever Morley chose to do among our crowd, or, indeed any group of his age in New York City in those days, was something that called for respectful imitation – not adverse criticism. Morley set the fashion for New York's foremost school for the four or five years that he and Gerald Canevin were buddies togther.

It was when we were sixteen that the Morley divorce case shrieked from the front pages of the yellow newspapers for the five weeks of its lurid course in the courts.

During that period I, who had been a constant visitor at the house on Madison Avenue where Williamson, an only son, lived with his parents, by some tacit sense of the fitness of things, refrained from dropping in Saturdays or after school hours. Subsequently, Mrs Morley, who had lost the case, removed to an apartment on Riverside Drive. Williamson accompanied his mother, and Mr Morley continued to occupy the former home.

It was a long time afterwards, a year or more, before Williamson talked of his family affairs with me. When he did begin it, it came with a rush, as though he had wanted to speak about it to a close friend for a long time and had been keeping away from the topic for decency's sake. I gathered from what he said that his mother was in no way to blame. This was not merely 'chivalry' on Williamson's part. He spoke reticently, but with a strong conviction. His father, it seemed, had always, as long as he could remember, been rather 'mean' to the kindest, most generous and whole-souled lady God had ever made. The attitude of Morley senior, as I gathered it, without, of course, hearing that gentleman's side of the affair, had always been distant and somewhat sarcastic, not only to Mrs Morley but to Williamson as well. It was, Williamson said, as though his father had disliked him from birth, thought of him as a kind of inferior being! This had been shown, uniformly, by a general attitude of contemptuous indifference to both mother and son as far back as Williamson's recollection of his father took him.

It was, according to him, the more offensive and unjust on his father's part, because, not long before his own birth, his mother had undergone a more than ordinarily harrowing experience, which, Williamson and I agreed, should have made any man that called himself a man considerate to half the woman Mrs Morley was, for the rest of his natural life!

The couple had, it appeared, been married about five years at the time, were as yet childless, and were living on the Island of Barbados in the Lower Caribbean. Their house was an estate-house, 'in the country', but quite close-in to the capital town, Bridgetown. Quite nearby, in the very next estate-house, in fact, was an eccentric old fellow, who was a retired animal collector. Mr Burgess, the neighbor, had been in the employ for many years before his retirement due to a bad clawing he had received in the wilds of Nepaul, of the Hagenbecks and Wombwells.

Mr Burgess's outstanding eccentricity was his devotion to 'Billy', a full-grown orang-utan which, like the fellow in Kipling's horrible story, *Bimi*, he treated like a man, had it at the table with him, had taught the creature to smoke – all that sort of thing. The negroes for miles around were in a state of sustained terror, Williamson said.

In fact, the *Bimi* story was nearly reënacted there in Barbados, only with a somewhat different slant. We boys at school read Kipling, and *Sherlock Holmes*, and Alfred Henry Lewis's *Wolfville* series those days, and *Bimi* was invoked as familiar to us both when Williamson told me what had happened.

It seems that the orang-utan and Mrs Morley were great friends. Old Burgess didn't like that very well, and Douglas Morley, Williamson's father, made a terrific to-do about it. He finally absolutely forbade his wife to go within a hundred yards of Burgess's place unless for the purpose of driving past!

Mrs Morley was a sensible woman. She listened to her husband's warnings about the treachery of the great apes, and the danger she subjected herself to in such matters as handing the orang-utan a cigarette, and willingly enough agreed to keep entirely away from their neighbor's place so long as the beast was maintained there at large and not, as Mr Morley formally demanded of Burgess, shut up in an adequate cage. Mr Morley even appealed to the law for the restraint of a dangerous wild beast, but could not, it appeared, secure the permanent caging of Burgess's strange pet.

Then, one night, coming home late from a Gentlemen's Party somewhere on the island, Mr Morley had walked into his house and discovered his wife unconscious, lying on the floor of the dining-room, most of her clothing torn off her, and great weals and bruises all over her where the orang-utan had attacked her, sitting alone in a small living-room next the dining-room.

Mrs Morley, hovering between life and death for days on end with a bad case of physiological shock, could give no account of what had occurred, beyond the startling apparition of 'Billy' in the open doorway, and his leap towards her. She had mercifully lost consciousness, and it was a couple of weeks before she was able to do so much as speak.

Meanwhile Morley, losing no time, had dug out a couple of his negroes from the estate-village, furnished them with hurricane-lanterns for light on a black and starless night, and, taking down his Martini-Henry elephant gun, and charging the magazine with explosive bullets, had gone out after the orang-utan, and blown the creature, quite justifiably of course, into a mound of bloody pulp. He had, again almost justifiably, it seemed to Williamson and me, been restrained only by his two Blacks disarming him lest he be hung by the neck until dead, from disposing of his neighbor, Burgess, with the last of the explosive cartridges. As it was, although Morley was not a man of any great physical force, being slightly built and always in somewhat precarious health, he had administered a chastising with his two hands to the fatuous ex-wild animal collector, which was long remembered in His Majesty King Edward's loyal colony of Barbados, B.W.I.

It was, as Williamson's maternal grandmother had confided to him, almost as though this horrible experience had unhinged Mr Morley's mind. Williamson himself had been born within a year, and Douglas Morley, who had in the meantime sold out the sugar estates in which most of his own and his young wife's money had been invested, had removed to New York where he instituted a Bond Brokerage business. This Williamson had inherited two years after his graduation from college, at the time of his father's death at the rather premature age of forty-seven.

Douglas Morley, according to his grandmother's report and his own experience, had included his son in the strange attitude of dislike and contemptuous indifference which the devastating experience with the orang-utan had seemed to bring into existence.

We were not out of school when Mrs Douglas Morley died, and Williamson went back to the Madison Avenue house to live with his father.

Mr Morley had a kind of apartment built in for him, quite separate from his own part of the house. He could not, it seemed, bear to have Williamson under his eye, even though his plain duty and ordinary usage and custom made it incumbent on him to share his home with his son. The two of them saw each other as little as possible. Williamson had inherited his mother's property, and this his father administered for him as I must record to his credit, in an admirably competent and painstaking manner, so that Williamson was already a rich man well before his father's death about doubled his material possessions.

I have gone into this detail largely because I want to accentuate how extremely regrettable, it seemed to me, was Sylvia's unaccountable attitude, which I have described, to one of the best and kindliest fellows on earth, after a childhood and youth such as he had been subjected to because of some obscure psychological slant of a very odd fish of a father for which, of course, he was in no way responsible himself.

Well, now Sylvia was gone, too, and Williamson Morley was once more alone in the world so far as the possession of near relatives went, and free to do about as he pleased.

His one comment, now that he was presumably settled down with me for the winter, about his late wife, I mean, was a very simple one, unconnected with anything that had been said or even alluded to, in answer to my carefully-phrased first personal word of regret for his loss.

'I did everything I knew how, Gerald.'

There was a world of meaning, a résumé of quiet suffering, patiently and I am sure bravely, borne in those few and simple words so characteristic of Williamson Morley.

He did, once, refer to his mother during his visit with me, which lasted for several months. It was apropos of his asking my help in classifying and arranging a brief-case full of papers, legal and otherwise, which he had brought along, the documentation connected with a final settlement of his financial affairs. He had disposed of his bond-brokerage business immediately after his wife's death.

There were various family records – wills, and suchlike – among these papers, and I noted among these as I sorted and helped arrange them for Morley, sitting opposite him at the big table on my West gallery, the recurring names of various kinsfolk of his – Parkers, Morleys, Graves, Putneys – but a total absence of the family name Williamson. I had asked him, without any particular purpose, hardly even curiosity over so small a matter, whether there were not some Williamson relatives, that being his own baptismal name.

'That's a curious thing, Gerald,' said Morley, reflectively, in his peculiarly deep and mellow voice. 'My poor mother always – well, simply *abominated* the name. I suppose that's how come I got it fastened on me – because she disliked it! You see, when I was born – it was in New York, in Roosevelt Hospital – my mother very nearly died. She was not a very big or strong person, and I was – er – rather a good-sized baby – weighed seventeen pounds or something outrageous at birth! Queer thing too – I nearly passed out during the first few days myself, they say! Undernourished. Sounds ridiculous, doesn't it. Yet, that was the verdict of three of New York's foremost obstetricians who were in on the case in consultation.

'Well, it seems, when I was about ten days old, and out of danger, my father came around in his car – it was a Winton, I believe in those days or perhaps, a Panhard – and carted me off to be baptized. My mother was still in a dangerous condition – they didn't let her up for a couple of weeks or so after that – and chose that name for me himself, so "Williamson" I've been, ever since!'

We had a really very pleasant time together. Morley was popular with the St Thomas crowd from the very beginning. He was too sensible to mope, and while he didn't exactly rush after entertainment, we went out a good deal, and there is a good deal to go out to in St Thomas, or was in those days, two years ago, before President Hoover's Economy Program took our Naval personnel out of St Thomas.

Morley's geniality, his fund of stories, his generous attitude to life, the outstanding kindliness and fellowship of the man, brought him a host of new friends, most of whom were my old friends. I was delighted that my prescription for poor old Morley – getting him to come down and stay with me that winter – was working so splendidly.

It was in company with no less than four of these new friends of Morley's, Naval Officers, all four of them, that he and I turned the corner around the Grand Hotel one morning about eleven o'clock and walked smack into trouble! The British sailorman of the Navy kind is, when normal, one of the most respectful and pleasant fellows alive. He is, as I have observed more than once, quite otherwise when drunk. The dozen or so British tars we encountered that moment, ashore from the Sloop-of-War *Amphitrite*, which lay in St Thomas's Harbor, were as nasty and truculent a group of human-beings as I have ever had the misfortune to encounter. There is no telling where they had acquired their present condition of semi-drunkenness, but there was no question whatever of their joint mood!

'Ho – plasterin' band o' brass-hat — — !' greeted the enormous cockney who seemed to be their natural leader, eyeing truculently the four white-drill tropical uniforms with their shoulder insignia, and rudely jostling Lieutenant Sankers, to whose house we were *en route* afoot that morning, 'fink ye owns the 'ole brasted universe, ye does. *I'll* show ye!!' and with that, the enormous bully, abetted by the salient jeers of his following which had, somehow, managed to elude their ship's Shore Police down to that moment, barged head first into Morley, seizing him first by both arms and leaving the soil-marks of a pair of very dirty hands on his immaculate white drill jacket. Then, as Morley quietly twisted himself loose without raising a hand against this attack, the big cockney swung an open hand, and landed a resounding slap across Morley's face.

This whole affair, of course, occupied no more than a few seconds. But I had time, and to spare, to note the red flush of a sudden, and I thought an unprecedented, anger in Morley's face; to observe the quick tightening of his tremendous muscles, the abrupt tensing of his long right arm, the beautifully-kept hand on the end of it hardening before my eyes into a great, menacing fist; the sudden glint in his deep-set dark-brown eyes, and then – then – I could hardly believe the evidence of my own two eyes – Williamson Morley, on his rather broad pair of feet, was trotting away, leaving his antagonist who had struck him in the face; leaving the rest of us together there in a tight little knot and an extremely unpleasant position on that corner. And then – well, the crisp 'quarter-deck' tones of Commander Anderson cut through that second's amazed silence which had fallen. Anderson had seized the psychological moment to turn-to these discipline-forgetting tars. He blistered them in a cutting vernacular in no way inferior to their own. He keel-hauled them, warming to his task.

Anderson had them standing at attention, several gaping-mouthed at his extraordinary skill in vituperation, by the time their double Shore Police squad came around the corner with truncheons in hand; and to the tender mercies of that businesslike and strictly sober group we left them.

We walked along in a complete silence, Morley's conduct as plainly dominating everything else in all our minds, as though we were five sandwich-men with his inexcusable cowardice blazoned on our fore-and-aft signboards.

We found him at the foot of the flight of curving steps with its really beautiful metal-wrought railing which leads up to the high entrance of Lieutenant Sankers's house. We went up the steps and into the house together, and when we had taken off our hats and gone into the 'hall', or living room, there fell upon us a silence so awkward as to transcend anything else of the kind in my experience.

I, for one, could not speak to save my life; could not, it seemed, so much as look at Morley. There was, too, running through my head a half-whispered bit of thick, native, negro, St Thomian speech, a dialect remark, made to herself, by an aged negress who had been standing, horrified, quite nearby, and who had witnessed our besetting and the fiasco of Morley's ignominious retreat after being struck full in the face. The old woman had muttered: 'Him actin' foo save him own soul, de mahn – Gahd keep de mahn stedfas'!'

And, as we stood there, and the piling-up silence was becoming simply unbearable, Morley, who quite certainly had not heard this comment of the pious old woman's, proceeded, calmly, in that mellow, deep baritone voice of his, to make a statement precisely bearing out the old woman's contention.

'You fellows are wondering at me, naturally. I'm not sure that even Canevin understands! You see, I've allowed myself to get really angry three times in my life, and the last time I took a resolution that nothing, nothing whatever, nothing *conceivable*, would ever do it to me again! I remembered barely in time this morning, gentlemen. The last time, you see, it cost me three weeks of suspense, nearly ruined me, waiting for a roughneck I had struck to die or recover – compound fracture – and I only tapped him, I thought! Look here!' as, looking about him, he saw a certain corporate lack of understanding on the five faces of his audience.

And, reaching up one of those inordinately long arms of his to where hung an old wrought-iron-barrelled musket, obviously an 'ornament' in Sankers's house, hired furnished, he took the thing down, and with no apparent effort at all, in his two hands, broke the stock away from the lock and barrel, and then, still merely with his hands, not using a knee for any pressure between them such as would be the obvious and natural method for any such feat attempted, with one sweep bent the heavy barrel into a right-angle.

He stood there, holding the strange-looking thing that resulted for us to look at, and then as we stood, speechless, fascinated, with another motion of his hands, and putting forth some effort this time – a herculean heave which made the veins of his forehead stand out abruptly and the sweat start up on his face on which the mark of the big cockney's hand now showed a bright crimson, Williamson Morley bent the gun-barrel back again into an approximate trueness and laid it down on Sankers' hall table.

'It's better the way it is, don't you think?' he remarked, quietly, dusting his hands together, 'rather than, probably to have killed that mucker out of Limehouse – maybe two or three of them, if they'd pitched in to help him.' Then, in a somewhat altered tone, a faintly perceptible trace of vehemence present in it, he added: 'I think you should agree with me, gentlemen!'

I think we were all too stultified at the incredible feat of brute strength we had just witnessed to get our minds very quickly off that. Sankers, our host for the time-being, came-to the quickest.

'Good God!' he cried out, 'of course – rather – Oh, very much so, Old Man! Good God! – Mere bones and cockney meat under those hands!'

And then the rest of them chimed in. It was a complete, almost a painful revulsion on the part of all of them. I, who had known Morley most of my life, had caught his point almost, as it happened, before he had begun to demonstrate it; about the time he had reached up after the old musket on the wall. I merely caught his eye and winked, aligning myself with him as against any possible adverse conclusion of the others.

This, of course, in the form of a choice story, was all over St Thomas, Black, White, and 'Coloured' St Thomas, within twenty-four hours, and people along the streets began to turn their heads to look after him, as the negroes had done since his arrival, whenever Morley passed among them.

I could hardly fail to catch the way in which my own household reacted to this new information about the physical strength of the stranger within its gates so soon as the grapevine route had apprized its dark-skinned members of the fact. Stephen Penn, the house-man, almost never looked at Morley now, except by the method known among West Indian negroes as 'cutting his eyes', which means a sidewise glance. Esmerelda, my extremely pious cook, appeared to add to the volume of her crooned hymn-tunes and frequently muttered prayers with which she accompanied her work. And once when my washer's pick'ny glimpsed him walking across the stone-flagged yard to the side entrance to the West gallery, that coal-black child's single garment lay stiff against the breeze generated by his flight towards the kitchen door and safety!

It was Esmerelda the cook who really brought about the set of conditions which solved the joint mysteries of Morley's father's attitude to him, his late wife's obvious feeling of dread, and the uniform reaction of every St Thomas negro whom I had seen in contact with Morley. The *dénouement* happened not very long after

Morley's demonstration in Lieutenant Sankers's house that morning of our encounter with the sailors.

Esmerelda had been trying-out coconut oil, a process, as performed in the West Indies, involving the boiling of a huge kettle of water. This, arranged outdoors, and watchfully presided over by my cook, had been going on for a couple of days at intervals. Into the boiling water Esmerelda would throw several panfuls of copra, the white meat dug out of the matured nuts. After the oil had been boiled out and when it was floating, this crude product would be skimmed off, and more copra put into the pot. The final process was managed indoors, with a much smaller kettle, in which the skimmed oil was 'boiled down' in a local refining process.

It was during this final stage in her preparation of the oil for the household that old Esmerelda, in some fashion of which I never, really heard the full account, permitted the oil to get on fire, and, in her endeavors to put out the blaze, got her dress afire. Her loud shrieks which expressed fright rather than pain, for the blazing oil did not actually reach the old soul's skin, brought Morley, who was alone at the moment on the gallery reading, around the house and to the kitchen door on the dead run. He visualized at once what had happened, and, seizing an old rag-work floor mat which Esmerelda kept near the doorway, advanced upon her to put out the fire.

At this she shrieked afresh, but Morley, not having the slightest idea that his abrupt answer to her yells for help had served to frighten the old woman almost into a fit, merely wrapped the floor-mat about her and smothered the flames. He got both hands badly burned in the process and Dr Pelletier dressed them with an immersion in more coconut oil and did them up in a pair of bandages about rubber tissue to keep them moist with the oil dressing inside, so that Morley's hands looked like a prize-fighter's with the gloves on. These pudding-like arrangements Dr Pelletier adjured his patient to leave on for at least forty-eight hours.

We drove home and I declined a dinner engagement for the next evening for Morley on the ground that he could not feed himself! He managed a bowl of soup between his hands at home that evening, and as he had a couple of fingers free outside the bandage on his left hand, assured me that he could manage undressing quite easily. I forgot all about his probable problem that evening, and did not go to his room to give him a hand as I had fully intended doing.

It was not until the next day at lunch that it dawned on me that Morley was fully dressed, although wearing pumps into which he could slip his feet, instead of shoes, and wondering how he had managed it. There were certain details, occurring to me, as quite out of the question for a man with hands muffled up all but the two outside fingers on the left hand as Morley was. Morley's tie was knotted with his usual careful precision; his hair, as always, was brushed with a meticulous exactitude. His belt-buckle was fastened.

I tried to imagine myself attending to all these details of dress with both thumbs and six of my eight fingers out of commission. I could not. It was too much for me.

I said nothing to Morley, but after lunch I asked Stephen Penn if he had assisted Mr Morley to dress.

Stephen said he had not. He had offered to do so, but Mr Morley had thanked him and replied it wasn't going to be necessary.

I was mystified.

The thing would not leave my mind all that afternoon while Morley sat out there on the West gallery with the bulk of the house between himself and the sun and read various magazines. I went out at last merely to watch him turn the pages. He managed that very easily, holding the magazine across his right forearm and grasping the upper, right-hand corner of a finished page between the two free fingers and the bandage itself whenever it became necessary to turn it over.

That comparatively simple affair, I saw, was no criterion.

The thing got to 'worrying' me. I waited, biding my time.

About ten minutes before dinner, carrying the silver swizzel-tray, with a clinking jug and a pair of tall, thin glasses, I proceeded to the door of Morley's room, tapped, rather awkwardly turned the door's handle, my other hand balancing the tray momentarily, and walked in on him. I had expected, you see, to catch him in the midst of dressing for dinner.

I caught him.

He was fully dressed, except for putting on his dinner jacket. He wore a silk soft shirt and his black tie was knotted beautifully, all his clothes adjusted with his accustomed careful attention to the detail of their precise fit.

I have said he was fully dressed, save for the jacket. Dressed, yes, *but not shod*. His black silk socks and the shining patent-leather pumps which would go on over them lay on the floor beside him, where he sat, in front of his bureau mirror, at the moment of my entrance brushing his ruddy-brown, rather coarse, but highly decorative hair with a pair of ebony-backed military brushes. Morley's hair had always been perhaps the best item of his general appearance. It was a magnificent crop, and of a sufficiently odd color to make it striking to look at without being grotesque or even especially conspicuous. Morley had managed a fine parting this evening in the usual place, a trifle to the right of the centre of his forehead. He was smoothing it down now, with the big, black-backed brushes with the long bristles, sitting, so to speak, on the small of his back in the chair.

With those pumps and socks not yet put on I saw Morley's feet for the first time in my life.

And seeing them I understood those dry rubs in the gymnasium when we were schoolboys together – that curious peculiarity of Morley's which caused him to take his rubs with his track shoes on! 'Curious peculiarity,' I have said. The phrase is fairly accurate, descriptive, I should be inclined to think, of those feet – feet with well-developed thumbs, like huge, broad hands – feet which he had left to clothe this evening until the last end of his dressing for dinner, because – well, because he had been using them to fasten his shirt at the neck, and tie that exquisite knot in his evening bow. He was using them now, in fact, as I looked dumbfounded, at him, to hold the big military brushes with which he was arranging that striking hair of his.

He caught me, of course, my entrance with the tray – which I managed not to drop – and at first he looked annoyed, and then, true to his lifelong form, Williamson Morley grinned at me in the looking-glass.

'O – good!' said he. 'That's great, Gerald. But, Old Man, I think I'll ask you to hold my glass for me, if you please. Brushing one's hair, you see – er – this way, is one thing. Taking a cocktail is, really, quite another.'

And then, quite suddenly, it dawned upon me, and very nearly made me drop that tray after all, why Morley's father had named him 'Williamson'.

I set the tray down, very carefully, avoiding Morley's embarrassed eyes, feeling abysmally ashamed of myself for what I, his host, had done – nothing, of course, farther from my mind than that I should run into any such oddment as this. I poured out the glasses. I wiped off a few drops I had spilled on the top of the table where I had set the tray. All this occupied some little time, and all through it I did not once glance in Morley's direction.

And when I did, at last, carry his glass over to him, and, looking at him, I am sure, with something like shame in my eyes wished him 'Good Health' after our West Indian fashion of taking a drink;

Morley needed my hand with his glass in it at his mouth, for the black silk socks and the shining, patent-leather pumps were on his feet now, and the slight flush of his embarrassment had faded entirely from his honest, good-natured face.

And, I thought down inside me, that, whatever his motive in his unique chagrin, Douglas Morley had honored him by naming him 'Williamson!' For Williamson Morley, as I had never doubted, and doubted just at that moment rather less than ever before, was a better man than his father – whichever way you care to take it.

The Shut Room

It was Sunday morning and I was coming out of All Saints' Church, Margaret Street, along with the other members of the hushed and reverent congregation, when, near the entrance doors, a hand fell lightly on my shoulder. Turning, I perceived that it was the Earl of Carruth. I nodded, without speaking, for there is that in the atmosphere of this great church, especially after one of its magnificent services and heart-searching sermons, which precludes anything like the hum of conversation which one meets with in many places of worship.

In these worldly and 'scientific' days it is unusual to meet with a person of Lord Carruth's intellectual and scientific attainments who troubles very much about religion. As for me, Gerald Canevin, I have always been a church-going fellow.

Carruth accompanied me in silence through the entrance doors and out into Margaret Street. Then, linking his arm in mine, he guided me, still in silence, to where his Rolls-Royce car stood at the curbstone.

'Have you any luncheon engagement, Mr Canevin?' he inquired, when we were just beside the car, the footman holding the door open.

'None whatever,' I replied.

'Then do me the pleasure of lunching with me,' invited Carruth.

'I was planning on driving from church to your rooms,' he explained, as soon as we were seated and the car whirling us noiselessly toward his town house in Mayfair. 'A rather extraordinary matter has come up, and Sir John has asked me to look into it. Should you care to hear about it?'

'Delighted,' I acquiesced, and settled myself to listen.

To my surprise, Lord Carruth began reciting a portion of the Nicene Creed, to which, sung very beautifully by All Saints' choir, we had recently been listening.

'Maker of Heaven and earth,' quoted Carruth, musingly, 'and of all things – visible and *invisible*.' I started forward in my seat. He had given a peculiar emphasis to the last word, 'invisible'.

'A fact,' I ejaculated, 'constantly forgotten by the critics of religion! The Church has always recognized the existence of the invisible creation.'

'Right, Mr Canevin. And – this invisible creation; it doesn't mean merely angels!'

'No one who has lived in the West Indies can doubt that,' I replied.

'Nor in India,' countered Carruth. 'The fact – that the Creed attributes to God the authorship of an invisible creation – is an interesting commentary on the much-quoted remark of Hamlet to Horatio: "There are more things in Heaven and earth, Horatio, than are dreamed of in your philosophy." Apparently, Horatio's philosophy, like that of the present day, took little account of the spiritual side of affairs; left out God *and what He had made*. Perhaps Horatio had recited the creed a thousand times, and never realized what that clause implies!'

'I have thought of it often, myself,' said I. 'And now – I am all curiosity – what, please, is the application?'

'It is an ocurrence in one of the old coaching inns,' began Carruth, 'on the Brighton Road; a very curious matter. It appears that the proprietor – a gentleman, by the way, Mr William Snow, purchased the inn for an investment just after the Armistice – has been having a rather unpleasant time of it. It has to do with shoes!'

'Shoes?' I inquired; 'shoes!' It seemed an abrupt transition from the Nicene Creed to shoes!

'Yes,' replied Carruth, 'and not only shoes but all sorts of leather affairs. In fact, the last and chief difficulty was about the disappearance of a commercial traveler's leather sample-case. But I perceive we are arriving home. We can continue the account at luncheon.'

During lunch he gave me a rather full account, with details, of what had happened at 'The Coach and Horses' Inn on the Brighton Road, an account which I will briefly summarize as follows.

Snow, the proprietor, had bought the old inn partly for business reasons, partly for sentimental. It had been a portion, up to about a century before, of his family's landed property. He had repaired and enlarged it, modernized it in some ways, and in general restored a much rundown institution, making 'The Coach and Horses' into a paying investment. He had retained, so far as possible, the antique architectural features of the old coaching inn, and before very long had built up a motor clientèle of large proportions by sound and careful management.

Everything, in fact, had prospered with the gentleman-innkeeper's affairs until there began, some four months back, a series of un-accountable disappearances. The objects which had, as it were, vanished into thin air, were all – and this seemed to me the most curious and bizarre feature of Carruth's recital – leather articles. Pair after pair of shoes or boots, left outside bedroom doors at night, would be gone the next morning. Naturally the 'boots' was suspected of theft. But the 'boots' had been able to prove his innocence easily enough. He was, it seemed, a rather intelligent broken-down jockey, of a keen wit. He had assured Mr Snow of his surprise as well as of his innocence, and suggested that he take a week's holiday to visit his aged mother in Kent and that a substitute 'boots', chosen by the proprietor, should take his place. Snow had acquiesced, and the disappearance of guests' footwear had continued, to the consternation of the substitute, a total stranger, obtained from a London agency.

That exonerated Billings, the jockey, who came back to his duties at the end of his holiday with his character as an honest servant intact. Moreover, the disappearances had not been confined to boots and shoes. Pocketbooks, leather luggage, bags, cigarette cases – all sorts of leather articles went the way of the earlier boots and shoes, and besides the expense and annoyance of replacing these, Mr Snow began to be seriously concerned about the reput-ation of his house. An inn in which one's leather belongings are known to be unsafe would not be a very strong financial asset. The matter had come to a head through the disappearance of the commercial traveler's sample-case, as noted by Carruth in his first brief account of this mystery. The main difficulty in this affair was that the traveler had been a salesman of jewelry, and Snow had been confronted with a bill for several hundred pounds, which he had felt constrained to pay. After that he had laid the mysterious matter before Sir John Scott, head of Scotland Yard, and Scott had called in Carruth because he recognized in Snow's story certain elements which caused him to believe this was no case for mere criminal investigation.

After lunch Carruth ordered the car again, and, after stopping at my rooms for some additional clothing and the other necessities for an over-night visit, we started along the Brighton Road for the scene of the difficulty.

We arrived about four that Sunday afternoon, and immediately went into conference with the proprietor.

Mr William Snow was a youngish middle-aged gentleman, very well dressed, and obviously a person of intelligence and natural attainments. He gave us all the information possible, repeating, with many details, the matters which I have already summarized, while we listened in silence. When he had finished: 'I should like to ask some questions,' said Carruth.

'I am prepared to answer anything you wish to enquire about,' Mr Snow assured us.

'Well, then, about the sentimental element in your purchase of the inn, Mr Snow – tell us, if you please, what you may know of the more ancient history of this old hostelry. I have no doubt there is history connected with it, situated where it is. Undoubtedly, in the coaching days of the Four Georges, it must have been the scene of many notable gatherings.'

'You are right, Lord Carruth. As you know, it was a portion of the property of my family. All the old registers are intact, and are at your disposal. It is an inn of very ancient foundation. It was, indeed, old in those days of the Four Georges, to whom you refer. The records go back well into the Sixteenth Century, in fact; and there was an inn here even before registers were kept. They are of comparatively modern origin, you know. Your ancient landlord kept, I imagine, only his "reckoning"; he was not concerned with records; even licenses are comparatively modern, you know.'

The registers were produced, a set of bulky, dry-smelling, calf-bound volumes. There were eight of them. Carruth and I looked at each other with a mutual shrug.

'I suggest,' said I, after a slight pause, 'that perhaps you, Mr Snow, may already be familiar with the contents of these. I should imagine it might require a week or two of pretty steady application even to go through them cursorily.'

Mr William Snow smiled. 'I was about to offer to mention the high points,' said he: 'I have made a careful study of these old volumes, and I can undoubtedly save you both a great deal of reading. The difficulty is – what shall I tell you? If only I knew what to put my finger upon – but I do not, you see!'

'Perhaps we can manage that,' threw in Carruth, 'but first, may we not have Billings in and question him?'

The former jockey, now the boots at 'The Coach and Horses,' was summoned and proved to be a wizened, copper-faced individual, with a keen eye and a deferential manner. Carruth invited him to a seat and he sat, gingerly, on the very edge of a chair while we talked with him. I will make so attempt to reproduce his accent, which is quite beyond me. His account was somewhat as follows, omitting the questions asked him both by Carruth and myself.

'At first it was only boots and shoes. Then other things began to go. The things always disappeared at night. Nothing ever disappeared before midnight, because I've sat up and watched many's the time. Yes, we tried everything: watching, even tying up leather things, traps! Yes, sir – steel traps, baited with a boot! Twice we did that. Both times the boot was gone in the morning, the trap not even sprung. No, sir – no one possibly among the servants. Yet, an "inside" job; it couldn't have been otherwise. From all over the house, yes. My old riding-boots – two pairs – gone completely; not a trace; right out of my room. That was when I was down in Kent as Mr Snow's told you, gentlemen. The man who took my place slept in my room, left the door open one night – boots gone in the morning, right under his nose.

'Seen anything? Well, sir, in a manner, yes – in a manner, no! To be precise, no. I can't say that I ever saw anything, that is, anybody; no, nor any apparatus as you might say, in a manner of speaking – no hooks no strings, nothing used to take hold of the things – but – ' Here Billings hesitated, glanced at his employer, looked down at his feet, and his coppery face turned a shade redder.

'Gentlemen,' said he, as though coming to a resolution, 'I can only tell you the God's truth about it. You may think me barmy – shouldn't blame you if you did! But – I'm as much interested in this 'ere thing as Mr Snow 'imself, barrin' that I 'aven't had to pay the score – make up the value of the things, I mean, as 'e 'as. I'll tell you – so 'elp me Gawd, gentlemen, it's a fact – I *ave* seen something, absurd as it'll seem to you. I've seen – '

Billings hesitated once more, dropped his eyes, looked distressed, glanced at all of us in the most shamefaced, deprecating manner imaginable, twiddled his hands together, looked, in short, as though he were about to own up to it that he was, after all, responsible for the mysterious disappearances; then finally said: 'I've seen things disappear – through the air! Now – it's hout! But it's a fact, gentlemen all – so 'elp me, it's the truth. Through the air, just as if someone were carrying them away – someone invisible I mean, in a manner of speaking – bloomin' pair of boots, swingin' along through the bloomin' air – enough to make a man say 'is prayers, for a fact!'

It took considerable assuring on the part of Carruth and myself to convince the man Billings that neither of us regarded him as demented, or, as he pithily expressed it, 'barmy'. We assured him, while our host sat looking at his servant with a slightly puzzled frown, that, on the contrary, we believed him implicitly, and furthermore that we regarded his statement as distinctly helpful. Mr Snow, obviously convinced that something in his diminutive servitor's mental works was unhinged, almost demurred to our request that we go, forthwith, and examine the place in the hotel where Billings alleged his marvel to have occurred.

We were conducted up two flights of winding steps to the story which had, in the inn's older days, plainly been an attic. There, Billings indicated, was the scene of the disappearance of the 'bloomin' boot, swingin' along – unaccompanied – through the bloomin' air'.

It was a sunny corridor, lighted by the spring sunlight through several quaint, old-fashioned, mullioned windows. Billings showed us where he had sat, on a stool in the corridor, watching; indicated the location of the boots, outside a doorway of one of the less expensive guest-rooms; traced for us the route taken by the disappearing boots.

This route led us around a corner of the corridor, a corner which, the honest 'boots' assured us, he had been 'too frightened' to negotiate on the dark night of the alleged marvel.

But we went around it, and there, in a small, right-angled hallway, it became at once apparent to us that the boots on that occasion must have gone through one of two doorways, opposite each other at either side, or else vanished into thin air.

Mr Snow, in answer to our remarks on this subject, threw open the door at the right. It led into a small, but sunny and very comfortable-looking bed-chamber, shining with honest cleanliness and decorated tastefully with chintz curtains with valances, and containing several articles of pleasant, antique furniture. This room, as the repository of air-traveling boots, seemed unpromising. We looked in in silence.

'And what is on the other side of this short corridor?' I enquired.

'The "shut room", ' replied Mr William Snow.

Carruth and I looked at each other.

'Explain, please,' said Carruth.

'It is merely a room which has been kept shut, except for an occasional cleaning,' replied our host, readily, 'for more than a century. There was, as a matter of fact, a murder committed in it in the year 1818, and it was, thereafter, disused. When I purchased the inn, I kept it shut, partly, I dare say, for sentimental reasons; partly, perhaps, because it seemed to me a kind of asset for an ancient hostelry. It has been known as "the shut room" for more than a hundred years. There was, otherwise, no reason why I should not have put the room in use. I am not in the least superstitious.'

'When was the room last opened?' I enquired.

'It was cleaned about ten days ago, I believe,' answered Mr Snow.

'May we examine it?' asked Carruth.

'Certainly,' agreed Snow, and forthwith sent Billings after the key.

'And may we hear the story – if you know the details – of the murder to which you referred?' Carruth asked.

'Certainly,' said Snow, again. 'But it is a long and rather complicated story. Perhaps it would do better during dinner.'

In this decision we acquiesced, and, Billings returning with the key, Snow unlocked the door and we looked into 'the shut room'. It was quite empty, and the blinds were drawn down over the two windows. Carruth raised these, letting in a flood of sunlight. The room was utterly characterless to all appearance, but – I confess to a certain 'sensitivity' in such matters – I 'felt' something like a faint, ominous chill. It was not, as the word I have used suggests, anything like physical cold. It was, so to express it, mentally cold. I despair of expressing what I mean more clearly. We looked over the entire room, an easy task as there was absolutely nothing to attract the eye. Both windows were in the wall at our right hand as we entered, and, save for the entrance door through which we had just come, the other three walls were quite blank.

Carruth stepped half-way out through the doorway and looked at the width of the wall in which the door was set. It was, perhaps, ten inches thick. He came back into the room, measured with his glance the distance from window-wall to the blank wall opposite the windows, again stepped outside, into the passageway this time, and along it until he came to the place where the short passage turned into the longer corridor from which we had entered it. He turned to his right this time, I following him curiously, that is, in the direction opposite that from which we had walked along the corridor, and tapped lightly on the wall there.

'About the same thickness, what?' he enquired of Snow.

'I believe so,' came the answer. 'We can easily measure it.'

'No, it will not be necessary, I think. We know that it is approximately the same.' Carruth ceased speaking and we followed him back into the room once more. He walked straight across it, rapped on the wall opposite the doorway.

'And how thick is this wall?' he enquired.

'It is impossible to say,' replied Snow, looking slightly mystified. 'You see, there are no rooms on that side, only the outer wall, and no window through which we could easily estimate the thickness. I suppose it is the same as the others, about ten inches I'd imagine.'

Carruth nodded, and led the way out into the hallway once more. Snow looked enquiringly at Carruth, then at me.

'It may as well be locked again,' offered Carruth, 'but – I'd be grateful if you'd allow me to keep the key until tomorrow.'

Snow handed him the key without comment, but a slight look of puzzlement was on his face as he did so. Carruth offered no comment, and I thought it wise to defer the question which was on my lips until later when we were alone. We started down the long corridor toward the staircase, Billings touching his forehead and stepping on ahead of us and disappearing rapidly down the stairs, doubtless to his interrupted duties in the scullery.

'It is time to think of which rooms you would prefer,' suggested our pleasant-voiced host as we neared the stairs. 'Suppose I show you some which are not occupied, and you may, of course, choose what suit you best.'

'On this floor, if you please,' said Carruth, positively.

'As you wish, of course,' agreed Snow, 'but, the better rooms are on the floor below. Would you not, perhaps, prefer – '

'Thank you no,' answered Carruth. 'We shall prefer to be up here if we may, and – if convenient – a large room with two beds.'

'That can be managed very easily,' agreed Snow. He stepped back a few paces along the corridor, and opened a door. A handsome, large room, very comfortably and well furnished, came to our view. Its excellence spoke well for the management of The Coach and Horses. The 'better' rooms must indeed be palatial if this were a fair sample of those somewhat less desirable.

'This will answer admirably,' said Carruth, directing an eyebrow at me. I nodded hastily. I was eager to acquiesce in anything he might have in mind.

'Then we shall call it settled,' remarked Snow. 'I shall have your things brought up at once. Perhaps you would like to remain here now?'

'Thank you,' said Carruth. 'What time do we dine?'

'At seven, if you please, or later if you prefer. I am having a private room for the three of us.'

'That will answer splendidly,' agreed Carruth, and I added a word of agreement. Mr Snow hurried off to attend to the sending up of our small luggage, and Carruth drew me at once into the room.

'I am a little more than anxious,' he began, 'to hear that tale of the murder. It is an extraordinary step forward – do you not agree with me? – that Billings's account of the disappearing boots – "through the air" – should fit so neatly and unexpectedly into their going around that corner of the corridor where "the shut room" is. It sets us forward, I imagine. What is your impression, Mr Canevin?'

'I agree with you heartily,' said I. 'The only point on which I am not clear is the matter of the thickness of the walls. Is there anything in that?'

'If you will allow me, I'll defer that explanation until we have had the account of the murder at dinner,' said Carruth, and, our things arriving at that moment, we set about preparing for dinner.

Dinner, in a small and beautifully furnished private room, did more, if anything more were needed, to convince me that Mr William Snow's reputation as a successful modern innkeeper had been well earned. It was a thoroughly delightful meal in all respects, but that, in a general way, is really all that I remember about it because my attention was wholly occupied in taking in every detail of the strange story which our host unfolded to us beginning with the fish course – I think it was a fried sole – and which ended only when we were sipping the best coffee I had tasted since my arrival in England from our United States.

'In the year 1818,' said Mr Snow, 'near the end of the long reign of King George III – the king, you will remember, Mr Canevin, who gave you Americans your Fourth of July – this house was kept by one James Titmarsh. Titmarsh was a very old man. It was his boast that he had taken over the landlordship in the year that His Most Gracious Majesty, George III, had come to the throne, and that he would last as long as the king reigned! That was in the year 1760, and George III had been reigning for fifty-eight years. Old Titmarsh, you see, must have been somewhere in the neighborhood of eighty, himself.

'Titmarsh was something of a "character". For some years the actual management of the inn had devolved upon his nephew, Oliver Titmarsh, who was middle-aged, and none too respectable, though, apparently, an able taverner. Old Titmarsh if tradition is to be believed, had many a row with his deputy, but, being himself childless, he was more or less dependent upon Oliver, who consorted with low company for choice, and did not bear the best of reputations in the community. Old Titmarsh's chief bugbear, in connection with Oliver, was the latter's friendship with Simon Forrester. Forrester lacked only a bard to be immortal. But – there was no Cowper to his John Gilpin, so to speak. No writer of the period, nor indeed since, has chosen to set forth Forrester's exploits. Nevertheless, these were highly notable. Forrester was the very king-pin of the highwaymen, operating with extraordinary success and daring along the much-traveled Brighton Road.

'Probably Old Titmarsh was philosopher enough to ignore his nephew's associations and acts so long as he attended to the business of the inn. The difficulty, in connection with Forrester, was that Forrester, an extraordinarily bold fellow, whose long immunity from the gallows had caused him to believe himself possessed of a kind of charmed life, constantly resorted to The Coach and Horses, which, partly because of its convenient location, and partly because of its good cheer, he made his house-of-call.

'During the evening of the first of June, in the year 1818, a Royal Courier paused at The Coach and Horses for some refreshment and a fresh mount. This gentleman carried one of the old king's peremptory messages to the Prince of Wales, then sojourning at Brighton, and who, under his sobriquet of "First Gentleman of Europe", was addicted to a life which sadly irked his royal parent at Whitehall. It was an open secret that only Prince George's import-ance to the realm as heir apparent to the throne prevented some very drastic action being taken against him for his innumerable follies and extravagances, on the part of king and parliament. This you will recall, was two years before the old king died and "The First Gentleman" came to the throne as George IV.

'The Royal Messenger, Sir William Greaves, arriving about nine in the evening after a hard ride, went into the coffee-room, to save the time which the engagement and preparation of a private room would involve, and when he paid his score, he showed a purse full of broad gold pieces. He did not know that Simon Forrester, sitting behind him over a great mug of mulled port, took careful note of this unconscious display of wealth in ready money. Sir William delayed no longer than necessary to eat a chop and drink a pot of "Six Ale". Then, his spurs clanking, he took his departure.

'He was barely out of the room before Forrester, his wits, perhaps, affected by the potations which he had been imbibing, called for his own mount, Black Bess, and rose, slightly stumbling to his feet, to speed the pot-boy on his way to the stables.

' "Ye'll not be harrying a Royal Messenger a-gad's sake, Simon," protested his companion, who was no less a person than Oliver Titmarsh, seizing his crony by his ruffled sleeve of laced satin.

' "Unhand me!" thundered Forrester; then, boastfully, "There's no power in England'll stay Sim Forrester when he chooses to take the road!"

'Somewhat unsteadily he strode to the door, and roared his commands to the stable-boy, who was not leading Black Bess rapidly enough to suit his drunken humor. Once in the saddle, the fumes of the wine he had drunk seemed to evaporate. Without a word Simon Forrester set out, sitting his good mare like a statue, in the wake of Sir William Greaves toward Brighton.

'The coffee-room – as Oliver Titmarsh turned back into it from the doorway whither he had accompanied Forrester – seethed into an uproar. Freed from the dominating presence of the truculent ruffian who would as soon slit a man's throat as look him in the eye along the sights of his horse-pistol from behind the black mask, the numerous guests, silent before, had found their tongues. Oliver Titmarsh sought to drown out their clamor of protest, but before he could succeed, Old Titmarsh, attracted by the unwonted noise, had hobbled down the short flight of steps from his private cubbyhole and entered the room.

'It required only a moment despite Oliver's now frantic efforts to stem the tide of comment, before the old man had grasped the purport of what was toward. Oliver secured comparative silence, then urged his aged uncle to retire. The old man did so, muttering helplessly, internally cursing his age and feebleness which made it out of the question for him to regulate this scandal which had originated in his inn. A King's Messenger, then as now, was sacred in the eyes of all decent citizens. A King's Messenger – to be called on to "stand and deliver" by the villainous Forrester! It was too much. Muttering and grumbling, the old man left the room, but, instead of going back to his easy-chair and his pipe and glass, he stepped out through the kitchens, and, without so much as a lantern to light his path, groped his way to the stables.

'A few minutes later the sound of horse's hoofs in the cobbled stable-yard brought a pause in the clamor which had once more broken out and now raged in the coffee-room. Listening, those in the coffee-room heard the animal trot out through the gate, and the diminishing sound of its galloping as it took the road toward Brighton. Oliver Titmarsh rushed to the door, but the horse and its rider were already out of sight. Then he ran up to his ancient uncle's room, only to find the crafty old man apparently dozing in his chair. He hastened to the stables. One of the grooms was gone, and the best saddle-horse. From the others, duly warned by Old Titmarsh, he could elicit nothing. He returned to the coffee-room in a towering rage and forthwith cleared it, driving his guests out before him in a protesting herd.

'Then he sat down, alone, a fresh bottle before him, to await developments.

'It was more than an hour later when he heard the distant beat of a galloping horse's hoofs through the quiet June night, and a few minutes later Simon Forrester rode into the stable-yard and cried out for an hostler for his Bess.

'He strode into the coffee-room a minute later, a smirk of satisfaction on his ugly, scarred face. Seeing his crony, Oliver, alone, he drew up a chair opposite him, removed his coat, hung it over the back of his chair, and placed over its back where the coat hung, the elaborate leather harness consisting of crossed straps and holsters which he always wore. From the holsters protruded the grips of "Jem and Jack", as Forrester had humorously named his twin horsepistols, huge weapons, splendidly kept, each of which threw an ounce ball. Then, drawing back the chair, he sprawled in it at his ease, fixing on Oliver Titmarsh an evil grin and bellowing loudly for wine.

' "For," he protested, "my throat is full of the dust of the road, Oliver, and, lad, there's enough to settle the score, never doubt me!" and out upon the table he cast the bulging purse which Sir William Greaves had momentarily displayed when he paid his score an hour and half back.

'Oliver Titmarsh, horrified at this evidence that his crony had actually dared to molest a King's Messenger, glanced hastily and fearfully about him, but the room, empty and silent save for their own presence, held no prying inimical informer. He began to urge upon Forrester the desirability of retiring. It was approaching eleven o'clock, and while the coffee-room was, fortunately, empty, no one knew who might enter from the road or come down from one of the guest-rooms at any moment. He shoved the bulging purse, heavy with its broad gold-pieces, across the table to his crony, beseeching him to pocket it, but Forrester, drunk with the pride of his exploit, which was unique among the depredations of the road's gentry, boasted loudly and tossed off glass after glass of the heavy port wine a trembling pot-boy had fetched him.

'Then Oliver's entreaties were supplemented from an unexpected source. Old Titmarsh, entering through a door in the rear wall of the coffee-room, came silently and leaned over the back of the ruffian's chair, and added a persuasive voice to his nephew's entreaties.

' "Best go up to bed, now, Simon, my lad," croaked the old man, wheedlingly, patting the bulky shoulders of the hulking ruffian with his palsied old hands.

'Forrester, surprised, turned his head and goggled at the gray-beard. Then, with a great laugh, and tossing off a final bumper, he rose unsteadily to his feet, and thrust his arms into the sleeves of the fine coat which old Titmarsh, having detached from the back of the chair, held out to him.

' "I'll go, I'll go, old Gaffer," he kept repeating as he struggled into his coat, with mock jocularity, "seeing you're so careful of me! Gad's hooks! I might as well! There be no more purses to rook this night, it seems!"

'And with this, pocketing the purse and taking over his arm the pistol-harness which the old man thrust at him, the villain lumbered up the stairs to his accustomed room.

' "Do thou go after him, Oliver," urged the old man. "I'll bide here and lock the doors. There'll likely be no further custom this night."

'Oliver Titmarsh, sobered, perhaps, by his fears, followed Forrester up the stairs, and the old man, crouched in one of the chairs, waited and listened, his ancient ears cocked against a certain sound he was expecting to hear.

'It came within a quarter of an hour – the distant beat of the hoofs of horses, many horses. It was, indeed, as though a considerable company approached The Coach and Horses along the Brighton Road. Old Titmarsh smiled to himself and crept toward the inn doorway. He laboriously opened the great oaken door and peered into the night. The sound of many hoofbeats was now clearer, plainer.

'Then, abruptly, the hoofbeats died on the calm June air. Old Titmarsh, somewhat puzzled, listened, tremblingly. Then he smiled in his beard once more. Strategy, this! Someone with a head on his shoulders was in command of that troop! They had stopped, at some distance, lest the hoofbeats should alarm their quarry.

'A few minutes later the old man heard the muffled sound of careful footfalls, and, within another minute, a King's Officer in his red coat had crept up beside him.

' "He's within," whispered Old Titmarsh, "and well gone by now in his damned drunkard's slumber. Summon the troopers, sir. I'll lead ye to where the villain sleeps. He hath the purse of His Majesty's Messenger upon him. What need ye of better evidence?"

' "Nay," replied the train-band captain in a similar whisper, "that evidence, even, is not required. We have but now taken up the dead body of Sir William Greaves beside the highroad, an ounce ball through his honest heart. 'Tis a case, this, of drawing and quartering, Titmarsh; thanks to your good offices in sending your boy for me."

'The troopers gradually assembled. When eight had arrived, the captain, preceded by Old Titmarsh and followed in turn by his trusty eight, mounted the steps to where Forrester slept. It was, as you have guessed, the empty room you examined this afternoon, "the shut room" of this house.

'At the foot of the upper stairs the captain addressed his men in a whisper: "A desperate man, this, lads. 'Ware bullets! Yet – he must needs be taken alive, for the assizes, and much credit to them that take him. He hath been a pest of the road as well ye know these many years agone. Upon him, then, ere he rises from his drunken sleep! He hath partaken heavily. Pounce upon him ere he rises."

'A mutter of acquiescence came from the troopers. They tightened their belts, and stepped alertly, silently, after their leader, preceded by their ancient guide carrying a pair of candles.

'Arrived at the door of the room the captain disposed his men and crying out "in the King's name!" four of these stout fellows threw themselves against the door. It gave at once under that massed impact, and the men rushed into the room, dimly lighted by Old Titmarsh's candles.

'Forrester, his eyes blinking evilly in the candle-light, was half-way out of bed when they got into the room. He slept, he was accustomed to boast, "with one eye open, drunk or sober!" Throwing off the coverlid, the highwayman leaped for the chair over the back of which hung his fine laced coat, the holsters uppermost. He plunged his hands into the holsters, and stood, for an instant, the very picture of baffled amazement.

'The holsters were empty!

'Then, as four stalwart troopers flung themselves upon him to bear him to the floor, there was heard Old Titmarsh's harsh, senile cackle.

' " 'Twas I that robbed ye, ye villain – took your pretty boys, your 'Jem' and your 'Jack' out the holsters whiles ye were strugglin' into your fine coat! Ye'll not abide in a decent house beyond this night, I'm thinking; and 'twas the old man who did for ye, murdering wretch that ye are!"

'A terrific struggle ensued. With or without his "Pretty Boys" Simon Forrester was a thoroughly tough customer, versed in every sleight of hand-to-hand fighting. He bit and kicked; he elbowed and gouged. He succeeded in hurling one of the troopers bodily against the blank wall, and the man sank there and lay still, a motionless heap. After a terrific struggle with the other three who had cast themselves upon him, the remaining troopers and their captain standing aside because there was not room to get at him in the mêlée, he succeeded in getting the forefinger of one of the troopers, who had reached for a face-hold upon him, between his teeth, and bit through it at the joint.

'Frantic with rage and pain this trooper, disengaging himself, and before he could be stopped, seized a heavy oaken bench and, swinging it through the air, brought it down on Simon Forrester's skull. No human bones, even Forrester's, could sustain that murderous assault. The tough wood crunched through his skull, and thereafter he lay quiet. Simon Forrester would never be drawn and quartered, nor even hanged. Simon Forrester, ignobly, as he had lived, was dead; and it remained for the troopers only to carry out the body and for their captain to indite his report.

'Thereafter, the room was stripped and closed by Old Titmarsh himself, who lived on for two more years, making good his frequent boast that his reign over The Coach and Horses would equal that of King George III over his realm. The old king died in 1820, and Old Titmarsh did not long survive him. Oliver, now a changed man, because of this occurrence, succeeded to the lease of the inn, and during his landlordship the room remained closed. It has been closed, out of use, ever since.'

Mr Snow brought his story, and his truly excellent dinner, to a close simultaneously. It was I who broke the little silence which followed his concluding words.

'I congratulate you, sir, upon the excellence of your narrative-gift. I hope that if I come to record this affair, as I have already done with respect to certain odd happenings which have come under my view, I shall be able, as nearly as possible, to reproduce your words.' I bowed to our host over my coffee cup.

'Excellent, excellent, indeed!' added Carruth, nodding and smiling pleasantly in Mr Snow's direction. 'And now – for the questions, if you don't mind. There are several which have occurred to me; doubtless also to Mr Canevin.'

Snow acquiesced affably. 'Anything you care to ask, of course.'

'Well, then,' it was Carruth, to whom I had indicated precedence in the questioning, 'tell us, if you please, Mr Snow – you seem to have every particular at your very fingers' ends – the purse with the gold? That, I suppose, was confiscated by the train-band captain and eventually found its way back to Sir William Greaves's heirs. That is the high probability, but – do you happen to know as a matter of fact?'

'The purse went back to Lady Greaves.'

'Ah! and Forrester's effects – I understand he used the room from time to time. Did he have anything, any personal property in it? If so, what became of it?'

'It was destroyed, burned. No one claimed his effects. Perhaps he had no relatives. Possibly no one dared to come forward. Everything in his possession was stolen, or, what is the same, the fruit of his thefts.'

'And – the pistols, "Jem and Jack?" Those names rather intrigued me! What disposition was made of them, if you happen to know? Old Titmarsh had them, of course, concealed somewhere; probably in that "cubby-hole" of his which you mentioned.'

'Ah,' said Mr Snow, rising, 'there I can really give you some evidence. The pistols are in my office – in the Chubbs' safe, along with the holster-apparatus, the harness which Forrester wore under his laced coat. I will bring them in.'

'Have you the connection, Mr Canevin?' Lord Carruth enquired of me as soon as Snow had left the dining-room.

'Yes,' said I, 'the connection is clear enough; clear as a pikestaff, to use one of your time-honored British expressions, although I confess never to have seen a pikestaff in my life! But – apart from the fact that the holsters are made of leather; the well-known background of the unfulfilled desire persisting after death; and the obvious connection between the point of disappearance of those "walking-boots" of Billings, with "the shut room", I must confess myself at a loss. The veriest tyro at this sort of thing would connect those points, I imagine. There it is, laid out for us, directly before our mental eyes, so to speak. But – what I fail to understand is not so much who takes them – that by a long stretch of the imagination might very well be the persistent "shade", "Ka", "projected embodiment" of Simon Forrester. No – what gets me is – *where does the carrier of boots and satchels and jewelers' sample-cases put them?* That room is utterly, absolutely, physically empty, and boots and shoes are material affairs, Lord Carruth.'

Carruth nodded gravely. 'You have put your finger on the main difficulty, Mr Canevin. I am not at all sure that I can explain it, or even that we shall be able to solve the mystery after all. My experience in India does not help. But – there is one very vague case, right here in England, which may be a parallel one. I suspect, not to put too fine a point upon the matter, that the abstracted things may very well be behind that rear-most wall, the wall opposite the doorway in "the shut room".'

'But,' I interjected, 'that is impossible, is it not? The wall is material – brick and stone and plaster. It is not subject to the strange laws of personality. How – ?'

The return of the gentleman-landlord of The Coach and Horses at this moment put an end to our conversation, but not to my wonder. I imagined that the 'case' alluded to by my companion would be that of the tortured 'ghost' of the jester which, with a revenge-motive, haunted a room in an ancient house and even managed to equip the room itself with some of its revengeful properties or motives. The case had been recorded by Mr Hodgson, and later Carruth told me that this was the one he had in mind. This, it seemed to me, was a very different matter. However –

Mr Snow laid the elaborate and beautifully made 'harness' of leather straps out on the table beside the after-dinner coffee service. The grips of 'Jem and Jack' peeped out of their holsters. The device was not unlike those used by our own American desperadoes, men like the famous Earp brothers and 'Doc' Holliday whose 'six-guns' were carried handily in slung holsters in front of the body. We examined these antique weapons, murderous-looking pistols of the 'bulldog' type, built for business, and Carruth ascertained that neither 'Jem' nor 'Jack' was loaded.

'Is there anyone on that top floor?' enquired Carruth.

'No one save yourselves, excepting some of the servants, who are in the other end of the house,' returned Snow.

'I am going to request you to let us take these pistols and the "harness" with us upstairs when we retire,' said Carruth, and again the obliging Snow agreed. 'Everything I have is at your disposal, gentlemen,' said he, 'in the hope that you will be able to end this annoyance for me. It is too early in the season at present for the inn to have many guests. Do precisely as you wish, in all ways.'

Shortly after nine o'clock, we took leave of our pleasant host, and, carrying the 'harness' and pistols divided between us, we mounted to our commodious bedchamber. A second bed had been moved into it, and the fire in the grate took off the slight chill of the spring evening. We began our preparations by carrying the high-powered electric torches we had obtained from Snow along the corridor and around the corner to 'the shut room'. We unlocked the door and ascertained that the two torches would be quite sufficient to work by. Then we closed but did not lock the door, and returned to our room.

Between us, we moved a solidly built oak table to a point diagonally across the corridor from our open bedroom door, and on this we placed the 'harness' and pistols. Then, well provided with smoke-materials, we sat down to wait, seated in such positions that both of us could command the view of our trap. It was during the conversation which followed that Carruth informed me that the case to which he had alluded was the one recorded by the occult writer, Hodgson. It was familiar to both of us. I will not cite it. It may be read by anybody who has the curiosity to examine it in the collection entitled *Carnacki the Ghost-Finder* by William Hope Hodgson. In that account it is the floor of the 'haunted' room which became adapted to the revenge-motive of the persistent 'shade' of the malignant court jester, tortured to death many years before his 'manifestation' by his fiendish lord and master.

We realized that, according to the man Billings's testimony, we need not be on the alert before midnight. Carruth therefore read from a small book which he had brought with him, and I busied myself in making the careful notes which I have consulted in recording Mr Snow's narrative of Simon Forrester, while that narrative was fresh in my memory. It was a quarter before midnight when I had finished. I took a turn about the room to refresh my somewhat cramped muscles, and returned to my comfortable chair.

Midnight struck from the French clock on our mantelpiece, and Carruth and I both, at that signal, began to give our entire attention to the articles on the table in the hallway out there.

It occurred to me that this joint watching, as intently as the circumstances seemed to warrant to both of us, might prove very wearing, and I suggested that we watch alternately, for about fifteen minutes each. We did so, I taking the first turn. Nothing occurred – not a sound, not the smallest indication that there might be anything untoward going on out there in the corridor.

At twelve-fifteen, Carruth began to watch the table, and it was, I should imagine, about five minutes later that his hand fell lightly on my arm, pressing it and arousing me to the keenest attention. I looked intently at the things on the table. The 'harness' was moving toward the left-hand edge of the table. We could both hear, now, the slight scraping sound made by the leather weighted by the twin pistols, and, even as we looked, the whole apparatus lifted itself – or so it appeared to us – from the supporting table, and began, as it were, to float through the air a distance of about four feet from the ground toward the turn which led to 'the shut room'.

We rose, simultaneously, for we had planned carefully on what we were to do, and followed. We were in time to see the articles 'float' around the corner, and, increasing our pace – for we had been puzzled about how anything material, like the boots, could get through the locked door – watched, in the rather dim light of that short hallway, what would happen.

What happened was that the 'harness' and pistols reached the door, and then the door opened. They went through, and the door shut behind them precisely as though someone, invisible to us, were carrying them. We heard distinctly the slight sound which a gently closed door makes as it came to, and there we were, standing outside in the hallway looking at each other. It is one thing to figure out, beforehand, the science of occult occurrences, even upon the basis of such experience as Carruth and I both possessed. It is, distinctly, another, to face the direct operation of something motivated by the Powers beyond the ordinary ken of humanity. I confess to certain 'cold chills', and Carruth's face was *very pale*.

We switched on our electric torches as we had arranged to do, and Carruth, with a firm hand which I admired if I did not, precisely, envy, reached out and turned the knob of the door. We walked into 'the shut room' . . .

Not all our joint experience had prepared us for what we saw. I could not forbear clutching Carruth's free arm, the one not engaged with the torch, as he stood beside me. And I testify that his arm was as still and firm as a rock. It steadied me to realize such fortitude, for the sight which was before us was enough to unnerve the most hardened investigator of the unearthly.

Directly in front of us, but facing the blank wall at the far end of the room, stood a half-materialized man. The gleam of my torch threw a faint shadow on the wall in front of him, the rays passing through him as though he were not there, and yet with a certain dimming. The shadow visibly increased in the few brief instants of our utter silence, and then we observed that the figure was struggling with something. Mechanically we concentrated both electric rays on the figure and then we saw clearly. A bulky man, with a bull-neck and close-cropped, iron-gray hair, wearing a fine satin coat and what were called, in their day, 'small cloths', or tight-fitting knee-trousers with silk stockings and heavy, buckled shoes, was raising and fitting about his waist, over the coat, the 'harness' with the pistols.

Abruptly, the materialization appearing to be now complete, he turned upon us, with an audible snarl and baleful, glaring little eyes like a pig's, deep set in a hideous, scarred face, and then he spoke – he spoke, and he had been dead for more than a century!

'Ah-h-h-h!' he snarled, evilly, 'ye would come in upon me, eh, my fine gents – into this my chamber, eh! I'll teach ye manners . . . ' and he ended this diatribe with a flood of the foulest language imaginable, stepping, with little, almost mincing, down-toed steps toward us all the time he poured out his filthy curses and revilings. I was completely at a loss what to do. I realized – these ideas went through my mind with the rapidity of thought – that the pistols were unloaded! I told myself that this was some weird hallucination – that the shade of no dead-and-gone desperado could harm us. Yet – it was a truly terrifying experience, be the man shade or true flesh and blood.

Then Carruth spoke to him, in quiet, persuasive tones.

'But – you have your pistols now, Simon Forrester. It was we who put them where you could find them, your pretty boys, "Jem and Jack". That was what you were trying to find, was it not? And now – you have them. There is nothing further for you to do – you have them, they are just under your hands where you can get at them whenever you wish.'

At this the specter, or materialization of Simon Forrester, blinked at us, a cunning light in his evil little eyes, and dropped his hands with which he had but now been gesticulating violently on the grips of the pistols. He grinned, evilly, and spat in a strange fashion, over his shoulder.

'Ay,' said he, more moderately now, 'ay – I have 'em – Jemmy and Jack, my trusties, my pretty boys.' He fondled the butts with his huge hands, hands that could have strangled an ox, and spat over his shoulder.

'There is no necessity for you to remain, then, is there?' said Carruth softly, persuasively.

The simulacrum of Simon Forrester frowned, looked a bit puzzled, then nodded its head several times.

'You can rest now – now that you have Jem and Jack,' suggested Carruth, almost in a whisper, and as he spoke, Forrester turned away and stepped over to the blank wall at the far side of the room, opposite the doorway, and I could hear Carruth draw in his breath softly and feel the iron grip of his fingers on my arm. 'Watch!' he whispered in my ear; 'watch now.'

The solid wall seemed to wave and buckle before Forrester, almost as though it were not a wall but a sheet of white cloth, held and waved by hands as cloth is waved in a theater to simulate waves. More and more cloth-like the wall became, and, as we gazed at this strange sight, the simulacrum of Simon Forrester seemed to become less opaque, to melt and blend in with the wavering wall, which gradually ceased to move, and then he was gone and the wall was as it had been before . . .

On Monday morning, at Carruth's urgent solicitation, Snow assembled a force of laborers, and we watched while they broke down the wall of 'the shut room' opposite the doorway. At last, as Carruth had expected, a pick went through, and, the interested workmen, laboring with a will, broke through into a small, narrow, cell-like room the plaster of which indicated that it had been walled up perhaps two centuries before, or even earlier – a 'priest's hole' in all probability, of the early post-reformation period near the end of the Sixteenth Century.

Carruth stopped the work as soon as it was plain what was here, and turned out the workmen, who went protestingly. Then, with only our host working beside us, and the door of the room locked on the inside, we continued the job. At last the aperture was large enough, and Carruth went through. We heard an exclamation from him, and then he began to hand out articles through the rough hole in the masonry – leather articles – boots innumerable, ladies' reticules, hand-luggage, the missing jeweler's sample case with its contents intact – innumerable other articles, and, last of all, the 'harness' with the pistols in the holsters.

Carruth explained the 'jester case' to Snow, who shook his head over it. 'It's quite beyond me, Lord Carruth,' said he, 'but, as you say this annoyance is at an end, I am quite satisfied; and – I'll take your advice and make sure by pulling down the whole room, breaking out the corridor walls, and joining it to the room across the way. I confess I can not make head or tail of your explanation – the unfulfilled wish, the "sympathetic pervasion" of the room as you call it, the "materialization", and the strange fact that this business began only a short time ago. But – I'll do exactly what you have recommended, about the room, that is. The restoration of the jeweler's case will undoubtedly make it possible for me to get back the sum I paid Messrs Hopkins and Barth of Liverpool when it disappeared in my house. Can you give any explanation of why the "shade" of Forrester remained quiet for a century and more and only started up the other day, so to speak?'

'It is because the power to materialize came very slowly,' answered Carruth, 'coupled as it undoubtedly was with the gradual breaking down of the room's material resistance. It is very difficult to realize the extraordinary force of an unfulfilled wish, on the part of a forceful, brutal, wholly selfish personality like Forrester's. It is, really, what we must call spiritual power, even though the "spirituality" was the reverse of what we commonly understand by that term. The wish and the force of Forrester's persistent desire, through the century, have been working steadily, and, as you have told us, the room has been out of use for more than a century. There were no common, everyday affairs to counteract that malign influence – no "interruptions", if I make myself clear.'

'Thank you,' said Mr Snow. 'I do not clearly understand. These matters are outside my province. But – I am exceedingly grateful – to you both.' Our host bowed courteously. 'Anything that I can possibly do, in return – '

'There is nothing – nothing whatever,' said Carruth quietly; 'but, Mr Snow, there is another problem on your hands which perhaps you will have some difficulty in solving, and concerning which, to our regret' – he looked gravely at me – 'I fear neither Mr Canevin with his experience, nor I with mine, will be able to assist you.'

'And what, pray, is that?' asked Mr Snow, turning slightly pale. He would, I perceive, be very well satisfied to have his problems behind him.

'The problem is,' said Carruth, even more gravely I imagined, 'it is – what disposal are you to make of fifty-eight pairs of assorted boots and shoes!'

And Snow's relieved laughter was the last of the impressions which I took with me as we rode back to London in Carruth's car, of The Coach and Horses inn on the Brighton Road.

The Left Eye

Pierre Godard was a French Canadian by descent, whose grand-father had departed the purlieus of Montreal for the good of his miserable hide in the days of Riel's Rebellion and settled in that indefinite area of scanty-soiled farmland along the western shore of Lake Champlain between Keeseville and Plattsburg.

The degenerate stock of the Godards, long impoverished since the era of its plebeian origins in France, did not recover in the descendants of the original fugitive. Pierre, the grandson, combined in his make-up the native cussedness of the lower class 'canuck' with the skinflint qualities which his lifelong residence among the narrow-minded yokels with whom he consorted had readily imparted. Shiftless, furtive, mean-souled, he eked out an existence on his few barren acres of poor land which was endurable only because there was neither in his heredity nor his experience any better standard by which he could realize to the full the utter meanness of everything that conspired to make up his life's record.

At nineteen Pierre had married Katie Burton, a flat-chested, sallow-faced slattern of his own age. At the end of five years of sordid married life, four brats of their begetting littered up the dirty kitchen of Pierre's cabin through the long, cold days of the north-ern New York winter, and spent their summers rolling about in the dirt at the roadside and making faces at the occupants of the automobiles which passed in a wavering, irregular string, all day and most of the early evening, along the State road between Keese-ville and Plattsburg.

That is, there were four brats – and Kathleen. To what ancestors of Pierre or Katie Kathleen could have been a 'throw-back' is one of those obscure ethnic mysteries which are so baffling when they emerge in the families of recognized people. In Kathleen's case, it baffled no one, since there was no one in particular to remark this fairy among the ugly gnomes who pretended to be her brothers and sisters, this glorious little swan among the rough ducklings of the Godard brood.

Kathleen had always been utterly different from the rest. By the time she was six or seven, her positive characteristics were already strongly developed. She stood out from the rest of her sordid family like a new-minted gold coin among pocket-worn pennies. By natural choice, and habitually, she was dainty and neat. Dirt never stuck to her, somehow. The rest of the brood were different from each other only in the varying ugliness of their budding dispositions and the equally variant qualities of their general detestability of appearance and habit. All the rest, for example, would fight at the drop of the hat to gain possession of anything that turned up unappropriated, that even vaguely suggested value to their joint scrutiny. In these snarling contests, Kathleen, coolly aloof, was uninterested. The rest possessed in common that coarse, scrubby hair of indeterminate color which characterizes the children of outdoor-living peasants the world over. Kathleen's, a shimmering glory of delicate ringlets, shone burnished copper in the afternoon sun when she swept off the rickety back porch or daintily threw a few grains of hard corn to Pierre's scraggly hens.

At sixteen she was as coolly aloof from the blandishments of the coarse young men of her neighborhood as ever she had been to the scrambling bickerings of her family. All such advances left her wholly uninterested. What dreams and aspirations lay behind those clear blue eyes, those eyes like the blue of the Caribbean at noon, no one had ever guessed, that is, no one except the good priest, Father Tracy, who came over from one of the neighboring towns for mass every Sunday morning, and on alternate Saturday nights and before First Fridays, to hear the confessions of his outlying portion of his difficult flock. To Father Tracy it had been some time clear that the lovely body of the little Kathleen harbored one of those rare souls, delicate and fragrant, which burn with the desire to offer themselves wholly to the Love of God. Here, the good father knew, or strongly suspected, was a budding vocation for the religious life, a vocation which it was one of his rewards to cultivate and foster.

As yet Kathleen was too young to leave her home, even if that had been feasible, and enter upon a novitiate with the good sisters at Plattsburg, or, perhaps better still, in her case, with some other good sisters much farther away from the place of her sordid origins, but for this vocation, as he watched it grow, at first weak and trembling up toward the dim light of a possible fulfillment, then later with a kind of thin, but pure and steady flame, Father Tracy said many novenas of thanks-giving. It was one of his chief sources of happiness, and, as was natural in such cases, Kathleen responded to his interest in her, and through his gentle, kindly leading of her soul, was beginning, as she fulfilled her maturity, to see the distant light more and more clearly.

This vision she cherished with all her heart, and if it begot in her an almost perceptible wistfulness, it did nothing to minimize the cheerful kindliness with which she went about the performance of her daily tasks, or the cultivated discretion with which she had laboriously learned to meet and neutralize the changeable moods of her vicious father and slatternly, loose-minded mother.

The wind-swept habitation for God which she had made of her pure little heart was rudely battered on a certain Thursday morning in the month of August in her seventeenth year.

Pierre, her father, who combined with the shiftless existence of a small peasant-farmer the more adventurous and profitable avocation of a bootlegger's runner for a Plattsburg operator, was frequently away from home at night and even for days at a time, when he was engaged in doing his part in bringing consignments of illicit merchandise down from unknown points in nearby Canada, either overland along the State road or by devious and rutted by-ways, or, what was an easier though somewhat less direct method much favored by 'the profession', 'up' the lake on dark nights, a process which was more lucrative because there were less people to bribe, and correspondingly somewhat more dangerous, as requiring a landing on the shores of Vermont across the lake, or somewhere on the New York side.

He had been away on one of these expeditions for two days, and had returned some time during the small hours Wednesday night. On that Thursday morning, after two nearly sleepless nights, unkempt, ugly as a bear with a sore nose, he pushed his way into the kitchen about nine o'clock and demanded something to eat.

Kathleen brought him his food and he ate in a brooding silence. She waited, sitting on the step below the open doorway, for him to finish, so that she might wash his dishes and tidy up the table after him, softly humming a tuneless little song, her mind entirely other-worldly.

Pierre, having finished his breakfast, came straight to the point of a certain matter which he had been cogitating for several weeks.

'Come here,' he said.

She rose and came to the table, expecting that he required another cup of coffee or something of the sort.

'Shut the door,' barked her father.

She closed the door leading into the small hallway out of the kitchen, wonderingly, and returned to her father's side.

'How old are you?' he asked, looking at her as though he were appraising her.

'Seventeen.'

'Seventeen, eh?' His eyes went over her again, in such fashion that, without knowing why, she felt suddenly choked.

'Ah, seventeen. Old enough! Now listen. That is old enough. You are going to marry Steve Benham. I got that all fixed, see. Me an' him, we talk about it a lot, and Steve is all right for it.'

The choking feeling nearly overcame her. The blood seemed to suffuse her whole body and then recede somewhere, leaving her icy cold and afraid. Marriage had never entered Kathleen's mind. And Steve Benham! Benham was a brutal-faced young tough who, with greater advantages such as are offered to the denizens of great cities in their worst aspects, might have shone as a criminal of the lower type – a yegg, a killer for hire, the ready and effective tool of some brutal organized gang. As it was, he had taken advantage of such opportunities as presented themselves to his somewhat restricted field of development. He was one of Levin's crowd in the bootlegging operations, a close associate of Pierre Godard's.

'What the hell's the matter with you, now?' roared Pierre, curbing his voice slightly in view of his desire for secrecy. This was his lookout, and none of Katie's business. He could handle his own girl all by himself without his wife's having any part in it. Benham had offered him two hundred dollars to put it through for him, and that two hundred he meant to have – as soon as possible, too.

'Steve's all right, ain't he? What's the matter with Steve? Now cut out this blubberin'.' Kathleen's lips were trembling in a colorless face, her eyes big and bright with the tears she was forcing to remain unshed. She knew the resources of this brute of a father which an inscrutably unkind Providence had inflicted upon her.

Pierre, his anger mounting by leaps and bounds, glared at her, his ugly face rendered hideous by a savage snarl, his clenched hand showing white at the knuckles as he gripped the table's edge.

'O daddy, I can't, I can't!'

Kathleen's restraint had broken down under this unexpected and crushing blow. She sank down in a chair at the side of the table, and buried her lovely head in her hands, her body shaken with convulsive sobs.

This weakening aroused all the half-latent brute in Godard. With a savage curse, he seized Kathleen by the hair, dragging her face up from the table, and with the back of the other hand dealt her several cruel and heavy blows.

She sank, as she shrank away, to the floor, a shuddering heap of misery and pain.

Pierre rose, his anger partially allayed, and looked down at her. He kicked her, but lightly, in the side.

'Get up out of that, an' get to hell out of here and clean yourself up. Steve's comin' in about noon, an' I'm goin' to tell him it's all set for him. Don't you dast do nothin' to spoil it, neither, you hear? Now git up, an' beat it along an' get yourself prettied up.'

He seized her roughly by the shoulder, dragged her to her feet and shoved her through the door into the hallway.

Upstairs in her tiny little room, she lay across the bed, bruised and shaken, trying to collect her wits. One refuge and one only occurred to her, for even under the stress of this unexpected manifestation of her father's known brutality she had no idea of giving in to his demand and receiving Steven Benham as a suitor.

Trembling, shaken in every fiber of her delicate body, but with her almost unformulated resolve burning within her like a bright, strong flame, she dragged herself resolutely to her feet, and began painfully to change her clothes. She had decided to go to Father Tracy for protection.

An hour later, very softly, she crept downstairs. It was past ten o'clock, and she would have to manage to elude her mother. Her brothers and sister had not been about the house, she remembered, since their breakfast time. Her mother would be below. She had been out in the chicken-yard when her father had come into the kitchen for his breakfast. He had gone out immediately after she had come up-stairs, probably to report progress to Benham! She shuddered, and crept down the stairs like a mouse.

She could hear her mother aimlessly pottering about in the kitchen. She slipped out of the seldom-used front door and out to the gate and along the road. As she turned the first corner, she met her sister Eunice, walking beside one of the town boys.

'Where you goin' all dressed up?' enquired Eunice, her pert face alive with interest in this unexpected apparition of Kathleen in her best dress and Sunday hat. Kathleen bit her lip. This was a wholly unexpected, and entirely unavoidable, misfortune. She was utterly unused to deceit. The truth was her only resource.

'I have to go over to Villanova to see Father Tracy,' she replied simply. Eunice's eyes opened wide in astonishment. She said nothing, and Kathleen, walking as rapidly as she could, passed the couple and continued on her way.

It was not until noon that Eunice arrived home, and Kathleen, with two hours' start, could not be overtaken.

Godard, on hearing of his daughter's destination, was, for the time being, nonplussed. He would have to think this over. It was a wholly unexpected move on Kathleen's part. Cursing her in his black heart, he betook himself, accompanied by a fresh bottle of Levine's commodity, to the barn, and spent the afternoon in consultation with the bottle.

About five o'clock, having had a brief nap, and awaking in an uglier mood than ever, he came back to the house for another bottle, and with that he disappeared until dark. He did not come into the house for his supper, and to the summons of his son Ernest he replied only with such fervent curses that Ernest, edified, returned to the house to warn the rest of the family to leave the 'old man' alone.

About ten o'clock, alone, he set out in his Ford car. The family heard him go, but this meant nothing to them. They were used to his blind rages and to his goings and comings at all hours.

Exercising that kind of low cunning which he had inherited from his disreputable ancestors and which had served him well in his many evasions of the officers of the law of the State of New York, he did not drive through the neighboring small village where Kathleen had met her sister walking, but took a devious way through obscure mountain roads to Villanova, the larger town which lay several miles inland from the lake shore and where Father Tracy lived.

He left his Ford several rods up a wood road at the foot of a mountain near the edge of the town, and threaded his way through the more obscure streets in the direction of the rectory.

Very few people were abroad, but when he arrived at the edge of the backyard of the parochial residence he observed with a certain satisfaction that the house was lighted in what he supposed to be the pastor's study on the first floor.

He had brought the automatic pistol which always accompanied his professional journeys over the Canadian border, but his ride in the pure Adirondack night air, and the necessity for concentration in driving over the rough mountain roads, had dissipated the effects of the two bottles of cut whisky which he had consumed, to that degree that as he approached the house with murder in his black heart, he did so with all the native cunning he possessed keyed to the last notch, and, indeed, in a state of almost preternatural caution. But within him, unleashed, burned the evil fires of rage, disappointment, and hatred against his daughter and this good priest, which had seared and hardened his evil soul to the point where he would stop at nothing.

Under the stress of this stimulation, he decided suddenly not to use the pistol, and he looked about the yard for a suitable weapon. The devil placed one to his hand. There, near the back porch, lay an ideal club, a section of thin gas-pipe left that very day by the local plumber who had fitted a new section to the hand-pump which supplied the kitchen. He picked up the pipe, which was about two feet in length, and balanced it in his hand, a devilish grin contorting his bleared features.

Very softly he approached the house on the side which lay in shadow, and took his stand under the lighted study window. Cautiously he raised himself to a level with the lower edge of the window, and peered through the transverse aperture left by an imperfectly pulled-down shade.

Kathleen sat with her back to him, within two feet of the open window. On the other side of the table sat the priest. Kathleen was speaking. He craned his neck to listen, his teeth now, unconsciously, bared.

'I think it would be better for me to go to the convent out there in the West, Father,' she was saying, 'for as you say, the farther away I go the safer I would feel.'

The priest made some reply, of acquiescence and approval, unintelligible to Godard, who was now busily engaged in removing with the delicate touch of a repairer of watches, the fasteners from the wire screen which separated him from his prey.

It came out in his hands without a sound, and before the priest had finished his remark, Godard was in the room. Cursing frenziedly, though still softly for he was still under the influence of his cautious obsession, he sprang like a tiger through the window, and with one terrific blow had crushed his daughter's lovely head like an eggshell.

Father Tracy, overcome with horror and momentarily helpless in the face of this berserk attack out of the calm mediocrity of his side-yard, was the next victim. With unspeakable blasphemies on his crusted lips, foam in the corners of his mouth, Godard was upon him, and the iron bar fell again and again until all human semblance was gone and a heap of huddled pulp on the rapidly crimsoning floor of his quiet study was all that remained mortal of the kindly priest of God.

Then, shivering under the fearful reaction of his holocaust, Godard, exercising the last remaining power of the stimulation of his low cunning, blew out the lamp, and as silently as a shadow slipped out through the opened window onto the grass beneath.

He turned back along the shadow of the house, but before he had reached the open yard behind, he bethought him abruptly of the detached wire screen which he had left leaning against the side of the house. He returned, catlike, and busied himself with refastening it. Just as he snicked home the last of the four patent fasteners, footsteps approached along the sidewalk from the farther side of the house, and he crouched like an animal against the side of the house in deep, protecting shadow. The footsteps, accompanied by two unconstrained voices, and punctuated by raucous laughs, continued past the house. Godard held his breath until it seemed to burn within his breast, and, furtively, catlike, watched with unwinking, small eyes the two uncertainly-outlined figures pass the house. At last they were gone, and noiselessly he slipped again along the side of the house in the protecting shadow, and disappeared in the tangle of weeds at the end of the yard.

Again, by back streets, he threaded his way tortuously toward the mountain road where he had concealed his car. As he stepped cautiously out onto the main road which led into the village of Villanova, he almost ran into two large men who were standing, smoking silently, at the roadside. Involuntarily he stopped, and the two turned toward him. A binding flash dazzled his eyes as one of the men turned the gleam of an electric flashlight in the direction of the furtive shape which had broken in upon their meditation. At once Godard was recognized.

It was the two men who had passed the rectory while he was replacing the wire screen in the window. Both hailed him by name.

'What you a-doin' 'way out here this time o' night, Pierre?' came the full bass of Martin Delaney.

'Goshamighty! Thought you was a ghost or somep'n!' It was the squeaky voice of Louis Le Grand.

Shaking in abject terror, the stimulation of his blood-lust entirely dissipated and no longer supporting him, Pierre Godard could only stand, his knees shaking and knocking, and goggle back at his interlocutors. At last, after the passage of several moments, and a new look, one of curiosity, having implanted itself on the faces of the two countrymen, Godard managed to gasp, in a dry throaty voice, not at all like his own, something about a piece of business here in Villanova; and not waiting to ascertain what effect his unusual preoccupation might have upon Delaney and Le Grand, he hastened at a kind of shambling trot down the main road toward his hidden car.

Both Delaney and Le Grand were very much mystified at Godard's unusual behavior. The two cronies, commonly bereft of all but the usual topics of local conversation, which were anything but interesting, made the most of this mild mystery. Therefore it was very firmly implanted in their rather obtuse minds that there could be only one possible author of the horrible crime which had been committed in the rectory, when the little town buzzed and seethed with it the next morning.

By ten o'clock of that Friday, a posse was out after Godard, under the direction of a deputy sheriff and equipped with three automobiles, and had traced him as far as Willsboro Point by an imperfection in one of his tires, when the search was abruptly terminated by finding the car itself, which he had abandoned at the side of the Point road, at the intersection of another road which led down to the shore of the lake. It did not require more than the very average intelligence of deputy sheriff Maclear to come to the obvious conclusion that he had got across the lake and into Vermont, a conclusion corroborated by the statement of an irate resident camper who had been searching during the past hour and a half for a missing St Lawrence skiff in which the camper had planned to go perch-fishing that morning, and which could nowhere be discovered.

The posse drove back to Willsboro station, and notified the Vermont authorities at Burlington, by telegraph. Then deputy sheriff Maclear reported to his superior, who got in touch with Albany asking requisition papers on the governor of the State of Vermont for a fugitive who had, the night before, brutally murdered his own daughter and a blameless priest of God.

But the Vermont authorities, although they took due action upon the telegraphed information, which contained an exact description of Godard, failed signally to get on the track of the fugitive from justice who had left the New York shore, unmistakably, from Willsboro Point. Every usual precaution was taken, and for some time it was surmised that Godard, familiar with the lake shores from a lifetime of contiguous residence and from his professional activities as a rum-runner, had managed to land on the Vermont side and make his escape into the mountains. The greatest puzzle was what could have become of that St Lawrence skiff which he had discovered so opportunely.

Some of the clearer-headed of those who set themselves to solve this problem came to the conclusion that Godard, desiring to conceal from his pursuers the point of his departure inland in Vermont, had scuttled the boat near the shore's edge, which he could easily have managed, either by smashing a hole or two after landing, weighting down the skiff with rocks, and shoving her out into the deep waters of the lake; or by doing the scuttling before landing, and swimming ashore. At any rate there was, on the Vermont side, no trace either of the fugitive or of the delicate little vessel in which he had left the New York side.

As Godard sped away from the vicinity of Villanova it required from him every particle of concentration he could summon to drive at all. He opened up his dingy little car, which had, despite its battered appearance, an excellent engine, and hitting the high spots of the twining, rough mountain roads, he concentrated every effort in the blind urge to put as many miles as possible between himself and the scene of his horrible crime.

It was only when after several miles of incredible bumping and swaying he had reached a State road, that a definite objective for his flight began to take form in his harassed and befuddled mind. As he gave fragmentary thought to this pressing problem, something of his native low-cunning reasserted itself. His evil mind began to function. It first became plain to him that he could not return to his squalid home. He had been seen, and recognized. His one hope was that the crushed and mangled bodies of his unfortunate victims might not be discovered until morning.

There was no good reason why they should be discovered. The priest, as he knew very well, lived alone except for a superannuated old woman who was his housekeeper, and this ancient crone had unquestionably retired for the night long before his arrival in Villanova. Being ancient, and decrepit, she could be trusted to sleep through everything until morning. Barring a night-call for Father Tracy, the chances were excellent that the bodies would not be discovered until some time the next morning. It was now a little after midnight. It would be light around four o'clock. He had something like four hours to work in.

He speeded up the car along the lake shore southward. He would go 'up the lake' – as the southerly direction, for some inexplicable reason, was called, locally – away from Canada. Canada had been his first lucid thought; but that, as he reasoned cunningly, would necessitate a wide detour or else passing through Plattsburg, and he wished to risk neither the loss of time, nor the dash through a good-sized city, even at one o'clock in the morning. Therefore he turned south, in the direction of Essex.

As he neared Willsboro, the town just north of Essex, a brand-new idea occurred to him. By abandoning his car somewhere here-abouts, he could get an earlier start for crossing the lake into Vermont. With every mile he traveled, the lake narrowed, but straight across from Willsboro it would be only four miles, and, he reasoned, he would rather be out on the lake in the dim dusk of early morning than attempting to conceal his car and steal a boat in anything approaching daylight. Some early-morning fisherman would be sure to see him!

A little past the Willsboro railroad station, therefore, his idea having begotten another, in his cunning brain, this time something in the nature of an inspiration, he turned his car sharply to the left, grinning evilly as he acted upon his newest hunch, and ran back, nearly at right angles with his previous course, down upon Wills-boro Point. This is a peninsula, several miles in length, running north-easterly – a section of fine farmland in the center, its two shores thickly populated by summer campers, city people for the most part. No one, pursuing, would ever imagine that he had turned off, he reasoned. Besides, the city people at the camps had canoes, and in a canoe, from somewhere near the Point's end, he could, with the greatest ease, make his unseen way out to one of the Four Brother Islands, conceal the canoe in some dense thicket of underbrush, and effectually hide out. There were, too, lake-gulls' eggs in abundance on the islands, and no one would suspect, until it was too late, that he had done otherwise than attempt to make his escape, either into Canada (his own first idea) or across the lake into Vermont.

The car was his immediate problem, but there was no way of solving that. There was, as he well knew, no water along the shore deep enough to permit his sending it at full speed over the edge into the lake, and so hiding it effectually.

He left it directly in the road, and slunk down to the lake shore at his right in search of a canoe.

His luck held. At the very first camp he reached he found not only canoes but a St Lawrence skiff, a staunch type of boat, round-bottomed, sharp-nosed at both ends, a boat capable, like a canoe, of being managed with a light paddle, but although equally fast, infinitely stauncher and less dangerous than any canoe.

Silently he launched out into the lake, and with swift, yet noiseless paddle-strokes shot his stolen skiff out into the black darkness in the direction of the Four Brothers . . .

These islands, 'Les Isles des Quatre Vents' of the voyageurs, are old haunts of the lake smugglers. They lie, from the viewpoint of one approaching them directly from the Point shore, in the order of a mouth, nose, and two eyes, roughly speaking. The nearest, called 'the mouth', was sighted after a few minutes of vigorous paddling by Godard, who passed it to the right or southerly direction. It had upon it a cabin, former residence of the keeper of the gulls, which are protected by state law. Godard was not looking for the comforts of cabins! He passed 'the nose', a low-lying, swampy island, and paddled on to the island which would correspond to the left eye. This, the most rarely visited of the islands, infested with gulls, presents, like its fellow 'eye', a precipitous shore all around, and is heavily forested with evergreens and thick virgin underbrush.

Guided precisely by the noise of the gulls, which are constantly bickering, and then by his own keen eyesight, Godard carefully navigated the little island, finally landing and drawing the skiff into a tiny bay which was little more than a cleft in the guano-covered rocks. He concealed the skiff, despite the darkness, with immense cleverness, and began the difficult ascent of the cliff.

At last, bruised, spent, and befouled with guano, he reached the summit, and half walked, half crawled through the tangled under-brush toward the almost impenetrable center.

In his ascent he had disturbed countless nesting gulls, and their din, to his trained and tautened nerves, was distracting, but the increased noise did not trouble him. The gulls were always at it, day and night, and such an increase would not be heard a mile and a half away on the sleeping Point. It was, curiously enough, the spider webs that really annoyed him. Undisturbed for centuries, these midnight spinners had worked and spun and plundered the air without hindrance.

As Godard pushed his precipitous way up the rocks and then again through the almost impenetrable underbrush, he was constantly brushing away long, clinging webs, which crossed and recrossed before his face and neck, and about his scratched and bleeding hands and wrists.

As he penetrated farther and farther toward the slightly conical center of this little island, it seemed to him that both the restraining pressure and the clinging tenacity of the webs were on the increase, but his native wit assured him that this impression was due to his fatigue and the reaction from the enormous amount of bad whisky he had imbibed during the afternoon.

He was, indeed, in the very depths of reactive depression. He cursed softly and bitterly, with a despairing note of self-pity, as the webs, ever thicker and stronger, as it seemed, appeared almost to reach out after him, to bar his way to effectual concealment.

At last, trembling in every limb, the salt sweat running into his parched mouth, shaking and weak, he observed that he was stepping slightly downhill. His progress since leaving the upper edge of the cliff had been slightly ascending. He had reached the approximate center of the island.

Wearily he paused, and almost sobbing out his bitter curses, tore fretfully, with trembling fingers, at a great mass of thick, silky web that had attached itself to his mouth.

As he looked about him through the darkness, and felt with his hands for a comparatively level place on which to sit down, he almost shrieked. He had put his hand down on something feathery, soft, and yielding to the touch. He looked, horrified, at the ground. Gibbering in mortal terror, he drew a box of matches from his pocket, and, cupping his hands, cautiously drew one across the side of the box. The flare of the safety-match revealed something white. He looked closer, stooping near the ground and carefully guarding the flame of his match, and he saw that it was the body of a gull.

Something, he thought, something that seemed as big as his two fists, scampered away through the underbrush, awkwardly, a lumpish kind of a thing. A mink, or weasel, his reason reassured him.

The match went out, burning his fingers, and a pall of sudden blackness fell upon him. Terrified, less moved with the caution of a lifelong habitude for concealment, now, he struck another match and examined the gull by its yellow flare.

From the bird's throat ran two thin streams of blood. The blood stained his hands as he picked it up. The gull was warm, living. It struggled, sinuously, faintly, in his hands. All about it, about its head and about its legs, and pinning its powerful wings close to its side, ran great, silken swaths of spider's web. The gull muttered, squeakingly, and writhed weakly between his hands. With a scream he could not suppress he hurled it from him and attempted to rush away from this place of horror.

But now, weakened by his exertions, his forces sapped by long debauchery, his nerves jangling from the terrific stress he had put upon them that night, he could not run. All about him the underbrush closed in, it seemed to him, as though bent malignantly upon imprisoning him here among these nameless, silent, spinning demons which had destroyed the gull.

He had hurled his matches away with that same flinging motion begotten of his horror. It was utterly impossible to recover them now.

The thick blackness had closed down upon him again at the burning out of the second match. He could feel the blood suffuse his entire body, and then recede, leaving him cold. He shivered, as he suddenly felt the sweat cold against his sodden body. Chill after chill raced down his spine. He whimpered and called suddenly upon God, the forgotten God of his erratic childhood.

But God, it seemed, had no answer for him. A soft touch came delicately upon the back of his clenched right hand. Something soft, clinging and silky, passed around it. Suddenly he shrieked again, and spasmodically tore his hand loose. But even as he struggled to free his hand, a terrible pain seared his leg, a pain as though he had stepped under water upon a sting-ray; a pain as though a red-hot poniard had been thrust far into his calf; and then something soft and clinging fell upon his head and he could feel the thick strands of silk being woven remorselessly through his hair and about his ears . . .

As he sank to the ground, his consciousness rapidly waning, the first clinging, composite, deliberate strands went across his eyes. His last conscious thought was of his daughter Kathleen's soft, silky hair . . .

It was not until nearly two weeks later that the skiff came to light, when four large rowboats slowly approached *Les Isles des Quatre Vents* from the direction of the lake side of the base of the Point. Crowded into the boats were the boys from Camp Cherokee making one of their annual boat-hikes to the four islands. Their course naturally brought them first to the island which has been called 'The Left Eye'.

The St Lawrence skiff, loosened from its primitive fastenings by a heavy storm which had intervened, had slipped out several feet from its concealing underbrush.

'Oh, look! Somebody's out here already!' shouted a sharp-eyed youngster in the bow of the foremost rowboat.

'Can't we land here, Mr Tanner?' asked one of the older boys when all eyes had sought out and discovered the skiff. 'We have plenty of time. Nobody ever comes to this island, they say, and most of us saw the others last year.'

Consulting his watch, his mind on lunch ashore, the counselor in charge of the boat-hike gave his consent, and the four rowboats drew in close to the spot where Godard had made his landing. Mr Tanner looked closely at the skiff.

'I shouldn't be a bit surprised,' he remarked, slowly, 'if that were the skiff that was stolen from down on the Point a couple of weeks ago!'

The boys chattered excitedly while the boats lay off the shore of 'The Left Eye', Mr Tanner considering. It was not impossible that the murderer, Godard, lay concealed on this island! No one had hitherto thought of such a possibility.

Mr Tanner came to a conclusion, after rapid thought. He would take the skiff, thus cutting off the murderer (if indeed he were concealed on the island) from any probable escape. So far it appeared a clear course.

Two reliable, older boys, placed in charge of the salvaged skiff, returned to its owners, who promptly telephoned the sheriff.

Mr Tanner conducted his protesting flotilla across to the island which has been called 'The Mouth' – the island on which stood the hut, and where the boys' temporary camp-site had been planned. The oars moved reluctantly, for the boys wanted to land and 'hunt the murderer'. Mr Tanner, whose responsibility lay in another direction than the apprehension of criminals, preferred to proceed according to schedule.

Two hours later a laden rowboat put off from the Point and approached The Four Brothers. The watching boys, thus, as it were, augmented by the authorities, could be restrained no longer.

Mr Tanner was able to manage it so that his four rowboats followed the official rowboat to 'The Left Eye'. Beyond that he could not control his Indians!

The boys nearly swamped their boats in their eagerness to disembark . . .

In the end it was one of them who did, actually, discover Godard's remains.

'Gosh!' the rest heard him shout. 'Look here, everybody! Here's a thing like a mummy!'

The spot was soon surrounded, the more agile boys distancing the slower-moving sheriff and constables.

Godard's body, easily identifiable from its clothing, lay, or, more precisely, hung, in the thickest tangle of all the tangled bushes and brush which made the central, highest point of the little island almost impenetrable. At first sight, it gave the impression of a bundle of clothes rather than a human body. It was, as the boy had cried out, virtually a mummy, though sodden through the draggled clothes (which Godard's progress through the tearing brush had greatly disarranged) by the effects of the heavy storm which had revealed the skiff.

It gave the appearance of a human body which, as though by some long process of time, had dried up to a mere fraction of its original bulk. It swayed, held free of the ground by the heavy brush, in the brisk breeze which was blowing 'up the lake' from the cold north.

The grayish appearance of this strange simulacrum of a human form, which at first puzzled the men when they approached to disengage it from the tangled bushes, was found to be due to innumerable heavy strands of broad opalescent silky webbing, webbing which had been wound about the head, about the hands and arms and legs, webbing now frayed and torn in places by the wind and the friction of the bushes.

One of the constables, a heavy, rather brutal-faced person, pulled at it and rubbed it from his hands on his canvas overalls.

'Looks for all the world like spider web,' he remarked laconically. 'What d'you s'pose it can be, Herb?' addressing the deputy sheriff in charge.

Herb Maclear, the sheriff, pushed his way through the brush close to the body. He, too, examined the web, touching it gingerly with his finger, and then rubbing his finger as though something uncanny, unwholesome, had touched him. The boys, sensing something dreadful, fell silent. Several pushed their way toward Mr Tanner, and stood near him.

Maclear, pale now, stooped and seemed to be looking at something near the ground. 'Gimme that stick!' he ordered. One of the constables handed him what he demanded, and with it the sheriff poked at something on the ground. Their curiosity overcoming the general sense of something queer about the whole proceeding, several of the boys and two of the constables shouldered through the brush toward the sheriff, now digging with his stick, his face red again from stooping and his exertions.

Those standing nearest observed that the sheriff was enlarging a hole that ran into the ground near the heavy root of one of the bushes, a hole about which were heavy wraps of the same gray, shimmering web.

The stick broke through a soft spot, and sank far into the enlarged hole.

'My God!' they heard the sheriff say.

He played delicately with the stick, as though working at something that the ground obscured. He twisted and worked it about in the hole.

At last he drew it up, still carefully, gingerly.

And on its end, transfixed, there came into the light of that morning a huge, frightful, maimed thing, of satiny loathsome black, like the fur of a bat, with glowing salmon-colored striping showing upon its hunched back – a spider as large as a prize peach, with great, waving, now ineffective, metal-like mandibles. They say its little burning eyes like harsh diamonds gleam once, before the sheriff, holding it on the ground with his stick, set his foot on the dreadful thing.

The wind blew cold from the north as the men, in a tight knot, half dragged, half carried the meager body of Pierre Godard hastily out through the retarding brush in silence, while a subdued and silent group of boys, closely gathered about their white-faced counselor, hurried down the declivity toward the edge of the cliff, below which they could see their boats, floating down there in the clean water.

Tea Leaves

The Spanish War had not yet broken in upon the late nineties when the great day came for Miss Abby Tucker – the day on which she deposited the last fifteen dollars which completed her Europe Fund. Five hundred dollars. At last the end of that desperate scrimping! Here was the price completed of a Cook's Tour, and an extra hundred for presents, every expenditure planned and polished to a hard brilliancy in the imagination-mill of a frugal little New England school-teacher.

Few people had heard of 'nervous reactions' in 1897, but Miss Abby had one as she stepped out of the bank. Perhaps a too-steady diet of bread and tea had something to do with it. But for all her meager little body, Miss Abby possessed a soul above nervous reactions. She stopped, and drew several deep breaths when her heart began to flutter and race, but she soon dispelled the effects of her 'turn' by the recollection that it was now only the beginning of the Easter vacation. She had three whole months left in which to arrange the last, fascinating detail of her tour!

There was, for example; the Tower of London. There was also Stratford-on-Avon. There was Vesuvius, and the Temples at Paestum. Miss Abby did hope they might go to Paestum. That was culture! She had steeped her soul in culture, at second-hand, chiefly through the works of Miss Constance Fenimore Woolson, of which Sophia Granniss approved strongly. Miss Granniss, who taught English Literature at the High School, insisted, too, on the necessity of a sojourn on or near the Grand Canal, the study of the Doge's Palace, and at least slight cultural familiarity – as she called it – with the great Church of Santa Maria della Salute. There were, too, the pigeons on the Piazza. That Piazza! Miss Abby's thoughts carried her happily to all these, and to other, anticipated delights. There was the Campanile, and the Four Bronze Horses of San Marco. Napoleon, she knew, had either brought them there or carried them away! She never could remember which. She must look that up. Anyhow, they were there now to be gazed at.

Sophia Granniss said that the glimpse one had of Monte Rosa over in Italy, as one traversed the Gemmi Pass from Spiess to Kandersteg, was 'sublime', and urged Miss Abby not to miss that whatever else she might do. 'You simply must take that walk, Miss Tucker,' she had remarked. 'If you don't, you'll live to regret it. Now mark my words!'

The nervous reaction had gone about its business. Miss Abby picked her careful way along the muddy street to her boarding-house. It would not be necessary to crimp quite so closely during the last school term before vacation in June. Miss Abby gained a pound and a quarter during that term.

It was a happy period for her, what with its constant references to the guide-books she got in turn from the public library of the little Vermont town, the minute arrangements for her departure, and especially, the high lights of certain necessary purchases. These included a steamer-rug, a shawl-strap with a leather handle, which Sophia Granniss had insisted upon, and a new valise. Then there was finally the almost suffocating experience of drawing the four hundred dollars for Thomas Cook and Sons and sending it off in four postal money orders at one fell swoop.

The next day after the closing of school she went to Boston to interview the agent of the steamship line about her accommodations. Sophia Granniss had insisted that 'the personal touch' in all such matters was absolutely necessary, and Miss Abby, feeling – a little goaded, went. She did not succeed in interviewing the steamship agent himself, although she inquired for him. She did see a very polite young English clerk, however. He was very polite indeed.

'I've come to see about my accommodations on board the *Ruritania* sailing the twenty-third, from Hoboken, New Jersey,' began Miss Abby. The clerk smiled delightfully, Miss Abby thought.

'I'm sorry. There are no accommodations on board the *Ruritania*. That is a "one-class" ship, you know, and Cook and Sons have booked her all up.'

'Yes, thank you, I know that. You see, I'm going with that – ah – group. I only wish to make the arrangements about my cabin.'

The clerk disclaimed responsibility.

'That, you see, is all arranged between the agency and the – that, ah – tou – their clients, you know. I mean to say we only make over the entire ship to them and they make the individual arrangements.'

Miss Abby was distinctly disappointed. The 'personal touch' then, would involve going on to New York and interviewing Messrs Cook and Sons. That was out of the question, impossible – financially impossible. She ruminated, a gloved finger against her lips.

'But I'm certain to have a cabin to myself, am I not?' she asked anxiously.

'Well, you see – I mean to say – that – ah – depends! Might I venture to inquire – ah – how much – hm! I – ah – mean to say – '

Miss Abby relieved the embarrassment of the young Englishman.

'I am paying four hundred dollars,' she informed him.

'I fear – I really am afraid – that you wouldn't have the sole use of a cabin. These tours are very popular, you know, and there will be a good many people. Probably they will pack you in, rather.'

Miss Abby thanked him, and took advantage of being in Boston to visit her married sister in Medford. She returned two days later, regretting the certainty that at the price she had paid she could not have the privacy of even the tiniest cabin, but resolved that, come what might, the strong-minded Miss Granniss should keep her finger out of the pie from then on! It was to be *her* tour; not Sophia Granniss's. Sophia Granniss had had hers!

At last the day of departure dawned. Several friends came to the station to see her off, proffering advice to the very last. The traveler for foreign parts sighed with relief as the train chug-chugged its deliberate way out of the railroad station with stentorian whoopings from the engine-whistle. She settled herself luxuriously to the perusal of a newly-bought magazine, but the perusal was sketchy for her heart was singing within her exultantly.

In a kind of happy daze she braved the unaccustomed terrors of crossing New York City, of threading the mazes of an uncharted Hoboken, of finding the right pier, and finally, of making herself known to the tour conductor. If anybody had taken especial notice of Miss Abby – which nobody did – while the liner was slipping down the bay with her nose to the open sea, such person would have caught a glimpse of a perfect, whole-souled happiness.

She was, indeed, far too happy to be seasick! She ate every meal with a sound appetite, and she liked everything but the coffee. That was, to her boarding-house nurtured palate, altogether too powerful a drink, and she soon reverted to her more accustomed tea.

Her attention to the tea leaves diverted her fellow travelers greatly. By long practice she had become accustomed to mixing the tea about with her spoon so that the tea leaves would accumulate on the bottom of the cup, and then, deftly she would drink the remaining tea and set the cup down with a kind of snap and peer at the picture on the bottom. She had acquired great skill in discerning the meanings in these omens! Now for the first time in her life however, the patterns puzzled her. The word 'bow' kept turning up with monotonous frequency. Sometimes it would be an arrangement of the tea leaves like a tied ribbon; sometimes the very letters themselves made their appearance. One day she blushed to herself over the implication which she found. A queer little homunculus near the side of the cup bowed grotesquely to the figure of a seated figure at the bottom, and 'beau' was inevitable! Miss Abby hastily disarranged this embarrassing scene with her teaspoon lest any prying, neighborly eye should see it too and, perhaps, think her somehow unmaidenly!

Then, too, the numbers four and seven would get themselves mixed in with the 'bow' pictures. Miss Abby went the length of publicity interpreting this to mean, under pressure of onlookers, that when *her* beau appeared he would be forty-seven years of age. 'Or,' said she archly, 'perhaps it means that I shall be forty-seven when he makes his appearance!' and she smiled at her fancy to the verge of blushing.

She enjoyed every minute of that propitious voyage.

At Gibraltar, she secured, after considerable bargaining with an opal-eyed nondescript, a lace mantilla for her cousin Emmaline in Bellow's Falls, and this at a price thirty-five cents less than she had planned on for Emmaline's present.

This securing of presents for relatives and friends was part of a long-made plan. From Salviati's in Venice she added largely to her store in the matter of mosaic brooches. In Bavaria she loaded up her luggage with somewhat bulkier gifts for the juvenile nieces and nephews in the shape of wooden toy-animals.

Nearly every place contributed its quota to this impedimenta, until as the tour neared its end the list at last became complete. Every single present was bought. Everybody had been remembered. The list was checked.

It was not, indeed, until that tour drew to a triumphant close with what has sometimes been described as 'Seeing England in Five Days', that it occurred to Miss Abby that in her concern for the others she had quite forgotten to expend the two dollars and a half which she had mentally set aside for the purchase of something for herself.

It was three days before the date set for sailing for home when this fact popped into her head. They were in London. The Tower had been viewed *en masse*. So had St Paul's Cathedral, The Houses of

Parliament, and Westminster Abbey, Poet's Corner and all! Hampton Court had got a glance. So had several other places of interest, which had passed under the breathless purview of those personally conducted. The next day they were to journey to Limehouse and London Docks. Miss Abby thought of her souvenir at luncheon. They had come back to their hotel direct from Trafalgar Square, the party joker, who had urged the conductor to show them Sherlock Holmes's house in Baker Street, having failed dismally! She decided that she would skip the regular program for the afternoon, and go shopping instead. It was the first item she had missed, that afternoon's fly-about.

At dinner, later, she seemed preoccupied. Bewildered among the riches of London town after a long shopping trip upon which she had looked at many things and had bought nothing, she had at last realized that she was 'as good as lost', and had enquired of a policeman the shortest route back to the hotel. He directed her, and the route led through a narrow, dingy street, little more than an alley, connecting two great thoroughfares. She had been much nearer the hotel than she had imagined. She had traversed this short-cut about halfway when she came before a small shop on the corner formed by the intersection of another alleyway. In the shop-window was displayed a miscellaneous collection of merchandise. There were ladies' watches, paper-cutters, bangles of many kinds, old rings, silver and wooden book-markers, pocketbooks, various set and unset semi-precious stones of dubious appearance, umbrellas, a lone lorgnette which appeared second-hand, and a bead necklace. This last caught Miss Abby's eye and she stopped to look at it. It was of medium-sized, pinkish beads. It was dusty and badly soiled, but it had a tiny gilt clasp which seemed to Miss Abby to set it off very well, and the beads themselves were well proportioned and nicely graded.

Miss Abby had always – all her life – wanted a pink bead necklace. Here was one, modest, commending itself therefore to the taste of a self-respecting spinster a little past the first bloom of youth. This, too, it was probable, would be inexpensive, and that was a strong recommendation for it!

Miss Abby, always a cautious soul, took rapid stock of the small shop, and decided that it appeared respectable. In this process she glanced at the doorway, which bore the number forty-seven. She smiled, remembering the omen of the tea-leaves. Across the alleyway her swiftly roving eye caught a street sign. It was dingy and the lettering was almost obliterated, but seeing it, Miss Abby came

very near to having one of her 'turns'. For the faded letters spelled
BOW LANE!

She gasped for breath, pressed her hand against her fluttering
heart, and entered the shop almost grimly. The proprietor, wiping
the crumbs of a tea-cake from his narrow face, and aroused by the
tinkle of the little bell which the opening of the door sounded in his
back room, emerged from that mysterious recess.

'I'd like to look at that necklace, please,' said Miss Abby, pointing
to it where it hung in the shop-window.

The shopkeeper detached the necklace from where it hung on a
wire, blew upon it to free it from the surface dust, and placed it on
the counter. Miss Abby picked it up and looked at it closely. Save that
it badly needed a good scouring it was precisely what she wanted.

'How much is it, please?' she enquired.

'Well now, nobody's asked to see that there necklace,' remarked
the proprietor, as he poked at it with a soiled forefinger, 'since I
bought this 'ere shop with its stock and fixtures, nineteen year now
come Michaelmas. It was one bit of the old stock at that, Miss. I'll let
you 'ave it for – well – say sixteen bob. 'Ow's that, Miss?'

Miss Abby did some mental arithmetic. Sixteen shillings! That
would be about four dollars – three eighty-four. That was rather
more than she had planned to spend on herself. Then she remembered that this was Old England and not New England! Here one
was expected to 'bargain'.

'I'll give you eight shillings,' she said, crisply . . .

They came to an agreement on the sum of twelve shillings, but
Miss Abby could not quite bring herself to the point of closing the
bargain and walking off with the necklace. She examined it again, the
shopkeeper waiting in silence. It was fifty cents, or thereabouts,
more than she had planned. Still! . . .

She bought it at last, counting out the money carefully lest she
make a mistake, and walked out with it wrapped up, in her pocket, in
whitey-brown paper.

She went straight to the hotel and took the necklace to her room.
There she prepared some warm suds and soaked it. She had to
change the water more than once. At last it was clean. She rinsed and
dried it thoroughly. It looked much better now. There was a kind of
shine to the beads which was very attractive. Then she polished the
tiny gilt clasp as well as she could. She laid it away after wrapping it
up, when she had it as clean as she could make it, and descended for
dinner on the dot. Three days later she was *en route* for home.

She took out her necklace several times aboard ship and looked at it. On the last evening aboard, the evening of The Concert, she wore it. No one noticed it, but that did not trouble Miss Abby. She had chosen it chiefly because it was plain and inconspicuous. She declared it with the rest of her purchases at the value of two dollars and eighty-eight cents. The inspector glanced at her and then took one perfunctory glance at the contents of her grip, now covered with 'etiquettes' and pasted his little paster on the end, and she was 'through'.

She was well settled into her accustomed routine by Christmas. Her tour had supplied her with culture enough and memories enough to last her for the lifetime of more or less sordid drudgery which was the best she could possibly anticipate for the future. But Miss Abby wasted no time over gloomy anticipations. She accepted all of the few joyful things that came in her way and she sang a little tune as she dressed for the Christmas party in her boarding-house. She put on the necklace last of all, and glanced at it with approval in the glass as it hung gracefully about her slim but by no means unbeautiful neck. Then, almost running, she went through the hallway and downstairs.

It was the usual country party. There were games, and a great deal of high-pitched conversation, and later, a substantial supper. It was long before the supper though that Miss Abby discovered the presence of a young man, a stranger to her, who seemed to glance at her in a certain way. She decided that the proper descriptive adjective was 'respectful'. He looked at her respectfully, with interest. She was strong-minded and she knew that she was thirty-seven, but when she caught him looking at her for the fourth time, she could feel her heart speed up again slightly, and she said 'Oh!' almost out loud!

For this was a very nice-looking young man, this stranger. He was, she considered, about her own age, perhaps a trifle more mature. He was still young, though! He was dressed quietly, in good taste, and his patent leather shoes gave him, Miss Abby considered, quite an urban touch. There was a suggestion of the man-of-the-world about those shoes – a look of sophistication. Miss Abby found herself cataloguing him. He looked like someone in a bank. He looked as though he might be, on Sunday, a Superintendent of a rather modern kind of Sunday School. That kind of a young man.

Miss Abby's heart gave an unmistakable flutter later when she observed the young man, in polite conversation with their hostess, and approaching her where she sat on a sofa, under the guardianship of a tall India-rubber plant.

'Let me make you acquainted with Miss Tucker,' said the landlady, on her arrival. 'Miss Tucker, Mr Leverett, of Bellow's Falls.'

Mr Leverett of Bellow's Falls bowed – a very nice bow, Miss Abby thought to herself. She murmured something appropriate to the introduction and Mr Leverett sat down beside her on the sofa and began to talk pleasantly.

They put each other at ease immediately, without any conscious effort on the part of either. Almost at once the talk fell into a confidential tone, as though each had many things to say to the other – some time! Miss Abby could not help telling herself that Mr Leverett's still entirely respectful gaze had something else behind it – something much more personal than the weather and the party, which topics had been so far exclusively discussed between them! There was a curious feeling, an indescribable kind of atmosphere, or glow, about those first few minutes of conversation, the kind of glow of which Romance is sometimes happily woven.

When Mr Leverett switched from the weather and the party and very respectfully enquired if he might ask 'a personal question', Miss Abby, while far from surprised, felt her heart give one of those little jumps which by now she had learned to associate with an 'experience'. She reassured herself with the consideration that there could hardly be any 'personal question' of any grave import which could well be asked after five minutes' conversation on first acquaintance!

'Why, certainly,' she replied, very brightly, and looked up at him almist quizzically.

Mr Leverett – he really was, said Miss Abby to herself, afterwards, a very nice young man – blushed, positively blushed.

'I thought, perhaps, you wouldn't mind my asking where you got that necklace you are wearing,' said Mr Leverett, without more than two stammers. 'You see, I'm in the jewelry business over at Bellow's Falls, and I'm very much interested in anything like that. It's rather odd, that necklace.'

Miss Abby, such is the human heart, was at once relieved and vaguely disappointed.

'It's only a little thing I bought last Summer in London,' she replied, taking it off and laying it, warm from her pretty throat, in Mr Leverett's hand. 'It's pretty, I think,' she continued as he looked closely at the necklace, 'but it was very inexpensive. It's only a trifle.'

'Hm!' remarked Mr Leverett, still looking closely at the necklace, 'do you happen to know what the beads are made of?'

'Why, really, I don't think I ever noticed exactly. But I've always supposed they were a kind of good imitation of coral, or perhaps of carnelian. I've thought several times I got a pretty good bargain, don't you?'

'I think they are something else. The beads are of a different texture from either coral or carnelian. I'd certainly like to look at them under a magnifying-glass. Would you, er – mind – ah – telling me . . . O please forgive me! You see I'm a jeweler, and I'm so much interested! I was actually going to ask you how much . . .'

Again Mr Leverett blushed.

'That's all right,' reassured Miss Abby, in an even tone. 'It's a perfectly proper question, I'm sure. I paid twelve shillings for them, about two dollars and eighty-eight cents.'

Mr Leverett peered at the necklace closely, with a kind of professional squint as though he were looking at the works of a watch.

'If it were not too preposterous,' he said, slowly, 'I'd say they were something like pearls, a very finely-made imitation of pearls, and colored, of course, artificially with that peculiar shade of pink which you naturally associated with coral or carnelian. Yes – very well made, indeed. You certainly got a tremendous bargain.'

'How much should you say they might be worth?' It was Miss Abby who blushed this time.

Mr Leverett cogitated this question, rolling the extended string of beads over and over in his hands.

'It's very hard to put a price on anything like these,' he remarked at last, judicially, 'as you can easily see. They are very fine workmanship, almost "ancient", I should say. Beautiful work – beautiful! It is real jewelers' handwork of the best quality. The clasp, and the metal string, and the exact piercing all show fine work. To get a set like these, made today, you would certainly have to pay – um – let me see! Well, I should be inclined to think, about five hundred dollars.' Then, as she exclaimed, 'I'll tell you what to do Miss Tucker. Why not take them to Boston and have them properly valued? You could take them into one of the great jewelry stores like Muffen's, where they would be in a position to give you a proper estimate; to look at them with good glasses and all that. You see, these might be worth even more than five hundred dollars. I only made a very rough guess.'

Miss Abby could hardly compose herself to sleep that night. Just suppose! Five hundred dollars! The complete expenses of her trip!

It wouldn't be right; it would not be fair to the man in the little shop there in Bow Lane, London! Miss Abby had a New England conscience – an old-fashioned one, in good working-order! Still, she was no fool. If they were of some considerable value, it was just the man's sheer carelessness that had not found it out. He had confessed to having the beads for nineteen years!

It occurred to her that she had several days before school started up again, and a little money in hand. She was not saving nowadays for a Europe Fund! It doesn't cost such a terrible lot of money to get to Boston, and she could stay with her sister in Medford. She made up her mind to go abruptly, and with this anticipated adventure clasped close, she fell quickly asleeep.

The next afternoon Miss Abby was asking for an interview with a member of the firm at Muffen's jewelry store in Boston. She was received by a gentleman named Mr Hay. He listened gravely to her story, took the necklace, and requested her to return the next morning at eleven.

She was promptly on hand and found Mr Hay wearing an expression of restrained enthusiasm. He was very cordial, and received her as though he had known her for some time! Miss Abby sat, tight-lipped, awaiting the verdict.

'I have made a very careful examination of your necklace,' said Mr Hay, with some deliberation. 'Two of our men in the store have also examined it at my request. We are at one in our conclusion. The necklace is of pink pearls, and these are among the most valuable of pearls when in perfect condition. A further and more exhaustive examination would have to be made, doubtless. But, as you said yesterday, you managed to get a real "bargain". I think I may tell you at once that we are prepared, in case you wish to dispose of the pearls, to give you our cheque for six thousand dollars.'

Miss Abby uttered a little gasp. Her eyes were shining. But she was careful, even in that overwhelming moment, not to interrupt Mr Hay, who had only paused, and seemed about to continue.

'At the same time,' he added, 'we feel unwilling to take any undue advantage of our comparative ignorance of the true value of the necklace. We therefore feel that we should advise you, definitely, to take this course – ' Mr Hay paused again, and continued.

'We suggest that you allow our offer to stand. We are ready to carry through that arrangement at any time. But we suggest to you that you take the necklace first to New York, to Dufane's, where Dr Schwartz, the pearl-expert is employed. Show the pearls to him and get his valuation. We do not imagine that it will be less than ours; it may very likely be more. In that case, it will be to your advantage to sell them elsewhere.'

Mr Hay bowed Miss Abby politely out, and she emerged upon the street walking on air. She wasted no time. This was sound advice and she knew it. The next morning she bade her relatives goodbye and took the early train to New York.

Her interview with the great pearl-expert proved a very simple matter. She went straight to Dufane's, and told the first person she saw that she was bringing some pearls from Muffen's in Boston to Dr Schwartz for valuation. She had not meant to deceive her inter-locutor, but he gathered the natural impression that she was in the employ of the Boston jewelers, and she was shown in to Dr Schwartz at once. He took the pearls and gave her an appointment for the next afternoon at two o'clock.

Leaving the great store she took, for the first time in her life, what she called 'herdic', or four-wheeler cab, and was driven to the Grand Union Hotel. After dinner there, being tired, she said her prayers and retired at eight o'clock.

The next morning dragged. She had arisen, according to her habit, bright and early, made her bed, eaten breakfast at an hour when no one else except an early-starting commercial traveler or two was in the dining-room, and was engaged in addressing picture-postal cards when the hotel chambermaid came in about ten o'clock. The maid gasped and beat hasty retreat, never before had she known a guest to 'do' her room herself!

Miss Abby, somewhat appalled at the prices in the hotel dining-room, took her lunch at a small restaurant, and shortly thereafter went to keep her appointment at Dufane's.

She was agreeably surprised on entering that great store to be addressed by name. Wondering somewhat at this distinction, she followed her guide to the sanctum of the pearl-expert. Here a sur-prising exercise was taking place. It was a good-sized room, up three flights in the elevator, and it was filled with men; filled almost uncomfortably. There were men with beards and men without; tall, thin men, and short, fat men. She counted nineteen, though she could not be certain she had included them all, for they kept moving about in the most extraordinary way. Little groups and knots of men kept forming, breaking up, and re-forming again. Everybody seemed to be talking in every imaginable language, including the Scandin-avian! But this was only the impression she got on her arrival. The talking and the group-shifting stopped abruptly at her arrival, and everybody present turned to stare at her. Miss Abby had never been so embarrassed in her life! Then Dr Schwartz rescued her and showed her to a seat at the end of the long table which ran down the length of the big room.

The pearl-expert coughed slightly and said, 'Will you please oblige us, Miss Tucker, by telling us about this necklace; and first, if you please, how it came into your possession?'

Miss Abby told them.

When she finished her brief and matter-of-fact recital there was a moment of silence, silence that is like the calm before the storm. Then the storm broke. A kind of roaring hum burst forth simultaneously from the throats of all the men present. Everyone was talking at once; nobody listening. Miss Abby tried to listen, but it was too much for her. She was completely nonplussed for the very first time in her life. It seemed to her that some of these men whom she had never seen or heard of before were shouting at her! It was dreadful! It was like being plunged suddenly into a meeting in a madhouse. The little groups formed afresh, only more rapidly now. Men gesticulated, and shouted at the tops of their voices. Two dark-skinned gentlemen who gesticulated more than any of the others seemed at one moment to be about to begin a duel, but they ended this demonstration very queerly, Miss Abby thought, by clasping each other in their arms and kissing each other! A phlegmatic gentleman with a thick, guttural accent, was waddling up and down the whole length of the room, much like a caged polar-bear, and waving his arms like flails all the time. He was rumbling, in his deep voice, 'incredible, incredible, incredible,' over and over again.

Even Dr Schwartz, to whom she looked as her anchor in this tumultuous sea – even Dr Schwartz was waving *his* arms about, and shouting with the rest!

It occurred to the distracted Miss Abby that perhaps she was going to faint. While she was wondering, Dr Schwartz, who had waved his arms and shouted, after all, to some purpose, succeeded in establishing something like quiet. 'Gentlemen, *Gentlemen* !' he was shouting.

At last he prevailed, and in the comparative silence which ensued he addressed Miss Abby a second time: 'You will understand,' he said, 'my dear lady, that an event like this does not occur every day among jewelers. These gentlemen and I have all examined your wonderful necklace. We are unanimous in our opinion. There is

indeed no room for doubt. This necklace is unique. Not one of us
was aware of its existence, that is for the past two centuries, since it
disappeared from the British Museum, in eighteen hundred and one.
There is, I may inform you, really no criterion by which it may be
properly valued. Will you look here for a moment; look through this
glass – ah, here is the adjustment – yes, like that. Do you see?'

Miss Abby saw. It came abruptly into focus as she turned gingerly
the adjustment-screw in the great magnifying instrument which
stood upon the table, below the sight of which the tiny, gilt clasp was
held in place by small clamps. She saw, but she could not speak. For
she was petrified. The inscription, far too fine even to be noticed
without the aid of a powerful magnifying agent, read:

ELIZABETH, FROM RALEIGH

Miss Abby took a deep, deliberate breath, and read it aloud, slowly,
in a tiny, clear and perfectly audible voice, not at all like her ordinary
voice, in the midst of a dead silence. Miss Abby felt again as though
she were going to faint. She could not be sure; she had never fainted
before! But she needed air, badly, just then. She did not faint. She
was too much interested to faint just then!

She listened very carefully to Dr Schwartz, who seemed to be
speaking in a very muffled, distant voice. He was saying:

' . . . So that Dufane and Company are prepared, in case you are
willing to dispose of this necklace, to pay the sum of two hundred
and fifty thousand dollars. We feel bound to inform you, however,
that if you care to hold it – your title is undoubtedly clear – and
decide to offer it to the British Museum, it is not unlikely that . . . '

Miss Abby did not wish to hear any more. She had heard enough,
she thought. With lightning-like rapidity she reviewed the various
estimates upon the value of the necklace: 'Sixteen bob.' – 'Well,
I should be inclined to think, about five hundred dollars.' – that
was Mr Leverett. Then Mr Hay: 'We are prepared . . . to give
you our cheque for six thousand . . . ' And now – 'Two hundred and
fifty thousand dollars!' And it had cost her twelve shillings, twelve
shillings, bargained for; argued over! She straightened up in her
chair, and looked Dr Schwartz in the eye.

'I will accept your offer,' she said simply. Then the bedlam broke
out afresh. Men were crowding about her, pressing towards her . . .
She fainted for the first – and last – time in her life.

The next evening she arrived home, tired out. The hotel bill had
been rather more than she had anticipated, and with that and the

railway fares nearly all her ready money was gone. In fact, she arrived at her boarding-house with precisely eight cents in coins and a certified cheque for two hundred and fifty-thousand dollars.

The first thing she did after removing her gloves, was to get a cup of tea. She needed the tea badly. When she had drunk it she noticed a large letter 'L' in the bottom of the cup. It looked rather like the shape of Lucerne outlined in its lights in the evening as one gazed down upon that city from the heights of Mt Pilatus – as Miss Abby had, in fact, looked down upon it three months previously. She sighed, reminiscently, and laid down her teacup.

In her bedroom she found a letter on the bureau. The postmark was Bellow's Falls. She opened and read it. It was from Mr Leverett. He wrote to ask if he might have the privilege of coming over soon to call upon her. He suggested the next Sunday afternoon, if she were not otherwise engaged then. Miss Abby was not otherwise engaged. 'I'll have those custom duties to pay,' she thought, irrelevantly, as she finished her letter.

She stood there in her bedroom with her letter in her hand. The eight cents and the certified cheque lay before her, side by side on the mean little bureau which had served her now continuously for some thirteen years. Miss Abby looked back over those thirteen years with her mind's eye, looked back, and shuddered. They had been dreary years, those thirteen. Then she ventured to look forward into the possible future – a tiny peep. She glanced appraisingly at the bureau and about her room and out the window. Then, without so much as removing her hat, she read Mr Leverett's letter through a second time, and glanced down at the coins and the cheque.

Miss Abby looked up from the very end of her letter, where Mr Leverett had signed his name, modestly, without any flourish, and in the glass. She caught herself blushing.

'I believe I shall marry him,' said she, in a whisper, and started to take the pins out of her hat.

The Trap

It was on a certain Thursday morning in December that the whole thing began with that unaccountable motion I thought I saw in my antique Copenhagen mirror. Something, it seemed to me, stirred – something reflected in the glass, though I was alone in my quarters. I paused and looked intently, then, deciding that the effect must be a pure illusion, resumed the interrupted brushing of my hair.

I had discovered the old mirror, covered with dust and cobwebs, in an outbuilding of an abandoned estate-house in Santa Cruz's sparsely settled Northside territory, and had brought it to the United States from the Virgin Islands. The venerable glass was dim from more than two hundred years' exposure to a tropical climate, and the graceful ornamentation along the top of the gilt frame had been badly smashed. I had had the detached pieces set back into the frame before placing it in storage with my other belongings.

Now, several years later, I was staying half as a guest and half as a tutor at the private school of my old friend Browne on a windy Connecticut hillside – occupying an unused wing in one of the dormitories, where I had two rooms and a hallway to myself. The old mirror, stowed securely in mattresses, was the first of my possessions to be unpacked on my arrival; and I had set it up majestically in the living-room, on top of an old rosewood console which had belonged to my great-grandmother.

The door of my bedroom was just opposite that of the living-room, with a hallway between; and I had noticed that by looking into my chiffonier glass I could see the larger mirror through the two doorways – which was exactly like glancing down an endless, though diminishing, corridor. On this Thursday morning I thought I saw a curious suggestion of motion down that normally empty corridor – but, as I have said, soon dismissed the notion.

When I reached the dining-room I found everyone complaining of the cold, and learned that the school's heating-plant was temporarily out of order. Being especially sensitive to low temperatures, I was myself an acute sufferer; and at once decided not to brave any freezing schoolroom that day. Accordingly I invited my class to come over to my living-room for an informal session around my grate-fire – a suggestion which the boys received enthusiastically.

After the session one of the boys, Robert Grandison, asked if he might remain; since he had no appointment for the second morning period. I told him to stay, and welcome. He sat down to study in front of the fireplace in a comfortable chair.

It was not long, however, before Robert moved to another chair somewhat farther away from the freshly replenished blaze, this change bringing him directly opposite the old mirror. From my own chair in another part of the room I noticed how fixedly he began to look at the dim, cloudy glass, and, wondering what so greatly interested him, was reminded of my own experience earlier that morning. As time passed he continued to gaze, a slight frown knitting his brows.

At last I quietly asked him what had attracted his attention. Slowly, and still wearing the puzzled frown, he looked over and replied rather cautiously: 'It's the corrugations in the glass – or whatever they are, Mr Canevin. I was noticing how they all seem to run from a certain point. Look – I'll show you what I mean.'

The boy jumped up, went over to the mirror, and placed his finger on a point near its lower left-hand corner.

'It's right here, sir,' he explained, turning to look toward me and keeping his finger on the chosen spot.

His musclar action in turning may have pressed his finger against the glass. Suddenly he withdrew his hand as though with some slight effort, and with a faintly muttered 'Ouch.' Then he looked at the glass in obvious mystification.

'What happened?' I asked, rising and approaching.

'Why – it – ' He seemed embarrassed. 'It – I – felt – well, as though it were pulling my finger into it. Seems – er – perfectly foolish, sir, but – well – it was a most peculiar sensation.' Robert had an unusual vocabulary for his fifteen years.

I came over and had him show me the exact spot he meant.

'You'll think I'm rather a fool sir,' he said shamefacedly, 'but – well, from right here I can't be absolutely sure. From the chair it seemed to be clear enough.'

Now thoroughly interested, I sat down in the chair Robert had occupied and looked at the spot he selected on the mirror. Instantly the thing 'jumped out at me'. Unmistakably, from that particular angle, all the many whorls in the ancient glass appeared to converge like a large number of spread strings held in one hand and radiating out in streams.

Getting up and crossing to the mirror, I could no longer see the curious spot. Only from certain angles, apparently, was it visible. Directly viewed, that portion of the mirror did not even give back a normal reflection – for I could not see my face in it. Manifestly I had a minor puzzle on my hands.

Presently the school gong sounded, and the fascinated Robert Grandison departed hurriedly, leaving me alone with my odd little problem in optics. I raised several window-shades, crossed the hallway, and sought for the spot in the chiffonier mirror's reflection. Finding it readily, I looked very intently and thought I again detected something of the 'motion'. I craned my neck, and at last, at a certain angle of vision, the thing again 'jumped out at me'.

The vague 'motion' was now positive and definite – an appearance of torsional movement, or of whirling; much like a minute yet intense whirlwind or waterspout, or a huddle of autumn leaves dancing circularly in an eddy of wind along a level lawn. It was, like the earth's, a double motion – around and around, and at the same time *inward*, as if the whorls poured themselves endlessly toward some point inside the glass. Fascinated, yet realizing that the thing must be an illusion, I grasped an impression of quite distinct *suction*, and thought of Robert's embarrassed explanation: '*I felt as though it were pulling my finger into it.*'

A kind of slight chill ran suddenly up and down my backbone. There was something here distinctly worth looking into. And as the idea of investigation came to me, I recalled the rather wistful expression of Robert Grandison when the gong called him to class. I remembered how he had looked back over his shoulder as he walked obediently out into the hallway, and resolved that he should be included in whatever analysis I might make of this little mystery.

Exciting events connected with that same Robert, however, were soon to chase all thoughts of the mirror from my consciousness for a time. I was away all that afternoon, and did not return to the school until the five-fifteen 'Call-over' – a general assembly at which the boys' attendance was compulsory. Dropping in at this function with the idea of picking Robert up for a session with the mirror, I was astonished and pained to find him absent – a very unusual and unaccountable thing in his case. That evening Browne told me that the boy had actually disappeared, a search in his room, in the gymnasium, and in all other accustomed places being unavailing, though all his belongings – including his outdoor clothing – were in their proper places.

He had not been encountered on the ice or with any of the hiking groups that afternoon, and telephone calls to all the school-catering merchants of the neighborhood were in vain. There was, in short, no record of his having been seen since the end of the lesson periods at two-fifteen; when he had turned up the stairs toward his room in Dormitory Number Three.

When the disappearance was fully realized, the resulting sensation was tremendous throughout the school. Browne, as headmaster, had to bear the brunt of it; and such an unprecedented occurrence in his well-regulated, highly-organized institution left him quite bewildered. It was learned that Robert had not run away to his home in western Pennsylvania, nor did any of the searching-parties of boys and masters find any trace of him in the snowy countryside around the school. So far as could be seen, he had simply vanished.

Robert's parents arrived on the afternoon of the second day after his disappearance. They took their trouble quietly, though of course they were staggered by this unexpected disaster. Browne looked ten years older for it, but there was absolutely nothing that could be done. By the fourth day the case had settled down in the opinion of the school as an insoluble mystery. Mr and Mrs Grandison went reluctantly back to their home, and on the following morning the ten days' Christmas vacation began.

Boys and masters departed in anything but the usual holiday spirit; and Browne and his wife were left, along with the servants, as my only fellow-occupants of the big place. Without the masters and boys it seemed a very hollow shell indeed.

That afternoon I sat in front of my grate-fire thinking about Robert's disappearance and evolving all sorts of fantastic theories to account for it. By evening I had acquired a bad headache, and ate a light supper accordingly. Then, after a brisk walk around the massed buildings, I returned to my living-room and took up the burden of thought once more.

A little after ten o'clock I awakened in my armchair, stiff and chilled, from a doze during which I had let the fire go out. I was physically uncomfortable, yet mentally aroused by a peculiar sensation of expectancy and possible hope. Of course it had to do with the problem that was harassing me. For I had started from that inadvertent nap with a curious, persistent idea – the odd idea that a tenuous, hardly recognizable Robert Grandison had been trying desperately to communicate with me. I finally went to bed with one conviction unreasoningly strong in my mind. Somehow I was sure that young Robert Grandison was still alive.

That I should be receptive of such a notion will not seem strange to those who know my long residence in the West Indies and my close contact with unexplained happenings there. It will not seem strange, either, that I fell asleep with an urgent desire to establish some sort of mental communication with the missing boy. Even the most prosaic scientists affirm, with Freud, Jung, and Adler, that the subconcious mind is most open to external impression in sleep; though such impressions are seldom carried over intact into the waking state.

Going a step further and granting the existence of telepathic forces, it follows that such forces must act most strongly on a sleeper; so that if I were ever to get a definite message from Robert, it would be during a period of profoundest slumber. Of course, I might lose the message in waking; but my aptitude for retaining such things has been sharpened by types of mental discipline picked up in various obscure corners of the globe.

I must have dropped asleep instantaneously, and from the vividness of my dreams and the absence of wakeful intervals I judge that my sleep was a very deep one. It was six-forty-five when I awakened, and there still lingered with me certain impressions which I knew were carried over from the world of somnolent cerebration. Filling my mind was the vision of Robert Grandison strangely transformed to a boy of a dull greenish dark-blue color; Robert desperately endeavoring to communicate with me by means of speech, yet finding some almost insuperable difficulty in so doing. A wall of curious spatial separation seemed to stand between him and me – a mysterious, invisible wall which completely baffled us both.

I had seen Robert as though at some distance, yet queerly enough he seemed at the same time to be just beside me. He was both larger and smaller than in real life, his apparent size varying *directly*, instead of *inversely*, with the distance as he advanced and retreated in the course of conversation. That is, he grew larger instead of smaller to my eye when he stepped away or backwards, and vice versa; as if the laws of perspective in his case had been wholly reversed. His aspect was misty and uncertain – as if he lacked sharp or permanent outlines; and the anomalies of his coloring and clothing baffled me utterly at first.

At some point in my dream Robert's vocal efforts had finally crystallized into audible speech – albeit speech of an abnormal thickness and dullness. I could not for a time understand anything he said, and even in the dream racked my brain for a clue to where he was, what he wanted to tell, and why his utterance was so clumsy and unintelligible. Then little by little I began to distinguish words and phrases, the very first of which sufficed to throw my dreaming self into the wildest excitement and to establish a certain mental connection which had previously refused to take conscious form because of the utter incredibility of what it implied.

I do not know how long I listened to those halting words amidst my deep slumber, but hours must have passed while the strangely remote speaker struggled on with his tale. There was revealed to me such a circumstance as I cannot hope to make others believe without the strongest corroborative evidence, yet which I was quite ready to accept as truth – both in the dream and after waking – because of my former contacts with uncanny things. The boy was obviously watching my face – mobile in receptive sleep – as he choked along; for about the time I began to comprehend him, his own expression brightened and gave signs of gratitude and hope.

Any attempt to hint at Robert's message, as it lingered in my ears after a sudden awakening in the cold, brings this narrative to a point where I must choose my words with the greatest care. Everything involved is so difficult to record that one tends to flounder helplessly. I have said that the revelation established in my mind a certain connection which reason had not allowed me to formulate consciously before. This connection, I need no longer hesitate to hint, had to do with the old Copenhagen mirror whose suggestions of motion had so impressed me on the morning of the disappearance, and whose whorl-like contours and apparent illusions of suction had later exerted such a disquieting fascination on both Robert and me.

Resolutely, though my outer consciousness had previously rejected what my intuition would have liked to imply, it could reject that stupendous conception no longer. What was fantasy in the tale of 'Alice' now came to me as a grave and immediate reality. That looking-glass had indeed possessed a malign, abnormal suction; and the struggling speaker in my dream made clear the extent to which it violated all the known precedents of human experience and all the age-old laws of our three sane dimensions. It was more than a mirror – it was a gate; a trap; a link with spatial recesses not meant for the denizens of our visible universe, and realizable only in terms of the most intricate non-Euclidean mathematics. *And in some outrageous fashion Robert Grandison had passed out of our ken into the glass and was there immured, waiting for release.*

It is significant that upon awakening I harbored no genuine doubt of the reality of the revelation. That I had actually held conversation with a transdimensional Robert, rather than evoked the whole episode from my broodings about his disappearance and about the old illusions of the mirror, was as certain to my utmost instincts as any of the instinctive certainties commonly recognized as valid.

The tale thus unfolded to me was of the most incredibly bizarre character. As had been clear on the morning of his disappearance, Robert was intensely fascinated by the ancient mirror. All through the hours of school, he had it in mind to come back to my living-room and examine it further. When he did arrive, after the close of the school day, it was somewhat later than two-twenty, and I was absent in town. Finding me out and knowing that I would not mind, he had come into my living-room and gone straight to the mirror; standing before it and studying the place where, as we had noted, the whorls appeared to converge.

Then, quite suddenly, there had come to him an overpowering urge to place his hand upon this whorl-center. Almost reluctantly, against his better judgement, he had done so; and upon making the contact had felt at once the strange, almost painful suction which had perplexed him that morning. Immediately thereafter – quite without warning, but with a wrench which seemed to twist and tear every bone and muscle in his body and to bulge and press and cut at every nerve – he had been abruptly *drawn through* and found himself *inside*.

Once through, the excruciatingly painful stress upon his entire system was suddenly released. He felt, he said, as though he had just been born – a feeling that made itself evident every time he tried to do anything; walk, stoop, turn his head, or utter speech. Everything about his body seemed a misfit.

These sensations wore off after a long while, Robert's body becoming an organized whole rather than a number of protesting parts. Of all the forms of expression, speech remained the most difficult; doubtless because it is complicated, bringing into play a number of different organs, muscles, and tendons. Robert's feet, on the other hand, were the first members to adjust themselves to the new conditions within the glass.

During the morning hours I rehearsed the whole reason-defying problem; correlating everything I had seen and heard, dismissing the natural scepticism of a man of sense, and scheming to devise possible plans for Robert's release from his incredible prison. As I did so a number of originally perplexing points became clear – or at least, clearer – to me.

There was, for example, the matter of Robert's coloring. His face and hands, as I have indicated, were a kind of dull greenish dark-blue; and I may add that his familiar blue Norfolk jacket had turned to a pale lemon-yellow while his trousers remained a neutral gray as before. Reflecting on this after waking, I found the circumstance closely allied to the reversal of perspective which made Robert seem to grow larger when receding and smaller when approaching. Here, too, was a physical *reversal* – for every detail of his coloring in the unknown dimension was the exact reverse or complement of the corresponding color detail in normal life. In physics the typical complementary colors are blue and yellow, and red and green. These pairs are opposites, and when mixed yield gray. Robert's natural color was a pinkish-buff, the opposite of which is the greenish-blue I saw. His blue coat had become yellow, while the gray trousers remained gray. This latter point baffled me until I remembered that gray is itself a mixture of opposites. There is no opposite for gray – or rather, it is its own opposite.

Another clarified point was that pertaining to Robert's curiously dulled and thickened speech – as well as to the general awkwardness and sense of misfit bodily parts of which he complained. This, at the outset, was a puzzle indeed; though after long thought the clue occurred to me. Here again was the same *reversal* which affected perspective and coloration. Anyone in the fourth dimension must necessarily be reversed in just this way – hands and feet, as well as colors and perspectives, being changed about. It would be the same with all the other dual organs, such as nostrils, ears, and eyes. Thus Robert had been talking with a reversed tongue, teeth, vocal cords, and kindred speech-apparatus; so that his difficulties in utterance were little to be wondered at.

As the morning wore on, my sense of the stark reality and maddening urgency of the dream-disclosed situation increased rather than decreased. More and more I felt that something must be done, yet realized that I could not seek advice or aid. Such a story as mine – a conviction based upon mere dreaming – could not conceivably bring me anything but ridicule or suspicions as to my mental state. And what, indeed, could I do, aided or unaided, with as little working data as my nocturnal impressions had provided? I must, I finally recognized, have more information before I could even think of a possible plan for releasing Robert. This could come only through the receptive conditions of sleep, and it heartened me to reflect that according to every probability my telepathic contact would be resumed the moment I fell into deep slumber again.

I accomplished sleeping that afternoon, after a midday dinner at which, through rigid self-control, I succeeded in concealing from Browne and his wife the tumultuous thoughts that crashed through my mind. Hardly had my eyes closed when a dim telepathic image began to appear; and I soon realized to my infinite excitement that it was identical with what I had seen before. If anything, it was more distinct; and when it began to speak I seemed able to grasp a greater proportion of the words.

During this sleep I found most of the morning's deductions confirmed, though the interview was mysteriously cut off long prior to my awakening. Robert had seemed apprehensive just before communication ceased, but had already told me that in his strange fourth-dimensional prison colors and spatial relationships were indeed reversed – black being white, distance increasing apparent size, and so on.

He had also intimated that, notwithstanding his possession of full physical form and sensations, most human vital properties seemed curiously suspended. Nutriment, for example, was quite unnecessary – a phenomenon really more singular than the omnipresent reversal of objects and attributes, since the latter was a reasonable and mathematically indicated state of things. Another significant piece of information was that the only exit from the glass to the world was the entrance-way, and that this was permanently barred and impenetrably sealed, so far as egress was concerned.

That night I had another visitation from Robert; nor did such impressions, received at odd intervals while I slept receptively-minded, cease during the entire period of his incarceration. His efforts to communicate were desperate and often pitiful; for at times the telepathic bond would weaken, while at other times fatigue, excitement, or fear of interruption would hamper and thicken his speech.

I may as well narrate as a continuous whole all that Robert told me throughout the whole series of transient mental contacts – perhaps supplementing it at certain points with facts directly related after his release. The telepathic information was fragmentary and often nearly inarticulate, but I studied it over and over during the waking intervals of three intense days; classifying and cogitating with feverish diligence, since it was all that I had to go upon if the boy were to be brought back into our world.

The fourth-dimensional region in which Robert found himself was not, as in scientific romance, an unknown and infinite realm of strange sights and fantastic denizens; but was rather a projection of certain limited parts of our own terrestrial sphere within an alien and normally inaccessible aspect or direction of space. It was a curiously fragmentary, intangible, and heterogeneous world – a series of apparently dissociated scenes merging indistinctly one into the other; their constituent details having an obviously different status from that of an object drawn into the ancient mirror as Robert had been drawn. These scenes were like dream-vistas or magic lantern images – elusive visual impressions of which the boy was not really a part, but which formed a sort of panoramic background or ethereal environment against which or amidst which he moved.

He could not touch any of the parts of these scenes – walls, trees, furniture, and the like – but whether this was because they were truly non-material, or because they always receded at his approach, he was singularly unable to determine. Everything seemed fluid, mutable, and unreal. When he walked, it appeared to be on whatever lower surface the visible scene might have – floor, path, greensward, or such; but upon analysis he always found that the contact was an illusion. There was never any difference in the resisting force met by his feet – and by his hands when he would stoop experimentally – no matter what changes of apparent surface might be involved. He could not describe this foundation or limiting plane on which he walked as anything more definite than a virtually abstract pressure balancing his gravity. Of definite tactile distinctiveness it had none, and supplementing it there seemed to be a kind of restricted levitational force which accomplished transfers of altitude. He could never actually climb stairs, yet would gradually walk up from a lower level to a higher.

Passage from one definite scene to another involved a sort of gliding through a region of shadow or blurred focus where the details of each scene mingled curiously. All the vistas were distinguished by the absence of transient objects, and the indefinite or ambiguous appearance of such semi-transient objects as furniture or details of vegetation. The lighting of every scene was diffuse and perplexing, and of course the scheme of reversed colors – bright red grass, yellow sky with confused black and gray cloud-forms, white tree-trunks, and green brick walls – gave to everything an air of unbelievable grotesquerie. There was an alternation of day and night, which turned out to be a reversal of the normal hours of light and darkness at whatever point on the earth the mirror might be hanging.

This seemingly irrelevant diversity of the scenes puzzled Robert until he realized that they comprised merely such places as had been reflected for long continuous periods in the ancient glass. This also explained the odd absence of transient objects, the generally arbitrary boundaries of vision, and the fact that all exteriors were framed by the outlines of doorways or windows. The glass, it appeared, had power to store up these intangible scenes through long exposure; though it could never absorb anything corporeally, as Robert had been absorbed, except by a very different and particular process.

But – to me at least – the most incredible aspect of the mad phenomenon was the monstrous subversion of our known laws of space involved in the relation of various illusory scenes to the actual terrestrial regions represented. I have spoken of the glass as storing up the images of these regions, but this is really an inexact definition. In truth, each of the mirror scenes formed a true and quasi-permanent fourth-dimensional projection of the corresponding mundane region; so that whenever Robert moved to a certain part of a certain scene, as he moved into the image of my room when sending his telepathic messages, *he was actually in that place itself, on earth* – though under spatial conditions which cut off all sensory communication, in either direction, between him and the present tri-dimensional aspect of the place.

Theoretically speaking, a prisoner in the glass could in a few moments go anywhere on our planet – into any place, that is, which had ever been reflected in the mirror's surface. This probably applied even to places where the mirror had not hung long enough to produce a clear illusory scene; the terrestrial region being then represented by a zone of more or less formless shadow. Outside the definite scenes was a seemingly limitless waste of neutral gray shadow about which Robert could never be certain, and into which he never dared stray far lest he become hopelessly lost to the real and mirror worlds alike.

Among the earliest particulars which Robert gave, was the fact that he was not alone in his confinement. Various others, all in antique garb, were in there with him – a corpulent middle-aged gentleman with tied queue and velvet knee-breeches who spoke English fluently though with a marked Scandinavian accent; a rather beautiful small girl with very blonde hair which appeared as glossy dark blue; two apparently mute Negroes whose features contrasted grotesquely with the pallor of their reversed-colored skins; three young men; one young woman; a very small child, almost an infant; and a lean, elderly Dane of extremely distinctive aspect and a kind of half-malign intellectuality of countenance.

This last named individual – Axel Holm, who wore the satin small-clothes, flared-skirted coat, and voluminous full-bottomed periwig of an age more than two centuries in the past – was notable among the little band as being the one responsible for the presence of them all. He it was who, skilled equally in the arts of magic and glass working, had long ago fashioned this strange dimensional prison in which himself, his slaves, and those whom he chose to invite or allure thither were immured unchangingly for as long as the mirror might endure.

Holm was born early in the seventeenth century, and had followed with tremendous competence and success the trade of a glass-blower and molder in Copenhagen. His glass, especially in the form of large drawing-room mirrors, was always at a premium. But the same bold mind which had made him the first glazier of Europe also served to carry his interests and ambitions far beyond the sphere of mere material craftsmanship. He had studied the world around him, and chafed at the limitations of human knowledge and capability. Eventually he sought for dark ways to overcome those limitations, and gained more success than is good for any mortal.

He had aspired to enjoy something like eternity, the mirror being his provision to secure this end. Serious study of the fourth dimension was far from beginning with Einstein in our own era; and Holm, more than erudite in all the methods of his day, knew that a bodily entrance into that hidden phase of space would prevent him from dying in the ordinary physical sense. Research showed him that the principle of reflection undoubtedly forms the chief gate to all dimensions beyond our familiar three; and chance placed in his hands a small and very ancient glass whose cryptic properties he believed he could turn to advantage. Once 'inside' this mirror according to the method he had envisaged, he felt that 'life' in the sense of form and consciousness would go on virtually forever, provided the mirror could be preserved indefinitely from breakage or deterioration.

Holm made a magnificent mirror, such as would be prized and carefully preserved; and in it deftly fused the strange whorl-configured relic he had acquired. Having thus prepared his refuge and his trap, he began to plan his mode of entrance and conditions of tenancy. He would have with him both servitors and companions; and as an experimental beginning he sent before him into the glass two dependable Negro slaves brought from the West Indies. What his sensations must have been upon beholding this first concrete demonstration of his theories, only imagination can conceive.

Undoubtedly a man of his knowledge realized that absence from the outside world if deferred beyond the natural span of life of those within, must mean instant dissolution at the first attempt to return to that world. But, barring that misfortune or accidental breakage, those within would remain forever as they were at the time of entrance. They would never grow old, and would need neither food nor drink.

To make his prison tolerable he sent ahead of him certain books and writing materials, a chair and table of stoutest workmanship, and a few other accessories. He knew that the images which the glass would reflect or absorb would not be tangible, but would merely extend around him like a background of dream. His own transition in 1687 was a momentous experience; and must have been attended by mixed sensations of triumph and terror. Had anything gone wrong, there were frightful possibilities of being lost in dark and inconceivable multiple dimensions.

For over fifty years he had been unable to secure any additions to the little company of himself and slaves, but later on he had perfected his telepathic method of visualizing small sections of the outside world close to the glass, and attracting certain individuals in those areas through the mirror's strange entrance. Thus Robert, influenced into a desire to press upon the 'door', had been lured within. Such visualizations depended wholly on telepathy, since no one inside the mirror could see out into the world of men.

It was in truth, a strange life that Holm and his company had lived inside the glass. Since the mirror had stood for fully a century with its face to the dusty stone wall of the shed where I found it, Robert was the first being to enter this limbo after all that interval. His arrival was a gala event, for he brought news of the outside world which must have been of the most startling impressiveness to the more thoughtful of those within. He, in his turn – young though he was – felt over-whelmingly the weirdness of meeting and talking with persons who had been alive in the seventeenth and eighteenth centuries.

The deadly monotony of life for the prisoners can only be vaguely conjectured. As mentioned, its extensive spatial variety was limited to localities which had been reflected in the mirror for long periods; and many of these had become dim and strange as tropical climates had made inroads on the surface. Certain localities were bright and beautiful, and in these the company usually gathered. But no scene could be fully satisfying, since the visible objects were all unreal and intangible, and often of perplexingly indefinite outline. When the tedious periods of darkness came, the general custom was to indulge in memories, reflections, or conversations. Each one of that strange, pathetic group had retained his or her personality unchanged and unchangeable, since becoming immune to the time effects of outside space.

The number of inanimate objects within the glass; aside from the clothing of the prisoners, was very small; being largely limited to the accessories Holm had provided for himself. The rest did without even furniture, since sleep and fatigue had vanished along with most other vital attributes. Such inorganic things as were present, seemed as exempt from decay as the living beings. The lower forms of animal life were wholly absent.

Robert derived most of his information from Herr Thiele, the gentleman who spoke English with a Scandinavian accent. This portly Dane had taken a fancy to him, and talked at considerable length. The others, too, had received him with courtesy and good-will; Holm himself, seeming well-disposed, had told him about various matters including the door of the trap.

The boy, as he told me later, was sensible enough never to attempt communication with me when Holm was nearby. Twice, while thus engaged, he had seen Holm appear; and had accordingly ceased at once. At no time could I see the world behind the mirror's surface. Robert's visual image, which included his bodily form and the clothing connected with it, was – like the aural image of his halting voice and like his own visualization of myself – a case of purely telepathic transmission; and did not involve true inter-dimensional sight. However, had Robert been as trained a telepathist as Holm, he might have transmitted a few strong images apart from his immediate person.

Throughout this period of revelation I had, of course, been desperately trying to devise a method for Robert's release. On the fourth day – the ninth after the disappearance – I hit on a solution. Everything considered, my laboriously formulated process was not a very complicated one; though I could not tell beforehand how it would work, while the possibility of ruinous consequences in case of a slip was appalling. This process depended, basically, on the fact that there was no possible exit from inside the glass. If Holm and his prisoners were permanently sealed in, then release must come wholly from outside. Other considerations included the disposal of the other prisoners, if any survived, and especially of Axel Holm. What Robert had told me of him was anything but reassuring; and I certainly did not wish him loose in my apartment, free once more to work his evil will upon the world. The telepathic messages had not made fully clear the effect of liberation on those who had entered the glass so long ago.

There was, too, a final though minor problem in case of success – that of getting Robert back into the routine of school life without having to explain the incredible. In case of failure, it was highly inadvisable to have witnesses present at the release operations – and lacking these, I simply could not attempt to relate the actual facts if I should succeed. Even to me the reality seemed a mad one whenever I let my mind turn from the data so compellingly presented in that tense series of dreams.

When I had thought these problems through as far as possible, I procured a large magnifying-glass from the school laboratory and studied minutely every square millimeter of that whorl-center which presumably marked the extent of the original ancient mirror used by Holm. Even with this aid I could not quite trace the exact boundary between the old area and the surface added by the Danish wizard; but after a long study decided on a conjectural oval boundary which I outlined very precisely with a soft blue pencil. I then made a trip to Stamford, where I procured a heavy glass-cutting tool; for my primary idea was to remove the ancient and magically potent mirror from its later setting.

My next step was to figure out the best time of day to make the crucial experiment. I finally settled on two-thirty a.m. – both because it was a good season for uninterrupted work, and because it was the 'opposite' of two-thirty p.m., the probable moment at which Robert had entered the mirror. This form of 'oppositeness' may or may not have been relevant, but I knew at least that the chosen hour was as good as any – and perhaps better than most.

I finally set to work in the early morning of the eleventh day after the disappearance, having drawn all the shades of my living-room and closed and locked the door into the hallway. Following with breathless care the elliptical line I had traced, I worked around the whorlsection with my steel-wheeled cutting tool. The ancient glass, half an inch thick, crackled cripsly under the firm, uniform pressure;

and upon completing the circuit I cut around it a second time, crunching the roller more deeply into the glass.

Then, very carefully indeed, I lifted the heavy mirror down from its console and leaned it face-inward against the wall, prying off two of the thin, narrow boards nailed to the back. With equal caution I smartly tapped the cut-around space with the heavy wooden handle of the glass-cutter.

At the very first tap the whorl-containing section of glass dropped out on the Bokhara rug beneath. I did not know what might happen, but was keyed up for anything, and took a deep involuntary breath. I was on my knees for convenience at the the moment, with my face quite near the newly made aperture; and as I breathed there poured into my nostrils a powerful *dusty* odor – a smell not comparable to any other I have ever encountered. Then everything within my range of vision suddenly turned to a dull gray before my failing eyesight as I felt myself overpowered by an invisible force which robbed my muscles of their power to function.

I remember grasping weakly and futilely at the edge of the nearest window drapery and feeling it rip loose from its fastening. Then I sank slowly to the floor as the darkness of oblivion passed over me.

When I regained consciousness I was lying on the Bokhara rug with my legs held unaccountably up in the air. The room was full of that hideous and inexplicable dusty smell – and as my eyes began to take in definite images I saw that Robert Grandison stood in front of me. It was he – fully in the flesh and with his coloring normal – who was holding my legs aloft to bring the blood back to my head as the school's first-aid course had taught him to do with persons who had fainted. For a moment I was struck mute by the stifling odor and by a bewilderment which quickly merged into a sense of triumph. Then I found myself able to move and speak collectedly.

I raised a tentative hand and waved feebly at Robert.

'All right, old man,' I murmured, 'you can let my legs down now. Many thanks. I'm all right again, I think. It was the smell – I imagine – that got me. Open that farthest window, please – wide – from the bottom. That's it – thanks. No – leave the shade down the way it was.'

I struggled to my feet, my disturbed circulation adjusting itself in waves, and stood upright hanging to the back of a big chair. I was still 'groggy', but a blast of fresh, bitterly cold air from the window revived me rapidly. I sat down in the big chair and looked at Robert, now walking toward me.

'First,' I said hurriedly, 'tell me, Robert – those others – Holm? What happened to *them*, when I – opened the exit?'

Robert paused half-way across the room and looked at me very gravely.

'I saw them fade away – into nothingness – Mr Canevin,' he said with solemnity; 'and with them – everything. There isn't any more "inside", sir – thank God, and you, sir!'

And young Robert, at last yielding to the sustained strain which he had borne through all those terrible eleven days, suddenly broke down like a little child and began to weep hysterically in great, stifling, dry sobs.

I picked him up and placed him gently on my davenport, threw a rug over him, sat down by his side, and put a calming hand on his forehead.

'Take it easy, old fellow,' I said soothingly.

The boy's sudden and very natural hysteria passed as quickly as it had come on as I talked to him reassuringly about my plans for his quiet restoration to the school. The interest of the situation and the need of concealing the incredible truth beneath a rational explanation took hold of his imagination as I had expected; and at last he sat up eagerly, telling the details of his release and listening to the instructions I had thought out. He had, it seems, been in the 'projected area' of my bedroom when I opened the way back, and had emerged in that actual room – hardly realizing that he was 'out'. Upon hearing a fall in the living-room he had hastened thither, finding me on the rug in my fainting spell.

I need mention only briefly my method of restoring Robert in a seemingly normal way – how I smuggled him out of the window in an old hat and sweater of mine, took him down the road in my quietly started car, coached him carefully in a tale I had devised, and returned to arouse Browne with the news of his discovery. He had, I explained, been walking alone on the afternoon of his disappearance; and had been offered a motor ride by two young men who, as a joke and over his protests that he could go no farther than Stamford and back, had begun to carry him past that town. Jumping from the car during a traffic stop with the intention of hitch-hiking back before Call-Over, he had been hit by another car just as the traffic was released – awakening ten days later in the Greenwich home of the people who had hit him. On learning the date, I added, he had immediately telephoned the school; and I, being the only one awake, had answered the call and hurried after him in my car without stopping to notify anyone.

Browne, who at once telephoned to Robert's parents, accepted my story without question; and forbore to interrogate the boy because of the latter's manifest exhaustion. It was arranged that he should remain at the school for a rest, under the expert care of Mrs Browne, a former trained nurse. I naturally saw a good deal of him during the remainder of the Christmas vacation, and was thus enabled to fill in certain gaps in his fragmentary dream-story.

Now and then we would almost doubt the actuality of what had occurred; wondering whether we had not both shared some monstrous delusion born of the mirror's glittering hypnotism, and whether the tale of the ride and accident were not after all the real truth. But whenever we did so we would be brought back to belief by some monstrous and haunting memory; with me, of Robert's dream-figure and its thick voice and inverted colors; with him, of the whole fantastic pageantry of ancient people and dead scenes that he had witnessed. And then there was that joint recollection of that damnable dusty odor . . . We knew what it meant: the instant dissolution of those who had entered an alien dimension a century and more ago.

There are, in addition, at least two lines of rather more positive evidence; one of which comes through my researches in Danish annals concerning the sorcerer, Axel Holm. Such a person, indeed, left many traces in folklore and written records; and diligent library sessions, plus conferences with various learned Danes, have shed much more light on his evil fame. At present I need say only that the Copenhagen glass-blower – born in 1612 – was a notorious Luciferian whose pursuits and final vanishing formed a matter of awed debate over two centuries ago. He had burned with a desire to know all things and to conquer every limitation of mankind – to which end he had delved deeply into occult and forbidden fields ever since he was a child.

He was commonly held to have joined a coven of the dreaded witchcult, and the vast lore of ancient Scandinavian myth – with its Loki the Sly One and the accursed Fenris-Wolf – was soon an open book to him. He had strange interests and objectives, few of which were definitely known, but some of which were recognized as intolerably evil. It is recorded that his two Negro helpers, originally slaves from the Danish West Indies, had become mute soon after their acquisition by him; and that they had disappeared not long before his own disappearance from the ken of mankind.

Near the close of an already long life the idea of a glass of immortality appears to have entered his mind. That he had acquired an enchanted mirror of inconceivable antiquity was a matter of common whispering; it being alleged that he had purloined it from a fellow-sorcerer who had entrusted it to him for polishing.

This mirror – according to popular tales a trophy as potent in its way as the better-known Aegis of Minerva or Hammer of Thor – was a small oval object called 'Loki's Glass', made of some polished fusible mineral and having magical properties which included the divination of the immediate future and the power to show the possessor his enemies. That it had deeper potential properties, realizable in the hands of an erudite magician, none of the common people doubted; and even educated persons attached much fearful importance to Holm's rumored attempts to incorporate it in a larger glass of immortality. Then had come the wizard's disappearance in 1687, and the final sale and dispersal of his goods amidst a growing cloud of fantastic legendry. It was, altogether, just such a story as one would laugh at if possessed of no particular key; yet to me, remembering those dream messages and having Robert Grandison's corroboration before me, it formed a positive confirmation of all the bewildering marvels that had been unfolded.

But as I have said, there is still another line of rather positive evidence – of a very different character – at my disposal. Two days after his release, as Robert, greatly improved in strength and appearance was placing a log on my living-room fire, I noticed a certain awkwardness in his motions and was struck by a persistent idea. Summoning him to my desk I suddenly asked him to pick up an inkstand – and was scarcely surprised to note that, despite lifelong right-handedness, he obeyed unconsciously with his left hand. Without alarming him, I then asked that he unbutton his coat and let me listen to his cardiac action. What I found upon placing my ear to his chest – and what I did not tell him for some time afterward – was that *his heart was beating on his right side*.

He had gone into the glass right-handed and with all organs in their normal positions. Now he was left-handed and with organs reversed, and would doubtless continue so for the rest of his life. Clearly, the dimensional transition had been no illusion – for this physical change was tangible and unmistakable. Had there been a natural exit from the glass, Robert would probably have undergone a thorough re-reversal and emerged in perfect normality – as indeed the color-scheme of his body and clothing did emerge. The forcible nature of his release, however, undoubtedly set something awry; so that dimensions no longer had a chance to right themselves as chromatic wave-frequencies still did.

I had not merely *opened* Holm's trap; I had *destroyed* it; and at the particular stage of destruction marked by Robert's escape some of the reversing properties had perished. It is significant that in escaping Robert had felt no pain comparable to that experienced in entering. Had the destruction been still more sudden, I shiver to think of the monstrosities of color the boy would always have been forced to bear. I may add that after discovering Robert's reversal I examined the rumpled and discarded clothing he had worn in the glass, and found, as I had expected, a complete reversal of pockets, buttons, and all other corresponding details.

At this moment Loki's Glass, just as it fell on my Bokhara rug from the now patched and harmless mirror, weighs down a sheaf of papers on my writing-table here in St Thomas, venerable capital of the Danish West Indies – now the American Virgin Islands. Various collectors of old Sandwich glass have mistaken it for an odd bit of that early American product – but I privately realize that my paperweight is an antique of far subtler and more paleologean craftsmanship. Still, I do not disillusion such enthusiasts.

The Napier Limousine

The nursemaid let go the handle of her perambulator, froze into an appearance of devastated horror and screamed.

Just what there might be about the sight of two gentlemen, dressed formally for the morning, stepping out of an impeccable town-car upon the curbstone in front of No. 12, Portman Terrace – one of an ultraconservative long row of solid family mansions in London's residential West End – to throw their only beholder into such a state of sudden, horrified terror, was a mystery. What drove home the startling implication that there was something rather dreadfully wrong, made a benumbing little chill course devastatingly up and down my spine, was the fact that I was one of them. My companion was James Rand, Earl of Carruth, back in London now after twenty years' continuous service in India as Chief of the British Government's Secret Service and armed with an experience which might well have filled the measure of life for a dozen ordinary men.

The beautifully-kept limousine had stopped with a jarless pause like the alighting of a poised hawk. Portman Terrace was empty of pedestrians with the exception of the liveried, middle-aged, sensible-looking servant with her glistening custom-built perambulator.

For my own part, if I had been alone, I suppose I should have followed my instinct, stopped, and made some attempt to restore to a normal condition this stricken fellow human being, inexplicably seized in the ruthless grasp of cold fear. But it took more than the eccentricity of a casual nursemaid to upset Lord Carruth's iron self-control. My companion glanced appraisingly at this strange disturbance of the King's Peace and led the way up the high flight of marble steps to the front doorway of No. 12, his normal expression of facial placidity altered by no more than a raised eyebrow. Still under the compulsion of our determination to meet the emergency with which we had hastened here to cope, I followed him across the broad sidewalk and ran up the steps just behind him.

Carruth's finger was already on the silver doorbell-button when I came up beside him, and this circumstance gave me my first occasion to turn and look behind me. I did so, at once, because it occurred to me that the very smart, gray-haired footman whom the car's owner had addressed as 'Baines', should have been there, pressing that button with an efficient black-gloved finger.

Below on the sidewalk the nursemaid was retreating as rapidly as she could walk, and, as she looked back over her shoulder, I saw that her apple cheeks had gone to a kind of oyster-gray, and that her terrified mouth hung open like a Greek tragic mask.

But the nursemaid, strange sight that she presented, got only a passing glance from me, for I brought my eyes around to the curb where we had alighted, a matter of seconds before, to see what had happened to the footman, Baines, who like any proper footman, should have been up the steps before us. It seemed inconceivable that such a man should be remiss in his duties and yet –

I brought my eyes around, I say, and looked down there, and – there was no Baines. Neither was there any driver beside the footman in the chauffeur's seat. There was no seat. *There was no car*! The limousine, an old-model Napier, was clean gone. The street in front of No. 12, Portman Terrace was entirely empty and deserted . . .

It is hard to set down in words how very serious a jar this discovery was. I *knew* that the car was still there before I turned around to look for Baines.

I knew that because I had not heard the inevitable slight sounds made in starting even by the most soundless of cars, under the ministrations of the most perfectly trained chauffeur such as ours had shown himself to be on our ride from in front of St Paul's Cathedral to Portman Terrace.

There it was, that empty street; the agitated back of the rapidly retreating nursemaid receding into the distance; the car gone, chauffeur, footman and all! My first sense of surprise rapidly mounted to the status of a slow shock. That car *must* be there! I could take my oath it had not started. It could not move off without some sound. It was unthinkable that I should not have heard it. Yet – it was not there. No. 12, Portman Terrace stands in its own grounds in the middle of a long block of solid houses. Starting with absolute noiselessness, even a racing car could not have reached the corner – either corner. And, to get to the nearer of the two corners, the car would have had to turn around. I looked up and down the broad, empty street in both directions. The Napier limousine, unmistakable in its custom-built lines, somewhat old-fashioned, conspicuous, was, simply, not there. I started to speak to Rand, but was interrupted by the opening of the door. A stout, florid, family-retainer of a butler stood there, bowing.

'The Earl of Carruth, and Mr Gerald Canevin,' said Rand, reaching for his card case, 'and it is imperative that we see Sir Harry Dacre immediately, in spite, even, of his possible orders that he is engaged.'

I followed Rand's motion for my card case mechanically and produced a card. The butler benignly ushered us within. He took our coats and hats and sticks. He showed us into a small drawing-room overlooking the square, just to the left of the entrance hall with its black marble paving.

'I will take your names to Sir Harry at once, m'Lord,' announced the butler urbanely, and disappeared up a wide flight of stairs.

This errand to Sir Henry Dacre, whom neither had ever seen, but who had been of late a familiar name to the newspaper-reading public, had been thrust upon Rand and myself in a somewhat remarkable manner. I had been, as it happened that morning, to my London tailor's, whose shop is in Jermyn Street, for a fitting. Finishing this minor ordeal and emerging upon Jermyn Street, the very first person I encountered was Rand. We had been together two nights previously, at a small men's dinner at Sir John Scott's. It was at Sir John's house that I had met him several months before. Anyone met there would be apt to be worth while. Sir John Scott presides over no less an institution than Scotland Yard. I had been immediately fascinated by Rand's grasp of the subject which has always more intrigued me – that of magical beliefs and occult practices among native peoples.

We had talked eagerly together, absorbingly, that first evening of our acquaintance. We talked, in fact, almost too late and too continuously for courtesy to one's host, even at a men's dinner. We outstayed our three other fellow guests. A brief note, received the next day from Sir John, had expressed – to my relief – his gratification that we had found so much to say to each other, had proved to be congenial. Rand, he explained briefly – as I, an Amercian, might not be aware – was the world's first authority on the subject I have named. He had been almost continuously away from England now for more than a score of years, serving the Empire in innumerable strange corners of its far-flung extent, but chiefly in India. A significant phrase of the note read: 'It is unquestionably due to Lord Carruth's remarkable abilities that the Indian Empire is now intact.' I considered that a very open admission for an Englishman, particularly one in Sir John Scott's position.

Meeting on the sidewalk that way, unexpectedly, we had stopped to chat for a moment, and, as it turned out that we were going in the same direction, we began to walk along together, arm in arm. As we came abreast of St Paul's Cathedral, an elderly lady, very well dressed in plain black, came diagonally down the steps directly towards us, meeting us precisely as she reached the bottom. She addressed Rand directly.

'Will you be good enough to spare me a minute of your time, Lord Carruth?' she inquired.

'Assuredly,' replied Rand, bowing. We paused, removing our hats.

'It is a very pressing matter, or I should not have put you to this trouble,' said the lady, in a very beautiful, softly modulated voice, in which was to be clearly discerned that unmistakable tone of a class born to rule through many generations: a tone of the utmost graciousness, but nevertheless attuned to command. She continued: 'I beg that you will go at once to Sir Harry Dacre. It is number 12, Portman Terrace. My car is here at your disposal, gentlemen.' She included me with a gracious glance. 'It is an emergency, a very pressing affair. If you will start at once, you will perhaps be in time to save him.'

As she spoke, the lady, without seeming to do so consciously, was approaching the curbstone, edging, and we with her, diagonally across the wide pavement. At the curb, as I now observed, stood a very beautifully kept and well appointed town car, a Napier of a dozen-years-ago model. The chauffeur, in a black livery, sat motionless at the wheel. A very smart-looking, alert though elderly footman – his close-cropped hair was quite white, I observed – stood at rigid attention beside the tonneau door, a carriage-rug, impeccably folded into a perfect rectangle, across his angular arm.

The footman saluted, snapped open the door of the car, and we were inside and the lady speaking to us through the open door almost before we realized what we were doing. Her last words were significant, and spoken with the utmost earnestness and conviction.

'I pray God,' said she, 'that you may be in time, Lord Carruth. Sir Harry Dacre's, Baines.' This last she spoke very crisply, her words carrying an unmistakable undernote of urgency. The footman saluted again, very smartly; he draped the rug with practised skill across our four knees; the door was snicked to; and the old but beautifully appointed car, glistening with polish and good care, started almost simultaneously, the elderly footman snapping into his seat beside the chauffeur with an altogether surprising agility, and coming into position there like a ramrod, his arms folded before him with stiff precision.

Through London's traffic now sped the Napier, as smoothly as a new car, the driving a very model of accuracy and sound form. It was plain that the unknown elderly lady was very well and promptly served. Not a single instant was lost, although there was no slightest feeling of being hurried such as ordinarily communicates itself to a person riding in an automobile when the driver is urged for time.

I glanced at Rand beside me. His ordinarily inscrutable, lean face was slightly puckered as though his mind were working hard.

'Who was the lady?' I ventured to inquire.

'That is what is puzzling me just now,' returned Rand. 'Frankly, I do not remember! And yet, at the same time, I'm quite sure I do know her, or know who she is. I simply cannot place her, although her face is familiar. She knew me, clearly enough. It is very unusual for me to forget like that.'

In a surprisingly short time after our start on this strange drive we had turned into Portman Terrace, stopped, had the door snapped open for us by the agile old footman and were out on the side-walk. My last glimpse of the equipage as a whole was the salute with which the footman dismissed us. Then the strange conduct of an otherwise commonplace nursemaid, to which I have alluded, took all my attention. The nursemaid acted in her crude manner, as nearly as I can manage to describe her motivation, precisely as though we had landed – the thought struck me even at that time – in front of her from nowhere, instead of having merely, as I have said, stepped to the curbstone beside her out of a very well appointed town-car.

I could see that nursemaid now on the far side of the street and at some distance, as we sat in Sir Harry Dacre's small drawing-room, through the large window which looked out upon Portman Terrace. I even got up and walked to the window for the purpose. She was now talking with animation to a policeman, a big fellow. I watched with very great interest. I could not, of course, because of the distance and through a closed window, hear what she was saying, but I could follow it almost as well as though I could, from her gestures and the expressions on both their faces.

The woman pantomimed the entire occurrence for the policeman, and I got it now from her point of view, very clearly and plainly. My first impression of her possible reason for having behaved so insanely was amply corroborated. She had been placidly wheeling her charge along the walk when *plop!* two gentlemen, out of no-where, had suddenly stepped on the curb in front of her! She had, of course, screamed. The gentlemen had looked at her as though surprised. They had then gone up the steps of Number 12, had rung and been admitted. These two visitors from Mars, or what-ever they were, were now in Sir Harry Dacre's house. Hadn't the policeman better go and ring the area bell and make sure the silver was safe?

The policeman, a respectable-looking middle-aged man, probably accustomed to the vagaries of nursemaids, and doubtless with women-folk of his own, sought to reassure her. Finally, not succeeding very well, he shrugged, left her expostulating and continued his dignified beat.

Learning in this way what had come over the nursemaid failed to make the mystery any clearer, however, than it had for the policeman, who had had the advantage of hearing her words. I was intensely puzzled. I turned away from the window and addressed Rand, who had been sitting there waiting in complete silence.

'Have you any idea what's wrong here?' said I. 'Here in this house, I mean.'

'You've read the papers, of course?' said Rand after a moment's consideration of my question.

'I know young Dacre's got himself rather heavily involved,' I replied. 'It's one of those infatuation affairs, is it not? A woman. She turns out to be mixed up, somehow, with Goddard, the impresario, or whatever he is. Isn't that about the case?'

Rand nodded. 'Yes. Apparently Goddard has him on toast. Rather a beast, that Goddard person. Goddard is not his name, by the way. A very clever person in the heavy-blackmail line. The Yard has never been able to "get anything on him", as you Americans put it. He has his various theatrical connections largely for a cover; but his real game is deeper, and blacker. It is rumored in certain circles that Goddard has ground poor Dacre here down to the very last straw in his garret; made him sign over all his holdings to avoid a show-up. Just how far he is committed with "The Princess Lillia" of the Gaieties, nobody seems to know. But that she is Goddard's wife, or at least that they are working together in close collusion, seems beyond question. That has not come out, of course. It is inside information.'

'But,' said I, 'just how, if I may ask, does that give them so com-plete a hold on Dacre? Why doesn't he simply repudiate them, now that he must know they set a trap for him? As nearly as I can figure it out from what I've seen in the papers and what you have just now told me, it's nothing more or less than an old-fashioned attempt at blackmail. And besides, it's had a certain amount of publicity already, hasn't it? Just what does Dacre stand to lose if Goddard does go to a show-down with him?'

'The point is,' explained Rand, 'that Dacre is engaged to be married to one of the loveliest girls in England. If it should really come out that "The Princess Lillia" is Goddard's wife, that would be off entirely. Lord Roxton would make that distinction very emphatically.

'To a man of his known views, a fine young fellow like Dacre would be more or less entitled to what Roxton would call "his fling". That would be typical, of course – British – to be expected. A well-to-do, unattached young man about town – and a lady from the Follies. Then the young blood really falls in love, drops his light-o'-love, is very devoted, marries, "settles down". But – if the lady from the Follies turns out to be the wife of somebody, somebody as much in the public eye as Leighton Goddard, and the matter of merely discontinuing that sort of thing is complicated by a law-suit brought by the outraged husband – you can see how ruinous it would be, can you not, Canevin? The more especially when one is dealing with one of those rather narrow, puritanical old hoddy-doddies like Lord Roxton, who is so consciously upright that he positively creaks with piety when he gets up or sits down. He would never allow his daughter to marry Dacre under those circumstances. He's the President of the Evangelican League, a reformer. Incidentally, he is one of the richest men in England; has tremendously strong views on how people should behave, you know. And Dacre's financial affairs, his investments, are to a considerable extent tied up with Lord Roxton's promotions and companies.'

This much of the background – though nothing whatever of the immediate urgency of the case which confronted us – we knew when the dignified butler returned with the announcement that Sir Harry Dacre would receive us at once. We followed the butler up a magnificent flight of stairs to the story above, and were shown into a kind of library-office, from behind whose enormous mahogany desk a handsome young fellow of about twenty-five rose to receive us. Sir Harry Dacre said nothing whatever, and I observed that his drawn face was lined and ghastly, plainly enough from the effects of lack of sleep. It was obvious to me that Lord Carruth's name alone had secured us admittance. The man whose abilities had served to keep the Indian Empire intact could hardly be gainsaid by anyone of Sir Harry Dacre's sort.

Rand went straight to the desk, and without any ceremony picked up and pocketed a .38 calibre American automatic pistol which lay directly in front of Sir Harry Dacre's chair.

'Perhaps you know I am accustomed to meeting emergencies half-way, sir,' said Rand, bluntly but not unkindly. 'I'll not ask you to forgive an intrusion, Sir Harry. I am Carruth; this is Mr Canevin, an American gentleman visiting in London.'

'Thanks,' said young Dacre, dully. 'I know you mean very well, Lord Carruth, and I appreciate your kindness in coming here. I have had the pleasure of reading Mr Canevin's remarkable tales,' he added, turning and bowing in my direction. We stood there, after that, in a momentarily tense, and indeed slightly strained silence.

'Suppose we all sit down, now that we are all together,' said our host. We followed the suggestion, making, as we sat, a triangle; Dacre behind his great desk; I facing him, with my back to the door through which we had entered the room; Rand at my right and facing a point between Dacre and me, and so commanding a view of him and also of the door.

'We are here to serve you, Sir Henry Dacre,' began Rand, without any preamble, 'and, judging by this,' – he indicated the automatic pistol – 'it appears that you need assistance and countenance. In a case like this it is rather futile to waste time on preliminaries or in beating about the bush. Tell us, if you will, precisely what we can do, and I assure you you may count upon us.'

'It is indeed very good of you,' returned Dacre, nodding his head. Then, with a wry and rueful smile: 'I do not see that there is anything that anybody can do! I suppose you know something of the situation. I am to marry the Lady Evelyn Haversham in a month's time. I have, I suppose, made a complete fool of myself, at least for practical purposes. As a matter of plain fact, there has been, really, nothing – nothing, that is, seriously to trouble one's conscience. But then, I'll not trouble to excuse myself. I am merely stating the facts. To put the matter plainly, this Goddard has me where he wants me – a very clever bit of work on his part. Here are the freeholds of every bit of property I own, piled up in front of me on this desk. He's coming for them this morning – eleven – should be here now. *That's* the price of his silence about the apparent situation, you see. "The Princess Lillia" is his wife, it appears.'

'But,' Rand put in, briskly, 'how about this?' Once more he indicated the pistol. The young man's face flushed a dull red.

'That was for him,' he said quietly, 'and afterwards' – he spread his
hands in a hopeless gesture – 'for me.'

'But, why, why?' urged Rand, leaning forward in his chair, his lean,
ascetic face eager, his eyes burning with intensity. 'Tell me – why
resort to such a means?'

'Because,' returned Sir Harry Dacre, 'there would be nothing left.
On the one hand, if I were to refuse Goddard's terms, he would bring
out the whole ugly business. Oh, they're clever: a case in court, one
of those ruinous things, and an action for alienation of his wife's
affections; a divorce case, with me as the villain-person. On the other
hand – don't you see? – I'm flatly ruined. These papers convey
everything I own to him in return for the release which lies here
ready for him to sign. Even with the release signed and in my
possession I could not go on with the marriage. I'd be, literally, a
pauper. It is, well, one of those things that one does not, cannot do.'

'Let me see the release,' said Rand, and rose, his hand outstretched.
He glanced through it, rapidly, nodding his head, and returned it to
its place on the desk. 'There is little time,' he continued. 'Will you do
precisely as I say?'

'Yes,' said Sir Harry Dacre laconically, but I could see no appearance of hope on his face.

'Go through with it precisely as arranged,' said Rand.

A rap fell on the door, and it was opened slightly.

'Mr Leighton Goddard,' announced the butler, and I saw Rand
stiffen in his chair. The look of hopeless despair deepened in the
lined face of the young man behind the desk. He had, I surmised, as
he had reasoned out this sordid affair, come to the last act. The
curtain was about to fall . . .

The man who now entered radiated personality. He was tall,
within half an inch or so of Rand's height, and Rand is two inches
over six feet. There was a suggestion of richness about him, sartorial
richness, an aura of something oriental which came into that Anglo-
Saxon room with him. One could not put a finger on anything wrong
in his really impeccable appearance. Bond Street was written upon
his perfect morning coat; but I would have guessed, I think, almost
instinctively, that his name was not really Goddard, even if no one
had suggested that to me. He glanced about the room, very much
self-possessed, and with an air almost proprietary, out of shining,
sloe-black eyes set in a face of vaguely Asiatic cast: a suggestion of

olive under the pale skin of the night-club habitué; a certain undue height of the cheekbones.

'Now, this isn't according to agreement, Dacre!' He addressed his host in a slightly bantering tone, almost genially, indeed; a tone underneath which I could feel depths of annoyance; of a poisonous, threatening malice. He had stopped between Rand and me.

'We merely dropped in,' said Rand, in a flat voice, and Goddard glanced around at him out of the corner of his eye. Dacre picked up the hint. 'This is Mr Gerald Canevin, the writer,' said he, and I rose and nodded to Goddard. As I did so, I caught Rand's eye, with warning in it. I thought I grasped his meaning. If he had formulated any definite plan for dealing with this ugly situation there had been no time to warn me of it before Goddard's rather abrupt arrival, several minutes late for his appointment. I did some very rapid thinking, came to a conclusion, and spoke quietly to Goddard in a tone of voice that was intentionally somewhat slow and deliberate.

'This is Mr Rand,' said I; and Rand flashed me a quick, commending look of relief. He did not want Goddard to know his true identity. That had been my conclusion from his warning look. Fortunately, I had struck the nail on the head that time. The two men nodded coolly to each other, and it seemed to me that suspicion loomed and smouldered in those oriental eyes.

Dacre came to the front.

'We can get our business over very easily,' said Dacre at this point. 'Here are the things you want, and here is the place to sign.' He stood up behind the desk, holding a sheaf of legal looking documents.

Goddard walked firmly over to the desk, took across it the papers out of Dacre's hand, glanced through them rapidly, nodded as he checked each mentally, and at last relaxing his tensely held body thrust them, all together, into the inside pocket of his morning coat. He smiled quickly, as though satisfied, took a step nearer the desk, stooped over, and, still standing, reached for a pen and scrawled his name on the paper Dacre indicated.

This done, he straightened up, though still retaining his slightly stooping position, and turned away from the desk. I was watching him narrowly and so, too, I knew, was Rand. Triumphant satisfaction was writ large on his unpleasant face. But that look was quickly dissipated. He turned away from the desk at last, and met Rand facing him, Dacre's pistol pointed straight at his heart. I, standing now behind Goddard, could look straight into Rand's face, and I do not care ever to have to look into such an expression of rigid determination and complete, utter self-confidence behind any weapon pointed in my direction.

'You will take those deeds out of your pocket, Wertheimer,' said Rand, in a deadly, cold, quiet voice, 'and drop them on the floor. Then you will go out of here without any further parley. Otherwise I shall take them from you; if necessary, kill you as you stand there; arrange the matter with Downing Street this afternoon, and so rid the world of a very annoying scoundrel. I am the Earl of Carruth. I came here without Dacre's knowledge, to deal with this situation. What you have to decide, rather quickly, is whether you will go on living on what you have already stolen, without this of Dacre's, or whether you will put me to the inconvenience of – removing you.'

From my position I could not, of course, see Goddard's – or Wertheimer's – face. But I did observe the telltale hunching of a shoulder, and cried out in time to warn Rand. But Rand needed no warning, as it happened. He met the rush of the big man with his disengaged hand, now a fist, and Wertheimer, catching that iron fist on the precise point of the chin, slithered to the floor, entirely harmless for the time being.

Rand looked down at the sprawled body, then walked over to the desk and laid the automatic pistol down on the place from which he had picked it up. Then, returning to the prostrate Wertheimer, he knelt beside him and removed the packet of deeds from the man's pocket. He rose, returned to the desk, and handed them to young Dacre, who, during the few seconds occupied by all these occurrences, had remained standing, silent and collected, behind his desk.

'The transaction, of course, was illegal,' remarked Rand, looking down at the crumpled torso of Wertheimer. 'You need have no compunction whatever, Dacre, my dear fellow, in retaining the release which he signed. "Goddard" is not his name, of course. But I imagine that fact would have no bearing upon the efficacy of the release. He has gone under that name and is thoroughly identified with it here in London, Sir John Scott informs me, for the past four or five years. You heard me call him "Wertheimer", but even that is not his real name. He is a Turk, and his right name is Abdulla Khan ben Majpat. However, he was a German spy during the War, and in Berlin he is very well known as "Wertheimer". I think I may say that you are now quite free from the complication which was distressing you.'

It was a very subdued Goddard-Wertheimer-ben Majpat who left the house a quarter of an hour later, after a few crisply spoken words of warning from Rand. And it was a correspondingly jubilant young man who besieged Rand with his reiterated thanks. Sir Harry Dacre was, indeed, almost beside himself. In the stimulating grip of a tremendous reaction such as he had just experienced, a man's everyday composure is apt to go to the winds. This unexpected release from his overpowering difficulties which Rand's intervention had brought about had, for the time being, caused Sir Harry Dacre to seem like a different person. There had not been any statements in the newspapers of sufficiently definite nature to injure his cause with his future wife or with his future father-in-law, the austere Lord Roxton, and now, as Rand took care to assure him, there would be no further press comment. The situation seemed entirely cleared up.

Young Dacre, looking years younger, with the lines of harassment and care almost visibly fading out of his face under the stimulation of his new freedom and the natural resiliency of his youth, would be quite all right again after a proper night's rest. He confessed to us that it was the best part of a week since he had so much as slept. His gratitude knew no bounds. It was almost effusive and really very touching. He pressed us to remain for luncheon. This we declined, but we could not very well refuse his request that we should have a Scotch and soda with him. While this refreshment was being brought by the butler, Rand stepped around to the other side of the desk and picked up a framed photograph which stood upon it.

'And who, if I may venture to ask, is this?' he inquired.

'It was my mother's sister, the Lady Mary Grosvenor,' said young Dacre. 'You may remember her, perhaps. It was she, you know, who organized the Red Cross at the beginning of the War. I was only a little chap of seven or eight then.' He took the photograph from Rand and stood looking at it with an expression of the deepest affection.

'A wonderful woman!' he added, 'and the best friend I ever had, Lord Carruth. She took me into her house here when I was a tiny little youngster. My own mother died when I was four. The house came to me in her will, eight years later. Dear Aunt Mary – her kindness and goodness never failed. She took me, a rather forlorn little creature, I dare say, into her care. She found time to do everything for me. She was a woman of manifold interests and activities, as you may remember, Lord Carruth, and even high in the counsels of the great, the affairs of the Empire. Cabinet members, even the

Prime Minister himself, sought her advice, kept her occupied with all kinds of difficult tasks. In spite of all these engagements, she was, as I have said, and in all ways, a mother to me – yes, more than a mother. I naturally revered her.'

Young Sir Harry Dacre paused, sitting there in his office-library, with his guests to whom he was thus opening his heart with sudden, wistful seriousness. When he spoke again it was in a much quieter tone than that of the little panegyric he had just ended.

'Do you know,' said he, 'I – I thank God that the dear soul was at least spared any knowledge of this – this dreadful affair which is – I can hardly realize, gentlemen, that it is over, done, a thing of the past.'

Again he paused, sat for a moment very quietly in a natural silence which neither Rand nor I desired to break.

Then, in a hushed tone, his words coming slowly and very reverently, he spoke again.

'And if,' he began, as though concluding a thought already partly uttered, ' – and if she *has* been enabled to see it all – from her place in Paradise, as one might say – she is rejoicing now, and thanking you. She would have moved Heaven and earth to help me.'

Then, as I looked into the face of Sir Harry Dacre, I saw a slow flush mounting upon it. That curious sense of shame which seems common to every Englishman who allows himself to show others something of his inmost feeling, had overtaken the young man. He resumed his discourse in an entirely different and rather restrained tone.

'But that, of course, is impossible,' said he. 'I hope that I have not made myself ridiculous. Naturally I should know better than to bore you in this way. Reasonable people should not allow themselves to be moved by such old sentimentality. And, I – I was educated Modern Side.'

'I do not think we are bored by what you have said,' remarked Rand, quietly, and added nothing to that.

Dacre paused, rose, and replaced on the desk the framed photograph which he had been holding and looking at while he spoke. As yet, except from the back, I had not had a view of it. Returning to where we were seated, Dacre took a chair between Carruth and me.

'Curious!' exclaimed our host, breaking a brief silence. 'I mean to say, my aunt, there, was very active in the War, you know. As a matter of fact, she visited every front, and never received as much as a scratch! People used to say that she seemed to bear a charmed life. Then back home here in England, driving one afternoon through Wolverhampton in her old town-car – it was just two days before the Armistice, in 1918 – I was just twelve at the time – a bomb from a raiding German airplane took her, poor lady; and along with her old Baines, her footman – been with her thirty-four years – and the chauffeur. Killed all three, snuffed 'em right out, and there wasn't enough of the old Napier town-car left to identify it! The way things happen . . . '

Carruth nodded, sympathetically. It was plain that young Dacre had been much moved by his recital. He must have had an extra-ordinarily high regard for the splendid woman who had mothered him. At this moment Dacre's butler appeared with a tray and bottles, ice, tall glasses and siphons of carbonated water.

While he was arranging these on a table, I walked over to the desk and took up the large framed photograph.

There, in the uniform of the British Red Cross, looked out at me the splendid face of a middle-aged lady, the face of a true aristocrat, of one born to command. It was kindly, though possessing a firm, almost a stern expression, the look of one who would never give up!

I replaced the photograph, my hands shaking. I turned about quickly and walked across the room. I wanted rather urgently to be quite close to living, breathing human beings like Carruth and our host – fellow-men, creatures of common, everyday flesh and blood. I stood there among them, between Rand and Dacre, and almost touching the urbane butler as he prepared our Scotch and soda with admirable professional deftness. I confess that I wanted something else, besides that sense of human companionship which had come upon me so compellingly that I had found my hands shaking as I set the framed photograph back into its original place on Sir Harry Dacre's desk.

Yes – I wanted that high cool, iced tumbler of Scotch whiskey and soda the butler was handing me. I barely waited, indeed, until the others had been served to raise it to my lips, to take a great, hasty drink which emptied the glass halfway to its bottom.

For – I had seen that photograph of Dacre's aunt, the Lady Mary Grosvenor, that firm gentlewoman who had, in the goodness of her noble heart, stolen precious time from the counsels of a great Empire to comfort a pathetic little motherless child; who would have moved Heaven and earth; a woman who would never give up . . .

' . . . old Baines, her footman – been with her thirty-four years . . . '

' . . . killed all three, snuffed 'em right out . . . '

' . . . not enough of the old Napier town-car left to identify it . . . '

And I had looked at that photograph.

I finished my Scotch and soda and set my glass down on the butler's silver tray. I drew in a deep breath. I was coming back satisfactorily to something like normal.

I raised my eyes and looked over at Rand. It had just occurred to me that he, too, was now aware of the identity of the lady who had sent us here in that old Napier with the two perfectly trained servants in its driving seat, to save Sir Harry Dacre. Rand had seen the photograph, too, well before I had picked it up and looked at it.

I found quite as usual the facial expression of the man who had held the Indian Empire together resolutely for twenty years – the man who had learned that iron composure facing courageously all forms of death and worse-than-death in the far, primitive places of the earth, places where transcendent evil goes hand in hand with ancient civilizations.

Even as I looked, James Rand, Lord Carruth, was turning to our host and addressed him in his firm, courteous, even voice.

'I take it that – with Mr Canevin to corroborate what I would say, speaking as an eye-witness – you would accept my word of honor – would you not, Dacre?'

Young Dacre stared at him, almost gulped with surprise when he replied to so unusual a question: 'Of course, Lord Carruth; certainly, sir. Your word of honor – Mr Canevin to corroborate! Of course such a thing would not be necessary, sir. Good Heavens! Of course, I'd believe anything you chose to say, sir, like the Gospel itself.'

'Well, then,' said Rand, smiling gravely, 'if it is agreeable to Mr Canevin, I think we shall change our minds and remain to luncheon with you. There is something I think you should know, and the period of luncheon will just give us time to tell you the circumstances behind our arrival here at about the right time for our business this morning.'

Rand looked over at me, and I nodded, eagerly.

'Splendid!' said Sir Harry Dacre, rising alertly and ringing the bell for the butler. 'I had, of course, been awfully keen to know about that. Hardly cared to ask, you know.'

'My reason for suggesting that we tell you,' said Rand gravely, 'goes rather deeper than merely satisfying a very reasonable curiosity. If by doing so we can accomplish what I have in mind, it will be, my dear fellow, a more important service in your behalf than ridding you of that Wertheimer.'

The butler came in and our host ordered the places set. Then, very soberly, he inquired: 'What, sir, if I may venture to ask, is the nature of that service?'

Rand answered only after a long and thoughtful interval.

'It may seem to you a rather odd answer, Dacre. I want to clear up in your mind, forever, the truth of what the religion we hold in common – the religion of our ancient Anglican Church here in England – teaches us about the souls in Paradise . . . '

The Ravel Pavane

In order to recount suitably the extraordinary case of the pianist Marie Boutácheff, it becomes necessary that I should set out first, in their order, certain facts. These are not without interest and are essential to its complete understanding. They have to do with the effects of sound upon a highly sensitive organism.

I first met Miss Boutácheff in the early Spring of the year 1928. I had come over from Santa Cruz, the southernmost of the Virgin Islands, to St Thomas, the colony's capital, after a Winter's residence on the other island. It was my intention to remain in St Thomas for about three weeks, to see the Spring tennis tournaments and for the renewal of social relationships with my friends in the capital. Then, about the first of June, I planned to take ship for continental United States, there to remain until my return to the Caribbean the following Autumn.

Miss Boutácheff had been spending the Winter in St Thomas, where she had been induced to come by several women friends, all painters. These friends of hers, as Rachel Manners, the landscapist assured me, had brought her, 'two jumps ahead of a nervous breakdown' from overwork, to our West Indian climate of spice and balm for the purpose of restoring her shattered health.

Miss Boutácheff, at that time very well known to and very greatly admired by a select circle of artistic people, was a serious artist, a pianist of great promise. She had, in fact, already 'arrived' professionally. She had given successful concerts in New York and elsewhere. She was a tall, blonde, rather slender woman of twenty-eight or twenty-nine, of that type which possesses enormous nervous energy coupled with a relatively low degree of physical vitality. She appeared, too, to be entirely free of that drawback which so frequently accompanies the make-up of people seriously engaged in the arts, and commonly named 'the artistic temperament'. In a very marked degree she possessed the intangible assets of charm and personality.

We took to each other at once. Miss Boutácheff had read everything of mine, she assured me. I had heard much about her and had even attended two of her concerts in Aeolian Hall. She had been making every effort not to think of music for five months!

'Hasn't that let your technic down?' I asked her.

'No, I do not think so. I hope not! You see, I have been using a clavier – a silent keyboard – all winter. That, being merely mechanical, does not trouble me. In fact it is soothing, restful. It is only sound, Mr Canevin, that – excuse me, if you please; let us talk of something else if you don't mind.'

It was I, as it happened, who started her later on, to 'thinking of music' again.

We were discussing *Pelléas et Mélisande*, and we got a little at cross-purposes because, to her, *Pelléas et Mélisande* meant the music of Claude Debussy and such performances as that splendid one of Mary Garden and the notable cast in that great seven nights' performance of the Hammerstein production in New York City; while to me, from the writer's viewpoint, most prominent was the written text of the story as it came from the hands of Maeterlinck. This, of course, as I might have known, Marie Boutácheff thought of merely as the *libretto*. We recognized at once that we were discussing two different problems of artistic expression.

'I grant you,' said she, 'that I do not know accurately the Maeterlinck text! I have never even read it through once. The story, yes, of course I know that; in a general way, as one knows the "plot" of any opera. One has to remember, though, that Maeterlinck is a symbolist. I confess I do not know, exactly, what he is trying to express in his "opus". I think it is jealousy; but, perhaps, it's something else! To be frank, Mr Canevin, I never gave the subject any particular thought.'

'From the writer's viewpoint,' I put in, 'it is difficult to know what he is up to! It has never been clear to me, for example, just why, at the very beginning, the castle doorkeeper is discovered struggling with a refractory door; or why the maid servants are assembling for the purpose of pouring water on the threshold! It is, undoubtedly, symbolism – it could hardly be anything else. But – what, please, does it symbolize?'

'I haven't the slightest idea!' said Marie Boutácheff, and we laughed together understandingly. Then she told me about a little group of six pieces by the composer Arnold Schönberg. She told me how she had studied these very carefully; and failed utterly to 'get' what the composer was trying to express. It was 'overtonal' composition, much, in fact, like Debussy's in *Pelléas et Mélisande*.

Then she proceeded (I recall clearly how the experience she related interested me then and later) to tell me how she had noticed their inclusion in a program played by the very famous *virtuoso* Orféo Mattaloni. The six little pieces required only a few minutes to play through. They were little scraps of expression; ideas; chiefly inter-woven phrases. She had gone to hear Mattaloni play them. She wanted, she said, to see if she could understand the composer's meaning by listening to them. She described her experience at that concert –

'Mattaloni paused just before that number on his program. He came down to the front of the platform and said to that big audience – it was in Carnegie Hall – "I beg that you will humor me! Keep silent, please, quite silent, *between* the numbers of this *suite* I am now going to play. No comment at all, if you will be so kind! I have studied them with the very greatest care. I will try to play them for you as they must be played. When I have finished all six – four minutes for them all – then, of course, such comment as you please."

'Then he sat down and played the six pieces through, very beauti-fully. He is a very great artist. They are, really, quite simple little things. And, do you know, perhaps it was merely my frame of mind at the moment, my "temperament" if you will! – I had come deliber-ately to find out Schönberg's meaning, you will remember – I closed my eyes and did not open them until Mattaloni had finished the six. I knew them all, of course, intimately. I had played them many, many times. Well I "got" six little pictures, Mr Canevin, like sketches; little, sharp, cleanly-etched line-drawings. Street, vista, sunset, a church! It was really extraordinary.

'And then when he had finished, there was quite an outbreak from the audience – boos; hisses even; applause, too; little murmurs and cheerings; several people in tears from their emotional reactions. The booings and hisses were for the composer; not for Mattaloni! He sat there and looked around at us, and smiled, inscrutably. That was all.

'Then he went on with his program; a very fine one. Everybody was delighted with it and it got very favorable notices in all the next morning's newspapers.

'But, here is the odd part of it, Mr Canevin: I "went behind"; Sylvia Manners, who was with me, and I; and I said to him: "There is a question I wish to ask you, Orféo. Tell me: had you those images – I named them all – or, if you do not mind my asking you, were you merely playing it, as Schönberg wrote it down, with that inimitable technic which is yours alone?"

'That pleased Mattaloni. He said: "I am very glad you have asked me that, Marie. No, not at all. No 'images'. I 'see' nothing; nothing whatever in them; no pictures. And, believe me, I have studied the things adequately – months of work and thought and consideration upon that little *suite* which requires only four minutes to play through, and which gives you 'sketches' as you say; *and*, which gave part of this audience what they think is reason to hiss Arnold Schönberg! It is curious, is it not? No, they mean nothing, nothing whatever to Orféo Mattaloni, except – perhaps, because of their technical construction – *a set of little children's plaything-puzzles!*" '

As for me, I could only shake my head over this account of Miss Boutácheff's experience. I appreciate the Moderns: Ravel, Stravinsky, Schönberg, Debussy; and the others. And yet, I should be the same as Signor Mattaloni. I do not, I fear, often understand what they mean to convey. It naturally interested me to learn that so great a musician as Mattaloni felt the same way about such compositions.

After a slight pause, and meaning merely to make conversation, I remarked, 'You know Mattaloni well, then, Miss Boutácheff?'

Miss Boutácheff forgot her convalescence. Her delicate, rather beautiful face lighted up with a sudden animation. She looked straight into my eyes.

'He is a very great artist,' she said. 'Yes, Mr Canevin, I know him very well.' Then at once she began to speak of Rachel Manners's remarkable work, a long series of highly-colored, florid, glowing canvases, drenched with light, made that winter under the dazzling West Indian sun; paintings which have since brought her fame.

It was not until I had had the opportunity somewhat to digest this peculiar susceptibility of Miss Boutácheff's for 'musical images' that she told me about the effect which another musical composition always had upon her.

This was Maurice Ravel's *Pavane*. The Ravel *Pavane* is a well-known composition, though rarely performed at concerts; and I think I need say no more about it here than that it is a very 'modern' musical treatment of an antique Italian dance. It is, to me, very beautiful. I imagine most audiences like it, even though it must be classed as purely intellectual music.

Marie Boutácheff said that one movement of this composition – the final movement which follows the *Grave Assai*, the suspended pause occuring on page six of the standard Schirmer edition – *she had never, really, heard* with what might be called her outward ears. When that movement began, that is, with anybody else playing the *Pavane*, and she listening, she 'passed out,' and, instead of hearing anything, got instead the mental *sensation of seeing a picture*. Near the conclusion of this particular movement, this 'picture' would disappear out of her consciousness, and she would again 'hear' the very end of the composition in a perfectly ordinary and normal manner.

She knew what were the musical *sounds* involved in this portion of the *Pavane*. She had played it herself many times and had studied it intensively. She always 'heard' every note clearly when she played it herself. So far in her career she had only practiced it. She had never included the Ravel *Pavane* in any of her own programs.

She knew, mentally, when hearing it played by somebody else, the precise sequence of the notes and chords, but, even when playing it herself, despite being able to hear every note, she nevertheless in some curious fashion 'passed out' in the same place and 'came to' in the same place.

Also – and here I could perceive the really *strange* element in the phenomenon – *the seeing impression was a growing and an increasing one*.

In other words, every time Marie Boutácheff 'saw' the picture which that particular section of the Ravel *Pavane* brought into her mind, that picture was more intense, clearer in its details, more real.

The 'picture' began with her outside the arched doorway which led into a vast ballroom in which the *Pavane* was being danced. She stood on a smooth marble flooring of square black and white tiles, looking in at the dancers.

Repetition had made it possible for her to get a clear and detailed idea of the appearance of the dancers; and every time she 'saw' the *Pavane, she was a trifle nearer the entrance-way.*

She had never been able to see all the dancers; only those just inside the arched doorway. But – there were other persons inside the ballroom around the corner, to her right, of whose presence there she was, somehow, certain.

Of the presence of those others she was thoroughly convinced. Delicate little snatches of conversation, in quaint, antique Italian, came out to her from the grouped dancers, as they made their formal bows to each other there inside the ballroom. Even *odors* as of some long-forgotten perfumes, floated out to her; scents of camphire and of bergamot. There was, too, in this composite set of sensations evoked by this portion of the *Pavane*, the feeling of a light, warm breeze, stirring the curtains of the gracious room; a little breeze which wafted itself out into the hallway where she stood looking in; entranced; breathless *with an ever-increasing, almost heart-breaking longing to get into the ballroom* – standing outside there on the cool, smooth, black and white marble tiles.

I have mentioned that Ravel's *Pavane* is rarely performed in public. But, not long after I got back to the Continental United States that Spring, having been on the lookout for its possible inclusion in some belated, end-of-the-season program, I discovered that Harold Bauer was to play the Ravel *Pavane* at his last concert, and I bought a ticket and went to Carnegie Hall for the particular purpose of hearing it.

It was a delightful, although a somewhat startling, experience!

Of course I had a certain psychological preparation for what happened. I was prepared, after what Marie Boutácheff had told me, to get mentally some kind of an 'image'. I got one! The little pause, noted in the musical score as *Grave Assai*, did, actually, give me a mental picture. I could 'see' it, intellectually, as it were (I had no clearly-defined visualization which could be literally described as a picture); four couples, dancing, as though at some distance; whether distance in space or time I can scarcely say. There were eight of the dancers in my 'picture'; four demure ladies, all young; four cavaliers attending them through the dance; handing them about the square figures of those sedate, grave measures, with a distinctively mediaeval courtesy; with gallant, studiously languid, bows.

Bauer gave a magnificent performance throughout. In the *Pavane* he accentuated the rhythm, bringing out, as Ravel clearly intends, the sense of an orchestra. I could clearly distinguish the violins, sawing along through the dignified cadences of the mellow old dance-measures. I was sure I could hear, too, in those marvellously harmonized dissonances wherein the composer speaks to the intellect in overtonal groupings of notes, the *viola da gamba*, gravely sobbing out the measured beats of melodic *ictus* – óne, two, thrée, four; óne, two, thrée, four.

It was a very interesting experience. I understood after it very much more clearly what Marie Boutácheff had meant to convey to me.

Very soon after the Bauer concert Marie Boutácheff, her health now greatly improved, came back to New York.

She called me up the day after her arrival, about ten in the morning. The New York musical season was over. It was well along in June, and those persons who, like myself, were for any reason lingering in the great city, were complaining of the heat. Marie asked me to come to tea at her studio the next day. When I got there, about four o'clock, several other people had already arrived. More came in after me. The tone of the gathering was congratulatory. These were Marie's friends, and they were outspokenly glad to see her so greatly restored. I, even, came in for a measure of their approval, as a person somehow associated with the place which had wrought such a salutary change.

Orféo Mattaloni was one of her guests. He was, it came out, to sail for Europe on the third or fourth day following.

At Marie's suggestion, hastily imparted between two admirable musical performances – and somewhat to my surprise, for I was only one of her new friends as compared with all these older and more intimate ones – I remained after the others had gone. She came back to me after seeing her other friends out of the studio, to where I sat on an enormous divan placed along the west wall of the big room. She was smiling and holding out her hands impulsively, as though I had only that moment arrived.

'O, Mr Canevin, it is indeed good to see you!' she cried, and settled herself beside me. Then at once she put into words what was in her mind, and I understood why she had asked me to remain.

'Do you know,' she said, eagerly, and turning an illuminated face towards me, 'I've had the most remarkable experience! It was only a day or so after you had sailed from St Thomas. There was an entertainment for the Municipal Hospital, a benefit. Probably you saw the notices before you left. They asked me to play. It was rather short notice, but I was quite willing, very happy indeed, really, to do that for them. I was feeling very well, you see. There was no program, no precise list of what was to be played. It was of course a very informal affair.

'I played several things; things I imagined the audience would appreciate. They liked them, and I was requested, near the end, to play again.

'*I played the Ravel Pavane*, Mr Canevin.' She paused, her eyes like stars.

'Mr Canevin – it was remarkable – extraordinary!!

'I was giving especial attention to emphasizing the rhythm – it suggests strings, you know: violins, a viola-like instrument or two, a harp, or perhaps a clavichord, accompaniment; when you analyze it, I mean. Everything went very well until that pause on page six of the manuscript; you know, the *Grave Assai* – we looked at it together there in St Thomas you remember, Mr Canevin – and then – then *I lost consciousness sitting there at the pianoforte*. I "came to" only at the somewhat abrupt ending; if you remember, there are merely a few concluding chords.

'I had played on, mechanically; played on, somehow, to the end. My mind carried me on, I suppose! Nobody noticed anything out of the ordinary. I suppose I gave no outward sign of any kind. There was applause. But – when I left the piano this time, I remembered clearly what I had seen. It was all there, chiselled sharply into my memory.

'I had been standing there outside the ballroom, as usual; only this time I felt a distinct sensation of anxiety. I wanted, oh, so acutely, to be inside the ballroom; to know if a certain person were also inside there; around the corner where I could not see. And, Mr Canevin, *I actually managed to walk several steps towards the doorway*. I was just on the very threshold when the *Pavane* ended.

'It was all clearer; more *alive*, somehow. There were the ladies; the cavaliers in their velvet cloaks and their slashed sleeves, and their rapiers – worn even while dancing; only, as I've said, it was vivid now, pulsing with life – it *was* life, Mr Canevin; and I was a part of it; and yet, somehow, not quite a part of it. And over it all was that consuming anxiety to know.

'I wanted to know if I – another self, so to speak, yet myself also – were inside there, and with someone else. It was harrowing while it lasted. The impression remained with me for days. It is not wholly gone even now. Everything depended on my knowing. Otherwise, I could not tell which of two courses to pursue. It was a question of all my happiness, Mr Canevin. I cannot describe how acute it was, how extremely vital to me.'

She paused, and relaxed her tense body, and slowly and with a gentle sigh sank back against the thick, soft cushions of the divan. Her eyes were closed; her breath was coming and going in audible, light sobs. It was plain that Marie Boutácheff had been through an extraordinary emotional experience. I sat very quietly, making no comment whatever, for several minutes – quite a long time, it seemed, under such circumstances!

Then, abruptly, Marie Boutácheff aroused herself, turned to me again with her eager animation. She said: 'What do you think of him, Mr Canevin?'

I was a trifle startled. I jumped to a conclusion which turned out to be the right one.

'You mean Signor Mattaloni?' I asked.

'Of course,' said Marie Boutácheff.

'I liked him immensely,' said I, at once, telling the exact truth. The big, handsome *virtuoso* had, indeed, impressed me very favorably.

'He is a great, a very great artist,' said Marie Boutácheff softly, and suddenly tears stood in her eyes. I began to suspect that she had a 'temperament' after all! She moved along the divan until she sat close beside me.

'I will tell you something, Mr Canevin,' she said, and was silent for a little space. She looked down at her hands lying in her lap. Then: 'It was Orféo Mattaloni whom I wanted to know about – *inside the ballroom*. He was the other person.'

I said nothing, but while I was turning over this unexpected statement in my mind, very quietly from where she sat close beside me, her voice now little more than a whisper, Marie Boutácheff began to tell me the story of that nervous breakdown. She had been, it appeared, and was still, very deeply and honestly in love with Mattaloni; and she had no means of knowing whether or not the *virtuoso* returned her love. Between the lines I discerned in Mattaloni a very noble character. Plainly the great *virtuoso* was a man of honor as well as that very great artist whom the entire musical world had already recognized and acclaimed. The Mattalonis, too, Miss Boutácheff had told me, had been great lords in Umbria in the Middle Ages.

He had been what might be called 'attentive' to her; had shown her that he thought very highly of her; but, whether as artist or woman, perhaps because of Mattaloni's punctiliousness, she had been quite unable definitely to ascertain.

And, now that the two of them were together once more in New York, it had begun all over again for her.

She ended with another allusion to her mental picture derived from the *Pavane* of Maurice Ravel.

'It is almost as though Orféo and I had lived over together similar events in that ancient setting. There was, in that experience of it, there in St Thomas after the benefit concert, the same type of anxiety which is making me unburden myself to you now. O, Mr Canevin, I know that *if I could once get into the ballroom* and see whether or not he and I are there together, I would know definitely what is in Orféo's heart! It will kill me if I do not know, Mr Canevin.'

She ended her story, her face now drawn and tragic. I waited for some time before saying anything. Then: 'Are you expecting to see him again before he sails for Europe?'

'He is coming to dinner here tomorrow. So is Rachel Manners. Will you make the fourth, Mr Canevin?'

'With great pleasure,' said I, and rose to take my departure. I had a dinner engagement that evening, and there was barely time for me to get back to my club and dress for it.

The dinner the next evening, with Orféo Mattaloni and Miss Manners as my fellow guests, was a thoroughly delightful one. Mattaloni was at his scintillating best. He shone as a conversationalist quite as brilliantly as at the pianoforte later. He played for us, one brilliant thing after another, the lovely, lucid notes rippling off his fingers like strings of pearls. He was, as Marie had said, a very great artist. Here, at his ease, away from the strain and stress of public performance, playing only for an audience in full appreciative *rapport* with him, his performance was truly magnificent. He ended with the *Fantasie Impromptu* of Chopin. There was a long pause after that. Mattaloni continued to sit at the grand piano, the three of us across the room from him, in a row on the divan.

I had an inspiration.

I spoke to him, very quietly. 'Will you play for us Ravel's *Pavane*, Signor Mattaloni?'

I could feel Marie Boutácheff's body go rigid on the long divan beside me, hear her utter a little smothered cry under her breath. She put her hands convulsively up over her face. Mattaloni did not notice any of this, in the dusk of the big room.

'Certainly – very willingly, Mr Canevin,' said he, and at once began it.

I closed my eyes, relaxed myself.

Clearly, distinctly, authoritatively, the strange, dissonant, mentally challenging chords followed one another. Mattaloni was playing very quietly, almost reflectively; precisely, I imagine, as Ravel intended his *Pavane* to be played. The *idea* of the old dance filled my mind; its rhythm exact, precise, as though under the baton of some ancient *kapellmeister* now dust these many centuries. There were the violins, the *viola da gamba*, the tinkling, precise clavichord. It was all there, beautifully clear and distinct; yet somehow distant, mellow with the dust of the fragrant centuries; an antique, a curiosity; to be sensed delicately, understandingly, with the intellect. It seemed a deliberate archaism; very beautiful, almost whimsical in certain of its nuances; steadily working on to accommodate the squares of slow-moving, graceful, formal dancers; complete to the very last measure – the last languid, formal bow of rapiered cavalier; the last deep, drooping *courtoisie* of demure *signorina* . . .

And then – there came the deliberate pause of the *Grave Assai*, the beginning of the final crucial, movement which ends with an abrupt, soft chord.

And then once more I 'saw' the dancers, this time more nearly as a literal picture than had been the case at the Bauer performance.

I became conscious of something very strange indeed.

I stood, mentally, as it were, leaning over a high stone gallery coping; and there, below me, was a black and white square-tiled floor, a graciously arched doorway with blowing curtains, the remote figures of slowly-treading dancers within. A faint, soft scent, perhaps of camphire and bergamot, was wafted up to me on the lift of the warm air from below; and there – paused, expectant, near the doorway, a woman, walking slowly towards the ballroom.

The woman was tall, slender, graceful, with very beautiful hands which she held clasped before her in a gesture indicative of some deep and carking anxiety.

I was entirely conscious of the firm notes, the dissonant chords, clear-cut under Mattaloni's masterful hands at Marie Boutácheff's pianoforte. I record definitely that I heard, plainly and clearly, every note. The two impressions, that of the eye and that of the ear, were synchronous, simultaneous; overlapping each other, so to express it. I could feel my scalp prickle, and the cold sweat starting out of the pores of my face. I was conscious of my own two hands gripped together in a vise-like clasp as I watched Marie Boutácheff down below me there, walking slowly, steadily, towards the ballroom doorway.

I was torn with a racking anxiety. Would Mattaloni's notes and chords continue long enough? Would there be *time* for her to reach the arched dorway – to go through it into the ballroom? Mattaloni's pearl-like notes, those clear-cut, precise chords of Maurice Ravel, followed one another in a relentlessly-timed procession. There were, I knew, only just so many of them.

She reached the doorway – *entered it*; and, abruptly, the sense of tenseness fell away from me; I felt myself relax, automatically. I unclasped my hands. There was no gallery, no ballroom. There was only Marie Boutácheff's studio. I let my head sink back against the deep cushion of the divan; and then I became aware of Rachel Manners speaking in a low voice, speaking to Mattaloni who had just struck the last firm, soft chord of the *Pavane's* abrupt ending: 'It was magnificent – magnificent!'

A deep silence followed Miss Manners' impulsive little speech. Mattaloni continued to sit at the piano, his leonine figure only dimly visible in the dusk of the high room. Very quietly, then, he began to speak.

'Had you remembered, perhaps, that the *Pavane* is dedicated "For a Dead Princess"? I think of her, always, when I play it. She was a Venetian, Rosabella Doria, daughter of the Doge Ludovico Doria. Her portrait, by Botticelli, is in the Louvre. She married my ancestor, the Prince Piero Mattaloni. That is how she became a Princess.

'She was very lovely – tall, blonde, slender – a woman of the most intense spirituality!'

Mattaloni paused there, and, as one could almost feel the palpable silence of the dim, quiet room restoring itself, turned about, slowly, on the piano-stool. Then quite abruptly, he threw out his long arms in a sudden, impulsive, purely Latin gesture towards the three of us, and said: 'It was of you, who are her very counterpart, my dear Marie, that I thought when I stood before the Donna Rosabella in the Louvre . . .'

Marie Boutácheff rose quietly and turned up the lights. I saw her face as she turned around. It was transfigured, rapturous!

There *is* a ballroom in that Umbrian castle of the ancient house of Mattaloni, a ballroom with an arched doorway after the manner of Torrigiano – another great artist, in stone and mortar. There are large, square, black and white marble tiles in the antechamber, and a daïs in the ballroom. I know because I asked Mattaloni when I went to see him and Marie off on the *Re Umberto*.

He was greatly moved, he assured me, by my very kind interest.

Sea Change

I

There were few secrets aboard the *Kestrel*, and her passenger Edward Renwick knew about the imminent typhoon almost as soon as the members of the crew. He had seen a kind of halo about the sun, which became more apparent as the day wore on. That was the first indication, and Captain Hansen had made no secret of its probable meaning. Hansen's noon observations confirmed his own suspicions on the day the halo first appeared, when they were some two hundred miles north of the Paumotus Group. The barometer was falling steadily, and light squalls had come spanking down during the night. Today the sea was smooth and marked with delicate ripples like a marshy millpond. When the swell began late in the afternoon, all precautions had been taken.

Hansen explained the course of a typhoon to Renwick in snatches. He spoke of cross-currents, atmospheric pressure, and various other indications. Renwick gathered that it was the accompanying 'revolving air-currents' which wrought the greatest damage to ships caught in these seasonal hurricanes of the South Seas.

Marian, his young wife, appeared unimpressed. She leaned over the rail to windward, her brown hair blowing in the freshening breeze, and Renwick retailed to her what he had gathered from Hansen's bits of nautical science. The sky had taken on a coppery glint which, despite its menace, allured them by its utter strangeness. Beneath, the sea seemed changed. One could no longer look down into its almost fathomless depths. It seemed deadened, obscure.

Everything had been made fast. Hatches were screwed down, lashings were renovated, and the davits examined. It was the provisioning of the three boats which first caused a catch at the girl's heart. Renwick reassured her. This was routine. It was only to save time. It would be an easy matter to reship the stores when the blow was over.

It was nearly nightfall when a heavy cloud-bank appeared out of the north-west, ominous and dreadful, soaring up out of the nothingness on the other side of the horizon like a huge, elongated funnel. It was very clearly marked even in the failing light which soon obscured it. They gazed at it, fascinated; but when they turned away from the rail they turned back to a changed ship. A foreboding of disaster had laid hold upon the crew. They went about their duties white-faced, subdued, as though profoundly disturbed by a sense of something imminent that could not be stayed or avoided . . .

The last thing they saw before they went below was two men removing the stores from the smallest of the three boats. On their way to their cabins below decks Captain Hansen gloomily admitted to Marian Renwick's question that this boat was unseaworthy. But there was ample room in the other boats, he assured her, if it should come to that!

They decided to remain awake and dressed during the night. They dined hastily on sandwiches and tea, and sat in their stuffy little cabin waiting for the typhoon to break.

The *Kestrel*'s sudden, wild swoop under its first impact came as a relief. The period of anxious waiting was over now. They were in for it.

The *Kestrel* wallowed, and the plunge seemed to the Renwicks more like the plunge of a frightened animal than anything a ship might do. Then, under careful guidance, she settled into a steady drive into the wind, her auxiliary engines doing their utmost.

It was Hansen's announced purpose to wear through until he could bear to the southward and 'get behind' the cyclone, and this policy he did his best to carry out. The stanch windjammer stood up bravely, and might indeed have weathered through had not the engines given out. The engines stopped. Her headway abruptly ceasing, the *Kestrel* was seized by the typhoon as though in monstrous and malignant arms and hurled and spun about in a chaos of mountainous waves.

In their cabin the two passengers were hurled together into a corner. They managed to seize and hold on to the edge of their lower bunk. They had been slung partly under it. Renwick braced his feet against the wall at the bunk's end and by main force held himself and his wife against this firm support. Beyond a few bruises neither had been hurt. Lurch and twist now as the *Kestrel* might, they fastened like limpets, spun with her. They were dizzy and sick when the *Kestrel* by an almost impish streak of luck righted herself and began to spin along with her keel down and her bow leading her. She had, after an incredible knocking about, in the course of the upheaval, gone completely about. She righted herself slowly and heavily and then scudded away before the mounting gale, naked to her sticks.

Some time after this comparative steadiness of motion had replaced the maddening upheavals, Renwick and his wife relaxed their grip on the bunkside and reassured themselves that they were able to stand upright. Marian was very giddy, and Renwick, after helping her into the lower bunk and wedging her in with bedding, staggered to the deck in search of information.

Hansen reassured him. How the *Kestrel* had lived he was unable to understand, still less to explain, but now they had more than a fair chance, he thought, to ride it out; as good a chance as any windjammer unequipped with auxiliary power. If only he had not trusted to the engines! No one would ever know what had happened. Both the engineer and his assistant were dead. They had been remorselessly jammed and crushed by the terrible tossing, there in their tiny engine-room. The engineer was unrecognizable. Five of the crew, too, were gone, washed away by the mountains of water that had been flung athwart the exposed decks.

There was comparatively little danger now. There were no leaks, though the house, all railings, and everything above decks was gone, that is, all save the masts, and, almost a miracle, the boats. All three boats were safe and, as hasty examination showed, intact, including the small boat that had been relieved of its provisions because of its unseaworthiness.

The *Kestrel* drove on through the night, under the slowly declining force of the typhoon, now blowing itself out. Food and coffee were served but no one thought of turning in.

The moon rose a little after four bells, flooding the pursuing waters and the deck of the *Kestrel*. It was full, and the light was clear and brilliant. Renwick and his young wife, on deck again, carefully worked their way to the small boat, where they clung to the rigging of the davits and looked outboard and aft where the long waves pursued relentlessly, like angry mountains.

'What's the matter with the boat?' asked Marian.

'I suppose it's been allowed to dry out too much. It seems sound enough to me, but naturally Hansen wouldn't have said it was no good unless he knew what he was talking about.'

They watched it swing. The davit rigging had been considerably loosened.

'Let's get into it!' suggested Marian, suddenly.

Renwick investigated. The canvas boat cover had not been replaced. There was no chock. He climbed gingerly into the boat, and with his help Marian managed it also. Then Renwick again descended to the deck and loosened the pully ropes and stays so that, with the swing of the level binnacle-lamp in his mind, the small boat might have a wider arc in which to swing and so keep them comparatively free from the pitching and tossing of the *Kestrel*.

It was a landsman's notion, a mere whimsy. A seaman would have scoffed at it, but, queerly enough, it seemed to work. He climbed back into the swinging boat and settled down in its bottom beside Marian.

The boat was, of course, swung inboard, and being small compared to the larger boats, both of which were chocked firmly, it swung free. Renwick felt that since the boat had been condemned they might make free with it, and he pulled some old cork lifepreservers out from under the thwarts and arranged them under Marian's head and his own. It was a weird sensation, lying there side by side looking up into the clear, moonlight sky, relatively motionless as the swinging boat accommodated itself to the rolling and pitching of the *Kestrel*.

They lay there and listened to the roar of the wind and sea. Both were dozing, fitfully, when the *Kestrel* struck.

Without warning there came a fearful, grinding crash forward. The *Kestrel* shivered and then appeared to crumple, her deck tilting to an abrupt angle. In the boat the impact was greatly modified, yet it would have been enough without that shattering crash ahead to have awakened people much more soundly asleep than Renwick and his wife. The masts snapped like pipestems.

The deck stayed on its perilous slant as the vessel hung on the teeth of the barrier reef on which she had struck bow on, while the great following waves roared over her in cascades. They lifted the small boat and tore it loose from its frayed tackle and carried it far forward, as with a tremendous and irresistible heave a huge following wave, overtopping its fellows, lifted the *Kestrel's* hull and heaved her forward for more than her own length and crushed her down upon the rocks. She parted like rotten cloth as she turned turtle and was engulfed in a mighty whirlpool of maddened water.

The small boat with two helpless wisps of humanity lying side by side upon her bottom, riding free, was borne forward on the resistless force of the rushing water.

2

When Edward Renwick's mother died he had the satisfaction of realizing that she passed out of the world forgetful of a remembered terror that had colored her thoughts as long as he could remember. His mother, left alone early in his life, had never once relaxed her vigilance over him. Now with her death he realized rather abruptly that no one remained to share the secret of what he knew.

Renwick himself knew it only as a matter of hearsay. His own memory did not extend to what they had called the Terrible Time, because then he had been little more than an infant.

His earliest days, he had been told, were like those of any other young child. It was not until he was two years old that The Change had begun.

He had always, since birth, slept more soundly than other children. Always his mother had been obliged to awaken him from a deep sleep like the inveterate slumbers of some young, hibernating animal. His growth had been regular, but slow.

They had always spent their summers at the ranch in those days. When he was two, just after they had arrived at the ranch, The Change began.

The child first lost his power of speech. His utterance became thicker, constantly, and less intelligible. Soon there remained only a few vague mutterings. Meantime he slept more and more soundly. It became correspondingly harder and harder to awaken him. His face began to grow expressionless, then repulsive. His skin became roughened and dry, and a waxy pallor overspread it. Wrinkles appeared on his forehead. The eyelids swelled. The nostrils flattened out, the ears thickened, and the fine baby hair, which had become harsh, like rough tow, fell out, leaving little pitiful bald patches. Then the child's teeth, which were small and irregular, blackened rapidly.

Finally, before the eyes of the distracted young parents, many miles distant from any center of even crude civilization, the child seemed to be shrinking in size, and his hands and feet to be turning in.

Nothing comparable to this shattering affliction lay within the utmost bounds of their understanding or experience. For several weeks their changeling continued to deteriorate. Then, at the end of their resources, in despair the father rode the thirty miles to the nearest telegraph office and sent an urgent message to their New York physician. The urgency of the message assured the doctor of an unusual need. He arranged his practise and journeyed to his friend.

The doctor spent several days, greatly puzzled, watching the child, now grotesquely deformed. He no longer recognized his mother. No longer had he the energy to sit upright.

Then the doctor, armed with photographs and other results of his investigations, went back to New York to consult specialists.

He did not return to the ranch, but he explained at length the findings of those whom he had consulted. The child, they said, had become a cretin. This, explained Dr Sturgis, meant that there had occurred one of those mystifying cases of failure of a gland. It was one of the ductless glands, probably the thyroid, in the lower portion of the throat. All the ductless glands were connected in some mysterious way. They operated in a human being somewhat like an interlocking directorate in business. One was dependent upon another. When anything like this silent, internal cataclysm occurred, the nicely adjusted balance was disturbed, and the victim became a monster.

What were the chances? The doctors were of the opinion that the case was not, necessarily, hopeless. He sent a preparation of the thyroid glands of sheep with directions for their administration and for the child's care. It was, further, the opinion of the specialists that so long as the child, if he recovered this time, continued to take thyroid, so long, in all probability, would he continue to grow and be normal. But they believed (all but one) that if the supply should be cut off, then that devastating process would repeat itself; and if the medication should be stopped, then the child would degenerate again until he had become a vegetative idiot. One doctor had been skeptical, Dr Sturgis wrote. He had approved the medication but had said that there was a possibility that the wasted gland might re-establish itself.

Confronted with the terrible alternative the doctor had described, it was no wonder that the young parents had made the daily capsule young Renwick's first duty, had impressed this upon him in season and out of season. The treatment worked. Within a few days the child's hands and feet were less cold. Other slight changes showed themselves daily. When three weeks had passed Edward was again noticing his surroundings. Gradually, through days and nights of anguished fears and a tentative, dawning hope, the young parents watched the return to normality. The child smiled, and attempted to play. He recognized his mother and father.

His growth became rapid. The remaining early teeth appeared and were firm, even, and white. A new growth of hair came in. By the end of summer the little boy was not only as well as he had ever been, but it was as though he had, in some magical fashion, been renewed. A new soul seemed to his mother to be looking out of his clear eyes.

In October, tremulous with thankfulness, they returned to their home in New York. Their friends commented freely on the child's remarkable growth.

When his mother died, he was twenty-five, alone in the world; alone with his queer secret. He had health and strength, a keen mind and a vigorous body. He was indistinguishable from any normal person – from any *other* normal person, as he liked to phrase the matter to himself. He could do precisely what anyone else might do. He might even marry, provided that he never omitted his daily capsule!

There was no reason, even of ordinary convenience, why he should ever omit it. Thyroid was easily procurable in these days. One could buy it in tablet form in any good drug store.

It was less than a year after his mother's death; he was twenty-six, when he became engaged to Marian. They were married five months later.

They had been drawn together by a community of tastes and interests. They possessed that indefinable happiness of being at ease with each other.

Among their common tastes was one that amounted to a positive longing – a yearning nostalgia for the sea. They discovered this very early in their acquaintance. They found that each had for long spent many hours on the Battery, smelling the smells of shipping, watching the ships as they faded serenely into the mists of the lower bay on their way to the varied ports of the outer world.

The peculiar glamors of Joseph Conrad, and of old Samuel Baker; Kipling's eery power to evoke a longing in his readers to go and join a ship's crew – these and many other glimpses of sea-things had laid their several holds upon their imaginations. They envisaged in their day-dreams tropic moons and palm-ringed atolls. Creaming blue surf, and white beaches blazing against turquoise sea had, somehow, got into his blood.

> Palms on blue sea's edge of coral,
> Driving gust and shrieking gale;
> Scudding, spindrift, decks a-creaking,
> Simoon's breath on baking sands,
> Buccaneers, and mission-compounds,
> Wrecks, and death in distant lands.

It was little wonder that, with their imaginations so hugely intrigued by the sea's fascination and its everlasting mystery, they had for their wedding journey engaged passage on the *Kestrel*. That was why they were in the South Pacific.

They satisfied each other profoundly, in a perfection of companionship for which the stanch old windjammer had proved to be the perfect setting. It was almost as though they had been born again, once their feet knew the swing of a deck. It seemed to them, like city-bred children drinking in the first invigorating, elusive breath of the salt sea, that it would always be impossible to encompass enough of that atmosphere. And if it was true that each felt this profound yearning for the breath of the salt winds stiffly glowing, it was true also that there ran through the fine fabric of their association something like a thin thread of somberness, almost of apprehension. It seemed to them too splendid and soul-filling to be true, or otherwise than the gossamer stuff of which dreams are made.

3

Not even a periodic missionary ever came to the tiny atoll. Most of its forty-four Polynesian inhabitants had had a hand at one time or another on the gunwales of the skiff when it was dragged through the surf of the inner reefs.

The 'unseaworthy' boat, the boat condemned as useless, had served Renwick and Marian well. Unconscious after that first mad ride away from the devils on the crest of a mountain of water, they had lain motionless, side by side in the boat's bottom, and so kept her trimmed as wave after great wave had successively carried them on and on through the torn waters of the reefs to the shallows within reach of the islanders.

Renwick's first half-conscious act when, from that fearful dream of grinding and hoarse cries of despair, and being smothered and hurled helplessly about, he awoke upon a pile of coco mats, was to reach into his pocket for the little metal box in which he carried his capsules. Then he thought of Marian, realizing dimly that he was, somehow, safe, and with a shudder, he reassured himself of her safety. She was sleeping peacefully, the sleep of utter exhaustion, on another pile of mats, near by. They were in a wattled hut. An intolerably bright sun was streaming through a low doorway and in at the lacelike interstices of the palm fronds that formed the roof.

He rose painfully to his feet, swaying with weakness, and took the little metal box out of his pocket and looked into it. There were eight of the capsules in the box.

Marian was safe. God be thanked! God was good, good, unbelievably good! Aching in every joint, Renwick stooped and passed out through the low doorway into the full, blinding glitter of the pouring sunlight.

A chirping mutter of many soft voices greeted him. The kindly islanders approached from every quarter. He saw them, bewilderedly, his hand shading his eyes from the glare.

A smiling woman placed a hat of plaited split grass upon his head. A fine, upstanding, elderly man addressed him in a strange parody of English, making him welcome. This native had been, it appeared, in the Paumotus. It was he who told what had happened: how they had come ashore; how the islanders had gone out through the surf to salvage an empty ship's boat, driving in through the jagged reefs; how he and his *vahine* had been found in the boat's bottom, 'asleep' side by side . . .

The rest of the *Kestrel's* company had found their 'death in distant lands'. Timber enough for several hut foundations was all that had come ashore.

Somewhere, out there beyond the distant farther reefs, lay the broken hull of the *Kestrel*; and somewhere within her submerged, inaccessible cabins, were the capsules that meant life . . .

He had eight. For one week and one day, then, he was safe. After that . . . A cold horror closed down upon him. He suddenly felt faint. Groping, overwhelmed, he re-entered the little hut. He threw himself down on the pile of mats. He covered his eyes with his hands. He tried to visualize what must happen. It had been dinned into his ears for a lifetime.

For a few days, perhaps even for a week or two, after he had taken all his tablets, there would probably be no perceptible change. Then he would begin gradually to slow down. He would find it harder and harder to awaken mornings. Then all that ghastly horror of degeneration would set in again. The new course of The Change would affect him, too, even more blastingly, if less rapidly, now that its victim was to be his adult and not his infant personality.

Marian! He groaned aloud, a groan choked suddenly by main force lest it disturb her sleeping peacefully over there on the mats in her corner of the little hut. He drew himself painfully to his feet and stood looking down upon her as she slept. It was like a farewell.

It was too much, this ravaging of all his hopes! This terrible fulfilment, in the very midst of his happiness, of all his life's direst dreads! But he wasted little time in anything like self-pity. It was Marian who filled his thoughts. He could not tell her! In his present weakened state he visualized a frightful purgatory, stretching out before him, and before Marian, when that change of Hell should set in here on a stage from which he might not so much as step for respite into the wings; a stage upon which he must otherwise play out the part of his incredible degradation before her horror-stricken eyes. Better, far better, to destroy himself . . .

A fresh aspect of the horror loomed before him, blackly. As the terrible spell wrought itself out, his own mind's powers would weaken, his faculties become numbed, and he would himself fail to understand the course of the disintegration that would be taking place within him. Then Marian, if unwarned beforehand, must witness with the same helpless terror that had set its mark on the lives of his young parents in those black days, his gradual and sickening change into Caliban . . .

4

Day by day he watched his capsules diminish. At the end of the sixth day, when only two were left, he suffered a revulsion. He would save these until some indications of the change appeared! When these came he would know of them before anyone else because he would be expecting them. In this way he would extend the period of his normality as long as possible, and then . . .

After that, life would be one growing terror concealed from Marian so long as his self-control should be left to him to exercise. Marian was occupied in alternations of sorrow over the loss of their shipmates and the eager happiness of a child confronted unexpectedly with an imagined paradise.

He went through one day without the thyroid: the first day within his recollection. The next day, at noon, engrained habit prevailing over his resolution, he took a tablet. The day following, after reasoning the problem out afresh, he swallowed his last tablet and flung the metal box far out among the creaming breakers of the nearest reef.

He stood, looking after it out to sea. Far beyond the breakers, beyond the great expanse of blue ocean which was their background, there swam into the scope of his vision the clear-cut outline of a spar. He lost it. He shaded his eyes with both hands against the intolerable glare. Again he picked it out standing up against the horizon. He wondered why he had not noticed it before. This was because, he reasoned, occupied with his introspections, he had glanced only indifferently out to sea. Besides, he had probably, he told himself, not looked in that precise direction. One looked out to sea from any spot on the tiny, almost circular, coral island.

Down under that spar, if chance had been only reasonably kind, lay the hull which supported it, and in the hull reposed in small, watertight cartons the thyroids which meant life, sanity, Marian!

Then, as he looked, his heart bounding with hope, all his young instincts stimulated to vigorous action, he saw, very faintly and indistinctly at that great distance, the unmistakable sign of the sea-wolves of the South Pacific – the rakish dorsal fins of great sharks. He looked long at them as they moved about in the vicinity of the spar, and shuddering, he turned inland and walked back to the hut.

Here on the island there was no means of procuring even crude thyroid. There were no animals. The atoll was utterly self-contained. Its simple inhabitants subsisted on fruit and fish. There was no settle-ment within hundreds of miles.

He interviewed the English-speaking islander. It had been the chance of a ship's crew putting in for water that had taken this man on his travels. Did such crews ever put in nowadays? Very seldom. Once in a year, perhaps, or two years – who could tell? The lull was a long chance. The sharks would go away when they had cleared up what was edible from the wreckage out there. At any rate there was the possibility of a solution out there; a solution first vaguely imagined, horrifically rejected, then avidly taken up again as Renwick tossed through the interminable tropic night on his coco matting, the night of the day on which he had taken his last capsule.

There was no help to be procured. He had sounded his friend the islander on the subject of summoning the men of the settlement with their primitive outriggers to go out there and loot the wreck. But the islander had said, indifferently, that there was no hurry about that. Some of it might come in anyway, as Renwick and Marian had come in, almost miraculously, through the jagged reefs. The sharks were thick out there now, and they would remain for some time. Time enough to go out there when they had dispersed and made it possible to dive! They might remain a week or a month. Who could explain the avidity or the patience of a shark? They would follow ships day after day in these seas, apparently subsisting on nothing, waiting!

There was something in that wreck they were waiting for now, and they would remain until they got it. Besides, it was far, almost too far for outriggers!

Renwick tried to argue. It was not so very far. One could see the spar. The islander only smiled. There appeared to be something unaccountably amusing to him in Renwick's idea of distance. But he did not explain. Perhaps what was clear enough to him was beyond his limited powers of expression, and realizing this, he only smiled.

Renwick was baffled. It appeared hopeless. But he laid his plans for his last resort with a steady mind. Marian must be spared at every cost. He broached to her the possibility of his reaching the sunken hull by swimming. He said nothing of the sharks, nothing of his conversation with the islander. He opened up the subject tentatively, delicately, with every resource of his strained finesse. He set her mind easily at rest about his going by harping upon the gentleness and kindly hospitality of the islanders. She would not mind remaining alone with them for a while?

Marian acquiesced easily, admiring her man's accustomed resource. Of course he might go out there if he wished! Why not? But he must not stay too long. He must come back soon – soon! He took her in his arms.

Four days later, as he awoke, he found that Marian was looking, smilingly, into his face. She had been shaking him. It was at least an hour after their usual time for rising.

Then he knew that *it* was beginning.

Almost at once he told Marian of his intention to swim out to the spar that afternoon. Of course she knew he was a wonderful swimmer! Wouldn't it be rather far, though? Her attention was diverted by the approach of an amber-colored baby, who waddled toward her, soft little murmurings on its lips, its tiny hands laden with hibiscus blooms.

She went with him down to the beach, his body glistening with coconut oil, a great coconut knife hanging by a lanyard about his neck. She waved to him when he stopped to tread water, turning about and shouting: 'Goodbye'. She could just hear his voice faintly because of the distant roar of the surf, a roar which rolled in for miles, even from the farthest breakers where a lone spar still hung aslant across the line of the horizon.

Then he swam straight out toward the spar where shadowy, black fins moved stealthily upon the mirror surface of the Pacific.

5

Once alone in the deep water, he settled himself to a steady, distance-devouring stroke. He had put everything in his past life definitely behind him. That now held for him, he knew, nothing that it was not altogether best to abandon. He would accomplish two ends in one, by failing to return. He would avoid the frightful process of disintegration and (infinitely nearer to his soul's desire) he would thus spare Marian all that concentrated horror which had so fearfully affected the lives of his parents. He was doing her, he reasoned, moreover, no wrong in depriving her of himself. He was only forcing the exchange between a horrible and long-drawn-out deprivation, and this sudden one which by comparison was merciful and kind.

His purpose was clear and definite. He would swim straight out to where the sea wolves moved restlessly back and forth about the wreck, and kill and rend with his great knife until he was overcome. It was not even suicide! There was a possibility that the sharks might not attack him, but would disappear upon his arrival. He knew, fragmentarily, something of sharks. One could never be certain what they might do. It was also possible that, even if attacked, the killing of one or two might divert the others; just as in Siberia travelers pursued by wolves sometimes escaped by shooting a wolf or two and so delaying the pack, which would stop to tear and devour.

He swam on steadily, these ideas uppermost in his mind. After what seemed a very long time, he raised himself, treading water, to make sure of his direction. He located the spar, straight in line with his course. To his surprise it seemed no nearer than when he had stood on the beach. This he attributed to the queer tricks of refraction, and resumed his swim.

After another long, steady period of progress in the same direction he repeated his lookout. Again he reassured himself as to his course. Once more he swam on, puzzled that the spar still seemed so distant. It was almost uncanny.

Suddenly, as this calamity usually comes, even to an expert swimmer, he began to tire. He rested, floating, for several minutes, and then, treading water, again oriented himself by the spar. He could perceive no difference in its appearance or nearness: For all the progress he had made he might as well have been standing on the beach! Then it came to him suddenly that his disintegration must have been making strides far more rapidly than he had imagined possible. He must have got only a little way from the island! How good it was – what a mercy – that it had this form, and not some other that would have been apparent to Marian.

Wearily he trod water again, and, locating the spar, turned himself directly around in the certainty of finding the island just at hand, his one hope being that he had got far enough away so that he might drown quietly here out of Marian's view. He hoped she might not have remained on the beach. If so she would be puzzled at his slight progress, and would be watching him intently . . . He could never reach the spar. He could not, of course, go back. The solution rested upon his not returning, unless (how absurd it seemed!) he should, by that saving chance which by its casuistry saved his act from deliberate self-destruction, manage in some way to drive off the sharks, and, by a lucky dive, succeed in lighting upon one of his cartons . . .

He could not see the island! He shaded his eyes with his hands, and looked carefully. Could that be it? It must be. There was no other island within hundreds of miles. But – could he possibly have come so far? The island appeared to him almost low on the horizon. He must have been swimming steadily for hours. He could see the island in its entirety; perspective had made it small and compact. And he had dreaded Marian's being on the beach to see!

Infinitely troubled, all his reasoning thrown askew, he rolled over upon his back and floated, trying to think consecutively. There was only one explanation for the apparently stationary spar. That must be the very common sea-mirage. That was what the islander had meant; what he could not explain! He, too, had seen the spar, had had it pointed out to him; and he had said it was almost too far for a company of men in the outriggers! How could he, in his decadent condition, have come such a distance as this toward it?

Then he recalled that he had been basing this present idea of decadence, of having covered only a short distance, on the fact that the spar had not appeared to grow in size. But that, as he had just rightly reasoned, was mirage! Reason allowed only one answer to the riddle. He had actually covered the great distance the time spent in the water would have permitted him to swim while in perfect condition.

He thought of his intended battle with the sharks. He shuddered, and imagined a shark just behind him, then laughed aloud at this fancy. Suddenly he sobered. He had laughed – laughed! A fitting conclusion to a perfectly normal sequence of ideas. He reasoned with himself afresh. What was the matter with him? This manner of thought, this great swim – these were not the ways of a cretin. He knew all about cretins! It was clearly, rather, what might be expected of a normal, healthily tired young man in magnificent physical condition, now floating for rest in this deep, very comfortable water, of high buoyancy; out here in the Pacific on a fool's errand.

That errand! What had he been thinking of? To attempt to do battle with a school of sharks, armed with a coconut knife! He was a fool! To be out here when he might be on shore – with Marian!

He remembered, with a queer feeling in his head, how he had planned never to see her again. That was because of The Change which had begun to come upon him. The Change! Nonsense! There had been no change. No man could have traveled this distance from shore and kept his direction as he had done unless he were in the very pink of condition, every nerve and sinew and muscle, and a perfectly sound brain, functioning and coördinating with a precision that spelled perfection. Why, he had actually been obliged to hunt about to locate the island, he had come out so far!

He floated for a few minutes more, the soft, invigorating water lapping gently over him, his hands clasped under his head. Tentatively he rubbed himself over with his hands. Every muscle was responding, working splendidly. He was not even fagged, but only slightly winded by an exceptionally long and vigorous swim.

He began to swim back toward the island. He went slowly at first, because now it was only a question of ordinary judgment to conserve his strength.

Strength! He had almost never put out his full strength! He shook his head vigorously in sheer exuberance, blowing the water away from his mouth right and left as he cut easily and swiftly through it.

The conviction grew upon him, as he swam, it seemed, more and more easily and strongly in a straight line toward the island, that there was nothing to mark him off from any normal man – from 'any *other* normal man', he repeated his old phrase to himself. What if he had, all these years, been deluding himself through bondservice to a fear which had no longer any substantial foundation; fear derived from his father and his dear mother, and Dr Sturgis?

There was nothing to distinguish him from an average man – nothing, that was, except his magnificent strength, energy, and endurance. None but a normal man could possess and retain this command over himself, his mind and body. It was no wonder, though, that he had given in to it so long. It had been dinned into his ears since as long ago as he could remember. He had simply acquiesced in a wrong idea, that was all. He had been frightened of a bogle, like a child! But he would give in to it no longer. He had left that ancient bogle of the imagination out there where he had been floating and thinking; left it out there to toss about or sink to the bottom. The sharks could have it! He laughed aloud in sheer glee, knowing that he was released from that old bondage of an overstressed idea. He swam on and on.

He walked up the beach at last, slowly, and a little stiffly and wearily from the tremendous swim, the water running in crooked trickles down his well-oiled body. The knife swung awkwardly against his broad chest. It annoyed him, and he unslung it and carried it in his hand, dangling by the lanyard. Then a glint of iridescent green and blue caught his eye as something moved across an exposed rock and caught the light from the afternoon sun now slanting far down toward the western horizon. It was a huge land-crab.

He hurled the knife at it, throwing from the point. It was a long throw, but the heavy knife, whirling as it flew, struck with a metallic clash fairly among the great crab's awkward legs. With a shout Renwick ran to his quarry, which, on its remaining sound legs, was attempting to drag itself away.

He picked it up, gingerly, and tied it to the lanyard, and then, with it swinging beside him, continued on his way.

He met Marian playing with some tiny children, her hair aureoled with flaming *flamboyant*. He held up the crab.

'The only booty from that voyage, I'm sorry to say,' he called out to her, 'and I didn't get *him* till after I was back on shore again. It was altogether too far. I'll have to try it in an outrigger some day.'

'Have you been swimming all this time?' asked Marian. 'I was beginning to worry about you a little!'

'Never worry about me! Lord, Marian, but I'm hungry! I haven't had a thing to eat since this morning.'

'Bring along your crab, then,' retorted Marian, rising from among the babies. 'I wish I had some mayonnaise! My goodness, what a blessing it is that I'm a "natural cook". I never saw such a caveman for food.'

Together they walked toward their hut, the great crab still struggling at the end of his string for the freedom he would never know again.

When the 'natural cook' had done her work and the crab, as such, had ceased to exist, Renwick, leaning back, addressed his wife.

'I hope you won't have to do this sort of thing very long, dear. Any time, of course, a ship may put in for water. Old "Parmenides" tells me there's one nearly every year; and they've never gone longer than two years without one.'

'But it's perfect! I could live here forever – well, a year anyhow.'

She placed her chin on her hands and looked at him, her eyes like stars.

'Then I'm satisfied,' said Renwick, as he rose to stretch mightily the growing stiffness of his overtaxed muscles. 'Let the ship sail in when she's ready. I'm dead-tired after that swim. Do you mind if I turn in?'

'I should think you would want to turn in, after that swim, and after last night. Do you realize that you sat out there in the moon-light, all by yourself, until after one o'clock by my wrist watch? It's never missed a tick, all through everything.'

She shuddered a little and returned to the subject of his dissipation.

'You may remember I had to wake you up this morning. You had only five hours of sleep!'

Just before he drifted into sleep that night he thought of the Caliban! He remembered his frightful delineation as the frontispiece of an old, leatherbound copy of *The Tempest*. It was something like that which had been at the back of his mind – his possible meta-morphosis into Caliban! So he had phrased it to himself. Caliban!

And now? What was it in Ariel's song? Something about a Change?

> He hath suffered a sea change
> Into something rich and strange!

The sea – the blessed sea! It had healed him, healed the wounds of his mind. He drifted into dreamless sleep with the sound of its distant thunder in his ears, like a great, kindly benediction.

The People of Pan

I, Gerald Canevin of Santa Cruz, have actually been down the ladder of thirteen hundred and twenty-six steps set into the masonry of the Great Cylinder of Saona; have marveled at the vast cathedral underground on that tropical island; have trembled under the menacing Horns of the Goat.

That this island, comparable in area with my own Santa Cruz, and lying as it does only an overnight's sail from Porto Rico's metropolis, San Juan, quite near the coast of Santo Domingo, and skirted almost daily by the vessels of the vast Caribbean trade – that such an island should have remained unexplored until our own day is, to me, the greatest of its many marvels. Through his discovery, Grosvenor is today the world's richest man.

How, under these conditions, it could have been inhabited by a cultured race for centuries, is not hard, however, to understand. The cylinder – but the reader will see that for himself; I must not anticipate. I would note that the insect life has been completely re-established since Grosvenor's well-nigh incredible adventure there. I can testify! I received my first (and only) centipede bite while on Saona with Grosvenor, from whose lips I obtained the extraordinary tale which follows . . .

'But,' protested Grosvenor, 'how about the lighthouse? Isn't there *anybody* there? Of course, I'm not questioning your word, Mr Lopez!'

'Automatic light.' The Insular Line agent spoke crisply. 'Even the birds avoid Saona! Here – ask Hansen. Come here, will you, Captain?'

Captain Hansen of the company's ship *Madeleine* came to the desk. 'Vot iss it?' he asked, steely blue eyes taking in Charles Grosvenor.

'Tell Mr Grosvenor about Saona, Captain. You pass it twice a week on your run to Santo Domingo. I won't say a word. You tell him!'

Captain Hansen lowered his bulk carefully into an office chair.

'It iss a funny place, Saona. Me, I'm neffer ashore there. Nothing to go ashore *for*. Flat, it iss; covered down to de beach with mahogany trees – millions of mahogany trees. Nodding else – only beach.

On one end, a liddle peninsula, and de automatic light. Nobody iss dere. De Dominican gofferment sends a boat vunce a month with oil for de light. Dat's all I could tell you – trees, sand, a dead leffel; nobody dere.'

The captain paused to light a long black cigar.

Grosvenor broke a silence. 'I have to go there, Captain. I am agent for a company which has bought a mahogany-cutting concession from the Dominican government. I have to look the place over – make a survey. Mr Lopez suggests that you put me ashore there on the beach.'

'Goot! Any time you made de arrangement here in de office, I put you on shore dere, and – I'll go ashore with you! In all de Seffen Seas neffer yet did I meet a man had been ashore on Saona. I t'ink dat yoost happens so. Dere iss noddings to go ashore for; so, efferybody sails past Saona.'

The captain rose, saluted the agent and Grosvenor gravely, and moved majestically toward the narrow stairs which led to the blazing sidewalk of San Juan below.

It required two weeks in *mañana*-land for Grosvenor to assemble his outfit for the sojourn on Saona. He was fortunate in discovering, out of work and looking for a job, a Barbadian negro who spoke English – the ancient island tongue of the buccaneers – and who labored under the name of Christian Fabio. Christian had been a ship's steward. He could cook, and like most Barbadians had some education and preferred long, polysyllabic words.

The *Madeleine* sailed out of San Juan promptly at three one blazing afternoon, with Grosvenor and Christian aboard.

Grosvenor had asked to be called at six, and when he came on deck the next morning the land off the *Madeleine's* starboard side was the shore of Saona. The *Madeleine* skirted this low-lying shore for several hours, and Grosvenor, on the bridge deck, scanned the island with the captain's Zeiss glass. He saw one dense mass of mahogany trees, dwarfed by perspective, appearing little more impressive than bushes.

At eight bells Captain Hansen rang for half-speed, and brought the *Madeleine* to anchor off a small bay skirted by a crescent of coconut palms. Greensward indicated the mouth of a fresh-water stream, and for this point in the bay Captain Hansen steered the ship's boat, in which he accompanied Grosvenor and Christian ashore. They were followed by another and larger boat, loaded to the gunwales with their supplies.

The trees, seen now close at hand, were much larger than they had appeared from the ship's deck. A fortune in hardwood stood there, untouched it seemed for centuries, ready for the cutting.

As soon as the stores were unloaded, Captain Hansen shook hands gravely with Grosvenor, was rowed back to his ship, and the *Madeleine* was immediately got under weigh and proceeded on her voyage. Long before the taint of her smoke had faded into nothingness in the blazing glare of the tropic sun, the two marooned inhabitants of Saona had pitched their tents and were settled into the task of establishing themselves for several weeks' sojourn.

Grosvenor started his explorations the next morning. His map of the island was somewhat sketchy. It did not show the slight rise toward the island's center which had been perceptible even from shipboard. Grosvenor's kit included an aluminum surveyor's transit, a thermos-flask of potato soup – one of the best of tropical foods – and the inevitable mosquito-net for the noon *siesta*.

He started along the line of the stream, straight inland. He was soon out of sight and hearing of his camp in a silence unbroken by so much as the hum of an insect. He found the trees farther inland, in the rich soil of centuries of undisturbed leafage, better grown than those nearer the sea. As they increased in size, the sun's heat diminished.

Grosvenor walked along slowly. The stream, as he had expected, narrowed and deepened after a few rods of travel, and even a short distance inland, rinsing out his mouth with an aluminum cupful of the water, he found it surprizingly cool. This indicated shelter for a great distance and that the island must be very heavily forested.

A quarter of a mile inland he set up his transit, laid out a square and counted the trees within it. The density of the wood was seventeen per cent greater than what the company had estimated upon. He whistled to himself with satisfaction. This promised a favorable report. He continued his walk inland.

Four times he laid out a similar square, counted the trees, measured the circumference of their bases a little above the ground, estimated their average height. The wood-area became steadily denser.

At twelve-thirty he stopped for lunch and a couple of hours' rest. It would take him less time to walk back because he would not have to stop to lay out his squares.

He drank his potato soup, ate two small sandwiches of sharp Porto Rico sausage, and boiled a cupful of the stream water over a sterno apparatus for tea.

Then he stretched himself out on the long grass of the stream's bank under his mosquito-netting. He drifted easily into sleep, to the accompaniment of the stream's small rustlings and the sough of the trade wind through the millions of small mahogany leaves.

He awakened, two hours later, a sense of foreboding heavily upon him. It was as though something weird and strange had been going on for some time – something of which he was, somehow, dimly conscious. As he started, uneasily, to throw off the net and get up, he noticed with surprise that there were no mosquitoes on the net's outer surface. Then he remembered Captain Hansen's remarks about the dearth of animal life on the island. There was rarely even a seagull, the captain had said, along the island's shore. Grosvenor recalled that he had not seen so much as an insect during his five hours on the trail. He threw off the net and rose to his feet.

The vague sense of something obscurely amiss with which he had awakened remained. He looked curiously about him. He listened, carefully. All was silent except for the dying breath of the trade wind.

Then, all at once, he realized that he was missing the sound of the little stream. He stepped toward it and saw that the water had sunk to a mere trickle. He sat down near the low bank and looked at it. There were the marks of the water, more than a foot higher than its present level.

He glanced at his watch. It was three-thirteen. He had slept for two hours, exactly as he had intended. He might have slept the clock around! Even so, twenty-six hours would hardly account for a drop like this. He wound his watch – seven and one-half twists. It was the same day! He looked at the water again. It was dropping almost visibly, like watching the hour-hand of a huge clock at close range. He stuck a twig at its present level, and started to roll up his net and gather his belongings into a pack. That finished, he lit a cigarette.

He smoked the cigarette out and went to look at his twig. The water was half an inch below it. The many slight sounds which make up the note of a brook were muted now; the little trickle of water gave off no sound.

Greatly puzzled, Grosvenor shouldered his pack and started back to camp.

The walk occupied an hour and a quarter. The water grew lower as he went downstream. Before he reached the edge of the mahogany forest it had dwindled into a shallow bit of fenland. At the edge of the coral sand it was quite dry. He found Christian getting supper and bubbling over with long words which emerged out of a puzzled countenance.

'Doubtless you have remarked the diminution of the stream,' began Christian. 'I was fortunate enough to observe its cessation two hours ago and I have filled various vessels with water. It was constitute a very serious menace to our comfort, sir, if we are deprived of water. We might signal the *Madeleine* on her return voyage tomorrow, but I fear that if the lowering of the stream is permanent we shall be obliged to ration ourselves as to ablutions!'

Having delivered this masterpiece, Christian fell silent.

When Grosvenor arose the next morning the stream was at the same level as on the previous morning. It was as though this stream were subject to a twenty-four-hour tide. There was no means of judging now whether this were the case, or whether some cataclysm of nature at the stream's source had affected it in this extraordinary way. Grosvenor's instinct was all for another trip upstream to the source to find out what he could.

He made more of his tree-tests that morning, and after lunch the stream began to fail again. The following morning it was once more at its high level. That day Grosvenor put his wish into execution. He had plenty of time for his surveys. He would go exploring on his own account today. He started after breakfast, taking only the materials for lunch this time. The mosquito-netting had proved to be useless. There were no mosquitoes!

At nine he reached the spot where he had taken the first *siesta*. He proceeded upstream, and half an hour later the ground began to rise. The stream shallowed and broadened. The trees in this moist area grew larger than any others he had seen on the island.

His pedometer informed him he was getting close to the island's center. The ground now mounted steadily. He came to a kind of clearing, where the trees were sparse and great whitish ricks replaced the soft coral soil. Through these, the stream, now again narrow and deep, ran a tortuous way, winding about the great boulders. On this broken ground, without much shade, the sun poured in intolerable brilliance. He wiped the sweat from his face as he climbed the last rise to the island's summit.

As he topped the rise an abrupt change took place. One moment he had been picking his way through broken ground among rocks. The next he was standing on smooth stone. He paused, and looked about him. He was at the top.

At his feet lay a smooth, round lake, enclosed by a stone parapet. Beyond, a gentle slope, heavily forested, ran down to the distant sea on the island's other side.

He stooped down, rubbed his hand over the level surface of the stone. It was masonry.

All was silent about him; not even a dragon-fly disturbed the calm surface of the circular pool. No insect droned its fervid note in the clear, warm air.

Very quietly now, for he felt that the silence of this place must not be disturbed by any unnecessary sound, he started around the lake's circular rim. In twenty steps he had reached the source of the stream. Here the edge of masonry was cut into a U through which the water flowed silently out. He resumed his walk, and the circuit occupied fifteen minutes. He reached his starting-point, sat down on the warm rock-edge, and looked intently into the pool. It must be fed by deep, subterranean springs, he judged, and these springs, possibly, ebbed and flowed, a rhythm reflected in a rise and fall of the pool's surface; a consequent rise and fall in the water of the stream.

The sun was almost intolerably hot. He walked off to the nearest mahogany grove, pitched his camp in its deep shade, and sat down to wait till noon. Here he prepared lunch, ate it, and returned to the basin's rim.

The reservoir was several feet lower, the water now barely trickling through its outlet. He watched the waters sink, fascinated. He leaned over the edge of masonry and gazed into their still depths. A cloud passed over the sun, throwing the great pool into shade.

No bottom was visible. Down, down, his gaze traveled, and as he looked the rate of the sinking water-level increased and there arose from the pool a dim, hollow sound as some incalculable suction drew the waters down into the cylinder's depths.

An almost irresistible desire came over him to descend with the water. His scrutiny traveled about the inner surface of the great cylinder now revealed by the sinking waters.

What was that? Something, a vertical line, toward the other side, broke the cementlike smoothness of the chiseled surface. He started toward the point, his heart jumping as what he had vaguely suspected, hoped, became an actuality before his eyes. The vertical line was a ladder down the inner surface of the cylinder, of broad, copper-colored metal insets extending far down until he lost it in the unfathomable darkness below.

The ladder's topmost inset step was some three feet below the top. Looking closely from the rim above it, he observed semi-circular ridges on the rim itself, handholds, obviously, shaped like the handles of a stone crock, cut deeply into the masonry. A thin, metal hand-rail of the same material as the steps ran down straight and true beside them.

The impulse to descend became overpowering. He muttered a brief, fragmentary prayer, and stooped down, clutching the stone handholds. He stepped over the rim and down inside, and felt for the topmost step of the ladder with his foot. The step, and the railing, as he closed a firm right hand about it, felt slippery. But steps and rail were rigid, firmly set as though installed the day before. The metal showed no corrosion.

With a deep breath, he took one last look at the tops of the mahogany trees and began to go down the ladder.

At first he felt carefully for each succeeding step, clutched the unyielding handrail grimly, as the dank coolness of the stone cylinder closed in around him. Then, with custom, his first nervous vigilance relaxed. The steps were at precisely regular intervals; the handrail firm. He descended beyond the penetrating light of the first fifty feet into a region of increasing coolness and dimness.

When he reached the two hundredth step, he paused, resting, and looked down. Only a vague, imponderable dimness, a suggestion of infinite depth, was revealed to him. He turned his head about and looked up. A clear blue, exact circle stood out. Within it he saw the stars.

He descended another hundred steps, and now all was black about him. The blue circle above had turned darker. The stars glowed brilliantly.

He felt no fear. He had steady nerves, fortitude, a fatalistic faith in something he named his destiny. If harm were to come to him, it would come, here or anywhere else. He reasoned that the water would not rise for many hours. In that blackness he resumed his descent. He went down and down, step after interminable step . . .

It was wholly dark now. The circle above was only the size of a small coin, the stars indistinguishable; only their flickering brightness over the surface of the tiny disk.

He had counted 1,326 steps when something happened to his left foot. He could not lower it from the step on which it rested. The very edge of a shadow of cold fear fell upon him, but resolutely he put it away. He lowered his right foot to the same step, and, resting his body's weight on the left foot attempted to lower the right. He could not!

Then it dawned upon him that he had reached the bottom of the ladder. Holding firmly to the rail with his left hand he reached for his flashlight with the other. By its light he looked about him. His feet were on a metal platform some twelve feet square. Just to his left, leading into the wall of the cylinder, was the outline of a lancet-shaped doorway. A great ring hung on a hinged knob near his hand.

He stepped out upon the platform, his muscles feeling strange after the long and unaccustomed strain of the descent. He took hold of the door-ring, twisted it to the left. It turned in his hand. He pulled, and a beam of light, soft and mellow, came through the vertical crack. He pulled the door half-open, and the soft light flooded the platform. He stepped over to its edge and looked down, leaning on the metal handrail which ran about the edge. Blackness there – sheer, utter blackness.

He turned again to the door. He had not come thus far to yield to misgivings as to what might lie behind it. He slipped through the opening and pulled the door to behind him. It shut, true and exactly flush with its surrounding walls and jambs, solidly.

He stood in a small, square room, of the same smooth masonry as the cylinder, floored with sheets of the coppery metal. The light came through from another doorway, open opposite the side where he stood. Resolutely he crossed the small room and looked through the door.

Vast space – a cathedral – was the first, breath-taking impression. Far above, a vast, vaulted arch of masonry. In the dim distance towered an amazing figure, so incredible that Grosvenor let out his breath in a long sigh and sat down weakly on the smooth floor.

The figure was that of an enormous goat, reared on a pair of colossal legs, the lowered head with sweeping horns pointing forward, some eighty feet in the air. About this astounding image hung such an air of menacing savagery that Grosvenor, weary with his long descent, covered his face with his hands to shut it out. He was aroused out of his momentary let-down by a sound.

He sat up, listened. It was a kind of faint, distant chanting. Suppressing a shudder he looked again toward the overpowering majesty of the colossus. A great concourse of people, dwarfed by the distance, danced rhythmically before the gigantic idol. The chant rose higher in measured cadence. Fascinated, Grosvenor rose and walked toward the distant dancers.

When he had traversed half the space between, the image took on a dignity not apparent from the greater distance. The craggy, bestial face was now benevolent, as it looked down upon its devotees. There was a grotesque air of benediction about the flare of the forehoofs as they seemed to wave in grave encouragement to the worshipers beneath. The attention of the throng was so occupied with their dance that Grosvenor remained unobserved. Clouds of incense rose before the image, making the head appear to nod, the forelegs to wave gravely.

Something more than its cadence seemed now to mingle with the chanting. There was something oddly familiar about it, and Grosvenor knitted his brows in the effort to place it. Then it came to him all at once. It was the words of the ancient Greek Chorus. Nearer and nearer he approached, his feet making no sound on the dull, russet-colored, metal flooring. It was like walking on solid lead. He stooped, at this thought, and with his sheath-knife scratched its surface, dulled with the wear of countless feet. A thin, wirelike splinter curled behind his scratching knife-point. It was bright yellow on the fresh surface. He tore the splinter loose, held it close. It was soft, like lead – virgin gold.

He placed the sliver in his jacket pocket and stood, dumfounded, his heart pounding tumultuously. Gold! . . .

The chanting ceased. A clear, woman's voice detached itself; was lifted in a paean – a hymn of praise. The words now came to him clear and full. He stopped dead, trying, straining all his faculties, to understand. The woman was singing in classical Greek!

Something of modern Greek he understood from a long professional sojourn in the Mediterranean island of Xante where once he had been employed by the owner of a group of currant-plantations, and where he had learned enough of the Italianized Greek of the island to make himself understood. He hastened forward, stopping quite near the rearmost worshipers. This was no dialect. This was Old Greek, Attic Greek, the tongue of Hellas, of classic days, as used to celebrate the Mysteries about the altars of Zeus and the Nature gods; in the Sacred Groves; at Elis, and Dodona, and before the shrines of Apollo – and in the worship of Pan. Pan! – the Goat. The beginnings of an understanding surged through his mind.

In the ancient tongue of Homer and Aeschylus, this recitative now began to take form in his mind. It was, he soon perceived, a hymn to Pan, to the patron god of woodlands and wild places; of glades and streams and hidden groves; of nymphs and dryads . . .

The people swayed to the cadences of the hymn, and at intervals the vast throng breathed out a few rhythmical words, a hushed, muted chorus, in which were recited the Attributes of Pan . . .

Grosvenor found himself swaying with them, the notes of the chorus somehow strangely familiar to him, as though remembered after a great interval, although he *knew* that he had never before in this life heard anything like this. He approached nearer, without concealment now, mingled with the multitude pouring out its corporate soul to the god of Nature.

The hymn ended. Then, to a thin, piping note – the note of a syrinx – and with no confusion, a dance began. Grosvenor danced naturally with a group of four, and the others, in a kind of gentle ecstasy, danced with him, a dance as old as trees and hills, the worship of the Great Powers which through the dignity and grace of the dance seemed to promise strange and unknown joys . . .

The dance ended, abruptly, on a note of the pan-pipes. Grosvenor, brought to himself, glanced quickly about him. He was conspicuous. The others were uniformly dressed in blue kirtles, sandals on their graceful feet. The people were very beautiful. Grace and dignity marked their every movement.

Behind the colossal image of the Goat a great recess was set off by an arch which towered aloft out of sight. Here stood an altar, about whose upper edge ran cameo-like figures: youths and girls bearing wreaths; garlanded oxen; children with torches; and, centrally placed, the grotesque figure of Pan with his goat's legs and small, crooked horns upon his forehead – Pan seated, his pipes at his lips.

Suddenly every eye turned to the altar.

There came from a recess a woman, tall and graceful, bearing in her hands a slender vase of white stone. From this, on reaching the altar, she poured out upon it a thin stream of golden-colored oil. An intense, reddish flame arose at once. The vast audience stood motionless.

Then a note on the pipe, and from the throng, quite close to Grosvenor, a young man stepped, and mounted broad, shallow steps to the altar. In his hand he carried a live beetle held delicately by the edge of elevated wings. Straight to the altar he proceeded and dropped the insect in the center of the flame. So silent was the motionless throng that the rackle of the flame devouring this inconsiderable offering was plainly heard. Bowing to the priestess, the young man returned to his place.

A sigh, such as proceeds from a large concourse of people who have been keeping silence, now arose from the throng, which forthwith broke up into conversing groups.

Then the first intimation of fear fell upon Grosvenor like a black mantle. For the first time since his arrival among this incredible company, a quarter of a mile underneath the surface of an 'uninhabited' West Indian island, he took sudden thought for his safety. It was late in the day to think of that! He was surrounded by these people, had intruded into their worship, a worship ancient when the Classics were composed. He was effectually cut off from any chance of escape, should they prove hostile. He saw a thickening group closing in about him – curious, incredulous, utterly taken by surprize at discovering this stranger in their midst . . .

By a great effort, and in a voice hardly more than a whisper – for his danger had made itself overwhelmingly apparent to him – he spoke in his best attempt at pure Greek.

'I give you greeting, in the name of Pan!' he said.

'And to you, greeting, O barbarian,' replied a deep and rich voice behind him.

The throng about him stirred – a movement of deference. He turned. The graceful priestess stood close to him. He bowed, prompted by an instinct for 'good manners'.

The priestess made a graceful inclination before him. Instinct prompted him a second time. He addressed her.

'I come to you in love and peace.' It was a phrase he had gathered from the hymn to Pan – that phrase 'love and peace'. He continued: 'I have sojourned in the Land of Hellas, the home of the great Pan, though no Hellene, as my speech declares.'

'Sojourn here, then, with Pan's people in love and peace,' returned the priestess with commanding dignity. She made him a summoning gesture.

'Come,' she said, and, turning, led the way back toward the altar.

He followed, into the blackening gloom of the sanctuary, and straight before him walked his conductress without so much as a glance right or left. They passed at last between two enormous curtains screening an aperture, and Grosvenor found himself in a very beautiful room, square, and unmistakably Greek in its appointments. Two long couches stood at each side, along the walls. In the center a chaste, rectangular table held a great vase of the yellow metal, heaped with pomegranates.

The priestess, pausing, motioned him gracefully to one of the seats, and reclined opposite him upon the other.

She clapped her hands, and a beautiful child ran into the room. After a round-eyed glance at the stranger, he stood before the priestess, who spoke rapidly to him. He left the room, and almost immediately returned with a vase and two small goblets of the ruddy gold. The drink proved to be pomegranate-juice mingled with cold water. Grosvenor found it very refreshing.

When they had drunk, the priestess began at once to speak to him.

'From where do you come, O barbarian?'

'From a region of cold climate, in the north, on the mainland.'

'You are not, then, of Hispaniola?'

'No. My countrymen are named "Americans". In my childhood my countrymen made war upon those of Hispaniola, driving them from a great island toward the lowering sun from this place, and which men name "Cuba". '

The priestess appeared impressed. She continued her questioning.

'Why are you here among the People of Pan?'

Grosvenor explained his mission to the island of Saona, and, as well as his limited knowledge of Greek permitted, recounted the course of his adventure to the present time. When he had finished: 'I understand you well,' said the priestess. 'Within man's memory none have been, save us of the People of Pan, upon this island's surface. I understand you are the forerunner of others, those who come to take of the wood of the surface. Are all your fellow-countrymen worshippers of Pan?'

Grosvenor was stuck! But his sense of humor came to his rescue and made an answer possible.

'We have a growing "cultus" of Pan and his worship,' he answered gravely. 'Much in our life comes from the same source as yours, and in spirit many of us follow Pan. This following grows fast. The words for it in our tongue are "nature-study", "camping", "scouting", "golf", and there are many other varieties of the cult of Pan.'

The priestess nodded.

'Again, I understand,' she vouchsafed. She leaned her beautiful head upon her hand and thought deeply.

It was Grosvenor who broke a long silence. 'Am I permitted to to make enquiries of you?' he asked.

'Ask!' commanded the priestess.

Grosvenor enquired about the rise and fall of the water in the great cylinder; the origin of the cylinder itself: was the metal of which the floors and steps and handrail were made common? Where did the People of Pan get the air they breathe; How long had they been here, a quarter of a mile beneath the earth's surface? On what kind of food did they live? How could fruit – he indicated the pomegranates – grow here in the bowels of the earth?

He stopped for sheer lack of breath. Again the priestess smiled, though gravely.

'Your questions are those of a man of knowledge, although you are an outlander. We are Hellenes and here we have lived always. All of us and our fathers and fathers' fathers were born here. But our tradition teaches us that in the years behind the years, in the very ancient past, in an era so remote that the earth's waters were in a different relation to the land, a frightful cataclysm overwhelmed our mother-continent, Antillea. That whole land sank into the sea, save only one Deucalion and his woman, one Pyrrha, and these from Atlantis, the sister continent in the North. These, so the legend relates, floated upon the waters in a vessel prepared for them with much food and drink, and these having reached the Great Land, their seed became the Hellenes.

'Our forebears dwelt in a colony of our mother continent, which men name Yucatan, a peninsula. There came upon our forebears men of warlike habit, men fierce and cruel, from a land adjacent to Hellas, named "Hispaniola". These interlopers drove out our people who had for eons followed the paths of love and peace; of flocks and herds; of song and the dance, and the love of fields and forest and grove, and the worship of Pan. Some of our people they slew and some they enslaved, and these destroyed themselves.

'But among our forebears, during this persecution, was a wise man, one Anaxagoras, and with him fled a colony to the great island in the South which lies near this island. There they settled and there would have carried on our worship and our ways of peace. But here they of Hispaniola likewise came, and would not permit our people to abide in peace and love.

'Then were our people indeed desperate. By night they fled on rafts and reached this low-lying place. Here they discovered the cylinder, and certain ones, greatly daring, cast themselves on the mercy of Pan and descended while the waters were sunken.

'Here, then, we have dwelt since that time, in peace and love.

'We know not why the waters fall and rise, but our philosophers tell us of great reservoirs far beneath the platform where man's foot had not stepped. In these, as the planet revolves, there is oscillation, and thus the waters flow and ebb once in the day and not twice as does the salt sea.

'We believe that in times past, beyond the power of man to measure or compute, the dwellers of these islands, which then were mountain-tops, ere the submersion of Antillea and its sister continent Atlantis, caused the waters of the sea to rise upon them, and whose descendants those of Hispaniola did name "Carib" were men of skill and know-ledge in mighty works, and that these men, like one Archimedes of the later Hellas, did plan to restore the earth's axis to its center, for this planet revolves not evenly but slantwise, as they who study the stars know well. We believe that it was those mighty men of learning and skill who built the cylinder.

'Vessels and the metal of the floor were here when we came, and this metal, being soft and of no difficulty in the craftsman's trade, we have used to replace the vessels as time destroys them and they wear thin. This metal, in vast quantities, surrounds our halls and vaults here below the surface of the land above.

'Our light is constant. It is of the gases which flow constantly from the bowels of the earth. Spouts confine it, fire placed at the mouths of the spouts ignites it. The spouts, of this metal, are very ancient. Upon their mouths are coverings which are taken away when fire is set there; replaced when the light is needed no more in that place.

'Our air we receive from shaft-ways from the surface of the earth above. Their ground openings are among the white rocks. Our philosophers think the yellow metal was melted by the earth's fires and forced up through certain of the ancient air-openings from below.'

The priestess finished her long recital, Grosvenor listening with all his faculties in order to understand her placid speech.

'I understand it all except the fruit,' said he.

The priestess smiled again, gravely.

'The marvels of nature make no difficulty for your mind, but this simple question of fruit is difficult for you! Come – I will show you our gardens.'

She rose; Grosvenor followed. They passed out through various chambers until they arrived at one whose outer wall was only a balustrade of white stone. An extraordinary sight met Grosvenor's eyes.

On a level piece of ground of many acres grew innumerable fruits: pineapples, mango-trees, oranges, pomegranates. Here were row upon row of sapodilla trees, yam-vines, egg-plants, bananas, lemon and grapefruit trees, even trellises of pale green wine-grapes.

At irregular intervals stood metal pipes of varying thickness and height, and from the tops of these, even, whitish flares of burning gas illuminated the 'gardens'. A dozen questions rose in Grosvenor's mind. 'How? Why?'

'What causes your failure to understand?' enquired the priestess, gently. 'Heat, light, moisture, good earth well tended! Here, all these are present. These fruits are planted from long ago, and constantly renewed; originally they grew on the earth's surface.'

They walked back through the rooms to the accompaniment of courteous inclinations from all whom they passed. They resumed their places in the first room. The priestess addressed Grosvenor.

'Many others will follow you; those who come to procure the wood of the forest above. Nothing we have is of any value to these people. Nothing they may bring do we desire. It would be well if they came and took their wood and departed knowing naught of us of the People of Pan here underground.

'We shall, therefore, make it impossible for them to descend should they desire so to do. We shall cut the topmost steps of the ladder away from the stone; replace them when your countrymen who drove the people of Hispaniola from Cuba have departed. I will ask you to swear by Pan that you will reveal nothing of what you have seen. Then remain with us if you so desire, and, when your countrymen have departed, come again in peace and love as behooveth a devotee of Pan.'

'I will swear by Pan, as you desire,' responded Grosvenor, his mind on the incalculable fortune in virgin gold which had here no value beyond that of its utility for vessels, and floors, and steps! Indeed he needed no oath to prevent his saying anything to his 'countrymen'! He might be trusted for that without an oath! A sudden idea struck him.

'The sacrifice,' said he, – 'the *thurìa*, or rather, I should say, the *holokautósis* – the burnt offering. Why was only an insect sacrificed to Pan?'

The priestess looked down at the burnished metal floor of the room and was silent. And as she spoke, Grosvenor saw tears standing in her eyes.

'The sinking and rise of the waters is not the only rhythm of this place. Four times each year the gases flow from within the earth. Then – every living thing upon this island's surface dies! At such seasons we here below are safe. Thus it happens that we have no beast worthy of an offering to Pan. Thus, at our festivals we may offer only inferior things. We eat no flesh. That is sacred to Pan, as it has been since our ancestors worshipped Him in the groves of Yucatan. That He may have His offering one or more of us journeys to the cylinder's top at full moon. Some form of life has always been found by diligent search. Somewhere some small creature survives. If we should not discover it, He would be angry, and, perhaps, slay us. We know not.'

'When does the gas flow upward again?' enquired Grosvenor. He was thinking of Christian Fabio waiting for him there on the beach.

'At the turning of the season. It seethes upward in three days from now.'

'Let me take my oath, then,' replied Grosvenor, 'and depart forthwith. Then I would speak concerning what I am to do with those others who follow me to this land.'

The priestess clapped her hands, and the little serving-lad entered. To him she gave a brief order, and he took his departure. Then with the priestess Grosvenor made his arrangement about the woodcutting force – a conversation which occupied perhaps a quarter of an hour. The little messenger returned as they were finishing. He bowed, spoke rapidly to the priestess, and retired.

'Rise, and follow me,' she directed Grosvenor.

Before the great idol the people were again gathering when they arrived beside the altar. They stood, and the priestess held out her arms in a sweeping gesture, commanding silence. An imponderable quiet followed.

His hands beneath hers on the altar of Pan, Grosvenor took his oath as she indicated it to him.

'By the great Pan, I swear – by hill and stream, by mountain and valley, by the air of the sky and the water of streams and ponds, by the sea and by fire which consumes all things – by these I swear to hold inviolate within me that which I have known here in this temple and among the People of Pan. And may He pursue me with His vengeance if I break this my oath, in this world and in the world to come, until water ceaseth to flow, earth to support the trees, air to be breathed, and fire to burn – by these and by the Horns and Hooves of Pan I swear, and I will not break my oath.'

Then, conducted by the priestess, Grosvenor walked through the people, who made a path for them, across the great expanse of the temple to the small anteroom beside the cylinder. Here the priestess placed her hands upon Grosvenor's head. 'I bless thee, in Pan's name,' she said, simply. He opened the door, passed through onto the metal platform, and pushed it shut behind him . . .

He found the ascent very wearing and his muscles ached severely before he could discern clearly the stars flaming in the disk above his head. At last he grasped the stone handles on the rim. Wearily he drew himself above ground, and stretched himself upon the level rim of the cylinder.

Before starting down the gentle slope for his camp under the shade of the mahogany forest's abundant leafage, he paused beside one of the white rocks, laboriously heaving it to one side. Beneath it was an aperture, running straight down, and lined with a curiously smooth, lavalike stone. He had seen one of the air-pipes which the priestess had described. He knew now that he had not been passing through some incredibly strange dream. He stepped away and was soon within the forest's grateful shade.

He reached camp and Christian Fabio a little before seven-thirty that evening, finding supper ready and the faithful Christian agog for news. This he proffered in Christian's kind of language, ending by the statement that the stream 'originated in a lake of indubitably prehistoric volcanic origin possessing superficial undulatory siphonage germane to seismic disturbance.'

Christian, pop-eyed at this unexpected exhibition of learning on his master's part, remarked only: 'How very extraordinary!' and thereafter maintained an awed silence.

The next day Grosvenor signaled the *Madeleine*, on her return trip, and taking Christian with him, returned to San Juan 'for certain necessary supplies which had been overlooked'.

From there he sent the company a long letter in which he enlarged on the danger of the periodic gas-escape and gave a favorable report on the island's forestation. He discharged Christian with a recommendation and a liberal bonus. Then he returned to Saona alone and completed his month's survey, doing his own cooking, and sleeping with no attention to non-existent insects. He did not visit the island's center again. He wished to expedite the woodcutting in every possible way, and disliked the loss of even a day.

The survey completed – in three weeks – he went back to San Juan, cabled his full report, and was at once instructed to assemble his gang and begin.

Within another month, despite the wails of '*mañana*' – tomorrow – a village, with himself as lawmaker, guide, philosopher, friend, and boss, was established on Saona. Cooks, camp roustabouts, woodcutters, and the paraphernalia of an American enterprise established themselves as though by magic, and the cutting began. Only trees in excess of a certain girth were to be taken down.

By almost superhuman efforts on Grosvenor's part, the entire job was finished well within the three-month period. Three days before the exact date when the gas was to be expected, every trace of the village except the space it had occupied was gone, and not a person was left on Saona's surface. The great collection of mahogany he had made he took, beginning a week later, by tugboat to San Juan, whence it was reshipped to New York and Boston, to Steinway, and Bristol and other boat-building centers; to Ohio to veneering plants; to Michigan to the enormous shops of the Greene and Postlewaithe Furniture Company.

Grosvenor's job was finished.

In response to his application to the company, he was granted a month's well-earned vacation, accompanied by a substantial bonus for his good work.

This time he did not travel by the *Madeleine* to Saona. Instead he took ship for Port-au-Prince, Haiti, thence by another vessel to Santo Domingo City; from that point, in a small, coastwise vessel, to San Pedro Macoris.

From Macoris, where he had quietly hired a small sailboat, he slipped away one moonless evening, alone. Thirty hours afterward, he reached Saona, and, making his boat fast in a small, landlocked inlet which he had discovered in the course of his surveys, and with a food-supply for two days, he walked along the beach half a mile to the mouth of the stream.

He followed the well-remembered path until he came to the edge of the woods. He had not brought his gang as far as this. There had been more than enough mahogany boles to satisfy the company without passing inland farther than the level ground.

He walked now, slowly, under the pouring sunlight of morning, across the broken ground to the cylinder's edge, and there, temporarily encamped, he waited until it began to sink. He watched it until it had gone down a dozen feet or more, and then walked around to the point where the ladder began.

The ladder was gone. Not so much as a mark in the smooth masonry indicated that there ever had been a ladder. Once more, with a sinking heart, he asked himself if his strange adventure had been a dream – a touch of sun, perhaps . . .

This was, dreams and sunstrokes apart, simply inexplicable. Twice, during the course of the wood-cutting operations, the People of Pan had communicated with him, at a spot agreed upon between him and the priestess. Both times had been early in the operations. It was nearly three months since he had seen any concrete evidence of the People's existence. But, according to their agreement, the ladder-steps should have been replaced immediately after the last of his gang had left Saona. This, plainly, had not been done. Had the People of Pan, underground there, played him false? He could not bring himself to believe that; yet – there was no ladder; no possible means of communicating with them. He was as effectually cut off from them as though they had been moon-dwellers.

Grosvenor's last man had left the island three days before the season's change – September twenty-first. It was now late in October.

Ingress and egress, as he knew, had been maintained by a clever, simple arrangement. Just below ground-level a small hole had been bored through the rim, near the U-shaped opening. Through this a thin, tough cord had run to a strong, thin, climbing rope long enough to reach the topmost step remaining. He remembered this. Perhaps the people below had left this arrangement.

He found the hole, pulled lightly on the string. The climbing-rope came to light. An ingenious system of a counter-pull string allowed the replacing of the climbing rope. Obviously the last person above ground from below had returned successfully, leaving everything shipshape here. To get down he would have to descend some thirty feet on this spindling rope to the topmost step. He tested the rope carefully. It was in good condition. There was no help for it. He must start down that way.

Very carefully he lowered himself hand over hand, his feet against the slippery inner surface of the stone cylinder. It was a ticklish job, but his fortitude sustained him. He found the step, and, holding the climbing-rope firmly, descended two more steps and groped for the handrail. He got it in his grasp, pulled the return-string until it was taut, then began the tedious descent, through its remembered stages of gradual darkening, the damp pressure of terrible depth upon the senses, the periodic glances at the lessening disk above, the strange glow of the stars . . .

At last he reached the platform, groped for the door-ring, drew open the door.

In the anteroom a terrible sense of foreboding shook him. The condition of the ladder might not be a misunderstanding. Something unforeseen, fearful, might have happened!

He pulled himself together, crossed the anteroom, looked in upon the vast temple.

A sense of physical emptiness bore down upon him. The illumination was as usual – that much was reassuring. Across the expanse the great idol reared its menacing bulk, the horned head menacingly lowered.

But before it bowed and swayed no thronged mass of worshippers. The temple was empty and silent.

Shaken, trembling, the sense of foreboding still weighing heavily upon him, he started toward the distant altar.

Soon his usual vigorous optimism came back to him. These had been unworthy fears! He looked about him as he proceeded, at the dun sidewalls rising, tier upon tier of vague masonry, up to the dim vault in the darkness above. Then the sense of evil sprang out again, and struck at his heart. His mouth went dry. He hastened his pace. He began to run.

As he approached the altar, something strange, something *different*, appeared before him. The line formed by the elevation of the chancel as it rose from the flooring, stone against dull, yellowish metal, a thousand paces ahead, should have been sharp and clear. Instead, it was blurred, uneven.

As he came nearer he saw that the statue's prancing legs were heaped about with piled stuff . . .

He ran on, waveringly, uncertain now. He did not want to see clearly what he suspected. He stumbled over something bulky. He stopped, turned to see what had lain in his way.

It was the body of a man, mummified – dry, leathery, brown; the blue kirtle grotesquely askew. He paused, reverently, and turned the body on its back. The expression on the face was quite peaceful, as though a natural and quiet death had overtaken the victim.

As he rose from his task, his face being near the floor's level, he saw, along it, innumerable other bodies lying about in varying postures. He stood upright and looked toward the image of the Goat. Bodies lay heaped in great mounds about the curved animal legs; more bodies lay heaped before the sanctuary.

Awestruck, but, now that he knew, something steadied by this wholesale calamity which had overtaken the peaceful People of Pan, he moved quietly forward at an even pace.

Something lay across the altar.

Picking his way carefully among the massed corpses he mounted the sanctuary steps. Across the altar lay the body of the priestess, her dead

arms outstretched toward the image of the Goat. She had died in her
appointed place, in the very attitude of making supplication for her
people who had died about her. Grosvenor, greatly moved, looked
closely into the once beautiful face. It was still strangely beautiful and
placid, noble in death; and upon it was an expression of profound
peace. Pan had taken his priestess and his people to Himself . . .

He had slightly raised the mummified body, and as he replaced it
reverently back across the altar, something fluttered from it to his
feet. He picked up a bit of parchment-like material. There was
writing on it. Holding it, he passed back through the sanctuary to the
room behind, where there would be a clearer light. The rooms were
empty. Nothing had been disturbed.

The parchment was addressed to him. He spelled out, carefully,
the antique, beautifully formed characters of the old literary Greek.

Hail to thee, and farewell, O stranger. I, Clytemnestra, priestess
of Pan the Merciful, address thee, that thou mayest understand.
Thou art freed from thy oath of silence.

'At the change of the seasons the sacrifice failed. Our search
revealed no living thing to offer to our god. Pan takes His
vengeance. My people abandon this life for Acheron, for upon us
has Pan loosed the poisonous airs of the underworld. As I write,
I faint, and I am the last to go.

'Thine, then, O kind barbarian, of the seed of them that drove
from Kuba the men of Hispaniola, are the treasures of Pan's
People. Of them take freely. I go now to my appointed place, at
the altar of the Great Pan who gathers us to Himself. In peace
and love, O barbarian of the North Continent, I greet thee. In
peace and love, farewell.

Grosvenor placed the parchment in his breast-pocket. He was
profoundly affected. He sat for a long time on the white stone couch.
At last he rose and passed reflectively out into the underground
gardens. The great flares of natural gas burned steadily at the tops of
the irregular pipes.

At once he was consumed in wonder. How could these continue
to burn without there having occurred a great conflagration? The
amount of free gas sufficient to asphyxiate and mummify the entire
population of this underground community would have ignited in one
heaving cataclysm which would have blown Saona out of the water!

But – perhaps that other gas was not inflammable. Then the true
explanation occurred to him abruptly. The destructive gas was

heavier than the air. It would lie along the ground, and be gradually dissipated as the fresh air from the pipes leading above diluted its deadly intensity. It would not mount to the tops of these illuminating pipes. The shortest of them, as he gaged it, was sixty feet high. Of course, he would never know, positively . . .

He looked about him through the lovely gardens, now *his* paradise. All about were the evidences of long neglect. Unshorn grass waved like standing hay in the light breeze which seemed to come from nowhere. Rotting fruit lay in heaps under the sapodilla trees.

He plucked a handful of drying grass as long as his arm, and began to twist it into the tough string of the Antilles' grass-rope. He made five or six feet of the string. He retraced his steps slowly back to the room where he had read his last message from the priestess of Pan. He passed the string through the handles of a massive golden fruit jar, emptied the liquefying mass of corrupt fruit which lay sodden in its bowl.

He slung the heavy jar on his back, returned through the sanctuary, threaded his way among the heaped bodies, began to walk back through the temple toward the anteroom.

From across that vast room he looked back. Through the dim perspective the monstrous figure of the Goat seemed to exult. With a slight shudder Charles Grosvenor passed out onto the platform. He grasped the handrail, planted his feet on the first round of the ladder, and began his long, weary climb to the top . . .

The Chadbourne Episode

Perhaps the most fortunate circumstance of the well-nigh incredible Chadbourne affair is that little Abby Chandler was not yet quite seven years of age on the evening when she came back home and told her mother her story about the old sow and the little pigs. It was July, and Abby with her big tin pail had been up on the high ridge near the Old Churchyard after low-bush blueberries. She had not even been especially frightened, her mother had said. That is what I mean by the fortunate aspect of it. Little Abby was altogether too young to be devastated, her sweet little soul permanently blasted, her mentality wrenched and twisted away from normality even by seeing with her round, China-blue eyes what she said she had seen up there on the steep hillside.

Little Abby had not noticed particularly the row of eight or nine pushing, squeaking, grunting little pigs at their early evening meal because her attention had been entirely concentrated on the curious appearance, as it seemed to her, of the source of that meal. That old sow, little Abby had told her mother, had had 'a lady's head . . . '

There was, of course, a *raison d'être* – a solution – back of this reported marvel. That solution occurred to Mrs Chandler almost at once. Abby must have heard something, in the course of her six and three-quarter years of life here in Chadbourne among the little town's permanent inhabitants, some old-wives' gossip for choice, about 'marked' people; whispered 'cases' of people born with some strange anatomical characteristics of a domestic animal – freaks – or even farm animals 'marked' with some human streak – a calf with a finger growing out of its left hind fetlock – things like that; animals quickly destroyed and buried out of sight. Such statements can be heard in many old New England rural settlements which have never wholly let go the oddments in tradition brought over from Cornwall and the West Country of Old England. Everybody has heard them.

Chadbourne would be no exception to anything like this. The old town lies nestling among the granite-bouldered ridges and dimpling hills of deep, rural, eastern Connecticut. In any such old New England town the older people talk much about all such affairs as Black Sabbaths, and Charmed Cattle, and Marked People.

All of that Mrs Chandler knew and sensed in her blood and bones. She had been a Grantham before she had married Silas Chandler, and the Grantham family had been quietly shrinking and deteriorating for nine generations in Chadbourne along with the process of the old town's gradual dry-rotting, despite the efforts of such of the old-time gentry as may have survived in such places.

For gentry there are, deeply imbedded in New England, people who have never forgotten the meaning of the old *noblesse oblige*, people who have never allowed their fine sense of duty and obligation to lapse. In Chadbourne we had such a family, the Merritts; *Mayflower* passengers to Plymouth in the Massachusetts Colony in 1620; officers and trustees for generations of Dartmouth College in New Hampshire and of Trinity College, Hartford, Connecticut. We Canevins, Virginians, were not, of course, of this stock. My father, Alexander Canevin, had bought up an abandoned farm on a Chadbourne ridge-top about the time of the Spanish War. In that high air, among those rugged hills and to the intoxicating summer scents of bayberry-blossoms and sweet-fern – which the Connecticut farmers name appropriately, 'hardhack' – I had sojourned summers since my early boyhood.

Tom Merritt and I had grown up together, and he, following the family tradition, had gone to Dartmouth, thence to the Harvard Medical School. At the time of little Abby's adventure he was serving his community well as the Chadbourne general practitioner. But for the four years previous to his coming back and settling down to this useful if humdrum professional career, Thomas Bradford Merritt, M.D., had been in the diplomatic service as a career consul, chiefly in Persia where, before his attachment as a step up to our legation in Teheran, he had held consular posts at Jask, a town in the far south on the Gulf of Oman; at Kut-el-Amara in the west, just south of Baghdad; and finally at Shiraz, where he had collected some magnificent rugs.

The autumn before little Abby Chandler's blueberrying expedition Tom, who acted as my agent, had rented my Chadbourne farmhouse just as I was leaving New York for my customary winter's sojourn in the West Indies. That my tenants were Persians had, it appeared, no connection at all with Tom's long residence in that land. They had been surprised, Tom told me, when they found out that the New England gentleman whose advertisement of my place they had answered from New York City was familiar with their country, had resided there, and even spoke its language passably.

In spite of this inducement to some sort of sociability, the Persian family, according to Tom, had comported themselves, toward him and everybody else in Chadbourne, with a high degree of reticence and reserve. The womenfolk had kept themselves altogether secluded, rarely leaving the house that winter. When they did venture forth they were always heavily muffled up – actually veiled, Tom thought – and only the edges, so to speak, of the mother and two daughters were ever to be observed by any inhabitant of Chadbourne curious to know how Persian ladies might look through the windows of Mr Rustum Dadh's big limousine.

Besides the stout mother and the two stout, 'yellowish-complected', sloe-eyed daughters, there was Mr Rustum Dadh himself, and two servants. These were the chauffeur, a square-built, tight-lipped, rather grim-looking fellow, who made all his own repairs to the big car and drove wrapped up in a fur-lined livery overcoat; and a woman, presumably the wife of the chauffeur, who never appeared outside at all, even on Friday nights when there was movies in Chadbourne's Palace Opera House.

All that I knew about my tenants Tom Merritt told me. I never saw any of the Rustum Dadh family from first to last. I had, in fact, completely forgotten all about them until I arrived in Chadbourne the following June some time after their departure and learned from Tom the bare facts I have set out here.

On a certain night in July that summer the Rustum Dadhs were farthest from my thoughts. It was nine o'clock, and I was sitting in the living-room reading. My telephone rang insistently. I laid down my book with a sigh at being interrupted. I found Thomas Bradford Merritt, M.D., on the other end of the wire.

'Come on down here as soon as you can, Gerald,' said Tom without any preliminaries, and there was a certain unusual urgency in his voice.

'What's happened?' I inquired.

'It may be – ah – something in your line, so to speak,' said Doctor Merritt; 'something – well – out of the ordinary. Bring that Männlicher rifle of yours!'

'I'll be right down,' said I, snapped up the receiver, got the Männlicher out of my case in the hall where it is in with my shotguns, and raced out to the garage. Here, of a certainty, was something quite strange and new for Chadbourne, where the nearest thing to anything like excitement from year's end to year's end would be an alter-cation between a couple of robins over a simultaneously discovered worm! 'Bring your rifle!' On the way down to the village I did not try to imagine what could possibly lie behind such a summons – from conservative Tom Merritt. I concentrated upon my driving, down the winding country road from my rugged hilltop into town, speeding on the short stretches, easing around treacherous turns at great speed . . .

I dashed into Tom's house eight minutes after hanging up the receiver. There was a light I had observed, in the library as well as in the office, and I went straight in there and found Tom sitting on the edge of a stiff chair, plainly waiting for my arrival.

'Here I am,' said I, and laid my rifle on the library table. Tom plunged into his story . . .

'I'm tied up – a confinement case. They'll be calling me now any minute. Listen to this, Gerald – this is probably a new one on you – what I've got to tell you – even in the face of all the queer things you know – your West Indian experiences; *vodu*; all the rest of it; some-thing *I* know, and – have always kept my mouth shut about! That is – if this is what I'm afraid it is. You'll have to take my word for it. I haven't lost my mind or anything of the sort – you'll probably think that if it turns out to be what I think it is – get this, now.

'Dan Curtiss's little boy, Truman, disappeared, late this afternoon, about sundown. Truman is five years old, a little fellow. He was last seen by some older kids coming back to town with berries from the Ridge, about suppertime. Little Truman, they said, was "with a lady", just outside the Old Cemetery.

'Two lambs and a calf have disappeared within the last week. Traced up there. A bone or two and a wisp of wool or so – the calf's ears, in different places, but both up there, and part of its tail; found 'em scattered around when they got up there to look.

'Some are saying "a cattymaount". Most of 'em say dogs.

'But – it isn't dogs, Gerald. "Sheep-killers" tear up their victims on the spot. They don't drag 'em three miles up a steep hill before they eat 'em. They run in a pack, too. Everybody knows that. Nothing like that has been seen – no pack, no evidences of a pack. Those lost animals have all disappeared singly – more evidence that it isn't "dogs". They've been taken up and, presumably, eaten, up on top of the Cemetery Ridge. Sheep-killing dogs don't take calves, either, and there's that calf to be accounted for. You see – I've been thinking it all out, pretty carefully. As for the catamount, well, catamounts don't, commonly, live – and eat – out in the open. A catamount would drag off a stolen animal far into the deep woods.'

I nodded.

'I've heard something about animals disappearing; only the way I heard it was that it's been going on for quite a long time, and somewhat more intensively during the past month or so.'

Tom Merritt nodded at that. 'Right,' said he. 'It's been going on ever since those Persians left, Gerald. All the time they were here – six months it was – they always bought their house supply of meat and poultry alive, "on the hoof". Presumably they preferred to kill and dress their meat themselves. I don't know, for a fact, of course. Anyhow, that was one of the peculiarities of the "foreigners up at the Canevin Place", and it got plenty of comment in the town, as you may well imagine. And – since they left – it hasn't been only lambs and calves. I know of at least four dogs. Cats, maybe, too! Nobody would keep much account of lost cats in Chadbourne.'

This, somehow, surprised me. I had failed to hear about the dogs and possible cats.

'Dogs, too, eh?' I remarked.

Then Tom Merritt got up abruptly, off his stiff chair, and came over and stood close behind me and spoke low and intensively, and very convincingly, directly into my ear.

'And now – it's a child, Gerald. That's too much – for this, or any other decent town. You've never lived in Persia. I have. I'm going to tell you in plain words what I think is going on. Try to believe me, Gerald. Literally, I mean. You've got to believe me – trust me – to do what you've got to do tonight because I can't come right now. It's going to be an ordeal for you. It would be for anybody. Listen to this, now.

'This situation only came to me, clearly, just before I called you up, Gerald. I'd been sitting here, after supper, tied up on this Grantham case – waiting for them to call me. It was little Truman Curtiss's disappearance that brought the thing to a head, of course. The whole town's buzzing with it, naturally. No such thing has ever happened here before. A child has always been perfectly safe in Chadbourne since they killed off the last Indian a hundred and fifty years ago. I hadn't seen the connection before. I've been worked to death for one thing. I naturally hadn't been very much steamed up about a few lambs and dogs dropping out of sight.

'That might mean a camp of tramps somewhere. But – tramps don't steal five-year-old kids. It isn't tramps that do kidnapping for ransom.

'It all fitted together as soon as I really put my mind on it. Those Rustum Dadhs and their unaccountable reticence – the live animals that went up to that house of yours all winter – what I'd heard, and even seen a glimpse of – out there in Kut and Shiraz – that grim-jawed, tight-lipped chauffeur of theirs, with the wife that nobody ever got a glimpse of – finally that story of little Abby Chandler – '

And the incredible remainder of what Doctor Thomas Merritt had to tell me was said literally in my ear, in a tense whisper, as though the teller were actually reluctant that the walls and chairs and books of that mellow old New England library should overhear the utterly monstrous thing he had to tell . . .

I was shaken when he had finished. I looked long into my lifelong friend Tom Merritt's honest eyes as he stood before me when he had finished, his two firm, capable hands resting on my two shoulders. There was conviction, certainty, in his look. There was no slightest doubt in my mind but that he believed what he had been telling me. But – could he, or anyone, by any possible chance, be right on the facts? Here, in Chadbourne, of all places on top of the globe!

'I've read about – them – in the *Arabian Nights*,' I managed to murmur.

Tom Merritt nodded decisively. 'I've seen – two,' he said, quietly. 'Get going, Gerald,' he added; 'it's action from now on.'

I stepped over to the table and picked up my rifle.

'And remember,' he added, as we walked across the room to the door, 'what I've told you about them. Shoot them down. Shoot to kill – if you see them. Don't hesitate. Don't wait. Don't – er – talk! No hesitation. That's the rule – in Persia. And remember how to prove it – *remember the marks*! You may have to prove it – to anybody who may be up there still, hunting for poor little Truman Curtiss.'

The office telephone rang.

Doctor Merritt opened the library door and looked out into the wide hallway. Then he shouted in the direction of the kitchen.

'Answer it, Mehitabel. Tell 'em I've left. It'll be Seymour Grantham, for his wife.' Then, to me: 'There are two search-parties up there, Gerald.'

And as we ran down the path from the front door to where our two cars were standing in the road I heard Doctor Merritt's elderly housekeeper at the telephone explaining in her high, nasal twang of the born Yankee, imparting the information that the doctor was on his way to the agitated Grantham family.

I drove up to the old cemetery on the Ridge even faster than I had come down from my own hill fifteen minutes earlier that evening.

The late July moon, one night away from full, bathed the fragrant hills in her clear, serene light. Half-way up the hill road to the Ridge I passed one search-party returning. I encountered the other coming out of the cemetery gate as I stopped my steaming engine and set my brakes in front of the entrance. The three men of this party, armed with a lantern, a rifle, and two sizable clubs, gathered around me. The youngest, Jed Peters, was the first to speak. It was precisely in the spirit of Chadbourne that this first remark should have no direct reference to the pressing affair motivating all of us. Jed had pointed to my rifle, interest registered plainly in his heavy, honest countenance.

'Some weepon – thet-thar, I'd reckon, Mr Canevin.'

I have had a long experience with my Chadbourne neighbors.

'It's a Männlicher,' said I, 'what is called "a weapon of precision". It is accurate to the point of nicking the head off a pin up to about fourteen hundred yards.'

These three fellows, one of them the uncle of the missing child, had discovered nothing. They turned back with me, however, without being asked. I could have excused them very gladly. After what Tom Merritt had told me, I should have preferred being left alone to deal with the situation unaided. There was no avoiding it, however. I suggested splitting up the party and had the satisfaction of seeing this suggestion put into effect. The three of them walked off slowly to the left while I waited, standing inside the cemetery gate, until I could just hear their voices.

Then I took up my stand with my back against the inside of the cemetery wall, directly opposite the big Merritt family mausoleum.

The strong moonlight made it stand out clearly. I leaned against the stone wall, my rifle cuddled in my arms, and waited. I made no attempt to watch the mausoleum continuously, but ranged with my eyes over the major portion of the cemetery, an area which, being only slightly shrubbed, and sloping upward gently from the entrance, was plainly visible. From time to time as I stood there, ready, I would catch a faint snatch of the continuous conversation going on among the three searchers, as they walked along on a long course which I had suggested to them, all the way around the cemetery, designed to cover territory which, in the local phraseology, ran 'down through', 'up across', and 'over around'. I had been waiting, and the three searchers had been meandering, for perhaps twenty minutes – the ancient town clock in the Congregational church tower had boomed ten about five minutes before – when I heard a soft, grating sound in the direction of the Merritt mausoleum. My eyes came back to it sharply.

There, directly before the now half-open bronze door, stood a strange, even a grotesque, figure. It was short, squat, thick-set. Upon it, I might say accurately, hung – as though pulled on in the most hurried and slack fashion imaginable – a coat and trousers. The moonlight showed it up clearly and it was plain, even in such a light, that these two were the only garments in use. The trousers hung slackly, bagging thickly over a pair of large bare feet. The coat, unbuttoned, sagged and slithered lopsidedly. The coat and trousers were the standardized, unmistakable, diagonal gray material of a chauffeur's livery. The head was bare and on it a heavy, bristle-like crop of unkempt hair stood out absurdly. The face was covered with an equally bristle-like growth, unshaven for a month by the appearance. About the tight-shut, menacing mouth which divided a pair of square, iron-like broad jaws, the facial hairs were merged or blended in what seemed from my viewpoint a kind of vague smear, as though the hair were there heavily matted.

From this sinister figure there then emerged a thick, guttural, repressed voice, as though the speaker were trying to express himself in words without opening his lips.

'Come – come he-ar. Come – I will show you what you look for.'

Through my head went everything that Tom Merritt had whispered in my ear. This was my test – my test, with a very great deal at stake – of my trust in what he had said – in him – in the rightness of his information; and it had been information, based on his deduction, such as few men have had to decide upon. I said a brief prayer in that space of a few instants. I observed that the figure was slowly approaching me.

'Come,' it repeated – 'come now – I show you – what you, a-seek – here.'

I pulled myself together. I placed my confidence, and my future, in Tom Merritt's hands.

I raised my Männlicher, took careful aim, pulled the trigger. I repeated the shot. Two sharp cracks rang out on that still summer air, and then I lowered the deadly little weapon and watched while the figure crumpled and sagged down, two little holes one beside the other in its forehead, from which a dark stain was spreading over the bristly face, matting it all together the way the region of the mouth had looked even before it lay quiet and crumpled up on the ground half-way between the mausoleum and where I stood.

I had done it. I had done what Tom Merritt had told me to do, ruthlessly, without any hesitation, the way Tom had said they did it in Persia around Teheran, the capital, and Shiraz, and in Kut-el-Amara, and down south in Jask.

And then, having burned my bridges, and, for all I knew positively, made myself eligible for a noose at Wethersfield, I walked across to the mausoleum, and straight up to the opened bronze door, and looked inside.

A frightful smell – a smell like all the decayed meat in the world all together in one place – took me by the throat. A wave of quick nausea invaded me. But I stood my ground, and forced myself to envisage what was inside; and when I had seen, despite my short retchings and coughings I resolutely raised my Männlicher and shot and shot and shot at moving, scampering targets; shot again and again and again, until nothing moved inside there. I had seen, besides those moving targets, something else; some things that I will not attempt to describe beyond using the word 'fragments'. Poor little five-year-old Truman Curtiss who had last been seen just outside the cemetery gate 'with a lady' would never climb that hill again, never pick any more blueberries in Chadbourn or any other place . . .

I looked without regret on the shambles I had wrought within the old Merritt tomb. The Männlicher is a weapon of precision . . .

I was brought to a sense of things going on outside the tomb by the sound of running feet, the insistent, clipping drawl of three excited voices asking questions. The three searchers, snapped out of their leisurely walk around the cemetery, and quite near by at the time my shooting had begun, had arrived on the scene of action.

'What's it all about, Mr Canevin?'

'We heard ye a-shootin' away.'

'Good Cripes! Gerald's shot a *man!*'

I blew the smoke out of the barrel of my Männlicher, withdrew the clip. I walked toward the group bending now over the crumpled figure on the ground halfway to the cemetery gate.

'Who's this man you shot, Gerald? Good Cripes! It's the fella that druv the car for them-there Persians. Good Cripes, Gerald – are ye crazy? You can't shoot down a man like that!'

'It's not a man,' said I, coming up to them and looking down on the figure.

There was a joint explosion at that. I waited, standing quietly by, until they had exhausted themselves. They were, plainly, more concerned with what consequences I should have to suffer than with the fate of the chauffeur.

'You say it ain't no man! Are ye crazy, Gerald?'

'It's not a man,' I repeated. 'Reach down and press his jaws together so that he opens his mouth, and you'll see what I mean.'

Then, as they naturally enough I suppose hesitated to fill this order, I stooped down, pressed together the buccinator muscles in the middle of the broad Mongol-like cheeks. The mouth came open, and thereat there was another chorus from the three. It was just as Tom Merritt had described it! The teeth were the teeth of one of the great carnivores, only flat, fang-like, like a shark's teeth. No mortal man ever wore such a set within his mouth, or ever needed such a set, the fangs of a tearer of flesh . . .

'Roll him over,' said I, 'and loosen that coat so you can see his back.'

To this task young Jed addressed himself.

'Good Cripes!' This from the Curtiss fellow, the lost child's uncle. Along the back, sewn thickly in the dark brown skin, ran a band of three-inch, coal-black bristles, longer and stiffer than those of any prize hog. We gazed down in silence for a long moment. Then: 'Come,' said I, 'and look inside the Merritt tomb – but – brace yourselves! It won't be any pleasant sight.'

I turned, led the way, the others falling in behind me. Then, from young Jed Peters: 'You say this-here ain't no man – an' – I believe ye, Mr Canevin! But – Cripes Almighty! – ef this'n hain't no man, what, a-God's Name, is it?'

'*It is a ghoul*,' said I over my shoulder, 'and inside the tomb there are ten more of them – the dam and nine whelps. And what is left of the poor little Curtiss child . . . '

Looking into the mausoleum that second time, in cold blood, so to speak, was a tough experience even for me who had wrought that havoc in there. As for the others – Eli Curtiss, the oldest of the three, was very sick. Bert Blatchford buried his face in his arms against the door's lintel, and when I shook him by the shoulder in fear lest he collapse, the face he turned to me was blank and ghastly, and his ruddy cheeks had gone the color of lead.

Only young Jed Peters really stood up to it. He simply swore roundly, repeating his 'Good Cripes!' over and over again – an articulate youth.

The whelps, with their flattish, human-like faces and heads, equipped with those same punishing, overmuscled jaws like their sire's – like the jaws of a fighting bulldog – their short, thick legs and arms, and their narrow, bristly backs, resembled young pigs more nearly than human infants. All, being of one litter, were of about the same size; all were sickeningly bloody-mouthed from their recent feast. These things lay scattered about the large, circular, marble-walled chamber where they had dropped under the merciless impacts of my bullets.

Near the entrance lay sprawled the repulsive, heavy carcass of the dam, her dreadful, fanged mouth open, her sow-like double row of dugs uppermost, these dragged flaccid and purplish and horrible from the recent nursing of that lately-weaned litter. All these unearthly-looking carcasses were naked. The frightful stench still prevailed, still poured out through the open doorway. Heaps and mounds of nauseous offal cluttered the place.

It was young Jed who grasped first and most firmly my suggestion that these horrors be buried out of sight, that a curtain of silence should be drawn down tight by the four of us, fastened permanently against any utterance of the dreadful things we had seen that night. It was young Jed who organized the three into a digging party, who fetched the grave tools from the unfastened cemetery shed.

We worked in a complete silence, as fast as we could. It was not until we were hastily throwing back the loose earth over what we had placed in the sizable pit we had made that the sound of a car's engine, coming up the hill, caused our first pause. We listened.

'It's Doctor Merritt's car,' I said, somewhat relieved. I looked at my wrist-watch. It was a quarter past midnight.

To the four of us, leaning there on our spades, Doctor Merritt repeated something of the history of the Persian tombs, a little of what he had come to know of those mysterious, semi-mythical dwellers among the half-forgotten crypts of ancient burial-grounds, eaters of the dead, which yet preferred the bodies of the living, furtive shapes shot down when glimpsed – in ancient, mysterious Persia . . .

I left my own car for the three fellows to get home in, young Jed promising to have it back in my garage later in the morning, and drove home with Doctor Merritt.

'There was another thing which I didn't take the time to tell you,' said Tom, as we slipped down the winding hill road under the pouring moonlight. 'That was that the Rustum Dadh's servants were never seen to leave Chadbourne; although, of course, it was assumed that they had done so. The family went by train. I went down to the station to see them off and I found old Rustum Dadh even less communicative than usual.

' "I suppose your man is driving your car down to New York," I said. It had arrived, six months before, when they came to Chadbourne, with both the servants in it, and the inside all piled up with the family's belongings. The old boy merely grunted unintelligibly, in a way he had.

'That afternoon, when I went up to your place to see that everything was ship-shape, there stood the car in the garage, empty. And, while I was wondering what had become of the chauffeur and his wife, and why they hadn't been sent off in the car the way they came, up drives Bartholomew Wade from his garage, and he has the car-key and a letter from Rustum Dadh with directions, and a check for ten dollars and his carfare back from New York. His instructions were to drive the car to New York and leave it there. He did so that afternoon.'

'What was the New York address?' I inquired. 'That might take some looking into, if you think – '

'I don't know what to think – about Rustum Dadh's connection with it all, Gerald,' said Tom. 'The address was merely the Cunard Line Docks. Whether Rustum Dadh and his family were – the same – there's simply no telling. There's the evidence of the live animals sent up to the house. That live meat may have been for the chauffer and his wife – seems unlikely, somehow. There was a rumor around town about some dispute or argument between the old man and his chauffeur, over their leaving all together – just a rumor, something picked up or overheard by some busybody. You can take that for what it's worth, of course. The two of 'em, desirous to break away from civilization, revert, here in Chadbourne – that, I imagine, is the probability. There are many times the number of people below ground in the three old cemeteries than going about their affairs – and other people's! – here in Chadbourne. But, whatever Rustum Dadh's connection with – what we know – whatever share of guilt rests on him – he's gone, Gerald, and we can make any one of the three or four possible guesses; but it won't get us anywhere.' Then, a little weariness showing in his voice, for Tom Merritt, too, had had a pretty strenuous evening, he added: 'I hired young Jed Peters to spend tomorrow cleaning out the old tombhouse of the ancestors!'

I cleaned my rifle before turning in that night. When I had got this job done and had taken a boiling-hot shower-bath, it was close to two o'clock a.m. before I rolled in between the sheets. I had been dreading a sleepless night with the edge of my mind, after that experience up there on the Old Cemetery Ridge. I lay in bed for a while, wakeful, going over snatches of it in my mind. Young Jed! No deterioration there at any rate. There was a fellow who would stand by you in a pinch. The old yeoman stock had not run down appreciably in young Jed.

I fell asleep at last after assuring myself all over again that I had done a thorough job up there on the hill. Ghouls! Not merely *Arabian Nights* creatures, like the Afreets and the Djinn. No. Real – those jaws! They shot them down, on sight, over there in Persia when they were descried coming out of their holes among the old tomb-places . . .

Little, reddish, half-gnawed bones, scattered about that fetid shambles – little bones that had never been torn out of the bodies of calves or lambs – little bones that had been –

I wonder if I shall ever be able to forget those little bones, those little, pitiful bones . . .

I awoke to the purr of an automobile engine in second speed, coming up the steep hill to my farmhouse, and it was a glorious late-summer New England morning. Young Jed Peters was arriving with my returned car.

I jumped out of bed, pulled on a bathrobe, stepped into a pair of slippers. It was seven-thirty. I went out to the garage and brought young Jed back inside with me for a cup of coffee. It started that new day propitiously to see the boy eat three fried eggs and seven pieces of breakfast bacon . . .

Scar-Tissue

'What is your opinion on the Atlantis question?' I asked my friend Dr Pelletier of the U. S. Navy. Pelletier, relaxed during the afternoon swizzel hour on my West Gallery, waved a deprecating hand.

'All the real evidence points to it, doesn't it, Canevin? The harbor here in St Thomas, for instance. Crater of a volcano. What could bring a crater down to sea-level like that, unless the submergence of quadrillions of tons of earth and rock, the submergence of a continent?'

Then: 'What made you ask me that, Canevin?'

'A case,' I replied. 'Picked him up yesterday morning just after he had jumped ship from that Spanish tramp, the *Bilbao*, that was coaling at the West India Docks night-before-last and yesterday morning. She pulled out this afternoon without him. Says his name is Joe Smith. A rough and tough bird, if I ever saw one. Up against it. They were crowding him pretty heavily, according to his story. Extra watches. Hazing. Down with the damned gringo! Looks as if he could handle himself, too – hard as nails. I've got him right here in the house.'

'What are you keeping him shut up for?' enquired Pelletier lazily. 'There isn't anybody on his trail now, is there?'

'No,' said I. 'But he was all shot to pieces from lack of sleep. Red rims around his eyes. He's upstairs, asleep, probably dead to the world. I looked in on him an hour ago.'

'What bearing has the alleged Joe Smith on Atlantis?' Pelletier's tone was still lazily curious.

'Well,' said I, having saved this up for my friend Pelletier to the last, 'Smith looks to me as though he had one of those dashes of "ancestral memory", like the fellow Kipling tells about, the one who "remembered" being a slave at the oars, and how a Roman galley was put together. Only, this isn't any measly two thousand years ago. This is – '

This brought Pelletier straight upright in his lounge-chair.

'Good God, Canevin! And he's here – in this house?'

'I'll see if he's awake,' said I, and went upstairs.

'He's getting cleaned up,' I reported on my return.

'That's in his favor, anyhow,' grunted Pelletier laconically.

Twenty minutes later Smith stepped out on the gallery. He looked vastly different from the beachcomber I had picked up near the St Thomas market-place the morning before. He was tall and spare, and my white drill clothes might have been made for him. He was cleanly shaved of a week's stubble that had disfigured his bronzed face. His step was alert. Plainly, Joe Smith, Able Seaman, had taken hold of himself.

Pelletier did most of the talking. He was establishing a quick footing with Smith with a view to getting his story of the 'buried memory' which the fellow had mentioned to me, and which pointed, he had hinted, at Atlantis. There might be a half-hour's entertainment in it, at the worst. At best, well, we would have to wait and see what Smith would have to say.

At the end of ten minutes or so, Pelletier surprised me.

'What was your college, Smith?' he enquired.

Smith's reply knocked my preconceived opinion of him into a cocked hat.

'Harvard, and Oxford,' he answered. 'Rhodes Scholar. Took my M.A. at Balliol. Yes, of course, Dr Pelletier. Ask me anything you like. This "buried memory" affair has come on me three different times, as a matter of fact. Always when I'm below par physically, a bit run down, vitality lower than normal. I mentioned it to Mr Canevin yesterday – sensed that he would be interested. I've read his stuff, you see, for the past dozen years or so!'

'Tell us about it,' invited Pelletier, and Joe Smith proceeded to do so, a tall tumbler of the iced swizzel on the table in front of him.

'It began when I was a small boy, after scarlet fever. I got up too soon and went swimming, and had a relapse, and the next three or four days, lying in bed, and all in, I "realized" that I was *memoriter familiar* with a life of skin clothes with the fur on, and stone-headed clubs, and the ability to run long distances and go up and down trees without much effort, and all of us getting around a bear and clubbing it to death, and incidentally being dirty as a pig! The thing passed off, dimmed out, although the recollection remains quite clear, as soon as I was well again.

'The second time was after the Spring track-meet with Yale when I was twenty-one. I had run in the 220, and then, half an hour later, I put everything I had into a gruelling quarter-mile, and won it. I was all in afterwards, didn't come back properly, and our trainer sent me for a week's rest to some people I knew who had their place open on the North Shore, at West Manchester, Massachusetts. I lay around and rested according to orders for a week – not even a book. There I "remembered" – not the cave-life this time – Africa. Portuguese and Negroes; enormous buildings, some of them with walls sixteen feet thick. Granite quarries and the Portuguese sweating the Blacks in some ancient gold mines. There were two rivers. I fished in them a great deal, with a big iron hook. They were called, the rivers, I mean, the Lindi and the Sobi.

'Curious kind of place. There was one enormous ruin, a circular tower on top of a round hill which was formed by an outcropping in the granite. There was a procession of bulls carved around the pediment. Yes, and the signs of the Zodiac. Curious place, no end!'

'Great Zimbábwe!' I cried out, 'in Southern Rhodesia. The Portuguese controlled it in the Fifteenth Century, before Columbus' time. Why, man, that place is the traditional site of Solomon's gold mines!'

'Click!' remarked Smith, turning an intelligent eye in my direction. 'It was pronounced, in those days – "Zim-baub-weh" – accent on the first syllable. I've often wondered if it wasn't the Romans who carved those bulls, they had the place first, called it Anaeropolis. Plenty of legionaries were Mithraists, and the bull was Mithras's symbol, you know.'

'And the last one, Smith,' Pelletier cut in. 'You mentioned Atlantis, Canevin tells me.'

'Well,' began Smith once more, 'the fact that it was Atlantis is, really, secondary. There is one item in *that* "memory" which is of very much greater interest, I should imagine.

'I don't want to be theatrical, gentlemen! But – well, I think the best way to begin telling you about it is to show you this.'

And Joe Smith, rising and loosening his belt, pulled up his shirt and singlet, exposing the skin of a bronzed torso, and showed us something that literally drew a gasp from us both.

Beginning a half-inch above his right hip-bone and extending straight across as though laid out with a ruler across the abdomen, there ran a great, livid, inch-wide scar; the kind that would result from a very deep knife or sword-cut, provided anyone receiving such a wound should survive long enough for the cut to form scar-tissue.

'Good God!' I muttered, really aghast at the dreadful thing.

Pelletier laughed. 'And – you're alive and standing there!' said he, almost caustically. Joe Smith tucked in his shirt, tightened his belt, and sat down again.

He lighted a cigarette, took a long sip from his tumbler of swizzel.

He crossed one knee over the other, leaned back in his chair, and looked at both of us, and blew out a reflective cloud of cigarette smoke.

'That's where it begins,' said he, and, as my house-man, Stephen Penn, appeared at this moment with the dinner-cocktails, he added: 'I'll tell you about it after dinner.'

It was Pelletier who started things off so soon as we were settled on the gallery again, the coffee and Chartreuse on the big table.

'I want to know, please, how you happen to be alive.'

Smith smiled wryly.

'I never told this before,' said he, 'and if I was somewhat pre-occupied during dinner it was because I've been figuring out how to put it all together for you.

'During the course of that last "recollection" I spoke of it went through my mind – no! that trite phrase doesn't give you the right idea. "Lived it over again" would be better. It's hard to put into words but we'll call it that! I was walking through a short enclosed passageway, rather wide, stone-flagged, and low-ceilinged. In front of me, beside me, and behind me walked eighteen or twenty others. We were all armed. Up in front of us in their bronze armor and closing our rear marched eight legionaries of the Ludektan army assigned to us as guards. We came out into the drenching sunlight of a great sanded arena. We followed our advance guard in a sharp turn to the right and wheeled to a right-face before a great awninged box full of the Ludektan nobles and dignitaries where we saluted, each after his own fashion with our variously assorted weapons.

'Do you get that picture? Lemurians, gentlemen, every man jack of us! Prisoners of war – yes, and here we were after a couple of months of the hardest training I have ever known, in the Ludekta gladiatorial school; about to shed our blood to make an Atlantean holiday! Yes, Ludekta was the southwestern province of Atlantis, the cultural center of the continent. There had been innumerable wars between the Atlanteans and Lemuria. Like Rome and Carthage.

'The really tough part of it was the uncertainty. I mean a fellow might be paired to fight to the death against some rather good pal, you know. I was one of the fortunate ones that day. I had the good luck to be paired with a Gamfron – a nearly black Atlantean mountain lion, an animal about the size and heft of an Indian black panther – Bagheera, in Kipling's Mowgli yarn! I had been armed with a short, sharp, double-edged sword and a small, bronze buckler. I had otherwise been given choice of my own accoutrement and I had selected greaves, a light breast-plate and a close-fitting helmet with a face-guard attachment with eye-holes, which covered practically my whole face and the back and sides of my neck.

'When it came my turn to step out on the sand and wait for my lion to be released, I asked the official in charge for permission to discard the buckler and use an additional weapon, a long dagger, in my left hand instead. I got the permission, and at the signal-blast which was made with a ram's horn, walked slowly straight towards the cage entrance from which my brute adversary would in a moment be released. I had noted that the sun was shining directly, full against that particular iron door.

'My strategy worked precisely as I had hoped.

'The great lithe beast came straight out and paused blinking. Before its great cat eyes had adjusted themselves to the glare I had begun the attack myself. I launched myself upon the beast, and when I sprang away the hilt of that left-hand dagger was all that showed sticking straight up out of the Gamfron's back, just within the shoulder attachment and in front of the foremost rib. The thirteen inches of steel were down inside that Gamfron to take up some of his attention! I had tried, you see, for a one-blow knockout – a thrust between the forward vertebrae, and I had missed it by half an inch. However, that first crack wasn't so bad! While I gathered myself for its probable spring, for which the animal was already crouched, the Gamfron suddenly relaxed and rolled over in the sand; hoping, I suppose, in this way to dislodge that inconveniently placed annoyance. The hilt was bent over, I noticed, when this lightening-like movement had been concluded and the Gamfron was again crouched for its leap at me, right side up once more, its steel and whalebone body and legs tensed, and a hellish blaze of pure beast anger in its great yellow eyes.

'And now it was sailing straight at me through the air, its set of enormous retractile claws protruding from its pads like menacing chisels. Its horrible red mouth with its great gleaming canine teeth seemed as big as a shark's! I side-stepped, and slashed with the sword, making a tearing wound along the animal's left side; but the impact knocked me spinning and the animal and I recovered ourselves at precisely the same instant, I bracing myself, and the Gamfron, spraying blood on the smooth sand, gathering itself for another of those deadly leaps.

'In the split seconds which intervened before it launched itself at me again I could hear as though from an enormous distance the wild tumult of applause from those massed thousands; I could see that vast crowd weave as it swayed hysterically – they were all standing now – at the spectacle they were getting.

'The effect of my tactics had shown me the virtual impossibility of disposing of the Gamfron by the side-step-and-slash method. The beast's heavy ribs made that impracticable. I could inflict no disabling wound in this way, and, the Gamfron's vitality being greater than mine, I realized that I should be very quickly worn down, even though all my side-stepping might be as effective as the first one had been. So I shifted my tactics.

'I side-stepped the same as before, but instead of trying another slash as that gleaming black streak went past me, I whirled, and as the great beast slithered along the sand under the impetus of its thirty-foot leap, gathering all my forces, I threw myself upon it and, thrusting my keen, double-edged sword under its momentarily sprawled head and neck, I sawed swiftly back and forth with every ounce of energy I possessed and felt my sword bite through the soft flesh, severing the jugulars and carotids. Then, my feet and legs wedged hard with a sudden motion under the animal's narrow flanks, and letting go the sword, I reached my bare hands under the two sides of the dew-lapped jaws and swinging backward from the fulcrum of my rigid lower legs and knees hauled the Gamfron's head backwards towards me.

'The snap of that tough-knit spine at the back of the neck could be heard about the arena. I could feel the great beast relax under me. I recovered my sword, stood up, placed my right foot upon the carcass and held up my sword toward the notables in a rigid salute.

'I was virtually blind in that glare with the salt sweat streaming into my eyes. My heart was pounding so violently from that lightning-like and terrific exertion that I could hear nothing except a vague roar.

'The next thing I was directly conscious of was a hand falling on my left shoulder. I relaxed, let down my sword, and heard the voice of the official in charge of the gladiators telling me that I was reprieved. I stumbled along beside him around the edge of the arena under a continuous shower of felt hats and gold and silver coin until I felt the grateful shade of that low-ceiling stone passage-way on my almost melting back, and a minute later, my armor off at last, I was being strigilled from head to foot after the buckets of cold water which had been dashed over me by one of the arena slaves, and quite my own man again.

'It was perhaps twenty minutes later when the chief of the officials in charge of the gladiators came into the small stone-flagged room where I was at the moment tying the thongs of my sandals. In the interim the gigantic Black who officiated at the stone slab had thoroughly kneaded all my muscles with oil, the usual process before and after a fight. I had been washed down again with hot water, strigilled and given a drying rub, and had just finished putting on my ordinary clothes.

' "The people demand your presence in the arena," announced the official from just inside the doorway. I rose and bowed in his direction. A public gladiator in Ludekta had the status of a slave. He was anything but a free man, like his modern equivalent the American professional ball player, or a matador. Then the official announced: "You have been chosen to fight Godbor as the day's concluding event – come!"

'Another fight! A sudden sense of hatred for those blood-lusting beasts out there surged over me. But I had no choice. The official turned on his heel and I followed him out towards the arena along the same passageway which I had traversed three quarters of an hour before.

'Half way along it the official stopped and turned abruptly towards me. He had dropped the rough tone of his official pronouncement. He smiled at me and grasped my hand. "It was a splendid fight – that against the animal!" Then, to my infinite surprise, he thrust an arm around behind my back, drew me close against him, and whispered with earnestness and vehemence directly into my ear. And when he had finished I was a new man! Gone now were all the feelings of rebellious hatred which his announcement at the rubbing-room door had raised up in me. He turned and led the way out into the arena. And I followed him now, gladly, eagerly, my head up and my heart beating high.

'A thunderous roar greeted our emergence, and the massed thou-sands rose in their seats like one man. A black slave stepping towards us from the barrier handed a bulging leather sack to the official. He took it and spoke to me over his shoulder. "These are your coins that were thrown into the ring. I will keep them safely for you."

'In the midst of that unanimous and sustained demonstration from what nowadays we would call the fans, we proceeded to a point directly before the great canopied enclosure of the nobles. Here, after saluting these gentry with my arms and hands straight up above my head and not giving their spokesman an opportunity to address me, I put into immediate effect what my unsuspected friend, the official, had whispered in my ear.

' "I will fight Godbor to the death," I announced.

'A simply deafening howl went up from the multitude, back of me to a man. I had been the commander of one of the Lemurian war-galleys and I was accustomed to making my commands heard on my ship! The entire amphitheatre had got my announcement. I waited quietly until the tumult died, and then as soon as I could be heard once more I addressed the nobles.

' "My Lords, I have proclaimed my willingness to please you despite the Ludektan Law which requires no man to fight twice in the arena on the same day. I beseech your nobility therefore, in return for this my good will to meet your desire, that you accord me my liberty, if I survive."

'There was a deathly silence about the arena, the people being agog with interest at this unusual speech of mine, and to hear the answer. As the group within the nobles' enclosure consulted together swiftly, an intense thin hum began to rise from every side of the amphitheatre, and, as I stood there, rigid, waiting for this decision which meant far more than life or death to me, I could see the right arms of the members of that vast concourse being raised in the Ludektan voting gesture of approval.

'Then as the Senator Bothon, who had been generalissimo of all the Ludektan armies, rose in his place to give me my answer, that sharp humming sound stilled and died and twenty thousand men and women leaned forward on their benches to hear the decision. The Senator Bothon was both terse and explicit.

' "The petition is granted," he announced in a voice no less carrying than my own sea-trained tones. Then, before the delighted mob could interrupt him, he added, "And a purse of gold."

'Then, remembering clearly all that the arena official had told me, I waited once more until I could be heard, and when that instant arrived I saluted the nobles and said: "I would gladly slay the traitorous dog Godbor without a reward, O illustrious, for not even yourselves, who deprived him of his Ludektan citizenship and condemned him to the arena, are better aware of his infamy than we of Lemuria who refused to profit by his treachery. I petition you that the rules which are to govern our combat be stated here, in his presence and mine, that there be no treachery but a fair fight."

'At this, which had been listened to in a dead silence that was almost painful, the mob on the benches broke out again. Watching the nobles' enclosure I saw the Senator Bothon turning his eyes from face to face of those about him. When he had gathered their unanimous acquiescence he turned to me and made the sign of approval. At that moment he could not have heard himself speak!

'Back in the preparation rooms with the chief official himself overlooking every detail, I got my self ready for my last fight in the arena. I was very well aware that I was now confronted with the most serious ordeal of my life. Not only had I spent some irrecoverable vitality in that short and intensive conflict with the wild beast, but also I was about to encounter in the traitor Godbor one of the most skillful and tricky hand-to-hand fighters that the Ludektan army had ever produced. He would be fresh, too, not having fought that day.

'I will pass over the details of that preparation – the testing out, by the chief official himself, of the double-edged sword which he selected for me, the complicated muscular treatment on the slab to which I once again submitted, the precise adjustment of the light armor. All this occupied at least half an hour.

'Then, at high noon, Godbor, who had been similarly prepared in another room, walking beside me in the usual formal procession, we proceeded out through the passageway and into that blinding glare and were shortly standing side by side listening to the Senator Bothon as in a pregnant silence he announced and then repeated the rules of the combat.

'And then on a great square of freshly pressed and dampened sand we two stood facing each other tensed for a conflict from which one or the other would never walk back again through the cool passage-way. I had decided to be the aggressor throughout. At the single blast from the herald's horn I leaped at my enemy. He had started forward at the same instant himself. I caught his descending blade squarely on the knop of my bronze buckler relaxing my left arm to lessen the shock of the blow, at the same time delivering a somewhat unusual thrust, above rather than below Godbor's buckler. My initial strategy proved to be sound. The fresh-ground razor-like point of my sword struck his left pectoral muscle near its upper or shoulder attachment, severing the tendon and rendering his left arm virtually useless. I made a lightning-like recovery, landing firmly on my feet, and the equally swift forward leap of Godbor brought him breast to breast with me. He had, with his extraordinary dexterity, managed to shift his sword in those split-seconds into the reverse or dagger-like position, and I was barely in time to divert the stabbing stroke which he aimed for the soft flesh under the ribs of my left side. Disentangling myself, I proceeded to the maneuver of running around him; but he whirled with me and faced me all the way.

'We backed away from each other at this point according to the stated rules of the combat, our initial attack-and-defense being completed. Then I lowered my sword – I had been a Lemurian officer – as I saw, watching Godbor, a look of sudden agony on his face, observed him drooping forward, his knees sagging under him, his eyes closing. I had not anticipated that the merely disabling wound I had inflicted would have such an effect upon so redoubtable a fighting-man as Godbor. And, I was still less suspecting that this incarnate demon, thus early in our fight, and utterly disregarding the twice-repeated rules, would resort to that same treachery which had lost him his coveted Ludektan citizenship. As I stood there, waiting for him to recover himself somewhat instead of closing in quickly and disposing of him at once, he suddenly dropped off the buckler from his left arm, and, launching himself forward, drove in a mighty impact the great bronze helmet which he wore against my chest, with the full momentum of his unexpected leap at me. Yes, those sagging knees which had moved my pity and a gentleman's sense of courtesy, had been bent under him in preparation for this foul attack.

'As I went down, crashing, under that terrific blow of the helmet against my chest, I could hear very clearly, rising above everything, the howl of rage which rose from the spectators on every side.

'And then, like a human avalanche, the huge bulk of Godbor was upon me, and mercilessly, deliberately, his evil face a distorted mask of bitter hatred, and while I, for that instant, lay stunned and helpless, the traitor Godbor thrust his sword down into the soft flesh between my right-hand hip bone and the lower and unprotected edge of my ribs, and drew the sword savagely across to the very edge of the left-hand ribs.

'A sudden, dull-red cloud descended upon me, obscuring my vision and crushing out my consciousness. My fast-dimming eyes caught the edge of the strange spectacle of the people of the benches leaping down on the sand in their dozens and scores and hundreds, pouring over the barriers into the arena like cascades.

'And, with the dull and dimming chorus of their massed roars of hate in my ears, I let go of life.'

Joe Smith ceased speaking, rose, walked over to the centre table. I noticed that his hands trembled as he poured himself out the second drink he had taken since he had been in my house. Deep lines, too, that had not shown before dinner, were in his clean-shaven face. It was evident that the telling of his strange tale had taken it out of him. He was settled in his chair again before either Pelletier or I offered any comment.

'I imagine Godbor didn't survive you very long,' said I. 'That mob probably took him apart.'

Smith nodded. 'He was very unpopular – execrated, in fact – there in Ludekta to begin with,' said he.

Pelletier's comments were in an entirely different vein.

'Don't, I beg of you, misunderstand me, Smith,' he began, 'but, most people would say: "That fellow is a damned good *raconteur!*" and let it go at that. It's a wonderful yarn, as a yarn, whatever else anyone might say or think! Atlantis, Zimbabwe, that cave-boy stuff! That scar of yours for a point of departure; well-known facts, open to any reader, about the ancestral memory theory; and all of 'em worked up into a yarn that is, I grant you, a corncracker! Exactly right, you see, for a couple of fellows like Canevin and me, known to be interested in out-of-the-ordinary matters. That, I say, is what the majority of people would say. I'm not insulting you by putting it that way myself. I merely call attention to the fact that there isn't a thing in it, my dear man, that couldn't have been put together by a clever storyteller.'

Smith, catching Pelletier's 'scientific' note in this somewhat caustic comment, merely nodded in agreement.

'Precisely as you put it,' said he, slowly, and a trifle wearily I thought. 'Precisely, except for this.'

And he rose from his chair, once again loosened his belt, and exposed that frightful scar.

Pelletier, the surgeon uppermost at once, got up, came over to Smith, and peered closely at the dreadful thing.

'Hm,' he remarked, 'the real mystery isn't in that yarn, Smith. It's in how you ever survived this. *That* lays over everything you have been telling us, even the Atlantis part of it that first interested Canevin so much. That breadth of this scar shows that the wound must have been several inches deep. It cut straight through the intestines and just about bisected the spleen. Such a cut would exsanguinate any man, kill him in a few minutes.'

'It did, as I told you,' said Smith, a little crisply.

'My dear man!' protestingly, from Pelletier.

But Joe Smith remained entirely unruffled.

'You know, of course, what scar-tissue feels like to the touch,' said he. 'Run your hand over this, Doctor. Then tell us if you ever felt any other scar-tissue like it. It *looks* like any other scar, of course.'

Pelletier did as requested, his attitude plainly doubtful, skeptical. He was acting in the obvious spirit of a person so open-minded as to try anything that will test the truth, to 'try anything once!'

But he straightened up from this tactile examination with a very different look on his face.

'Good God!' he exploded. 'There's nothing to feel! This thing only *looks* like scar-tissue! What – ?'

Smith carefully tucked in his shirt.

'It's precisely, literally, the way I told it to you,' said he, quietly. 'I was born without any appearance of a scar, although it falls within the classification of "birth-marks", so-called, or the stigmata. It did not begin to appear until I was twenty-seven. That was my age when I died there in the arena, from that wound in the same place, just as I told you, God knows how many thousands of years ago.'

Pelletier looked at Joe Smith who had sat down again and lighted a cigarette. Then, after a couple of minutes' blank silence, Pelletier asked, 'Did you have it on you during those two other "memory-experiences" you spoke of, as a cave-boy, or there in Africa in the Fifteenth Century?'

'No,' replied Smith. 'At least I have no conscious recollection of them as including an abdominal scar. I suppose the reason is that I was not yet twenty-seven years of age in either of those two experiences.'

'Well, I'll take your word for it all, Smith,' said Pelletier. 'It's been mighty interesting. Nothing personal, you know. But I'm not credulous!'

And the two of them bowed to each other, Pelletier smiling whimsically, Joe Smith's tired, lined face inscrutable.

' "Handsomely spoken, my man!" ' quoted Smith, dryly, and we all laughed. Just after this Pelletier took his departure, very cordially.

Half an hour later – it must have been about eleven – Smith rapped on the door of my bedroom. He was in pajamas and bathrobe, and wearing a pair of my spare slippers.

'Would you like to hear the rest of it?' said Smith, from the open doorway.

'Until thirty-two o'clock p.m.!' said I, 'if it's anything like the rest of what Pelletier called your "yarn".'

Smith came in and took a chair. He placed something he had been carrying beside him on the wide chair's cushion.

'There isn't much more of it,' he remarked, 'but I'd rather like you to hear it all together, so to speak.'

'Fire away,' I invited, and settled myself to listen.

'That "birth-mark" of mine,' he began, 'isn't the only thing I could have shown you two fellows this evening. I had this around my waist, too!'

Smith reached down beside him and picked up and unrolled the thing he had brought into my room. It was a pigskin money-belt.

'There's between seven and eight hundred pounds in this,' he remarked, laying it on the table beside him, 'in Bank of England notes. I thought you might put it in your safe until tomorrow, and then I'll put it in the bank I noticed down there by the market where you first ran into me. And now, here's the rest of the "yarn".

'I have only one "polite accomplishment". I paint. I was in Spain making sketches for future working out, up to the end of the summer. I was in Valencia first, and then I made a long jump up north-side, to Santander where there is a peculiar, hard, clear light afternoons that makes everything stand out rather remarkably.

'I stayed on in Santander for more than three weeks altogether, and I had nine or ten rather satisfactory "block-ins" done. I stayed at a small waterfront inn all the time I was there; not any too respectable, I imagine, but exactly convenient for me. I was making waterfront sketches, you see, and my material was right there handy.

'I'm going to make this short, Canevin – merely state the facts. It doesn't need any narrative skill, or whatever it was our friend Pelletier called it – my telling of the first part of it, I mean. These are the bare facts, and they'll speak for themselves.

'I'd been on board the *Bilbao* nearly two months when we struck this port of St Thomas to coal. It was, to be precise, the fourteenth of August when I went on board her, there in Santander. Three days before that, while I was sitting eating my dinner (the Spanish are the worst of the world's cooks, you know – haven't learned anything about preparing food since Cervantes' day!), a great big fellow came in and took a table across the room from me. I didn't particularly take note of him except that he was big. I was gnawing away at a chicken – one of Noah's – and when I happened to glance over in the big man's direction, I noticed that he was glowering at me. His extremely ugly face seemed vaguely familiar, which, of course, fitting in with his really personal expression of dislike, made me wonder who he could be.

'Canevin, I said I'd make it short. I mulled over that not very interesting problem of the man's identity until, quite suddenly, it broke upon me. I had, I knew, seen him somewhere, and there was something quite definitely unpleasant connected with that face and that huge bulk.

'It was "Godbor", Canevin – Godbor to the life.

'That was where I "remembered" him, facing me with those drooping knees and false face full of pretended pain, there in the arena in Ludekta. The whole thing – just as I told it to you and Pelletier this evening – came back to me. I felt sick. I could not eat any more. I sat there, with the queerest feelings imaginable. I can't really put it into words. It was, well, as though an inescapable fate had dropped down on me out of a clear sky – something inevitable, predestined, inescapable.

'I sat there, and just sweated. I remember putting my face between my hands, my elbows on the table, and feeling just plain sick at heart.

'There was something hopeless, grim, really dreadful about it.

'And then, down beside me on a chair dropped this fellow who had been glowering at me, and a big, thick, guttural voice, such as would go naturally with that gross body, was speaking to me.

'He was civil enough. His name was Fernando Lopez. He was the first mate of the *Bilbao*, just arrived in Santander harbor, expecting to clear for Buenos Aires three or four days from then.

'Lopez proposed that we, being the only persons of quality in the inn, should take our meals together. The man sickened me. His mere presence, the fact that he existed, had a most devastating effect upon a set of otherwise sound and untroubled nerves.

'I told him that I was painting and required as much time to myself, including meal-times, as I could get, without social engagements or interruptions! I spoke, of course, with a civility equal, at least, to his. I imagined that any Latin would understand that refusal. They instinctively respect any kind of an artist, as everybody knows.

'But it had no effect on Fernando Lopez! He was the grossest, the most thick-skinned individual you could possibly imagine. Nothing could daunt the fellow, put aside or deter the tremendous admiration my work – he had seen me painting on the wharves, he alleged; had looked more than once on tiptoes over my shoulder – had inspired in him. He would take no refusal.

'There was no shaking him off, you see. Try it, literally, I mean, with a person entirely impervious to snubs, silence, direct statements of one's unwillingness to associate with him and anything else you can think of to get him out from under one's feet, and you'll see what I mean.

'In and out of season, this Old-Man-of-the-Sea hung on my flank, so to speak! He was always beseeching me to come on board his vessel to visit him. Well, I'll make it short, as I said I would.

'The morning of the day the *Bilbao* was to clear from Santander, about seven o'clock, I found my money-belt gone. Fernando Lopez, too, was gone. He would be on board very early, I figured, getting ready for the ship's departure, and I had found out that she was to sail about eight o'clock. I suspected no one else. I hurried down to the docks and went on board.

'There he was, waiting for me, his ugly grin which I had grown to hate and loathe, heavily in evidence. I charged him flatly with the theft. He made no bones about it, said he had taken the money-belt out of my room about five that morning, had it down in his cabin, was ready to give it back to me – no, not a joke – a device to get me to visit him; his last resort. He was quite frank about these statements.

'I went down to his cabin with him, thoroughly disgusted. But, of course, I had to get that money-belt back. All I had with me was in it.

'He stood aside at his cabin door with an elaborate gesture of courtesy which made me squirm internally, and I walked in and he after me, and the next thing I knew, after the blow which he struck me over the head with a blackjack or something of the sort, was coming to in a berth, my hands ironed, and a head that ached and throbbed so that I could barely move.

'The rest of it is simple enough, until we came in sight of St Thomas three days ago. I was sweated and hazed through a period that is like a black nightmare. I was forced to sign on with two men – one of them Lopez – holding my hands. I was given extra watches.

'The captain, an old man named Chico Perez, was Lopez's uncle. He left everything to his nephew, who was cock of the walk on board the *Bilbao*.

'They ironed me again the day we put into Buenos Aires. Lopez was taking no chances on my jumping the ship and reporting him, you see. And, two days after we had cleared from there, the old captain disappeared. I have no doubts in my own mind about what happened to him. Lopez probably broke his neck, or knifed him, and threw the body overboard.

'That fact, I imagine, saved me. You see, the entire crew had sailed with the old man, who was a part owner of the ship, for voyage after voyage. Lopez, as I well knew from the conversations among the members of the crew, was strongly suspected of having made away with him. He commanded the *Bilbao* now, and he did not, I think, quite dare to risk something like a mutiny if another member of the ship's company "disappeared" in the same manner. Otherwise, I haven't the slightest doubt, I'd have had the same treatment.

'We made four or five other South American ports, Cartagena last of all, and then we were to put in to St Thomas for coal. This was the first American port of the voyage. I plucked up a little hope. It wouldn't have done very much good even if I could have made my escape in one of the other places. We Americans are anything but popular down below there, as you know. Here it would be different. I did some figuring and kept my own counsel.

'We were actually in sight of St Thomas when I got my chance, according to what I had planned out.

'It was about five o'clock in the evening, four days ago. I was on deck, and we had just made our landfall. Lopez, and a member of the crew carrying the irons, came towards me across the deck. I had always submitted before. This time I took him by surprise. I simply waited until the two of them had got within a few feet of me, and then without warning I landed as hard as I knew how on Lopez' jaw.

'It knocked him over flat on the deck, but what would have been a clean knockout for a normal man, had little effect on his brute vitality. He was up like a rubber ball, and at me, a knife in his hand and a look of deadly hatred on his beast-face such as I had only faced once before – back there in the Ludekta arena, Canevin, before Godbor.

'I figured that it was all up with me now, and I was fixing to go over on my back and try to catch him amidships with a double-footed kick as my only possible chance, when I felt a knife-hilt thrust into my hand. It was the fellow who had been carrying the irons.

'Then, enormously heartened, I crouched and met Lopez' attack.

'I've described two fights already this evening. I'm not going into the particulars of this one beyond saying that I got Lopez across the arms with my first slash, sideways as I ducked that first rush of his; and I must have severed a tendon, for he slowed and paused and shifted his knife into his other hand.

'I was on him like a cat at this opportunity. I was fighting for my life, and I knew it, and knew besides that I could expect no quarter.

'I simply plunged at him, and struck, and felt the long, keen knife go home in soft flesh, and I sliced with it, and felt his great brutal body relax and then – he was lying on his back, cut clean across the stomach, and a great ooze of blood spreading over the deck.

'I stood there, looking down on the havoc I had made, and became conscious that four or five of the *Bilbao*'s crew were gathered nearby looking on. Neither of the remaining ship's officers was in sight, one being on the bridge and the other probably asleep between watches. Then I began to be conscious of the comments from the crew members.

' "It was well and quickly done!" "He can 'disappear' like old Chico, as well as not." "He is where he put old Chico – the *sine verguenza*!! *Saco la mandonga*!! The Gringo has cut the tripe out of him!!!"

'I felt the knife being quietly withdrawn from my hand, and the fellow who had passed it to me remarked, in my ear – "As well that I take it back now, Señor, and clear it of that hog's blood. You will not need it further, Señor!"

'And then, with many a furtive glance for possible witnesses other than the five or six like-minded fellows who had seen the disposal of Fernando Lopez, that person's hulking carcass was quietly heaved overboard, and a dozen pails of water effectually cleansed the deck of his coagulating blood.

'Nothing whatever was done to me, or even said to me. I have no doubt the officer who automatically succeeded to the command of the *Bilbao* made some kind of innocuous entry in his logbook. There was no report, and no investigation after they reached their anchorage in St Thomas Harbor, so far as I know.

'I had gone straight down to Lopez's cabin after the money-belt, got it, put it on, and come back on deck. I knew exactly where it was, you see, because Lopez had sent for me to his cabin half a dozen times, and taken it out, and gibed me about it during the past couple of months.

'It was the easiest possible affair to come ashore here. No one stopped me or even questioned me. I imagine that that ship's family was only too glad to get rid of the fellow who had relieved them of Fernando Lopez. The rest of it you know, Canevin. I might add that I haven't the smallest possible regret over "removing" Lopez. If those "ancestral memories" of mine are authentic, I have killed before, but never in "this life", certainly. There isn't a single qualm! And if there's any poetry in justice, as some imagine, it's interesting to note that Lopez got the same wound that finished me there in the arena, delivered by his double, maybe twelve thousand years ago.'

Joe Smith sat silent, and I sat across from him and looked at him. The only thing I could think of to say seemed an incongruity after what I had listened to that day! However, by some strange perversity, the question I had on the end of my tongue, however irrelevant, would not down. Almost desperately, I blurted it out.

'What is your real name, Smith?' I enquired.

The fellow stared at me.

'Joe Smith,' said he.

'O.K.,' said I. 'I'll put your money in the safe and we'll go to the bank with it in the morning.'

'Good-night, Canevin, and thank you again,' said my guest.

I saw him out, and picked up the money-belt from the table and carried it over to my old-fashioned, wrought-iron West Indian house-safe which stands in the corner of my bedroom and opens and locks with an enormous key with elaborate filed wards.

I opened the old safe and was about to lay the belt inside when I felt something rough against my hand. I turned it about and looked. A name was embossed upon the fine pigskin leather of the other side. I held it up to the light to read it. I read:

'Josephus Troy Smith.'

I put the belt inside and closed and locked the safe.

Then I came back and sat down in the chair wherein I had listened to my guest's recital of his recent adventures aboard the Spanish tramp steamer *Bilbao*.

Josephus Troy Smith. It wasn't so vastly different from 'Joe Smith', and yet what a different viewpoint that full name had given me! Josephus Troy Smith, as most of the cultivated world is aware, is

America's foremost landscapist. Josephus Troy Smith was a modest chap. I realized that, now. 'I have only one polite accomplishment,' he had said, when he was explaining what he was doing there in northern Spain. A polite accomplishment!

Well, at any rate I had one on Pelletier, and I knew whom I was having the honor of entertaining here in my house on Denmark Hill, St Thomas, Virgin Islands of the U. S. A. Perhaps he would become interested in St Thomas, and stay awhile and make some paintings. Anyway, there were all the colors in the rainbow here, and there is no brighter sunlight in all the world.

' – In Case of Disaster Only'

It was not Sir Austin Fynes, who occupied Suite A with his stout wife, a trained nurse who had given up the training, who told us the story. Sir Austin Fynes uses affairs like thought-transference every day in that 'mental-and-nervous' practice of his which had made him the light of Harley Street, that physician's paradise of London. No, it was a quiet big fellow who, as so often happens in such cases, had sat over to one side of the ship's smoking-room, at one of the separate, small tables beside a mug of beer which he had allowed to grow stale, listening to the rest of us. The big fellow was a native West Indian, with an accent you could cut with a knife, a Barbados brogue. He was 'in sugar'; or, maybe – now that cane isn't so good any more what with the Tariff and Beetroot, and the German bounty, 'in mules'; or perhaps 'in' what is commercially known in the market as 'Cuban beef'.

That big fellow got off the ship early the next morning, and I, for one, never even learned his name. He got off at St John, Antigua, where, I dare say, he lived, and bossed his plantation-hands, and rode around his plantation early mornings, and ate fresh-killed tough meat and drank too-strong tea after noon, alternated with swizzels of antique rum.

It had been the subject of telepathy on which our talk had turned towards midnight. It was about last-order time, when the smoking-room steward makes his final rounds to see what you'll take before he locks up his little cubby-hole of a bar with its swizzel-stick and its green limes, and its staple of *Prunier* for the French-Island passengers and the even more numerous British calls for 'B. & S.'s.'

Sir Austin had contributed his bit, about the therapeutic use of 'suggestion' in mental-and-nervous and 'borderline' cases. The whole field had been pretty thoroughly covered, in fact. Even I had put in a word or two. I'm no scientist but I had read my *Laws of Psychic Phenomena* by Thompson W. Hudson, Ph.D. Some book, that one! Gives you pretty much all the dope. Shows, incidentally, what's 'Science' and what's just merely plain blah. Lot of people wouldn't know the difference, I dare say, me for a good example! The big fellow hitched around in his chair when that midnight lull came, and started in in his big beefy, British voice.

'Do any of you chaps by any chance know Reuter, in St Thomas – Clinton Reuter? No? Sorry. An exceedingly good chap, Reuter. In 1926 he was in the States, and was rather hastily summoned back to St Thomas. Took the first ship he could get – sailed that same afternoon in rather a rush. It was a tramp, carrying a few pasengers – the *Bonaventure*.'

Then, the big fellow, having caught everybody's attention, went on to tell what happened to Clinton Reuter on that voyage from New York to St Thomas, in the Virgin Islands. St Thomas is the first port of call going 'down the Islands' from New York. We had been there two days before. It's about the best-looking town in the Lesser Antilles, way ahead of the rest of them, although Bridgetown, the capital of Barbados, and Port-of-Spain down on Trinidad are a lot bigger and a lot busier.

It was some story, and the big fellow told it right: very simply. It was the only real story we had had that evening, although there had, of course, been a number of instances brought up, as there always are when people get together on a subject like telepathy.

I'm not reproducing the English-West Indian's yarn. It would be a dialect-story, for one thing, with that brogue of his, and besides, I didn't believe the big fellow's yarn for sour apples. I handed it to him for a well-told tale, coming in on that general conversation at precisely the right time to click and get a lot of plausibility in such a setting. It didn't, to tell the truth, impress me, otherwise.

And then, seven months afterwards, by a kind of dumb luck I came back on the *Bonaventure* myself.

Mr Sills, who had been the Third Officer on Reuter's voyage, was still with the ship. He was Number One now. That company operated a number of vessels, it seemed, and followed a policy of shifting its men around, Captain Sills told me.

That wasn't all the genial young Captain told me, however, sitting evenings in his pleasant cabin over a jugfull of mild Martinique rum swizzel with plenty of lime juice in it. Of course, I told him what the big West Indian had told us in that brogue of his, and Sills, one of the least superstitious seamen I have ever encountered, came back at me that the West Indian had not altered the facts in one single particular; had not stretched the plain truth; had not been pulling our leg that night in the smoking-room.

Here, then, is the story.

When Reuter stepped across the sill of his stateroom on the *Bonaventure* the first thing he saw was a sign, which read:

Alarm-Bell – To Be Used In Case of Disaster Only
When this Bell Rings, Go On Deck At Once

Just above the sign was a gong, painted white with ship's paint. Reuter had never seen just such an arrangement, and when the steward, just behind him with the hand-luggage, spoke, he had to repeat himself because Reuter had his eyes on the sign and had to pull them away, as it were!

He had a large stateroom to himself. He stowed his luggage, put on a cap, and went up on deck. He took an overcoat, too, it was late October and chilly. He stood up on deck and watched the last of the lading.

The stevedores, like bees, swarmed above and below the opened hatches. The winches creaked and groaned incessantly to the usual accompaniment of various bellowed directions, commands, and counter-commands. Both the forward hatches had already been closed because the lading forward had been finished. Now the First Officer, a chap named Pollard, was driving the work aft. A cold wind blew up the Hudson River where the ship was docked.

Reuter looked on at all this, and, I dare say, anyone watching him might have supposed him immensely interested. But, as a matter of fact, he had been at sea a good bit and such affairs were an old story to him. His mind was really in St Thomas. He looked at the maneuvers of two tugboats which hovered out in the river off the *Bonaventure's* stern, flannel-shirted captains with peaked caps aslant over their eyes leaning nonchalantly out of their respective pilot-houses, spinning the great wheels as though negligently, jockeying skillfully about among the thick and varied traffic of the river.

Only that morning he had received Morrison's letter from St Thomas. Morrison was his partner. When he had grasped its purport he had dropped everything else abruptly, hurriedly telephoned to the steamship office, and cabled Morrison of his sailing at once. It was his singular good fortune that there happened to be this vessel sailing late that afternoon. Because of that stroke of luck he would be able to arrive in St Thomas at the end of six days, even though the *Bonaventure* was no more than a slow tramp which carried passengers only incidentally. There had been no time to await a reply to his cabled message; cables had to be relayed through Porto Rico.

Morrison should, of course, have cabled him in the first place instead of writing. The mails were very slow. Perhaps, though, poor old Morrison had not realized the gravity of his own condition. Reuter had been obliged to use his instinct over that letter. The information it contained and his knowledge of the tropics and of Morrison all had conspired to make him realize the necessity for this hastily undertaken voyage.

Morrison had written that he was coming down again with another attack of pneumonia. His letter had been written in the Municipal Hospital. This attack, Reuter knew, would be likely to finish him. If he were to see Morrison alive – if their affairs were not to dissolve in sudden ruin, now that they were in their most critical state of development – he must go, and go at once; be standing by to see poor Morrison out if he should last until his arrival, and then immediately take over the control of affairs himself. One thing was certain; Morrison was still alive. Otherwise he would have had a cable. It was peculiarly unfortunate that Morrison had come down ill at this particular time. Their business required constant, personal attention, Morrison on one end, in St Thomas; he on the other, in New York.

A sudden, general movement among the stevedores aroused Reuter out of his thoughts to watch what was going on below him on deck. The stevedores, their task finished, were collecting their coats, swarming over the ship's side onto the dock. Under the direction of a ship's officer the crew now turned to at getting the tarpaulins over the closed hatches; the wedges were already being driven home on one of them. Hawsers were being cast off. The two tugboats were no longer weaving in and out among the traffic out in the river. Both were attached, now, and hauling skillfully.

The ship was beginning to move. Reuter watched the careful process of backing out into the stream, but his mind was still on Morrison. Poor old Morrison! Well, if he passed out in the meantime, he would be getting a message, after three days at sea, at about the extreme range of the St Thomas wireless station. He arranged for that in his cable. He could not keep his mind off Morrison, somehow. Well, that was natural enough. He sighed deeply, turned, and went forward to the boat-deck. The *Bonaventure* was well out in the river now, her bows swinging towards the open sea. The tugs dropped off. The breeze from the lower bay began to blow. The voyage had begun.

When Reuter went back to his stateroom afer the early dinner which the occasional passengers on his line took with the ship's officers, the alarm-bell and its accompanying sign again struck his eye. He read through the sign again, carefully, his mind still pre-occupied with Morrison.

After a short evening spent arranging his cabin for the voyage, and tired out by the unusual exertions of that very busy day ashore, he turned in not long after eight bells. It was a comfort to settle down in the narrow berth and relax. Just before switching off the light he paused and read the sign through once more. Then he shut his eyes and slept like the dead until a smiling black steward carrying hot black coffee awakened him at six bells in the morning, announcing: 'Breakfast in half an hour, sir.'

The voyage was entirely uneventful. For three days and nights the *Bonaventure* plowed along at a steady ten knots S.S.E. through the deepening blue of the ocean. Every day, at first as they traversed the Gulf Stream, then later, to the south'ard of it, the hue of the water became more intense until it took on that perfect indigo color which artists find easy to paint, and viewers of their pictures who have not seen the West Indian waters, find hard to credit. About the ship the trailing edge-weed of the Atlantic Sargasso wavered out in long strings, indicating the direction of the current wind to the least knowing landsman. Reuter noted the first of the flying fish in the late afternoon of the second day, and on the early morning of the third a few of the snouted porpoises which suggest to the beholder the dolphins of antique pictorial art.

Every evening, before retiring, he read through gravely the sign below the bell in his cabin. Every morning when he awakened it was always, somehow, the first object to catch his eye. It was as though some vague premonition, connected inexplicably with the alarm-bell, had laid its strong hold upon his imagination. Once, after he had switched off the light and slipped into his bunk, so strongly did this feeling persist, that he could not get asleep. Rather shamefacedly he rose, turned on the light, drew out and dusted a life-preserver, and tried it on. Rather grimly he smiled at his reflection, wearing it, in the small mirror before he replaced it and turned in again.

On the stroke of six bells – three o'clock in the early morning – of the fourth day at sea, he was abruptly wrenched into full wakefulness by a deep, insistent clanging beside him. *The alarm-bell*!

He rolled hastily out of his bunk and fumbled for the light. When he had found it and switched it on, and struggled to adjust his suddenly blinded eyes to its glare, he noted the bell had ceased ringing, though clearly in his mind still sounded its harsh note of clangorous, insistent warning.

He reached up and rapped the gong smartly with his seal ring. It answered with the note which had awakened him. Though that made it unmistakable, he wondered vaguely why it had ceased ringing. It should, he supposed, have continued automatically. He wondered what disaster could have overtaken the ship. As he tugged on his bathrobe and thrust his feet hurriedly into his slippers, and reached to the rack for a life-preserver, he heard, clearly, the steady throb of the engines. Disaster? What had happened? Well, the directions on the sign – (did he not know them by heart?) – were to go on deck at once. Out there, of course, he would find out in short order.

He opened his cabin door, expecting to meet he knew not what. He stepped carefully over the high iron door-sill, life-preserver hanging over his left arm. He turned aft at once and made his way, rapidly for the semi-darkness, along the covered-in passageway on which his door opened, towards the ladder leading to the deck above. It was there that the lifeboats stood in their chocks. As he mounted the ladder he remembered, inconsequently, that he had always wanted to see just how efficiently those new-fashioned leaning davits worked in the actual launching of a lifeboat. Now, probably, he was to find out!

He found the boat-deck deserted. A slight breeze, the very north-ernmost edge of the early-morning Trade, freshly blowing, was just beginning to make itself felt. Above, in a perfectly cloudless sky, the great stars flamed and glowed. There was no moon, but the reflection of Venus lay to starboard like a thin, unbroken bar of faint moonlight along the smooth sea. The *Bonaventure* forged steadily onward, her engines throbbing monotonously in their incessant, sustained beat.

Somewhat bewildered now, he walked farther forward along the boat-deck. He paused under a broad canvas awning just below the extension of the bridge on the port side. There was no motion except the slight, undulating pitch of the vessel as she responded to the long Atlantic swell of Latitude 28. In the soft and silent calm of this subtropic night the footfalls, regular and unhurried, of the slowly pacing officer on duty came delicately to his ears. It would be Mr Sills, the Third Officer, at this hour.

Reuter spoke hesitantly up the bridge companionway.

'Good morning, Mr Sills.'

The officer on the bridge paused in his steady walk. Doubtless he would think it somewhat strange for a passenger to be up on the boat-deck at this unusual hour. That bell!

'Good morning, Mr Reuter,' came Sill's voice. 'Very bright star-light this morning. Did you notice Venus?'

'Remarkably clear – yes! I was noticing Venus particularly. Shows up quite like a regular little moon, doesn't she?'

The officer remained to chat for a moment, then resumed his duty-tramp along the bridge, his tread leisurely – no indication here of anything out of the ordinary. Disaster!

Reuter glanced down at his life-preserver, dangling awkwardly from his arm. He hoped Mr Sills had not noticed it. The life-preserver seemed an incongruity on this perfect night.

That bell!

Could this, perhaps, be one of those cases such as one read about occasionally – an assumed, reassuring calm on the part of the officers, a professionally false calm to keep the passengers from a stampede in the face of imminent danger? No! Hardly that, here, under these circumstances. There were only two or three passengers aboard the tramp besides himself, all men. He was alone on this deck where the lifeboats, stood, still in their chocks, belted down, their rigging coiled as though no one ever expected to disturb it. This, of course, was no passenger ship. The ringing of the alarm-bell at this time of night could have no possible meaning except public and necess-ary announcement of disaster. Even on passenger vessels boat-drills always came day-times at convenient hours. The wording of the sign was explicit and unmistakable.

To Reuter's now thoroughly alert mind only one explanation was possible. He must have dreamed, vividly, of the bell's ringing. Such an explanation seemed absurd, ridiculous. But that would at least account for its silence after he had switched on his light and noticed that it was ringing no longer. Perhaps, he reminded himself, the sign had made, in his state of preoccupation about poor Morrison, an absurdly strong impression on his mind. It was curious, though, that the *note* of the bell, as he had heard it – in his sleep, if that were the true explanation – had exactly corresponded to its actual note; the sound it had given out when he had rapped it with his ring. He had never tried ringing it before. He had no previous knowledge of the gong's note.

He remained there on the boat-deck a few minutes longer, greatly puzzled. He looked out at the slightly phosphorescent sea and upward at the serene stars. Disaster! Well – it had been a very queer experience for him, in his matter-of-fact existence; something to think about, surely – it would supply him with a story to tell . . .

He went below, almost reluctantly, now, because of the charm of this warm night out here on deck, and the soft early-morning breeze, which was now coming in little puffs from the West, the land side – somewhere off Florida they would be now – back to his cabin. He looked first at the sign and the bell, half fascinated, his brows heavily puckered in his deep puzzlement. He did not tap the bell again before putting out the light and turning in. Contrary to his expectation, for he felt very completely awake, he fell asleep immediately. He slept straight through until the arrival of the steward with the morning coffee aroused him at seven.

After his shower and breakfast he settled himself in a deck chair on the shady starboard side of the boat-deck, away from the blazing morning sun. Idly he ran through the unread portions and even the advertisements of a magazine hastily purchased just before coming aboard four days before. It was here, about the middle of the morning that the wireless operator found him and handed him a message just received. It was from St Thomas, from the Chief Municipal Physician, at the hospital, Commander Joseph Carver of the Navy. The message was explicit and terse, Navy style.

MORRISON DIED THREE THIS MORNING. – CARVER.

Poor old Morrison! Always careful and considerate, Morrison. He, of course, had provided for the sending of this message in case he was called West before Reuter's ship arrived.

He would not even be able to get there in time for the funeral! Two full days, possibly a third, must necessarily intervene before the *Bonaventure* could tie up to the West India Docks in St Thomas harbor. In the Islands they buried people, usually, the same day on which they died. Reuter looked at his watch. It was ten thirty-three now. Morrison had been dead more than seven hours.

He had gone out at three o'clock! Abruptly it flashed into Reuter's mind – that was when he had heard the 'disaster' bell. He could feel little chills now running up and down his spine . . .

He pulled himself together. He stood up, thrust the wireless message into the pocket of his drill coat. There would be a tremendous lot for him to attend to when he arrived. Too bad he could not be at the funeral! That could not be helped. Thinking of the endless details that would be piled up for him on his arrival, an anxious frown on his forehead, he walked aft, descended the ladder, and entered his stateroom.

The sign took his first glance, held it. He stood there, just inside the stateroom door, looking at it fixedly, as though fascinated. Had it actually rung or not? Would he ever, really, know? He walked the length of the room and looked closely at the bell. It was, of course, no more than an inanimate thing, a mechanical device, glistening in its white ship's paint. He could recall, as though it were only a few moments ago, the precise tone of it, as it had sounded, recording itself in his sleep-ridden brain; that had been nearly eight hours ago, just at the time when Morrison had passed out, hundreds of miles away down there in St Thomas.

Abruptly he reached up and inserted his index finger under the gong's heavy spherical clapper. As he tried to raise it he encountered a stiff resistance. He thrust a little harder with a muscular finger. He saw that he was only bending the wire by which the globular copper ball was attached to the make-and-break electrical appliance which rang the gong. Then, very carefully, he straightened the bent wire. He took hold of the rectangular piece of metal to which the wire was attached at its other end. He tried to force this up. Again he encountered resistance. It would not budge. *The gong was not in working order*! He stepped on the metal railing of the lower bunk. He peered at the apparatus, his head bent close.

Successive coatings of the ship's paint had fastened down the gong's clapper rigidly. Reuter took out his knife and pried under the paint, hard now as cement. Flakes of it came away under the knife blade. He had the clapper entirely freed now. Probably it had not rung the gong since its original installation. It moved stiffly, grating back and forth reluctantly under his hand. He lifted it up forcibly, then let it fall back into place upon the gong's rim with a solid impact . . .

The gong sounded in the very middle of the note that had been ringing in his mind; the note he had been expecting; the note that had been stamped into his mind at three o'clock that morning, when Morrison had died.

Disaster.

He stepped down slowly to the stateroom's deck, dusting off white flaked particles and chippings of ancient paint from his hands and the front of his coat. He stood in the middle of the room, his feet wide apart, and read the sign through once more. Unconscious of his own action, he shook his head, doubtfully. He remained standing there for a long time, balancing himself to the ship's slow roll, in a musing daze.

At last he lowered his eyes, turned, and walked slowly out of his stateroom, mounted to the deck, resumed his chair, and picked up the abandoned magazine.

But he did not open the magazine. Instead he laid it across his knees to serve as a writing desk. It had occurred to him that he ought to jot down as many things as he could think of – it would be wise to have them clearly in mind – the many things that would have to be attended to as soon as the *Bonaventure* had made fast alongside the West India Company's docks in St Thomas.

Bothon

Powers Meredith, at his shower-bath before dinner in the bathroom adjoining his room in his New York City club, allowed the cake of soap to drop on the tiled floor. Stooping to recover it he rapped the side of his head smartly against the marble sidewall. The resulting bruise was very painful, and almost at once puffed up into a noticeable lump. Meredith dined in the grill that evening. Having no after-dinner engagement he went into the quiet library of the club, empty at this hour, and settled himself with a new book beside a softly-shaded reading lamp.

From time to time a slight, inadvertent pressure of his head against the chair's leather-upholstered back would remind him unpleasantly of his accident in the shower-bath. This, after it happened several times, became an annoyance, and Meredith shifted himself into a preventive attitude with his legs draped over one of the big chair's rounded arms.

No one else came into the library. Faint, clicking noises came in from the nearby billiard-room where a couple of men were playing, but, absorbed in his book, he did not notice these. The only perceptible sound was that of the gentle, steady rain outside. This, in the form of a soothing, continuous murmur, came through the partly-opened, high windows. He read, interestedly, on and on in his book.

As he turned over the ninety-sixth page of his book, at precisely that instant's brief and almost unnoticed interruption of the thread of the story which this mechanical act involved, he heard a dull, overwhelmingly heavy sound, like a very large explosion plainly coming from a vast distance. It was the kind of deep booming dull roar which would accompany the destruction of several city blocks simultaneously.

Suddenly alert now, his finger holding his place in the book, he listened, horrified, for the aftermath – some stupendous crashing of falling masonry.

After several apprehensive instants, his mind entirely engaged with that keen process of listening, he heard it, almost with relief. It was a rumbling roar as though of countless tons of wrecked masonry; falling; falling; clearly, unmistakably, the remote thunder of some catastrophic ruin. He dropped his book, and, obeying his most prominent reactive impulse, literally leaped to his feet and started for the door.

He met nobody as he rushed down the stairs. At the coat-room, which he had to pass on his way to the doorway, two fellow members were chatting urbanely together as they took their checks. Meredith glanced at them, surprised at their callousness. He rushed on, to the doorway, and out into the street, where he paused. An empty street! As he shoved his way impatiently through the heavy revolving door an imperturbable doorman checked him out on the club-membership list-board beside his standing desk. Meredith thought, fleetingly, of the sentinel of Pompeii! He turned automatically, naturally, to the right, in the general direction from which that terrific sound had appeared to come. He had been visualizing streets thronged with horror-stricken people crowding westward; mad rush of fire apparatus, clanging raucously westward along crosstown streets; platoons of reserve police moving at the double in the same direction in their disciplined, orderly ranks. He half expected to see some lurid glow, searing the heavens over towards the Hudson River.

There was, strangely, as it seemed to him, disappointingly, almost startlingly – none of these things. The rain, reduced now to the merest light drizzle, made the asphalt of the street shimmer as it reflected upwards innumerable slightly distorted lights. Over towards Broadway, certainly, there was clamor. On this his expectant mind seized avidly. But, as he analyzed this automatically, it reduced itself to an accustomed note, heightened and intensified, now, by the emptying of the theaters. It was only the compound eleven o'clock bedlam of Times Square.

Along Sixth Avenue as he approached it with hurried strides, a pace just short of running, countless weaving taxicabs in a many-hued stream jockeyed for position in the maelstrom of the night-traffic about the Hippodrome. On the corner, a solitary, conspicuous figure, a rubber-coated and helmeted policeman, swinging long efficient arms like a pair of mechanical semaphores, skillfully directed the hypersensitive, crawling traffic, soundless on its multi-tudinous rubber tires save for the sustained, growling, compound cachinnation of shifting gears and squawking protesting brakes. Against him, as he stood now irresolutely on the curb, scores of hustling pedestrians jostled unheedingly. To his ever-increasing wonderment, all these seemed uniformly to be unmoved, to be totally unconcerned, by what, he supposed, must of necessity be one of the major destructive calamities of modern times.

Now thoroughly disturbed, vastly perplexed and reeling under this sense of quite inexplicable incongruity, Meredith turned and walked back towards the club. He was at a complete loss now, his mind at a standstill as though reason itself had failed to function. He sought for refuge, to find quickly some mental relief in palliative explanations – the terrific explosion he had heard might, of course, have taken place at some very great distance. On that grand scale one could not easily determine either the source or the direction of sound. The lower end of Manhattan Island might have given way! Like everyone else he had read from time to time varying predictions of such a possible calamity in the pseudo-scientific write-ups which now and again and at almost regular intervals made their appearance in the Magazine Sections of the Sunday newspapers. That vast, pro-gravitational, and ever-increasing accumulation of pressure from the crowding sky-scrapers – the well-nigh incalculable massed weight of towering structural steel and heavy stone blocks always encroaching more and more upon the uncalculated supporting strength of the island's lower stratum of bedrock – the reckless undermining of that same solid bedrock by more and more tunnels and subways!

A new idea, a possible explanation! The sudden blowing up of one of the great manufacturing plants across the Hudson in New Jersey! All that territory was to the west and there were many such manu-factories far inland. One of them, an ammunition-plant, had blown up during the War. He remembered that that explosion, although some twenty miles away, had blown out windows right here in New York City.

He came abreast of the club entrance, hesitated, a deep frown corrugating his puzzled brow, mounted the three steps hesitatingly, and entered. He paused at the door-man's desk. No, that liveried automaton, his whole attention, as always, concentrated upon his duties, had heard of nothing. Neither had the somewhat sleepy clerk at the cigar counter.

'Send me up an "extra", please, if one comes out,' Meredith requested of the other clerk at the mail desk. He went up in the elevator to his bedroom completely nonplussed.

Half an hour later as he lay in bed wakeful and trying to compose in his thoughts the varying, incongruous aspects of this strange affair, he was all at once acutely conscious of a distant, thin, confused, roaring hum apparently the resultant of several composite sounds. These were such sounds as would be made under the stress of a common excitement by a huge concourse of people at a vast distance. The most prominent element in this sound was the deep, soft, and insistently penetrating blending of countless voices. Through it ran a kind of dominant note – a note of horror. The sound positively chilled his blood. It was horrible, eerie. He found himself holding his breath as he listened, straining every faculty to take in that faint, distant, terrible clamor of fear and despair.

Of just when he fell asleep he had no recollection but when he awakened the next morning there hung over his mind a shadow of remembered horror, not wholly dissipated until he had bathed and begun to dress. He heard none of the sounds at the time of his awakening.

No 'extra' lay outside his bedroom door, and a little later at breakfast he opened expectantly and scanned several newspapers vainly and with a mounting sense of wonderment for any account of a catastrophe which could have caused the sounds. The implication grew upon him staggeringly. He had, actually, heard the convincing, unmistakable evidence of such a catastrophe – *and no one else knew anything about it*!

He reasoned himself deliberately away from the mist of something like cold fear that gripped chillingly at his heart with a kind of internal chill. There was quite a variety of news in the papers that morning, too. He glanced through the headings – crimes of violence; the execution of a famous criminal; the earthquake in Tokyo; several divorces; a notable prize-fight; the simultaneous crises of two European cabinets. But there was literally nothing which would account for what he, alone, apparently, had heard.

Strange dreams, the details gone, dissipated, the vague, devastating general recollection only remaining now, adumbrated in his mind in the form of an intense, horrific recollection. He had been one of those intimately, indeed poignantly, concerned in some vast and deep, some almost cosmic, cataclysm.

The dreadful thing, vague, disquieting memories of which had seared his mind and heart in those broken, horrific dreams, was not – and this element was entirely clear in his waking thoughts – was not as yet consummated. It was as though in the dream-state, he had been living – that phase of it was also very clear and unmistakable; stamped into his mind – an extraordinarily vivid, tense, and active life in some great urban community, wherein the utter certainty of some forthcoming and inevitable catastrophe was surely impending, a cataclysm the general knowledge of which had keyed up to the boiling-point the whole activity and the entire mental outlook of that community in which he had found himself, and in which he seemed to have been living for a long time under some kind of handicapping condition very irksome to him.

The one element of the horror and disturbance which lingered on, coloring powerfully that overhanging sense of destruction and sheer, paralyzing terror which had shadowed his waking day, was a sound – a vast, ear-filling, nerve-shattering dull roar as of the rising, menacing commotion of all the waters of the world.

Much more vaguely, a visual memory, the memory of a view point, lingered in the very back of Meredith's mind, bound up with, and seemingly a part of the general setting of those horrible dreams. He had been, somehow, under physical restraint in his dreams. It had been through great, massive walls all about him that the roar of impending catastrophe had come, muffled and dreadful, to his ear. And it was not wholly eradicated from his waking consciousness that he had seen through a barred aperture a flaming, red sky and had glimpses of tall towers tottering to the aural accompaniment of soul-shattering detonations, against that awful sound-background of the preternatural roaring of the fury-lashed, earth-shaking, near but unseen ocean.

He did his sensible best to account for these dreams of horror by attributing their outstanding features to his reading of the now detailed accounts of the great earthquake which had occurred in the Japanese capital, a catastrophe which had aroused the horror and sympathy of the whole civilized world. This, he told himself, was the necessary, the obvious, explanation of such dreams. So very keen and vivid had been the dreams' import in his mind, that although he attached no significance to the fact, he had to repeat this process of self-assurance, of every-day, material-background explanation to himself, again and again, throughout a day colored by an ever-recurrent, inescapable preoccupation with those night-dreams of dread, and horror, and impending destruction.

That evening, with his fianceé, Lois Harding, he had a dinner-and-dance engagement. Miss Harding thought him preoccupied; told him he was working too hard.

It was late when he came home to the club afterwards. He was physically tired and he fell asleep immediately after turning in. The following morning was Sunday. The reading-room was full and he carried his book up to his bedroom after late breakfast to read the rest of it in peace. He was soon immersed in it. Some time later his attention was distracted by the tapping of a window-shade, blown in and out by the breeze. It was annoying and he paused in his reading, intending to rise and adjust the shade.

As he withdrew his eyes, and part of his attention, from his book, all at once he heard a new sound. It was precisely as though a distant, sound-proof door had been abruptly opened. The new and different sound came through that imaginary door in the form of the composite noise of a distant battle. The details were vague but not so vague as to impair the certainty that what he was hearing now was conflict, the secondary or accompanying element in the compound aural impact being as unmistakably the sounds of con-flagration – the crackle and roar of seething, devouring flame, rampant, uncontrollable. And back of these sound-elements, and carrying with it the recrudescence of the dreams' well-remembered aspect of a communal terror, the deep, underlying, dominating roar of a merciless, barbaric sea.

A mental picture leaped forthwith into his mind, the precise visual 'atmosphere' of those dreams of Friday night.

As he listened, fascinated, there came back to him and grew upon him a paralyzing, cold fear. There was no stopping it now. It was the fear of *that which cannot be related to any previous experience*; the fear of the unknown; the fear of certain and imminent destruction.

Cold sweat suddenly beaded his forehead. The faint penumbra of a slight nausea shook him. He could distinguish overtones now, high tones, cries of battle; the impact of a charge against a resistant horde; noise of plied weapons.

The window-shade tapped again against the window casing. He snapped back into the familiar environment of his bedroom. He felt a little sick and weak. He rose, rather shakily, walked across the room and into the bathroom, and, noisily splashing the water about, washed his trembling hands and his face. Anything, to disperse those dreadful, haunting sounds from that incalculable world; that No Man's Land of rending destruction which had begun to project its echoes of cosmic calamity into his mind.

He paused, suddenly to listen again, a towel gripped between his shaking hands. But he could 'hear' nothing now, nothing except the tapping of that window-shade in the fresh breeze blowing through the open window. He hung the towel on its porcelain rod and walked back to his chair. He had seen his face, ghastly, in the bathroom mirror.

It was an hour too early for lunch, but he wanted urgently to be where there were people about, even waiters, people who were not 'hearing things'!

In order to prolong his companionship with old Cavanagh, the only other early luncher, Meredith ate somewhat more than usual. The unaccustomed heavy meal at such an hour made him drowsy and after lunch he stretched out on a davenport before one of the two open fireplaces in the now unoccupied reading-room, and fell at once into an uneasy sleep.

A little before three he awakened, stale, and as he came to conscious wakefulness he began to 'hear', at first quite distinctly, and then with increasing loudness and clarity as though a steady hand were opening up a loudspeaker, that same sound of fire and human conflict, and the dreadful, menacing roar of a thunderous ocean's incalculable anger.

Then, Old Cavanagh, napping on the other davenport, struggled with senile deliberation to his feet with many accompanying 'hums' and 'ha's', and began lumbering across the room towards him.

Meredith pulled himself together, forced away from him the idea that his sanity was dissolving into something like imbecility, and sat up; but his face, as his fellow club-member saw it, was again drawn and ghastly. Old Cavanagh plopped down beside him on the davenport. The old gentleman's kindly, florid face puffed with startled emotion. His eyes goggled. His mouth opened slackly.

'Lord's sake, what's the matter?' he demanded.

Kindly goodwill looked out of the old man's distorted countenance. Meredith, as though a spring within him had been released, stammered out his incredible story, the older man studying him narrowly as he talked and nodding sympathetically from time to time.

'Hm! mighty queer!' was his comment when Meredith had ended. He produced, lighted deliberately, and puffed upon an enormous cigar. He seemed to cogitate as the two sat side by side in a pregnant silence of many minutes. At last he spoke.

'You're upset, my boy, naturally. But, you can hear everything that's going on around you, can't you? Your actual hearing's all right, then. Hm! This other "hearing" starts up and goes on only when everything's perfectly quiet. First time, you were here reading; second time, in bed; third time, reading again; this time – if I wasn't snoring – you were in perfect quiet once more. Let's test that out, now. Keep perfectly still, and I'll do the same. Let's see if you hear anything.'

They fell silent once more, and for a while Meredith could hear nothing of the strange sounds. Then, as the silence deepened, once again came that complex of sounds indicating devastatingly battle, murder, and sudden death.

He nodded silently at Cavanagh, and at the old man's acquiescent murmur the sounds ceased abruptly.

It took urging before Meredith could be persuaded to consult an aurist. Medical men, Cavanagh reminded him, would keep quiet about anything strange or embarrassing. Professional ethics . . .

They went uptown together that afternoon to Dr Gatefield, a noted specialist. The doctor heard the story with close-lipped, professional attention. Then he tested Meredith's hearing with various delicate instruments. Finally he gave an opinion.

'We are familiar with various "ear-noises", Mr Meredith. In some cases the location of one of the arteries too close to the ear-drum gives "roaring" noises. There are others, similar. I have eliminated everything of that kind. Your physical organism is in excellent condition, and unusually acute. There is nothing wrong with your hearing. This is a case for a psychiatrist.

'I am not suggesting anything like mental derangement, you will please understand! But I recommend Dr Cowlington. This seems to be a clear case of what is sometimes called "clairaudience", or something similar – his department; not mine. The aural equivalent of "clairvoyance" is what I am indicating, you see what I mean. "Second-sight" has to do with the eyes, of course, but it is mental, although there is often some physical background. I have no knowledge of those phenomena. I hope you will take my advice and allow Dr Cowling – '

'All right!' interrupted Meredith. 'Where does he live? I might as well go through with the thing now as later.'

Dr Gatefield showed traces of sympathy under his rather frosty professional exterior. He dropped the diagnostician, became the obliging, courteous gentleman. He telephoned to his colleague, the psychiatrist, and then surprised both Meredith and Cavanagh by accompanying them to Dr Cowlington's. The psychiatrist proved to be a tall, thin, and rather kindly person, with heavy, complex spectacles on a prominent nose, and then, sand-colored wisps of hair in a complication of cowlicks. He showed marked interest in the case from the start. After hearing Meredith's story and the aurist's report he subjected Meredith to an examination of more than an hour from which, feeling more or less as though he had been dissected, he nevertheless derived a considerable sense of relief.

It was decided that Meredith should arrange at once to take several days off, come to Dr Cowlington's house, and remain 'under observation'.

He arrived at the doctor's the next morning and was given a pleasant, upstairs room, with many books and a comfortable davenport on which, in a recumbent position, the psychiatrist suggested, he should spend most of his waking hours reading.

During Monday and Tuesday, Meredith, now after Dr Cowlington's skillful reassurances no longer upset at 'hearing' the strange sounds, listened carefully for whatever might reach him from what seemed like another – and very restless – world! He 'heard' as he 'listened' for long periods uninterrupted by any aural distractions, the drama of a great community in the paralyzing grip of fear – fighting for its corporate life – against irresistable, impending, dreadful doom.

He began, about this time, at Dr Cowlington's suggestion, to write down some of the syllabification of the cries and shouts as well as he could manage it, on a purely phonetic basis. The sounds corresponded to no language known to him. The words and phrases were blurred and marred by the continuous uproar of the fury of waters. This was invariably, and continued to be, the sustained, distinctive background for every sound he heard during the periods while he remained passive and quiet. The various words and phrases were entirely unintelligible. His notes looked like nothing which either he or Cowlington could relate to any modern or ancient tongue. When read aloud they made nothing but gibberish.

The strange terms were studied over very carefully by Dr Cowlington, by Meredith himself, and by no less than three professors, of Archaeology and Comparative Philology, one of whom, the Archaeologist, was a friend of Cowlington's and the other two called in by him. All of these experts on ancient and obsolete languages listened with the greatest courtesy to Meredith's attempt to explain the apparent setting of the sounds – most of them were in the nature of battle-cries and what Meredith took to be fragments of desperately uttered prayer – some of the material having come to him in the form of uncouth, raucous howls – and with the greatest interest to his attempts at reproducing them orally. They studied his written notes with the most meticulous care. The verdict was unanimous, even emphatic on the part of the younger and more dogmatic philologist. These sounds were quite utterly at variance with, entirely different from, any known speech, including Sanskrit, Indo-Iranian and even the conjectural Akkadian and Sumerian spoken tongues. The transcribed syllables corresponded to nothing in any known language, ancient or modern. Emphatically they were not Japanese.

The three professors took their departure, the younger philologist showing almost plainly his opinion that Meredith was either slightly demented or trying to put something over on him!

Meredith and the psychiatrist Dr Cowlington went over the list again after the experts had taken their departure. They had to agree that the words heard were probably unique in the history of human speech.

Meredith had written: 'Iï, Iï, Iï, Iï – R'ly-eh! – Ieh nya – Ieh nya – Zoh, zoh-an-nuh!' These strange words and various others quite as uncouth occurred mostly as monosyllabic exclamations. There was only one grouping of the words which formed anything like a section of continuous speech, or sentence, and which Meredith had been able to capture more or less intact and write down – 'Ióth, Ióth – Natcal-o, do yan kho thút-thut.'

There were many other cries and, as he believed, desperately uttered prayers quite as strange and off the beaten tracks of recognized human speech as those noted down.

It was quite possibly because of his concentration on this affair of the remembered words – his own interest in them being naturally enhanced by Dr Cowlington's and that of the three experts – that Meredith's dream-state impressions just at this time, and suddenly, became markedly acute. These dreams had been continuous and consecutive since their beginning several nights before, but on this night after the rather elaborate investigation of the words and syllables, Meredith began in earnest, so to speak, upon getting the affair of his environment in the strange city of the flames and conflicts and confusion and of a roaring ocean, cleared up with a startling abruptness. His dream impression that night was so utterly vivid; so acutely identical with the terms of the waking state; so entirely free of the blurred penumbras which accompany nightmares, as to cause him suddenly to feel the cold sweat running down his back when he paused on the way to his shower-bath, in the middle of his bedroom floor, confronted without warning with the unexpected question which sprang into his mind: 'Which of these two is my real life!!!'

Everything that he had derived mentally out of that night's sleep was clearly and definitely present in his mind. It seemed to him precisely as though he had not been asleep; that he had not emerged from an ordinary night's rest into the accustomed circumstances of an early morning's awakening. It was, rather, as though he had very abruptly passed out of one quite definite life into another; as though, as it came to him afterwards, he had walked out of a theatre (where his interest in a scene being enacted had so thoroughly absorbed his attention as to identify him with it as an active participant), into the wholly unrelated after-theatre life of Times Square.

One of the radical phases of this situation was not only that the succession of dream experiences had been continuous, with time-allowances for the intervening periods of those days-in-between which he had spent here in Dr Cowlington's quiet house; not only that, extraordinary as this realization seemed to him. The nearly consecutive dream experiences *had been the events of the past few days in a life of thirty-two years*, spent in that same environment and civilization of which the cataclysmic conditions which he had been envisaging appeared to presage a direful end.

He was, to set out plainly what he had brought out of that last night's dream-experience, one Bothon, general of the military forces of the great district of Ludekta, the south-westerly provincial division of the continent of Atlantis, which had been colonized, as every Atlantean school child was well aware, some eighteen hundred years before by a series of emigrations from the mother continent. The Naacal language – with minor variations not unlike the differences between American speech and 'English English' – was the common language of both continents. From his native Ludekta the General Bothon had made several voyages to the mother land. The first of these had been to Ghua, the central eastern province, a kind of grand tour made just after his finishing, at the age of twenty-two, his professional course in the Ludekta College of Military Training. He was thus familiar by experience, as were many other cultivated Atlanteans of the upper classes, with the very highly developed civilization of the mother continent. These cultural contacts had been aided by his second visit, and further enhanced not long before the present period of the dream-experiences when, at the age of thirty-one, Bothon, already of the rank of general, had been sent out as Ambassador to Aglad-Dho, joint capital of the confederated south-eastern provinces of

Yish, Knan, and Buathon, one of the most strategic diplomatic posts and the second most important provincial confederation of the mother continent.

He had served in his ambassadorial capacity for only four months, and then had been abruptly recalled without explanation, but, as he had soon discovered upon his arrival home, because of the privately communicated request of the Emperor himself. His diplomatic superiors at home offered him no censure. Such Imperial requests were not unknown. These gentlemen were, actually, quite unaware of the reasons behind the Imperial request. No explanations had been given them, but there had been no Imperial censure of any kind.

But the General, Bothon, knew the reasons very well, although he kept them strictly to himself. There was, indeed, only one reason, as he was acutely and very well aware.

The requirements of his office had taken him rather frequently to Alu, the continental capital, metropolis of the civilized world.

Here in the great city of Alu were assembled from all known parts of the terrestrial globe the world's diplomats, artists, philosophers, traders and ship-masters. Here in the great ware-houses of solid stone and along the innumerable wharves were piled the world's goods – fabrics and perfumes; strange animals for the delectation of the untravelled curious. Here in the endless stalls and markets were dyed stuffs and silks; tubas and cymbals and musical rattles and lyres; choice woods and implements for the toilet – strigils, and curiously carved hand-fitting little blocks of soap-stone, and oils innumerable for the freshening of beards and the anointing of bodies. Here were tunics and sandals and belts and thongs of soft-tanned, variously perfumed leathers. Here were displayed carved and cunningly wrought pieces of household furniture – glowing, burnished wall-mirrors of copper and tin and steel, bedsteads of an infinite range and design, cushions of swans' feathers, tables of plain and polished artizanship and of intarsia with metal scrolls set flush to their levels; marquetry work of contrasting woods – chairs and stools and cupboards and chests and foot-rests. Here were ornaments innumerable – fire-screens, and spindles for parchment-rolls, and tongs, and shades for lamps made of the scraped skins of animals; metal lamps of every design, and vegetable oils for the lamps in earthenware jars of many sizes and shapes. Here were foods and wines and dried fruits, and honey of many flavors; grains and dried meats and loaves of barley and wheat-meal past computation. Here in the great street of the armorers were maces and axes and swords and daggers of all the world's varieties and designs; armor of plate and chain – hauberks, and greaves, and bassinets, and shelves with rows and rows of the heavy plate and helmets standardized for the use of such fighting men as Bothon himself commanded in their thousands.

Here were to be seen and examined costly canopies and the elaborate litters in which the slaves of the rich carried their masters through the narrow streets and broad, airy avenues of Alu. Rugs there were in an endless profusion of size and shape and design; rugs from distant Lemuria and from Atlantis and from tropical Antillea, and from the mountainous interior regions of the mother continent itself, where thousands of cunning weavers of fabrics worked at their looms; ordinary rugs of pressed felt, and gorgeous glowing rugs of silk from the southern regions where the mulberry trees grew; rugs, too, and thin, soft draperies of complex patterns made of the wool of lambs and of the long, silk-like hair of the mountain sheep.

Here in Alu, center of the world's culture, were philosophers with their groups of disciples, small or great, propounding their systems on the corners of streets and in the public squares, wrangling incessantly over the end of man, and the greatest good, and the origin of material things. Here were vast libraries containing the essence of all that had been written down concerning science and religion and engineering and the innumerable fine arts, of the civilization of forty thousand years. Here were the temples of religion where the hierarchs propounded the principles of life, colleges of priests studying incessantly more and more deeply into the mysteries of the four principles; teaching the people the endless applications of these esoteric affairs to their conduct and daily lives.

Into this fascinating treasure house of a great civilization the ambassador Bothon had penetrated as often as possible. The excellence of his family background, his own character and personal qualities, and his official position, all combined to make him a welcome guest in the mansions of the members of the emperor's court and of the highest stratum of social life in Alu.

An impressionable young man, most of whose life previous to his appointment as ambassador had been spent in hard training for his military duties and in the rigorous prosecution of those as he rose rapidly grade by grade by hard man's work in camp and field during his many campaigns in the standing army of Ludekta, the general, Bothon, revelled in these many high social contacts. Very soon he found within himself and growing apace, the strong and indeed natural desire for a type of life to which his backgrounds and achievements had amply entitled him, but of which he had been, so far, deprived because of the well-nigh incessant demands upon him of his almost continuous military service.

In short, the ambassador from Ludekta very greatly came to desire marriage, with some lady of his own caste, and, preferably, of this metropolitan city of Alu with its sophistication and wide culture; a lady who might preside graciously over his ambassadorial establishment; who, when his term of office was concluded, would return with him to his native Ludekta in Atlantis, there permanently to grace the fine residence he had in his mind's eye when, a little later, he should retire from the Ludektan army and settle down as a senator into the type of life which he envisaged for his middle years.

He had been both fortunate and unfortunate in his actual falling in love. The lady, who reciprocated his ardent advances, was the Netvissa Ledda, a daughter of the Netvis Toldon who was the emperor's brother. The fortunate aspect of this intense and sudden love affair which set all social Alu to commenting upon it, was the altogether human one of a virtually perfect compatability between the two. Their initial mutual attraction had become a settled regard for each other almost overnight. Within a few days thereafter they were very deeply in love. Humanly considered, the affair was perfection itself. Every circumstance save one, and that a merely artificial side of the case, gave promise of an ideal union.

The single difficulty in the way of this marriage was, however, most unfortunately, an insuperable one. The Netvissa Ledda, niece of the emperor, belonged of right to the very highest social caste of the empire. The rank and degree of Netvis lay next to Royalty itself and in the case of the family of the Netvis Toldon partook of royalty. Against this fact, basic in the structure of the empire's long-established custom, the Ambassador, General Bothon of Ludekta – although a gentleman of the very highest attainments, character, and worth, whose family records reached back a thousand years into the dim past before the colonization of Atlantis, whose reputation was second to none in the empire – the General, Bothon, was a commoner. As such, according to the rigid system prevalent at the court in Alu, capital of the Empire, he was hopelessly ineligible. The marriage was simply out of the question.

The Emperor, being called upon to settle this awkward affair, acted summarily, quite in the spirit of one who destroys a hopelessly wounded and suffering creature as an act of mercy. The Emperor took the one course open to him under these circumstances, and the General, Bothon, without any choice being open to him save submission to an Imperial request which had the force of law, took ship for Ludekta, leaving behind him in Alu the highest and dearest hope of his life, irreparably shattered.

For the subsequent conduct of the General Bothon, recently Ludektan Ambassador to Aglad-Dho, there were three very definite contributing reasons. Of these the first and most prominent was the depth and intensity and genuineness of his love for the Netvissa Ledda. Beyond all possible things, he wanted her; and the proud soul of Bothon was very grievously racked and torn at the sudden unexpected and arbitrary separation from her which the Imperial request had brought about.

The voyage from Aglad-Dho to Ludekta, across the two sections of the globe's great oceans and through the ship canals and lakes which bisected the southern continent of the western hemisphere, occupied seven weeks. During this period of enforced inaction the bitter chagrin and deep disappointment of Bothon crystallized itself by means of the sustained reflection inevitable under the circumstances. General Bothon arrived in Ludekta in a state of mind which made him ready for anything, provided only it was action. This state of mind was the second of these contributory factors.

The third was the immediate satisfaction of his desire for activity. During the course of his voyage home the ghoulish and, indeed, subhuman factory slaves, the shockingly Simian Gyaa-Hua, had inaugurated a revolt. This had spread, by the time of Bothon's arrival, throughout the entire province of Ludekta. The state sorely needed the efficient services of this, the youngest and most brilliant of its generals, and his reception on landing was more nearly that of a savior of his country than what a virtually disgraced diplomat might expect.

Into this campaign, which he prosecuted with the utmost rigor and a thoroughgoing military effectiveness, Bothon threw himself with an abounding energy which even his most ardent Ludektan admirers had not anticipated. At the end of an intensive campaign of less than three weeks, with this very dangerous revolt completely crushed and the leaders of the Gyaa-Hua to a man hanging by great hooks through their neck muscles in dreadful rows along the outer city walls on either side of the great archway that pierced the defense of Ludekta's capital, the General Bothon found himself the hero of

Ludekta and the idol of his admiring troops. A rigid disciplinarian, the attitude of the officers and men of the Ludektan standing army towards this general had hitherto been based upon the respect which his great abilities had always commanded. Now he found himself the recipient of something almost like worship because of this last brilliant campaign of his. It had been a *tour de force*.

Although it is highly probable that they would have advanced him because of this achievement in any event, the actual occasion for the action of the Ludektan Senate in rewarding Bothon with the supreme command of the standing army was the speech before that body of the aging generalissimo Tarba. Old Tarba ended his notable panegyric by laying his truncheon, emblem of the supreme command, on the great marble slab before the presiding senator, with a dramatic gesture.

Bothon thus found himself suddenly possessed of that intensive hero worship which would cause the state to acquiesce in anything which its object might suggest. He was, at the same time, in supreme command of the largest sectional standing army of the entire continent of Atlantis; an army, thanks chiefly to his own efficiency, probably the best trained and most effective fighting unit then extant.

Under the combined effect of the contributing causes and his new authority General Bothon made up his mind. On the eleventh day after his triumphal entry into Ludekta's capital city forty-seven Ludektan war vessels freshly outfitted, their oar-slaves supplemented by a reserve of the Gyaa-Hua, selected for the power and endurance of their gorilla-like bodies, with new skin sails throughout the fleet, and the flower of the Ludektan army on board, sailed out from Ludekta westward for Alu under the command of the General Bothon.

It was precisely simultaneous with the arrival of this war fleet off the shores of the great city of Alu that there began unprecedented natural disturbances affecting the entire area of the mother continent. These were comparable to nothing recorded in the capital's carefully kept slate and parchment records, which went back over a period of thousands of years.

The first presage of these impending calamities took the form of a coppery tinge which replaced the blue of the sky. Without any premonitory warnings the long ground-swell of this Western Ocean changed abruptly, along with the color of the water, into a kind of dull brick-grey, to short, choppy, spray-capped waves. These tossed even the great Ludektan war galleys so violently as to shatter many of the sweeps. The wind, to the consternation of several of Bothon's captains, appeared to come from every quarter at once! It tore the heavy skin sails of the Ludektan galleys away from their copper rings and bolts in some cases. In others it split the sails in clean straight lines as though they had been slit with sharp knives.

Undaunted by these manifestations and the reports of his augurs who had cast their lots and slain their sheep and fowls in a hasty series of divinations to account, if possible, for this unfavorable reception at the hands of the elements, the indomitable will of Bothon forced his fleet to an orderly landing. He sent forthwith as his herald to the Emperor himself, his highest ranking sub-general, accompanied by an imposing guard of honor. On slate tablets Bothon had set forth his demand in his own hand. This was in the form of a set of alternatives. The emperor was asked to receive him as Generalissimo of the military forces of Ludekta, and to consent to his immediate marriage with the Netvissa Ledda; or, he, Bothon, would proceed forthwith to the siege of Alu and take the lady of his heart by force and arms.

The message prayed the Emperor to elect the first alternative. It also set forth briefly and in formal heraldic terms the status of the ancient family of Bothon.

The Emperor had been very seriously annoyed at this challenge, as he chose to regard it. He felt that his office and dignity had been outraged. He crucified Bothon's entire delegation.

The siege of Alu began forthwith under that menacing copper-tinted sky and to the accompaniment of a rumbling series of little earthquakes.

Not only not within the memory of living men, but, as the records indicated, during its entire history over thousands of years as the metropolis of the civilized world, had there been any previous hostile manifestations against the great city of Alu. That anything like this terrible campaign which the renowned General Bothon of Ludekta set in motion against her might come to pass, had never even remotely occurred to anyone in Alu. So promptly did Bothon launch his attack that the tortured bodies of the members of his delegation to the Emperor had not yet ceased writhing on their row of crosses before he had penetrated, at the head of his trained legionaries, to a point within two squares of the Imperial Palace which stood at the center of the great city.

There had been virtually no resistance. This intensive campaign would have been triumphantly concluded within twenty minutes, the Emperor probably captured along with all his Palace guards and household, the person of the Lady Ledda secured by this ardent lover of hers, and the entire objective of the expedition accomplished, save for what in modern legal phraseology would have been described as 'An Act of God'.

The premonitory earth-shakings which had accompanied this armed invasion culminated, at that point in the advance of Bothon's army, in a terrific seismic cataclysm. The stone-paved streets opened in great gaping fissures. Massive buildings crashed tumultuously all about and upon the triumphantly advancing Ludektans. The General, Bothon, at the head of his troops, dazed and deafened and hurled violently upon the ground, retained consciousness long enough to see three quarters of his devoted following engulfed, smashed, torn to fragments, crushed into unrecognizable heaps of bloody pulp; and this holocaust swiftly and mercifully obliterated from before his failing vision by the drifting dust from millions of tons of crumbled masonry.

He awakened in the innermost keep of the dungeon in Alu's citadel.

Coming quietly into Meredith's bedroom about ten o'clock in the morning, Dr Cowlington, who had made up his mind overnight on a certain matter, quietly led his initial conversation with his observation-patient around to the subject which had been most prominent in his mind since their conference of yesterday over the strange linguistic terms which Meredith had noted down.

'It has occurred to me that I might very well tell you about something quite out of the ordinary which came under my notice seven or eight years ago. It happened while I was chief intern in the Connecticut State Hospital for the Insane. I served there for two years under Dr Floyd Haviland before I went into private practice. We had a few private patients in the hospital, and one of these, who was in my particular charge, was a gentleman of middle-age who had come to us because of Haviland's enormous reputation, without commitment. This gentleman, whom I will call "Smith", was neither legally nor actually "insane". His difficulty, which had interfered very seriously with the course of his life and affairs, would ordinarily be classified as "delusions". He was with us for nearly two months. As a voluntary patient of the institution, and being a man of means, he had private rooms. He was in every way normal except for his intensive mental preoccupation with what I have called his delusions. In daily contact with him during this period I became convinced *that Mr Smith was not suffering from anything like a delusive affection of the mind.*

'I diagnosed his difficulty – and Dr Haviland agreed with me – that this patient, Smith, *was suffering mentally from the effects of an ancestral memory.*

'Such a case is so rare as to be virtually unique. The average psychiatrist would go through a lifetime working at his specialty without encountering anything of the sort. There are, however, recorded cases. We were able to send our patient home in a mental condition of almost complete normality. As sometimes occurs in mental cases, his virtual cure was accomplished by making our diagnosis very clear to him – impresssing upon his mind through reiterated and very positive statements that he was in no sense of the word demented, and that his condition, while unusual, was not outside the range and limitations of complete normality.'

'It must have been a very interesting case,' said Meredith. His reply was dictated by nothing deeper than a desire to be courteous. For his mind was full of the affairs of the General, Bothon, raging now in his prison-chamber; his mind harried, anxious over the fate of his surviving soldiers; that lurid glare, dimmed by the remoteness of his flame-tinted prison-chamber, in his eyes; his mind tortured and his keen sense of hearing stultified by the sustained, dreadful roaring of that implacable sea. He, Meredith, for reasons far too deep for his own analysis, felt utterly incapable of telling Dr Cowlington what was transpiring in those dreams of his. All his inmost basic instincts were warning him, though subconsciously, that what he might tell now, if he would, could not possibly be believed! Dr Cowlington, looking at his patient, saw a face drawn and lined as though from some devastating mental stress; a deeply introspective expression in the eyes, which professionally speaking, he did not like. The doctor considered a moment before resuming, erect in his chair, his knees crossed, his finger-tips joined in a somewhat judicial attitude.

'Frankly, Meredith, I emphasized the fact that the man I have called Smith was in no sense insane because I feel that I must go farther and tell you that the nature of his apparent "delusions" was, in one striking particular, related to your own case. I did not wish to give you the slightest alarm over the perfect soundness of your own mentality! To put the matter plainly, Mr Smith "remembered", although rather vaguely and dimly, certain phases of those ancestral memories I mentioned, and was able to reproduce a number of the terms of some unknown and apparently prehistoric language. Meredith – ' the doctor turned and looked intensely into the eyes of his now interested patient, ' – *there were three or four of Smith's words identical with yours!*'

'Good God!' exclaimed Meredith, now thoroughly aroused. Then, after a minute's anxious reflection: 'What were the words, Doctor? Did you make notes of them?'

'Yes, I have them here,' answered the psychiatrist, and brought a thin sheaf of papers out of his breast-pocket.

Meredith was out of his chair and leaning eagerly over the doctor's shoulder long before Cowlington had his papers arranged. He gazed with a consuming intensity at the words and phrases carefully typed on several sheets of foolscap; listened, with an almost tremulous attention, while Dr Cowlington carefully reproduced the sounds of these uncouth terms. Then, taking the sheets and resuming his chair, he read through all that had been written down, pronouncing the words, though very quietly, under his breath, his lips barely moving.

He was pale, and shaking from head to foot when he rose at last and handed back, hands trembling, the thin fascicle of papers to its owner. Dr Cowlington looked at him anxiously, his professional mind alert, his fears somewhat aroused over the wisdom of this experiment of his in bringing his former case thus abruptly to his patient's attention. Dr Cowlington felt, if he had cared to put his impression into words, somewhat baffled. He could not, despite his long and careful training in dealing with mental, nervous, and 'borderline' cases, quite put his acute professional finger upon just which one of the known simple and complex emotions was, for this moment, dominating this very interesting patient of his.

Dr Cowlington would have been even more completely puzzled if he had known.

For Meredith, reading through the strange babblings of the patient, Smith, had recognized all the words and terms, and had lit upon the phrase –

'Our beloved Bothon has disappeared.'

Dr Cowlington, sensing accurately that it might be unwise to prolong this particular interview, concluded wisely that Meredith would most readily regain his normal poise and equanimity if left alone to cope with whatever, for the time being, held possession of his mind, rose quietly and walked over to the bedroom door.

He paused there, however, for an instant, before leaving the room, and looked back at the man now introspectively relaxed in a comfortable lounge-chair. Meredith had not, apparently, so much as noted the doctor's movements towards departure. His mind, very obviously, was turned inward. He was, it appeared, entirely oblivious to his surroundings.

And Dr Cowlington, whose professional outward deportment, acquired through years of contact with abnormal people, had not wholly obliterated a kindly disposition, noted with a certain emotion of his own that there were unchecked tears plainly visible in his patient's inward-gazing eyes.

Summoned back to Meredith's room an hour later by one of his house nurses, Dr Cowlington found his patient restored to his accustomed urbane normality.

'I asked you to come up for a moment, Doctor,' began Meredith, 'because I wanted to inquire if there is anything that you would care to give a patient to induce sleep.' Then, with a deprecating smile: 'The only such things I know about are morphine and laudanum! I don't know very much about medicine and naturally you wouldn't want to give me one of those any more than I would want to take it.'

Dr Cowlington resumed his judicial manner. He thought rapidly about this unexpected request. He took into consideration how his story about the patient, Smith, had appeared to upset Meredith. He deliberately refrained from inquiring why Meredith wanted a sleeping potion. Then he nodded his head.

'I use constantly a very simple preparation,' said he; 'it is non-habit-forming; based on a rather dangerous drug, chloral; but, as I use it for my patients, compounded with an aromatic syrup and diluted with half a tumbler of water, it works very well. I will send some up to you at once, and you can take it yourself. Remember, please, four teaspoonfuls of the syrup is the outside dose. Two will probably be enough. Never more than four at any time, and not more than one dose in twenty-four hours.'

Dr Cowlington rose, came over to Meredith, and looked at the place where he had struck the side of his head against the marble wall of his shower-bath. The bruise was still swollen. The doctor passed his fingers lightly over this contusion.

'It's beginning to go down,' he remarked. 'It's just at the posterior edge of the mastoid process of the temporal bone. You're fortunate, I think, that we didn't have to put you through an operation for mastoiditis. A bruise over the network of little laminated bones that are under that spot is always a risk, you know.'

The doctor smiled pleasantly, again nodded his head at Meredith, and started to leave. Meredith stopped him as he was about to go out of the room.

'Yes?' said the doctor inquiringly, as he turned, his hand on the bedroom door-handle.

'I wanted to ask you,' said Meredith – and the acute-minded Cowlington suspected a faint note of diffidence in his patient's tone – 'I wanted to ask you, Doctor, if you would be willing to put me in touch with the man to whom you referred as "Smith".'

The doctor shook his head. 'I'm sorry, Mr Smith died two years ago.'

In ten minutes the house nurse fetched in a small tray. On it was a tumbler, a mixing spoon, and a freshly put up eight-ounce bottle containing a reddish colored, pleasant-tasting syrup.

Twenty minutes later, Meredith, who had compromised on three teaspoons, was deeply asleep on his bed; and the General, Bothon, in the innermost dungeon-chamber of the great citadel of Alu, was standing poised in the center of that dungeon's smooth stone floor, tensed to leap in any direction; while all about him the rending crashes of thousands of tons of the riven and falling masonry of the citadel itself was deafening him against all other sounds except the incessant and indescribably thunderous fury of the now utterly maddened ocean. The lurid glare of the fires from without had been markedly heightened. Detonation after rending detonation came to Bothon's ears at frequent intervals. The Aluans were blowing up this central portion of their great city, as he was able quite easily to guess, in order to check the advance of the terrific conflagration which had raged for days and nights and was utterly beyond control. These detonations seemed actually faint to the alert man in that prison room against the hideous crashing of the sections of the citadel itself, and the well-nigh unbearable sustained roar of the ocean.

Abruptly the crisis for which he had been waiting arrived. The stone flooring beneath his feet buckled and sagged at his right. He whirled about and leaped far in the other direction, pressing himself, hands and arms stretched out above his head, against the wall of the prison-chamber, his heart pounding wildly, his breath coming in great gasps and sobs as the stifling, earthquake-deadened air about him shrank to a sudden and devastating attenuation. Then the solid wall opposite split in a tearing gap from top to bottom; and an even more stifling cloud of fine white dust sifted abruptly through the room as the ceiling was riven asunder.

Stifling, choking, fighting for breath and life, the General, Bothon, lowered his arms and whirled about again in the direction of this thunderous breakage, and groped his way across the now precarious flooring in the faint hope of discovering an avenue of escape. He struggled up a steep mound of *débris* through the grey darkness of the hanging dust where a few seconds before had been a level floor of solid masonry. He groped his way through thicker clouds of the drifting, settling stone-dust, skirted the irregular edges of yawning holes and toiled up and down mounded heaps of rubble, far past the place where the confining wall of his dungeon had stood, onward and forward resolutely towards that vague goal of freedom.

At last, the resources of his mighty body well-nigh spent, himself a solid grey from hair to sandals from the thickly clinging dust, his eyes two tortured red holes, his mouth and throat one searing pain, his heart and lungs well-nigh bursting, the General, Bothon, emerged across the last hill of rubbish which had been the citadel of Alu, and came out upon the corner edge of one of the largest of the city's great public squares.

For the first time in the course of his progress out of that death trap, unscathed save for a long shallow gash where in the darkness he had scraped the upper portion of his right thigh sharply against the rough cutting-edge of a great chunk of granite, but now barely able either to see or breath, Bothon suddenly trod on something soft and yielding. He paused. He could hardly see, and he crouched and felt with his hands, under the thickly mounded dust. It was the body of a man, in chain mail. The General, Bothon, exhaled a painful breath of satisfaction. He rolled the body over, freeing it from the pounds of dust upon it, and slid his hand along the copper-studded leather belt to where a short, heavy, one-handed battle-axe was attached. This he drew from its sheath. Then from the dead man's silken tunic which his hand had encountered he tore off a large section and with this cleansed his eyes and mouth and wiped the sweat-caked dust from his face and arms and hands. Finally he took from the corpse a heavy leathern purse. He sensed that this nook where he had discovered his unknown benefactor was a secluded spot where the dust had concealed the body from looters or the horrible attentions of the ghoulish Gyaa-Hua, mobs of which creatures, freed as he had been from their strict confinement, had added to the city's horrors their bestial chitterings and unspeakable feastings on the bodies of the dead. He lay down for a few moments beside the dead soldier on the soft dust for a brief respite and to rest the tissues of his body and to permit his tear and salivary glands to readjust themselves to their normal functions and so somewhat to relieve the burning torture of his mouth and nose and eyes.

Some ten minutes later he rose to his feet, wiped his lips and the now freely flowing tears from his restored eyes, stretched himself mightily, tested the heavy axe with three or four singing strokes through the clearing air, and dusted out and readjusted his garments, finally tightening a loosened sandal thong. General Bothon, inured to mere physical hardships by the many years of rigid military activity, was his own man again. He stood now free in the center of Alu. He was adequately armed. A great gust of energy surged through him. He oriented himself; then he turned with an instinct as sure as a homing bee's in the direction he had been seeking, and began to march at the unhurrying, space-devouring pace of a Ludektan legionary, straight for the Imperial Palace.

Bothon had thoroughly settled in his mind the answer to a question which, for the first few days of his captivity had puzzled him greatly. Why had he been left alone and undisturbed in that confinement; food and water brought him at regular intervals in accordance with the ordinary routine of the citadel? Why, to put the matter plainly, having been obviously captured by the Emperor's retainers while lying unconscious within two squares of the Imperial Palace, had he not been summarily crucified? His keen trained mind had apprised him that the answer was to be found in the hideous turmoil of the raging sea and in the fearful sounds of a disintegrating city. The Emperor had been too greatly occupied by those cataclysms even to command the punishment of this leader of such an armed attack against the world's metropolis as had not been known in all the long history of the mother continent.

Skirting its enormous outer walls, Bothon came at last to the massive chief entrance-way to the Imperial Palace. This enormous structure, its basic walls eight feet thick, stood massive, magnificent, intact. Without any hesitation he began mounting the many broad steps straight towards the magnificent entrance-gates of copper and gold and porphyry. Before these gates, in a rigid line and under the command of an officer beneath whose corselet appeared the pale blue tunic of the Emperor's household-guards, stood a dozen fully armed soldiers. One of these, at a word from the officer, ran down the steps to turn back this intruder. Bothon slew him with a single crashing stroke and continued to mount the steps. At this a shouted command of the officer sent the entire troop down the steps upon him in close order. Bothon paused, and, waiting until the foremost was no more than the space of two of the broad steps above him, leaped lightly to his right. Then as the foremost four of the soldiers passed beyond him under the impetus of their downward charge, Bothon as lightly leaped back again, his heavy axe fairly singing now as he fell upon the troop's flank with deadly, short, quick-swinging blows. Before they could collect themselves the officer and five of his men lay dead upon the steps. Leaving the demoralized remainder to gather themselves together as best they might, Bothon leaped up the intervening steps and was through the great entrance-doors, and, with a pair of lightning-like right-and-left strokes of his axe, had disposed of the two men-at-arms; stationed just inside the doorway.

His way into the Palace now entirely unobstructed, Bothon sped through well-remembered rooms and along broad corridors into the very heart of the Imperial Palace of Alu.

Traversing the very last of these, that leading to the quarter of the palace occupied by the Netvis Toldon, brother of the Emperor, with his family, it abruptly occurred to Bothon that the deafening intensity of the long-sustained roaring of the ocean and the crashing clamor from the city had lessened. His hearing, after many days of that unspeakable bedlam, had, as he realized, necessarily become adjusted to the incessant impact of the conglomerate thunderings. Might it be breaking down now under the strain of such unwonted continuity? He dismissed that solution as merely improbable. In every respect the terrific complex clamors continued, only there was that general and quite obvious softening in their general effect to be accounted for. Lowered vitality from the wound in his thigh? His long military training had brought that possible solution uppermost. His common-sense dismissed it, together with the problem itself, from his mind. He had something of greater import to tax his energies than troubling his mind over a question of acoustics.

Within thirty seconds he had located the entrance to the Netvis Toldon's apartments, and had passed through the doorway.

He discovered the family reclining about the horseshoe-shaped table in the refectory, for it was the hour of the evening meal. He paused in the refectory doorway, was met with a semicircular row of surprised glances, bowed low to the Netvis Toldon.

'I beseech you to pardon this intrusion, my Lord Netvis. It were inexcusable under other circumstances, at a more favorable time.'

The utterly stultified nobleman returned no answer, only stared in the throes of his paralysis of surprise. Then, the dear lady of his heart, the Netvissa Ledda, rose to her feet from her place at her father's table, her eyes wide with wonderment, and a dawning realization of what this strange invasion might mean, her lovely face suddenly of the hue of the Aluan roses. She looked at this heroically formed lover of hers, her whole soul in her eyes.

'Come, my Lady Ledda!' said Bothon quickly, and as lightly as a deer the Netvissa Ledda ran to him.

He took her arm, very quietly, and, before the assembled members of the family of Toldon had recovered from their utter stupefaction, the two were hastening along the corridor towards the palace entrance.

From around the first corner before them came then abrupt sounds of armed men, hastening, the authoritative voices of military commands. They paused, listening, and Bothon shifted his axe into his right hand and stepped before the Lady Ledda to meet whatever force might come into sight within the instant.

But the Netvissa Ledda laid firm hands upon his left arm. 'This way, swiftly!' she whispered, and led him down a narrow passage-way at the wide corridor's left. This they traversed in haste, and had barely negotiated a sharp turn when they heard the guard-troop rush along the main corridor, and a voice, insistent, commanding: 'To the apartment of my Lord, the Netvis Toldon!'

The narrow passage-way led them past cook-rooms and scullery-chambers, and ended at a small door which opened upon a narrow court. Rapidly traversing this, they emerged upon a square at the west side of the palace, and well before any pursuit could have traced their course, were indistinguishable among the vast concourse of the people who thronged the wide avenues of Alu.

Bothon now resumed the direction of their course of escape, with a few low and hurried words of thanks to his companion for her timely guidance out of the palace to the freedom of the streets. Leading the way across a larger adjacent square, he reached the secluded corner, mounded about with *débris*, where he had secured his weapon. It was not yet past the early dusk of a mid-summer evening, and now there was nothing to interfere with his keen vision.

Yes, it was as he had guessed from the quality of that torn fragment of silken tunic with which he had wiped his tortured eyes free of the stone-dust. The dead man was an officer of one of the Imperial Legions.

Seating the Lady Ledda upon a block of granite and requesting her to watch for any intrusion on their comparative privacy, Bothon knelt swiftly beside the dead body and busied himself upon it energetically with his two large and capable hands.

At the end of two intensive minutes the Netvissa Ledda looked up at his light summoning touch upon her shoulder to see her lover for whom she had unhesitatingly abandoned all else that life held dear to her, apparelled from head to foot in the uniform, armor, and accoutrements of an Elton of the Imperial Legion of the Hawk.

Then they hurried southward, side by side, across the great square with its desolation of shattered buildings, towards one of the few remaining residences of the rich before which four coal-black slaves in the livery of their household were lowering an ornamental litter to the ground.

From the luxurious vehicle, as they arrived beside it, there emerged a stout citizen who stared at them enquiringly, his initial obvious fear of molestation disappearing at his recognition of the Emperor's niece and the uniform of an Imperial Legion.

'We request the loan of your litter, my Lord,' said Bothon.

'Most willingly,' returned the citizen, smirking and flattered at this form of address.

Bothon expressed hearty thanks, handed his companion into the litter, distributed a handful of silver among the four slaves, and gave the destination to the Negro who stood beside the forward left-hand pole. Then he climbed in himself and drew the red silk curtains together.

The strong litter-poles strained and creaked as the load was hoisted to four brawny shoulders, and then the litter swung away from the residence of its still bowing and smirking owner towards the military enclosure which housed and guarded the flying-vessels of the Aluvian standing army.

'You may have observed how very completely I have entrusted my Imperial person to you,' remarked the Netvissa Ledda, smiling. She was very well aware of the reasons for the Imperial request which had sent Bothon back to Ludekta, and for the first armed invasion against the Aluvian metropolis. 'I have not so much as enquired our destination!'

'It is my intention to seek safety to the northwest,' answered Bothon gravely. 'I have become convinced, I may say to you plainly, my beloved, that the prediction of Bal, Lord of Fields, as to the destruction of the Mother Continent, is not a mere classic to be learned, as we learned it in our childhood, as a formal exercise in rhetoric. Here, all about us, is the evidence. More, my four augurs warned me of the continent's danger ere I brought my war-galleys up upon the beaches of Alu. The four great forces, they insisted, were in collusion to that end. Do we not see and hear them at their work? Fire raging through the land; earth shaking mightily; winds such as never were encountered hitherto upon the planet, else the old records lie! Water, the commotion of which surpasses all experience – is it not so, my beloved? Am I not constrained to speak thus to be heard amidst this hellish tumult?'

The Lady Ledda nodded, grave now in her turn.

'There are many deafened in the palace,' she remarked. 'Where are we to go for refuge?'

'We depart straight this night, for the great mountains of 'A-Wah-Ii,' answered Bothon, 'if so be the four great forces allow us possession of a war-chariot. And, to that end, your ring, my beloved.'

The Lady Ledda nodded again, understandingly, and removed from the middle finger of her right hand the ring of the two suns and the eight-pointed star which, as a member of the Royal Family, she was entitled to wear. Bothon received it, and slipped it upon the little finger of his right hand.

The sentinel on guard before the barracks of the officer commanding the military enclosure of the Aluvian supply-barracks saluted the commanding-looking Elton of the Legion of the Hawk who stepped down from the gorgeously ornamented litter at the entrance to that military residence. The Elton addressed him in formal military phrases. It was evident to the sentinel that this officer was here on official duty.

'Report at once to the Ka-Kalbo Netro, the arrival of the Elton Barko of the Legion of the Hawk, conveying a member of the Imperial household into exile. I am requisitioning one battle-chariot of capacity for two persons, and officer's rations sufficient for fourteen days, together with the medicinal supply for a full kit-va of men. My authority, the Imperial Signet. Behold!'

The sentinel saluted the sun-and-star ring of the Emperor, repeated his orders like an efficient automaton, saluted the Elton of the Hawk Legion, and departed at the double to fetch the commandant, the Ka-Kalbo Netro.

The Ka-Kalbo arrived promptly in answer to this summons. He saluted the Imperial Signet, and, as a Ka-Kalbo outranked an Elton by one full grade, was punctiliously saluted according to military usage by the Elton Barko of the Legion of the Hawk, an officer whose personal acquaintance he had not previously made. Within ten minutes the Netvissa Ledda had been ceremoniously carried to and placed upon her seat in the commandeered battle-chariot, and the Elton Barko had taken his place beside her. Then, the dozen sweating mechanicians who had carried out their commandant's orders in record time, standing in a stiff, saluting row, the battle-chariot started off at a stiff gallop, the driver standing and plying his long thong with loud, snapping reports over the horses' backs, while at the great chariot's rear the spare-horse leader whistled continuously to the four relay animals which galloped behind. The empty litter, its bearers freshly rewarded with another heaping handful of coins by this generous officer, swung swiftly through the dust-heaped streets and square towards its owner's residence.

The heights of 'A-Wah-Ii, to the northwest, gave some promise, in Bothon's opinion, of security from the anciently predicted submersion of the continent. Those towering mountains would, at least, be among the last sections to sink, should the gas belts, hypothecated by the scientists of the mother continent, explode, and remove the underseas support of this great land of the globe's most ancient and noble civilization.

Shortly after daybreak, and accurately, according to the map and careful explanations of the painstaking Ka-Kalbo Netro, the chariot paused in the centre of a great level table-land one quarter of the way to his destination. The country hereabouts was utterly uninhabited. They were relatively safe here in a region only lightly visited by the earthquakes, and not at all by fires. The roar of the north wind troubled the Netvissa Ledda severely. Bothon barely noticed it. He was now convinced that he was losing his sense of hearing.

They ate and slept and resumed their journey at noon after a re-adjustment of the provisions and a change of the now rested animals.

Their four days' journey steadily northwest was uneventful. The charioteer drove onward steadily. On the fourth day, as the coppery ball which was the smoking sun reached and touched a flat horizon, they caught their first view of the lofty summits of the 'A-Wah-Ii region, goal of a possible immunity.

Dr Cowlington, an anxious look in his face, was standing beside Meredith's bed when he awakened in the middle morning. He had slept twenty hours. However, what the doctor thought of as his patient's 'mental condition' was so entirely normal, and his cheerfulness so pronounced after his protracted sleep, that Dr Cowlington was reassured, and changed his mind about removing the bottle of sleeping medicine. Plainly it had had an excellent effect on Meredith.

Stretched out in his usual quiet-inducing attitude on the davenport just before lunch, Meredith suddenly ceased reading and laid down his magazine. It had occurred to him that he had 'heard' none of the turmoil of Alu during that waking period. He sat up, puzzled. Bothon, he remembered, had been hearing the sounds about him only dimly, a strange, perhaps a significant, coincidence.

He felt the bruise behind his right ear. It was no longer even slightly painful to the touch. He pressed his finger-tips firmly against the place. The contusion was now barely perceptible to the sense of touch.

He reported the apparent loss of what the ear-specialist Gatefield had named his 'clairaudience' to Dr Cowlington after lunch.

'Your bruise is going down,' said the doctor significantly. He examined the posterior edge of Meredith's right temporal area.

'I thought so,' remarked the doctor, nodding. 'Your secondary "hearing" began with that injury to your head. As it goes down, some obscure stimulation of the auditory apparatus, which accounts for your ability to "hear" those sounds, diminishes accordingly. You could probably "hear" only some stupendous sound from "there" now. And in a day or so I predict that you will be "hearing" nothing more, and then you can go home!'

And, within an hour came the 'stupendous sound' in very truth. It broke in upon Meredith's quiet reading once more as though someone had opened that sound-proof door.

A curious, secondary mental vision accompanied it. It was as though Meredith, in his own proper person, yet through the strange connection of his personality with the General, Bothon, stood on the heights of Tharan-Yud, overlooking the stricken city of Alu. The utter fury of mountainous waves accompanied the now titanic rumblings of malignant earth, the wholesale crashing of the cyclopean masonry of Alu as the vast city crumbled and melted beneath his horrified eyes. With these hellish horrors went the wild roaring of ravaging flame, and the despairing, hysterical cacophony of Alu's doomed millions.

Then there came, at last, a sound as of the veritable yawning of the nethermost watery gulf of earth, and the high sun itself was blotted out by a monstrous green wall of advancing death. The sea rose up and fell upon accursed Alu, drowning forever the shrieks of utter despair, the piping and chittering of the obscurely gnawing Gyaa-Hua distracted at last from their loathsome banquet – hissings, roarings, shriekings, whinings, tearings, seethings – a cacophony more than human ears might bear, a sight of utter devastation more onerous than man might look upon, and live.

There came to Meredith a merciful stupor, as the waters of Mu-ladon closed in forever over the mother continent, and as his consciousness failed him, he emerged once more out of that quiet bedroom – away from his overlooking of the world's major catastrophe, and as Bothon, walked beside the Lady Ledda along a wooded ravine in 'A-Wah-Ii, goal of safety, among laden fruit trees, yet not, it seemed, upon the towering heights of those noble mountains but upon an *island* about the shores of which rolled and roared a brown and viscid ocean choked with the mud which had been the soil of the mother continent.

'We are safe here, it would appear, my Bothon,' said the Netvissa Ledda. 'Let us lie down and sleep, for I am very weary.'

And after watching for a little space while the Lady Ledda reclined and slept, Bothon lay down beside her and fell at once into the deep and dreamless slumber of utter physical exhaustion.

Meredith awakened on his davenport. The room was dark, and when he had risen, switched on the lights and looked at his watch, he found that it was four o'clock in the morning. He undressed and went to bed and awakened three hours later without having dreamed.

A world and an era had come to its cataclysmic end, and he had been witness of it.

The contusion on his head had disappeared, Dr Cowlington observed later in the morning.

'I think you can go home now,' said the doctor, in his judicial manner. 'By the way, Meredith, what, if anything, was the name of that "mother continent" of yours?'

'We called it Mu,' said Meredith.

The doctor was silent for a while; then he nodded his head. He had made up his mind. 'I thought so,' said he, gravely.

'Why?' asked Meredith, intrigued.

'Because "Smith" called it that,' replied the doctor.

Meredith returned home that afternoon, his mind at rest. He has had no recurrence of his 'clairaudience'; there has been no resumption of the vivid, life-like dreams.

And he is, probably, since 'Smith' is dead, the only person who knows, at first-hand, of the existence and of the high civilization, and of the utter ultimate destruction of that vast continent of the Pacific, mother of all the world's subsequent civilizations, whose traces are manifold, whose very physical fragments survive in fair Hawaii, through whose fruited ravines walked Bothon and the Lady Ledda; in eikon-shadowed Easter Island; in Megalithic Ponape, brooding cryptically under the drenching Polynesian sunlight. There, from the midst of that indigo sea twenty millennia in the past, departed mighty Mu, which colonized the world and ruled imperially from Alu the Great City, until the four great forces conspired to end her glory in cataclysmic doom.

The Great Circle

The transition from those hours-on-end of looking down on the dark-green jungle of virgin forest was startling in its abruptness. We had observed this one break in the monotonous terrain, of course, well before we were directly over it. Then Wilkes, the pilot, slowed and began to circle. I think he felt it, the element I have referred to as startling; for, even from the first – before we landed, I mean – there was something – an atmosphere – of strangeness about this vast circular space entirely bare of trees with the exception of the giant which crowned the very slight elevation at its exact center.

I know at any rate that I felt it; and Dr Pelletier told me afterward that it had seemed to lay hold on him like a quite definite physical sensation. Wilkes did not circle very long. There was no need for it and I think he continued the process, as though looking for a landing place, as long as he did, on account of that eeriness rather than because of any necessity for prolonged observation.

At last, almost, I thought, as though reluctantly, he shut off his engine – 'cut his gun' as airmen express it – and brought the plane down to an easy landing on the level greensward within a hundred yards of the great tree standing there in its majestic, lonely grandeur. The great circular space about it was like a billiard table, like an English deer park. The great tree looked, too, for all the world like an ash, itself an anomaly here in the uncharted wilderness of Quintana Roo.

We sat there in the plane and looked about us. On every side, for a radius of more than half a mile from the center where we were, the level grassy plain stretched away in every direction and down an almost imperceptible gradual slope to the horizon of dense forest which encircled it.

There was not a breath of air stirring. No blade of the fine short grass moved. The tree, dominating everything, its foliage equally motionless, drew our gaze. We all looked at it at the same time. It was Wilkes the pilot who spoke first, his outstretched arm indicating the tree.

'Might be a thousand years old!' said Wilkes, in a hushed voice. There was something about this place which made all of us, I think, lower our voices.

'Or even two thousand,' remarked Pelletier.

We had taken off that morning at ten from Belize. It was now one o'clock in the afternoon. We had flown due north for the first eighty miles or so, first over the blue waters of landlocked Chetumal Bay, leaving Ambergris Cay on our right, and then Xkalok, the south-eastern point of Quintana Roo; then over dry land, leaving the constricted northern point of the bay behind where parallel 19, north latitude, crosses the 88th meridian of longitude. Thence still due north until we had turned west at Santa Cruz de Bravo, and continued in that direction, glimpsing the hard, metallic luster of the noon sun on Lake China-haucanab, and then, veering south-west in the direction of Xkanba and skirting a tremendous wooden plateau on our left, we had been attracted, after cursory, down-looking views of innumerable architectural remains among the dense forestation, to our landing place by the abrupt conspicuousness of its treeless circularity.

That summarizes the geography of our flight. Our object, the general interest of the outlook rather than anything definitely scientific, was occasioned by Pelletier's vacation, as per the regulations of the U. S. Navy, of whose Medical Corps he is one of the chief ornaments, from his duties as Chief of the Naval Hospital in St Thomas, Virgin Islands. Pelletier wanted to get over to Central America for this vacation. He talked it over with me several times on the cool gallery of my house on Denmark Hill. Almost incidentally he asked me to accompany him. I think he knew that I would come along.

We started, through San Juan, Porto Rico, in which great port we found accommodation in the Bull Line's *Catherine* with our friend Captain Rumberg, who is a Finn, as far as Santo Domingo City. From there we trekked, across the lofty intervening mountains, with a guide and pack burros, into Haiti. At Port au Prince we secured accommodations as the sole passengers on a tramp going to Belize in British Honduras, which made only one stop, at Kingston, Jamaica.

It was between Kingston and Belize that the idea of this air voyage occurred to Pelletier. The idea of looking down comfortably upon the Maya remains, those cities buried in impenetrable jungles, grew upon him and he waxed eloquent out of what proved an encyclopedic fund of knowledge of Maya history. I learned more about these antiquities than I had acquired in my entire life previously! One aspect of that rather mysterious history, it seemed, had intrigued Pelletier. This was the abrupt and unaccountable disappearance of what he called the earliest of major civilizations. The superior race which had built the innumerable temples, palaces and other elaborate and ornate structures now slowly decaying in the jungles of the Yucatan Peninsula, had been, apparently, wiped out in a very brief period. They had, it seemed, merely disappeared. Science, said Pelletier, had been unable to account for this catastrophe. I had, of course, read of it before, but Pelletier's enthusiasm made it vastly intriguing.

Our two-men-and-hired-pilot expedition into this unexplored region of vast architectural ruins and endless forestation had landed, as though by the merest chance, here in a section presenting topographical features such as no previous explorers had reported upon! We were, perhaps, two hours by air, from Belize and civilization – two months, at least, had we been traveling afoot through the thick jungles, however well equipped with food, guides, and the machetes which all previous adventurers into the Yucatan jungles report as the first essential for such travel.

Pelletier, with those small verbal creakings and gruntings which invariably punctuate the shifting of position in his case, was the first to move. He heaved his ungainly bulk laboriously out of the plane and stood on the grassy level ground looking up at Wilkes and me. The sun beat down pitilessly on the three of us. His first remark was entirely practical.

'Let's get into the shade of that tree, and eat,' said Dr Pelletier.

Ten minutes later we had the lunch basket unpacked, the lunch spread out, and were starting to eat, there in the heart of Quintana Roo. And, to all appearances, we might have been sitting down picnicking in Kent, or Connecticut!

I remember, with a vivid clarity which is burned indelibly into my mind, Wilkes reaching for a tongue sandwich, when the wind came.

Abruptly, without any warning, it came, a sudden, violent gust out of nowhere, like an unexpected blow from behind, upsetting our peaceful little session there, sociably, on the grass in the quiet shade of the ancient tree which looked like an English ash. It shredded to filaments the paper napkin I was holding. It caused the squat mustard bottle to land twenty feet away. It sucked dry the brine out of the saucerful of stuffed olives. It sent Pelletier lumbering after a rapidly rolling pith sun helmet. And it carried the pilot Wilkes's somewhat soiled and grimy Shantung silk jacket – which he had doubled up and was using to sit on, and had released by virtue of half rising to reach for that tongue sandwich – and blew it, fluttering, folding and unfolding, arms now stiffly extended, now rolled up into a close ball, up, off the ground, and then, in a curve upward and flattened out and into the tree's lower branches, and then straight up among these, out of our sight.

Having accomplished all these things, and scattered items of lunch broadcast, the sudden wind died a natural death, and everything was precisely as it had been before, save for the disorganization of our lunch – and save, too, for us!

I will not attempt to depart from the strict truth: we were, all of us, quite definitely startled. Wilkes swore picturesquely at the disappearance of his jacket, and continued to reach, with a kind of baffled ineptitude which was quite definitely comic, after the now scattered tongue sandwiches. Pelletier, returning with the rescued sun helmet, wore a vastly puzzled expression on his heavy face, much like an injured child who does not know quite what has happened to him. As for me, I dare say I presented an equally absurd appearance. That gust had caught me as I was pouring limeade from a quart thermos into three of those half-pint paper cups which are so difficult to manage as soon as filled. I found myself now gazing ruefully at the plate of cold sliced ham, inundated with the cup's contents.

Pelletier sat down again in the place he had vacated a moment before, turned to me, and remarked: 'Now where did *that* come from?'

I shook my head. I had no answer to that. I was wondering myself. It was Wilkes who answered, Wilkes goaded to a high pitch of annoyance over the jacket, Wilkes unaware of the singular appropriateness of his reply.

'Right out of the corner of hell!' said Wilkes, rather sourly, as he rose to walk over to that enormous trunk and to look up into the branches, seeking vainly for some glimpse of Shantung silk with motor grease on it.

'Hm!' remarked Pelletier, as he bit, reflectively, into one of the sandwiches. I said nothing. I was trying at the moment to divide what was left of the cold limeade evenly among three half-pint paper cups.

It was nearly a full hour later, after we had eaten heartily and cleared up the remains of the lunch, and smoked, that Wilkes prepared to climb the tree. I know because I looked at my watch. It was two fourteen – another fact burned into my brain; I was estimating when, starting then, we should get back to Belize, where I had a dinner engagement at seven. I thought about five or five-fifteen.

'The damned thing is up there somewhere,' said Wilkes, looking up into the branches and leaves. 'It certainly hasn't come down. I suppose I'll have to go up after it!'

I gave him a pair of hands up, his foot on them and a quick heave, a lower limb deftly caught, an overhand pull; and then our Belize pilot was climbing like a cat up into the great tree's heart after his elusive and badly soiled garment.

The repacked lunch basket had to be put in the plane, some hundred yards away from the tree. I attended to that while Pelletier busied himself with his notebook, sitting cross-legged in the shade.

I sauntered back after disposing of the lunch basket. I glanced over at the tree, expecting to see Wilkes descending about then with the rescued jacket. He was still up there, however. There was nothing to take note of except a slight – a very slight – movement of the leaves, which, looking up the tree and seeing, I remarked as unusual because not a single breath of air was stirring anywhere. I recall thinking, whimsically, that it was as though the great tree were laughing at us, very quietly and softly, over the trouble it was making for Wilkes.

I sat down beside Pelletier, and he began to speak, perhaps for the third or fourth time, about that strange clap of wind. That had made a very powerful impression on Pelletier, it seemed. After this comment Pelletier paused, frowned, looked at his watch and then at the tree, and remarked: 'Where is that fellow? He's been up there ten minutes!' We walked over to the tree's foot and looked up among the branches. The great tree stood there inscrutable, a faint movement barely perceptible among its leaves. I remembered that imagined note of derision which this delicate movement had suggested to me, and I smiled to myself.

Pelletier shouted up the tree: 'Wilkes! Wilkes – can't you find the coat?'

Then again: 'Wilkes! Wilkes – we've got to get started back pretty soon!'

But there was no answer from Wilkes, only that almost imperceptible movement of the leaves, as though there were a little breeze up there; as though indeed the tree were quietly laughing at us. And there was something – something remotely sinister, derisive, like a sneer, in that small, dry, rustling chuckle.

Pelletier and I looked at each other, and there was no smile in the eyes of either one of us.

We sat down on the grass then as though by agreement. Again we looked at each other. I seemed to feel the tree's derision;

more openly now, less like a delicate hint, a nuance. It seemed to me quite open now, like a slap in the face! Here indeed was an unprecedented predicament. We were all ready to depart, and we had no pilot. Our pilot had merely performed a commonplace act. He had climbed a tree.

But – he had not come down – that was all.

It seemed simple to state it to oneself that way, as I did, to myself. And yet, the implications of that simple statement involved – well, what *did* they involve? The thing, barring an accident: Wilkes having fallen into a decay-cavity or something of the sort; or a joke: Wilkes hiding from us like a child among the upper branches – barring those explanations for his continued absence up there and his refusal to answer when called to, the thing was – well, impossible.

Wilkes was a grown man. It was inconceivable that he should be hiding from us up there. If caught, somehow, and so deterred from descending, at least he could have replied to Pelletier's hail, explained his possible predicament. He had, too, gone far up into the tree. I had seen him go up agilely after my initial helping hand. He was, indeed, well up and going higher far above the lower trunk area of possible decay-cavities, when I had left him to put the lunch basket back in the plane. He had been up nearly twenty minutes now, and had not come down. We could not see him. A slightly cold sensation up and down my spine came like a presage, a warning. There seemed – it was borne in abruptly upon me – something sinister here, something menacing, deadly. I looked over at Pelletier to see if anything of this feeling might be reflected in his expression, and as I looked, he spoke.

'Canevin, did you notice that this deforested area is circular?'

I nodded.

'Does that suggest anything to you?'

I paused, took thought. It suggested several things, in the light of my recent, my current, feeling about this place centered about its great tree. It was, for one thing, apparently an unique formation in the topography of this peninsula. The circularity suggested an area set off from the rest, and by design – somebody's design. The 'ring' idea next came uppermost in my mind. The ring plays a large part in the occult, the preternatural: the elves' ring; dancing rings (they were grassy places, too); the Norman cromlechs; Stonehenge; the Druidical rites; protective rings, beyond the perimeter of which the Powers of Evil, beleaguering, might not penetrate . . . I looked up from these thoughts again at Pelletier.

'Good God, Pelletier! Yes – do you imagine . . . ?'

Pelletier waved one of his big, awkward-looking hands, those hands which so often skirted death, defeated death, at his operating table.

'It's significant,' he muttered, and nodded his head several times. Then: 'That gust of wind, Canevin – remember? It was *that* which took Wilkes's coat up there, made him climb after it; and now – well, where is he?'

I shook my head slowly. There seemed no answer to Pelletier's question. Then: 'What is it, Pelletier?'

Pelletier replied, as was usual with him, only after some additional reflection and with a certain deliberateness. He was measuring every word, it seemed.

'Every indication, so far, points to – an air-elemental.'

'An air-elemental?' The term, with whatever idea or spiritual entity, or vague, unusual superstition underlay its possible meaning, was familiar to me, but who – except Pelletier, whose range of knowledge I certainly had never plumbed – would think of such a thing in this connection?

'What is an air-elemental?' I asked him, hoping for some higher information.

Pelletier waved his hand in a gesture common to him.

'It would be a little difficult to make it clear, right off the bat, so to speak, Canevin,' said he, a heavy frown engendered by his own inability to express what might be in that strange, full mind of his, corrugating his broad forehead. 'And even if I had it at my tongue's end,' he continued, 'it would take an unconscionable time.' He paused and looked at me, smiling wryly.

'I'll tell you, Canevin, all about them, if we ever get the chance.' Then, as I nodded, necessarily acquiescing in this unsatisfactory explanation, he added: 'That is, what little, what very little, I, or indeed anybody, knows about them!'

And with that I had, perforce, to be satisfied.

It seemed to my taunted senses, attuned now to this suggested atmosphere of menace which I was beginning to sense all about us, that an intensified rustle came from the tree's leaves. An involuntary shudder ran over my body. From that moment, quite definitely, I felt it: the certain, unmistakable knowledge that we three stood alone, encircled, hemmed in, by something; something vast, powerful beyond all comprehension, like the incalculable power of a god, or a demigod; something elemental and, I felt, old with a hoary antiquity; something established here from beyond the ken of humanity; something utterly inhuman, overwhelmingly hostile, inimical, to us. I felt that we were on Its ground, and that It had, so far, merely shown us, contemptuously, the outer edge of Its malice and of Its power. It had, quietly, unobtrusively, taken Wilkes. Now, biding Its time, It was watching, as though amused; certain of Its malignant, Its overwhelming, power; watching us, waiting for Its own good time to close in on us . . .

I stood up, to break the strain, and walked a few steps toward the edge of the tree's nearly circular shade. From there I looked down that gentle slope across the motionless short grass through the shimmering heat waves of that airless afternoon to the tree-horizon.

What was that? I shaded my hands and strained my vision through those pulsating heat waves which intervened; then, astonished, incredulous, I ran over to the plane and reached in over the side and brought out the high-powered Lomb-Zeiss binoculars which Bishop Dunn at Belize had loaned me the evening before. I put them to my eyes without waiting to go back into the shade near Pelletier. I wanted to test, to verify, what I thought I had seen down there at the edge of the encircling forest; to assure myself at the same time that I was still sane.

There at the jungle's edge, clear and distinct now, as I focused those admirable binoculars, I saw, milling about, crowding upon each other, gesticulating wildly – shouting, too, soundlessly of course, at that distance from my ears – evidencing in short the very apogee of extreme agitation; swarming in their hundreds – their thousands, indeed – a countless horde of those dull-witted brown Indians, still named Mayas, some four hundred thousand of which constitute the native population of the Peninsula of Yucatan – Yucatan province, Campeche, and Quintana Roo.

All of them, apparently, were concentrated, pointing, gesticulating, upon the center of the great circle of grassland, upon the giant tree – upon us.

And, as I looked, shifting my glasses along great arcs and sections of the jungle-edged circle, fascinated by this wholly bizarre configuration, abruptly, with a kind of cold chill of conviction, I suddenly perceived that, despite their manifest agitation, which was positively violent, all those excited Indians were keeping themselves rigidly within the shelter of the woods. Not one stepped so much as his foot over that line which demarcated the forested perimeter of the circle, upon that short grass.

I lowered the glasses at last and walked back to Pelletier. He had not moved. He raised to me a very serious face as I approached.

'What did you see down there, Canevin?' He indicated the distant rim of trees.

He listened to my account as thought preoccupied, nodding from time to time. He only became outwardly attentive when I mentioned how the Indians kept back to the line of trees. He allowed a brief, explosive 'Ha!' to escape him when I got to that.

When I had finished: 'Canevin,' said he, gravely, 'we are in a very tight place.' He looked up at me still gravely, as though to ascertain whether or not I realized the situation he had in mind. I nodded, glanced at my watch.

'Yes,' said I, 'I realize that, of course. It is five minutes to three. Wilkes has been gone up there, three-quarters of an hour. That's one thing, explain it as you may. Neither of us can pilot a plane; and, even if we were able to do so, Pelletier, we couldn't, naturally, go back to Belize without Wilkes. We couldn't account for his disappearance: "Yes, Mr Commissioner, he went up a tree and never came down!" We should be taken for idiots, or murderers! Then there's that – er – horde of Indians, surrounding us. We are hemmed in, Pelletier, and there are, I'd say, thousands of them. The moment they make up their minds to rush us – well, we're finished, Pelletier,' I ended these remarks and found myself glancing apprehensively toward the rim of jungle.

'Right enough, so far!' said Pelletier, grimly. 'We're "hemmed in", as you put it, Canevin, only perhaps a little differently from the way you mean. Those Indians' – his long arm swept our horizon – 'will never attack us. Put that quite out of your mind, my dear fellow. Except for the fact that there's probably only food enough left for one scant meal, you've summed up the – er – material difficulties. However – '

I interrupted.

'That mob, Pelletier, I tell you, there are thousands of them. Why should they surround us if – '

'They won't attack us. It isn't *us* they're surrounding, even though our being here is, in a way, the occasion for their assembly down there. They aren't in any mood to attack anybody, Canevin – *they're frightened.*'

'Frightened?' I barked out. 'Frightened! About what, for God's sake?' This idea seemed to me so utterly far-fetched, so intrinsically absurd, at first hearing – after all, it was I who had watched them through the binoculars, not Pelletier who sat here so calmly and assured me of what seemed a basic improbability. 'It doesn't seem to make sense to me, Pelletier,' I continued. 'And besides, you spoke just now of the "material" difficulties. What others are there?'

Pelletier looked at me for quite a long time before answering, a period long enough for me to recapitulate those eerier matters which I had lost sight of in what seemed the imminent danger from those massed Indians. Then: 'Where do you imagine Wilkes is?' inquired Pelletier. 'Can you – er – see him up there?' He pointed over his shoulder with his thumb, as artists and surgeons point.

'Good God, Pelletier, you don't mean . . . ?'

'Take a good look up into the tree,' said Pelletier, calmly. 'Shout up to him; see if he answers now. You heard me do it. Wilkes isn't deaf!'

I stood and looked at my friend sitting there on the grass, his ungainly bulk sprawled awkwardly. I said nothing. I confess to a whole series of prickly small chills up and down my spine. At last I went over close to the enormous bole and looked up. I called: 'Wilkes! Oh *Wilkes*!' at the top of my voice, several times. I desisted just in time, I think, to keep an hysterical note out of that stentorian shouting.

For no human voice had answered from up there – only, as it seemed to me, a now clearly derisive rustle, a kind of thin cacophony, from those damnable fluttering leaves which moved without wind. Not a breath stirred anywhere. To that I can take oath. Yet those leaves . . .

The sweat induced by my slight exertions even in the tree's shade, ran cold off my forehead into my eyes; down my body inside my white drill clothes. I had seen no trace of Wilkes in the tree, and yet the tree's foliage for all its huge bulk was not so dense as to prevent seeing up into every part of it. Wilkes had been up there now for nearly an hour. It was as though he had disappeared from off the face of the earth. I knew now, clearly, what Pelletier had had in mind when he distinguished between our 'material' and other difficulties. I walked slowly back to him.

Pelletier had a somber look on his face.

'Did you see him?' he asked. 'Did he answer you?' But, it seemed, these were only rhetorical questions. Pelletier did not pause for any reply from me. Instead, he proceeded to ask more questions.

'Did you see any ants on the trunk? You were quite close to it.' Then, not pausing: 'Have you been troubled by any insects since we came down here, Canevin? Notice any at lunch, or when you took the lunch basket back to the plane?' Finally, with a sweeping, upward gesture: 'Do you see any birds, Canevin?'

I shook my head in one composite reply to these questions. I had noticed no ants or any other insects. No bird was in flight. I could not recall, now that my attention had been drawn to the fact, seeing any living thing here besides ourselves. Pelletier broke in upon this momentary meditation.

'The place is tabu, Canevin, and not only to those Indians down there in the trees – to everything living, man! – to the very birds, to the ground game, to the insects!' He lowered his voice suddenly to a deep significant resonance which was purely tragic.

'Canevin, this is a theater of very ancient Evil,' said Dr Pelletier, 'and we have intruded upon it.'

After that blunt statement, coming as it did from a man like Dr Pelletier, I felt, strange as it seems, better. That may appear the reverse of reason; yet, it is strictly, utterly true. For, after that, I knew where we stood. Those eery sensations which I have mentioned, and which I had well-nigh forgotten in the face of the supposed danger from that massed horde of semi-savages in the forest, crystallized now into the certainty that we stood confronted with some malign menace, not human, not of this world, something not to be gaged or measured by everyday standards of safety. And when I, Gerald Canevin, know where I stand in anything like a pinch, when I know to what I am opposed, when all doubt, in other words, is removed, I act!

But first I wanted to know rather more about what Pelletier had in that experienced head of his; Pelletier, who had looked all kinds of danger in the face in China, in Haiti, in this same Central American territory, in many other sections of the world.

'Tell me what you think it is, Pelletier,' I said, quietly, and stood there waiting for him to begin. He did not keep me waiting.

'Before Harvey discovered the circulation of the blood, Canevin, and so set anatomy on the road to its present modern status, the older anatomists said that the human body contained four humours. Do you remember that? They were called the Melancholic, the Sanguine, the Phlegmatic, and the Choleric Humours – imaginary fluids! These, or the supposed combination of them, in various proportions, were supposed to determine the state and disposition of the medical patient. That was "science" – in the days of Nicholas Culpepper, Canevin! Now, in the days of the Mayo Brothers, that sort of thing is merely archaic, historical, something to smile at! But, never forget, Canevin, it *was* modern science – once! And, notice how basically true it is! Even though there are no such definite fluids in the human body – speculative science it was, you know, not empirical, not based on observation like ours of today, not experimental – just notice how those four do actually correspond to the various human temperaments. We still say such-and-such a person is "sanguine" or "phlegmatic", or even "choleric"! We attribute a lot of temperament today to the ductless glands with their equally obscure fluids; and, Canevin, one is just about as close to the truth as the other!

'Now, an analogy! I reminded you of that old anatomy to compare it with something else. Long before modern natural science came into its own, the old-timers, Copernicus, Duns Scotus, Bacon, the scientists of their day, even Ptolemy, had their four elements: air, earth, water and fire. Those four are still elements, Canevin. The main difference between now and then is the so-called "elemental" behind each of them – a thing with intelligence, Canevin, a kind of demigod. It goes back, that idea, to the Gnostics of the second and third centuries; and the Gnostics went back for the origins of such speculations to the once modern science of Alexandria; of Sumer and Accad; to Egypt, to Phrygia, to Pontus and Commagene! That gust of wind, Canevin – do you – '

'You think,' I interrupted, 'that an air-elemental is . . . ?'

'What more probable, Canevin? Or, what the ancients meant by an air-elemental, a directing intelligence, let us say. You wouldn't attribute all this, Wilkes's disappearance, all the rest of it, so far – ' Pelletier indicated in one comprehensive gesture the tree, the circle of short grass, even the insectless ground and the birdless air – 'to everyday, modern, material causes; to things that Millikan and the rest could classify and measure, and compute about – would you, Canevin?'

I shook my head.

'I'm going up that tree after Wilkes,' I said, and dropped my drill coat on the grass beside Pelletier. I laid my own sun-helmet on the ground beside him. I tightened my belt a hole. Then I started for the tree. I expected some sort of protest or warning from Pelletier. He merely said: 'Wilkes got caught, somehow, up there, because he was taken off his guard, I should surmise. You know, more or less, what to expect!'

I did not know what to expect, but I was quite sure there would be something, up there. I was prepared. This was not the first time Gerald Canevin had been called upon to face the Powers of Darkness, the preternatural. I sent up a brief and fervent prayer to the

Author of this universe, to Him Who made all things, 'visible and invisible' as the Nicene Creed expresses it. He, Their Author, was more powerful than They. If He were on my side . . .

I jumped for the limb up to which I had boosted Wilkes, caught it, got both hands around it, hauled myself up, and then, taking a deep breath, I started up among those still dryly rustling leaves in an atmosphere of deep and heavy shade where no breath of air moved . . .

I perceive clearly enough that in case this account of what happened to Wilkes and Pelletier and me ever has a reader other than myself – and, of course, Pelletier if he should care to peruse what I have set down here; Wilkes, poor fellow, crashed over the Andes, less than three months ago as I write this – I perceive that, although the foregoing portion of this narrative does not wholly transcend ordinary strangeness, yet, that the portion which is now to follow will necessarily appear implausible; will, in other words, strain severely that same hypothetical reader's credulity to the utmost.

For, what I found when I went up the tree after Wilkes – spiritually prepared, in a sense, but without any knowledge of what I might encounter – was – well, it is probable that some two millennia, two thousand years or thereabouts had rolled over the jungles since that background Power has been directly exorcised. And yet, the memory of It had persisted without lapse among those semi-savage inhabitants such as howled and leaped in their agitation down there at the jungle's rim at that very moment; had so persisted for perhaps sixty generations.

I went up, I should estimate, about as far as the exact center of the great tree. Nothing whatever had happened so far. My mind, of course, was at least partly occupied by the purely physical affair of climbing. At about that point in my progress upward among the branches and leaves I paused and looked down. There stood Pelletier, looking up at me, a bulky, lonely figure. My heart went out to him. I could see him, oddly foreshortened, as I looked straight down; his contour somewhat obscured by the intervening foliage and branches. I waved, and called out to him, and Pelletier waved back to me reassuringly, saying nothing. I resumed my climb.

I had got myself perhaps some fifteen feet or more higher up the tree – I could see the blue vault above as I looked straight up – when, quite as abruptly as that inexplicable wind-clap which had scattered our lunch, the entire top of the tree began suddenly, yet as though with a sentient deliberation, to constrict itself, to close in on me. The best description of the process I can give is to say that those upper branches, from about the tree's midst upward, suddenly squeezed themselves together. This movement coming up toward me from below, and catching up with me, and pressing me upon all sides, in a kind of vertical peristalsis, pushed me straight upward like a fragment of paste through a collapsible tube!

I slid along the cylinder formed by these upper branches as they yielded and turned themselves upward under the impact of some irresistible pressure. My pace upward under this mechanical compulsion was very rapidly accelerated, and, in much less time than is required to set it down, I flew straight up; almost literally burst out from among the slender topmost twigs and leaves as though propelled through the barrel of some monstrous air-gun; and, once clear of the tree's hindering foliage and twigs, a column of upward-rushing air supporting me, I shot straight up into the blue empyrean.

I could feel my senses slipping from my control as the mad pace increased! I closed my eyes against the quick nausea which ensued, and fell into a kind of blank apathy which lasted I know not how long, but out of which I was abruptly snatched with a jar which seemed to wrench every bone and muscle and nerve and sinew in my body.

Unaccountably, as my metabolism slowly readjusted itself, I felt firm support beneath me. I opened my eyes.

I found myself in a sitting position, the wrenching sensations of the jar of landing rapidly dissipating themselves, no feeling of nausea, and, indeed, incongruous as such a word must sound under the circumstances being related, actually comfortable! Whatever substance supported me was comparatively soft and yielding, like thick turf, like a pneumatic cushion. Above me stretched a cloudless sky, the tropical sky of late afternoon, in these accustomed latitudes. Almost automatically I put down my hand to feel what I was resting upon. My eyes, as naturally, followed my hand's motion. My hand encountered something that felt like roughly corrugated rubber, my eyes envisaged a buff-colored ground-surface entirely devoid of vegetation, a surface which, as I turned my head about curiously, stretched away in every direction to an irregular horizon at an immense distance. This ground was not precisely level, as a lawn is level. Yet it showed neither sharp elevations nor any marked depressions. Quite nearby, on my right as I sat there taking in my novel surroundings, two shallow ravines of considerable breadth crossed each other. In one direction, about due south I estimated from the sun's position, three distant, vast, and rounded elevations or hummocks raised themselves against the horizon; and beyond them, dim in the far distance, there appeared to extend farther south vague heights upon four gradually rising plateaus, barely perceptible from where I sat. I was in the approximate center of an enormous plain the lowest point of which, the center of a saucer-like terrain, was my immediate environment; the reverse conformation, so to speak, of the great circle about the tree.

'Good God!' said a voice behind me. 'It's Canevin!'

I turned sharply to the one direction my few seconds' scrutiny had failed to include. There, not twenty feet away, sat Wilkes the pilot. He had found his jacket! He was wearing it, in fact. That, queerly enough, was my first mental reaction to having a companion in this weird world to which I had been transported. I noted at that moment, simultaneously with seeing Wilkes, that from somewhere far beneath the surface of the ground there came at regular intervals a kind of throbbing resonance as though from some colossal engine or machine. This pulsing, rhythmical beat was not audible. It came to me – and to Wilkes, as I checked the matter over with him later – through the sense of feeling alone. It continued, I may as well record here, through our entire stay in this world of increasing strangeness.

'I see you have recovered your coat,' said I, as Wilkes rose and stepped toward me.

'No doubt about it!' returned Wilkes, and squared his angular shoulders as though to demonstrate how well the jacket fitted his slender figure.

'And what do you make of – this?' he asked, with a comprehensive gesture including the irregular, vegetationless, buff-colored terrain all about us.

'Are we in the so-called "fourth dimension", or what?'

'Later,' said I, 'if you don't mind, after I get a chance to think a bit. I've just been shot into this place, and I'm not quite oriented!' Then: 'And how did you manage to get yourself up here? I suppose, of course, it's *up*!'

There is no occasion to repeat here Wilkes's account of his experience in the tree and later. It was identical with mine which I have already described. Of that fact I assured Wilkes as soon as he had ended describing it to me.

'This – er – ground is queer enough,' remarked Wilkes. 'Look at this!'

He opened his clasp-knife, squatted down, jabbed the knife into the ground half an inch or so, and then cut a long gash in what he had referred to as the 'ground'. In all conscience it was utterly different from anything forming a surface or topsoil that I had ever encountered. Certainly it was not earth as we know it. Wilkes cut another parallel gash, close beside his first incision, drew the two together with his knife at the cut's end, and pried loose and then tore up a long narrow sliver. This, held by one thin end, hung from his hand much as a similarly shaped slice of fresh-cut kitchen linoleum might hang. It looked, indeed, much like linoleum, except that it was both more pliable and also translucent.

'I have another sliver in my pocket,' said Wilkes, handing this fresh one to me. I took the thing and looked at it closely.

'May I see yours?' I asked Wilkes.

Wilkes fished his strip out of a pocket in that soiled silk jacket and handed it to me. He had it rolled up, and it did not unroll easily. I stretched it out between my hands, holding it by both ends. I compared the two specimens. His was considerably dryer than mine, much less pliable. I said nothing. I merely rolled up Wilkes's strip and handed it back to him.

'I've stuck right here,' remarked Wilkes, 'ever since I landed in this Godforsaken place, if it is a place, because, well, because there simply didn't seem to be anything else to do. The sun has been terrific. There's no shade of any kind, you see, not a single spot, as far as you can see; not any at all on the entire damned planet – or whatever it is we've struck! Now that you've "joined up", what say to a trek? I'd agree with anyone who insisted that anything at all beats standing here in one spot! How about it?'

'Right,' I agreed. 'Let's make it either north or south – in the direction of those hummocks, or, up to the top of that plateau region to the south'ard.'

'O. K. with me,' agreed Wilkes. 'Did you, by any blessed chance, bring any water along when you came barging through?'

I had no water, and Wilkes had been here more than an hour in that pitiless glare without any before my arrival. He shook his head ruefully.

'Barring a shower we'll have to grin and bear it, I imagine. Well, let's go. Is it north, or south? I don't care.'

'South, then,' said I, and we started.

Our way took us directly across one of the intersecting depressions in the ground which I have mentioned. The walking was resilient, the ground's surface neither exactly soft nor precisely hard. It was, I remember thinking, very much like a very coarse crêpe-rubber sole such as is used extensively in tennis and similar sports shoes. As we went down the gradual slope of that ravine the footing changed gradually, the color of underfoot being heightened by an increasingly reddish or pinkish tinge, and the surface becoming smoother as this coloration intensified itself. In places where the more general corrugations almost disappeared, it was so smooth as to shine in the sun's declining rays like something polished. In such stretches as we traversed it was entirely firm, however, and not in the least slippery, as it appeared to be to the eye.

A cool breeze began to blow from the south, in our faces as we walked. This, and a refreshing shower which overtook us about six o'clock, served to revive us just at a point in our journey when we had really begun to suffer from the well-nigh intolerable effects of the broiling sun overhead and the lack of drinking water. The sun's decline put the finishing touch upon our comparative comfort. As for the actual walking, both of us were as tough as pine knots, both salted thoroughly to the tropics, both in the very pink of physical condition. Nevertheless, we felt very grateful for these several reliefs.

The sun went down, this being the month of February, just as we were near the top of the gentle slope which led out of the ravine's farther side. Two miles or so farther along as we continued to trek southward, the stars were out and we were able to keep our course by means of that occasional glance into the heavens which night travelers in the open spaces make automatically.

We pressed on and on, the resilient underfooting favoring our stride, the cool breeze, which grew gradually stronger as we walked into it, blowing refreshingly into our faces. This steady breeze was precisely like the evening trade wind as we know it who live in the Lesser Antilles of the Caribbean.

There was some little talk between us as we proceeded, steadily, due south in the direction of a rising, still distant, mounded tableland, from the summit of which – this had been my original idea in choosing this direction – I thought that we might be enabled to secure a general view of this strange, vegetationless land into which we two had been so singularly precipitated. The tableland, too, was considerably less distant from our starting point than those bolder hummocks to the north which I have mentioned.

From time to time, every couple of miles or so, we sat down and rested for a few minutes.

At about four in the morning, when we had been walking for more than eleven hours by these easy stages, the ground before us began gradually to rise, and, under the now pouring moonlight, we were able to see that a kind of cleft or valley, running almost exactly north and south, was opening out before us. Along the bottom of this, and up a very gradual rise, we mounted for the next two hours. We estimated that we had gone up several thousand feet from what I might call the mean level of our starting point. For this final stage of our journey, the walking conditions had been especially pleasant. Neither of us was particularly tired.

As we mounted the last of the acclivity, my mind was heavily occupied with Pelletier, left there alone under the tree, with the useless plane nearby and those swarming savages all about him in their great numbers. Also I thought, somewhat ruefully, of my abandoned dinner engagement in Belize. I wondered, in passing, if I should ever sit down to a dinner table again! It seemed, I must admit, rather unlikely just then. Quite likely they would send out some sort of rescue expedition after us; probably another plane following the route which we had placed on file at the airport.

Of such matters, I say, I was thinking, rather than what might be the result, if any, of our all night walk. Just then the abrupt, bright dawn of the tropics broke over at our left in the east. We looked ahead from the summit we had just gained in its blazing, clarifying effulgence, over the crown of the great ridge.

We looked out.

No human being save Wilkes and me, Gerald Canevin, has seen, in modern times at least, what we saw. And, so long as the earth's civilization and science endure, so long as there remains the procession of the equinoxes, so long, indeed, as the galaxy roars its invincible way through unsounded space toward imponderable Hercules, no man born of woman shall ever again see what opened there before our stultified senses, our dazzled eyes . . .

Before us the ground beyond the great ridge began to slope abruptly downward in one vast, regular curve. It pitched down beyond this parabola in an increasingly steep declivity, such as an ocean might form as it poured its incalculable volume over the edge of the imagined geoplanarian earth-edge of the ancients! Down, down, down to well-nigh the extreme range of our vision it cascaded, down through miles and miles of naked space to a sheer verticalness – a toboggan slide for Titans.

The surface of this downward-pitching slope, beginning some distance below the level upon which we stood there awestruck, was in one respect different from the land as we had so far seen it. For there, well down that awful slope, we could easily perceive the first vegetation, or what corresponded to vegetation, that we had observed. Down there and extending out of our range of vision for things of that size, there arose from the ground's surface, and growing thicker and more closely together as the eye followed them down, many great columnar structures, irregularly placed with relation to each other, yet of practically uniform height, thickness, and color. This last was a glossy, almost metallic, black. These things were branchless and showed no foliage of any kind. They were narrowed to points at their tops, and these tapering upper portions waved in the strong breeze which blew up from below precisely as the tops of trees moved under the impulse of an earthly breeze. I say 'earthly' advisedly. I will proceed to indicate why!

It was not, primarily, the inherent majesty of the unique topography which I am attempting to describe which rooted Wilkes and me, appalled, to that spot at the ridge's summit. No. It was the clear sight of our planet, earth, as though seen from an airplane many miles high in the earth's atmosphere, which, in its unexpectedness, caused the sophisticated Wilkes to bury his face in his arms like a frightened child at its mother's lap, caused me to turn my head away. It was the first, demonstrative proof that we had been separated from earth; that we stood, indeed, 'up', and with a vengeance, miles away from its friendly surface.

It was then, and not before, that the sense of our utter separation, our almost cosmic loneliness, came to us in an almost overwhelming surge of uncontrollable emotion. The morning sun shone clear and bright down there upon our earth, as it shone here where we were so strangely marooned. We saw just there, most prominently presented to our rapt gaze, the northeast section of South America, along the lower edge of our familiar Caribbean, the Guianas, Venezuela, the skirting islands, Margherita, Los Roques, Bonaire, and, a trifle less clear, the lower isles of my own Lesser Antilles: Trinidad, Barbados on the horizon's very edge, the little shadow I knew to be Tobago.

I shall not attempt further to tell here how that unexpected, yet confirmatory sight, shook the two of us; how small and unimportant it made us feel, how cut off from everything that formed our joint backgrounds. Yet, however detached we felt, however stultifying was the vision of earth down there, it was, literally, as nothing, even counting in our conviction of being mere animated, unimportant specks among the soulless particles of space – even that devastating certainty was as nothing to the climactic focus of what we were to behold.

I sat down beside Wilkes, and, speaking low to each other, we managed gradually to recover those shreds of our manhood which had partly escaped us, to get back some of that indomitable courage which sustains the sons of men and makes us, when all is said and done, the ultimate masters of our destinies.

When we were somewhat recovered – readjusted perhaps is the better word – we stood up and once more looked down over the edge of this alien world, down that soul-dizzying slope, our unaided eyes gradually accommodating themselves to seeing more and more clearly its distant reaches and the continentlike section which lay, dim and vague from distance, below it. We observed now what we had failed to perceive before, that the enormous area of that land-pitch was, in its form, roughly rounded, that it sloped to right and left, as well as directly away from us; that it was, in short, a tremendous, slanted column, like a vast circular bridge between the level upon which we then stood and that continent-like mass of territory down below there in the vague distance. As the sun rose higher and higher the fresh breeze died to a trickle of air, then ceased. Those cylindrical, black, tree-like growths no longer waved their spikes. They stood now like rigid metallic columns at variant, irregular angles. In the increasing light the real character of what I had mentally named the Continent below became more nearly apparent. It was changing out of its remote vagueness, taking form. I think it dawned upon me before Wilkes had succeeded in placing what was slowly emerging, mentally. For, just before I turned my head away at the impact of the shock which that dawning realization brought to my mind and senses, the last thing I observed clearly was Wilkes, rigid, gazing below there, staring down that frightful declivity, a mounting horror spreading over the set face above the square-cut jaw . . .

Realization of the rewards of this world as dross had come, two millennia ago, to Him Who stood beside the Tempter, upon the pinnacles of the Temple, viewing the kingdoms of the world. In some such fashion – if I may so describe the process without any intentional irreverence – there came to me the blasting conviction which then overtook me, forced itself into my protesting mentality, turned all my ideas upside-down.

For it was not a continent that we had been gazing down upon. It was no continent. It was not land – ground. *It was a face* – a face of such colossal majesty, emerging there, taking form in the rays of the revealing sunlight, as utterly to stagger mind and senses attuned to earthly things, adjusted for a lifetime to earthly proportions; a face ageless in its serene, calm, inhumaneness; its conviction of immeasurable power; its ab-human inscrutability.

I reeled away, my face turned from this incredible catastrophe of thought; and, as I sank down upon the ground, my back turned toward the marge of this declivity, I knew that I had dared to look straight into the countenance of a Great Power, such as the ancients had known. And I realized, suddenly sick at heart, that this presence, too, was looking out of eyes like level, elliptical seas, up into my eyes, deep into my very inmost soul.

But this conviction, so monstrous, so devastating, so incredible, was not all! Along with it there went the heart-shaking realization that what we had visualized as that great slope was the columnar, incredible arm of that cosmic Colossus – that our night-long trek had been made across a portion of the palm of his uplifted hand!

Overhead the cloudless sky began to glow a coppery brown. An ominous, wedge-shaped tinge spread fast, gathering clouds together out of nowhere as it sped into the north. And now the sun-drenched air seemed heavy, of a sudden difficult to breathe under that pitiless, oppressive sun which glared out of the bland, cerulean corner of the sky in which it burned. A menacing sultriness filled the atmosphere, pressed down upon us like a relentless hand. A hand! I shuddered involuntarily, and turned to Wilkes and spoke, my hand on his shoulder. It was a matter of seconds before the stark horror died out of his eyes. He interrupted my almost whispered words.

'Did you see It, Canevin?'

I nodded.

'I think we'll have to get back from the edge,' I repeated my warning he had failed to hear, 'down into that – ravine – again. There's the making of a typhoon up topside, I'm afraid.'

Wilkes shot a quick, weatherwise glance aloft.

'Right-o,' said he, and we started together toward that slight shelter of the shallow valley up which we had toiled as dawn was breaking.

But the wind-storm from out of the north broke upon us long before we had gained this questionable refuge. A blasting hurricane smote down upon us out of that coppery, distorted sky. We had not a chance. The first blast picked us up as though we had been specks of flotsam lint, carried us straight to the brink, and over, and down; and then, side by side, so long as we retained our senses under the stress of that terrific friction, we were hurled at a dizzyingly increasing rate down that titanic toboggan slide as its sheer vertical pitch fell away under our spinning bodies, always faster and faster, with the roar of ten Niagaras rending the very welkin above – down, down, down into the quick oblivion which seemed to shut out all life and all understanding and all persisting hope in one final, mercifully quick-ended horror of ultimate destruction.

Somehow, I carried with me into that disintegration of the senses and ultimate coma, the thought of Pelletier.

In order to achieve in this strange narrative which I am setting down as best I can, some sense of order and a reasonable brevity, I have, from time to time, summarized my account. I have, for example, mentioned once that engine-like beat, that regular pulsation to be felt here. I have said, to avoid reference to it, that it continued throughout our sojourn in the 'place' which I have described. That is what I mean by summarizing. I have, indeed, omitted much, very much, which, now that I am writing at leisure, I feel would burden my account with needless detail, unnecessary recording of my emotional reaction to what was happening. In this category lies all that long conversation between Wilkes and me, as we strode along, side by side, on that long night walk.

But, of all such matters, the most prominent to me was the pre-occupation – a natural one, I believe – with that good friend whom I had left looking up into the tree which looked like an English ash, as I climbed away from him into what neither of us could possibly visualize or anticipate, away, as it transpired, from our very planet earth, and into a setting, a set of conditions, quite utterly diverse from anything the mind of modern man could possibly conceive or invent.

This preoccupation of mine with Pelletier had been virtually con-tinuous. I had never had him wholly out of my mind. He had uttered, it will be remembered, no protest at my leaving him down there alone. That, at the time, had surprised me considerably. But on reflection I came to see that such an attitude on his part was entirely natural. It was part of that tremendous fortitude of his, almost fatalism, which was an integral part of his character. I have known few men better balanced than that ungainly, big-hearted naval surgeon friend of mine. Pelletier was the man I should choose, beyond all others, to have beside me in a pinch.

And here we were, Wilkes and I, in a situation which I have endeavored to make as clear as possible, perhaps as tight a pinch as any human beings have ever been in, and the efficient and reliable Pelletier not only miles away from us, as we would think of the separation in earthly terms, but, actually, as our sight down that slope had devastatingly revealed, as effectively cut off from us as though we two human atoms had been standing on the planet Jupiter! There had been no moment, I testify truly, since I had been drawn into that tree-vortex and hurled regardless into this monstrous environment, when I had not wanted that tried and true friend beside me.

For, in that same desire to keep this narrative free from the extraneous, to avoid labored repetitions, I see that I have said nothing, so far at least, of what I must name the atmosphere of terror, the sense of malign pressure against my mind, and against Wilkes's, which had been literally continuous; which by now, under the successive impacts of shock to which both of us had been subjected, had soared hauntingly to the status of a sustained horror, a sense of helplessness well-nigh intolerable, as it became borne in upon us what we had to face.

We were like a pair of sparrows in a great, incalculable grip.

Against that dread Power there seemed to be no possible defense. We were, and increasingly realizing the fact, completely, hopelessly, Its prey. Whenever It decided to close in upon us, It would strike – at intruders, as the canny Pelletier, sensing our status on Its ground, had phrased the matter. It had us, and we knew it! And there was nothing we could do, men of action though both of us were; nothing, that is, that any man of whatever degree of fortitude could do. Therein lay the oppressive horror of the situation.

When I opened my eyes my first impression was a mental one; to wit, that an enormous period of time had elapsed since last I had looked upon the world and its sky above it. This curious delusion, I have since learned, is due to the degree of unconsciousness which has been sustained. The impression, I will note in passing, shortly wore off. My second, immediately subsequent, impression was a physical one. I ached in every bone, muscle tendon and sinew of a body which all my life I have kept in the highest possible degree of physical fitness. I felt sorely bruised. Every inch of me protested as I attempted to move, holding me back. And, immediately after this realization, that old preoccupation with Pelletier reëstablished itself in my mind and became abruptly paramount. I could, so to speak, think of nothing, just then, but Pelletier.

Into this cogitation there broke a suppressed groan. With a wrenching effort, I rolled over, and there, behind me, lay Wilkes. We were, it seemed, still together! Whatever the strange Power might be planning and executing upon us, was upon us both. Very slowly and carefully, Wilkes sat up, and, with a rueful glance over at me, began laboriously to feel about over his body.

'I'm merely one enormous bruise,' said Wilkes, 'and I'm a bit surprised that either of us is – '

'Alive at all,' I finished for him, and we nodded, rather dully, at each other.

'Yes, after that last dash they gave us,' added Wilkes. Then, slowly: 'What do you suppose it's all about, Canevin? Who, what is it? Is it – er – Allah – or – what?'

'I'm none too agile myself,' I said, after a pause spent going over various muscles and joints. 'I'm intact, it seems, and I've got to agree with you, old man! I don't in the least understand why we're not in small fragments, "little heaps of huddled pulp", as I once heard it put! However, if It can use a typhoon to move us about, of course It can temper the typhoon, land us gently, keep us off the ground – undoubtedly It did, for some good reason of Its own! However, the main point is that we're still here – but where *are* we now?'

It was not Wilkes who answered. The answer came – I am recording precisely what happened, exaggerating nothing, omitting nothing salient from this unprecedented adventure – the reply came to me mentally, as though by some unanticipated telepathy, quite clearly enunciated, registering itself unmistakably in my inner-consciousness.

'*Sit tight*!' it said. 'I'm with you here on this end of things.'

And the 'voice' which recorded itself in my brain, a calm, efficient kind of voice, a voice which reached out its intense helpfulness and sympathy to us, waifs of some inchoate void, a voice replete with reassurance, with steady confidence, a voice which healed the raw wounds of the beleaguered soul – was the voice of Pelletier.

Pelletier standing by! I cannot hope to reproduce and set down here the immeasurable comfort of it.

I stood up, Wilkes rising groaningly at the same time, a laborious, painful process, and, reeling on my two feet as I struggled for and finally established my normal balance, looked about me.

We stood, to my mounting surprise, on a stone-flagged pavement. About us rose inner walls of smoothed stone. We were in a room about sixteen by twenty feet in size, lighted by an open doorway and by six windows symmetrically placed along the side walls, and unglazed. The light which flooded the room through these vents was plainly that of late afternoon. Simultaneously we stepped over to the wide-open doorway and looked out.

Before us waved the dignified foliage of a mahogany grove, thickly interspersed with ceiba trees, its near edge gracious with the brave show of flowering shrubs in full blossom – small white flowers which smelled like the Cape jessamine. I had only just taken in these features when I felt Wilkes's grip on my arm from where we stood, just behind me and a little to one side. His voice was little more than a whisper.

'We're – Oh, God! – Canevin! Look, Canevin, look! We're back on earth!' His whispered words broke in a succession of hysterical dry sobs, and, as I laid my arm about the poor fellow's heaving shoulders, I felt the unchecked tears running down my own face.

We stepped out side by side after a minute or two, and stood here, once more on true earth, in the pleasant silence of late afternoon and with the fragrance of those flowering shrubs pouring itself over everything. It was a delicate aroma, grateful and refreshing. We said nothing. We spent this quiet interval in some sort of silent thanksgiving.

And, curiously, Wilkes's oddly phrased question came forcibly into my mind: 'Is it Allah – or what?' I remembered, standing there in that pleasant, remote garden with its white flowers, an evening spent over a pair of pipes in the austere study of an old friend, Professor Harvey Vanderbogart, a brilliant young Orientalist, since dead. Vanderbogart, I remembered very clearly, had been speaking of one of the Moslem theologians, Al Ghazzali. He had quoted me a strange passage from the magnum opus of that medieval Saracen, a treatise well known to scholars as *The Precious Pearl*. I could even call back into my mind with the smell of the tobacco and the breeze blowing Vanderbogart's dull reddish window curtains, the resonance of his serious, declaiming voice.

' . . . the soul of man passeth out of his body, and this soul is of the shape and size of a bee . . . The Lord Allah holdeth this soul of man between His thumb and finger, and Allah bringeth it close before His eyes, and Allah holdeth it at the length of His arm, and Allah saith: "Some are in the Garden – and I care not; and some are in the Fire – and I care not . . . " '

Poor Vanderbogart had been dead many years, a most worthy and lovable fellow and a fine scholar. May he rest in peace! Doubtless he is reaping his reward of a blameless life, in the Garden.

And here, somewhere on earth, which was, for the time being, quite enough for us to know, stood Wilkes and I, also in a garden, tremulously grateful to be alive, and on our Mother Earth, glad indeed of this respite as it seemed to us; free, for the time being, of the malevolent caprice of that Power from Whose baleful control, we, poor fools, supposed that we might have been, as it were carelessly, released.

Our momentary illusion of security was strangely shattered.

Without any preliminary warning of any kind, those great trees before us on the other edge of the row of flowering bushes made deep obeisance all together in their deeply rooted rows, in our direction, as a great wind tore rudely through them, hurling us backwards like chips of cork before a hurricane, whipping us savagely with the strong twigs of the uprooted shrubs pelting us, ironically, with a myriad detached blossoms. This fearsome surge of living air smote us back through the wide doorway and landed us in the middle of that compact stone room, and died as abruptly, leaving us, almost literally breathless, and reeling after our dislocated balance.

There was, it occurred to me fragmentarily and with a poignant acuteness, a disastrous certainty brooking no mental denial, none of the benign carelessness of Allah about this Adversary of ours! His was, plainly enough, an active maleficence. He had no intention of allowing us quietly, unobtrusively, to slip away. If we had been landed once more on earth, it was in no sense a release – no more than the cat releases the mouse save to add some infinitesimal mental torture to that pitiful little creature's dash for freedom, ending in the thrust of those ruthless retractile claws.

Brief respites, the subsequent crushing of our very souls by that imponderable Force!

We pulled ourselves together, Wilkes and I, there in that austere little stone room, and, in the breathless calm which had followed that astounding clap of air-force, we found ourselves racked to a very high degree of nervous tension. We stood there, and pumped laboriously the dead, heavy air into our laboring lungs in great gasping breaths. It was as though a vacuum had, for long moments, replaced the warm fresh air of a tropical midafternoon. The stone room's floor was thickly sewn with those delicate white blooms, their odor now no longer refreshing; rather an overpowering additional element now, in the sultry burning air.

Then the center of the rearmost end wall began to move, revealing another doorway the size of that which led outside into the little garden now denuded of its blooms. As the first heavy, grating crunching ushered this new fact into our keyed-up joint consciousness, we turned sharply toward that wall, now parting, moving back as though on itself.

We looked through, into what seemed an endless, dim-lit vaulted arena of some forgotten worship, into the lofty nave of a titanic cathedral, through dim, dust-laden distances along a level floor of stone to where at an immense distance shimmered such an altar as the Titans might have erected to Jupiter, an altar of shining white stone and flanked by a chiseled figure of a young man, kneeling on one knee, and holding poised on that knee a vast cornucopia-like jar, for all the world, as I envisaged it, like a statute of zodiacal Aquarius.

Greatly intrigued, Wilkes and I walked through the doorway out of our stone anteroom, into the colossal structure which towered far, far above into dimness, and straight across the stone-flagged nave toward this unexpected and alluring shrine; glowing up ahead there in all the comeliness of its ancient chaste beauty.

That the architecture here, including the elaborate ornamentation, was that of those same early Mayas concerning whom Pelletier had discoursed so learnedly, there could be no possible question. Here, plainly, was a very ancient and thoroughly authentic survival, intact, of the notable building propensity of that early people, The First Mayas of the High Culture, the founders of the predecessors of the present surviving and degenerate inhabitants. Here, about us, remained the work of that cryptic civilization which had so unaccountably disappeared off this planet's face, leaving their enduring stone monuments, their veritable handiwork, developed, sophisticated, with its strange wealth of ornamentation behind them as an insoluble riddle for the archeologists.

That this stupendous structure was a survival from a hoary antiquity there was all about us abundant and convincing evidence. I knew enough of the general subject to be acutely aware of that, that this represented the building principles of the earliest period – the high point, as I iderstood the matter, of the most notable of the successive Maya civilizations. That the building had stood empty and unused for some incalculable period in time was equally evidenced by various facts. One of these, unmistakable, was the thick blanket of fine dust which lay, literally inches thick, over everything; dust through which we were obliged to plod as though over the trackless surface of some roofed and ceiled Sahara; dust which rose in choking clouds behind and about us as we pressed forward toward that distant altar and its glorious statue.

That figure of the youth with his votive jar towered up ahead of us there, white, glistening, beautiful – and the dust of uncounted centuries which lay inches thick upon its many upper, bearing, surfaces such as offered support to its impalpability, caused the heroic figure to stand out in a deeply enhanced and accentuated perspective, lending to it strange highlights in shining contrast to the very dust's thick, quasi-shadows; a veritable perfection of shading such as no sculptor of this world could hope to rival.

We walked, necessarily rather slowly, on and forward toward the altar and statue, their beauty and symmetry becoming more and more clearly apparent as our progress brought them closer and closer within the middle range of our vision.

Naturally enough, I had pondered deeply upon the whole affair in which we were involved, in those intervals – such as our long night walk – as had been afforded us between the various actual 'attacks' of the Power that held us in its grip. I had, of course, put two and two together again and again in the unceasing human mental process of effort to make problematical two-and-two yield the satisfying four of a solution.

This process, had, of course, included the consideration of many matters, such as the possible connection between the existence of the Great Power and that same ancient Maya civilization; the basic facts, the original reasons back of the terror of those massed aborigines swarming in their forest cover all about the tree-circle; the placing in their appropriate categories of the phenomena of the Great Body; that mechanical regular pulsation which could only be the throbbing of Its circulatory fluids – Ichor was the classical term, I remembered, for the blood of a god; the 'ravines' which crossed each other like shallow valleys and which were the 'lines' upon that primordial palm; the hirsute growth adorning that titanic forearm which had glistened like metallic tree-boles as the morning sun shone down that slope, and which moved their tapering tops in the breeze from the cosmic nostrils.

All such as these, and various other details, I had, I say, attempted mentally to resolve, to adjust to their right and logical places and settings; to work, that is, mentally, into some coherent unity, literal or cosmic.

The process had included the element of worship. The gods and demigods of deep antiquity had had their worshipers, their devotees diabolic or human, and this as an integral part, an essential, of their now only vaguely comprehended existence; since day and night struggled for primordial precedence in the dim gestation of time.

That those prehistoric, highly civilized Maya forebears might have been worshipers of this particular Power (which, as we had had forced upon our attention, had somehow localized Its last stand here in these modern times – that Great Circle; the tree in its center as Its bridge to and from this world of ours) was a possibility which had long since occurred to me. That such a possibility might have some bearing upon that scientific puzzle which centered about their remote and simultaneous disappearance, had, I am sure, also occurred to me at that time. To that problem, which had barely come under my mental scrutiny because it was not central in terms of our predicament, I had, I am equally sure, given no particular thought.

That there could, in the nature of the case, be any evidence – 'documentary' or merely archeological – had not entered my mind. I did wonder about it now, however, as we two plodded forward through those choking dust clouds, slowly yet surely onward toward what seemed to have been a major shrine of such forgotten worship, if, indeed, what I suspected had ever had its place upon this planet.

For one thing, the worshipers themselves would by now have been dust these twenty centuries; perhaps, indeed, the once-animated basis of this very powder which swirled and eddied about us two, up from underfoot as we pushed forward laboriously toward the shrine. There, in its forgotten heyday, that worship had sent swirling and eddying upward in active spirals incense compounded of the native tree-gums; the balsams and *olibana*, the styrax and powdered sweet-leaves of the environing forests; incense bearing upward in its votive clouds the aspirations of an antiquity as remote as that of the Roman Augurs, and to a deity fiercer, more inscrutable, than Olympian Jove.

It would, indeed, have been a relief to us to see some worshipers now, human beings, even though, devoted as they might be to their deity in Whose hostile power we were held, such personages should prove correspondingly hostile to us. This unrelenting, unrelieved god-and-victim situation was a truly desperate one. Within its terms – as I have elsewhere tried to make clear – we felt ourselves helpless. There was nothing to strike against! A man, however resolute, cannot, in the very nature of things, contend with a Power of this kind! Useless mere courage, fortitude. Even the possession of a body stalwart, inured by exercise and constant usage against conflict and the deadly fatigue of intensive competitive effort, is no match for hurricanes – powerless against a Force which could be mistaken for a major geographical division of land!

Despite the fact that we had gone without rest or sleep, to say nothing of food and water, for a much longer period than was our common custom; apart, too, from the fact that these sound bodies of ours were just then rather severely strained and racked from the cosmic manhandling to which we had been subjected; leaving wholly out of consideration the stresses which had worn thin our nervous resistance – taking into consideration all these factors which told against us, I know that both of us would have welcomed any contact, even though it should involve conflict of the most drastic kind, with human beings, people like ourselves. They might be, for all of us, out of any age, past or present; of any degree of rudeness, of any lack of civilization, in any numbers – just so that they be human.

We did not know then – certainly I did not, and Wilkes was saying nothing – what lay in wait for us, just around the corner of time, so to speak!

We had by now traversed about half of the distance between the anteroom and the altar. Behind us, a heavy, weaving, tenuous cloud of the fine dust we had disturbed hung like a gray, nebulous curtain between us and the towering rearward end wall of that enormous fane. Ahead now the altar glowed, jewel-like, in the slanting rays of a declining sun, rays which appeared to fall through some high opening as yet invisible to us. The genuflecting figure I have named Aquarius gleamed, too, gloriously, in its refined, heroic contours – a thing of such pure beauty as to cause the beholder to catch his breath.

About us all things were utterly silent, a dead stillness, like the settled, lifeless quiet of some abandoned tomb. Even our own foot-falls, muffled in the thick dust of marching centuries, registered no audible sound.

An then, with the rude abruptness which seemed to characterize every manifestation of that anachronistic divinity, that survival out of an unfriendly past, there came without any warning the deep, soul-stirring, contrapuntal beat of a vast gong. This tremendous note poured itself into this dead world, this arid arena of a forgotten worship; the sudden, pulsing atmosphere of renewal, of life itself.

We stopped there in our tracks and the fine dust rose all about us like gray cumulus. We looked, we listened, and all about us the quickening air became alive. Then the vibrating, metallic clangor reverberated afresh and the atmosphere was electrified into pulsing animation; an unmistakable, palpable sense of fervid, hastening act-ivity. We stood there, in that altered environment, tense, strained, every nerve and every faculty aroused as though by an unmistakable abrupt challenge. The altar seemed to coruscate in this new atmosphere. The zodiacal figure of Aquarius gleamed afresh in the sun's slanting rays with a poignant, unearthly beauty.

The slow, shattering sub-bass of the gong reverberated a third time, its mighty, overtonic echoes jarring the revived air with a challenging summons; and, before these had wholly died away and silence above the dust clouds established itself, out from some point beside and beyond the altar there emerged a slow-moving procession of men in long, dignified garments, in hierarchical vesture, walking gravely, two and two.

We watched breathlessly. Here, at long last, was the fulfilment of that half-formulated wish. Human beings! Here were worshipers: tall, stalwart men; great, bearded men, warriors in seeming; bronzed, great-thewed hierophants, bearing strange instruments, the paraphernalia of some remote ritual – wands and metal cressets; chained thuribles, naviculae, long cornucopiae, like that upon the flexed knee of Aquarius; harsh-sounding systra, tinkling triangles, netted rattles strung with small, sweet-chiming bells; salsalim, castanets, clanging cymbals; great rams' horns banded with plates of shining fresh gold; enormous, fanlike implements of a substance like elephants' hide; a gilt canopy, swaying on ebony poles, ponderous, its fringes powdered with jewels, sheltering a votive bullock, its wide horns buried beneath looped garlands. This procession moved gravely toward the altar, an endless stream of grave, bearded men, until, as we watched, stultified, wondering, the space about it became finally filled, and the slow-moving, endless-seeming throng, women and girls among the men now, turned toward us, pouring deliberately into the forepart of the nave.

It was, after this change in the course of the procession's objective, only a matter of seconds before we were seen. There was no possibility of retreat, nothing whatever behind which we might have concealed ourselves. We could, of course, have lain down, burrowing in the dust, and so, perhaps, have delayed the instant of discovery. But that did not occur to either of us. Such a course would, too, have been quite futile. Enormous as was this vast fane – built, it appeared, to accommodate worshipers in their thousands – there were here, thronging in endlessly, more than enough to fill it to suffocation.

There was, once we were observed, not so much as an instant's hesitation, a moment's respite for us. Between the instant when the foremost of that great throng perceived us, strangers, outlanders, and the instantaneous corporate cry of rage which rose from a thousand throats, there was not time for us to clasp hands in a futile gesture of farewell. They rushed us without any other preliminary than that roar of fierce, primitive anger. The dust under that mass movement of sandeled feet rose in an opaque cloud which obscured the altar. Out of that thick, mephitic cloud they came at us, brandishing thick, metallic, macelike clubs, great bronze swords, obvious, menacing, in that dust-dim air, the rapidly-failing light of the sun – deadly blades, thirsting for our blood.

'Back to back, as soon as they surround us,' I hurled in Wilkes's ear, but I had not completed that brief counsel of despair when Wilkes, who produced from somewhere a small, flat automatic pistol, had abruptly dropped in his tracks a huge bearded warrior, who, by reason of a greatly superior fleetness of foot, had by far outdistanced the others. This giant fell within fifteen feet of us. The nearest of the others, also bounding along well in advance of the pack, was perhaps thirty feet distant. I had time to plunge forward and seize out of a great hairy fist the enormous bronze sword of this our first casualty. With this it was my plan to rush back to where Wilkes stood, sighting calmly along his pistol barrel, as I glimpsed him, and make together some sort of stand.

The second runner was nearly on top of me, however, before I could straighten up and try to fell him with this untried weapon. Wilkes shot him through the middle precisely as he was about to bring down his macelike weapon across my skull. I secured the mace before any of the others out of that frenzied horde was within striking distance, and leaped back through the now boiling dust clouds to Wilkes's side. This was a trifle better, though obviously hopeless against those odds. I straightened myself, caught my balance, turned to face the rush beside Wilkes.

'Good for five more, anyhow!' said Wilkes calmly, firing past me twice in quick succession. I was turned about and again facing the oncoming rush in time to see two more of them sinking down. I thrust choice of the two primitive weapons I had secured toward Wilkes. He snatched the mace in his left hand, fired his remaining three shots, hurled the pistol into the thick of the vanguard; and then, shifting the mace to his right hand while I made my huge sword sing through the dust, we faced the attack.

We possessed jointly the single advantage of comparative lightness. Our massed opponents were uniformly men of literally huge stature, heroic-looking fellows, stalwart, bulky, deadly serious in this business of killing!

Unquestionably, as I think back over that conflict, too much emphasis cannot be placed upon this single advantage of lightness, mobility, to which I have just alluded. Otherwise, had we not been able to move about very much more rapidly than our opponents, that fight would have been finished, with our offhand slaughter, in a matter of seconds! The odds were – 'overwhelming' is not the word. 'Ridiculous' comes nearer to it. Probably a thousand of the enormous warriors were using their utmost endeavor to close in upon and slaughter two men. But they necessarily got inextricably tangled up together for that very reason. If they had delegated two or three of their number to attend to Wilkes and me while the others merely stood by, there can be no question but what they would have accomplished their end, and in a very brief period of time.

The bulk, and the consequent relative awkwardness of the individual warriors, too, counted powerfully in our favor. We were, thus, both jointly infinitely more mobile than the huddled phalanx which we confronted, and individually as well when compared, man for man, to even the lightest of our opponents when considered singly. They got into each others' way through the sheer directness of their massed attack, and of this circumstance which counted so heavily in our favor we took the fullest advantage. The great warriors, too, appeared to pay no attention either to their own dead, which began to pile up after a few moments of that intensive affray, and these, as they increased, served to protect us and to cause them, intent only on reaching us, to stumble broadcast. They seemed to know nothing of defensive fighting.

We plunged, both of us, into that fight, berserk, with no other idea but that this was the inevitable, the predestined end; no other idea than that we were going out like men – and with as much company as possible for whatever Stygian process might await us beyond the doors of that imminent death.

It was like a preface to Valhalla, that fight! In that remote edge of my brain which people call 'the back of the mind', I remember the thought cropping up that such combat as this was an affair of utter futility! We had no shadow of misunderstanding with these towering, swarming legionaries out of some unguessed backwater of antiquity. They, certainly, apart from their primitive urges, had no reason for attacking us. Yet, I confess, I went into that shambles with a sense of relief, with a quite definite satisfaction, a gusto! These great, truculent, brown, bearded creatures were subjects of, part and parcel with, that hostile demigod, that basic anachronism, Who was persecuting us. Striking at them, His Myrmidons, meant blows at Him – shrewd blows they were . . .

We struck out, Wilkes and I. I found my great awkward-looking weapon surprisingly well-balanced and keen. It was only after I had sheared through that first torso, clear through the big neck muscles and ribs of my first actual opponent, that I realized what a sword could be! I set my teeth. Vague, hereditary instincts burgeoned in my blood-quickened mentality. I went half mad with the urge to slay. I exulted as my great sword found its mark, struck home again and yet again. Half-articulate cries burst through my compressed lips; terrible thoughts, a fearful, supporting self-confidence boiled in my mind as I fought, and thrust, and swung; vague instincts freshly quickened into seething life and power; the inheritance from count-less Nordic forebears, men who were men indeed, heroes of song and saga, men of my clan who had fought their relentless way to chieftainship, men who fought with claymores.

There came over me a terrible swift surge of security, of certainty, of appalling confidence. I was more than a man. I, too, was a god, empowered with the achievements of those old Canevins who had feared neither man nor devil in the ancient eras of the clan's glory in the field of red battle – a sense of strange happiness, of fulfilment, of some deep destiny coming into its own like the surging up of a great tide. This, I suppose, is what people name the blood-lust. I do not know. I only know that I settled down to fighting, my brain alert, my arm wielding the sword tirelessly, my feet and legs balancing me for the great shearing strokes with which I cleared space after recurrent space about me and caused the mounded dead to make a bulwark between me and those indefatigable huge brutes who pressed on and on, filling up the ranks of their cloven, sinking colleagues.

Heredity laid its heavy hand upon me as I slew right and left and always before me. It was like some destiny, I say, fulfilling itself. Strange cries, deep, primitive slogans burst from my lips. I pressed upon those before me – we were, of course, surrounded – and, feeling the comradeship of Wilkes at my back as he swung and lashed out with that metal club taking his toll of brains and crackling skulls, I surged into a song, a vast war shout, rushing upon the ever-renewed front of my enemies, flailing the great sword through yielding flesh and resistant bone and sinew, forward, ever forward into a very fulfilment and epitome of slaughter. From time to time one or another would reach, and wound me, but the blood of the ancient fighting clan of Canevin heeded not.

My bronze sword drank deep as it sheared insatiable through tissue and tendon. Before me, an oriflamme, flared a blood-red mist in that dank shambles where blood mingled with paralyzing dust clouds. It was basic; hand to hand; pure conflict. My soul exulted and sang as I ploughed forward into the thick of it, Wilkes's staccato 'Ha!' as his metal club went home, punctuating the rhythm of my terrible strokes against that herded phalanx. I struck and struck, and the sword drank and drank.

I strode among heaped bodies now, seeking foot leverage, a greater purchase for my blows. Against these heart-lifting odds, heedless of death, feeling none of the gashes and bruises I received, I strove, in a still-mounting fury of utter destruction. I drove them before me in scores, in hundreds . . .

Then, insistent, paralyzing, came the last stroke, the shattering reverberation of the great gong.

With that compelling stroke, like the call of Fate, the conflict died all about me. The tense, striving fury dropped away from the distorted faces before me. Their weapons fell. I heard Wilkes's quick 'Ha!' as his last blow went home on a crumpling skull, and then my sword hung idle all at once in my scarlet hand; the pressure of the circle about us relaxed, fell away to nothing. I breathed again without those choking gasps through air fouled with the fetor of dust and blood – old dust, newly-shed blood. We stood together, still back to back, our strained hearts pumping wildly, our red vision clearing. We stood near the very rearmost wall now, such had been the pressure into the nave.

We turned, as though by an agreement, and looked into each other's eyes. Then, as a surge of chanted song far up by the altar inaugurated this worship which was beginning, which had taken from us the attention of that mad horde, we slipped quietly out through the anteroom, and into the garden now tremulous with the verge of dusk upon it; side by side, on the short grass, we lay down upon our faces, and relaxed our sorely taxed bodies, turned, and spoke quietly to each other, and gazed up at the friendly stars, and closed our eyes, and fell at once into the quick deep sleep of complete and utter exhaustion.

It was Wilkes who shook me awake. It was pitch dark, or nearly so, the moon being at the moment obscured under clouds. A light, refreshing rain was falling, and my soaking wetness from head to foot evidenced a heavier shower through which both of us had slept. My wounds and bruises from that terrific mêlée ached and burned and throbbed. Yet I had lost little blood, it appeared, and when I stood up and had moved about somewhat, my usual agility seemed quite fully restored. The phosphorus-painted dial of my wrist-watch – which had survived that shambles intact – showed that it was half past four in the morning.

'I've been scouting around,' explained Wilkes. 'It isn't so bad in this light after you've got used to it a bit. I've discovered a sapodilla tree. That's why I awakened you, Canevin – thought you could do with a bit to eat, what?'

He held out four of the round, dull-brown fruits which look like Irish potatoes. I took them eagerly, the first food in many hours. I do not recall a more satisfactory meal at any time in my life.

Greatly refreshed, I washed my hands in the rain and wiped them clean on the short wet grass. Wilkes was speaking again.

'Those people, Canevin! There are no such people in the world, today – except here, I believe. What do you think? That is, if you've had time to think after that. Good God, man, were you a gladiator in some past existence? But, to get back to those people in there. It seems to me that – well, either those are the old-time Mayas, surviving just in this spot, wherever it may be, or else – do you suppose He could – er – make them immortal, something of the sort, what? Sounds ridiculous. I grant you that, of course, but then, this whole affair is . . . ' He paused, leaving me to fill in the adjective. I stepped on something hard. I stooped down, picked up the enormous sword which I had carried out here to the garden when we had left the temple last night. I balanced it in my hand. I looked at Wilkes in the still dim light.

'It's really, in a sense, the greatest puzzle of all,' I said reflectively. 'You're right, of course. No question about it, man! Those people were – well, anything but what I'd call contemporaries of ours. I'd almost be inclined to say that the immortality alternative gets my vote.'

'Let's go back and take a look for ourselves,' said Wilkes. 'We don't seem, somehow, to have very much choice, this trip. Now seems to be one of the slack moments. Let's go back inside there, get up behind that altar and statue, and see what's there, in that place they all marched out from, what? Everything seems quieted down now inside; has been for hours on end, I'd say. We weren't molested while we slept through all that rain.'

I nodded. A man can only die once, and the Power could, certainly, do as it wished with us. The rain ended, as tropical showers end, abruptly. The sweet odor of some flowering shrub poured itself out. The clouds passed from before the moon.

'Right,' said I. 'Let's get going.' And, without another word, we entered the stone anteroom, walked across it to where the doorway had opened into the temple, and – stopped there. The door was shut now. It was not, in the dim moonlight which filtered through the openings, even perceptible now. There was simply nothing to be seen there, not so much as a chink in the solid masonry of the wall, to indicate that there was a door.

'We'll have to work around to it from the outside,' said Wilkes, after we had stood awhile in baffled silence. 'There must be a way.'

I laughed. 'They say that "where there's a will there's a way", ' I quoted. "Well, let's try it, outside," answered Wilkes; and we walked out into the garden again.

There was no particular difficulty about finding that 'way'. We simply walked around the end of the small structure I have called the anteroom and followed along the almost endlessly high, blank stone-mason work of the temple's outside sheathing. The walking was not difficult, the growth being chiefly low shrubs. At last we came to the end of the temple wall, and turned the sharp corner it made at the beginning of a slight slope which ran down very gradually in the same direction in which we had been walking.

To our considerable surprise, for we had thought of nothing like this, there stretched away from us, farther than we could see in the moonlight broken by small, drifting clouds of the cirrus variety, a succession of other buildings, all of them obviously of that same early-civilization period of the first Maya empire, rounded structures for the most part, carrying the typical stone arrangement and orna-mentation. Enormous as was the great temple, the area occupied by these massed and crowded buildings, close-standing, majestic in their heavy, solid grandeur, was far greater. The nearest, less than half the height of the towering temple side walls, was joined onto the temple itself, and stretched away virtually out of our sight. We stood and looked up at this.

'Undoubtedly,' I agreed, standing beside him and looking up at the solid masonry, its massive lines somewhat broken, dignified and beautiful in the fickle, transient moonlight.

Not a sound, not a whisper, even from a night insect, broke the deathly stillness. I remembered the Great Circle.

'It's His territory, right enough,' I murmured; and Wilkes nodded.

'Closed for the season!' he said lightly, and lit a cigarette.

I sat down beside Wilkes and looked for my cigarette case. I had left it in the pocket of my drill jacket when I took it off and laid it on the ground beside Pelletier before going up the tree. Curiously, in all this time that had elapsed I had not thought of smoking. Wilkes handed me his case, and we sat there side by side saying nothing. A glance down at the heavy sword which I had laid across my knees reminded me of our current mission.

'We'll have to go all the way to the end of this masonry-work at least,' I said, 'before we can get into the inclosure!'

Wilkes tossed away the stub of his cigarette, stood up, and stretched his arms.

'All right,' said he, 'let's do it.'

It took us a quarter of an hour of steady walking before we came to a corner. We turned this, walked past that enormous building's end, and emerged in a kind of open space much like the quadrangle of a modern university, only many times larger in area, surround by more buildings dim in the present light, one side bounded by the edge of the great structure we had been skirting. The moonlight shone somewhat brighter on this side, against that long plain wall of masonry.

Suddenly Wilkes caught me by the arm. He uttered a typically British expletive.

'My hat!' said Wilkes, 'Look, Canevin! There isn't a window in the place!'

We stood looking up at the building.

'Curious,' commented Wilkes. 'Other old Maya architecture has windows – that little anteroom effect we called in at before going into the temple has windows, both sides. Why not this?'

'Perhaps it's a kind of store-house,' I suggested. 'If so, it wouldn't need windows.'

'I doubt that – sort of instinct, perhaps,' returned Wilkes. 'All along I've had the idea that the – er – congregation came out of this into the temple. It's attached – we saw that outside there, built right onto it; we had to walk around it on just that account.'

'If you're right,' I said, reflecting, 'if there are people in there – well, then they don't need windows – light.'

'If so, why? threw out Wilkes; and I had no answer.

We stood staring up at the blank, unornamental, solid wall.

'Curious!' vouchsafed Wilkes again. 'Curious, no end!' Then: 'Might bear out my idea, rather – you remember, Canevin? That "immortality" idea I mean. If He has them – er – preserved, so to speak, ready to be revived, started going when He wants them, or *needs* them, what? As you remarked, they weren't exactly "contemporaries" of ours! He's been going at this whole affair His own way, all through; not the way we human being would go at it. If you ask me, He – er – needed them to scrag us in there, in the temple I mean. They tried, you know! Failed, rather! We're still on deck, Canevin! And, back of that – why, for the sake of argument, did He set us down here, on earth once more, but not at the same old stand, not where we parked the old bus, in that circle of grass, under that tree? Perhaps it's a small matter but – well, why, Canevin? Why here, I mean to say, rather than there? It's a point to consider at any rate. Looks to me, if you ask me, as though He were trying, in His own peculiar way, to do us in, and had, so far, failed.'

I pondered over this long speech of Wilkes's, the longest I had heard him make. He was, like many engineering fellows, inclined to be monosyllabic rather than garrulous. It was, I thought, a curious piece of reasoning. Yet, anything coming from this staunch comrade in a pinch such as he had proved himself to be, was worth consideration. It might be what he called 'instinct', or indeed, anything. It might be the truth.

I was very far from realizing at that moment – and so, too, I think, was Wilkes himself, despite this curiously suggestive set of ideas – that within a very short time this utterly strange adventure upon which we were embarked was to give us its final, and, thoughtfully considered, perhaps its most poignant, surprise. Even warned as I should have been by Wilkes's strange surmise, I was quite unprepared for what we found inside.

We proceeded slowly along what I have called the inner wall of the vast structure which joined the temple at its farther end. We walked for minute after minute along beside it, always glancing up at it, constantly on the lookout for an entrance. The walls remained entirely blank, without either apertures or ornamentation. The huge building might, to all appearances, have been some prehistoric warehouse or granary.

At last we came to its end, the end structurally joined onto the temple's rearmost wall. We walked directly up to this point, where the two structures made a sharp corner.

There was no entrance except, presumably, through the temple, from the inside, there behind the altar. We had had half an hour's walk around these massive survivals of ancient architecture for nothing. It was five-three by my watch in the moon's clear light. The clouds had retreated toward the horizon by now, as we stood there at that corner, baffled.

We turned, rather wearily now, away at right angles from our course just finished, and plodded along the grassy ground under the towering rear wall of the temple.

And, halfway along it, we came to an opening, an arched doorway without a door. We stopped, point-blank, and looked at each other.

'Shall we . . . ?' whispered Wilkes.

I nodded, and stepped through, the great sword, which I had been carrying like a musket over my shoulder, now gripped, business-fashion, in my right hand.

We stepped through into an ambulatory, a semicircular passage-way behind the altar. We turned to our left, in the direction of the temple's corner against which was built the building we had been encircling, walking once more through heaped dust such as had clogged the nave, our footfalls soundless in an equally soundless environment.

Emerging from that semicircular course at the altar's side, we were able to see from this coign of vantage the overhead opening through which the rays of the late-afternoon sun had streamed down the day before. This was a wide space left vacant in the roofing, far above, overhung by what seemed another roof-structure twenty or thirty feet higher up, an arrangement plainly designed to keep out the rain while letting in the rays of the declining sun.

Now, in the moonlight of pre-dawn, both altar and statue took on an unearthly beauty. We stood rapt, looking along the altar directly toward the face of the statue.

This time it was I who jogged Wilkes's elbow.

'It's a quarter past five,' I warned him. 'If we're going to get a look at those people, we'd better do it now, before daylight. We haven't very long. And if they're – well, regular people, ordinary human beings, a segregated nation and *not* – er – "embalmed", or whatever it is you had in mind, we'd best take a quick glance and get away before they are awake!'

We turned away from those shimmering, pale glories which were the altar and the statue, the one jeweled, the other shining, resplendent, toward the predicated passageway that must lead out of the temple to where its erstwhile worshipers took their repose.

We could have told where it began if we had been blind men, by the feel of the heavily-trodden dust under our feet, dust not heaped and soft as we had experienced it – dust matted into the consistency of felt by the pressure of ten thousand feet.

Along that carpet over the stone flooring of a wide passageway we walked, warily now, not knowing what we might confront, toward a high, wide archway which marked the entrance proper into the windowless barrack or storehouse we had so lately scrutinized.

Here the moonlight shone scantily. We could not see very far before us, but we could see far enough to show us what kind of place it was into whose purlieus we had penetrated. We paused, just beyond the archway, paused and looked . . .

There, in that storehouse laid out before us as far as the dim moonlight permitted our vision to reach, straight before us until their regular ranks were no longer visible except to the agitated eye of the mind, lay endless, regularly spaced rows of bodies, endless rows, rank upon serried rank; still, motionless, mummy-like, in the ineffable calm of latency; life suspended; life merged into one vast, incalculable coma. This was a storehouse indeed, in very fact: the last abiding place of those old Mayas of the first civilization, that classical puzzle of the archeologists – a puzzle no longer to Wilkes and me of all modern men; a civilization, a nation, in bond to the Power that still held us in an ironical, unrelenting, grasp – to that One Whom these very ancients worshiped and propitiated, the Prince of the Powers of the Air . . .

Without a word we hastened out of that grim house of a living death and back into the temple, and, with no more than a glance toward the altar and statue, hurried silently back through the ambulatory and out through the doorless archway again into the breaking dawn of another day, under the fading stars of a new morning.

And, as we emerged, toward us, diagonally across what I have called the 'quadrangle', in regular formation, disciplined, there marched unfaltering, resolute, a vast horde of tall, brown men, led by two figures who stepped gravely in their van, ahead of those serried thousands. He on the left was a tall, brown man of majestic carriage, bearing in his hand a small burning torch, young, yet of a commanding dignity as one used to rule. Upon the right marched beside him a heavy, lumbering figure, who walked wearily; yet not without a certain heavy dignity of his own, a figure of a certain familiarity – the figure of Pelletier!

My immediate instinct was to cry in sudden relief, to rush incontinently forward. I felt suddenly as though my heart would burst. Pelletier, of all the men this old planet could possibly produce, here! Pelletier, the most welcome sight . . .

I could not have done so, however, even though I had actually yielded to that impulse I have named. For Pelletier was calling out to me, in a curious kind of voice, I noted at once, with some puzzlement – in a kind of rude, improvised chant.

'Steady, Canevin, steady does it, as the British Navy says! Walk toward us, both of you, side by side; stand up straight; make it as dignified as you know how – slow; like two big guns conferring a favor on the populace. Pay no attention to anybody but me. Stop in front of me. We'll bow to each other; not too low. Then, when *He* bows, put your hands on his head – like a blessing, do you understand? On this big fellow beside me, I mean. Don't botch it now either of you. It's important . . . Good! That's the ticket! Keep it up now; carry the whole works through just the way I'm telling you.'

We carried out these amazing instructions to the letter. They were, of course, apart from the general idea of making an impression on Pelletier's inexplicable following, quite unintelligible to us. But, we went through with them precisely according to these weird, chanted instructions – like the directions of some madman, a paranoiac for choice! 'Delusions of grandeur!' The old phrase came inevitably into my mind. Even the young chieftain did his part, kneeling with gravity before us as soon as we had finished our salutation to Pelletier, and he had majestically returned it.

Immediately after these ceremonial performances which were received in a solemn silence by the army – for the orderly ranks were numerous enough to deserve such a distinctive title – Pelletier drew us aside and spoke with haste tempering his gravity.

'I'll explain all this later. Tell me, first, how long have you been in this place?'

We told him we had spent the night here and started to outline our adventures, but Pelletier cut in.

'Another time,' he said curtly. 'This is vital, pressing. Is there anything here – I don't know, precisely, how to make clear exactly what I mean; you'll have to use your wits; I haven't the time to hold a long palaver now, and we mustn't waste a minute – anything, I mean, that would correspond to that tree you fellows went up; something, in other words, that would serve – er – Him as a bridge, a means of access to the earth? I don't know how to make it any clearer. Maybe you catch what I mean.'

'There's a temple back of us,' said Wilkes, 'with an altar – '

'And a statue,' I finished for him, 'a magnificent thing, heroic in size; looks for all the world like the figure of Aquarius in the signs of the zodiac. Possibly – '

'Take us straight to it,' commanded Pelletier, and turned and spoke rapidly to the brown chieftain in sonorous Spanish. He told him to detach one hundred or more of his most reliable warriors and follow us without the least delay, and to this task the young leader forthwith addressed himself. Within two minutes, so unquestioned appeared to be his authority, this picked company was following us at the double back to the temple entrance, back along the curving ambulatory, back to the vicinity of the altar and statue.

We paused at the point where these first became visible, and Pelletier looked at the statue for a long instant.

'The perfect focus!' he muttered, and turned and addressed the chieftain once more.

'Advance with us in close order,' he commanded, 'to the figure of the man holding the vessel. Draw up the men beside it, on this side, and when I give you the signal, push it over on its side!'

This order, immediately passed on to the Indians, was set in motion without delay, the stalwart fellows crowding toward the statue eagerly.

We were almost beside the statue when the sudden roar of the great gong, almost beside us, shattered the quiet air. I winced, and so did Wilkes, and the Indians stopped in their tracks. Automatically I gripped the hilt of my bronze sword as I felt Wilkes's steadying hand close on my shoulder.

Then Pelletier raised his great booming voice and began to sing in Spanish, something about 'the conquering fire'! He almost literally pushed that group of Indians toward their appointed task. Not without a certain hesitation, a reluctance, I thought, they lined up beside the statue obediently, yet with rolled eyes and fearful glances in all directions, indicating that panic lay only a little way below their corporate surface of strict obedience. Then, at Pelletier's spoken signal, the massed group heaved, all together. The great statue moved, gratingly, on its solid foundation.

'Again!' cried Pelletier, and hurled his own weight and bulk into the balance.

The statue swayed this time, hung balanced precariously, then toppled over on its farther side in a shattering crash which detached the cornucopia and the beautifully modeled arms and hands which held it, at the very instant of the gong's second, deep, reverberant note.

Pelletier surveyed the damage he had wrought; turned with the rest of us toward the entering procession that came marching in from that arched opening, precisely as we had seen them enter at yesterday's fall of dusk. It was now, however, the fresh, clear light of early morning, and in this better illumination I confess that I gasped at what I had not observed the day before.

Upon the garments, yes, upon the very jutting, powerful features of the members of that hierarchical company gravely advancing now towards us, upon their hair and their beards, even their shaggy eyebrows, hung the clotted dust of the centuries!

But, Wilkes and I did not hesitate over this strange sight. We knew why He had summoned once again these Myrmidons of His from their sleep-like-death in those storerooms of His, those slave pens.

'Out, for God's sake, out, as quick as you can get them going!' I cried out to Pelletier. 'There are thousands of them!' And he, not hesitating now that he had accomplished what he had come here to do, over any idea of conflict against the overwhelming odds which I had indicated, passed swiftly to his Indians the word of command and retreat.

But even this immediate response of his to my warning was not swift enough. We had been observed, and already as he shouted to the chieftain, that corporate roar of rage and fury was rising, multiplying itself, as more and more voices joined in upon its fearsome volume. Already the foremost hierophants of this now-desecrated shrine were parting their ranks to let through and at us the massed warriors who pressed eagerly to the attack.

I was deadly weary. Yet, something of that old fighting blood call of the Canevins, some stavistic battle lust derived from those ancient fighting forebears of mine, nerved me of sudden. Those ancestors of mine had shirked no conflict, if tradition spoke truly down the ages. I swung up the great bronze sword, a strange, vague, yet unmistakable call from dim departed ages of red battle stirring my blood to fire. With a shout on my lips I stepped out before that company of ours, prepared to meet the oncoming rush, if need be, alone.

But I was frustrated in this mad instinctive gesture – frustrated, I say, and in the strangest manner imaginable. For I was not the only one who stepped out into the open space between our group and the rush of oncoming fighting men of a revived antiquity. No. Beside me, towering tall, slender, commanding, pressed the noble figure of that young chieftain, unarmed, his long arms held straight up before him, the palms of his hands held forward in an immemorial gesture of authority.

Then from his lips there burst a veritable torrent of some strange, sonorous speech, at the sound of which the oncoming fighting men stopped dead.

I paused, amazed at this wholly unexpected occurrence. I lowered my sword automatically as I saw the menacing weapons brandished by the others likewise lowered.

On and on went that authoritative speech, until of a sudden it stopped as abruptly as it had been begun, and the young chieftain lowered his hands, folded his arms, and stood facing the now silent throng of brown, bearded warriors and the priests of their strange cult behind them, all of them equally motionless before him, their massed attention directed to him alone, standing there like a group carved out of stone.

And then, out of the midst of them, came one great bearded giant. This man, evidently their leader, walked straight toward us where we stood grouped behind the orator, paused before him, and then this statuesque warrior flung down his bronze sword, clanging, and prostrated himself. The young chieftain took two grave steps forward, and placed his sandaled foot upon the prostrate figure's neck. Inspired, I stepped over to him and placed my own great bronze sword in his hand.

Of how we traveled back to the Great Circle through a mahogany forest interspersed with ceiba, Otaheite, and Guinea-tamarind trees, I shall say but little. We traversed levels and dips and toiled up slopes and skirted marshlands. We traveled faint trails which had to be negotiated single file. We passed through clearing recently cut free of the clinging bush and trailing liana vines. Occasionally small, tapir-like quadrupeds started up almost under our feet, disturbed at their early-morning browsing in that thick jungle. We stepped along now and again through stretches fragrant with the odors of frangipane blooms, and the rich, attar-like sweetness of the flowering vanilla orchid.

And at last we came to the edge of the Great Circle once more, at a quarter before nine o'clock by my faithful wrist-watch which had not missed a tick throughout all these alarums and excursions. Here

Pelletier paused, and in a brief, emphatic speech, in Spanish, took leave of and dismissed his army, which melted away, after profound salaams in our direction, into the deeper forests forming the hinterlands of that horizon of jungle. Forty or more hostages, brought with us from the company of those Ancient Ones who had accepted the overlordship of that remarkable young chief, departed with them. They were seen no more by us.

I was far too weary – and poor Wilkes was literally tottering in his tracks – to listen very closely to what Pelletier said to the Indians. As soon as the last of them had disappeared out of our sight, the three of us started across the stretch of short grass, up the slight slope toward the center where our plane still rested on the ground. Pelletier forged ahead to get his first-aid satchel for our wounds.

The great tree was gone!

It was nearly ten o'clock when at last we sank down in the grateful shade of the plane's broad wings, and the last thing that I remember before falling into the sleep from which I was awakened an hour and a half later, was Pelletier holding to my mouth one of our canteens, and feeling the comfort to my parched throat of the stale, tepid water it contained.

It was the roar of the rescuing plane which awakened me, at eleven-thirty.

We reached Belize a few minutes before two. I had slept part of the way in the air, which is no mean feat considering the thunderous roar of the engine. I stumbled up to my bedroom in the hotel, and did not move until seven the following morning.

When I did awaken, raw with weariness, Pelletier was standing beside my bed.

'I thought I'd better tell you as soon as possible,' said he genially, 'that I did all the necessary talking to that rescue party. You and Wilkes had been scouting around, making discoveries, and had got yourselves pretty well worn in the process. They swallowed that easily enough. It was ordinary engine trouble that dished us, out there where they found us. We were out of gas, too. There was the empty tank to prove it. I'll tell you later where that gasoline went to. I'm responsible for that. You'd better stick to the same simple yarn, too. I've already told Wilkes.'

I nodded, and fell asleep again, after drinking without question the glassful of stuff Pelletier handed me. I do not even remember the taste, and I have no idea what the concoction was. But just before noon, when I awakened again, I was myself once more. I got up, bathed thoroughly, and gave myself a very much-needed shave. After lunch I called on the Bishop of British Honduras, and returned to him the binoculars he had considerately loaned me with the thanks of the party.

On the following morning Pelletier and I made our farewells to the splendid Wilkes, and to our other Belize friends and aquaintances. We had secured passage in a fruiter clearing that noon for Kingston, the first leg of our journey home to St Thomas.

About four p.m. that afternoon Pelletier, whom I had not seen since luncheon on board, lumbered along the deck and stopped at my chair.

'Would you like to hear my end of it all now – or would it do better later?' he inquired. He grinned down at me.

'Later – in St Thomas preferably, if it's all the same to you, Pelletier,' I answered him. 'I'd rather get my mind clean off it all and keep it off for the present. Later, by all means, with the home things, the home atmosphere all about me, if you don't mind. Just now I'd rather do nothing and think nothing, and hear nothing beyond ice water, and eating fruit, and sleeping!'

'I don't blame you,' threw back Pelletier as he shuffled ponderously away, the smoke from his big black cigar trailing behind him. We were making ten knots or so, with the wind abaft us, a following wind. I had spoken truly to Pelletier. I did not feel just then, nor indeed, for some time later, that I could easily bear more than casual reference to that experience, all of which, it will be remembered, had been crowded into less than two twenty-four-hour days.

I drank ice water. I ate fruit. I slept. And by easy stages, as we had gone to the coast of Central America, we came back again to the settled peace and comfort of the Lesser Antilles; to the kindly sophistication which is the lovely little city of St Thomas; to the quiet efficiency of my good servants in my house on Denmark Hill. Only then, it seemed to me, could I quite bear to open my mind again to those affairs in the deep jungle of Quintana Roo, where He had established his 'foci' as from time immemorial; where that had happened, with me as active participant, which the structure of our modern minds bears ill in reminiscence . . .

For it is not always good for a man to see the things that had fallen to Wilkes and myself to see; to have to do what we had done. There were times, even after I had got back and was settled into my accustomed routines, in St Thomas, when I would lie awake in bed, with the scent of the tuberoses and of Cape jessamine pouring in through my windows, and fail of ready sleep, and wonder what really had happened out there; whether or not certain aspects of that adventure were not basically incredible; whether, perhaps, my imagination had not tricked me – in other words, whether or not the whole madhouse affair had actually occurred in very truth; and if I, Gerald Canevin, occasional weaver of tales based upon the somewhat strange affairs of these islands of the Lesser Antilles, might not have suffered some eldritch change.

At such times, I found, it was salutary to change over my attention, when this proved possible, to something else, something as radically different as possible.

I played a good deal of contract bridge, I remember, during that interval of doubt and some distress mentally. I accepted more invit-ations than was usual with me. I wanted, in general, to be with people, sane, everyday, ordinary people, my neighbors and friends, as much as possible. I took off some weight, I remember.

It was not, I think, until Pelletier had related to me his account of how he had spent the period beginning with my disappearance up the tree – it had been removed, I remembered, on my arrival back at the Great Circle, and I had not asked Pelletier what had become of it – until he marched across that 'quadrangle' at the head of his army, that the whole affair, somehow, resolved itself, and ceased troubling me.

'I'll try to tell you my end of it,' said Pelletier. He was in a characteristic attitude, sprawled out over the full length of my Chinese rattan lounge-chair on my cool west gallery, a silver swizzel-jug, freshly concocted by my house man, Stephen Penn, placed between us beside two greenish glasses, the ice-beads all over the outside of it; cigarettes going; myself, just after having done the honors, in another chair; both of us in fresh, white drill, cool and comfortable.

'I had very little to go on,' continued Pelletier, after a healthy sip out of his long, green glass and an accompanying slight grunt of creature satisfaction, 'as you may imagine, Canevin, very little indeed. And yet, it all straightened out, cleared itself up in a kind of natural way. It was, I suppose, partly instinct, a kind of sixth sense if you like. For I had no more idea than you or Wilkes that we were running into a – well, a survival, when I looked down out of the plane and first saw that Circle sticking up to the eye out of that jungle like, like a sore thumb!

'The first definite indication, the first clue, was of course that original crack of wind "out of the corner of hell", as Wilkes put it. Wind is air, and my mind, naturally enough, stuck to that. It was not especially brilliant to deduce an air-elemental, or, at least to have that in my mind all the way through the various happenings; before you started up the tree I mean: that wind out of nowhere; the disappearance of Wilkes; the absence of animal and insect life; those Indians getting around us. It all fitted together, somehow, under the circumstances, and after what both of us have seen of the present-day survival of magic – two-thirds of the world's population believing in it, practicing it: Lord, look at Haiti – well, I thought, if it *were* something supernatural, something not quite of this world, why, then, Canevin, the logic of it all pointed toward the one possibly surviving elemental rather than in some other direction.

'For – don't you see? – man has ousted those others, by his own control of the three other elements, earth, fire, water! The whole land surface of this planet, practically, has been subjected to human use – agriculture, mines, cities built on it – and water the same. We have dominated the element of water, reduced to its allotted sphere in this man-ruled world – ships, submarines, steam – Lord, there's no end to our use of water! Fire, too, Canevin. We have it – er – harnessed, working for us, in every ship's engine room, every dynamo and factory, in every blast-furnace, cook-stove, campfire, automobile.

'And in all this civilization-long process, the one single element that has remained unsubdued, untamed, is air. We are a long way from what people smugly call "the conquest of air", Canevin, a mighty long way, even though we have started in on that, too. Even fire is controllable. Fires do not start by themselves. There is no such thing as "spontaneous combustion"! But who, Canevin, can control the winds of heaven?

'Maybe there's more in what I've just said than appears on the surface. Take astrology for example. Modern science laughs at astrology, puts it in the same category as those Bodily Humours, the Melancholic, and the rest of them! Astronomers nowadays, scientists busy measuring light-years, the chemistry of Antares, whether or not there is barium on Mars, the probable weight of Eros, or the "new" one, Pluto – those fellows tell us the old beliefs about the stars are so much junk. Why? Well, because, they say, the old ideas of things like zodiacal groups and so forth are "unscientific", formulated on the basis of how the stars look from the earth's surface, merely! Artificial, unscientific! The stars must be looked at mathematically, they tell us, not as they appear from your gallery at night.

'But, Canevin, which of those modern sharps has told us where one *should* stand, to view the heavens? And – speaking pragmatically; that's a good scientific word! – which of them has done more than figure out weights, distances – what of them, dry approximations of alleged facts, Canevin? – a lot of formulas like the inside of an algebra book. Which of them, the modern scientific astronomers, from my good old Professor Pickering at Harvard down – for he was the king-pin of them all – has given humanity one single, practical, useful fact, out of all their up-to-the minute modern science? Answer: not one, Canevin!

'And here's the red meat in that account – think of this, Canevin, in the light of relativity, or the Quantum Theory if you like; that's "modern" and "scientific" enough, God knows: the astrological approach is the normal approach, Canevin, *for the people living on this planet*. We have to view the heavens from here, because that's where Almighty God Who made us and them put us. That's the only viewpoint we have, Canevin, and – it works; it possesses the – er – pragmatic sanction of commonsense!

'Well, now, to get down to the brass tacks of this thing, the thing we've been through together, I mean: what is it, as we human beings, constrained to live on earth and meet earth conditions know it, that upsets our schemes, plans and calculations as we deal with the three elements that we *have* brought under control, subdued? It's air, Canevin.

'It's air and air alone that sends hurricanes into these latitudes and knocks out the work and hopes of decades of effort; takes crops, animals, buildings. It's the air that just this season smashed things to pieces right nearby here, in Nicaragua; knocked old Santo Domingo City into a cocked hat. Plants can't grow, leaf-plants especially, without air. Without air fire itself refuses to burn. That's the principle of all the workable fire extinguishers. Without air man and animals can't breathe, and die like fish out of water, painfully. Without air – but what's the use of carrying it further, Canevin?

'I had, of course, the first day and night, alone, to think in. All that, and a lot more besides, went into those cogitations of mine under that tree in the Great Circle both before and after I was there all by myself; mostly after, when I had nothing else to do but think. You see? It wasn't so very hard to figure out, after all.

'But figuring it out was less than half the battle. I was appalled, Canevin, there with my merely human brain figuring out the possible combinations, at what He could do, if He happened to take it into His head. His head! Why, He could merely draw away the breathable air from around us three intruders, and we'd flop over and pass out then and there. He could blast us into matchwood with a hurricane at any moment. He could – well, there's no use going over all the things I figured that He could do. The ways of the gods and the demigods have never been the ways of men, Canevin. All literature affirms that. Well, He didn't do any of those things. He was going at it His way. How to circumvent Him, in time! *That* was the real problem.

'I had, theoretically at least, all three of the other elements to use against Him, the same as every man has – such as a dugout of earth, out there in Kansas, against a tornado of wind; a log fire, to get over the effects of a New England blizzard. I put my mind on it, Canevin, and decided to use Fire – *to burn down the tree*! I did it, toward dusk of the second day.

'I soaked it, all over the trunk and lower part, and as far up as I could reach and throw, with the gasoline from the plane's tanks. I used it all. I was counting, you see, on the rescue plane following our route the next morning when we hadn't shown up in Belize; but, if I couldn't get you and Wilkes back I was pretty thoroughly dished anyhow, and so, of course, were you two fellows.

'I lighted it and ran, Canevin, ran out of the shade – there wouldn't be any left in a short time anyhow – and over to the plane and sat down under the farther wing where I could get a good look through the binoculars at those savages down yonder. I wanted to see how the idea of my fighting one element with another would strike them.

'It struck them right enough!

'There had been plenty of gasoline. The fire roared up the dry tree. It was blazing in every twig, it seemed, inside two minutes after I had set it going. Talk of a study in primitive fear! Psychology! I had it right there, all around me. The only kick I had coming was that I couldn't watch it all at once. It was like trying to take in a forty-ring circus with one pair of eyes!

'They liked it, Canevin! That much was clear enough anyhow.

'It was a medium-sized limb, burned halfway through, which broke off and fell between me and the main blaze, that suddenly gave me the big idea. So far I hadn't planned beyond destroying the tree, His bridge between the earth and wherever He was. But then it suddenly flashed through my mind that here was a chance to enlist those aborigines, while they were all together, and in the mood, so to speak. I went over and picked up that blazing limb. It made a magnificent torch, and, holding it above my head where it blazed as I walked in the falling dusk, I proceeded, slow and-dignified, down toward the place at the jungle's rim where they seemed to be most thickly congregated.

'I had the wit to sing, Canevin! Never knew I could sing, did you? I did then, all the way, the best stab I could make at a kind of paean of victory. Do you get the idea? I walked along steadily, roaring out at the top of my voice. There weren't any particular words – only a lot of volume to it!

'It occurred to me halfway down that out of those thousands some certainly would know Spanish. The idea took hold of me, and by the time I had got near enough to make them understand I had some sentences framed up that would turn them inside-out if it got across to their primitive minds! I stopped, and raised the torch up high over my head, and called it out like old Cortez ordering a charge!

'For a few instants right afterwards I waited to see the effect, if any. They seemed to be milling around more or less in groups and bunches. That, I figured, would be the fellows who understood Spanish telling the others! Then – then it worked, Canevin! They prostrated themselves, in rows, in battalions, in tribes! And every one of them, I was careful to notice, still kept within the safe shelter of the woods. I had, you see, told them who I was, Canevin! I was the Lord of the Fire, that was all, the Great Friend of mankind, the Lord, the Destroyer, the Big Buckaroo and High Cockalorum of all the Elements, and pretty much everything else besides. Spanish lends itself, somehow, to those broad, general statements!

'And then, once again, I had an inspiration. I gathered myself together after that first blast that I had turned loose on them, and let go another! This time I informed them that I was destroying my enemy the Ruler of the Air, who was their enemy as well – I gathered that, of course, from their fear of the Circle – Who had been having His own way with them for a couple of thousand years or thereabouts; that they could see for themselves that I was right here on the tabu place the Circle, and unharmed; and then I called for volunteers to come out of the woods and *stand beside me in the Circle*!

'Canevin, there was a silence that you could have cut with a knife. It lasted and lasted, and lasted! I began to get afraid that perhaps I had gone too far, in some unrealizable way – with savages, you know: not a single, solitary sound, not a whisper, from that mob weighed down with sixty generations of fear.

Then – to a rising murmur which grew into a solid roar of astonishment – one of them, an upstanding young man with an intelligent face, stepped out toward me. I suppose that fellow and his descendants will have epic songs sung about them for the next sixty generations, nights of the full moon.

'I had the general idea, you see, of getting this mob convinced: the new harmlessness of the ancient tabu-ground for conclusive evidence; and then enlisting them. Precisely what I was going to do with them, what to set them at doing, wasn't so clear as the general idea of getting them back of me.

'And right then, when it was working, everything coming my way, I very nearly dropped my authoritative torch, my symbol of the firepower! I went cold, Canevin, from head to foot; positively sick, with plain, shaking, shivering fear! Did they all suddenly start after me with their throw-sticks and blow-guns? Did an unexpected hurricane tear down on me? No. Nothing like that. I had merely thought, quite suddenly, out of nowhere, of something! The air was as calm around me as ever. Not an Indian made a hostile gesture. It was an idea that had occurred to me – fool, idiot, moron!

'It had just struck me, amidships, that in destroying the tree, His bridge to earth, I might have cut you and Wilkes off forever from getting back! That was what made the quick, cold sweat run down into my eyes; that was what sent waves of nausea over me.

'I stood there and sweated and trembled from head to foot. It was only by sheer will power that I kept the torch up in the air, a proper front before those still thousands. My mind reeled with the trouble of it. And then, after a sudden silence, they started yelling themselves blue once more, with enthusiasm over that champion of champions who had dared to step out on the forbidden ground; to enter the Circle for the first time in history – their history.

'That paladin was close to me now, coming on steadily, confidently, quite nearby. My eyes went around to him He was a fine, clean-cut-looking person. He stopped, and raised his hands over his head, and made me a kind of salaam.

'The whole yowling mob quieted down again at that – wanted to see what I'd do to him, I suppose.

'I stepped over to him and handed him the torch. He took it, and looked me in the eye. He was some fellow, that young Indian!

'I spoke to him, in Spanish: "Exalted Servant of the Fire, indicate to me now the direction of the other forbidden place, where He of the Wind places his foot upon the earth." Every chance the three of us had in the world was staked on that question, Canevin; on the idea that lay behind it; on the possibility that there was more than one bridge-place like this Great Circle where we stood. It was, of course, merely a piece of guesswork.

'And, Canevin, he raised his other arm, the one that was not holding the torch, and pointed and answered: "Straight to the south, Lord of Fire!" '

'Canevin, I could have kissed that Indian! Another chance! I went up to him and hugged him like a bear. I don't know what he thought of that. I didn't give him time to think, to make up his mind. I held him off at arms' length as though he had been my favorite brother-in-law that I hadn't seen for a couple of years! I said to him: "Speak, heroic Servant of the Fire – name your reward!"

'He never hesitated an instant. He knew what he wanted, that fellow – saw this was his big chance. He breathed hard. I could see his big chest go in and out. He'll go a long way, believe me, Canevin!

' "The lordship over – these!" he said, with a little gasp, and pointed with the torch, around the circle. I raised both my hands over my head and called out: "Hearken, men of this nation! Behold your overlord who with his descendants shall rule over all your nations and tribes and peoples to the end of time. Down – and salute your lord!"

A little later, when they got it, as they dropped in rows on their faces, Canevin, I turned to that fellow holding the torch, and said: "Call them together; make them sit in a circle around us here. Then the first thing you are to do is to pick out the men you want to help you govern them. After that, tell them they are to listen to me!"

'He looked me in the eye again, and nodded. Oh, he was an intelligent one, that fellow! To make a long story short, he did just that; and you can picture us there in the moonlight, for the moon had a chance to get going long before the Indians were arranged the way I had said, the new king bossing them all as though he had never done anything else, with me standing there in the center and haranguing them – I'd had plenty of time, you see, to get that speech together – and, as I palavered, the interpreters relayed it to the rest.

'The upshot of it all was that we started off for the place, the other place where He could "put his foot upon the earth" as I had said, the place where we found you. It took us all night, even with that willing mob swinging their machetes.'

I thanked Pelletier for his story. He had already heard the outline of mine, such as I have recounted here somewhat more fully. I let his account sink in, and then, as I have said, I was able to be myself again. Perhaps Pelletier's very commonplace sanity, the matter-of-factness of his account, may have had something to do with this desirable effect. I do not know, but I am glad to be able to record the fact.

'There is one thing not quite clear in my mind,' said I, after Pelletier had finished.

'Yes?' said Pelletier, encouragingly.

'That figure in the temple – Aquarius,' I explained. 'Just how did you happen to fasten on that? I understand, of course, why you destroyed it. It was, like the tree, one of His "foci", a "bridge" to earth. By wiping those out, as I understand the matter, you broke what I might call his earth-power; you cut off his points of access. It's mysterious enough, yet clear in a way. But how did you know that *that* was the focal point, so to speak? Why the statue? Why not, for example, the altar?'

Pelletier nodded, considering my questions. Then he smiled whimsically.

'That's because you do not know your astrology, Canevin!' he said, propping his bulk up on one arm, for emphasis, and looking straight at me. He grinned broadly, like a mischievous boy. Then: 'You remember – I touched on that – how important it is, or should be, as an element in a modern education! Aquarius would fool you; would puzzle anybody, I'll grant you – anybody, that is, who doesn't know his astrology! You'd think from his name that he was allied with the element of water, wouldn't you, Canevin? The name practically says so: "Aquarius" – water-bearer. You'd think so, unless, as I say, you knew your astrology!'

'What do you mean?' I asked. 'It's too much for me, Pelletier. You'll have to tell me, I'm afraid.' It was plain that Pelletier held some joker up his sleeve.

'Did you ever see a picture of Aquarius, Canevin, in which – stop and think a moment – he is not represented as *pouring water out* of that vessel of his? Aquarius is not the personage who *represents* water, Canevin. Quite the contrary, in fact. He's the fellow who is getting rid of the water to make way for the air. Aquarius, in spite of his name, is the zodiacal symbol for *air*, not water, as you'd imagine if you didn't know your astrology, Canevin! He is represented always as *pouring out water*, getting rid of it! Aquarius is *not* the protagonist of water. He is the precursor, the forerunner of air!' As he said this, Dr Pelletier waved one of his big, awkward-looking hands – sure sign of something on his mind. I laughed. I admitted freely that my education had been neglected.

'And what next?' I asked, smiling at my big friend. He laughed that big contagious laugh of his.

'Canevin,' said he, wagging his head at me, 'I'm wondering which of the archaeologists, or maybe some rank outsider, who will go to the top on it, and get D. Sc.'s all the way from Harvard to the University of Upsala – which of 'em will be the first to "discover" that the first Maya civilization is *not* defunct; knock the very best modern archaeological science endwise all over again, the way it's constantly being done in every "scientific" field, from Darwin to Kirsopp Lake! An "epoch-making discovery"!'

Then, musing, seriously, yet with a twinkle in his kindly brown eyes: 'I have great hopes of the leadership they're going to get; that they're getting, right now, Canevin. That was some up-and-coming boy, some fellow, that new king in Quintana Roo, the one I appointed, the new ruler of the jungle! Did you see him, Canevin, standing there, telling them what was what?

'Do you know, I never even found out his name! He's one of the very few, by the way – told me about it on the trek back to the Circle – who had learned the old language. It's come down, you know, through the priests, here and there, intact, just as they used to speak it a couple of thousand years ago. Well, you heard him use it! Quite a group, I believe, keep it up, in and around Chichen-Itza particularly. He told them, he said, how fire had prevailed over their traditional air – Aquarius lying there, toppled off his pedestal, to prove it!'

I was glad I had given the young chieftain my bronze sword. Perhaps its possession will help him in establishing his authority over those Old Ones: that giant from whose hand I originally snatched it there in the temple may very well have been their head man. He was big enough, and fast enough on his feet; had the primitive leadership qualities, in all conscience. He had been mightily impressive as he came bounding ahead of his followers, charging upon us through the clouds of dust.

I have kept the sliver Wilkes, poor fellow, cut from the palm of the great Hand. I discovered it, rolled up and quite hardened and stiff, in the pocket of my trousers there in the hotel in Belize when I was changing to fresh clothes.

I keep it in a drawer of my bureau, in my bedroom. Nobody sees it there; nobody asks what it is.

'Yes – a sliver cut from the superficial scarf-skin of one of the ancient classical demigods! Yes – interesting, isn't it!'

I'd rather not have to describe that sliver. Probably my hearers would say nothing much. People are courteous, especially here in St Thomas where there is a tradition to that effect. But they could hardly visualize, as I still do – yet, fortunately, at decreasing intervals – that cosmic Entity of the high atmosphere, presiding over His element of air; menacing, colossal; His vast heart beating on eternally as, stupendous, incredible, He towers there inscrutable among the unchanging stars.

Obi in the Caribbean

Shortly before the annual Christmas horse-races on the American West Indian Island of Santa Cruz, in 1922, a young colored man named Anduze, living in Christiansted, was murdered, and the murderer was subsequently convicted in the American district court. The object of this murder was to procure Anduze's heart and liver. An obi-doctor had been engaged to work voodoo on one of the racehorses owned by a black man, and the heart and liver were the necessary materials for the magicking.

The horse in question, which had been 'obi-doctored', happened to win the race. Immediately afterward one of the gentleman-planters of Santa Cruz went over to Porto Rico to purchase a first-class racehorse with which to make certain that the obi horse should be beaten at the Easter races. The new horse won his race against the 'doctored' horse, and what gave promise of a recrudescence of black African magic on this island of Uncle Sam's newest colony, the Virgin Islands, died a natural death.

Obi bottles hanging on fruit trees, particularly those which bear the nutritious avocado pear, are common sights in the West Indies. These are ordinary bottles, ornamented weirdly with seeds, bits of string, scraps of red flannel, etc. These obi bottles are usually effective deterrents against theft of the ripening fruit. They are tabu signs, which, if disturbed, will arouse the malicious anger of Jumbee!

Of course only the black people use magic, although belief in it is not wholly confined to the ignorant black population of those jewel-like islands which form the sweeping northern boundary of the Caribbean Sea. There is something weirdly approaching the 'sacramental' about the West Indian magical practices. Here is a perverted application of the principle of the outward and visible being bound up with the inwardness – the 'spirituality' – of affairs. The invisible creation of God, as the black African West Indian sees the matter, may be either good or evil – like the visible creation – and may be invoked and even compelled. The West Indian hills are full of this magic – obi (obeah). It is part of the very atmosphere breathed by West Indians. The black shadow of obeah and voodoo ('bad' magic, i.e., deleterious) lies, a great cloud, over the minds of the blacks, once, of course, the slave-population of these incredibly fruitful and lovely isles.

'T'ank Gahd it drap!' A bit of food has fallen from the hand in eating. It means that Jumbee wants that bit of food – is favoring the eater. Therefore he thanks God for Jumbee's favor, a characteristic anomaly.

Cabin doors are carefully closed at nightfall, lest Jumbee plague the sleepers. It is better to swelter through an airless night than to risk Jumbee's pranks or malice. 'Jumbee,' so visitors may be assured, 'was invented by the old planters to keep the blacks indoors after nightfall.' Belief in him seems nearly universal through the islands. In the French islands of Guadeloupe and Martinique, he is 'Zombi', a close philological relative. Probably Jumbee originated on the African west coast, in the hinterlands all the way from Dakar to the Congo Basin. He is one of the most important personages in the West Indies. He is a kind of demon – any kind. The term is generic. On Martinique and elsewhere among French-speaking Negroes, one of his varieties is the 'Zomblesse'. A Zomblesse is half man (or woman), half demon, a person able, like Stevenson's Thrawn Janet, to shed his skin, hang it on a nail, and go out marauding after nightfall when the tropic dark ushers in the myrmidons of Eblis, to plague Ham's sons. Finding and salting the skin renders the discoverer immune from any subsequent injury from that particular Zomblesse.

On the doors of Negro cabins 'in the country', i.e., outside the towns, crosses may be seen, much like those the Hebrews made with the blood of the Passover lamb. This is 'to keep out de wolf'. The werewolf, especially inimical to prospective mothers, may also be kept out by placing sand on the cabin roof, since the marauder must, by the nature of his being, pause to count the grains before proceeding to tear up the roof. This is 'wolf curiosity', and that is almost an epithet! All the usual characteristics of the werewolf are also present in the West Indian variety.

There is 'canicanthropy' as well as lycanthropy extant. The central figure of this belief takes the form of a little black woman who transforms herself into a little white dog, which bounds up steps. Touching the dog with any part of the body is certain, immediate death. A blow from a stick will turn the dog, which increases in size and fierceness with every step upward, and then the little old woman may be heard pattering away howling with the pain of the blow.

Under certain ancient tamarinds and up sundry canefield ranges lurks the dread Sow with Seven Pigs. It is a dreadful portent if these run across the path of a late-returning reveller.

Many varieties of West Indian obi cannot be described, and these include not the least interesting from the viewpoint of the ethnologist. In them, definite phobias are invoked, more or less successfully. It is a question of beliefs, '*les ideés fixes*'.

'Snake-Cut' (recently described in *Harper's Magazine* by an eye-witness) is still practised in the Guiana hinterlands, though I think it is unknown in the West India Islands proper. There back of French, British and Dutch Guiana, is a little transplanted Africa, and Africa changeth not! In the police court at Frederiksted, Virgin Islands, in October, 1925, before the late Justice J. L. Curry, a case of slander was tried. One old woman had entitled another, 'to me face, Yer Honor!' a 'wuthless old Cartagène!' That means 'a Carthaginian', i.e., a pirate, a marauder. It was Cato the Elder who enunciated '*delenda est Carthago*' so insistently before his *confrères* in the Roman Senate, in the second century, B.C. But to this day black West Indians call each other 'Carthaginians' when they desire denunciatory emphasis. Carthage was an African seaport!

Readers of William Palgrave's *Ulysses*, which is a more profitable book than James Joyce's similarly entitled obscenities, will note that Queen Victoria's consul-general at St Thomas during part of Mr Seitz's Dreadful Decade has nothing to say about the Danish West Indies (now the Virgin Islands) though he gives very full accounts of his various other appointments in the British consular service. The fact is that Palgrave, who had published in the *Corn-hill Magazine* certain animadversions on the ways of St Thomas society, was literally driven out by a song made by the blacks about him during their spring 'magicking' in the hills back of the town:

> Weelum Palgrave is a cha-cha, bal'hoo;
> He is a kind of a-half-a-Jew!
>
> . . . .
> Him go back to Trebizond.

He did! There had been certainty – hypnotism – 'put' into that silly little song, which contains delicate ironies quite imperceptible on its surface, which penetrated Her Britannic Majesty's consul-general's head and literally drove him out, so that St Thomas society was rid of its gadfly.

Love-philtres, curative 'simples' made from common West Indian herbs, and 'charms' of every description are in common, every-day use among the blacks, as well as the practices deriving from all the usual superstitions. Many authentic cures are recorded, for obi means both good and bad magic, obeah being, strictly, the good or curative variety.

Next to interior Africa, Haiti is probably the most magic-infested place in the world. There even the continental, European-educated intellectuals appear to believe in magic, and Haiti has always labored under the dead weight of these beliefs. It is not uncommon for a qualified physician to be called in and requested to demonstrate on a cadaver by means of a bodkin thrust through the heart that the dead person actually is dead. The belief back of this practice is in the magic of being 'near-dead'. This state is attributed to some enemy or to the papaloi (witch-doctor) himself, who will, after the obsequies, dig up the 'dead' person, restore animation, and hold him in slavery for the rest of his life. Slavery is the bugaboo of which all West Indian blacks stand in fear.

A 'toof from a dead' is the equivalent of the American rabbit's foot. Armed with this trophy a gambler is supposed to be consist-ently lucky. Having a dead man's hand in the possession renders a thief more bold, or immune to capture, or even invisible! Various other members of the human body are believed to possess magical properties. A piece of string is often tied about a great-toe to cause the toe to 'see', and so prevent stumbling. The psychology here is simple and really practicable. The person who devoutly, unques-tionably, believes that his toe can be made to see, will usually correct automatically a propensity to stumble.

Under the mental burden of these characteristic superstitions the blacks of the West Indies live continuously. It is a part, and a very important part, of their lives. It is only too frequently concealed beneath the honest piety of primitive people, their genuine religious conviction and the regular practice of their religion.

In the minds of these simple people there is being waged always a silent, desperate battle between 'Gahd' and His good angels, and the powers of darkness. This is no dry theological belief, of the sort ordinarily shelved in the minds of persons preoccupied otherwise by daily affairs, and with scant inclination to consider the matters of the spirit, whether good or evil. It is, rather, the literal condition under which ordinary life is lived. In the West Indies God and Satan are fighting out the destiny of mankind hand to hand, and the strange echoes of that desperate, incessant conflict resound in the preoccupied minds of the Negroes. In the daytime, under the glorious, reassuring sunlight of the Antilles, God reigns, in the minds of a grave but happy and carefree people. But after nightfall, even under the Caribbean moon, which seems twice as large and twice as near as the American moon, the evil powers come forth from their lurking dens variously to plague the children of Ham, accursed with a lingering, nameless fear – because their ancestor once dared to be so bold as to break a commandment and laugh at Noah, his father.

JUMBEE

and other Voodoo Tales

Jumbee

Mr Granville Lee, a Virginian of Virginians, coming out of the World War with a lung wasted and scorched by mustard gas, was recommended by his physician to spend a winter in the spice-and-balm climate of the Lesser Antilles – the lower islands of the West Indian archipelago. He chose one of the American islands, St Croix, the old Santa Cruz – Island of the Holy Cross – named by Columbus himself on his second voyage, once famous for its rum.

It was to Jaffray Da Silva that Mr Lee at last turned for definite information about the local magic; information which, after a two months' residence, accompanied with marked improvement in his general health, he had come to regard as imperative, from the whetting glimpses he had received of its persistence on the island.

Contact with local customs, too, had sufficiently blunted his inherited sensibilities, to make him almost comfortable, as he sat with Mr Da Silva on the cool gallery of that gentleman's beautiful house, in the shade of forty years' growth of bougainvillea, on a certain afternoon. It was the restful gossipy period between five o'clock and dinnertime. A glass jug of foaming rum-swizzel stood on the table between them.

'But, tell me, Mr Da Silva,' he urged, as he absorbed his second glass of the cooling, mild drink, 'have you ever, actually, been confronted with a "Jumbee"? – ever really seen one? You say, quite frankly, that you believe in them!'

This was not the first question about Jumbees that Mr Lee had asked. He had consulted planters; he had spoken of the matter of Jumbees with courteous, intelligent, colored store-keepers about the town, and even in Christiansted, St Croix's other and larger town on the north side of the island. He had even mentioned the matter to one or two coal-black sugar-field laborers; for he had been on the island just long enough to begin to understand – a little – the weird jargon of speech which Lafcadio Hearn, when he visited St Croix many years before, had not recognized as 'English'!

There had been marked differences in what he had been told. The planters and storekeepers had smiled, though with varying degrees of intensity, and had replied that the Danes had invented Jumbees, to keep their estate-laborers indoors after nightfall, thus ensuring a proper night's sleep for them, and minimizing the depredations upon growing crops. The laborers whom he had asked, had rolled their eyes somewhat, but, it being broad daylight at the time of the inquiries, they had broken their impassive gravity with smiles, and sought to impress Mr Lee with their lofty contempt for the beliefs of their fellow blacks, and with queerly-phrased assurances that Jumbee is a figment of the imagination.

Nevertheless, Mr Lee was not satisfied. There was something here that he seemed to be missing – something extremely interesting, too, it appeared to him; something very different from 'Bre'r Rabbit' and similar tales of his own remembered childhood in Virginia.

Once, too, he had been reading a book about Martinique and Guadeloupe, those ancient jewels of France's crown, and he had not read far before he met the word 'Zombi'. After that, he knew, at least, that the Danes had not 'invented' the Jumbee. He heard, though vaguely, of the laborers' belief that Sven Garik, who had long ago gone back to his home in Sweden, and Garrity, one of the smaller planters now on the island, were 'wolves'! Lycanthropy, animal-metamorphosis, it appeared, formed part of this strange texture of local belief.

Mr Jaffray Da Silva was one-eighth African. He was, therefore, by island usage, 'colored', which is as different from being 'black' in the West Indies as anything that can be imagined. Mr Da Silva had been educated in the continental European manner. In his every word and action, he reflected European forebears. By every right and custom of West Indian society, Mr Da Silva was a colored gentleman, whose social status was as clear-cut and definite as a cameo.

These islands are largely populated by persons like Mr Da Silva. Despite the difference in their status from what it would be in North America, in the islands it has its advantages – among them that of logic. To the West Indian mind, a man whose heredity is seven-eighths derived from gentry, as like as not with authentic coats-of-arms, is entitled to be treated accordingly. That is why Mr Da Silva's many clerks, and everybody else who knew him, treated him with deference, addressed him as 'sir', and doffed their hats in continental fashion when meeting; salutes which, of course, Mr

Da Silva invariably returned, even to the humblest, which is one of the marks of a gentleman anywhere.

Jaffray Da Silva shifted one thin leg, draped in spotless white drill, over the other, and lighted a fresh cigarette.

'Even my friends smile at me, Mr Lee,' he replied, with a tolerant smile, which lightened for an instant his melancholy, ivory-white countenance. 'They laugh at me more or less because I admit I believe in Jumbees. It is possible that everybody with even a small amount of African blood possesses that streak of belief in magic and the like. I seem, though, to have a peculiar aptitude for it! It is a matter of *experience* with me, sir, and my friends are free to smile at me if they wish. Most of them – well, they do not admit their beliefs as freely as I, perhaps!'

Mr Lee took another sip of the cold swizzel. He had heard how difficult it was to get Jaffray Da Silva to speak of his 'experiences', and he suspected that under his host's even courtesy lay that austere pride which resents anything like ridicule, despite that tolerant smile.

'Please proceed, sir,' urged. Mr Lee, and was quite unconscious that he had just used a word which, in his native South, is reserved for gentlemen of pure Caucasian blood.

'When I was a young man,' began Mr Da Silva, 'about 1894, there was a friend of mine named Hilmar Iversen, a Dane, who lived here in the town, up near the Moravian Church on what the people call "Foun'-Out Hill". Iversen had a position under the government, a clerk's job, and his office was in the Fort. On his way home he used to stop here almost every afternoon for a swizzel and a chat. We were great friends, close friends. He was then a man a little past fifty, a butter-tub of a fellow, very stout, and, like many of that build, he suffered from heart attacks.

'One night a boy came here for me. It was eleven o'clock, and I was just arranging the mosquito-net on my bed, ready to turn in. The servants had all gone home, so I went to the door myself, in shirt and trousers, and carrying a lamp, to see what was wanted – or, rather, I knew perfectly well what it was – a messenger to tell me Iversen was dead!'

Mr Lee suddenly sat bolt-upright.

'How could you know that?' he inquired, his eyes wide.

Mr Da Silva threw away the remains of his cigarette.

'I sometimes know things like that,' he answered, slowly. 'In this case, Iversen and I had been close friends for years. He and I had talked about magic and that sort of thing a great deal, occult powers, manifestations – that sort of thing. It is a very general topic here, as you may have seen. You would hear more of it if you continued to live here and settled into the ways of the island. In fact, Mr Lee, Iversen and I had made a compact together. The one of us who "went out" first, was to try to warn the other of it. You see, Mr Lee, I had received Iversen's warning less than an hour before.

'I had been sitting out here on the gallery until ten o'clock or so. I was in that very chair you are occupying. Iversen had been having a heart attack. I had been to see him that afternoon. He looked just as he always did when he was recovering from an attack. In fact he intended to return to his office the following morning. Neither of us, I am sure, had given a thought to the possibility of a sudden sinking spell. We had not even referred to our agreement.

'Well, it was about ten, as I've said, when all of a sudden I heard Iversen coming along through the yard below there, toward the house along that gravel path. He had, apparently, come through the gate from the Kongensgade – the King Street, as they call it nowadays – and I could hear his heavy step on the gravel very plainly. He had a slight limp. "Heavy crunch – light crunch; plod-plod – plod-plod"; old Iversen to the life; there was no mistaking his step. There was no moon that night. The half of a waning moon was due to show itself an hour and a half later, but just then it was virtually pitch-black down there in the garden.

'I got up out of my chair and walked over to the top of the steps. To tell you the truth, Mr Lee, I rather suspected – I have a kind of aptitude for that sort of thing – that it was not Iversen himself; how shall I express it? I had the idea from somewhere inside me, that it was Iversen trying to keep our agreement. My instinct assured me that he had just died. I cannot tell you how I knew it, but such was the case, Mr Lee.

'So I waited, over there just behind you, at the top of the steps. The footfalls came along steadily. At the foot of the steps, out of the shadow of the hibiscus bushes, it was a trifle less black than farther down the path. There was a faint illumination, too, from a lamp inside the house. I knew that if it were Iversen, himself, I should be able to see him when the footsteps passed out of the deep shadow of the bushes. I did not speak.

'The footfalls came along toward that point, and passed it. I strained my eyes through the gloom, and I could see nothing. Then

I knew, Mr Lee, that Iversen had died, and that he was keeping his agreement.

'I came back here and sat down in my chair, and waited. The footfalls began to come up the steps. They came along the floor of the gallery, straight toward me. They stopped here, Mr Lee, just beside me. I could *feel* Iversen standing here, Mr Lee.' Mr Da Silva pointed to the floor with his slim, rather elegant hand.

'Suddenly, in the dead quiet, I could feel my hair stand up all over my scalp, straight and stiff. The chills started to run down my back, and up again, Mr Lee. I shook like a man with the ague, sitting here in my chair.

'I said: "Iversen, I understand! Iversen, I'm afraid!" My teeth were chattering like castanets, Mr Lee. I said: "Iversen, please go! You have kept the agreement. I am sorry I am afraid, Iversen. The flesh is weak! I am not afraid of *you*, Iversen, old friend. But you will understand, man! It's not ordinary fear. My intellect is all right, Iversen, but I'm badly panic-stricken, so please go, my friend."

'There had been silence, Mr Lee, as I said, before I began to speak to Iversen, for the footsteps had stopped here beside me. But when I said that, and asked my friend to go, I could *feel* that he went at once, and I knew that he had understood how I meant it! It was, suddenly, Mr Lee, as though there had never been any footsteps, if you see what I mean. It is hard to put into words. I dare say, if I had been one of the laborers, I should have been halfway to Christiansted through the estates, Mr Lee, but I was not so frightened that I could not stand my ground.

'After I had recovered myself a little, and my scalp had ceased its prickling, and the chills were no longer running up and down my spine, I rose, and I felt extremely weary, Mr Lee. It had been exhausting. I came into the house and drank a large tot of French brandy, and then I felt better, more like myself. I took my hurricane-lantern and lighted it, and stepped down the path toward the gate leading to the Kongensgade. There was one thing I wished to see down there at the end of the garden. I wanted to see if the gate was fastened, Mr Lee. It was. That huge iron staple that you noticed, was in place. It has been used to fasten that old gate since some time in the eighteenth century, I imagine. I had not supposed anyone had opened the gate, Mr Lee, but now I knew. There were no footprints in the gravel, Mr Lee. I looked, carefully. The marks of the bushbroom where the house-boy had swept the path on his way back from closing the gate were undisturbed, Mr Lee.

'I was satisfied, and no longer even a little frightened. I came back here and sat down, and thought about my long friendship with old Iversen. I felt very sad to know that I should not see him again alive. He would never stop here again afternoons for a swizzel and a chat. About eleven o'clock I went inside the house and was preparing for bed when the rapping came at the front door. You see, Mr Lee, I knew at once what it would mean.

'I went to the door, in shirt and trousers and stockinged feet, carrying a lamp. We did not have electric light in those days. At the door stood Iversen's house-boy, a young fellow about eighteen. He was half-asleep, and very much upset. He "cut his eyes" at me, and said nothing.

' "What is it, mon?" I asked the boy.

' "Mistress Iversen send ax yo' sir, please come to de house. Mr Iversen die, sir."

' "What time Mr Iversen die, mon – you hear?"

' "I ain' able to say what o'clock, sir. Mistress Iversen come wake me where I sleep in a room in the yard, sir, an' sen' me please cahl you, – I t'ink he die aboht an hour ago, sir."

'I put on my shoes again, and the rest of my clothes, and picked up a St Kitts supplejack – I'll get you one; it's one of those limber, grapevine walking sticks, a handy thing on a dark night – and started with the boy for Iversen's house.

'When we had arrived almost at the Moravian Church, I saw something ahead, near the roadside. It was then about eleven-fifteen, and the streets were deserted. What I saw made me curious to test something. I paused, and told the boy to run on ahead and tell Mrs Iversen I would be there shortly. The boy started to trot ahead. He was pure black, Mr Lee, but he went past what I saw without noticing it. He swerved a little away from it, and I think, perhaps, he slightly quickened his pace just at that point, but that was all.'

'What did you see?' asked Mr Lee, interrupting. He spoke a trifle breathlessly. His left lung was, as yet, far from being healed.

'The "Hanging Jumbee",' replied Mr Da Silva, in his usual tones.

'Yes! There at the side of the road were three Jumbees. There's a reference to that in *The History of Stewart McCann*. Perhaps you've run across that, eh?'

Mr Lee nodded, and Mr Da Silva quoted:

> There they hung, though no ladder's rung
> Supported their dangling feet.

'And there's another line in *The History*,' he continued, smiling, 'which describes a typical group of Hanging Jumbee.

Maiden, man-child, and shrew.

'Well, there were the usual three Jumbees, apparently hanging in the air. It wasn't very light, but I could make out a boy of about twelve, a young girl, and a shriveled old woman – what the author of *The History of Stewart McCann* meant by the word "shrew". He told me himself, by the way, Mr Lee, that he had put feet on his Jumbees mostly for the sake of a convenient rime – poetic license! The Hanging Jumbee have no feet. It is one of their peculiarities. Their legs stop at the ankles. They have abnormally long, thin legs – African legs. They are always black, you know. Their feet – if they have them – are always hidden in a kind of mist that lies along the ground wherever one sees them. They shift and "weave", as a full-blooded African does – standing on one foot and resting the other – you've noticed that, of course – or scratching the supporting ankle with the toes of the other foot. They do not swing in the sense that they seem to be swung on a rope – that is not what it means; they do not twirl about. But they do – always – face the oncomer . . .

'I walked on, slowly, and passed them; and they kept their faces to me as they always do. I'm used to that . . .

'I went up the steps of the house to the front gallery, and found Mrs Iversen waiting for me. Her sister was with her, too. I remained sitting with them for the best part of an hour. Then two old black women who had been sent for, into the country, arrived. These were two old women who were accustomed to prepare the dead for burial. Then I persuaded the ladies to retire, and started to come home myself.

'It was a little past midnight, perhaps twelve-fifteen. I picked out my own hat from two or three of poor old Iversen's that were hanging on the rack, took my supplejack, and stepped out of the door onto the little stone gallery at the head of the steps.

'There are about twelve or thirteen steps from the gallery down to the street. As I started down them I noticed a third old black woman sitting, all huddled together, on the bottom step, with her back to me. I thought at once that this must be some old crone who lived with the other two – the preparers of the dead. I imagined that she had been afraid to remain alone in their cabin, and so had accompanied them into the town – they are like children, you know, in some ways – and that, feeling too humble to come into the house, she had sat down to wait on the step and had fallen asleep. You've heard their proverbs, have you not? There's one that exactly fits this situation that I had imagined: "Cockroach no wear crockin' boot when he creep in fowl-house!" It means: "Be very reserved when in the presence of your betters!" Quaint, rather! The poor souls!

'I started to walk down the steps toward the old woman. That scant half-moon had come up into the sky while I had been sitting with the ladies, and by its light everything was fairly sharply defined. I could see that old woman as plainly as I can see you now, Mr Lee. In fact, I was looking directly at the poor old creature as I came down the steps, and fumbling in my pocket for a few coppers for her – for tobacco and sugar, as they say! I was wondering, indeed, why she was not by this time on her feet and making one of their queer little bobbing bows – "cockroach bow to fowl", as they might say! It seemed this old woman must have fallen into a very deep sleep, for she had not moved at all, although ordinarily she would have heard me, for the night was deathly still, and their hearing is extraordinarily acute, like a cat's, or a dog's. I remember that the fragrance from Mrs Iversen's tuberoses, in pots on the gallery railing, was pouring out in a stream that night, "making a greeting for the moon"! It was almost overpowering.

'Just as I was putting my foot on the fifth step, there came a tiny little puff of fresh breeze from somewhere in the hills behind Iversen's house. It rustled the dry fronds of a palm-tree that was growing beside the steps. I turned my head in that direction for an instant.

'Mr Lee, when I looked back, down the steps, after what must have been a fifth of a second's inattention, that little old black woman who had been huddled up there on the lowest step, apparently sound asleep, was gone. She had vanished utterly – and, Mr Lee, a little white dog, about the size of a French poodle, was bounding up the steps toward me. With every bound, a step at a leap, the dog increased in size. It seemed to swell out there before my very eyes.

'Then I was, really, frightened – thoroughly, utterly frightened. I knew if that "animal" so much as touched me, it meant death, Mr Lee – absolute, certain death. The little old woman was a "sheen" – *chien*, of course. You know of lycanthropy – wolf-change – of course. Well, this was one of our varieties of it. I do not know what it would be

called, I'm sure. "Canicanthropy", perhaps. I don't know, but something – something first-cousin-once-removed from lycanthropy, and
on the downward scale, Mr Lee. The old woman was a were-dog!

'Of course, I had no time to think, only to use my instinct. I swung
my supplejack with all my might and brought it down squarely on
that beast's head. It was only a step below me, then, and I could see
the faint moonlight sparkle on the slaver about its mouth. It was
then, it seemed to me, about the size of a medium-sized dog – nearly
wolf-size, Mr Lee, and a kind of deathly white. I was desperate, and
the force with which I struck caused me to lose my balance. I did not
fall, but it required a moment or two for me to regain my equi-
librium. When I felt my feet firm under me again, I looked about,
frantically, on all sides, for the "dog". But it, too, Mr Lee, like the old
woman, had quite disappeared. I looked all about, you may well
imagine, after that experience, in the clear, thin moonlight. For
yards about the foot of the steps, there was no place – not even a
small nook – where either the "dog" or the old woman could have
been concealed. Neither was on the gallery, which was only a few
feet square, a mere landing.

'But there came to my ears, sharpened by that night's experiences,
from far out among the plantations at the rear of Iversen's house,
the pad-pad of naked feet. Someone – something – was running,
desperately, off in the direction of the center of the island, back into
the hills, into the deep "bush".

'Then, behind me, out of the house onto the gallery rushed the
two old women who had been preparing Iversen's body for its burial.
They were enormously excited, and they shouted at me unintelligibly. I will have to render their words for you.

' "O, de Good Gahd protec' you, Marster Jaffray, sir – de Joombie,
de Joombie! De "Sheen", Marster Jaffray! He go, sir?"

'I reassured the poor old souls, and went back home.'

Mr Da Silva fell abruptly silent. He slowly shifted his position in
his chair, and reached for, and lighted, a fresh cigarette.

Mr Lee was absolutely silent. He did not move. Mr Da Silva
resumed, deliberately, after obtaining a light.

'You see, Mr Lee, the West Indies are different from any other
place in the world, I verily believe, sir. I've said so, anyhow, many a
time, although I have never been out of the islands except when I was
a young man, to Copenhagen. I've told you, exactly, what happened
that particular night.'

Mr Lee heaved a sigh.

'Thank you, Mr Da Silva, very much indeed, sir,' said he, thought-fully, and made as though to rise. His service wrist-watch indicated six o'clock.

'Let us have a fresh swizzel, at least, before you go,' suggested Mr Da Silva. 'We have a saying here in the island, that "a man can't travel on one leg"! Perhaps you've heard it already.'

'I have,' said Mr Lee.

'Knud, Knud! You hear, mon? Knud – tell Charlotte to mash up another bal' of ice – you hear? Quickly now,' commanded Mr Da Silva.

Cassius

My house-man, Stephen Penn, who presided over the staff of my residence in St Thomas, was not, strictly speaking, a native of that city. Penn came from the neighboring island of St Jan. It is one of the ancient West Indian names, although there remain in the islands nowadays no Caucasians to bear that honorable cognomen.

Stephen's travels, however, had not been limited to the crossing from St Jan – which, incidentally, is the authentic scene of R. L. Stevenson's *Treasure Island* – which lies little more than a rowboat's journey away from the capital of the Virgin Islands. Stephen had been 'down the Islands', which means that he had been actually as far from home as Trinidad or, perhaps, British Guiana, down through the great sweep of former mountaintops, submerged by some vast, cataclysmic, prehistoric inundation and named the Bow of Ulysses by some fanciful, antique geographer. That odyssey of humble Stephen Penn had taken place because of his love for ships. He had had various jobs afloat and his exact knowledge of the house-man's art had been learned under various man-driving ship's stewards.

During this preliminary training for his life's work, Stephen had made many acquaintances. One of these, an upstanding, slim, parchment-colored Negro of thirty or so, was Brutus Hellman. Brutus, like Stephen, had settled down in St Thomas as a house-man. It was, in fact, Stephen who had talked him into leaving his native British Antigua, to try his luck in our American Virgin Islands. Stephen had secured for him his first job in St Thomas, in the household of a naval officer.

For this friend of his youthful days, Stephen continued to feel a certain sense of responsibility; because, when Brutus happened to be abruptly thrown out of employment by the sudden illness and removal by the Naval Department of his employer in the middle of the winter season in St Thomas, Stephen came to me and requested that his friend Brutus be allowed to come to me 'on board-wages' until he was able to secure another place.

I acquiesced. I knew Brutus as a first-rate house-man. I was glad to give him a hand, to oblige the always agreeable and highly efficient Stephen, and, indeed, to have so skilful a servant added to my little staff in my bachelor quarters. I arranged for something more substantial than the remuneration asked for, and Brutus Hellman added his skilled services to those of the admirable Stephen. I was very well served that season and never had any occasion to regret what both men alluded to as my 'very great kindness'!

It was not long after Brutus Hellman had moved his simple belongings into one of the servants'-quarters cabins in my stone-paved yard, that I had another opportunity to do something for him. It was Stephen once more who presented his friend's case to me. Brutus, it appeared, had need of a minor operation, and, Negro-like, the two of them, talking the matter over between themselves, had decided to ask me, their present patron, to arrange it.

I did so, with my friend, Dr Pelletier, Chief Surgeon, in charge of our Naval Station Hospital and regarded in Naval circles as the best man in the Medical Corps. I had not inquired about the nature of Brutus's affliction. Stephen had stressed the minor aspect of the required surgery, and that was all I mentioned to Dr Pelletier.

It is quite possible that if Dr Pelletier had not been going to Porto Rico on Thursday of that week, this narrative, the record of one of the most curious experiences I have ever had, would never have been set down. If Pelletier, his mind set on sailing at eleven, had not merely walked out of his operating-room as soon as he had finished with Brutus a little after eight that Thursday morning, leaving the dressing of the slight wound upon Brutus's groin to be performed by his assistants, then that incredible affair which I can only describe as the persecution of the unfortunate Brutus Hellman would never have taken place.

It was on Wednesday, about two p.m., that I telephoned to Dr Pelletier to ask him to perform an operation on Brutus.

'Send him over to the hospital this afternoon,' Pelletier had answered, 'and I'll look him over about five and operate the first thing in the morning – if there is any need for an operation! I'm leaving for San Juan at eleven, for a week.'

I thanked him and went upstairs to my siesta, after giving Stephen the message to Brutus, who started off for the hospital about an hour later. He remained in the hospital until the following Sunday afternoon. He was entirely recovered from the operation, he reported. It had been a very slight affair, really, merely the removal of some kind of growth. He thanked me for my part in it when he came to announce dinner while I was reading on the gallery.

It was on the Saturday morning, the day before Brutus got back, that I discovered something very curious in an obscure corner of my house-yard, just around the corner of the wall of the three small cabins which occupy its north side. These cabins were tenantless except for the one at the east end of the row. That one was Brutus Hellman's. Stephen Penn, like my cook, washer, and scullery-maid, lived somewhere in the town.

I had been looking over the yard which was paved with old-fashioned flagging. I found it in excellent condition, weeded, freshly swept, and clean. The three stone servants'-cubicles had been recently whitewashed and glistened like cake-icing in the morning sun. I looked over this portion of my domain with approval, for I like things shipshape. I glanced into the two narrow air spaces between the little, two-room houses. There were no cobwebs visible. Then I took a look around the east corner of Brutus Hellman's little house where there was a narrow passageway between the house and the high wall of antique Dutch brick, and there, well in towards the north wall, I saw on the ground what I first took to be a discarded toy which some child had thrown there, probably, it occurred to me, over the wall at the back of the stone cabins.

It looked like a doll's house, which, if it had been thrown there, had happened to land right-side-up. It looked more or less like one of the quaint old-fashioned beehives one still sees occasionally in the conservative Lesser Antilles. But it could hardly be a beehive. It was far too small.

My curiosity mildly aroused, I stepped into the alleyway and looked down at the odd little thing. Seen from where I stopped it rewarded scrutiny. For it was, although made in a somewhat bungling way, a reproduction of an African village hut, thatched, circular, conical. The thatching, I suspected, had formerly been most of the business-end of a small house-broom of tine twigs tied together around the end of a stick. The little house's upright 'logs' were a heterogenous medley of little round sticks among which I recognized three dilapidated lead pencils and the broken-off handle of a tooth-brush. These details will serve to indicate its size and to justify my original conclusion that the thing was a rather cleverly made child's toy. How such a thing had got into my yard unless over the wall, was an unimportant little mystery. The little hut, from the ground up to its thatched peak, stood about seven inches in height. Its diameter was, perhaps, eight or nine inches.

My first reaction was to pick it up, look at it more closely, and then throw it into the wire cage in another corner of the yard where Stephen burned up waste paper and scraps at frequent intervals. The thing was plainly a discarded toy, and had no business cluttering up my spotless yard. Then I suddenly remembered the washer's pick'ny, a small, silent, very black child of six or seven, who sometimes played quietly in the yard while his stout mother toiled over the washtub set up on a backless chair near the kitchen door where she could keep up a continuous stream of chatter with my cook.

I stayed my hand accordingly. Quite likely this little thatched hut was a valued item of that pick'ny's possessions. Thinking pleasantly to surprise little Aesculapius, or whatever the child's name might be, I took from my pocket a fifty-bit piece – value ten cents – intending to place the coin inside the little house, through its rounded, low entranceway.

Stooping down, I shoved the coin through the doorway, and, as I did so, something suddenly scuttered about inside the hut, and pinched viciously at the ends of my thumb and forefinger.

I was, naturally, startled. I snatched my fingers away, and stood hastily erect. A mouse, perhaps even a rat, inside there! I glanced at my fingers. There were no marks on them. The skin was not broken. The rodent's vicious little sharp teeth had fortunately missed their grip as he snapped at me, intruding on his sacred privacy. Wondering a little I stepped out of the alleyway and into the sunny, open yard, somewhat upset at this Lilliputian *contretemps*, and resolved upon telling Stephen to see to it that there was no ugly rodent there when next little Aesculapius should retrieve his plaything.

But when I arrived at the gallery steps my friend Colonel Lorriquer's car was just drawing up before the house, and, in hastening to greet welcome early-morning callers and later in accepting Mrs Lorriquer's invitation to dinner and contract at their house that evening, the little hut and its unpleasant inhabitant were driven wholly out of my mind.

I did not think of it again until several days later, on the night when my premises had become the theater for one of the most inexplicable, terrifying and uncanny happenings I have ever experienced.

My gallery is a very pleasant place to sit evenings, except in that spring period during which the West Indian candle-moths hatch in their myriads and, for several successive days, make it impossible to sit outdoors in any lighted, unscreened place.

It was much too early for the candle-moths, however, at the time I am speaking of, and on the evening of that Sunday upon which Brutus Hellman returned from the hospital, a party of four persons, including myself, occupied the gallery.

The other man was Arthur Carswell, over from Haiti on a short visit. The two ladies were Mrs Spencer, Colonel Lorriquer's widowed daughter, and her friend, Mrs Squire. We had dined an hour previously at the Grand Hotel as guests of Carswell, and, having taken our coffee at my house, were remaining outdoors on the gallery 'for a breath of air' on a rather warm and sultry February evening. We were sitting, quietly talking in a rather desultory manner, all of us unspokenly reluctant to move inside the house for a projected evening at contract.

It was, as I recall the hour, about nine o'clock, the night warm, as I have said, and very still. Above, in a cloudless sky of luminous indigo, the tropical stars glowed enormous. The intoxicating sweet odors of white jessamine and tuberoses made the still air redolent. No sound, except an occasional rather languid remark from one of ourselves, broke the exquisite, balmy stillness.

Then, all at once, without any warning and with an abruptness which caused Carswell and me to stand up, the exquisite perfection of the night was rudely shattered by an appalling, sustained scream of sheer mortal terror.

That scream inaugurated what seems to me as I look back upon the next few days, to be one of the most unnerving, devastating, and generally horrible periods I can recall in a lifetime not devoid of adventure. I formulated at that time, and still retain, mentally, a phrase descriptive of it. It was 'the Reign of Terror'.

Carswell and I, following the direction of the scream, rushed down the outer gallery steps and back through the yard toward the Negro-cabins. As I have mentioned, only one of these was occupied, Brutus Hellman's. As we rounded the corner of the house a faint light – it was Brutus's oil lamp – appeared in the form of a wide vertical strip at the entrance of the occupied cabin. To that we ran as to a beacon, and pushed into the room.

The lamp, newly lighted, and smoking, its glass chimney set on askew as though in great haste, dimly illuminated a strange scene.

Doubled up and sitting on the side of his bed, the bedclothes near the bed's foot lumped together where he had flung them, cowered Brutus. His face was a dull, ashen gray in the smokey light, his back was bent, his hands clasped tightly about his shin. And, from between those clenched hands, a steady stream of blood stained the white sheet which hung over the bed's edge and spread below into a small pool on the cabin room's stone-paved floor.

Brutus, groaning dismally, rocked back and forth, clutching his leg. The lamp smoked steadily, defiling the close air, while, incongruously, through the now open doorway poured streams and great pulsing breaths of night-blooming tropical flowers, mingling strangely with the hot, acrid odor of the smoking lampwick.

Carswell went directly to the lamp, straightened the chimney, turned down the flame. The lamp ceased its ugly reek and the air of the cabin cleared as Carswell, turning away from the lamp, threw wide the shutters of the large window which, like most West Indian Negroes, Brutus had closed against the 'night air' when he retired.

I gave my attention directly to the man, and by the time the air had cleared somewhat I had him over on his back in a reclining position, and with a great strip torn from one of his bedsheets, was binding up the ugly deep little wound in the lower muscle of his leg just at the outside of the shinbone. I pulled the improvised bandage tight, and the flow of blood ceased, and Brutus, his mind probably somewhat relieved by this timely aid, put an end to his moaning, and turned his ashen face up to mine.

'Did you see it, sar?' he inquired, biting back the trembling of his mouth.

I paid practically no attention to this remark. Indeed, I barely heard it. I was, you see, very busily engaged in staunching the flow of blood. Brutus had already lost a considerable quantity, and my rough bandaging was directed entirely to the end of stopping this. Instead of replying to Brutus's question I turned to Carswell, who had finished with the lamp and the window, and now stood by, ready to lend a hand in his efficient way.

'Run up to the bathroom, will you, Carswell, and bring me a couple of rolls of bandage, from the medicine closet, and a bottle of mercurochrome.' Carswell disappeared on this errand and I sat, holding my hands tightly around Brutus's leg, just above the bandage. Then he repeated his question, and this time I paid attention to what he was saying.

'See what, Brutus?' I inquired, and looked at him, almost for the first time – into his eyes, I mean. Hitherto I had been looking at my bandaging.

I saw a stark terror in those eyes.

'It,' said Brutus; 'de T'ing, sar.'

I sat on the side of the bed and looked at him. I was, naturally, puzzled.

'What thing, Brutus?' I asked, very quietly, almost soothingly. Such terror possessed my second house-man that, I considered, he must, for the time being, be treated like a frightened child.

'De T'ing what attack me, sar,' explained Brutus.

'What was it like?' I countered. 'Do you mean it is still here – in your room?'

At that Brutus very nearly collapsed. His eyes rolled up and their irises nearly disappeared; he shuddered as though with a violent chill, from head to foot. I let go his leg. The blood would be no longer flowing, I felt sure, under that tight bandaging of mine. I turned back the bedclothes, rolled poor Brutus under them, tucked him in. I took his limp hands and rubbed them smartly. At this instant Carswell came in through the still open doorway, his hands full of first-aid material. This he laid without a word on the bed beside me, and stood, looking at Brutus, slightly shaking his head. I turned to him.

'And would you mind bringing some brandy, old man? He's rather down and out, I'm afraid – trembling from head to foot.'

'It's the reaction, of course,' remarked Carswell quietly. 'I have the brandy here.' The efficient fellow drew a small flask from his jacket pocket, uncorked it, and poured out a dose in the small silver cup which covered the patent stopper.

I raised Brutus's head from the pillow, his teeth audibly chattering as I did so, and just as I was getting the brandy between his lips, there came a slight scuttering sound from under the bed, and something, a small, dark, sinister-looking animal of about the size of a mongoose, dashed on all fours across the open space between the bed's corner and the still open doorway and disappeared into the night outside. Without a word Carswell ran after it, turning sharply to the left and running past the open window. I dropped the empty brandy cup, lowered Brutus's head hastily to its pillow, and dashed out of the cabin. Carswell was at the end of the cabins, his flashlight stabbing the narrow alleyway where I had found the miniature African hut. I ran up to him.

'It went up here,' said Carswell laconically.

I stood beside him in silence, my hand on his shoulder. He brightened every nook and cranny of the narrow alleyway with his light. There was nothing, nothing alive, to be seen. The Thing had had, of course, ample time to turn some hidden corner behind the cabins, to bury itself out of sight in some accustomed hiding-place, even to climb over the high, rough-surfaced back wall. Carswell brought his flashlight to rest finally on the little hut-like thing which still stood in the alleyway.

'What's that?' he inquired. 'Looks like some child's toy.'

'That's what I supposed when I discovered it,' I answered. 'I imagine it belongs to the washer's pickaninny.' We stepped into the alleyway. It was not quite wide enough for us to walk abreast. Carswell followed me in. I turned over the little hut with my foot. There was nothing under it. I dare say the possibility of this as a cache for the Thing had occurred to Carswell and me simultaneously. The Thing, mongoose, or whatever it was, had got clean away.

We returned to the cabin and found Brutus recovering from his ague-like trembling fit. His eyes were calmer now. The reassurance of our presence, the bandaging, had had their effect. Brutus proceeded to thank us for what we had done for him.

Helped by Carswell, I gingerly removed my rough bandage. The blood about that ugly bite – for a bite it certainly was, with unmistakable tooth-marks around its badly torn edges – was clotted now. The flow had ceased. We poured mercurochrome over and through the wound, disinfecting it, and then I placed two entire rolls of three-inch bandage about Brutus's wounded ankle. Then, with various encouragements and reassurances, we left him, the lamp still burning at his request, and went back to the ladies.

Our contract game was, somehow, a jumpy one, the ladies having been considerably upset by the scare down there in the yard, and we concluded it early, Carswell driving Mrs Spencer home and I walking down the hill with Mrs Squire to the Grand Hotel where she was spending that winter.

It was still several minutes short of midnight when I returned, after a slow walk up the hill, to my house. I had been thinking of the incident all the way up the hill. I determined to look in upon Brutus Hellman before retiring, but first I went up to my bedroom and loaded a small automatic pistol, and this I carried with me when I went down to the cabins in the yard. Brutus's light was still going, and he was awake, for he responded instantly to my tap on his door.

I went in and talked with the man for a few minutes. I left him the gun, which he placed carefully under his pillow. At the door I turned and addressed him.

'How do you suppose the Thing – whatever it was that attacked you, Brutus – could have got in, with everything closed up tight?'

Brutus replied that he had been thinking of this himself and had come to the conclusion that 'de T'ing' had concealed itself in the cabin before he had retired and closed the window and door. He expressed himself as uneasy with the window open, as Carswell and I had left it.

'But, man, you should have the fresh air while you sleep. You don't want your place closed up like a field-laborer's, do you?' said I, rallyingly. Brutus grinned.

'No, sar,' said he, slowly, 'ain't dat I be afeared of de Jumbee! I dare say it born in de blood, sar. I is close up everyt'ing by instinct! Besides, sar, now dat de T'ing attackin' me, p'raps bes' to have the window close up tightly. Den de T'ing cyant possibly mek an entrance 'pon me!'

I assured Brutus that the most agile mongoose could hardly clamber up that smooth, whitewashed wall outside and come in that window. Brutus smiled, but shook his head nevertheless.

' 'Tain't a mongoose, nor a rat, neither, sar,' he remarked, as he settled himself for rest under the bedclothes.

'What do you think it is, then?' I inquired.

'Only de good Gawd know, sar,' replied Brutus cryptically.

I was perhaps half-way across the house-yard on my way to turn in when my ears were assailed by precisely one of those suppressed combinations of squeals and grunts which John Masefield describes as presaging an animal tragedy under the hedge of an English countryside on a moonlit summer night. Something – a brief, ruthless combat for food or blood, between two small ground animals – was going on somewhere in the vicinity. I paused, listened, my senses the more readily attuned to this bitter duel because of what had happened in Brutus's cabin. As I paused, the squeals of the fighting animals abruptly ceased. One combatant, apparently, had given up the ghost! A grunting noise persisted for a few instants, however, and it made me shudder involuntarily. These sounds were low, essentially bestial, commonplace. Yet there was in them something so savage, albeit on the small scale of our everyday West Indian fauna, as to give me pause. I could feel the beginning of a cold shudder run down my spine under my white drill jacket!

I turned about, almost reluctantly, drawn somehow, in spite of myself, to the scene of combat. The grunts had ceased now, and to my ears, in the quiet of that perfect night of soft airs and moonlight, there came the even more horrible little sound of the tearing of flesh! It was gruesome, quite horrible, well-nigh unbearable. I paused again, a little shaken, it must be confessed, my nerves a trifle unstrung. I was facing in the direction of the ripping sounds now. Then there was silence – complete, tranquil, absolute!

Then I stepped towards the scene of this small conflict, my flash-light sweeping that corner of the yard nearest the small alleyway.

It picked up the victim almost at once, and I thought – I could not be quite sure – that I saw at the very edge of the circle of illumination, the scrambling flight of the victor. The victim was commonplace. It was the body, still slightly palpitating, of a large, well-nourished rat. The dead rat lay well out in the yard, its freshly drawn vital fluid staining a wide smear on the flagstone which supported it – a ghastly-looking affair. I looked down at it curiously. It had, indeed, been a ruthless attack to which this lowly creature had succumbed. Its throat was torn out, it was disembowelled, riven terrifically. I stepped back to Brutus's cabin, went in, and picked up from a pile of them on his bureau a copy of one of our small-sheet local newspapers. With this, nodding smilingly at Brutus I proceeded once more to the scene of carnage. I had an idea. I laid the paper down, kicked the body of the rat upon it with my foot, and, picking up the paper, carried the dead rat into Brutus's cabin. I turned up his lamp and carried it over to the bedside.

'Do you suppose this was your animal, Brutus?' I asked. 'If so, you seem to be pretty well avenged!'

Brutus grinned and looked closely at the riven animal. Then: 'No, sar,' he said, slowly, ' 'Twas no rat whut attacked me, sar. See de t'roat, please, sar. Him ahl tore out, mos' effectively! No, sar. But – I surmise – from de appearance of dis t'roat, de mouf which maim me on de laig was de same mouf whut completely ruin dis rat!'

And, indeed, judging from the appearance of the rat Brutus's judgment might well be sound.

I wrapped the paper about it, said good night once more to Hellman, carried it out with me, threw it into the metal waste basket in which the house-trash is burned every morning, and went to bed.

At three minutes past four the next morning I was snatched out of my comfortable bed and a deep sleep by the rattle of successive shots from the wicked little automatic I had left with Brutus. I jumped into my bathrobe, thrust my feet into my slippers, and was downstairs on the run, almost before the remnants of sleep were out of my eyes and brain. I ran out through the kitchen, as the nearest way, and was inside Brutus's cabin before the empty pistol, still clutched in his hand and pointed towards the open window, had ceased smoking. My first words were: 'Did you get it, Brutus?' I was thinking of the thing in terms of 'It'.

'Yes, sar,' returned Brutus, lowering his pistol. 'I t'ink I scotch him, sar. Be please to look on de window-sill. P'raps some blood in evidence, sar.'

I did so, and found that Brutus's marksmanship was better than I had anticipated when I entrusted him with the gun. To be sure, he had fired off all seven bullets, and, apparently, scored only one hit. A small, single drop of fresh blood lay on the white-painted wooden window-sill. No other trace of the attacker was in evidence. My flashlight revealed no marks, and the smooth, freshly-whitewashed wall outside was unscathed. Unless the Thing had wings – something suddenly touched me on the forehead, something light and delicate. I reached up, grasping. My hand closed around something like a string. I turned the flashlight up and there hung a thin strand of liana stem. I pulled it. It was firmly fastened somewhere up above there. I stepped outside, with one of Brutus's chairs, placed this against the outer wall under the window, and standing on it, raked the eaves with the flashlight. The upper end of the liana stem was looped about a small projection in the gutter, just above the window.

The Thing, apparently, knew enough to resort to this mechanical method for its second attack that night.

Inside, Brutus, somewhat excited over his exploit, found a certain difficulty in describing just what it was that had drawn his aim.

'It hav de appearance of a frog, sar,' he vouchsafed. 'I is wide awake when de T'ing land himse'f 'pon de sill, an' I have opportunity for takin' an excellent aim, sar.' That was the best I could get out of Brutus. I tried to visualize a 'Thing' which looked like a frog, being able to master one of our big, ferocious rats and tear out its inner parts and go off with them, not to mention liana stems with loop-knots in them to swing from a roof to an open window, and which could make a wound like the one above Brutus Hellman's ankle. It was rather too much for me. But – the Reign of Terror had begun, and no mistake!

Running over this summary in my mind as I stood and listened to Brutus telling about his marksmanship, there occurred to me – in a somewhat fantastic light, I must admit – the idea of calling in 'science' to our aid, forming the fantastic element – that the Thing had left a clue which might well be unmistakable; something which, suitably managed, might easily clear up the mounting mystery.

I went back to the house, broached my medicine closet, and returned to the cabin with a pair of glass microscopic slides. Between these I made a smear of the still fresh and fluid blood on the window-sill, and went back to my room, intending to send the smear later in the morning to Dr Pelletier's laboratory-man at the Municipal Hospital.

I left the slides there myself, requesting Dr Brownell to make me an analysis of the specimen with a view to determining its place in the gamut of West Indian fauna, and that afternoon, shortly after the siesta hour, I received a telephone call from the young physician. Dr Brownell had a certain whimsical cast apparent in his voice which was new to me. He spoke, I thought, rather banteringly.

'Where did you get your specimen, Mr Canevin?' he inquired. 'I understood you to say it was the blood of some kind of lower animal.'

'Yes,' said I, 'That was what *I* understood, Dr Brownell. Is there something peculiar about it?'

'Well – ' said Dr Brownell slowly, and somewhat banteringly, 'yes – and no. The only queer thing about it is that it's – human blood, probably a Negro's.'

I managed to thank him, even to say that I did not want the specimen returned, in answer to his query, and we rang off.

The plot, it seemed to me, was, in the language of the tradition of strange occurrences, thickening! This, then, must be Brutus's blood. Brutus's statement, that he had shot at and struck the marauder at his open window, must be imagination – Negro talk! But, even allowing that it was Brutus's blood – there was, certainly, no one else about to supply that drop of fresh fluid which I had so carefully scraped up on my two glass slides – how had he got blood, from his wounded lower leg, presumably, on that high window-sill? To what end would the man lie to me on such a subject? Besides, certainly he had shot at something – the pistol was smoking when I got to his room. And then – the liana stem? How was that to be accounted for?

Dr Brownell's report made the whole thing more complicated than it had been before. Science, which I had so cheerfully invoked, had only served to make this mystery deeper and more inexplicable.

Handicapped by nothing more than a slight limp Brutus Hellman was up and attending to his duties about the house the next day. In response to my careful questioning, he had repeated the story of his shooting in all particulars just as he had recounted that incident to me in the gray hours of the early morning. He had even added a particular which fitted in with the liana stem as the means of ingress. The Thing, he said, had appeared to *swing down* onto the window-sill from above, as he, awake for the time being between catnaps, had first seen it and reached for the pistol underneath his pillow and then opened fire.

Nothing happened throughout the day; nor, indeed, during the Reign of Terror as I have called it, did anything untoward occur throughout, except at night. That evening, shortly after eight o'clock, Brutus retired, and Stephen Penn, who had accompanied him to his cabin, reported to me that, in accordance with my suggestion, the two of them had made an exhaustive search for any concealed 'Thing' which might have secreted itself about Brutus's premises. They had found nothing, and Brutus, his window open, but provided with a tight-fitting screen which had been installed during the day, had fallen asleep before Stephen left. Penn had carefully closed the cabin door behind him, making sure that it was properly latched.

The attack that night – I had been sleeping 'with one eye open' – did not come until two o'clock in the morning. This time Brutus had no opportunity to use the gun, and so I was not awakened until it was all over. It was, indeed, Brutus calling me softly from the yard at a quarter past two that brought me to my feet and to the window.

'Yes,' said I, 'what is it, Brutus?'

'You axed me to inform you, sar, of anything,' explained Brutus from the yard.

'Right! What happened? Wait, Brutus, I'll come down,' and I hurriedly stepped into bathrobe and slippers.

Brutus was waiting for me at the kitchen door, a hand to his left cheek, holding a handkerchief rolled into a ball. Even in the moon-light I could see that this makeshift dressing was bright red. Brutus, it appeared, had suffered another attack of some kind. I took him into the house and upstairs, and dressed the three wounds in his left cheek in my bathroom. He had been awakened without warning, fifteen minutes before, with a sudden hurt, had straightened up in bed, but not before two more stabs, directly through the cheek, had been delivered. He had only just seen the Thing scrambling down over the foot of the bed, as he came awake under the impetus of these stabs, and, after a hasty search for the attacker had wisely devoted himself to staunching his bleeding face. Then, trembling in every limb, he had stepped out into the yard and come under my window to call me.

The three holes through the man's cheek were of equal size and similar appearance, obviously inflicted by some stabbing implement of about the diameter of a quarter-inch. The first stab, Brutus thought, had been the one highest up, and this one had not only penetrated into the mouth like the others, but had severely scratched the gum of the upper jaw just above his eye-tooth. I talked to him as I dressed these three wounds. 'So the Thing must have been concealed inside your room, you think, Brutus?'

'Undoubtedly, sar,' returned Brutus. 'There was no possible way for it to crawl in 'pon me – de door shut tight, de window-screen undisturb', sar.'

The poor fellow was trembling from head to foot with shock and fear, and I accompanied him back to his cabin. He had not lighted his lamp. It was only by the light of the moon that he had seen his assailant disappear over the foot of the bed. He had seized the handkerchief and run out into the yard in his pajamas.

I lit the lamp, determining to have electricity put into the cabin the next day, and, with Brutus's assistance, looked carefully over the room. Nothing, apparently, was hidden anywhere; there was only a little space to search through; Brutus had few belongings; the cabin furniture was adequate but scanty. There were no superfluities, no place, in other words, in which the Thing could hide itself.

Whatever had attacked Brutus was indeed going about its work with vicious cunning and determination.

Brutus turned in, and after sitting beside him for a while, I left the lamp turned down, closed the door, and took my departure.

Brutus did not turn up in the morning, and Stephen Penn, returning from an investigatory visit to the cabin, came to me on the gallery about nine o'clock with a face as gray as ashes. He had found Brutus unconscious, the bed soaked in blood, and, along the great pectoral muscle where the right arm joins the body, a long and deep gash from which the unfortunate fellow had, apparently, lost literally quarts of blood. I telephoned for a doctor and hurried to the cabin.

Brutus was conscious upon my arrival, but so weakened from loss of blood as to be quite unable to speak. On the floor, beside the bed, apparently where it had fallen, lay a medium-sized pocket knife, its largest blade open, soaked in blood. Apparently this had been the instrument with which he had been wounded.

The doctor, soon after his arrival, declared a blood-transfusion to be necessary, and this operation was performed at eleven o'clock in the cabin, Stephen contributing a portion of the blood, a young Negro from the town, paid for his service, the rest. After that, and the administration of a nourishing drink, Brutus was able to tell us what had happened.

Against his own expectations, he had fallen asleep immediately after my departure, and curiously, had been awakened not by any attack upon him, but by the booming of a *rata* drum from somewhere up in the hills back of the town where some of the Negroes were, doubtless, 'making magic', a common enough occurrence in any of the *vodu*-ridden West India islands. But this, according to Brutus, was no ordinary awakening.

No – for, on the floor, beside his bed, *dancing to the distant drumbeats*, he had seen – It!

That Brutus had possessed some idea of the identity or character of his assailant, I had, previous to this occurrence of his most serious wound, strongly suspected. I had gathered this impression from half a dozen little things, such as his fervid denial that the creature which had bitten him was either a rat or a mongoose; his 'Gawd know' when I had asked him what the Thing was like.

Now I understood, clearly of course, that Brutus knew what kind of creature had concealed itself in his room. I even elicited the fact, discovered by him, just how I am quite unaware, that the Thing had hidden under a loose floor-board beneath his bed and so escaped detection on the several previous searches.

But to find out from Brutus – the only person who knew – that, indeed, was quite another affair. There can be, I surmise, no human being as consistently and completely shut-mouthed as a West Indian Negro, once such a person has definitely made up his mind to silence on a given subject! And on this subject, Brutus had, it appeared, quite definitely made up his mind. No questions, no cajolery, no urging – even with tears, on the part of his lifelong friend Stephen Penn –

could elicit from him the slightest remark bearing on the description or identity of the Thing. I myself used every argument which logic and common-sense presented to my Caucasian mind. I urged his subsequent safety upon Brutus, my earnest desire to protect him, the logical necessity of co-operating, in the stubborn fellow's own obvious interest, with us who had his welfare at heart. Stephen, as I have said, even wept! But all these efforts on our parts, were of no avail. Brutus Hellman resolutely refused to add a single word to what he had already said. He had awakened to the muted booming of the distant drum. He had seen the Thing dancing beside his bed. He had, it appeared, fainted from this shock, whatever the precise nature of that shock may have been, and knew nothing more until he came slowly to a vastly weakened consciousness between Stephen Penn's visit to him late in the morning, and mine which followed it almost at once.

There was one fortunate circumstance. The deep and wide cut which had, apparently, been inflicted upon him with his own pocket-knife – which had been lying, open, by mere chance, on a small tabouret beside his bed – had been delivered lengthwise of the pectoral muscle, not across the muscle. Otherwise the fellow's right arm would have been seriously crippled for life. The major damage he had suffered in this last and most serious attack had been the loss of blood, and this, through my employment of one donor of blood and Stephen Penn's devotion in giving him the remainder, had been virtually repaired.

However, whether he spoke or kept silent, it was plain to me that I had a very definite duty towards Brutus Hellman. I could not, if anything were to be done to prevent it, have him attacked in this way while in my service and living on my premises.

The electricity went in that afternoon, with a pull-switch placed near the hand of whoever slept in the bed, and, later in the day, Stephen Penn brought up on a donkey cart from his town lodging-place, his own bedstead, which he set up in Brutus's room, and his bureau containing the major portion of his belongings, which he placed in the newly-swept and garnished cabin next door. If the Thing repeated its attack that night, it would have Stephen, as well as Brutus, to deal with.

One contribution to our knowledge Stephen made, even before he had actually moved into my yard. This was the instrument with which Brutus had been stabbed through the cheek. He found it cached in the floor-space underneath that loose board where the Thing had hidden itself. He brought it to me, covered with dried blood. It was a rough, small-scale reproduction of an African 'assegai', or stabbing-spear. It was made out of an ordinary butcher's hardwood meat-skewer, its head a splinter of pointed glass such as might be picked up anywhere about the town. The head – and this was what caused the resemblance to an 'assegai' – was very exactly and neatly bound on to the cleft end of the skewer, with fishline. On the whole, and considered as a piece of work, the 'assegai' was a highly creditable job.

It was on the morning of this last-recorded attack on Brutus Hellman during the period between my visit to him and the arrival of the doctor with the man for the blood-transfusion, that I sat down, at my desk, in an attempt to figure out some conclusion from the facts already known. I had progressed somewhat with my theoretical investigation at that time. When later, after Brutus could talk, he mentioned the circumstance of the Thing's dancing there on his cabin floor, to the notes of a drum, in the pouring moon-light which came through his screened window and gave its illum-ination to the little room, I came to some sort of indeterminate decision. I will recount the steps – they are very brief – which led up to this.

The facts, as I noted them down on paper that day, pointed to a pair of alternatives. Either Brutus Hellman was demented, and had invented his 'attacks', having inflicted them upon himself for some inscrutable reason; or – the Thing was possessed of qualities not common among the lower animals! I set the two groups of facts side by side, and compared them.

Carswell and I had actually seen the Thing as it ran out of the cabin that first night. Something, presumably the same Thing, had torn a large rat to pieces. The same Thing had bitten savagely Brutus's lower leg. Brutus's description of it was that it looked 'like a frog'. Those four facts seemed to indicate one of the lower animals, though its genus and the motive for its attacks were unknown!

On the other hand, there was a divergent set of facts. The Thing had used mechanical means, a liana stem with a looped knot in it, to get into Brutus's cabin through the window. It had used some stabbing instrument, later found, and proving to be a manufactured affair. Again, later, it had used Brutus's knife in its final attack. All these facts pointed to some such animal as a small monkey. This theory was strengthened by the shape of the bites on Brutus's leg and on the rat's throat.

That it was *not* a monkey, however, there was excellent evidence. The Thing looked like a frog. A frog is a very different-looking creature from any known kind of monkey. There were, so far as I knew, no monkeys at the time on the island of St Thomas.

I added to these sets of facts two other matters: The blood alleged to be drawn from the Thing had, on analysis, turned out to be human blood. This single circumstance pointed very strongly to the insanity theory. On the other hand, Brutus could hardly have placed the fresh blood which I had myself scraped up on my slides, on the window-sill where I found it. Still, he might have done so, if his 'insanity' were such as to allow for an elaborately 'planted' hoax or something of the kind. He could have placed the drop of blood there, drawn from his own body by means of a pin-prick, before he fired the seven cartridges that night. It was possible. But, knowing Brutus, it was so improbable as to be quite absurd.

The final circumstance was the little 'African' hut. That, somehow, seemed to fit in with the 'assegai'. The two naturally went together.

It was a jumble, a puzzle. The more I contrasted and compared these clues, the more impossible the situation became.

Well, there was one door open, at least. I decided to go through that door and see where it led me. I sent for Stephen. It was several hours after the blood-transfusion. I had to get some of Brutus's blood for my experiment, but it must be blood drawn previous to the transfusion. Stephen came to see what I wanted.

'Stephen,' said I, 'I want you to secure from Hellman's soiled things one of those very bloody sheets which you changed on his bed today, and bring it here.'

Stephen goggled at me, but went at once on this extraordinary errand. He brought me the sheet. On one of its corners, there was an especially heavy mass of clotted blood. From the underside of this I managed to secure a fresh enough smear on a pair of glass slides, and with these I stepped into my car and ran down to the hospital and asked for Dr Brownell.

I gave him the slides and asked him to make for me an analysis for the purpose of comparing this blood with the specimen I had given him two days before. My only worry was whether or not they had kept a record of the former analysis, it being a private job and not part of the hospital routine. They had recorded it, however, and Dr Brownell obligingly made the test for me then and there. Half an hour after he had stepped into the laboratory he came back to me.

'Here are the records,' he said. 'The two specimens are un-questionably from the same person, presumably a Negro. They are virtually identical.'

The blood alleged to be the Thing's, then, was merely Brutus's blood. The strong presumption was, therefore, that Brutus had lost his mind.

Into this necessary conclusion, I attempted to fit the remaining facts. Unfortunately for the sake of any solution, they did not fit! Brutus might, for some insane reason, have inflicted the three sets of wounds upon himself. But Brutus had not made the 'African' hut, which had turned up before he was back from the hospital. He had not, presumably, fastened that liana stem outside his window. He had not, certainly, slain that rat, nor could he have 'invented' the creature which both Carswell and I had seen, however vaguely, running out of his cabin that night of the first attack.

At the end of all my cogitations, I knew absolutely nothing, except what my own senses had conveyed to me; and these discordant facts I have already set down in their order and sequence, precisely and accurately, as they occurred.

To these I now add the additional fact that upon the night following the last recorded attack on Brutus Hellman nothing whatever happened. Neither he nor Stephen Penn, sleeping side by side in their two beds in the cabin room, was in any way disturbed.

I wished, fervently, that Dr Pelletier were at hand. I needed someone like him to talk to. Carswell would not answer, somehow. No one would answer. I needed Pelletier, with his incisive mind, his scientific training, his vast knowledge of the West Indies, his open-mindedness to facts wherever these and their contemplation might lead the investigator. I needed Pelletier very badly indeed!

And Pelletier was still over in Porto Rico.

Only one further circumstance, and that, apparently, an irrelevant one, can be added to the facts already narrated – those incongruous facts which did not appear to have any reasonable connection with one another and seemed to be mystifyingly contradictory. The circum-stance was related to me by Stephen Penn, and it was nothing more or less than the record of a word, a proper name. This, Stephen alleged, Brutus had repeated, over and over, as, under the effects of the two degrees of temperature which he was carrying as the result of his shock and of the blood-transfusion, he had tossed about restlessly during a portion of the night. That name was, in a sense, a singularly appropriate one for Brutus to utter, even though one would hardly suspect the fellow of having any acquaintance with Roman history, or, indeed, with the works of William Shakespeare!

The name was – Cassius!

I figured that anyone bearing the Christian name, Brutus, must, in the course of a lifetime, have got wind of the original Brutus's side-partner. The two names naturally go together, of course, like Damon and Pythias, David and Jonathan! However, I said nothing about this to Brutus.

I was on the concrete wharf beside the Naval Administration Building long before the *Grebe* arrived from San Juan on the Thursday morning a week after Brutus Hellman's operation.

I wanted to get Pelletier's ear at the earliest possible moment. Nearby, in the waiting line against the wall of the Navy building, Stephen Penn at the wheel, stood my car. I had telephoned Pelletier's man that he need not meet the doctor. I was going to do that myself, to get what facts, whatever explanation Pelletier might have to offer as I drove him through the town and up the precipitous roadways of Denmark Hill to his house at its summit.

My bulky, hard-boiled, genial naval surgeon friend, of the keen, analytical brain and the skillful hands which so often skirted the very edges of death in his operating-room, was unable, however, to accompany me at once upon his arrival. I had to wait more than twenty minutes for him, while others, who had prior claims upon him, interviewed him. At last he broke away from the important ones and heaved his unwieldy bulk into the back seat of my car beside me. Among those who had waylaid him, I recognized Doctors Roots and Maguire, both naval surgeons.

I had not finished my account of the persecution to which Brutus Hellman had been subjected by the time we arrived at the doctor's hilltop abode. I told Stephen to wait for me and finished the story inside the house while Pelletier's house-man was unpacking his travelling valises. Pelletier heard me through in virtual silence, only occasionally interrupting with a pertinent question. When I had finished he lay back in his chair, his eyes closed.

He said nothing for several minutes. Then, his eyes still shut, he raised and slightly waved his big, awkward-looking hand, that hand of such uncanny skill when it held a knife, and began to speak, very slowly and reflectively.

'Dr Roots mentioned a peculiar circumstance on the wharf.'

'Yes?' said I.

'Yes,' said Dr Pelletier. He shifted his ungainly bulk in his big chair, opened his eyes and looked at me. Then, very deliberately: 'Roots reported the disappearance of the thing – it was a parasitic growth – that I removed from your house-man's side a week ago. When they had dressed the fellow and sent him back to the ward Roots intended to look the thing over in the laboratory. It was quite unusual. I'll come to that in a minute. But when he turned to pick it up, it was gone; had quite disappeared. The nurse, Miss Charles, and he looked all over for it, made a very thorough search. That was one of the things he came down for this morning – to report that to me.'

Once again Pelletier paused, looked at me searchingly, as though studying me carefully. Then he said: 'I understand you to say that the Thing, as you call it, is still at large?'

The incredible possible implication of this statement of the disappearance of the 'growth' removed from Hellman's body and the doctor's question, stunned me for an instant. Could he possibly mean to imply – ? I stared at him, blankly, for an instant.

'Yes,' said I, 'it is still at large, and poor Hellman is barricaded in his cabin. As I have told you, I have dressed those bites and gashes myself. He absolutely refuses to go to the hospital again. He lies there, muttering to himself, ash-gray with fear.'

'Hm,' vouchsafed Dr Pelletier. 'How big would you say the Thing is, Canevin, judging from your glimpse of it and the marks it leaves?'

'About the size, say, of a rat,' I answered, 'and black. We had that one sight of it, that first night. Carswell and I both saw it scuttering out of Hellman's cabin right under our feet when this horrible business first started.'

Dr Pelletier nodded, slowly. Then he made another remark, apparently irrelevant.

'I had breakfast this morning on board the *Grebe*. Could you give me lunch?' He looked at his watch.

'Of course,' I returned. 'Are you thinking of – '

'Let's get going,' said Dr Pelletier, heaving himself to his feet.

We started at once, the doctor calling out to his servants that he would not be back for one o'clock 'breakfast', and Stephen Penn who had driven us up the hill drove us down again. Arrived at my house we proceeded straight to Hellman's cabin. Dr Pelletier talked soothingly to the poor fellow while examining those ugly wounds. On several he placed fresh dressings from his professional black bag. When he had finished he drew me outside.

'You did well, Canevin,' he remarked, reflectively, 'in not calling in anybody, dressing those wounds yourself! What people don't know, er – won't hurt 'em!'

He paused after a few steps away from the cabin.

'Show me,' he commanded, 'which way the Thing ran, that first night.'

I indicated the direction, and we walked along the line of it, Pelletier forging ahead, his black bag in his big hand. We reached the corner of the cabin in a few steps, and Pelletier glanced up the alleyway between the cabin's side and the high yard-wall. The little toy house, looking somewhat dilapidated now, still stood where it had been, since I first discovered it. Pelletier did not enter the alleyway. He looked in at the queer little miniature hut.

'Hm,' he remarked, his forehead puckered into a thick frowning wrinkle. Then, turning abruptly to me: 'I suppose it must have occurred to you that the Thing lived in that,' said he, challengingly.

'Yes – naturally; after it went for my fingers – whatever *that* creature may have been. Three or four times I've gone in there with a flashlight after one of the attacks on Brutus Hellman; picked it up, even, and looked inside – '

'And the Thing is never there,' finished Dr Pelletier, nodding sagaciously.

'Never,' I corroborated.

'Come on up to the gallery,' said the doctor, 'and I'll tell you what I think.'

We proceeded to the gallery at once and Dr Pelletier, laying down his black bag, caused a lounge-chair to groan and creak beneath his recumbent weight while I went into the house to command the usual West Indian preliminary to a meal.

A few minutes later Dr Pelletier told me what he thought, according to his promise. His opening remark was in the form of a question; about the very last question anyone in his senses would have regarded as pertinent to the subject in hand.

'Do you know anything about twins, Canevin?' he inquired.

'Twins?' said I. 'Twins!' I was greatly puzzled. I had not been expecting any remarks about twins.

'Well,' said I, as Dr Pelletier stared at me gravely, 'only what everybody knows about them, I imagine. What about them?'

'There are two types of twins, Canevin – and I don't mean the difference arising out of being separate or attached-at-birth, the "Siamese" or ordinary types. I mean something far more basic than that accidental division into categories; more fundamental – deeper than that kind of distinction. The two kinds of twins I have reference to are called in biological terminology "monozygotic" and "dizygotic", respectively; those which originate, that is, from one cell, or from two.'

'The distinction,' I threw in, 'which Johannes Lange makes in his study of criminal determinism, his book *Crime and Destiny*. The one-cell-originated twins, he contends, have identical motives and personalities. If one is a thief, the other has to be! He sets out to prove – and that pompous ass, Haldane, who wrote the foreword, believes it, too – that there is no freewill; that man's moral course is predetermined, inescapable – a kind of scientific Calvinism.'

'Precisely, just that,' said Dr Pelletier. 'Anyhow, you understand that distinction.' I looked at him, still somewhat puzzled.

'Yes,' said I, 'but still, I don't see its application to this nasty business of Brutus Hellman.'

'I was leading up to telling you,' said Dr Pelletier, in his matter-of-fact, forthright fashion of speech; 'to telling you, Canevin, that the Thing is undoubtedly, the parasitic "Siamese-twin" that I cut away from Brutus Hellman last Thursday morning, and which disappeared out of the operating-room. Also, from the evidence. I'd be inclined to think it is of the "dizygotic" type. That would not occur, in the case of "attached" twins, more than once in ten million times!'

He paused at this and looked at me. For my part, after that amazing, that utterly incredible statement, so calmly made, so dispassionately uttered, I could do nothing but sit limply in my chair and gaze woodenly at my guest. I was so astounded that I was incapable of uttering a word. But I did not have to say anything. Dr Pelletier was speaking again, developing his thesis.

'Put together the known facts, Canevin. It is the scientific method, the only satisfactory method, when you are confronted with a situation like this one. You can do so quite easily, almost at random, here. To begin with, you never found the Thing in that little thatched hut after one of its attacks – did you?'

'No,' I managed to murmur, out of a strangely dry mouth. Pelletier's theory held me stultified by its unexpectedness, its utter, weird strangeness. The name, 'Cassius', smote my brain. That identical blood –

'If the Thing had been, say a rat,' he continued, 'as you supposed when it went for your fingers, it would have gone straight from its attacks on Brutus Hellman to its diggings – the refuge-instinct; "holing-up". But it didn't. You investigated several times and it wasn't inside the little house, although it ran toward it, as you believed, after seeing it start that way the first night; although the creature that went for your hand was there, inside, *before it suspected pursuit*. You see? That gives us a lead, a clue. The Thing possesses a much higher level of intelligence than that of a mere rodent. Do you grasp that significant point, Canevin? The Thing, anticipating pursuit, avoided capture by instinctively outguessing the pursuer. It went toward its diggings but deferred entrance until the pursuer had investigated and gone away. Do you get it?'

I nodded, not desiring to interrupt. I was following Pelletier's thesis eagerly now. He resumed: 'Next – consider those wounds, those bites, on Brutus Hellman. They were never made by any small, ground-dwelling animal, a rodent, like a rat or a mongoose. No; those teeth-marks are those of – well, say, a marmoset or any very small monkey; or, Canevin, of *an unbelievably small human being!*'

Pelletier and I sat and looked at each other. I think that, after an appreciable interval, I was able to nod my head in his direction. Pelletier continued. 'The next point we come to – before going on to something a great deal deeper, Canevin – is the *color* of the Thing. You saw it. It was only a momentary glimpse, as you say, but you secured enough of an impression to seem pretty positive on that question of its color. Didn't you?'

'Yes,' said I, slowly. 'It was as black as a derby hat, Pelletier.'

'There you have one point definitely settled, then.' The doctor was speaking with a judicial note in his voice, the scientist in full stride now. 'The well-established ethnic rule, the biological certainty in cases of miscegenation between Caucasians or quasi-Caucasians and the Negro or negroid types is that the offspring is never darker than the darker of the two parents. The "black-baby" tradition, as a "throwback" being produced by mulatto or nearly Caucasian parents is a bugaboo, Canevin, sheer bosh! It doesn't happen that way. It *cannot* happen. It is a biological impossibility, my dear man. Although widely believed, that idea falls into the same category as the ostrich burying its head in the sand and thinking it is concealed! It falls in with the Amazon myth! The "Amazons" were merely long-haired Scythians, those "women-warriors" of antiquity. Why, damn it, Canevin, it's like believing in the Centaur to swallow a thing like that.'

The doctor had become quite excited over his expression of biological orthodoxy. He glared at me, or appeared to, and lighted a fresh cigarette. Then, considering for a moment, while he inhaled a few preliminary puffs, he resumed. 'You see what that proves, don't you, Canevin?' he inquired, somewhat more calmly now.

'It seems to show,' I answered, 'since Brutus is very "clear-colored", as the Negroes would say, that one of his parents was a black; the other very considerably lighter, perhaps even a pure Caucasian.'

'Right, so far,' acquiesced the doctor. 'And the other inference, in the case of twins – what?'

'That the twins were "dizygotic", even though attached,' said I, slowly, as the conclusion came clear in my mind after Pelletier's preparatory speech. 'Otherwise, of course, if they were the other kind, the mono-cellular or "monozygotic", they would have the same coloration, derived from either the dark or the light-skinned parent.'

'Precisely,' exclaimed Dr Pelletier. 'Now – '

'You mentioned certain other facts,' I interrupted, ' "more deep-seated", I think you said. What – '

'I was just coming to those, Canevin. There are, actually, two such considerations which occur to me. First – why did the Thing degenerate, undoubtedly after birth, of course, if there were no pre-natal process of degeneration? They would have been nearly of a size, anyway, when born, I'd suppose. Why did "It" shrink up into a withered, apparently lifeless little homunculus, while its fellow twin, Brutus Hellman, attained to a normal manhood? There are some pretty deep matters involved in those queries, Canevin. It was comatose, shrunken, virtually dead while attached.'

'Let's see if we can't make a guess at them,' I threw in.

'What would you say?' countered Dr Pelletier.

I nodded, and sat silently for several minutes trying to put what was in my mind together in some coherent form so as to express it adequately. Then: 'A couple of possibilities occur to me,' I began. 'One or both of them might account for the divergence. First, the failure of one or more of the ductless glands, very early in the Thing's life after birth. It's the pituitary gland, isn't it, that regulates the physical growth of an infant – that makes him grow normally? If that fails before it has done its full work, about the end of the child's second year, you get a midget. If, on the other hand, it keeps on too long – does not dry up as it should, and cease functioning, its normal task finished – the result is a giant; the child simply goes on growing, bigger and bigger! Am I right, so far? And, I suppose, the cutting process released it from its coma.'

'Score one!' said Dr Pelletier, wagging his head at me. 'Go on –
what else? There are many cases, of course, of bloodletting ending a
coma.'

'The second guess is that Brutus had the stronger constitution, and
outstripped the other one. It doesn't sound especially scientific, but
that sort of thing does happen as I understand it. Beyond those two
possible explanations I shouldn't care to risk any more guesses.'

'I think both those causes have been operative in this case,' said
Dr Pelletier, reflectively. 'And, having performed that operation,
you see, I think I might add a third, Canevin. It is purely conjectural.
I'll admit that frankly, but one outstanding circumstance supports
it. I'll come back to that shortly. In short, Canevin, I imagine –
my instinct tells me – that almost from the beginning, quite unconsciously, of course, and in the automatic processes of outstrip-
ping his twin in physical growth, *Brutus absorbed the other's share of
nutriments*.

'I can figure that out, in fact, from several possible angles. The
early nursing, for instance! The mother – she was, undoubtedly, the
black parent – proud of her "clear" child, would favor it, nurse it first.
There is, besides, always some more or less obscure interplay, some
balanced adjustment, between physically attached twins. In this
case, God knows how, that invariable "balance" became disadjusted;
the adjustment became unbalanced, if you prefer it that way. The
mother, too, from whose side the dark twin probably derived its
constitution, may very well have been a small, weakly woman. The
fair-skinned other parent was probably robust, physically. But, whatever the underlying causes, we know that Brutus grew up to be
normal and fully mature, and I know, from that operation, that the
Thing I cut away from him was his twin brother, degenerated into an
apparently lifeless homunculus, a mere appendage of Brutus, something which, *apparently, had quite lost nearly everything of its basic
humanity*; even most of its appearance, Canevin – a Thing to be
removed surgically, like a wen.'

'It is a terrible idea,' said I, slowly, and after an interval. 'But, it
seems to be the only way to explain, er – the facts! Now tell me, if
you please, what is that "outstanding circumstance" you mentioned
which corroborates this, er – theory of yours.'

'It is the Thing's *motive*, Canevin,' said Dr Pelletier, very gravely,
'allowing, of course, that we are right – that I am right – in assuming
for lack of a better hypothesis that what I cut away from Hellman had
life in it; that it "escaped"; that it is now – well, trying to get at a thing

like that, under the circumstances, I'd be inclined to say, we touch bottom!'

'Good God – the *motive*!' I almost whispered. 'Why, it's horrible, Pelletier; it's positively uncanny. The Thing becomes, quite definitely, a horror. The motive – in that Thing! You're right, old man. Psychologically speaking, it "touches bottom", as you say.'

'And humanly speaking,' added Dr Pelletier, in a very quiet voice.

Stephen came out and announced breakfast. It was one o'clock. We went in and ate rather silently. As Stephen was serving the dessert Dr Pelletier spoke to him. 'Was Hellman's father a white man, do you happen to know, Stephen?'

'De man was an engineer on board an English trading vessel, sar.'

'What about his mother?' probed the doctor.

'Her a resident of Antigua, sar,' replied Stephen promptly, 'and is yet alive. I am acquainted with her. Hellman ahlways send her some portion of his earnings, sar, very regularly. At de time Hellman born, her a 'ooman which do washing for ships' crews, an' make an excellent living. Nowadays, de poor soul liddle more than a piteous invalid, sar. Her ahlways a small liddle 'ooman, not too strong.'

'I take it she is a dark woman?' remarked the doctor, smiling at Stephen.

Stephen, who is a medium brown young man, a 'Zambo', as they say in the English islands like St Kitts and Montserrat and Antigua, grinned broadly at this, displaying a set of magnificent, glistening teeth.

'Sar,' he replied, 'Hellman's mother de precisely identical hue of dis fella,' and Stephen touched with his index finger the neat black bow-tie which set off the snowy whiteness of his immaculate drill house-man's jacket. Pelletier and I exchanged glances as we smiled at Stephen's little joke.

On the gallery immediately after lunch, over coffee, we came back to that bizarre topic which Dr Pelletier had called the 'motive'. Considered quite apart from the weird aspect of attributing a motive to a quasi-human creature of the size of a rat, the matter was clear enough. The Thing had relentlessly attacked Brutus Hellman again and again, with an implacable fiendishness; its brutal, single-minded efforts being limited in their disastrous effects only by its diminutive size and relative dsficiency of strength. Even so, it had succeeded in driving a full-grown man, its victim, into a condition not very far removed from imbecility.

What obscure processes had gone on piling up cumulatively to a fixed purpose of pure destruction in that primitive, degenerated organ that served the Thing for a brain! What dreadful weeks and months and years of semi-conscious brooding, of existence endured parasitically as an appendage upon the instinctively loathed body of the normal brother! What savage hatred had burned itself into that minute, distorted personality! What incalculable instincts, deep buried in the backgrounds of the black heredity through the mother, had come into play – as evidenced by the Thing's construction of the typical African hut as its habitation – once it had come, after the separation, into active consciousness, the new-born, freshly realized freedom to exercise and release all that acrid, seething hatred upon him who had usurped its powers of self-expression, its very life itself! What manifold thwarted instincts had, by the processes of sub-stitution, crystallized themselves into one overwhelming, driving desire – the consuming instinct for revenge!

I shuddered as all this clarified itself in my mind, as I formed, vaguely, some kind of mental image of that personality. Dr Pelletier was speaking again. I forced my engrossed mind to listen to him. He seemed very grave and determined, I noticed . . .

'We must put an end to all this, Canevin,' he was saying. 'Yes, we must put an end to it.'

Ever since that first Sunday evening when the attacks began, as I look back over that hectic period, it seems to me that I had had in mind primarily the idea of capture and destruction of what had crystallized in my mind as 'The Thing'. Now a new and totally bizarre idea came in to cause some mental conflict with the destruction element in that vague plan. This was the almost inescapable conviction that the Thing had been originally – whatever it might be properly named now – a human being. As such, knowing well, as I did, the habits of the blacks of our Lesser Antilles, it had, unquestionably, been received into the Church by the initial process of baptism. That indescribable creature which had been an appendage on Brutus Hell-man's body, had been, *was now*, according to the teaching of the Church, a Christian. The idea popped into my mind along with various other sidelights on the situation, stimulated into being by the discussion with Dr Pelletier which I have just recorded.

The idea itself was distressing enough, to one who, like myself, has always kept up the teachings of my own childhood, who has never found it necessary, in these days of mental unrest, to doubt, still less to abandon, his religion. One of the concomitants of this idea was that the destruction of the Thing after its problematical capture, would be an awkward affair upon my conscience, for, however far departed the Thing had got from its original status as 'A child of God – an Inheritor of the Kingdom of Heaven', it must retain, in some obscure fashion, its human, indeed its Christian, standing. There are those, doubtless, who might well regard this scruple of mine as quite utterly ridiculous, who would lay all the stress on the plain necessity of stopping the Thing's destructive malignancy without reference to any such apparently far-fetched and artificial considerations. Nevertheless this aspect of our immediate problem, Pelletier's gravely enunciated dictum: 'We must put an end to all this', weighed heavily on my burdened mind. It must be remembered that I had put in a dreadful week over the affair.

I mention this 'scruple' of mine because it throws up into relief, in a sense, those events which followed very shortly after Dr Pelletier had summed up what necessarily lay before us, in that phrase of his.

We sat on the gallery and cogitated ways and means, and it was in the midst of this discussion that the scruple alluded to occurred to me. I did not mention it to Pelletier. I mentally conceded, of course, the necessity of capture. The subsequent disposal of the Thing could wait on that.

We had pretty well decided, on the evidence, that the Thing had been lying low during the day in the little hut-like arrangement which it appeared to have built for itself. Its attacks so far had occurred only at night. If we were correct, the capture would be a comparatively simple affair. There was, as part of the equipment in my house, a small bait net, of the circular closing-in-from-the-bottom kind, used occasionally when I took guests on a deep-sea fishing excursion out to Congo or Levango Bays. This I unearthed, and looked over. It was intact, recently mended, without any holes in the tightly meshed netting designed to capture and retain small fish to be used later as live bait.

Armed with this, our simple plan readily in mind, we proceeded together to the alleyway about half past two that afternoon, or, to be more precise, we were just at that moment starting down the gallery steps leading into my yard, when our ears were assailed by a succession of piercing, childish screams from the vicinity of the house's rear.

I rushed down the steps, four at a time, the more unwieldy Pelletier following me as closely as his propulsive apparatus would allow. I was in time to see, when I reached the corner of the house, nearly everything that was happening, almost from its beginning. It was a scene which, reproduced in a drawing accurately limned, would appear wholly comic. Little Aesculapius, the washer's small, black child, his eyes popping nearly from his head, his diminutive black legs twinkling under his single flying garment, his voice uttering blood-curdling yowls of pure terror, raced diagonally across the yard in the direction of his mother's wash-tub near the kitchen door, the very embodiment of crude, ungovernable fright, a veritable caricature, a figure of fun.

And behind him, coming on implacably, for all the world like a misshapen black frog, bounded the Thing, in hot pursuit, Its red tongue lolling out of Its gash of a mouth, Its diminutive blubbery lips drawn back in a wide snarl through which a murderous row of teeth flashed viciously in the pouring afternoon sunlight. Little Aesculapius was making good the promise of his relatively long, thin legs, fright driving him. He outdistanced the Thing hopelessly, yet It forged ahead in a rolling, leaping series of bounds, using hands and arms, frog-like, as well as Its strange, withered, yet strangely powerful bandied legs.

The sight, grotesque as it would have been to anyone unfamiliar with the Thing's history and identity, positively sickened me. My impulse was to cover my face with my hands, in the realization of its underlying horror. I could feel a faint nausea creeping over me, beginning to dim my senses. My washer-woman's screams had added to the confusion within a second or two after those of the child had begun, and now, as I hesitated in my course toward the scene of confusion, those of the cook and scullery-maid were added to the cacophonous din in my back yard. Little Aesculapius, his garment stiff against the breeze of his own progress, disappeared around the rear-most corner of the house to comparative safety through the open kitchen door. He had, as I learned some time afterwards, been playing about the yard and had happened upon the little hut in its obscure and seldom-visited alleyway. He had stopped, and picked it up. 'The Thing' – the child used that precise term to describe It – lay, curled up, asleep within. It had leaped to Its splayed feet with a snarl of rage, and gone straight for the little Negro's foot.

Thereafter the primitive instinct for self-preservation and Aesculapius' excellent footwork had solved his problem. He reached the kitchen door, around the corner and out of our sight, plunged within, and took immediate refuge atop the shelf of a kitchen cabinet well out of reach of that malignant, unheard-of demon like a big black frog which was pursuing him and which, doubtless, would haunt his dreams for the rest of his existence. So much for little Aesculapius, who thus happily passes out of the affair.

My halting was, of course, only momentary. I paused, as I have mentioned, but for so brief a period as not to allow Dr Pelletier to catch up with me. I ran, then, with the net open in my hands, diagonally across the straight course being pursued by the Thing. My mind was made up to intercept it, entangle it in the meshes. This should not be difficult considering its smallness and the comparative shortness of its arms and legs; and, having rendered it helpless, to face the ultimate problem of its later disposal.

But this plan of mine was abruptly interfered with. Precisely as the flying body of the pursued pick'ny disappeared around the corner of the house, my cook's cat, a ratter with a neighborhood reputation and now, although for the moment I failed to realize it, quite clearly an instrument of that Providence responsible for my 'scruple', came upon the scene with violence, precision, and that uncanny accuracy which actuates the feline in all its physical manifestations.

This avatar, which, according to a long-established custom, had been sunning itself demurely on the edge of the rain-water piping which ran along the low eaves of the three yard cabins, aroused by the discordant yells of the child and the three women in four distinct keys, had arisen, taken a brief, preliminary stretch, and condescended to turn its head towards the scene below ...

The momentum of the cat's leap arrested instantaneously the Thing's course of pursuit, bore it, sprawled out and flattened, to the ground, and twenty sharp powerful retractile claws sank simultaneously into the prone little body.

The Thing never moved again. A more merciful snuffing out would be difficult to imagine.

It was a matter of no difficulty to drive Junius, the cat, away from his kill. I am on terms of pleasant intimacy with Junius. He allowed me to take the now limp and flaccid little body away from him quite without protest, and sat down where he was, licking his paws and readjusting his rumpled fur.

And thus, unexpectedly, without intervention on our part, Pelletier and I saw brought to its sudden end, the tragical dénouement of what seems to me to be one of the most outlandish and most distressing affairs which could ever have been evolved out of the mad mentality of Satan, who dwells in his own place to distress the children of men.

And that night, under a flagstone in the alleyway, quite near where the Thing's strange habitation had been taken up, I buried the mangled leathery little body of that unspeakable grotesque homunculus which had once been the twin brother of my house-man, Brutus Hellman. In consideration of my own scruple which I have mentioned, and because, in all probability, this handful of strange material which I lowered gently into its last resting-place had once been a Christian, I repeated the Prayer of Committal from the Book of Common Prayer. It may have been – doubtless was, in one sense – a grotesque act on my part. But I cherish the conviction that I did what was right.

Black Tancrède

It is true that Black Tancrède did not curse Hans De Groot as his mangled body collapsed on the rack, and that he did curse Gardelin. But, it must be remembered, Governor Gardelin went home, to Denmark, and so escaped – whatever it was that happened to Achilles Mendoza and Julius Mohrs; and Black Tancrède, who always kept his word, they said, had cursed three!

The Grand Hotel of St Thomas in the Virgin Islands glistens in the almost intolerable brilliance of the Caribbean sunlight, because that great edifice is whitewashed in every corner, every winter. Built somewhat more than a century ago, it is a noble example of that tropical architecture which depends, for its style, upon the structural necessity for resistance to summer hurricanes. Its massive walls of stone, brick, and heavy cement are thick and ponderous. The ceilings of its huge, square rooms are eighteen feet high. Despite its solidity, the 1916 hurricane took the top story off the main building and this has never been replaced. The fact that the hotel is now uniformly a two-story structure somewhat mars its original symmetry, but it is still as impressive as in the days when the Danish Colonial High Court sat in one of its sections; when its 'slave-pens' were especially noted for their safety.

Built alongside the great courtyard which its bulk surrounds, and toward the harbor, once the crater of a volcano in that era when Atlantis and its companion continent, Antillea, reared their proud civilizations in the central Atlantic, stand two houses, added, it is believed, some time after the construction of the original building. On this point the St Thomas wiseacres continue to dispute. Nevertheless, under the house nearest to the hotel, and built with connecting steps leading to its great gallery, are those very slave-pens, converted nowadays into one enormous workroom where the hotel washing and ironing goes on, remorselessly, all the year around. During its early history, the hotel was called 'Hôtel du Commerce'.

In that nearer, and slightly smaller of the two houses, I was installed for the winter. I took this house because I was accompanied that winter by Stephen de Lesseps, my young cousin, a boy of four-teen. Stephen's parents (his mother is my cousin Marie de Lesseps) had persuaded me to take him with me for the change of climate. Stephen is an agreeable young fellow. I gave him daily 'lessons' and he read much himself, so that his education out of books was not neglected, and that major portion derived otherwise was enhanced. Stephen turned out on close association to be so manly, sensible, and generally companionable, that I congratulated myself upon yielding to my cousin Marie's suggestion.

In the middle of that winter, Marie and her sister Suzanne paid us a visit of a month. Mr Joseph Reynolds, the American proprietor of the Grand Hotel, assigned them Room 4, a huge, double room, opening off the enormous hotel ballroom in which the major social functions of the Virgin Island capital are usually held. I am obliged to mention this background for the extraordinary story I have to tell. If I had not had Stephen along, I should not have remained in St Thomas. I did so on his account. The capital, rather than my beloved island of Santa Cruz, was a better place for his education. Don Pablo Salazar, a famous teacher of Spanish, is resident there; the director of education lived in the neighboring house – there were many reasons.

And, if I had not had Stephen with me, Marie and Suzanne would not have made that visit, and so could not have spent a month in Number 4, and so this tale would never, perhaps, have been told.

The ladies arrived early in January, after a sweeping tour of 'the lower islands' – those historic sea-jewels where England and France fought out the supremacy of the seas a century ago. They were delighted with Number 4. They slept on vast mahogany four-posters; they were entertained by everybody; they patronized St Thomas's alluring shops; they reveled in the midsummer warmth of midwinter in this climate of balm and spice; they exclaimed over Stephen's growth and rejoiced over the fine edge with which one of the world's politest communities had ornamented the boy's natur-ally excellent manners. In brief, my lady cousins enjoyed their month tremendously and went home enthusiastic over the quaint charm and magnificent hospitality of the capital of the Virgin Islands, our Uncle Sam's most recent colonial acquisition, once the historic Danish West Indies.

Only one fly, it appeared, had agitated the ointment of their enjoyment. Neither, they eventually reported, could get proper sleep in Number 4 in spite of its airiness, its splendid beds, and its conveniences. At night, one or the other, and, as I learned later, sometimes both simultaneously, would be awakened out of refreshing sleep at that most unpropitious of all night hours, four o'clock in the morning.

They said very little of this to me. I found out later that they were extremely chary of admitting that anything whatever had been interfering with their enjoyment of my hospitality. But later, after they were gone, I did recall that Suzanne had mentioned, though lightly, how she had heard knocks at the double-doors of their big room, just at that hour. It had made little impression upon me at the time.

Long afterward, questioning them, I discovered that they had been awakened nearly every morning by the same thing! They had mentioned it to their room-maid, a black girl, who had appeared 'stupid' about it; had only rolled her eyes, Marie said. They tried several explanations – brooms carelessly handled in the early morning; a permanent early 'call' for some guest, perhaps an officer of marines who had to get to his duties very early. They rejected both those theories, and finally settled down to the explanation that some pious fellow-guest was accustomed to attend the earliest religious service of the day, which, in both the Anglican and Roman Catholic churches in St Thomas, is at five in the morning. They knew, because they had several times answered the knocks, that there was never anybody at the door when they opened it. They reconciled their ultimate explanation with the discrepancy that the knocks were on *their* door, by the supposition that there was involved some strange, auditory illusion.

As I have said, these ladies were fascinated with St Thomas, and they did not allow one minor disturbing element to interfere with their enjoyment of its many strange sights; the weird speech of the blacks; the magnificent hospitality; the Old World furniture; the street lamps; the delightful little vistas; the Caribbean's incredible indigo; especially, I think, with the many strange tales which they heard more or less incidentally.

For St Thomas, the very home and heart of old romance, is full of strange tales. Here, in September 1824, the pirate Fawcett with his two mates was publicly hanged. To this very day, great steel doors guard most St Thomas stores, and particularly the funds of the Dansk Vestindiske Nationalbank, from marauders, as anciently those same doors guarded them from the frequent raids of the buccaneers. St Thomas's streets have more than once run red with human blood; for, like Panama, it is a town which has been sacked, though never burned like Frederiksted on the neighboring island of Santa Cruz.

Among these many tales was that of Black Tancrède. This Negro, a Dahomeyan, so said tradition, had lived for a while in one of those very slave-pens under my house. He had been, strangely enough, a Haitian refugee, although a full-blooded black African. Many Caucasian refugees from Haiti had come to St Thomas in the days of Dessalines, Toussaint l'Ouverture, and Henry Cristophe, the black king of Northwestern Haiti, the bloody days of that wise despot whose marvelous citadel still towers incredibly on the hills behind Cap Haitien and who is chiefly remembered for his tyrannies, but who is probably the only person who ever made millions out of the 'free' labor of his fellow blacks!

Tancrède had, so said tradition, incurred the enmity of Cristophe, and that in the days of his power was a fearsome thing for any man. But, unlike other known unfortunates who had risked that terrible anger, Tancrède had escaped Cristophe's executioner. That personage boasted that he had had so much practise with the broadsword that he could remove a head without soiling the victim's collar!

By some hook or crook, hidden probably in the stinking, rat-infested hold of some early nineteenth-century sailing vessel, perhaps buried under goathides or bales of *bacalhao*, Tancrède had shivered and sweated his way to the Danish refuge of St Thomas. There he fell swiftly into inescapable debt, for he was a fighting-man from a warlike tribe, and no bargainer. Therefore he had become the property of one Julius Mohrs, and because of that his connection with the old hotel had begun. Black Tancrède had been lodged, for safe keeping, in one of those same slave-pens under my house.

He had soon escaped from that servitude, for his strong, bitter soul could not brook it, and made his way to the neighbouring Danish island of St Jan. There he is next heard of as a 'free laborer' on the sugar estates of Erasmus Espersen. In the 'Rising' of 1833 he was prominent as a leader of those who revolted against the harsh laws of Governor Gardelin. Later, whether by the French troops from Martinique who came in to help the Danes put down their Slave War, or by the Spanish troops from Porto Rico, Black Tancrède had been captured alive, which was a grave error of judgment on his part, and brought back to St Thomas in chains, there to be tortured to death.

That sentence was delivered in the Danish colonial high court, sitting in its own quarters in the hotel, by Governor Gardelin's judge.

First Black Tancrède's hands had been cut off, one a day. Then he suffered the crushing of his feet (after 'three pinches with a hot iron instrument'), a punishment consummated with a heavy bar of iron in the hands of Achilles Mendoza, the executioner, himself a black slave. The iron sheared through his leg-bones, and he was 'pinched', and his hands chopped off, because he had been so unfortunate as to be caught in insurrection, bearing weapons, and he was therefore to be made an example by a governor whose name is even now execrated among the black people.

With his last expiring breath Black Tancrède cursed his tormentors. He cursed Achilles Mendoza. He cursed Julius Mohrs. He cursed Governor Gardelin. They buried his shattered body in quicklime in the courtyard of the fort, and with it went his left hand, which was clutched so firmly about the wooden crossbar of the rack that it could not be pried loose. Mendoza therefore broke off the crossbar with the hand attached, and threw it into the limepit. The other hand, chopped off the day before, had disappeared, and no effort was made to recover it. Such items in those 'good old days' were not infrequently picked up and kept by onlookers as interesting souvenirs.

Four months after the execution, Julius Mohrs was found strangled in bed one morning. Even the lash failed to elicit any testimony from his household. No one has ever known who committed that murder. Mohrs, like Governor Gardelin, had the reputation of being harsh with slaves.

Achilles Mendoza died 'of a fit' in the year 1835, in the open air. He was, in fact, crossing the courtyard of the hotel at the time and was not more than a few steps from the doors leading into the slave-pens. Many bystanders saw him fall, although it was at night, for the full moon of the Caribbee Islands – by whose light I have myself read print – was shining overhead. Indeed, so much light comes from the Caribbean moon that illuminates these latitudes – degree seventeen runs through Santa Cruz, eighteen through St Thomas – that on full moonlight nights in the 'good old days', the capital itself saved the cost of street-lights; and that is the custom even today in the Santa Crucian towns.

Some of the black people at first believed that Mendoza had strangled himself! This foolish idea was doubtless derived from the fact that both the executioner's hands had gone to his throat even before he fell, gasping and foaming at the mouth, and they were found clasped unbreakably together, the great muscles of his mighty arms rigid in death with the effort, when his now worthless body was unceremoniously gathered up and carted away for early morning burial.

Naturally, everybody who remembered Black Tancrède and his curses, and his character – that is, everybody who believed in black magic as well as in Black Tancrède – was certain that that malefactor, murderer, leader of revolt, had consummated a posthumous revenge. Perhaps Julius Mohrs, too –

The Danes pooh-poohed this solution of the two unaccountable deaths in the capital of their West Indian colony, but that did not affect black belief in the slightest degree. Black Quashee was in those days only a generation removed from Black Africa, where such matters are commonplaces. Such beliefs, and the practises which accompany them, had come in through Cartagena and other routes, deviously and direct, into the West Indies from the Gold Coast, from Dahomey and Ashantee and the Bight of Benin – all the way, indeed, from Dakar to the Congo mouth regions – into the West Indies indeed, where Quashee's sheer fecundity, now that the 'good old days' are no more, and Quashee is a Christian of one kind or another, and often a high school or even a college graduate, has caused him vastly to outnumber his erstwhile white masters. White people are now Quashee's masters no longer, though they still live beside him in the West Indies, in a constantly diminishing proportion, under that same bright moon, that same glowing sun, in the shade of the mighty tamarinds, beside the eye-scorching scarlet of the hibiscus, the glaring purple and magenta of the bougainvillea.

Governor Gardelin returned to Denmark very soon after the Slave War of 1883, where, so far as one may know from perusal of the old records, he died in his bed full of years and honors.

As I have mentioned, my cousins, Marie and Suzanne, returned to the continental United States. They left about the tenth of February, and Stephen and I, regretting their departure, settled down for the rest of that winter, planning to return the middle of May.

One morning, a few weeks after their departure, Reynolds, the proprietor, asked me a question.

'Did you hear the uproar last night, or, rather, early this morning?'

'No,' said I. 'What was "the uproar?" If it was out in the streets I might have heard it, but if it happened inside the hotel, my house is so detached that I should probably have heard nothing of it and gone right on sleeping.'

'It was inside,' said Reynolds, 'so you probably wouldn't have noticed it. The servants are all chattering about it this morning, though. They believe it is another manifestation of the Jumbee in Number 4. By the way, Mr Canevin, your cousins were in that room. Did they ever mention any disturbance to you?'

'Why, yes, now that you speak of it. My cousin Suzanne spoke of somebody knocking on their door; about four in the morning I believe it happened. I think it happened more than once. They imagined it was somebody being "called" very early, and the servant knocking on the wrong door or something of that kind. They didn't say much about it to me. What is "the Jumbee in Number 4"? That intrigues me. I never happened to hear that one!'

Now a 'Jumbee' is, of course, a West Indian ghost. In the French islands the word is 'Zombi'. Jumbees have various characteristics, which I will not pause to enumerate, but one of these is that a Jumbee is always black. White persons, apparently, do not 'walk' after death, although I have personally known three white gentlemen planters who were believed to be werewolves! Among the West Indian black population occurs every belief, every imaginable practise of the occult, which is interwoven closely into their lives and thoughts; everything from mere 'charms' to active necromancy; from the use of the deadly *Vaudoux* to the 'toof from a dead', which last renders a gambler lucky! Jumbee is a generic word. It means virtually any kind of a ghost, apparition, or *revenant*. I was not in the least surprised to learn that Number 4, Grand Hotel, had its other-worldly attendant. My sole ground for wonder was that I had not heard of it before now! Now that I recalled the matter, something *had* disturbed Marie and Suzanne in that room.

'Tell me about it, please, Mr Reynolds,' I requested.

Mr Reynolds smiled. He is a man of education and he, too, knows his West Indies.

'In this case it is only a general belief,' he answered. The only specific information about "the Jumbee in Number 4" is that it wakes occupants up early in the morning. There has, it seems, "always been a Jumbee" connected with that room. I dare say the very frying-pans in the kitchen have their particular Jumbees, if they happen to be old enough! That rumpus this morning was only that we had a tourist, a Mr Ledwith, staying overnight – came over from Porto Rico in the *Catherine* and left this morning for "down the islands" on the *Dominica*. He came in pretty late last night from a party with friends in the town. He explained later that he couldn't sleep because of somebody knocking on his door. He called out several times, got no answer; the knocking went on, and then he lost his temper. He reached out of bed and picked up the earthen-ware water-jug. His aim was excellent, even though he may have had a drop too much at his party. He hit the door-handle, smashed the jug into fragments, and then, really aroused, got up, flung open the door, found nobody there, and took it into his head that some-body was having a joke on him. Absurd! The man was a total stranger to everybody in the hotel.

'He raged around the ballroom and woke up the Gilbertsons and Mrs Peck – you know they have rooms on that side – and at last he awakened me and I got up and persuaded him to go back to bed. He said there were no more knocks after that. I was afraid it might have disturbed you and Stephen. I'm glad it didn't. Of course such a rumpus is very unusual in the hotel at any time.'

'Hm,' said I, 'well, well!' I had been thinking while Mr Reynolds made this long speech about the nocturnal activities of the unknown Mr Ledwith. I could not talk with him. He had already sailed that morning.

I was really intrigued by now – that occurence coupled with the experience of my cousins! Of course I knew very little about that, for they had said almost nothing. But it was enough to arouse my interest in 'the Jumbee in Number 4'.

That was the only time Mr Reynolds and I spoke of the matter, and for some time, although I kept my ears open, I heard nothing further about Number 4. When the 'trouble' did start up again, I was in Number 4 myself. That came about in this manner.

An American family named Barnes, permanent residents of St Thomas – I believe Barnes was a minor official of the public works or the agricultural departmant of the Virgin Island government – let their house-lease expire and decided to move into the hotel at family-rates-by-the-month for the convenience. Mrs Barnes had two young children, and was tired of household cares. She had employed, I think, some rather inferior servants, which always mean a heavy burden in the West Indies. One of the two hotel houses would suit them exactly. The other was occupied, by the year, by the director of education and his family, delightful Americans.

It was the first of May, and as Stephen and I were booked to sail on the twelfth for New York, I proposed to Mr Reynolds that we give up our house to Mr and Mrs Barnes, and he could put us into one of the huge double rooms for the remainder of our stay. Mr Reynolds put us into Number 4, probably the best of all the rooms, and which was, fortunately, vacant at the moment.

It happened that on our first night in our new quarters, I was out very late. I had gone, with the colonel in command of the naval station marines and his wife, to meet an incoming ship on which a certain Major Upton was returning to St Thomas from a month's leave. Two days before the arrival of the ship, a cable had informed the colonel of Mrs Upton's sudden death in Virginia. We did not know whether or not Upton had learned of his unexpected bereavement by wireless aboard ship, and we rather thought he had not. The ship was reported due at one a.m. She came in a little after two, and after meeting Upton – who had, fortunately, received a wireless – and making his arrival as pleasant as we could for him under the circumstances, I got back to the hotel about three-thirty in the morning.

I came in at the side door, which is always open, walked softly along the great length of the ballroom, and very quietly opened the door of Number 4. By the streaming moonlight which was pouring in through the open jalousies of the great room, I could see Stephen's outlines, dimly, through the cloud of mosquito-netting which covered his enormous four-poster. I undressed silently, so that I should not disturb my young cousin. I was just ready to turn in, my soiled drill clothes in the washbag, my white buckskin shoes neatly treed, my other things laid away where they belonged – for I am a rather fussy fellow about such matters – and it was within a minute or two to four o'clock in the morning; I know I was beastly tired; when, just beside me, on the door leading in from the ballroom, came an abrupt, unmistakable rap-rap-rap! There could be no possible doubt about it. I was standing within three feet of the door at the moment the raps were delivered. I, Gerald Canevin, am a teller of the truth. I admit that I felt the cold chills which are characteristic of sudden, almost uncontrollable, paralyzing fear, run swiftly up and down my spine; that acute prickling at the hair roots which is called one's hair standing on end.

But, if Gerald Canevin is a trifle old maidish about the arrangement of his personal belongings, and, even damagingly, truthful, he may boast, and justly, that no man living can call him a poltroon.

I took one firm step to that door and flung it open, and – so help me God! – as I turned the small, old-fashioned brass knob, the last of the raps – for the summons was repeated, just as the convivial Led-with had alleged – sounded within three inches of my hand, on the other side of the door.

The great-ghostly still ballroom stood silent and empty. Not a sound, not a movement disturbed its early-morning, dead, serene emptiness. I raked the room with my scrutiny. Everything was visible because the vivid moonlight – the moon had been full two nights before – came flooding in from the gallery with its nine Moorish arches, overlooking the harbor.

There was nothing – absolutely, literally, nothing – to be seen or heard. I glanced back over my shoulder along the wall through which the door of Number 4 opens. What was that? I could feel my heart skip a beat, then start pounding. A dim something, the merest shadowy outline, it seemed, in the form of a gigantic Negro was moving along the wall toward the passageway, curtained from the ballroom, which leads to the main entrance of the hotel below.

Even as I looked, the strange form seemed to melt and vanish, and there came a hard, dull thud from the direction where I imagined I had seen it slipping furtively along the wall.

I looked narrowly, my heart still pounding, and there, on the floor moving rapidly from me in the same direction I had imagined that sinister figure following, and with a queer, awkward movement suggestive of a crab's sidelong gait, but moving in utter silence, there ran along the bare floor something about the size of a baseball.

I was barefooted and in thin, China-silk pajamas, but I started, weaponless, after the thing. It was, I surmised, the biggest tarantula I had ever seen in or out of the West Indies. Certainly it was no crab, although its size and even its gait would suggest one of our boxlike, compact land-crabs. But a crab, running away like that, would make a distinctive, identifying, hard rattle with its shell-covered feet on that hard, wooden floor, and this thing ran silently, like velvet.

What I should do with, or to, the tarantula if I caught it, I did not stop to consider. I suppose it was a kind of instinct that sent me in pursuit. I gained on it, but it slipped past the curtains ahead of me and was lost to sight in the broad passageway on the other side of the stairs' head. As soon as I had passed the curtain I saw that any attempt to catch the thing would be an impossibility. There would be innumerable hiding-places; the main entrance doors were closed tight down below there, and the stair-well was as dark as the inside of Jonah's whale.

I turned back, perforce, and re-entered Number 4, shut the door quietly behind me, and turned in upon my own gigantic four-poster and tucked the mosquito-netting under the edge of the mattress. I slept at once and did not awaken until five and one-half hours later, at nine-thirty in the morning. The excellent Stephen, realizing the situation, had repaid my pussyfooting in his interest of the earlier morning by getting dressed in silence and ordering my breakfast sent in at this hour.

That was Saturday morning, and there were no lessons for Stephen. I took advantage of that fact to put in a very much occupied day at my typewriter, and I got such a start on what I was then engaged in writing that I determined, if possible, to finish it the next day in time for the New York mail which goes out through Porto Rico every week. A brief, unaccustomed siesta Saturday afternoon helped make up for some lack of sleep. I decided to get up and go to that horribly 'early' service at five on Sunday morning. That would give me a reason for early rising – which I have always secretly abominated! – and a good day's start. Stephen and I retired that evening as soon as he returned from his movingpictures at the naval station; that was about nine-thirty.

I must have grown wearier than I had realized, sitting up for Major Upton's ship, and accompanying him to the colonel's quarters afterward; for I slept like the dead, and had my usual fight with myself to get up and shut off an insistent alarm-clock at four-fifteen. I got to church in time, and was back again a few minutes before six. It was barely dawn when I came in at the side entrance and up the stairs.

As I walked along the still dim ballroom toward Number 4, the tarantula, or land-crab, or whatever the thing might prove to be, came sidling in that same awkward fashion which I had noted along the edge of the sidewall, toward me this time. It was as though the creature were returning from the hiding-place whither I had chased him Saturday morning.

I was carrying a tough, resilient walking-stick, of native black wattle, cut by myself on Estate Ham's Bay, over on Santa Cruz, two years before. I stepped faster toward the oncoming thing, with this stick poised in my hand. I saw now in the rapidly brightening dawn what was wrong with the spider – it was obvious now that it was no land-crab. The thing was maimed. It had, apparently, lost several of its legs, and so proceeded in the odd, crablike fashion which I had noted before. A spider should have eight legs, as most people know. This one came hunching and sidling along on five or six.

The thing, moving rapidly despite its paucity of legs, was almost at the door to Number 4. I ran toward it, for the door stood slightly open, and I did not want that horrible creature to go into my room on account of Stephen. I struck at it, viciously, but it eluded my black wattle and slipped in under the conch-shell which served as a door-chock.

Conches have many uses in the West Indies. In the Bahamas their contents serve as a food-staple. They occasionally yield 'pearls', which have some value to jewelers. One sees the shells everywhere – bordering garden paths, outlining cemetery plots, built, with cement, into ornamental courses like shining pink bricks. In the Grand Hotel every door has a conch for a chock. The one at my door was a very old one, painted, in a dark brown color, to preserve it from disintegration due to the strong, salt air.

I approached the shell, now covering the huge tarantula, with some caution. The bite of our native tarantulas in St Thomas is rarely or never fatal, but it can put the human victim into the hospital for several days, and this fellow, as I have said, was the largest I had ever seen, in or out of St Thomas. I poked the end of my stick under the lip-edge of the shell, and turned it suddenly over. The spider had disappeared. Obviously it had crawled inside the shell. There is a lot of room inside a good-sized conch. I decided to take a chance. I did not want that thing about the place, certainly.

Keeping my eye on the upturned shell, I stepped over to the center of the ballroom and picked up a week-old Sunday supplement roto-gravure section of one of the New York newspapers, crumpled it, folded it into a kind of wad, and with this, very gingerly – for the tarantula is a fighter and no timid beast – effectually stopped up the long triangular entrance to the shell's inside. Then, picking it up, I carried it outside onto the stone-flagged gallery.

Here things were appreciably lighter. The dawn was brightening into the tropic day every instant, and I could now see everything clearly.

I raised the conch-shell and brought it down crashing on the tessellated floor.

As I had expected, the old shell smashed into many fragments, and I stood by, my black wattle raised and ready to strike at the tarantula as it attempted to run away. I had figured, not unnaturally, that the experience of having its rocklike refuge suddenly picked up, carried away, and then crashing to pieces about itself, would, from the tarantula's viewpoint, prove at least momentarily disconcerting, and I should have a chance to slay the loathsome thing at my leisure. But, to my surprise, nothing ran out of the shattered shell.

I bent and looked closer. The fragments were relatively both large and small, from powdery dust all the way to a few chunks as big as my two fists. I poked at one of these, of an extraordinary and arresting shape, a strangely suggestive shape, though colored a dirty pink like the rest of the conch's lining. I turned it over with the end of my stick.

It was the hand of a Negro, which, lying palm upward, had at first seemed pink. The palm of the hand of the blackest of black Africans is pink. So is the sole of the foot. But there was no mistaking the back of that sooty, claw-like thing. It was a severed hand, and it had originally grown upon an owner who had no admixture of any blood other than that of Africa. The name 'Tancrède' leapt to my mind. Had he not, even among his fellow slaves, been called 'Black Tancrède'? He had, and my knowledge of that ancient tale and the sooty duskiness of this ancient relic conspired forthwith to cause me to leap to that outrageous, that incredible conclusion. The hand of Black Tancrède – this was a right hand, and so, said tradition, was the one which had first been severed and then disappeared – or, at least, the veritable hand of some intensely dark Negro, lay there before me on the gallery floor, among the debris of an ancient conch-shell.

I drew a deep breath, for it was an unsettling experience, stooped, and picked the thing up. It was as dry and hard as so much conch-shell, and surprisingly heavy. I looked at it carefully, turning it about and examining it thoroughly; for I was alone on the gallery. Nobody was stirring in the hotel; even the kitchen was silent.

I slipped the hand into the pocket of my drill jacket, and returned to Number 4. I laid the hand down on the marble-topped table which stands in the room's center, and looked at it. Stephen, I had noted at once, was absent. He had got up, and was now, doubtless, in his shower-bath.

I had not been looking at it very long, before an explanation, too far-fetched to be dwelt upon or even to be seriously entertained, was invading my dazed mind. Something on five or six 'legs' had run under that conch-shell. Nothing, save this, had been there when I smashed the shell. There were the surface facts, and I was my own witness. There was no hearsay about it. This was no black Quashee tale of marvels and wonderment.

I heard a pad-pad outside, like slippered feet, and I had the thing in my pocket again when Stephen came in, glowing from his shower. I did not want to explain that hand to the boy.

'Good morning, Cousin Gerald,' said Stephen. 'You got off early, didn't you? I heard your alarm-clock but I turned over and went to sleep again.'

'Yes,' I answered. 'You see, I have a lot of work to get through today.'

'I'd have gone with you,' continued Stephen halfway into his fresh clothes by now, 'if you'd waked me up! I'm going to six o'clock church if I can make it.'

He dressed rapidly, and with another pleasant, hasty word or two, the boy was off, running. The 'English Church' is quite near by.

I got up, left Number 4 empty, crossed the ballroom diagonally, and entered Mr Reynolds's sanctum at its western extremity. I had thought of something. I *must* do what I could to clear up, or put away forever, if possible, that explanation, the details of which were invading my excited mind, pressing into it remorselessly.

I went to the lowest shelf of one of his bookcases, and took out the three heavy, calf-bound, ancient registers of the Hôtel du Commerce. I must find out, on the off-chance that the room numbers had not been changed since then, who had occupied Room 4 at the time of Black Tancrède's execution and cursings. That, for the moment, seemed to me absolutely the salient fact, the key to the whole situation . . .

I could hardly believe my eyes when the faded entry, the ink brown, the handwriting oddly curlycued, jumped out at me.

For all of the years 1832, 1833, and most of 1834 besides, Room 4, Hôtel du Commerce, Raoul Patit, proprietor, had been occupied by one Hans de Groot. Hans de Groot had been Governor Gardelin's judge of the Danish Colonial high court. Hans de Groot had condemned Black Tancrède to death, by amputation of hands, pinching, and breaking on the rack.

I had my explanation . . .

If only this were a romance, I should proceed to tell how thereafter I had applied, in the traditional method for the laying of this kind of ghost – a ghost with an unfulfilled desire, promise, or curse – how I had applied for permission to restore the hand to the resting-place of Black Tancrède. I should recite the examination of old records, the location of the lime-pit in the Fort yard; I might even have the horrible thing which lay in my jacket pocket 'escape' to wreak devastation upon me after unavailing efforts on my part to avoid destruction; a final twist of luck, the destruction of the hand . . .

But this is not romance, and I am not attempting to make 'quite a tale' of these sober facts.

What I did was to proceed straight to the hotel kitchen, where fat Lucinda the cook was cutting breakfast bacon at a table, and two dusky assistants were preparing grapefruit and orange-juice against the hour for breakfast.

'Good morning, Lucinda,' I began; 'is your fire going?'

'Marnin', Mars' Canevin, sar,' returned Lucinda, 'hot, good'n hot, sar. Is yo' desirous to cook someting?'

Both handmaidens giggled at this, and I smiled with them.

'I only have something I wish to burn,' said I, explaining my early-morning visit.

I approached the glowing stove, anticipating Lucinda, and waving her back to her bacon-cutting, lifted a lid, and dropped the horrible, mummified thing into the very heart of a bed of cherry-colored coals.

It twisted in the heat, as though alive and protesting. It gave off a faint, strange odor of burning, like very old leather. But within a few moments the dry and brittle skin and the calcined bones were only scraps of shapeless, glowing embers.

I replaced the stove lid. I was satisfied. I would now satisfy Lucinda, if not her very natural curiosity. I handed her with an engaging smile one of the small, brown, five-franc currency bills which are still issued by the Dansk Vestindiske Nationalbank, and are legal tender in our Uncle Sam's Virgin Islands.

'May t'anks, sar; Gahd bless yo', Mars' Canevin, sar,' muttered the delighted Lucinda.

I nodded to them and walked out of the kitchen reasonably certain that the Jumbee of Number 4 would trouble guests no more at four o'clock in the morning, nor at any other hour; that eternity had now swallowed Black Tancrède, who, tradition alleged, was a very persevering man and always kept his word . . .

It is true, as I remarked at the beginning of this narrative, that Black Tancrède did not curse Hans de Groot, but that Governor Gardelin went home to Denmark and so escaped – whatever whatever it was that happened to Achilles Mendoza and Julius Mohrs. Perhaps the persevering shade of Black Tancrède was limited, in the scope of its revengeful 'projection' through that severed hand, to the island on which he died. I do not know, although there are almost fixed rules for these things; rules in which Quashee believes religiously.

But, since that morning, I, truthful Gerald Canevin, confess, I have never seen any large spider without at least an internal shudder. I can understand, I think, what that strange mental aberration called 'spider fear' is like . . .

For I *saw* that thing which ran along the floor of the Grand Hotel ballroom like a maimed spider – I saw it go under that conch-shell. And it did not come out as it went in . . .

The Shadows

I did not begin to see the shadows until I had lived in Old Morris's house for more than a week. Old Morris, dead and gone these many years, had been the scion of a still earlier Irish settler in Santa Cruz, of a family which had come into the Island when the Danes, failing to colonize its rich acres, had opened it, in the middle of the eighteenth century, to colonists; and younger sons of Irish, Scottish, and English gentry had taken up sugar estates and commenced that baronial life which lasted for a century and which declined after the abolition of slavery and the German bounty on beet sugar had started the long process of West Indian commercial decadence. Mr Morris's youth had been spent in the French islands.

The shadows were at first so vague that I attributed them wholly to the slight weakness which began to affect my eyes in early childhood, and which, while never materially interfering with the enjoyment of life in general, had necessitated the use of glasses when I used my eyes to read or write. My first experience of them was about one o'clock in the morning. I had been at a 'Gentlemen's Party' at Hacker's house, 'Emerald', as some poetic-minded ancestor of Hacker's had named the family estate three miles out of Christiansted, the northerly town, built on the site of the ancient abandoned French town of Bassin.

I had come home from the party and was undressing in my bedroom, which is one of two rooms on the westerly side of the house which stands at the edge of the old 'Sunday Market'. These two bedrooms open on the market-place, and I had chosen them, rather than the more airy rooms on the other side, because of the space outside. I like to look out on trees in the early mornings, whenever possible, and the ancient market-place is overshadowed with the foliage of hundred-year-old mahogany trees, and a few gnarled 'otaheites' and Chinese-bean trees.

I had nearly finished undressing, had noted that my servant had let down and properly fastened the mosquito netting, and had stepped into the other bedroom to open the jalousies so that I might get as much of the night-breeze as possible circulating through the house. I was coming back through the doorway between the two bedrooms, and taking off my dressing gown, at the moment when the first faint perception of what I have called 'the shadows' made itself apparent. It was very dark, just after switching off the electric light in that front bedroom. I had, in fact, to feel for the doorway. In this I experienced some difficulty, and my eyes had not fully adjusted themselves to the thin starlight seeping in through the slanted jalousies of my own room when I passed through the doorway and groped my way toward the great mahogany four-poster in which I was about to lie down for my belated rest.

I saw the nearest post looming before me, closer than I had expected. Putting out my hand, I grasped – nothing. I blinked in some surprise, and peered through the slightly increasing light, as my eyes adjusted themselves to the sudden change. Yes, surely – there was the corner of the bedstead just in front of my face! By now my eyes were sufficiently attuned to the amount of light from outside to see a little plainer. I was puzzled. The bed was not where I had supposed it to be. What could have happened? That the servants should have moved my bed without orders to do so was incredible. Besides, I had undressed, in full electric light in that room, not more than a few minutes ago, and then the bed was standing exactly where it had been since I had had it moved into that room a week before. I kicked, gently, before me with a slippered foot, against the place where that bedpost appeared to be standing – and my foot met no resistance.

I stepped over to the light in my own room, and snapped the button. In the sudden glare, everything readjusted itself to normal. There stood my bed, and here in their accustomed places about the room were ranged the chairs, the polished wardrobe (we do not use cupboards in the West India Islands), the mahogany dressing table – even my clothes which I had hung over a chair where Albertina my servant would find them in the morning and put them (they were of white drill) into the soiled-clothes bag in the morning.

I shook my head. Light and shadow in these islands seem, some-how, different from what they are like at home in the United States! The tricks they play are different tricks, somehow.

I snapped off the light again, and in the ensuing dead blackness, I crawled in under the loose edge of the mosquito netting, tucked it along under the edge of the mattress on that side, adjusted my pillows and the sheets, and settled myself for a good sleep. Even to a

moderate man, these gentlemen's parties are rather wearing sometimes. They invariably last too long. I closed my eyes and was asleep
before I could have put these last ideas into words.

In the morning the recollection of the experience with the bed-
being-in-the-wrong-place was gone. I jumped out of bed and into
my shower bath at half past six, for I had promised O'Brien, captain
of the U.S. Marines, to go out with him to the rifle range at La
Grande Princesse that morning and look over the butts with him. I
like O'Brien, and I am not uninterested in the efficiency of Uncle
Sam's Marines, but my chief objective was to watch the pelicans.
Out there on the glorious beach of Estate Grande Princesse ('Big
Princess' as the Black People call it), a colony of pelicans make their
home, and it is a never-ending source of amusement to me to watch
them fish. A Caribbean pelican is probably the most graceful flier
we have in these latitudes – barring not even the hurricane bird,
that describer of noble arcs and parabolas – and the most insanely,
absurdly awkward creature on land that Providence has cared in a
light-hearted moment to create!

I expressed my interest in Captain O'Brien's latest improve-
ments, and while he was talking shop to one of his lieutenants
and half a dozen enlisted men he has camped out there, I slipped
down to the beach to watch the pelicans fish. Three or four of
them were describing curves and turns of indescribable complexity
and perfect grace over the green water of the reef-enclosed white
beach. Ever and again one would stop short in the air, fold himself
up like a jackknife, turn head downward, his great pouched bill
extended like the head of a cruel spear, and drop like a plummet
into the water, emerging an instant later with the pouch distended
with a fish.

I stayed a trifle too long – for my eyes. Driving back I observed that
I had picked up several sun-spots, and when I arrived home I polished
a set of yellowish sun-spectacles I keep for such emergencies and put
them on.

The east side of the house had been shaded against the pouring
morning sunlight, and in this double shade I looked to see my eyes clear
up. The sun-spots persisted, however, in that annoying, recurrent way
they have – almost disappearing and then returning in undiminished
kaleidoscopic grotesqueness – those strange blocks and parcels of pure
color changing as one blinks from indigo to brown and from brown to
orange and then to a blinding turquoise-blue, according to some eery
natural law of physics, within the fluids of the eye itself.

The sun-spots were so persistent that morning that I decided to keep my eyes closed for some considerable time and see if that would allow them to run their course and wear themselves out. Blue and mauve grotesques of the vague, general shape of diving pelicans swam and jumped inside my eyes. It was very annoying. I called to Albertina.

'Albertina,' said I, when she had come to the door, 'please go into my bedroom and close all the jalousies tight. Keep out all the light you can, please.'

'Ahl roight, sir,' replied the obedient Albertina, and I heard her slapping the jalousie-blinds together with sharp little clicks.

'De jalousie ahl close, sir,' reported Albertina. I thanked her, and proceeded with half-shut eyes into the bedroom, which, not yet invaded with afternoon's sunlight and closely shuttered, offered an appearance of deep twilight. I lay, face down, across the bed, a pillow under my face, and my eyes buried in darkness.

Very gracefully, the diving pelicans faded out, to a cube, to a dim, recurrent blur, to nothingness. I raised my head and rolled over on my side, placing the pillow back where it belonged. And as I opened my eyes on the dim room, there stood, in faint, shadowy outline, in the opposite corner of the room, away from the outside wall on the market-place side, the huge, Danish bedstead I had vaguely noted the night before, or rather, early that morning.

It was the most curious sensation, looking at that bed in the dimness of the room. I was reminded of those fourth-dimensional tales which are so popular nowadays, for the bed impinged, spatially, on my large bureau, and the curious thing was that I could see the bureau at the same time! I rubbed my eyes, a little unwisely, but not enough to bring back the pelican sun-spots into them, for I remembered and desisted pretty promptly. I looked, fixedly, at the great bed, and it blurred and dimmed and faded out of my vision.

Again, I was greatly puzzled, and I went over to where it seemed to stand and walked through it – it being no longer visible to my now restored vision, free of the effects of the sun-spots – and then I went out into the 'hall' – a West Indian drawing room is called 'the hall' – and sat down to think over this strange phenomenon. I could not account for it. If it had been poor Prentice, now! Prentice attended all the 'gentlemen's parties' to which he was invited with a kind of religious regularity, and had to be helped into his car with a similar regularity, a regularity which was verging on the monotonous nowadays, as the invitations became more and more strained. No – in my case it was, if there was anything certain about it, assuredly not the effects of strong liquors, for barring an occasional sociable swizzel I retained here in my West Indian residence my American convictions that moderation in such matters was a reasonable virtue. I reasoned out the matter of the phantom bedstead – for so I was already thinking of it – as far as I was able. That it was a phantom of defective eyesight I had no reasonable doubt. I had had my eyes examined in New York three months before, and the oculist had pleased me greatly by assuring me that there were no visible indications of deterioration. In fact, Dr Jusserand had said at that time that my eyes were stronger, sounder, than when he had made his last examination six months before.

Perhaps this conviction – that the appearance was due to my own physical shortcoming – accounts for the fact that I was not (what shall I say?) *disturbed* by what I saw, or thought I saw. Confront the most thoroughgoing materialist with a ghost, and he will act precisely like anyone else; like any normal human being who believes in the material world as the outward and visible sign of something which animates it. All normal human beings, it seems to me, are sacramentalists!

I was, for this reason, able to think clearly about the phenomenon. My mind was not clouded and bemused with fear, and its known physiological effects. I can, quite easily, record what I 'saw' in the course of the next few days. The bed was clearer to my vision and apprehension than it had been. It seemed to have grown in visibility; in a kind of substantialness, if there is such a word! It appeared more *material* than it had before, less shadowy.

I looked about the room and saw other furniture: a huge, old-fashioned mahogany bureau with men's heads carved on the knuckles of the front legs, Danish fashion. There is precisely such carving on pieces in the museum in Copenhagen, they tell me, those who have seen my drawing of it. I was actually able to do that, and had completed a kind of plan-picture of the room, putting in all the shadow-furniture, and leaving my own, actual furniture out. Thank the God in whom I devoutly believe – and know to be more powerful than the Powers of Evil – I was able to finish that rather elaborate drawing before . . . Well, I must not 'run ahead of my story'.

That night when I was ready to retire, and had once more opened up the jalousies of the front bedroom, and had switched off the light, I looked, naturally enough under the circumstances, for the outlines of that ghostly furniture. They were much clearer now. I studied them with a certain sense of almost 'scientific' detachment. It was, even then, apparent to me that no weakness of the strange complexity which is the human eye could reasonably account for the presence of a well-defined set of mahogany furniture in a room already furnished with real furniture! But I was by now sufficiently accustomed to it to be able to examine it all without that always-disturbing element of fear – strangeness. I looked at the bedstead and the 'roll-back' chairs, and the great bureau, and a ghostly, huge, and quaintly carved wardrobe, studying their outlines, noting their relative positions. It was on that occasion that it occurred to me that it would be of interest to make some kind of drawing of them. I looked the harder after that, fixing the details and the relations of them all in my mind, and then I went into the hall and got some paper and a pencil and set to work.

It was hard work, this task of reproducing something which I was well aware was some kind of an 'apparition', especially after looking at the furniture in the dark bedroom, switching on the light in another room and then trying to reproduce. I could not, of course, make a direct comparison. I mean it was impossible to look at my drawing and then look at the furniture. There was always a necessary interval between the two processes. I persisted through several evenings, and even for a couple of evenings fell into the custom of going into my bedroom in the evening's darkness, looking at what was there, and then attempting to reproduce it. After five or six days, I had a fair plan, in considerable detail, of the arrangement of this strange furniture in my bedroom – a plan or drawing which would be recognizable if there were anyone now alive who remembered such an arrangement of such furniture. It will be apparent that a story had been growing up in my mind, or, at least, that I had come to some kind of conviction that what I 'saw' was a reproduction of something that had once existed in that same detail and that precise order!

On the seventh night, there came an interruption.

I had, by that time, finished my work, pretty well. I had drawn the room as it would have looked with that furniture in it, and had gone over the whole with India ink, very carefully. As a drawing, the thing was finished, so far as my indifferent skill as a draftsman would permit.

That seventh evening, I was looking over the appearance of the room, such qualms as the eeriness of the situation might have otherwise produced reduced to next-to-nothing partly by my interest, in part by having become accustomed to it all. I was making, this evening, as careful a comparison as possible between my remembered work on paper and the detailed appearance of the room. By now, the furniture stood out clearly, in a kind of light of its own which I can roughly compare only to 'phosphorescence'. It was not, quite, that. But that will serve, lame as it is, and trite perhaps, to indicate what I mean. I suppose the appearance of the room was something like what a cat 'sees' when she arches her back – as Algernon Blackwood has pointed out, in *John Silence* – and rubs against the imaginary legs of some personage entirely invisible to the man in the armchair who idly wonders what has taken possession of his house-pet.

I was, as I say, studying the detail. I could not find that I had left out anything salient. The detail was, too, quite clear now. There were no blurred outlines as there had been on the first few nights. My own, material furniture had, so to speak, sunk back into invisibility, which was sensible enough, seeing that I had put the room in as nearly perfect darkness as I could, and there was no moon to interfere, those nights.

I had run my eyes all round it, up and down the twisted legs of the great bureau, along the carved ornamentation of the top of the wardrobe, along the lines of the chairs, and had come back to the bed. It was at this point of my checking up that I got what I must describe as the first 'shock' of the entire experience.

Something moved, beside the bed.

I peered, carefully, straining my eyes to catch what it might be. It had been something bulky, a slow-moving object, on the far side of the bed, blurred, somewhat, just as the original outlines had been blurred in the beginning of my week's experience. The now strong and clear outlines of the bed, and what I might describe as its ethereal substance, stood between me and it. Besides, the vision of the slow-moving mass was further obscured by a ghostly mosquito-net, which had been one of the last of the details to come into the scope of my strange night-vision.

Those folds of the mosquito-netting moved – waved, before my eyes.

Someone, it might almost be imagined, was getting into that bed!

I sat, petrified. This was a bit too much for me. I could feel the little chills run up and down my spine. My scalp prickled. I put my hands on my knees, and pressed hard. I drew several deep breaths. 'All-overish' is an old New England expression, once much used by spinsters, I believe, resident in that intellectual section of the United States. Whatever the precise connotation of the term, that was the way I felt. I could feel the reactive sensation, I mean, of that particular portion of the whole experience, in every part of my being – body, mind, and soul! It was – paralyzing. I reached up a hand that was trembling violently – I could barely control it, and the fingers, when they touched the hard-rubber button, felt numb – and switched on the bedroom light, and spent the next ten minutes recovering.

That night, when I came to retire, I dreaded – actually dreaded – what might come to my vision when I snapped off the light. This, however, I managed to reason out with myself. I used several arguments – nothing had so far occurred to annoy or injure me; if this were to be a cumulative experience, if something were to be 'revealed' to me by this deliberate process of slow materialization which had been progressing for the last week or so, then it might as well be for some good and useful purpose. I might be, in a sense, the agent of Providence! If it were otherwise; if it were the evil work of some discarnate spirit, or something of the sort, well, every Sunday since my childhood, in church, I had recited the Creed, and so admitted, along with the clergy and the rest of the congregation, that God our Father had created all things – visible *and invisible*! If it were this part of His creation at work, for *any* purpose, then He was stronger than they. I said a brief prayer before turning off that light, and put my trust in Him. It may appear to some a bit old-fashioned – even Victorian! But He does not change along with the current fashions of human thought about Him, and this 'human thought', and 'the modern mind', and all the rest of it, does not mean the vast, the overwhelming majority of people. It involves only a few dozen prideful 'intellectuals' at best, or worst!

I switched off the light, and, already clearer, I saw what must have been Old Morris, getting into bed.

I had interviewed old Mr Bonesteel, the chief government surveyor, a gentleman of parts and much experience, a West Indian born on this island. Mr Bonesteel, in response to my guarded inquiries – for I had, of course, already suspected Old Morris; was not my house still called his? – had stated that he remembered Old Morris well, in his own remote youth. His description of that personage and this apparition tallied. This, undoubtedly, was Old Morris. That it was *someone*, was apparent. I felt, somehow, rather relieved to realize that it was he. I knew something about him, you see. Mr Bonesteel had given me a good description and many anecdotes, quite freely, and as though he enjoyed being called on for information about one of the old-timers like Morris. He had been more reticent, guarded, in fact, when I pressed him for details of Morris's end. That there had been some obscurity – intentional or otherwise, I could never ascertain – about the old man, I had already known. Such casual inquiries as I had made on other occasions through natural interest in the person whose name still clung to my house sixty years or more since he had lived in it, had never got me anywhere. I had only gathered what Mr Bonesteel's more ample account corroborated: that Morris had been eccentric, in some ways, amusingly so. That he had been extraordinarily well-to-do. That he gave occasional large parties, which, contrary to the custom of the hospitable island of St Croix, were always required to come to a conclusion well before midnight. Why, there was a story of Old Morris almost literally getting rid of a few reluctant guests, by one device or another, from these parties, a circumstance on which hinged several of the amusing anecdotes of that eccentric person!

Old Morris, as I knew, had not always lived on St Croix. His youth had been spent in Martinique, in the then smaller and less important town of Fort-de-France. That, of course, was many years before the terrific calamity of the destruction of St Pierre had taken place, by the eruption of Mt Pelée. Old Morris, coming to St Croix in young middle age – forty-five or thereabouts – had already been accounted a rich man. He had been engaged in no business. He was not a planter, not a storekeeper, had no profession. Where he produced his affluence was one of the local mysteries. His age, it seemed, was the other.

'I suppose,' Mr Bonesteel had said, 'that Morris was nearer a hundred than ninety, when he – ah – died. I was a child of about eight at that time. I shall be seventy next August-month. That, you see, would be about sixty-two years ago, about 1861, or about the time your Civil War was beginning. Now my father has told me – he died when I was nineteen – that Old Morris looked exactly the same when he was a boy! Extraordinary. The Black People used to say – ' Mr Bonesteel fell silent, and his eyes had an old man's dim, far-away look.

'The Black People have some very strange beliefs, Mr Bonesteel,' said I, attempting to prompt him. 'A good many of them I have heard about myself, and they interest me very much. What particular – '

Mr Bonesteel turned his mild, blue eyes upon me, reflectively.

'You must drop in at my house one of these days, Mr Stewart,' said he, mildly. 'I have some rare old rum that I'd be glad to have you sample, sir! There's not much of it on the island these days, since Uncle Sam turned his prohibition laws loose on us in 1922.'

'Thank you very much indeed, Mr Bonesteel,' I replied. 'I shall take the first occasion to do so, sir; not that I care especially for "old rum" except a spoonful in a cup of tea, or in pudding sauce, perhaps; but the pleasure of your company, sir, is always an inducement.'

Mr Bonesteel bowed to me gravely, and I returned his bow from where I sat in his airy office in Government House.

'Would you object to mentioning what that "belief" was, sir?'

A slightly pained expression replaced my old friend's look of hospitality.

'All that is a lot of foolishness!' said he, with something like asperity. He looked at me, contemplatively.

'Not that I believe in such things, you must understand. Still, a man sees a good many things in these islands, in a lifetime, you know! Well, the Black People – ' Mr Bonesteel looked apprehensively about him, as though reluctant to have one of his clerks overhear what he was about to say, and leaned toward me from his chair, lowering his voice to a whisper.

'They said – it was a remark here and a kind of hint there, you must understand; nothing definite – that Morris had interfered, down there in Martinique, with some of their queer doings – offended the Zombi – something of the kind; that Morris had made some kind of conditions – oh, it was very vague, and probably all mixed up! – you know, whereby he was to have a long life and all the money he wanted – something like that – and afterward . . .

'Well, Mr Stewart, you just ask somebody, sometime, about Morris's death.'

Not another word about Old Morris could I extract out of Mr Bonesteel.

But of course he had me aroused. I tried Despard, who lives on the other end of the island, a man educated at the Sorbonne, and who knows, it is said, everything there is to know about the island and its affairs.

It was much the same with Mr Despard, who is an entirely different kind of person; younger, for one thing, than my old friend the government surveyor.

Mr Despard smiled, a kind of wry smile. 'Old Morris!' said he, reflectively, and paused.

'Might I venture to ask – no offense, my dear sir! – why you wish to rake up such an old matter as Old Morris's death?'

I was a bit nonplussed, I confess. Mr Despard had been perfectly courteous, as he always is, but, somehow, I had not expected such an intervention on his part.

'Why,' said I, 'I should find it hard to tell you, precisely, Mr Despard. It is not that I am averse to being frank in the face of such an inquiry as yours, sir. I was not aware that there was anything important – serious, as your tone implies – about that matter. Put it down to mere curiosity if you will, and answer or not, as you wish, sir.'

I was, perhaps, a little nettled at this unexpected, and, as it then seemed to me, finicky obstruction being placed in my way. What could there be in such a case for this formal reticence – these verbal safeguards? If it were a 'jumbee' story, there was no importance to it. If otherwise, well, I might be regarded by Despard as a person of reasonable discretion. Perhaps Despard was some relative of Old Morris, and there was something a bit off-color about his death. That, too, might account for Mr Bonesteel's reticence.

'By the way,' I inquired, noting Despard's reticence, 'might I ask another question, Mr Despard?'

'Certainly, Mr Stewart.'

'I do not wish to impress you as idly or unduly curious, but – are you and Mr Bonesteel related in any way?'

'No, sir. We are not related in any way at all, sir.'

'Thank you, Mr Despard,' said I, and, bowing to each other after the fashion set here by the Danes, we parted.

I had not learned a thing about Old Morris's death.

I went in to see Mrs Heidenklang. Here, if anywhere, I should find out what was intriguing me.

Mrs Heidenklang is an ancient Creole lady, relict of a prosperous storekeeper, who lives, surrounded by a certain state of her own, propped up in bed in an environment of a stupendous quantity of lacy things and gauzy ruffles. I did not intend to mention Old Morris to her, but only to get some information about the Zombi, if that should be possible.

I found the old lady, surrounded by her ruffles and lace things, in one of her good days. Her health has been precarious for twenty years!

It was not difficult to get her talking about the Zombi.

'Yes,' said Mrs Heidenklang, 'it is extraordinary how the old beliefs and the old words cling in their minds! Why, Mr Stewart, I was hearing about a trial in the police court a few days ago. One old Black woman had summoned another for abusive language. On the witness stand the complaining old woman said: "She cahl me a wuthless ole Cartagene, sir!" Now, think of that! Carthage was destroyed 'way back in the days of Cato the Elder, you know, Mr Stewart! The greatest town of all Africa. To be a Carthaginian meant to be a sea-robber – a pirate; that is, a thief. One old woman on this island, more than two thousand years afterward, wishes to call another a thief, and the word "Cartagene" is the word she naturally uses! I suppose that has persisted on the West Coast and throughout all those village dialects in Africa without a break, all these centuries! The Zombi of the French islands? Yes, Mr Stewart. There are some extraordinary beliefs. Why, perhaps you've heard mention made of Old Morris, Mr Stewart. He used to live in your house, you know?'

I held my breath. Here was a possible trove. I nodded my head. I did not dare to speak!

'Well, Old Morris, you see, lived most of his earlier days in Martinique, and, it is said, he had a somewhat adventurous life there, Mr Stewart. Just what he did or how he got himself involved, seems never to have been made clear, but – in some way, Mr Stewart, the Black People believe, Morris got himself involved with a very powerful "Jumbee", and that is where what I said about the persistence of ancient beliefs comes in. Look on that table there, among those photographs, Mr Stewart. There! that's the place. I wish I were able to get up and assist you. These maids! Everything askew, I have no doubt! Do you observe a kind of fish-headed thing, about as big as the palm of your hand? Yes! That is it!'

I found the 'fish-headed thing' and carried it over to Mrs Heiden-klang. She took it in her hand and looked at it. It lacked a nose, but otherwise it was intact, a strange, uncouth-looking little godling, made of anciently-polished volcanic stone, with huge, protruding eyes, small, human-like ears, and what must have been a nose like a Tortola jackfish, or a black witch-bird, with its parrot beak.

'Now that,' continued Mrs Heidenklang, 'is one of the very ancient household gods of the aborigines of Martinique and you will observe the likeness in the idea to the *Lares* and *Penates* of your school-Latin days. Whether this is a *lar* or a *penate*, I can not tell,' and the old lady paused to smile at her little joke, 'but at any rate he is a representation of something very powerful – a fish-god of the Caribs. There's something Egyptian about the idea, too, I've always suspected; and, Mr Stewart, a Carib or an Arawak Indian – there were both in these islands, you know – looked much like an ancient Egyptian; perhaps half like your Zuñi or Aztec Indians, and half Egyptian, would be a fair statement of his appearance. These fish-gods had men's bodies, you see, precisely like the hawk-headed and jackal-headed deities of ancient Egypt.

'It was one of those, the Black People say, with which Mr Morris got himself mixed up – "Gahd knows" as they say – how! And, Mr Stewart, they say, his death was terrible! The particulars I've never heard, but my father knew, and he was sick for several days, after seeing Mr Morris's body. Extraordinary, isn't it? And when are you coming this way again, Mr Stewart? Do drop in and call on an old lady.'

I felt that I was progressing.

The next time I saw Mr Bonesteel, which was that very evening, I stopped him on the street and asked for a word with him.

'What was the date, or the approximate date, Mr Bonesteel, of Mr Morris's death? Could you recall that, sir?'

Mr Bonesteel paused and considered.

'It was just before Christmas,' said he. 'I remember it not so much by Christmas as by the races, which always take place the day after Christmas. Morris had entered his sorrel mare Santurce, and, as he left no heirs, there was no one who "owned" Santurce, and she had to be withdrawn from the races. It affected the betting very materially and a good many persons were annoyed about it, but there wasn't anything that could be done.'

I thanked Mr Bonesteel, and not without reason, for his answer had fitted into something that had been growing in my mind. Christmas was only eight days off. This drama of the furniture and Old Morris getting into bed, I had thought (and not unnaturally, it seems to me), might be a kind of reenactment of the tragedy of his death. If I had the courage to watch, night after night, I might be relieved of the necessity of asking any questions. I might witness whatever had occurred, in some weird reproduction, engineered God knows how!

For three nights now, I had seen the phenomenon of Old Morris getting into bed repeated, and each time it was clearer. I had sketched him into my drawing, a short, squat figure, rather stooped and fat, but possessed of a strange, gorillalike energy. His movements, as he walked toward the bed, seized the edge of the mosquito-netting and climbed in, were, somehow, full of *power*, which was the more apparent since these were ordinary motions. One could not help imagining that Old Morris would have been a tough customer to tackle, for all his alleged age!

This evening, at the hour when this phenomenon was accustomed to enact itself, that is, about eleven o'clock, I watched again. The scene was very much clearer, and I observed something I had not noticed before. Old Morris's *simulacrum* paused just before seizing the edge of the netting, raised its eyes, and began, with its right hand, a motion precisely like one who is about to sign himself with the cross. The motion was abruptly arrested, however, only the first of the four touches on the body being made.

I saw, too, something of the expression of the face that night, for the first time. At the moment of making the arrested sign, it was one of despairing horror. Immediately afterward, as this motion appeared to be abandoned for the abrupt clutching of the lower edge of the mosquito-net, it changed into a look of ferocious stubbornness, of almost savage self-confidence. I lost the facial expression as the appearance sank down upon the bed and pulled the ghostly bedclothes over itself.

Three nights later, when all this had become as greatly intensified as had the clearing-up process that had affected the furniture, I observed another motion, or what might be taken for the faint fore-shadowing of another motion. This was not on the part of Old Morris. It made itself apparent as lightly and elusively as the swift flight of a moth across the reflection of a lamp, over near the bed-room door (the doors in my house are more than ten feet high, in fourteen-foot-high walls), a mere flicker of something – something entering the room. I looked, and peered at that corner, straining my eyes, but nothing could I see save what I might describe as an intensification of the black shadow in that corner near the door, vaguely formed like a slim human figure, though grossly out of all human proportion. The vague shadow looked purple against the black. It was about ten feet high, and otherwise as though cast by an incredibly tall, thin human being.

I made nothing of it then; and again, despite all this cumulative experience with the strange shadows of my bedroom, attributed this last phenomenon to my eyes. It was too vague to be at that time accounted otherwise than as a mere subjective effect.

But the night following, I watched for it at the proper moment in the sequence of Old Morris's movements as he got into bed, and this time it was distinctly clearer. The shadow, it was, of some monstrous shape, ten feet tall, long, angular, of vaguely human appearance, though even in its merely shadowed form, somehow cruelly, strangely inhuman! I cannot describe the cold horror of its realization. The head-part was, relatively to the proportions of the body, short and broad, like a pumpkin head of a 'man' made of sticks by boys, to frighten passers-by on Hallowe'en.

The next evening I was out again to an entertainment at the residence of one of my hospitable friends, and arrived home after midnight. There stood the ghostly furniture, there on the bed was the form of the apparently sleeping Old Morris, and there in the corner stood the shadow, little changed from last night's appearance.

The next night would be pretty close to the date of Old Morris's death. It would be that night, or the next at latest, according to Mr Bonesteel's statement. The next day I could not avoid the sensation of something impending!

I entered my room and turned off the light a little before eleven, seated myself, and waited.

The furniture tonight was, to my vision, absolutely indistinguishable from reality. This statement may sound somewhat strange, for it will be remembered that I was sitting in the dark. Approximating terms again, I may say, however, that the furniture was visible in a light of its own, a kind of 'phosphorescence', which apparently emanated from it. Certainly there was no natural source of light. Perhaps I may express the matter thus: that light and darkness were *reversed* in the case of this ghostly bed, bureau, wardrobe, and chairs. When actual light was turned on, they disappeared. In darkness, which, of course, is the absence of physical light, they emerged. That is the nearest I can get to it. At any rate, tonight the furniture was entirely, perfectly, visible to me.

Old Morris came in at the usual time. I could see him with a clarity exactly comparable to what I have said about the furniture. He made his slight pause, his arrested motion of the right hand, and then, as usual, cast from him, according to his expression, the desire for that protective gesture, and reached a hard-looking, gnarled fist out to take hold of the mosquito-netting.

As he did so, a fearful thing leaped upon him, a thing out of the corner by the high doorway – the dreadful, purplish shadow-thing. I had not been looking in that direction, and while I had not forgotten this newest of the strange items in this phantasmagoria which had been repeating itself before my eyes for many nights, I was wholly unprepared for its sudden appearance and malignant activity.

I have said the shadow was purplish against black. Now that it had taken form, as the furniture and Old Morris himself had taken form, I observed that this purplish coloration was actual. It was a glistening, humanlike, almost metallic-appearing thing, certainly ten feet high, completely covered with great, iridescent fish-scales, each perhaps four square inches in area, which shimmered as it leaped across the room. I saw it for only a matter of a second or two. I saw it clutch surely and with a deadly malignity, the hunched body of Old Morris, from behind, just, you will remember, as the old man was about to climb into his bed. The dreadful thing turned him about as a wasp turns a fly, in great, flail-like, glistening arms, and never, to the day of my death, do I ever expect to be free of the look on Old Morris's face – a look of a lost soul who knows that there is no hope for him in this world or the next – as the great, squat, rounded head, a head precisely like that of Mrs Heidenklang's little fish-jumbee, descended, revealing to my horrified sight one glimpse of a huge, scythelike parrot-beak which it used, with a nodding motion of the ugly head, to plunge into its writhing victim's breast, with a tearing motion like the barracuda when it attacks and tears . . .

I fainted then, for that was the last of the fearful picture which I can remember.

I awakened a little after one o'clock, in a dark and empty room, peopled by no ghosts, and with my own, more common-place, mahogany furniture thinly outlined in the faint light of the new moon which was shining cleanly in a starry sky. The fresh night-wind stirred the netting of my bed. I rose, shakily, and went and leaned out of the window, and lit and puffed rapidly at a cigarette, which perhaps did something to settle my jangling nerves.

The next morning, with a feeling of loathing which has gradually worn itself out in the course of the months which have now elapsed since my dreadful experience, I took up my drawing again, and added as well as I could the fearful scene I had witnessed. The completed picture was a horror, crude as is my work in this direction. I wanted to destroy it, but I did not, and I laid it away under some unused clothing in one of the large drawers of my bedroom wardrobe.

Three days later, just after Christmas, I observed Mr Despard's car driving through the streets, the driver being alone. I stopped the boy and asked him where Mr Despard was at the moment. The driver told me Mr Despard was having breakfast – the West Indian midday meal – with Mr Bonesteel at that gentleman's house on the Prince's Cross Street. I thanked him and went home. I took out the drawing, folded it, and placed it in the inside breast pocket of my coat, and started for Bonesteel's house.

I arrived fifteen minutes or so before the breakfast hour, and was pleasantly received by my old friend and his guest. Mr Bonesteel pressed me to join them at breakfast, but I declined.

Mr Bonesteel brought in a swizzel, compounded of his very old rum, and after partaking of this in ceremonious fashion, I engaged the attention of both gentlemen.

'Gentlemen,' said I, 'I trust that you will not regard me as too much of a bore, but I have, I believe, a legitimate reason for asking you if you will tell me the manner in which the gentleman known as Old Morris, who once occupied my house, met his death.'

I stopped there, and immediately discovered that I had thrown my kind old host into a state of embarrassed confusion. Glancing at Mr Despard, I saw at once that if I had not actually offended him, I had, by my question, at least put him 'on his dignity'. He was looking at me severely, rather, and I confess that for a moment I felt a bit like a schoolboy. Mr Bonesteel caught something of this atmosphere, and looked helplessly at Despard. Both men shifted uneasily in their chairs; each waited for the other to speak.

Despard, at last, cleared his throat.

'You will excuse me, Mr Stewart,' said he, slowly, 'but you have asked a question which for certain reasons, no one, aware of the circumstances, would desire to answer. The reasons are, briefly, that Mr Morris, in certain respects, was – what shall I say, not to do the matter an injustice? – well, perhaps I might say he was abnormal. I do not mean that he was crazy. He was, though, eccentric. His end was such that stating it would open up a considerable argument, one which agitated this island for a long time after he was found dead. By a kind of general consent, that matter is taboo on the island. That will explain to you why no one wishes to answer your question. I am free to say that Mr Bonesteel here, in considerable distress, told me that you had asked it of him. You also asked me about it not long ago. I can add only that the manner of Mr Morris's end was such that – '

Mr Despard hesitated, and looked down, a frown on his brow, at his shoe, which he tapped nervously on the tiled floor of the gallery where we were seated.

'Old Morris, Mr Stewart,' he resumed, after a moment's reflection, in which, I imagined, he was carefully choosing his words, 'was, to put it plainly, murdered! There was much discussion over the identity of the murderer, but the most of it, the unpleasant part of the discussion, was rather whether he was killed by human agency or not! Perhaps you will see now, sir, the difficulty of the matter. To admit that he was murdered by an ordinary murderer is, to my mind, an impossibility. To assert that some other agency, something abhuman, killed him, opens up the question of one's belief, one's credulity. "Magic" and occult agencies are, as you are aware, strongly intrenched in the minds of the ignorant people of these islands. None of us cares to admit a similar belief. Does that satisfy you, Mr Stewart, and will you let the matter rest there, sir?'

I drew out the picture, and, without unfolding it, laid it across my knees. I nodded to Mr Despard, and, turning to our host, asked: 'As a child, Mr Bonesteel, were you familiar with the arrangement of Mr Morris's bedroom?'

'Yes, sir,' replied Mr Bonesteel, and added: 'Everybody was! Persons who had never been in the old man's house, crowded in when – ' I intercepted a kind of warning look passing from Despard to the speaker. Mr Bonesteel, looking much embarrassed, looked at me in that helpless fashion I have already mentioned, and remarked that it was hot weather these days!

'Then,' said I, 'perhaps you will recognize its arrangement and even some of the details of its furnishing,' and I unfolded the picture and handed it to Mr Bonesteel.

If I had anticipated its effect upon the old man, I would have been more discreet, but I confess I was nettled by their attitude. By handing it to Mr Bonesteel (I could not give it to both of them at once) I did the natural thing, for he was our host. The old man looked at what I had handed him, and (this is the only way I can describe what happened) became, suddenly, as though petrified. His eyes bulged out of his head, his lower jaw dropped and hung open. The paper slipped from his nerveless grasp and fluttered and zig-zagged to the floor, landing at Despard's feet. Despard stooped and picked it up, ostensibly to restore it to me, but in doing so, he glanced at it, and had *his* reaction. He leaped frantically to his feet, and positively goggled at the picture, then at me. Oh, I was having my little revenge for their reticence, right enough!

'My God!' shouted Despard. 'My God, Mr Stewart, where did you get such a thing?'

Mr Bonesteel drew in a deep breath, the first, it seemed, for sixty seconds, and added his word.

'Oh my God!' muttered the old man, shakily, 'Mr Stewart, Mr Stewart! What is it, what is it? Where – '

'It is a Martinique fish-zombi, what is known to professional occult investigators like Elliott O'Donnell and William Hope Hodgson as an "elemental",' I explained, calmly. 'It is a representation of how poor Mr Morris actually met his death; until now, as I understand it, a purely conjectural matter. Christiansted is built on the ruins of French Bassin, you will remember,' I added. 'It is a very likely spot for an "elemental"!'

'But, but,' almost shouted Mr Despard, 'Mr Stewart, where did you get this, it's – '

'I made it,' said I, quietly, folding up the picture and placing it back in my inside pocket.

'But how – ?' this from both Despard and Bonesteel, speaking in unison.

'I saw it happen, you see,' I replied, taking my hat, bowing formally to both gentlemen, and murmuring my regret at not being able to remain for breakfast, I departed.

And as I reached the bottom of Mr Bonesteel's gallery steps and turned along the street in the direction of Old Morris's house, where I live, I could hear their voices speaking together.

'But how, how – ?' This was Bonesteel.

'Why, why – ?' And that was Despard.

Sweet Grass

A tale, this, of the Black Obayi of Ashantee . . . Nybladh, administrator for the Copenhagen Company of the Rasmussen Centràl,
allotted Estate Fairfield to young Cornelis Hansen, just out from
Denmark to the Danish West Indies to begin the life of a sugar
planter. Cornelis, tall, straight, ruddy-cheeked, twenty-two, fell in
love with the island of Santa Cruz and with his pretty little house.

Nybladh had indeed used diplomacy in that allotment. An inexper-
ienced estate manager could do little harm at Fairfield. The house
stood, quite near the sea, at the western end of the Centràl's many
properties, among dimpling hills. Hillside cane was a losing venture.
Very little was grown at Fairfield, and that on its small proportion
of level bottom-land. Then, Cornelis could be promoted as soon
as he became accustomed to the practicalities. That would mean a
favorable report to Old Strach, Cornelis' uncle in Copenhagen. Old
Strach owned the Centràl.

Cornelis proved to be a social success from the very start. The Santa
Crucian gentry drove up to call on him in their family carriages,
to the little stone house glistening frostily in the Caribbean sunlight.
It had been freshly whitewashed – Crucian wash, held together
with molasses, and now baked to the appearance of alabaster by the
relentless sun.

At their own houses Cornelis met the resident planters, chiefly
Scottish and Irish gentlefolk and their sons and daughters. Also he
became acquainted with the officers at the three Danish garrisons –
at Christiansted, Frederiksted, and Kingshill. Many visitors, too,
came over from St Thomas, the capital, forty-three miles away;
others, too, from the English Islands – Antigua, St Kitts, even sometimes from Montserrat or St Lucia. There was never any lack of good
company on Santa Cruz. This tropical life was vastly different from
Copenhagen. Cornelis was never home-sick. He did not want to go
back to cold Copenhagen. There, it seemed now to Cornelis, he had
been spending a beginningless eternity, absorbed in his chemistry,
his English, and other dull studies. All that had been to fit him to

take his place here in this pleasant, short-houred, expensive life of a tropical planter in the sugar-trade. He enjoyed the new life from its very beginning. Yet, in spite of his pleasant housing, his hospitable entertainment, his unaccustomed freedom to come and go, he was, sometimes poignantly, lonesome.

His new friends did not, perhaps, realize the overpowering effect of the sudden change upon this northern-bred man; the effects of the moonlight and the soft tradewind; the life of love which surrounded him here. Love from the palm fronds, rustling dryly in the continuous breeze; love was telegraphed through the shy, bovine eyes of the brown girls in his estate-house village; love assailed him in the breath of the honeylike sweet grass, undulating all day and all night under the white moonlight of the Caribbees, pouring over him intoxicatingly through his opened jalousies as he lay, often sleeping, through long nights of spice and balm smells on his mahogany bedstead – pale grass, looking like snow under the moon.

The half-formulated yearnings which these sights and sounds were begetting were quite new and fresh in his experience. Here fresh instincts, newly released, stirred, flared up, at the glare of early-afternoon sunlight, at the painful scarlet of the hibiscus blooms, the incredible indigo of the sea – all these flames of vividness through burning days, wilting into a caressing coolness, abruptly, at the fall of the brief, tropic dusk. The fundament of his crystallizing desire was for companionship in the blazing life of this place of rapid growth and early fading, where time slipped away so fast.

At first he had wondered, vaguely, how other men had met this primal urge. Very soon he saw that the answer to that was all about him, here in his own estate-village. Here were ruddy *zambos*, pale-brown mulattos, cream-colored octoroons – *mestizos* of every type, of every shade of skin. That was one answer; that had been the great answer, here in the West Indies, from time immemorial; the answer here on Santa Cruz of the Spaniards and the Dutch, as many names showed; of the French and of his own people, the Danes. He wondered, whimsically, what had been the answer in the case of those austere Knights of Malta who had owned the island for a season.

But, for Cornelis, fastidiousness intervened. Across the edge of that solution hung the barrier of his inertia, his resistance, his pride of a Caucasian. The barrier seemed insurmountable to Cornelis.

Marriage? Was he not young for that? He asked himself that question many times. One did not marry, ideally, without love; love true and deep and trustful; love founded on acquaintance, appreciation, some conviction of permanence. Those were the backgrounds of marriage.

Some daughter of one of the gentry planters, perhaps? Those girls had the domestic virtues. But – he was comfortable enough with his good servants at Fairfield House. His yearnings had little relation to somebody to preside over his household. Somehow, to Cornelis, these young ladies of the planter gentry were not alluring, vital. The most attractive of them, Honoria Macartney, he could hardly imagine beside him perpetually. Honoria had the dead-white skin of the Caucasian Creole lady whose face has been screened from the sun since infancy.

'And how are you enjoying the island?' she had asked him on an afternoon when he had been visiting the Macartneys, eating some of Honoria's perfect small frosted cakes; drinking her rather too-strong tea on the east gallery of her father's estate-house near Christiansted.

Cornelis reassured her. He was enjoying himself very much indeed. Everything Honoria said, did, wore – he felt instinctively – was – *suitable*. That was the English word for it. Yes.

Looking at her, as he had looked at her various other afternoons, Cornelis was certain his mother in Copenhagen would approve of her as a daughter-in-law. Most of the Crucian young gentry ladies were like that. Suitable – that was the precise word . . .

That night he lay, sleepless, on the mahogany bed. The grass on the rolling hillsides seen through the opened jalousies under the full moon of February was at its palest, more than ever suggesting snow. That he had observed driving up the straight road from the sea to his house less than an hour before. He had dined with the Macartneys – a placid, uneventful evening. Mrs Macartney had mentioned that Honoria had made the dessert. It had been a Danish dessert, for him: 'red grout' – sago pudding stained purple with cactus-fruit. Honoria had made it perfectly. He had complimented her upon her pudding.

The warm, pulsing breath of the sweet grass surged through the open windows in a fashion to turn the head of a stone image. It was exotic, too sweet, exaggerated, like everything else in this climate! Cornelis turned over again, seeking a cool place on the broad bed. Then he sat up in bed, impatiently throwing off the sheet. A thin streak of moonlight edged the bed below his feet. He slipped out of bed, walked over to a window. He leaned out, looking down at the acres of undulating grass. There seemed to be some strange, hypnotic rhythm to it, some vague magic, as it swayed in the night wind. The scent poured over him in great, pulsing breaths. He shut his eyes and drew it in, abandoning his senses to its effect.

Instinctively, without thought or plan, he walked out of his open bedroom door, down the stairs, out upon the south gallery below. The smooth tiles there felt caressingly cool to his bare feet. Jessamine here mingled with the sweet grass. He drew a light cane chair to the gallery's edge and sat, leaning his arms on the stone coping, his shadow sharply defined in the cold moonlight. He looked out at the sea a long time. Then he shut his eyes, drinking in the intoxicating, mixed odors.

A sound secured his attention. He raised his head, looked down his narrow private road toward the sea. Clearly outlined in the moonlight a girl, possibly fifteen, came along the road toward him. About her lithe body hung a loose slip, and around her head, carelessly twined, turban-wise, was draped a white towel. She was quite close, making no sound on the sandy road with her bare feet.

His shadow moving slightly, perhaps, startled her. She paused in her languorous stride, a slender neck bearing erect a fawnlike head, nostrils wide, eyes open, taken unawares.

Then the girl recognized him and curtsied, her sudden smile revealing white, regular teeth set in a delicate, wide mouth, a mouth made for love. In the transforming magic of the moonlight her pale brown skin showed like cream.

'Bathing in de sea,' she murmured explanatorily.

Lingeringly, as though with reluctance, she resumed her sedate, slow walk, the muscles flowing, rippling, as though to pass around the house to the village at the rear. Her eyes she kept fixed on Cornelis.

Cornelis, startled, had felt suddenly cold at the unexpected, wraith-like sight of her. Now his blood surged back, his heart pumping tumultuously. A turbulent wave of sea air sweetened from acres of sweet grass surged over him. He closed his eyes.

'Come!' he whispered, almost inaudibly.

But the girl heard. She paused, looked up at him, hesitating. He managed to nod his head at her. The blood pounded in his veins; he felt detached, weak, drowned in the odor of sweet grass and jessamine.

The girl ran lightly up the gallery's stone steps. The pattern of the small jessamine leaves played grotesquely upon her when she paused, as moonlight filtered through them and they moved in the light, irregular sea breeze.

Cornelis rose and looked down into the girl's eyes. Their amber irises were very wide and eery light played in them; a kind of luminous glow, a softening . . .

Trembling, he placed a tentative hand on her shoulder, gently. She leaned toward him; his arms went about her firm, slender body. Young Cornelis Hansen felt, for the first time, a girl's heart tumultuously beating against his breast.

A hush enveloped the quiet of the pure, clear night. No dog muttered from the sleeping estate-village. A fresh breath, enervating, redolent of the acres of waving grass, fanned the gallery. A delicate beam of moonlight seemed, to young Cornelis, entranced, bewitched, to usher them into the open doorway of his house . . .

Then, suddenly, almost brutally it seemed, even to him, he thrust this pale, brown girl of gossamer and moonlight away from him. He stood clear of her, no longer bemused by the witchery of the breeze and the moonlight's magic.

With more of gentleness he laid again his hand on the delicate, rounded shoulder. As gently he turned the girl about and marched her, resolutely – like a Dane – toward the gallery steps. His fastidiousness had reasserted itself.

'Good night – my child,' said Cornelis.

The girl looked up at him shyly, out of the corners of her eyes, puzzled and resentful.

'Good night, sar,' she murmured, and slipped down the steps and like a shadow around the corner of the house.

Cornelis walked firmly into his house and shut the door behind him. He went into his dining-room and poured himself a glass of French brandy and rinsed out the glass from the earthenware water-gugglet, throwing the water onto the stone floor. Then he mounted the stairs to his bedroom, got into bed, rolled over on his side, and went to sleep.

In the morning, after his tea, he was riding about his fields so early that he was finished with his managerial inspection before nine. Ten o'clock saw him, very carefully shaved, and wearing spotless white drill and his best Danish straw hat instead of a sun helmet, driving a pair of horses in the light phaeton toward Christiansted.

That same afternoon, during the period devoted to swizzels of old rum or brandy and, especially among the Danes, tea and coffee and cakes – the period of sociability before the company at the various great houses broke up before its various dinner-parties – Cornelis called at the Nybladhs'. The Administrator and his wife were pleased to see him, as always. Several others were present, quite a company in fact, for the swizzel-hour at Nybladhs' was almost an official occasion.

After a quarter of an hour, Cornelis drew the Administrator aside and they spoke together briefly, then returned to the company gathered about an enormous mahogany table which held the silver swizzel jug and the afternoon's lunch.

At the next pause in the conversation Nybladh rose, focusing his guests' attention upon himself. He held up his glass.

'Be pleased to fill all glasses,' he commanded, importantly.

There was a considerable bustle about the great round table. Nybladh noted the fulfilling of his command. Servants hurried about among the guests. When all were freshly served he cleared his throat and waved his own glass ceremoniously.

'I announce' – he paused, impressively, all eyes dutifully upon him. 'I announce – the engagement of Herr Hansen and Miss Honoria Macartney. Skoal!' He boomed it out sonorously. Every glass was raised.

Cornelis bowed from the waist, deeply, to each of his pledgers, as they drank the health of himself and his bride-to-be.

Thus did Honoria, daughter of the great Irish-West Indian family of the Fighting Macartneys, become the Fru Hansen, after an exceptionally brief engagement, and leave her father's house to live at Estate Fairfield with her husband who was the nephew of Old Strach.

A West Indian family does not pick up titles from the populace by knocking about their estates and doing nothing. The Fighting Macartneys were well worthy of theirs. Even Saul Macartney, their ancient black sheep, who had paid the penalty of piracy by hanging in St Thomas in 1824 along with the notorious Fawcett, his chief, and who, as some believed, had been strangely magicked even after his death by his cousin Camilla Lanigan who was believed to practise obeah and was immensely respected by the Negroes – even the disgraced Saul was no poltroon. The jewels Saul and Captain Fawcett buried under Melbourne House, Saul's Santa Cruz mansion, had not been handed that miscreant over the counter!

This young Honoria was of that sanguine blood, even though her sheltered life had made her walk somewhat mincingly and there was no color in her cheeks. She began her reign at Fairfield like a sensible young housewife, studying Cornelis' likes and dislikes, satisfying him profoundly, beyond his very moderate expectations. The ardent yet self-contained young man had linked to himself something compounded of fire and silk. Honoria brought to her housekeeping, too, great skill and knowledge, from her young life-time in her mother's great house near Christiansted.

She was a jewel of a wife, this young Honoria Hansen, born Macartney. Cornelis came suddenly to love her with an ardency which even he had never dreamed of as possible, like flame. Then their love was tempered in a fearful happening.

One morning when Cornelis was riding early about his sugar fields, it came to him, traversing a cane-range on his black mare, Aase, that never, before or since that sleepless night when he had called the girl to him on the gallery, had he laid eyes upon that girl. That he would recognize the girl whom, for a moment of abandoned forgetfulness of his fastidious reserve, he had held in his arms, whose body had lain against his heart, was beyond question in his mind. Then it occurred to him that he had thought of the girl as living in his village. That night when he had dismissed her, she had walked away around the house toward the cabins at the rear. He shuddered – those cabins!

Yet the fact remained that, cogitate the matter as he might, riding along at Aase's delicate walking pace, he could not recollect having laid eyes upon her, either before or since that night when he had sent her away. It was very curious, inexplicable indeed – if the girl lived in his village. There was really no way to inquire. Well, it did not greatly matter, of course! A brown girl was – a brown girl. They were all alike. Cornelis rode on to another canefield.

Telepathy, perhaps! When he arrived at Fairfield House toward eleven under the mounting brilliance of the late-morning sunlight, and tossed his bridle-reins to Alonzo his groom at the front gallery steps, the girl stood beside the door of Fairfield House, inside the high hallway. She curtsied gravely to him as he passed within.

Cornelis' mouth went dry. He managed to nod at the girl, who reached for his sun helmet and hung it on the hallway hatrack.

'Mistress say de brekfuss prepare' in few moments, sar,' announced the girl.

Honoria, in his absence, it appeared, had engaged this girl as a house servant. There was no other explanation of her presence in the house. She had been carefully dressed, rustling with starch, the very picture of demureness. Cornelis strode upstairs to wash before late breakfast, which came at eleven.

His equanimity was sufficiently restored after breakfast to inquire of Honoria about the new housemaid. The girl had been engaged that morning, taking the place of one Anastasia Holmquist, a Black girl, who had sent a message, by this girl, Julietta Aagaard, that she was leaving the service of Fru Hansen, and had obtained Julietta to take her place.

'She seems a very quiet, good girl,' added Honoria, 'and she knows her duties.'

'She is not of our village, eh?' inquired Cornelis, tentatively.

'No. She says she lives with her mother, somewhere up in the hills,' Honoria indicated with a gesture the section of the island behind Fairfield.

Cornelis found his mind relieved. The girl was not of his village. Only one thing remained to be explained. He understood now why he had not observed the girl about the estate. But what had she been doing 'bathing in the sea' at night? Such a practise was unheard of among the Negroes. Few, indeed, would venture abroad or even out of their houses, unless necessity compelled, after dark. The houses themselves were closed up tightly, at nightfall, the doors of the cabins marked with crosses to keep out jumbee – ghosts; their corrugated-iron roofs strewed with handfuls of sea-sand, the counting of which delayed the werewolf marauding nightly. A vast superstition ruled the lives of the Santa Crucian Negroes with chains of iron. They believed in necromancy, witchcraft; they practised the obeah for sickness among themselves, took their vengeances with the aid of the Vauxdoux; practises brought in through Cartagena and Jamaica; from Dakar to the Congo mouths in the slave days; Obayi from Ashantee; Vauxdoux, worship of the Snake with its attendant horrors, through the savage Dahomeyans who had slaved for King Christophe in the sugar fields of Black Haiti.

To go from up in the hills to the sea, at night, for a bath – it was simply unheard of. Yet, the girl, seeing him there on the gallery, had been plainly startled. She had come from the sea. Her lithe body, the towel about her head, had been sea-damp that night. It was unheard of, unless – Cornelis had learned something in the six months of his residence on Santa Cruz.

'Who is Julietta's mother?' he inquired suddenly.

Honoria did not know anything about Julietta's mother. This was the West End of Santa Cruz, and Honoria had lived all her life near Christiansted.

But, three days later, from a brow-beaten Alonzo, Cornelis learned the truth. The deference with which the young Julietta had been treated by the other servants, the Black People of his village, had been marked. Reluctantly Alonzo told his master the truth. Julietta's mother was the *mamaloi*, the witch-woman, of this portion of the island.

Beyond satisfying his curiosity, this news meant little to Cornelis. He was too much a product of civilization, too much Caucasian, for the possible inferences to have their full effect upon him. It was not until some days later, when he surprised the look of sullen hatred in Julietta's swiftly drooped eyes, that it recurred to him; that the thought crossed his mind that Julietta had come into service in Fairfield House to retaliate upon him for her rejection. Hell hath no fury like a woman scorned! There was no Danish equivalent to the English proverb, or if there was, it lay outside Cornelis' knowledge. Yet, although a European Dane – despite the fact that his residence on Santa Cruz had not been long enough for him to realize what such deadly dislike as he had surprised in Julietta's glance might mean – Cornelis, no imbecile, did realize at the least a certain sense of discomfort.

Honoria, born on the island, could have helped the situation. But – there was no developed 'situation'. Cornelis wished this girl at the bottom of the sea; transplanted to another and distant island of the archipelago, but beyond that there was no more than the sense of discomfort at the girl's quiet, efficient presence about her duties in his house. He could not, of course, explain to his young wife his reason for wishing lithe Julietta away.

But the sense of discomfort, somehow, persisted strangely. He could not see Julietta, demure, neat, submissive to her young mistress, without being unpleasantly reminded of what he came to think of as his folly.

Then, without rime or reason, the sense of discomfort localized itself. Cornelis, annoyed during the night by a vague itching on his upper arms, discovered in the early-morning light a slight rash. Prickly heat, he told himself, and anointed his burning arms with salve. Useless. The rash persisted, annoyed him all through his morning field-inspection.

That late-morning, in his shower bath after his ride among the cane-fields, he noticed that the rash was spreading. It ran now below his elbows, was coming out about his neck. It burned detestably. He was obliged to towel himself very softly on the arms and neck that morning before he dressed for breakfast in his spotless white drill.

Julietta, waiting on table, did not look at him; went about her duties like a cleverly made automaton, her look distant, introspective.

Honoria reported an annoyance. One of Cornelis' shirts had disappeared. They discussed it briefly over breakfast.

'But – it must turn up.' Cornelis dismissed the topic, spoke of his plowing of the field abutting on Högensborg.

That night he was nearly frantic with his itching. Pustules, small, hard, reddish knobs that burned like fire, covered his arms and neck, were spreading across the firm pectoral muscles of his chest, down his sides.

Honoria offered sympathy, and some salve for prickly heat she had brought from her father's house. Together they anointed Cornelis' burning skin.

'You must drive in to Frederiksted and see Dr Schaff in the morning,' commanded Honoria. She dusted her husband's body with her own lady-like rice-powder.

The dawn after a sleepless night discovered Cornelis' torso a mass of the small, red, hard pustules. He was in agony. Honoria it was who drove in the five miles to Frederiksted, fetched Dr Schaff from his duties at his municipal hospital, leaving his assistant, Dr Malling-Holm, in charge of the cases there assembled. Cornelis, Old Strach's nephew, must not be kept waiting. Besides, Honoria had been insistent. She had seen something of the suffering of her man.

Schaff had been on the island five years; had earned his promotion there to be Chief Municipal Physician. He knew much about tropical mischances in his field of medicine. He looked with interest at the pustules. Cold-bloodedly he punctured several. He wanted an analysis. He left a new kind of salve, drove back to the hospital with his specimens.

He drove back late in the afternoon, when the hospital day's rush was over. He found Cornelis writhing in bed, his body tortured with the solid spread of the infection. Curiously, his hands and face were free of the now solidly massed red pustules. They stopped at his wrists, and again at his neck. Below the waist, at the sides, his body was free of the infection, which extended, however, down the front and back of his thighs.

'It iss verree curious, this!' commented the doctor, speaking English on Honoria's account. 'It iss as though he had worn an infected shirt.'

Cornelis, through his three degrees of fever, spoke to Honoria.

'Have you discovered my shirt? You said there was a shirt gone.'

'Ha – so-o-o!' muttered the doctor. 'And where?'

'I cannot say,' said Honoria, her lips suddenly dry. She and the doctor looked at each other.

'A servant, perhaps?'

'It must be.' Honoria nodded. 'No one else – '

Honoria disappeared while the doctor anointed Cornelis, writhing, afresh; soothed him with a long, bitter draft.

Below, Honoria had resolutely summoned all the servants. They stood before her, expressionless.

'The master's shirt is to be returned this night,' commanded Honoria imperiously. 'I shall expect to find it – on the south gallery by nine o'clock. Otherwise' – she looked about her at each expressionless face – 'otherwise – the fort. There will be a dark room for every one of you – no food, no sleep, until it is confessed. I will have none of this in my house. That is all.'

She came upstairs again, helped the doctor assiduously. At the door when he took his departure, she whispered: 'I have ordered them to return the shirt by nine tonight.'

The doctor looked at her meaningly, an eyebrow lifted. 'So! You understand, then, eh? It is bad, bad, this Black "stupidness". Burn the shirt.'

'Yes – of course,' said Honoria.

At nine she descended the stairs, went out upon the south gallery among the scents of the white-flowering jessamine; the sweet grass. All was silent. The servants had left the house, as usual, about an hour before.

The shirt hung over the stone gallery-coping. She ran down the steps, found a stick, lifted the crumpled shirt on its end, carefully, carried it into the house. It bore no marks, save the crumpling. It had been soiled before its disappearance.

She carried it into the kitchen, carefully lowered the corner of the thin garment until it caught fire from the embers of a charcoal-pot. The thin linen flamed up, and with her stick she manipulated it until every particle of it was consumed, and then stirred the embers. A few sparks came out. The shirt was completely burned.

Her face drawn, she returned to the bedroom above. Cornelis was asleep. She sat beside his bed for two hours; then, after a long look at his flushed face, she departed silently for her own room.

In the morning the fever was broken. Many of the smaller pustules had disappeared. The remaining rash was going down. Cornelis, at her beseeching, remained in bed. At noon he arose. He felt perfectly well, he said.

'All that vexation about a little prickly heat!' Honoria sighed. She had four brothers. Men! They were much alike. How often had she heard her mother, and other mature women, say that!

That night Cornelis' skin was entirely restored. It was as though there had been no interval of burning agony. Cornelis, apparently, had forgotten that painful interval. But the reaction had made him especially cheerful at dinner-time. He laughed and joked rather more than usual. He did not even notice Julietta as she waited, silently, on the table.

Two nights later, at the dinner-table, Cornelis collapsed forward in the middle of a phrase. He went deathly white, his lips suddenly dry, a searing pain like the thrust of a carving-knife through and through his chest. Sudden froth stood at the corners of his mouth. The table-edge athwart him alone kept him from falling prone. He hung there, in intolerable agony, for seconds. Then, slowly, as it had 'gone in', the white-hot 'knife' was withdrawn. He drew in a labored breath, and Honoria supported him upright. She had flown to him around the table.

As she stood upright propping him back into his chair, she saw Julietta. The brown girl's lips were drawn back from her even, beautiful teeth, her wide mouth in an animal-like snarl, her amber eyes boring into Cornelis' face, a very Greek-mask of hatred. An instant afterward, Julietta's face was that of the blank, submissive housemaid. But Honoria had seen.

At a bound her hands were clenched tight about the girl's slender arms and Julietta was being shaken like a willow wand, in a great, gale. Her tray, with glasses, shot resoundingly to the stone floor, to a tinkle of smashed glass. The Fighting Macartney blood showed red in Honoria's pallid face.

'It's you, then, you deadly creature, is it, eh? You who have done this devilish thing to your master! You – in my house! It was you, then, who made the rash, with your double-damned "magic"!'

In the primitive urge of her fury at one who had struck at her man, Honoria had the slim brown girl against the room's wall now, holding her helpless in a grasp like steel with her own slender arms.

Cornelis, faint after that surge of unbearable, deadly pain, struggled to speak, there in his chair. Well-nigh helpless, he looked on at this unaccountable struggle. At last he found his voice, a voice faint and weak.

'What is it? – What is it, Honoria, my dear?'

'It's this witch!' cried Honoria, through clenched teeth. 'It is she who has put the *obeah* on you.' Then, 'You she-devil, you will "take it off" or I'll kill you here and now. Take it off, then! Take it off!'

Honoria's voice had risen to a menacing scream. The girl cowered, wiltingly, under her fierce attack.

'Ooh Gahd – me mistress! Ooh, Gahd! 'Taint I, ma'am, I swear to Gahd – I ain't do it, ma'am. Ooh, Gahd – me boans! Yo' break me, mistress. Fo' Gahd-love leave me to go!'

But Honoria, unrelaxed, the fighting-blood of her clan aroused, held the brown girl relentlessly.

'Take it off!' came, ever and again, through her small, clenched teeth. The brown girl began to struggle, ineffectually, gave it up, submitted to be held against the wall, her eyes now wide, frightened at this unexpected, sudden violence.

'What is it that you tell her to do?' This from Cornelis, recovering, shocked, puzzled.

'It is their damnable "obi",' hissed Honoria. 'I will make her "take it off" you or I'll kill her.'

'It is her mother,' said Cornelis, suddenly inspired. 'I know about her mother. I asked. Her mother, this girl's mother, there in the hills – it is the girl's mother who does this wickedness.'

Honoria suddenly shifted her desperate grip upon the girl's numb arms. She twisted, and Julietta's slender body, yielding, collapsed limply to the floor. With a lightning-like motion, back and then forward again, Honoria menaced her with the great carving-knife, snatched from before her husband.

'Get up!' Her voice was low now, deadly. 'Get up, you devil, and lead me to your mother's house.'

Julietta, trembling, silent, dragged herself to her feet. Honoria pointed to the door with the knife's great shining blade. In silence the girl slipped out, Honoria following. Cornelis sat, still numb with that fearful reaction after his unbearable pain, slumped forward now in his mahogany armchair at the head of his table. His bones felt like water. His head sank forward on his arms. He remained motionless until Alonzo, the groom, summoned from the village by the frightened, gray-faced cook, who had overheard, roused him, supported him upstairs.

The two women passed around the corner of Fairfield House, skirted the huddled cabins of the estate-village in silence, began to mount the steep hill at the back. Through tangled brush and twining, resistant guinea-grass, a slender trail wound abruptly upward into the deeper hills beyond. Up, and always up they went, the Caucasian lady grim and silent, the great knife held menacingly behind the unseeing back of the brown girl who stepped around turns and avoided roots and small rocks with the ease of custom.

At the head of the second ravine Honoria's conductress turned sharply to the right and led the way along the hill's edge toward a small clearing among the mahogany and tibet tree scrub. A dingy cabin, of wood, with the inevitable corrugated-iron roof, hung perilously on the hill's seaward edge. Straight to its door walked Julietta, paused, tapped, opened the door and, pressed close by Honoria, entered.

A dark brown woman peered at them across a small table. With her thumb, Honoria noted, she was rubbing very carefully the side of a small waxlike thing, which glistened dully in the illumination of a small, smoky oil lamp standing on the table. The woman, her eyes glassy as though from the effects of some narcotic drug, peered dully at the intruders.

Honoria, her left hand clenched tightly on Julietta's wincing shoulder, confronted her, the knife's point resting on the table beside the brown hand which held the wax. This was molded, Honoria observed, to the rough simulacrum of a human being.

'That is my husband!' announced Honoria without preamble. 'You will take your "obi" off now. Otherwise I will kill you both.'

A long, blackened needle lay beside the brown woman's hand on the table. She looked up into Honoria's face, dully.

'Yes, me mistress,' she acquiesced in a singsong voice.

'You will do that at once!' Honoria tapped her knife-blade on the table decisively. 'I am Fru Hansen. I was Honoria Macartney. I mean what I say. Come!'

The brown woman laid the wax image carefully down on the table. She rose, dreamily, fumbled about in the semidarkness of the cabin. She returned carrying a shining, new tin, half filled with water. This, as carefully as she had handled the wax image, she set down beside it. Then, as gingerly, she picked up the image, muttered a string of unintelligible words in the old Crucian Creole, thickly interspersed with Dahomeyan. Honoria recognized several of the words – 'caffoón', 'shandràmadan' – but the sequence she could not grasp.

The brown woman ended her speech, plunged the image into the water. She washed it carefully, as though it had been an incredibly tiny infant and she fearful of doing it some injury by clumsy handling. She removed it from the tin of water, the drops running down its surface of oily wax. She handed the image, with a suggestion of relaxed care now, to Honoria.

'Him aff, now, me mistress; I swear-yo', him aff! I swear yo' be Gahd, an' help me de Jesus!'

Honoria took the image into her hand, looked at it curiously in that dim light, made upon it with her thumb the sign of the cross. Then she slowly broke it into pieces, the sweat standing in beads on her face. She turned, without another word, and walked out of the cabin. As she proceeded down the trail, laboriously now, her legs weak in her high-heeled slippers, she cast crumbling bits of the wax right and left into the dense scrub among the bushes at the trail's sides. Her mouth and throat felt strangely dry. She murmured inarticulate prayers.

She limped into Fairfield House half an hour later and found Cornelis entirely restored. He asked her many questions, and to these she returned somewhat evasive answers. Yes – she had gone to Julietta's mother's cabin up the hill. Yes – the 'stupidness' of these people needed a lifetime to realize. No – there had been no difficulty. Julietta's mother was a 'stupid' old creature. There would be no more trouble, she was sure. It was extraordinary what effects they could produce. They brought it with them from Africa, of course – stupidness, wickedness – and handed it down from generation to generation . . .

She might have her own thoughts – men were very much alike, as her mother had said – as the days wore into weeks, the weeks into the placid years which lay before her, with her man, here at Fairfield for a while, later, perhaps, in some larger house, in a more important position.

What had caused that devilish little Julietta to contrive such a thing? Those eyes! That mouth! Honoria had seen the hatred in her face.

She would, of course, never ask Cornelis. Best to leave such matters alone. Men! She had fought for this man – her man.

She would give him of her full devotion. There would be children in time. She would have, to replace Julietta, a new housemaid. There was one she remembered, near Christiansted. She would drive over tomorrow. The affairs of a Santa Crucian wife!

Cornelis plainly loved her. He was hers. There would be deviled land-crabs, sprinkled with port wine, dusted with herbs, baked in the stone oven for breakfast . . .

The Tree-Man

My first sight of Fabricius, the tree-man, was within a week of my first arrival on the island of Santa Cruz not long after the United States had purchased the Danish West Indies and officially re-named its new colony the Virgin Islands of the United States.

My ship came into Frederiksted harbor on the west coast of the island just at dusk and I saw for the first time a half-moon of white sand beach with the charming little town in its middle. In the midst of the bustle incident to anchoring in the roadstead, there came over the side an upstanding gentleman in a glistening white drill uniform who came up to me, bowed in a manner to commend itself to kings, and said: 'I am honored to welcome you to Santa Cruz, Mr Canevin. I am Director Despard of the Police Department. The police boat is at your disposal when you are ready to go ashore. May I see to your luggage?'

This was a welcome indeed. I was nearly knocked off my feet by such an unexpected reception. I thanked Director Despard and before many minutes my trunks were overside, my luggage bestowed in the police boat waiting at the foot of the ladder-gangway, and I was seated beside him in the boat's sternsheets, he holding the tiller-ropes while four coal-black convicts rowed us ashore with lusty pulls at their long sweeps.

Through the lowering dusk as we approached the landing I observed that the wharf was crowded with black people. Behind these stood half a dozen knots of white people, conversing together. A long row of cars stood against the background of waterfront buildings. I remarked to the Police Director: 'Isn't it unusual for so many persons to be on the docks for the arrival of a vessel, Mr Director?'

'It is not usual,' replied the dignified gentleman beside me. 'It is for you, Mr Canevin.'

'For me?' said I. 'Extraordinary! What – for me? Certainly – my dear sir – certainly not for me. Why, it's ... '

Mr Despard turned about and smiled at me.

'You are Captain McMillin's great-nephew, you know, Mr Canevin.'

So that was it. My great-uncle, one of my Scots kinsfolk, my great-uncle who had died many years before I had seen the light of day, my grandfather's oldest brother, the one who had been in the British Army and later a planter here on Santa Cruz. He had been the very last person I should have thought of, and now –

The police boat landed smartly at the concrete jetty. Mr Despard and I landed, and in the lowering dusk I could not help noticing the quietly-expressed but very genuine interest of the thousand or more Negroes who thronged the wharf as they courteously parted a way for us while we proceeded toward the groups of white people, thronging forward now with a unanimous and unmistakable greeting shining from dozens of kindly faces.

I will pass over the rest of that first evening ashore. At the end of it and its lavish hospitality I found myself comfortably installed in a small private hotel pending the final preparations to my own hired residence. I found every estate-house on Santa Cruz open to me. Hospitalities were showered upon me to the point of embarrassment, kindnesses galore, considerate and timely bits of information, help of every imaginable kind. I learned in this process much about my late great-uncle, all of which information was new to me, and it was not long after my arrival when it was arranged for me to visit his estate, Great Fountain.

I went with Hans Grumbach, in his Ford car, a bumpy journey of more than three hours up hills and through ravines and along precipitous trails on old roads incredibly roundabout and primitive.

All the way Hans Grumbach talked about this section of the island, now rarely visited. Here, up to ten years before, Grumbach had lived as the last of a long line of estate-managers which the old place had had in residence since the day, in 1879, when my Scottish relatives had sold their Santa Crucian holdings. It was now the property of the largest of the local sugar-growing corporations, known as the Copenhagen Concern. Because of its inaccessibility cultivation on it had finally been abandoned and Hans Grumbach had come to live in Frederiksted, married the daughter of a respectable Creole family, and settled down to keeping store on one of the town's side streets.

But, it came out, Grumbach had wanted for all those ten years, to go back to the northern hills. This trip to the old place stimulated his loquacity. He sang its praises: the beauty of its configuration, its magnificent views and vistas, the amazing fertility of its soil.

We arrived at last. All about us the vegetation had grown to be ideally tropical, the 'tropical' of old-fashioned pictures on calendars! The soil appeared to be rich, blackish 'bottomland'.

The old estate was in a sad state of rack and ruin. We walked over a good part of it under the convoy of the courteous black caretaker, and looked out over its rolling domain from various angles and coigns of vantage. The Negro village was half tumbled-down. The cabins remaining were all out of repair. The characteristic quick tropical inroads upon land 'turned out' of active cultivation were everywhere apparent. The ancient Great House was entirely gone. The farm buildings, though built of sound stone and mortar, were terribly dilapidated.

On that visit to Great Fountain I had my first experience of the 'grapevine' method of communication among Africans. I had been perhaps four days on the island, and it is reasonably certain that none of these people had ever so much as heard of me before; these obscure village Negroes cut off here in the hills from others the nearest of whom lived miles away. Yet, we had hardly come within a stone's throw of the remains of the village before we were surrounded by the total population, of perhaps twenty adults, and at least as many children of all ages.

As one would expect, these blacks were of very crude appearance; not only 'country Negroes' but that in an exaggerated form. Negroes in the West Indies have some tendency to live on the land where they originated, and as it happened most of these Negroes had been born up here and several generations of their forebears before them.

We had brought our lunch along, and this Hans Grumbach and I ate sitting in the Ford under the shade of a grove of magnificent old mahogany trees, and afterwards Grumbach took me up along a ravine to see the 'fountain' from which the old estate had originally derived its title.

The 'fountain' itself was a delicate natural waterfall, streaming thinly over the edge of a high rock. It was when we were coming back, by a slightly different route, for Grumbach wanted me to take in everything possible, that I saw the tree-man.

He stood, a youngish, coal-black Negro, of about twenty-five years, scantily dressed in a tattered shirt and a sketchy pair of trousers, about ten yards away from the field-path we were following and from which a clear view of a portion of the estate was obtained, and beside him, towering over him, was a magnificent coconut-palm. The Negro stood motionless. I thought, in fact, that he had gone asleep standing there, both arms clasped about the tree's smooth, elegant trunk, the right side of his face pressed against it.

He was not, however, asleep, because I looked back at him and his eyes – rather intelligent eyes, they seemed to me – were wide open, although to my surprise he had not changed his position, nor even the direction of his gaze, to glance at us; and, I was quite sure, he had not been in that village group when we had stood among them just before our lunch.

Grumbach did not speak to him, as he had done to every other Negro we had seen. Indeed, I observed that his face looked a trifle – well, apprehensive; and I thought he very slightly quickened his pace. I stepped nearer to him as we walked past the man and the tree, and then I noticed that his lips were moving, and when I came closer I observed that he was muttering to himself. I said, very quietly, almost in his ear: 'What's the matter with that fellow, Grumbach?'

Grumbach glanced at me out of the corner of his eye, and my impression that he was disturbed grew upon me.

'He's listening!' was all that I got out of Grumbach. I supposed, of course, that there was something odd about the fellow; perhaps he was slightly demented and might be an annoyance; and I supposed that Grumbach meant to convey that the young fellow was 'listening' for our possible comment upon him and his strange behaviour. Later, after we had said good-bye to the courteous caretaker and he had seen us off down the first hillside road, with its many ruts, I brought up the subject of the young black fellow at the tree.

'You mentioned that he was listening,' said I, 'so I dropped the matter, but, why does he do that, Grumbach – I mean, why does he stand against the tree in that unusual manner? Why, he didn't even gee his eyes to look at us, and that surprised me. They don't have visitors up here every day, I understand.'

'He was listening – *to his tree*!' said Hans Grumbach, as though reluctantly. '*That* was what I meant, Mr Canevin.' And he drew my attention to an extraordinarily picturesque ruined windmill, the kind once used for the grinding of cane in the old days of 'muscovado' sugar, which dominated a cone-like hillside off to our left as we bumped over the road. It was not until months later, when I had gained the confidence of Hans Grumbach, that that individual gave me any further enlightenment on the subject of the man and his tree.

Then I learned that, along with his nostalgia for the life of an agriculturist – an incurable matter with some persons I have found – there was mixed in with his feelings about the Great Fountain estate a kind of inconsistent thankfulness that he was no longer stationed there! This inconsistency, this being dragged sentimentally in two opposite directions, rather intrigued me. I saw something of Grumbach and got rather well acquainted with him as the months passed that first year of my residence. Bit by bit, in his reluctant manner of speech, it came out.

To put the whole picture of his mind on this subject together, I got the idea that Grumbach, while always suffering from a faint nostalgia for his deep-country residence and the joys of tilling the soil, felt, somehow, *safe* here in the town. If he chafed, mildly, at the restrictions of town life and his storekeeping, there was yet the certainty that 'something' – a vague matter at first, as it came out – was always hanging over him; something connected with a lingering fear.

The Negroes, it appeared – this came to me very gradually, of course – up there at Great Fountain, were not, quite, like the rest of the island's black population; in the two towns; out on the many sugar-estates; even those residues of village communities which continued to live, in that mild, beneficent climate, on 'turned-out' estate land because there was no one sufficiently interested to eject these squatters. No – the Great Fountain village was, somehow, at least in Hans Grumbach's dark hints, different; *sui generis*; a peculiar people.

They were, to begin with, almost purely of Dahomeyan stock. These Dahomeyans had drifted 'down the islands' from Haiti, beginning soon after the revolt against France in the early nineteenth century. They were tall, very black, extremely clannish blacks. And just as the Loromantyn slaves in British Jamaica had brought to the West Indies their Obay-i-, or herb-magic, so, it seemed, had the Dahomeyans carried with them from Guinea their *vodu*, which properly defined, means the practices accompanying the worship of 'the Snake'.

This worship, grown into a vast localized *cultus* in unfettered Hayti and in the Guiana hinterlands down in South America, is very imperfectly understood. But its accompaniments, all the charms, *ouangas*, philtres, potions, talismans, amulets, 'doctoring' and whatnot, have spread all through the West India islands, and these are thoroughly established in highly developed and widely variant forms. Haiti is its West Indian home, of course. But down in French Martinique its extent and intensity is a fair rival to the Haitian supremacy. It is rife on Dominica, Guadeloupe, even on British Montserrat. Indeed, one might name every island from Cuba to Trinidad, and, allowing for the variations, the local preferences, and all such matters, one might say, and truly, that the *vodu*, generically described by the blacks themselves as 'obi', is very thoroughly established.

According to Grumbach, the handful of villagers at Great Fountain was very deeply involved in this sort of thing. Left to themselves as they had been for many years, forming a little, self-sustaining community of nearly pure-blooded Dahomeyans, they had, it seemed, reverted very nearly to their African type; and this, Grumbach alleged, was the fact despite their easy kindliness, their use of 'English', and the various other outward appearances which caused them to seem not greatly different from other 'country Negroes' on this island of Santa Cruz.

Grumbach had known Silvio Fabricius since he had been a pick'ny on the estate. He knew, so far as his limited understanding of black people's magic extended, all about Silvio. He had been estate-manager at the time the boy had begun his attentions to the great coconut palm. He had heard and seen what he called the 'stupidness' which had attended the setting apart of this neophyte. There had been three days – and nights; particularly the nights – when not a single plantation-hand would do a piece of work for any consideration. It was, as Grumbach bitterly remembered it all, 'the crop season'. His employers, not sensing, businessmen as they were, any underlying reason for no work done when they needed the cane from Great Fountain for their grinding-mill, had been hard on him. They had, in Santa Crucian phraseology, 'pressed him' for cane deliveries. And there, in his village, quite utterly ignoring his authority as estate-manager, those blacks had danced and pounded drums, and burned flares, and weaved back and forth in their interminable ceremonies – 'stupidness' – for three strategic days and nights, over something which had Silvio Fabricius, then a rising pick-ny of twelve or thirteen, as its apparent center and underlying cause. It was no wonder that Hans Grumbach raved and probably swore mightily and threatened the estate-hands.

But his anger and annoyance, the threats and cajolings, the offers of 'snaps' of rum, and pay for piece-work; all these efforts to get his ripe cane cut and delivered had come to nothing. The carts stood empty. The mules gravely ate the long guinea-grass. The canetops waved in the soft breath of the North-East Trade Wind, while those three days stretched themselves out to their conclusion.

This conclusion, which was ceremonial, took place in the daytime, about ten o'clock in the morning of the fourth day. After that, which was a very brief and apparently meaningless matter indeed, the hands sheepishly resumed the driving of their mule-carts and the swinging of their cane-bills, and once more the Fountain cane travelled slowly down the rutted hill road toward the factory below. On that morning, before resuming their work, the whole village had accompanied young Silvio Fabricius in silence as he walked ahead of them up toward the source of the perennial stream, stepped out into the field, and clasped his arms about a young, but tall and promising coconut palm which stood there as though accidentally in solitary towering grandeur. There the villagers had left the little black boy when they turned away and filed slowly and silently back to the village and to their interrupted labor.

And there, beside his tree, Grumbach said, Silvio Fabricius had stood ever since, only occasionally coming in to the village and then at any hour of the day or night, apparently 'reporting' something to the oldest inhabitant, a gnarled, ancient grandfather with pure white wool. After such a brief visit Fabricius would at once, and with an unshaken gravity, return to his tree. Food, said Grumbach, was always carried out to him from the village. He toiled not, neither spun! There, day and night, under the blazing sun, through showers and drenching downpours, erect, apparently unsleeping – unless he slept standing up against his tree as Grumbach suspected – stood Silvio Fabricius, and there he had stood, except when he climbed the tree to trim out the 'cloth' or chase out a rat intent on nesting up there, or to gather the coconuts, for eleven years.

The coconuts, it seemed, were his perquisite. They were, Grumbach said, absolutely *tabu* to anybody else. It was over the question of some green coconuts from this superior tree that Grumbach himself, with all his authority as estate-manager behind his demand, had come to grips with Silvio Fabricius; or, to be more precise, with the entire estate-village.

I never succeeded in getting this story in detail from Grumbach, who was plainly reluctant to tell it. It reflected, you see, upon him; his authority as estate-manager, his pride, were here heavily involved. But, as I gathered it, his house-man, sent to that particular tree for a basket of green coconuts – Grumbach was entertaining some friends and wanted the coconut-water and jelly to put in a Danish concoction based on Holland gin – had returned half an hour later, delivered the coconuts, and later, it came out that he had gone *down* the hill to a neighbouring estate for the nuts. Taken to task for this duplicity, the house-man had balked, 'gone stupid' over the affair, and upon the dispute which followed the village itself had joined in. The conclusion, as Grumbach gathered it, to his great mystification, was that the coconut tree 'belonged to' young Silvio Fabricius, was *tabu*, and that the village was solid against him on the issue. He, the manager, with control of everything, could not get coconuts from the best tree on the estate! This, attributed to the usual black 'stupidness', had rankled. It also more or less accounted for Grumbach's attitude toward Silvio Fabricius, an attitude which I myself had witnessed. That his 'fear' of this young Negro went deeper than that, I sensed, however. I was, later, to see that suspicion justified.

For a long time I had no occasion to revisit Great Fountain. But six years later, while in the States during the summer, I made the acquaintance of a man named Carrington who wanted to know 'all about the Virgin Islands' with a view to investing some money there in a proposal to grow pineapples on a large scale. I talked with Mr Carrington at some length, and in the course of our discussions it occurred to me that Great Fountain estate would be virtually ideal for his purpose. Here was a very considerable acreage of rich land: the Copenhagen Company would probably rent it out for a period of ten years for a very reasonable price since it was bringing them in nothing. I spread before Carrington these advantages, and he traveled down on the ship with me that autumn to make an investigation in person.

Carrington, a trained fruit-grower, spent a day with me on the estate, and thereafter with characteristic American energy started in to put his plan into practice. A lease was easily secured, the village was repaired and the fallen stone cabins rebuilt, and within a few weeks cultivating machinery of the most modern type began to arrive on the Frederiksted wharf.

After a considerable consultation with Hans Grumbach, to whose lamentations over the restrictions of town-life I had been listening for years, I recommended him to Mr Carrington as manager of the laborers, and Hans, after going over the matter with his good wife and coming to an amicable understanding, went back to Great Fountain where a manager's house had been thrown up for him on the foundation of one of the ruined buildings. At Carrington's direction, Grumbach set the estate laborers at work on the job of repairing the roads; and, as the village cabins went up, one after another, laborers, enticed by the prospect of good wages, filled them up and ancient Great Fountain became once more a busy scene of industry.

During these preparatory works I spent a good deal of time on the estate because I was naturally interested in Joseph Carrington's venture being a success. I had, indeed, put several thousand dollars into it myself, not solely because it looked like a good investment, but in part for sentimental reasons connected with my great-uncle. Being by then thoroughly familiar with the odd native speech, I made it a point to visit the village and talk at length with the 'people'. They were courteous to me, markedly so; deferential would be a better word to describe their attitude. This, of course, was wholly due to the family connection. Only a very few of them, and those the oldest, had any personal recollection of Captain McMillin, but his memory was decidedly green among them. The old gentleman had been greatly beloved by the Negroes of the island.

In the course of my reading I had run across the peculiar affair of a 'tree-man'. I understood, therefore, the status of Silvio Fabricius in that queer little black community; why he had been 'devoted' to the tree; what were the underlying reasons for that strange sacrifice.

It was, on the part of that handful of nearly pure-blooded Daho-meyan villagers there at my great-uncle's old place, a revival of a custom probably as old as African civilization. For – the African *has* a civilization. He is at a vast disadvantage when among Caucasians, competing, as he necessarily must, with Caucasian 'cultures'. His native problems are entirely different, utterly diverse, from the white man's. The African's whole history among us Caucasians is a history of more or less successful adaptation. Place an average American business man in the heart of 'uncivilized' Africa, in the Liberian hinterland, for example, and what will he do – how survive? The answer is simple. He will perish miserably, confronted with the black jungle night, the venomous reptilian and insect life, the attacks of wild beasts, the basic problems of how to feed and warm himself – for even this last is an African problem. I know. I have been on safari in Uganda, in British East Africa, in Somali-land. I speak from experience.

Africans, supposedly static in cultural matters, have solved all these problems. And, very prominent among these, especially as it con-cerns the agricultural peoples – for there are, perhaps, as many black nations, kindreds, peoples, tongues, as there are Caucasian – is, of course, the question of weather.

Hence, the 'tree-man'.

Set apart with ceremonies which were ancient when Hammurabi sat on his throne in Babylon, a young boy is dedicated to a forest tree. Thereafter he spends his life beside that tree, cares for it, tends it, listens to it; becomes 'the-brother-of-the-tree' in time. He is truly 'set apart'. To the tree he devotes his entire life, dying at last beside it, in its shade. And – this is African 'culture' if you will; a culture of which we Caucasians get, perhaps, the faint reactions in the (to us) meaningless jumble of Negro superstition which we sense all about us; the 'stupidness' of the West Indies; faint, incomprehensible reflections of a system as practical, as dogmatic, as utilitarian, as the now well-nigh universal system of synthetic exercise for the tired businessman which goes by the name of golf!

These Negroes at Great Fountain were, primarily, agriculturists. They had the use of the soil bred deeply in their blood and bones. That, indeed, is why the canny French brought their Hispaniola slaves from Dahomey. Left to themselves at the old estate in the north central hills of Santa Cruz the little community rapidly reverted to their African ways. They tilled the soil, sporadically, it is true, yet they tilled it. They needed a weather prognosticator. There are sudden storms in summer throughout the vast sweep of the West India Islands, devastating storms, hurricanes indeed; long, wasting periods of drought. They needed a tree-man up there. They set apart Silvio Fabricius.

That fact made the young fellow what a white man would call 'sacred'. Not for nothing had they danced and performed their 'stupid' rites those three long days and nights to the detriment of Hans Grumbach's deliveries. No. Silvio Fabricius, from the moment he had clasped his arms about that growing coconut-palm, was as much a person 'set apart', dedicated, as any white man's pundit, priest, or yogi. Hence the various *tabus* which, like the case of the green coconuts, had puzzled Hans Grumbach. He must never take his attention away from the tree. There, beside it, he was consecrated to live and to die. When he departed from his 'brother' the tree, it was only for the purpose of reporting something which the tribe should know; something, that is, which his brother the tree had told him! There would be drenching rain the second day following. A plague of small green flies would, the third day later, come to annoy the animals. The banana grove must be propped forthwith. Otherwise, a high wind, two days hence, would nullify all the work of its planting and care.

Such were the messages that Silvio Fabricius, austere, introspective, unnoticing, his mind fully preoccupied with his brotherhood to the tree, brought to his tribe; proceeding, the message delivered, austerely back to his station beside the magnificent palm.

All this, because of my status as the great-nephew of an old Bukra whom he remembered with love and reverence, and because he discovered that I knew about tree-men and many other matters usually sealed books to Bukras, the old fellow who was the village patriarch, who, by right of his seniority, received and passed on from Silvio the messages from Silvio's brother the tree, amply substantiated. There was nothing secretive about him, once he knew my interest in these things. Such procedure as securing the possession of a tree-man for his tribe seemed to the old man entirely reasonable; there was no necessary secret about it, certainly not from sympathetic me, the 'yoong marster' of Great Fountain Estate.

And Hans Grumbach, once he had finished with his road-work, not being aware of all this, but sensing something out of the ordinary and hence to be feared about Silvio Fabricius and his palm tree, decided to end the stupidness out there. Grumbach decided to cut down the tree.

If I had had any inkling of this intention I could have saved Grumbach. It would have been a comparatively simple matter for me to have said enough to Carrington to have him forbid it; or, indeed, as a partner in the control of the estate, to forbid it myself. But I knew nothing about it, and have in my statement of his intention to destroy the tree supplied my own conception of his motives.

Grumback, although virtually Caucasian in appearance, was of mixed blood, and quite without the Caucasian background of superior quality which makes the educated West Indian *mestizo* the splendid citizen he is in so many notable instances. His white ancestry was derived from a grandfather, a Schleswig-Holsteiner, who had been a sergeant of the Danish troops stationed on Santa Cruz and who, after the term of his enlistment had expired, had married into a respectable colored family, and remained on the island. Grumbach was without the Caucasian aristocrat's tolerance for the preoccupations of the blacks. To him such affairs were 'stupidness', merely. Like others of his kind he held the black people in a kind of contempt; was wholly, I imagine, without sympathy for them, though a worthy fellow enough in his limited way. And, perhaps, he had not enough Negro in him to understand instinctively even so much as what Silvio Fabricius, the tree-man, stood for in his community.

I had, too, you will remember, known something in those six years, of his viewpoints, his reactions to the 'stupidness', and, specifically, some knowledge at least of his direct reaction, his pique and resentment, as these arose from his contacts with the tree-man. As I have indicated, the element of fear colored this attitude.

He chose, cannily, one of the periods when Fabricius was away from his tree, reporting to the village. It was early in the afternoon, and Grumbach, having finished his roadwork several days before, was directing a group of laborers who were grubbing ancient 'bush' – heavy undergrowth, brush, rank weeds, small trees – from along the winding trail which led from the village to the fountain or waterfall. This was now feeding a tumbling stream which Carrington intended to dam, lower down, for a central reserve reservoir.

The majority, if not all, of these laborers under his eye at the moment were new to the village; members of the increasing group which were coming into the restored stone cabins as fast as these became habitable. They were cutting out the brush with machetes, canebills, and knives; and, for the small trees, a couple of axes were being used from time to time. This work was being done quite near the great tree, and from his position in the roadway overlooking his gang, Grumbach must have seen the tree-man leave his station and start toward the village with one of his 'messages'.

This opportunity – he had, unquestionably, made up his mind about it all – was too good to be lost. As I learned from the two men whom he detached from his grubbing-gang and took with him, Silvio Fabricius was hardly out of sight over the sweep of the lower portion of the great field near the upper edge of which the coconut-palm towered, when Grumbach called to the two axe-men to follow him, and, with a word to the rest of the gang, led the way across the field's edge to the tree.

About this time Carrington and I were returning from one of our inspections of the fountain. We had been up there several times of late, since the scheme for the dam had been working in our minds. We were returning toward the village and the construction work progressing there along the same pathway through the big field from which, years before, I had had my first sight of the tree-man.

As we came in sight of the tree, toward which I invariably looked when I was near it, I saw, of course, that Fabricius was not there. Grumbach and his two laborers stood under it, Grumbach talking to the men. One of them as we approached – we were still perhaps a hundred yards distant – shook his head emphatically. He told me later that Grumbach had led them straight to the tree and com-manded them to chop it down.

Both men had demurred. They were not of the village, it is true, not, certainly, Dahomeyans. But – they had some idea, even after generations away from 'Guinea', that here was something strange;

something over which the suitable course was to 'go stupid'. Both men, therefore, 'went stupid' forthwith.

Grumbach, as was usual with him, poor fellow, was vastly annoyed by this process. I could hear him barge out at the laborers; see him gesticulate. Then from the nearest, he seized the axe and attacked the tree himself. He struck a savage blow at it, then, gathering himself together, for he was stout like the middle-aged of all his class, and unused to such work, he struck again, somewhat above the place where the first axe-blow had landed on the tree.

'You'd better stop him, Carrington,' said I, 'and I will explain my reasons to you afterward.'

Carrington cupped his hands and shouted, and both Negroes looked toward us. But Grumbach, apparently, had not heard, or, if he had, supposed that the words were directed to somebody other than himself. Thus, everybody within view was occupied, you will note – Carrington looking at Grumbach; the two laborers looking toward us; Grumbach intent upon making an impression on the tough coconut wood. I alone, for some instinctive reason, thought suddenly of Silvio Fabricius, and directed my gaze toward the point, down the long field, over which horizon he would appear when returning.

Perhaps it was the sound of the axe's impact against his brother the tree apprehended by a set of senses for seventeen years attuned to the tree's moods and rustlings, to the 'messages' which his brother the tree imparted to him; perhaps some uncanny instinct merely, that arrested him in his course toward the village down there, carrying the current 'message' from the tree about tomorrow's weather.

As I looked, Silvio Fabricius, running lightly, erect, came over the distant horizon of the lower field's bosomed slope. He stopped there, a distant figure, but clearly within my view. Without taking my eyes off him I spoke again to Carrington.

'You must stop Grumbach, Carrington – there's more in this than you know. Stop him – at once!'

And, as Carrington shouted a second time, Grumbach raised the axe for the third blow at the tree, the blow which did not land.

As the axe came up, Silvio Fabricius, a distant figure down there, reached for the small sharp canebill which hung beside him from his trouser-belt, a cutting tool with which he smoothed the bark of his brother the tree on occasion, cut out annually the choking mass of 'cloth' from its top, removed fading fronds as soon as their decay reached the stage where they were no longer benefiting the tree, cut his coconuts. I could see the hot sunlight flash against the wide blade of the canebill as though it had been a small heliograph-mirror. Fabricius was about a thousand yards away. He raised the canebill empty in the air, and with it made a sudden, cutting, pulling motion downward; a grave, almost a symbolic movement. Fascin-ated, I watched him return the canebill to its place, on its hook, fastened to the belt at the left side.

But, abruptly, my attention was distracted to what was going on nearer at hand. Carrington's shout died, half-uttered. Simultan-eously I heard the yells of uncontrollable sudden terror from the two laborers at the tree's foot. My eyes, snatched away from the distant tree-man, turned to Carrington beside me, glimpsing a look of terrified apprehension; then, with the speed of thought, toward the tree where one laborer was in the act of falling face-downward on the ground – I caught the terrified white gleam of his rolled eyes – the other, twisting himself away from the tree toward us, the very personification of crude horror, his hands over his eyes. And my glance was turned just in time to see the great coconut which, detached from its heavy, fibrous cordage up there, sixty feet about the ground, struck Grumbach full and true on the wide pitch helmet which he affected, planterwise, against the sun.

He seemed almost to be driven into the ground by the impact. The axe flew off at an angle past the tree.

He never moved. And when, with the help of the two laborers, Carrington and I, having summoned a cart from the nearby road-gang cutting bushes, lifted the body, the head which had been that poor devil Grumbach's, was merely a mass of sodden pulp.

We took the body down the road in the cart, toward his newly erected manager's house. And a few yards along our way Silvio Fabricius passed us, running erectly, his somber face expressionless, his stride a kind of dignified lope, glancing not to right or left, speeding straight to his brother the tree which had been injured in his absence.

Looking back, where the road took a turn, I saw him, leaning now close beside the tree, his long fingers probing the two gashes which Hans Grumbach, who would never swing another axe, had made there, about two feet above the ground; while aloft the glorious fronds of the massive tree burgeoned like great sails in the afternoon Trade.

Later that afternoon we sent the mortal remains of Hans Grum-bach down the long hill road to Frederiksted in a cart, decently disposed, after telephoning his wife's relatives to break the sorrowful news to her. It was Carrington who telephoned, at my suggestion. I told him that they would appreciate it, he being the head of the company. Such *nuances* have their meaning in the West Indies where the finer shades are of an importance. He explained that it was an accident, gave the particulars as he had seen them with his own eyes – Grumbach had been working under a tall coconut-palm and a heavy coconut, falling, had struck him and killed him instantly. It had been a quite merciful death.

The next morning, I walked up toward the fountain again, alone, after a sleepless night of cogitation. I walked across the section of field between the newly-grubbed roadside and the great tree. I walked straight up to the tree-man, stood beside him. He paid no attention to me whatever. I spoke to him.

'Fabricius,' said I, 'it is necessary that I should speak to you.'

The tree-man turned his gaze upon me gravely. Seen thus, face to face, he was a remarkably handsome fellow, now about thirty years of age, his features regular, his expression calm, inscrutable; wise with a wisdom certainly not Caucasian, such as to put into my mind the phrase: 'not of this world'. He bowed, gravely, as though assuring me of his attention.

I said: 'I was looking at you yesterday afternoon when you came back to your tree, over the lower end of the field – down there.' I indicated where he had stood with a gesture. Again he bowed, without any change of expression.

'I wish to have you know,' I continued, 'that I understand; that no one else besides me saw you, saw what you did – with the canebill, I mean. I wish you to know that what I saw I am keeping to myself. That is all.'

Silvio Fabricius the tree-man continued to look into my face, without any visible change whatever in his expression. For the third time he nodded, presumably to indicate that he understood what I had said, but utterly without any emotion whatever. Then, in a deep, resonant voice, he spoke to me, the first and last time I have ever heard him utter a word.

'Yo' loike to know, yoong marster,' said he, with an impressive gravity, 'me brudda' – he placed a hand against the tree's smooth trunk – ''t'ink hoighly 'bout yo', sar. Ahlso 'bout de enterprise fo' pineopples. Him please', sar. Ahlso marster; him indicate-me yo' course be serene an' ahlso of a profit.' The tree-man bowed again, and without another word or so much as a glance in my direction, detaching his attention from me as deliberately as he had given it when I first spoke to him, he turned toward his brother the tree, laid his face against its bark, and slowly encircled the massive trunk with his two great muscular black arms.

I arrived on the island in the middle of October 1928, coming down as usual from New York after my summer in the States. Great Fountain had suffered severely in the hurricane of the previous month, and when I arrived there I found Carrington well along with the processes of restoration. Many precautions had been taken beforehand and our property had been damaged because of these much less than the other estates. I had told Carrington, who had a certain respect for my familiarity with 'native manners and customs', enough about the tree-man and his functions tribally to cause him to heed the warning, transmitted by the now nearly helpless old patriarch of the village, and brought in by the tree-man four days before the hurricane broke – and two days before the government cable-advice had reached the island.

Silvio Fabricius had stayed beside his tree. On the third day, when it was for the first time possible for the villagers to get as far as the upper end of the great field near the fountain, he had been found, Carrington reported to me, lying in the field, dead, his face composed inscrutably, the great trunk of his brother the tree across his chest which had been crushed by its great weight when it had been uprooted by the wind and fallen.

And until they wore off there had been smears of earth, Carrington said, on the heads and faces of all the original Dahomeyan villagers and upon the heads and faces of several of the newer laborer families as well.

Passing of a God

'You say that when Carswell came into your hospital over in Port au Prince his fingers looked as though they had been wound with string,' said I, encouragingly.

'It is a very ugly story, that, Canevin,' replied Doctor Pelletier, still reluctant, it appeared.

'You promised to tell me,' I threw in.

'I know it, Canevin,' admitted Doctor Pelletier of the U.S. Navy Medical Corps, now stationed here in the Virgin Islands. 'But,' he proceeded, 'you couldn't use this story, anyhow. There are editorial *tabus*, aren't there? The thing is too – what shall I say? – too outrageous, too incredible.'

'Yes,' I admitted in turn, 'there are *tabus*, plenty of them. Still, after hearing about those fingers, as though wound with string – why not give me the story, Pelletier; leave it to me whether or not I "use" it. It's the story I want, mostly. I'm burning up for it!'

'I suppose it's your lookout,' said my guest. 'If you find it too gruesome for you, tell me and I'll quit.'

I plucked up hope once more. I had been trying for this story, after getting little scraps of it which allured and intrigued me, for weeks.

'Start in,' I ventured, soothingly, pushing the silver swizzle-jug after the humidor of cigarettes from which Pelletier was even now making a selection. Pelletier helped himself to the swizzle frowningly. Evidently he was torn between the desire to pour out the story of Arthur Carswell and some complication of feelings against doing so. I sat back in my wicker lounge-chair and waited.

Pelletier moved his large bulk about in his chair. Plainly now he was cogitating how to open the tale. He began, meditatively: 'I don't know as I ever heard public discussion of the malignant bodily growths except among medical people. Science knows little about them. The fact of such diseases, though, is well known to everybody, through campaigns of prevention, the life insurance companies, appeals for funds –

'Well, Carswell's case, primarily, is one of those cases.'

He paused and gazed into the glowing end of his cigarette.

' "Primarily"?' I threw in encouragingly.

'Yes. Speaking as a surgeon, that's where this thing begins, I suppose.'

I kept still, waiting.

'Have you read Seabrook's book, *The Magic Island*, Canevin?' asked Pelletier suddenly.

'Yes,' I answered. 'What about it?'

'Then I suppose that from your own experience knocking around the West Indies and your study of it all, a good bit of that stuff of Seabrook's is familiar to you, isn't it? – the *vodu*, and the hill customs, and all the rest of it, especially over in Haiti – you could check up on a writer like Seabrook, couldn't you, more or less?'

'Yes,' said I, 'practically all of it was an old story to me – a very fine piece of work, however, the thing clicks all the way through – an honest and thorough piece of investigation.'

'Anything in it new to you?'

'Yes – Seabrook's statement that there was an exchange of personalities between the sacrificial goat – at the "baptism" – and the young Black girl, the chapter he calls: *Girl-Cry – Goat-Cry*. That, at least, was a new one on me, I admit.'

'You will recall, if you read it carefully, that he attributed that phenomenon to his own personal "slant" on the thing. Isn't that the case, Canevin?'

'Yes,' I agreed, 'I think that is the way he put it.'

'Then,' resumed Doctor Pelletier, 'I take it that all that material of his – I notice that there have been a lot of story-writers using his terms lately! – is sufficiently familiar to you so that you have some clear idea of the Haitian-African demigods, like Ogoun Badagris, Damballa, and the others, taking up their residence for a short time in some devotee?'

'The idea is very well understood,' said I. 'Mr Seabrook mentions it among a number of other local phenomena. It was an old Negro who came up to him while he was eating, thrust his soiled hands into the dishes of food, surprised him considerably – then was surrounded by worshippers who took him to the nearest *houmfort* or *vodu*-house, let him sit on the altar, brought him food, hung all their jewelry on him, worshipped him for the time being; then, characteristically, quite utterly ignored the original old fellow after the "possession" on the part of the "deity" ceased and reduced him to an unimportant old pantaloon as he was before.'

'That summarizes it exactly,' agreed Doctor Pelletier. 'That, Can-evin, that kind of thing, I mean, is the real starting-place of this dreadful matter of Arthur Carswell.'

'You mean – ?' I barged out at Pelletier, vastly intrigued. I had had no idea that there was *vodu* mixed in with the case.

'I mean that Arthur Carswell's first intimation that there was anything pressingly wrong with him was just such a "possession" as the one you have recounted.'

'But – but,' I protested, 'I had supposed – I had every reason to believe, that it was a surgical matter! Why, you just objected to telling about it on the ground that – '

'Precisely,' said Doctor Pelletier, calmly. 'It was such a surgical case, but, as I say, it *began* in much the same way as the "occupation" of that old Negro's body by Ogoun Badagris or whichever one of their devilish deities that happened to be, just as, you say, is well known to fellows like yourself who go in for such things, and just as Seabrook recorded it.'

'Well,' said I, 'you go ahead in your own way, Pelletier. I'll do my best to listen. Do you mind an occasional question?'

'Not in the least,' said Doctor Pelletier considerately, shifted him-self to a still more pronouncedly recumbent position in my Chinese rattan lounge-chair, lit a fresh cigarette, and proceeded: 'Carswell had worked up a considerable intimacy with the snake-worship of interior Haiti, all the sort of thing familiar to you; the sort of thing set out, probably for the first time, in English at least, in Seabrook's book; at the gatherings, and the "baptism", and the sacrifices of the fowls and the bull, and the goats; the orgies of the worshippers, the boom and thrill of the *rata* drums – all that strange, incomprehensible, rather silly-surfaced, deadly-underneathed worship of "the Snake" which the Dahomeyans brought with them to old Hispaniola, now Haiti and the Dominican Republic.

'He had been there, as you may have heard, for a number of years; went there in the first place because everybody thought he was a kind of failure at home; made a good living, too; in a way nobody but an original-minded fellow like him would have thought of – shot ducks on the Léogane marshes, dried them, and exported them to New York and San Francisco to the United States's two largest Chinatowns!

'For a "failure", too, Carswell was a particularly smart-looking chap, in the English sense of that word. He was one of those fellows who was always shaved, clean, freshly groomed, even under the rather adverse conditions of his living, there in Léogane by the salt marshes; and of his trade, which was to kill and dry ducks. A fellow can get pretty careless and let himself go at that sort of thing, away from "home"; away, too, from such niceties as there are in a place like Port au Prince.

'He looked, in fact, like a fellow just off somebody's yacht the first time I saw him, there in the hospital in Port au Prince, and that, too, was right after a rather singular experience which would have unnerved or unsettled pretty nearly anybody.

'But not so old Carswell. No, indeed. I speak of him as "Old Carswell", Canevin. That, though, is a kind of affectionate term. He was somewhere about forty-five then; it was two years ago, you see, and, in addition to his being very spick and span, well groomed, you know, he looked surprisingly young, somehow. One of those faces which showed experience, but, along with the experience, a philosophy. The lines in his face were *good* lines, if you get what I mean – lines of humor and courage; no dissipation, no let down kind of lines, nothing of slackness such as you would see in the face of even a comparatively young beach-comber. No, as he strode into my office, almost jauntily, there in the hospital, there was nothing, nothing whatever, about him, to suggest anything else but a prosperous fellow American, a professional chap, for choice, who might, as I say, have just come ashore from somebody's yacht.

'And yet – good God, Canevin, the story that came out – '

Naval surgeon though he was, with service in Haiti, at sea, in Nicaragua, the China Station to his credit, Doctor Pelletier rose at this point, and, almost agitatedly, walked up and down my gallery. Then he sat down and lit a fresh cigarette.

'There is,' he said, reflectively, and as though weighing his words carefully, 'there is, Canevin, among various others, a somewhat "wild" theory that somebody put forward several years ago, about the origin of malignant tumors. It never gained very much approval among the medical profession, but it has, at least, the merit of originality, and – it was new. Because of those facts, it had a certain amount of currency, and there are those, in and out of medicine, who still believe in it. It is that there are certain *nuclei*, certain masses, so to speak, of the bodily material which have persisted – not generally, you understand, but in certain cases – among certain persons, the kind who are "susceptible" to this horrible disease, which, in the prenatal state, did not develop fully or normally – little places in the bodily structure, that is – if I make myself clear – which remain undeveloped.

'Something, according to this hypothesis, something like a sudden jar, or a bruise, a kick, a blow with the fist, the result of a fall, or what not, causes traumatism – physical injury, that is, you know – to one of the focus-places, and the undeveloped little mass of material *starts in to grow*, and so displaces the normal tissue which surrounds it.

'One objection to the theory is that there are at least two varieties, well-known and recognized scientifically; the carcinoma, which is itself subdivided into two kinds, the hard and the soft carcinomae, and the sarcoma, which is a soft thing, like what is popularly understood by a "tumor". Of course they are all "tumors", particular kinds of tumors, malignant tumors. What lends a certain credibility to the theory I have just mentioned is the malignancy, the growing element. For, whatever the underlying reason, they grow, Canevin, as is well recognized, and this explanation I have been talking about gives a reason for the growth. The "malignancy" is, really, that one of the things seems to have, as it were, its own life. All this, probably, you know?'

I nodded. I did not wish to interrupt. I could see that this side-issue on a scientific by-path must have something to do with the story of Carswell.

'Now,' resumed Pelletier, 'notice this fact, Canevin. Let me put it in the form of a question, like this: To what kind, or type, of *vodu* worshipper, does the "possession" by one of their deities occur – from your own knowledge of such things, what would you say?'

'To the incomplete; the abnormal, to an *old* man, or woman,' said I, slowly, reflecting, 'or – to a child, or, perhaps, to an idiot. Idiots, ancient crones, backward children, "town-fools" and the like, all over Europe, are supposed to be in some mysterious way *en rapport* with deity – or with Satan! It is an established peasant belief. Even among the Mahometans, the moron or idiot is "the afflicted of God". There is no other better-established belief along such lines of thought.'

'Precisely!' exclaimed Pelletier. 'And Canevin, go back once more to Seabrook's instance that we spoke about. What type of person was "possessed"?'

'An old doddering man,' said I, 'one well gone in his dotage apparently.'

'Right once more! Note now, two things. First, I will admit to you, Canevin, that that theory I have just been expounding never made much of a hit with me. It might be true, but – very few first-rate men in our profession thought much of it, and I followed that negative lead and didn't think much of it, or, indeed, much about it. I put it down to the vaporings of the theorist who first thought it out and published it, and let it go at that. Now, Canevin, *I am convinced that it is true*! The second thing, then: When Carswell came into my office in the hospital over there in Port au Prince, the first thing I noticed about him – I had never seen him before, you see – was a peculiar, almost an indescribable, discrepancy. It was between his general appearance of weather-worn cleanliness, general fitness, his "smart" appearance in his clothes – all that, which fitted together about the clean-cut, open character of the fellow; and what I can only describe as a pursiness. He seemed in good condition, I mean to say, and yet – there was something, somehow, *flabby* somewhere in his makeup. I couldn't put my finger on it, but – it was there, a suggestion of something that detracted from the impression he gave as being an upstanding fellow, a good-fellow-to-have-beside-you-in-a-pinch – that kind of person.

'The second thing I noticed, it was just after he had taken a chair beside my desk, was his fingers, and thumbs. They were swollen, Canevin, looked sore, as though they had been wound with string. That was the first thing I thought of, being wound with string. He saw me looking at them, held them out to me abruptly, laid them side by side, his hands I mean, on my desk, and smiled at me.

' "I see you have noticed them, Doctor," he remarked, almost jovially. "That makes it a little easier for me to tell you what I'm here for. It's – well, you might put it down as a 'Symptom'."

'I looked at his fingers and thumbs; every one of them was affected in the same way; and ended up with putting a magnifying glass over them.

'They were all bruised and reddened, and here and there on several of them, the skin was abraded, broken, *circularly* – it was a most curious-looking set of digits. My new patient was addressing me again.

' "I'm not here to ask you riddles, Doctor," he said, gravely, this time, "but – would you care to make a guess at what did that to those fingers and thumbs of mine?"

' "Well," I came back at him, "without knowing what's happened, it *looks* as if you'd been trying to wear about a hundred rings, all at one time, and most of them didn't fit!"

'Carswell nodded his head at me. "Score one for the medico," said he, and laughed. "Even numerically you're almost on the dot, sir. The precise number was one hundred and six!"

'I confess, I stared at him then. But he wasn't fooling. It was a cold, sober, serious fact that he was stating; only, he saw that it had a humorous side, and that intrigued him, as anything humorous always did, I found out after I got to know Carswell a lot better than I did then.'

'You said you wouldn't mind a few questions, Pelletier,' I interjected.

'Fire away,' said Pelletier. 'Do you see any light, so far?'

'I was naturally figuring along with you, as you told about it all,' said I. 'Do I infer correctly that Carswell, having lived there – how long, four or five years or so – ?'

'Seven, to be exact,' put in Pelletier.

' – that Carswell, being pretty familiar with the native doings, had mixed into things, got the confidence of his Black neighbors in and around Léogane, become somewhat "adept", had the run of the *houmforts*, so to speak – "*votre bougie, M'sieu*" – the fortune-telling at the festivals, and so forth, and – had been "visited" by one of the Black deities? That, apparently, if I'm any judge of tendencies, is what your account seems to be leading up to. Those bruised fingers – the one hundred and six rings – good heavens, man, is it really possible?'

'Carswell told me all about that end of it, a little later – yes, that was, precisely, what happened – but that, surprising, incredible as it seems, is only the small end of it all. You just wait – '

'Go ahead,' said I, 'I am all ears, I assure you!'

'Well, Carswell took his hands off the desk after I had looked at them through my magnifying glass, and then waved one of them at me in a kind of deprecating gesture.

' "I'll go into all that, if you're interested to hear about it, Doctor," he assured me, "but that isn't what I'm here about." His face grew suddenly very grave. "Have you plenty of time?" he asked. "I don't want to let my case interfere with anything."

' "Fire ahead," says I, and he leaned forward in his chair.

' "Doctor," says he, "I don't know whether or not you ever heard of me before. My name's Carswell, and I live over Léogane way. I'm an American, like yourself, as you can probably see, and, even after seven years of it, out there, duck-hunting, mostly, with virtually no White-man's doings for a pretty long time, I haven't 'gone native' or anything of the sort. I wouldn't want you to think I'm one of those wasters." He looked up at me inquiringly for my estimate of him. He had been by himself a good deal; perhaps too much. I nodded at him. He looked me in the eye, squarely, and nodded back. "I guess we understand each other," he said. Then he went on.

' "Seven years ago, it was, I came down here. I've lived over there even since. What few people know about me regard me as a kind of failure, I dare say. But – Doctor, there was a reason for that, a pretty definite reason. I won't go into it beyond your end of it – the medical end, I mean. I came down because of this."

'He stood up then, and I saw what made that "discrepancy" I spoke about, that "flabbiness" which went so ill with the general cut of the man. He turned up the lower ends of his white drill jacket and put his hand a little to the left of the middle of his stomach. "Just notice this," he said, and stepped toward me.

'There, just over the left center of that area and extending up toward the spleen, on the left side, you know, there was a protuberance. Seen closely it was apparent that here was some sort of internal growth. It was that which had made him look flabby, stomachish.

' "This was diagnosed for me in New York," Carswell explained, "a little more than seven years ago. They told me it was inoperable then. After seven years, probably, I dare say it's worse, if anything. To put the thing in a nutshell, Doctor, I had to 'let go' then. I got out of a promising business, broke off my engagement, came here. I won't expatiate on it all, but – it was pretty tough, Doctor, pretty tough. I've lasted all right, so far. It hasn't troubled me – until just lately. That's why I drove in this afternoon, to see you, to see if anything could be done."

' "Has it been kicking up lately?" I asked him.

' "Yes," said Carswell, simply. "They said it would kill me, probably within a year or so, as it grew. It hasn't grown – much. I've lasted a little more than seven years, so far."

' "Come into the operating-room," I invited him, "and take your clothes off, and let's get a good look at it."

' "Anything you say," returned Carswell, and followed me back into the operating-room then and there.

'I had a good look at Carswell, first, superficially. That preliminary examination revealed a growth quite typical, the self-contained, not the "fibrous" type, in the location I've already described, and about the size of an average man's head. It lay imbedded, fairly deep.

It was what we call "encapsulated". That, of course, is what had kept Carswell alive.

'Then we put the X-rays on it, fore-and-aft, and sidewise. One of those things doesn't always respond very well to skiagraphic examination, to the X-ray that is, but this one showed clearly enough. Inside it appeared a kind of dark, triangular mass, with the small end at the top. When Doctor Smithson and I had looked him over thoroughly, I asked Carswell whether or not he wanted to stay with us, to come into the hospital as a patient, for treatment.

' "I'm quite in your hands, Doctor," he told me. "I'll stay, or do whatever you want me to. But, first," and for the first time he looked a trifle embarrassed, "I think I'd better tell you the story that goes with my coming here! However, speaking plainly, do you think I have a chance?"

' "Well," said I, "speaking plainly, yes, there is a chance, maybe a 'fifty-fifty' chance, maybe a little less. On the one hand, this thing has been let alone for seven years since original diagnosis. It's probably less operable than it was when you were in New York. On the other hand, we know a lot more, not about these things, Mr Carswell, but about surgical technique, than they did seven years ago. On the whole, I'd advise you to stay and get ready for an operation, and, say about 'forty-sixty' you'll go back to Léogane, or back to New York if you feel like it, several pounds lighter in weight and a new man. If it takes you, on the table, well, you've had a lot more time out there gunning for ducks in Léogane than those New York fellows allowed you."

' "I'm with you," said Carswell, and we assigned him a room, took his "history", and began to get him ready for his operation.

'We did the operation two days later, at ten-thirty in the morning, and in the meantime Carswell told me his "story" about it.

'It seems that he had made quite a place for himself, there in Léogane, among the Negroes and the ducks. In seven years a man like Carswell, with his mental and dispositional equipment, can go quite a long way, anywhere. He had managed to make quite a good thing out of his duck-drying industry, employed five or six "hands" in his little wooden "factory", rebuilt a rather good house he had secured there for a song right after he had arrived, collected local antiques to add to the equipment he had brought along with him, made himself a real home of a peculiar, bachelor kind, and, above all, got in solid with the Black People all around him. Almost incidentally I gathered from him – he had no gift of narrative, and I had to question him a great deal – he had got onto, and into, the know in the *vodu* thing. There wasn't, as far as I could get it, any aspect of it all that he hadn't been in on, except, that is, "*la chèvre sans cornes*" – the goat without horns, you know – the human sacrifice on great occasions. In fact, he strenuously denied that the *voduists* resorted to that; said it was a canard against them; that they never, really, did such things, never had, unless back in prehistoric times, in Guinea – Africa.

'But, there wasn't anything about it all that he hadn't at his very finger ends, and at first-hand, too. The man was a walking encyclopedia of the native beliefs, customs, and practises. He knew, too, every turn and twist of their speech. He hadn't, as he had said at first, "gone native" in the slightest degree, and yet, without lowering his White Man's dignity by a trifle, he had got it all.

'That brings us to the specific happening, the "story" which, he had said, went along with his reason for coming in to the hospital in Port au Prince, to us.

'It appears that his sarcoma had never, practically, troubled him. Beyond noting a very gradual increase in its size from year to year, he said, he "wouldn't know he had one". In other words, characteristically, it never gave him any pain or direct annoyance beyond the sense of the wretched thing being there, and increasing on him, and always drawing him closer to that end of life which the New York doctors had warned him about.

'Then, it had happened only three days before he came to the hospital, he had gone suddenly unconscious one afternoon, as he was walking down his shell path to his gateway. The last thing he remembered then was being "about four steps from the gate". When he woke up, it was dark. He was seated in a big chair on his own front gallery, and the first thing he noticed was that his fingers and thumbs were sore and ached very painfully. The next thing was that there were flares burning all along the edge of the gallery, and down in the front yard, and along the road outside the paling fence that divides his property from the road, and in the light of these flares, there swarmed literally hundreds of Negroes, gathered about him and mostly on their knees; lined along the gallery and on the grounds below it; prostrating themselves, chanting, putting earth and sand on their heads; and, when he leaned back in his chair, something hurt the back of his neck, and he found that he was being nearly choked with the necklaces, strings of beads, gold and silver coin-strings, and other kinds, that had been draped over his head. His fingers, and the thumbs as well, were covered with gold and silver rings, many of them jammed on so as to stop the circulation.

'From his knowledge of their beliefs, he recognized what had happened to him. He had, he figured, probably fainted, although such a thing was not at all common with him, going down the pathway to the yard gate, and the Blacks had supposed him to be "possessed" as he had several times seen Black people, children, old men and women, morons, chiefly, similarly "possessed". He knew that, now that he was recovered from whatever had happened to him, the "worship" ought to cease and if he simply sat quiet and took what was coming to him, they would, as soon as they realized he was "himself" once more, leave him alone and he would get some relief from this uncomfortable set of surroundings; get rid of the necklaces and the rings; get a little privacy.

'But – the queer part of it all was that they didn't quit. No, the mob around the house and on the gallery increased rather than diminished, and at last he was put to it, from sheer discomfort – he said he came to the point where he felt he couldn't stand it all another instant – to speak up and ask the people to leave him in peace.

'They left him, he says, at that, right off the bat, immediately, without a protesting voice, but – and here was what started him on his major puzzlement – they didn't take off the necklaces and rings. No – they left the whole set of that metallic drapery which they had hung and thrust upon him right there, and, after he had been left alone, as he had requested, and had gone into his house, and lifted off the necklaces and worked the rings loose, the *next* thing that happened was that old Pa'p Josef, the local *papaloi*, together with three or four other neighboring *papalois*, witch-doctors from nearby villages, and followed by a very old man who was known to Carswell as the *hougan*, or head witch-doctor of the whole countryside thereabouts, came in to him in a kind of procession, and knelt down all around him on the floor of his living-room, and laid down gourds of cream and bottles of red rum and cooked chickens, and even a big china bowl of Tannia soup – a dish he abominated, said it always tasted like soapy water to him! – and then backed out leaving him to these comestibles.

'He said that this sort of attention persisted in his case, right through the three days that he remained in his house in Léogane, before he started out for the hospital; would, apparently, be still going on if he hadn't come in to Port au Prince to us.

'But – his coming in was not, in the least, because of this. It had puzzled him a great deal, for there was nothing like it in his experience, nor, so far as he could gather from their attitude, in the experience of the people about him, of the *papalois*, or even of the *hougan* himself. They acted, in other words, precisely as though the "deity" supposed to have taken up his abode within him had remained there, although there seemed no precedent for such an occurrence, and, so far as he knew, he felt precisely just as he had felt right along, that is, fully awake, and, certainly, not in anything like an abnormal condition, and, very positively, not in anything like a fainting-fit!

'That is to say – he felt precisely the same as usual except that – he attributed it to the probability that he must have fallen on the ground that time when he lost consciousness going down the pathway to the gate (he had been told that passers-by had picked him up and carried him to the gallery where he had awakened, later, these Good Samaritans meanwhile recognizing that one of the "deities" had indwelt him) – he felt the same except for recurrent, almost unbearable pains in the vicinity of his lower abdominal region.

'There was nothing surprising to him in this accession of the new painfulness. He had been warned that that would be the beginning of the end. It was in the rather faint hope that something might be done that he had come in to the hospital. It speaks volumes for the man's fortitude, for his strength of character, that he came in so cheerfully; acquiesced in what we suggested to him to do; remained with us, facing those comparatively slim chances with complete cheerfulness.

'For – we did not deceive Carswell – the chances were somewhat slim. "Sixty-forty" I had said, but as I afterward made clear to him, the favorable chances, as gleaned from the mortality tables, were a good deal less than that.

'He went to the table in a state of mind quite unchanged from his accustomed cheerfulness. He shook hands good-bye with Doctor Smithson and me, "in case", and also with Doctor Jackson, who acted as anesthetist.

'Carswell took an enormous amount of ether to get him off. His consciousness persisted longer, perhaps, than that of any surgical patient I can remember. At last, however, Doctor Jackson intimated to me that I might begin, and, Doctor Smithson standing by with the retracting forceps, I made the first incision. It was my intention, after careful study of the X-ray plates, to open it up from in front, in an

up-and-down direction, establish drainage directly, and, leaving the
wound in the sound tissue in front of it open, to attempt to get it
healed up after removing its contents. Such is the technique of the
major portion of successful operations.

'It was a comparatively simple matter to expose the outer wall.
This accomplished, and after a few words of consultation with
my colleague, I very carefully opened it. We recalled that the X-ray
had shown, as I mentioned, a triangular-shaped mass within. This
apparent content we attributed to some obscure chemical coloration
of the contents. I made my incisions with the greatest care and
delicacy, of course. The critical part of the operation lay right at this
point, and the greatest exactitude was indicated, of course.

'At last the outer coats of it were cut through, and retracted, and
with renewed caution I made the incision through the inmost wall of
tissue. To my surprise, and to Doctor Smithson's, the inside was
comparatively dry. The gauze which the nurse attending had caused
to follow the path of the knife, was hardly moistened. I ran my knife
down below the original scope of the last incision, then upward from
its upper extremity, greatly lengthening the incision as a whole, if
you are following me.

'Then, reaching my gloved hand within this long up-and-down
aperture, I felt about and at once discovered that I could get my
fingers in around the inner containing wall quite easily. I reached
and worked my fingers in farther and farther, finally getting both
hands inside and at last feeling my fingers touch inside the posterior
or rear wall. Rapidly, now, I ran the edges of my hands around inside,
and, quite easily, lifted out the "inside". This, a mass weighing
several pounds, of more or less solid material, was laid aside on the
small table beside the operating-table, and, again pausing to consult
with Doctor Smithson – the operation was going, you see, a lot
better than either of us had dared to anticipate – and being encour-
aged by him to proceed to a radical step which we had not hoped
to be able to take, I began the dissection from the surrounding,
normal tissue, of the now collapsed walls. This, a long, difficult, and
harassing job, was accomplished at the end of, perhaps, ten or twelve
minutes of gruelling work, and the bag-like thing, now completely
severed from the tissues in which it had been for so long imbedded,
was placed also on the side table.

'Doctor Jackson reporting favorably on our patient's condition
under the anesthetic, I now proceeded to dress the large aperture,
and to close the body-wound. This was accomplished in a routine

manner, and then, together, we bandaged Carswell, and he was taken back to his room to await awakening from the ether.

'Carswell disposed of, Doctor Jackson and Doctor Smithson left the operating-room and the nurse started in cleaning up after the operation; dropping the instruments into the boiler, and so on – a routine set of duties. As for me, I picked up the shell in a pair of forceps, turned it about under the strong electric operating-light, and laid it down again. It presented nothing of interest for a possible laboratory examination.

'Then I picked up the more or less solid contents which I had laid, very hastily, and without looking at it – you see, my actual removal of it had been done inside, in the dark for the most part and by the sense of feeling, with my hands, you will remember – I picked it up; I still had my operating-gloves on to prevent infection when looking over these specimens, and, still, not looking at it particularly, carried it out into the laboratory.

'Canevin' – Doctor Pelletier looked at me somberly through the very gradually fading light of late afternoon, the period just before the abrupt falling of our tropic dusk – 'Canevin,' he repeated, 'honestly, I don't know how to tell you! Listen now, old man, do something for me, will you?'

'Why, yes – of course,' said I, considerably mystified. 'What is it you want me to do, Pelletier?'

'My car is out in front of the house. Come on home with me, up to my house, will you? Let's say I want to give you a cocktail! Anyhow, maybe you'll understand better when you are there, *I want to tell you the rest up at the house, not here.* Will you please come, Canevin?'

I looked at him closely. This seemed to me a very strange, an abrupt, request. Still, there was nothing whatever unreasonable about such a sudden whim on Pelletier's part.

'Why, yes, certainly I'll go with you, Pelletier, if you want me to.'

'Come on, then,' said Pelletier, and we started for his car.

The doctor drove himself, and after we had taken the first turn in the rather complicated route from my house to his, on the extreme airy top of Denmark Hill, he said, in a quiet voice: 'Put together, now, Canevin, certain points, if you please, in this story. Note, kindly, how the Black People over in Léogane acted, according to Carswell's story. Note, too, that theory I was telling you about; do you recollect it clearly?'

'Yes,' said I, still more mystified.

'Just keep those two points in mind, then,' added Doctor Pelletier, and devoted himself to navigating sharp turns and plodding up two steep roadways for the rest of the drive to his house.

We went in and found his houseboy laying the table for his dinner. Doctor Pelletier is unmarried, keeps a hospitable bachelor establishment. He ordered cocktails, and the houseboy departed on this errand. Then he led me into a kind of office, littered with medical and surgical paraphernalia. He lifted some papers off a chair, motioned me into it, and took another near by. 'Listen, now!' he said, and held up a finger at me.

'I took that thing, as I mentioned, into the laboratory,' said he. 'I carried it in my hand, with my gloves still on, as aforesaid. I laid it down on a table and turned on a powerful light over it. It was only then that I took a good look at it. It weighed several pounds at least, was about the bulk and heft of a full-grown coconut, and about the same color as a hulled coconut, that is, a kind of medium brown. As I looked at it, I saw that it was, as the X-ray had indicated, vaguely triangular in shape. It lay over on one of its sides under that powerful light, and – Canevin, so help me God' – Doctor Pelletier leaned toward me, his face working, a great seriousness in his eyes – 'it moved, Canevin,' he murmured, 'and, as I looked – the thing *breathed!* I was just plain dumbfounded. A biological specimen like that – does not move, Canevin! I shook all over, suddenly. I felt my hair prickle on the roots of my scalp. I felt chills go down my spine. Then I remembered that here I was, after an operation, in my own biological laboratory. I came close to the thing and propped it up, on what might be called its logical base, if you see what I mean, so that it stood as nearly upright as its triangular conformation permitted.

'And then I saw that it had faint yellowish markings over the brown, and that what you might call its skin was moving, and – as I stared at the thing, Canevin – two things like little arms began to move, and the top of it gave a kind of convulsive shudder, and it opened straight at me, Canevin, a pair of eyes and looked me in the face.

'Those eyes – my God, Canevin, those eyes! They were eyes of something more than human, Canevin, something incredibly evil, something vastly old, sophisticated, cold, immune from anything except pure evil, the eyes of something that had been worshipped, Canevin, from ages and ages out of a past that went back before all known human calculation, eyes that showed all the deliberate, lurking wickedness that has ever been in the world. The eyes closed, Canevin, and the thing sank over onto its side, and heaved and shuddered convulsively.

'*It was sick, Canevin*; and now, emboldened, holding myself together, repeating over and over to myself that I had a case of the quavers, of post-operative "nerves", I forced myself to look closer, and as I did so I got from it a faint whiff of ether. Two tiny, ape-like nostrils, over a clamped-shut slit of a mouth, were exhaling and inhaling; drawing in the good, pure air, exhaling ether fumes. It popped into my head that Carswell had consumed a terrific amount of ether before he went under; we had commented on that, Doctor Jackson particularly. I put two and two together, Canevin, remembered we were in Haiti, where things are not like New York, or Boston, or Baltimore! Those Negroes had believed that the "deity" had not come out of Carswell, do you see? *That* was the thing that held the edge of my mind. The thing stirred uneasily, put out one of its "arms", groped about, stiffened.

'I reached for a nearby specimen-jar, Canevin, reasoning, almost blindly, that if this thing were susceptible to ether, it would be susceptible to – well, my gloves were still on my hands, and – now shuddering so that I could hardly move at all, I had to force every motion – I reached out and took hold of the thing – it felt like moist leather – and dropped it into the jar. Then I carried the carboy of preserving alcohol over to the table and poured it in till the ghastly thing was entirely covered, the alcohol near the top of the jar. It writhed once, then rolled over on its "back", and lay still, the mouth now open. Do you believe me, Canevin?'

'I have always said that I would believe anything on proper evidence,' said I, slowly, 'and I would be the last to question a statement of yours, Pelletier. However, although I have, as you say, looked into some of these things perhaps more than most, it seems, well – '

Doctor Pelletier said nothing. Then he slowly got up out of his chair. He stepped over to a wall-cupboard and returned, a wide-mouthed specimen-jar in his hand. He laid the jar down before me, in silence.

I looked into it, through the slightly discolored alcohol with which the jar, tightly sealed with rubber-tape and sealing-wax, was filled nearly to the brim. There, on the jar's bottom, lay such a thing as Pelletier had described (a thing which, if it had been 'seated', upright, would somewhat have resembled that representation of the happy little godling 'Billiken' which was popular twenty years ago as a desk ornament), a thing suggesting the sinister, the unearthly, even in this desiccated form. I looked long at the thing.

'Excuse me for even seeming to hesitate, Pelletier,' said I, reflectively.

'I can't say that I blame you,' returned the genial doctor. 'It is, by the way, the first and only time I have ever tried to tell the story to anybody.'

'And Carswell?' I asked. 'I've been intrigued with that good fellow and his difficulties. How did he come out of it all?'

'He made a magnificent recovery from the operation,' said Pelletier, 'and afterward, when he went back to Léogane, he told me that the Negroes, while glad to see him quite usual, had quite lost interest in him as the throne of a "divinity".'

'H'm,' I remarked, 'it would seem, that, to bear out – '

'Yes,' said Pelletier, 'I have always regarded that fact as absolutely conclusive. Indeed, how otherwise could one possibly account for – *this*?' He indicated the contents of the laboratory jar.

I nodded my head, in agreement with him. 'I can only say that – if you won't feel insulted, Pelletier – that you are singularly openminded, for a man of science! What, by the way, became of Carswell?'

The houseboy came in with a tray, and Pelletier and I drank to each other's good health.

'He came in to Port au Prince,' replied Pelletier after he had done the honors. 'He did not want to go back to the States, he said. The lady to whom he had been engaged had died a couple of years before; he felt that he would be out of touch with American business. The fact is – he had stayed out here too long, too continuously. But, he remains an "authority" on Haitian native affairs, and is consulted by the High Commissioner. He knows, literally, more about Haiti than the Haitians themselves. I wish you might meet him; you'd have a lot in common.'

'I'll hope to do that,' said I, and rose to leave. The houseboy appeared at the door, smiling in my direction.

The table is set for two, sar,' said he.

Doctor Pelletier led the way into the dining-room, taking it for granted that I would remain and dine with him. We are informal in St Thomas, about such matters. I telephoned home and sat down with him.

Pelletier suddenly laughed – he was halfway through his soup at the moment. I looked up inquiringly. He put down his soup spoon and looked across the table at me.

'It's a bit odd,' he remarked, 'when you stop to think of it! There's one thing Carswell doesn't know about Haiti and what happens there!'

'What's that?' I inquired.

'That – thing – in there,' said Pelletier, indicating the office with his thumb in the way artists and surgeons do. 'I thought he'd had troubles enough without *that* on his mind, too.'

I nodded in agreement and resumed my soup. Pelletier has a cook in a thousand.

Hill Drums

When Mr William Palgrave, British consul-general at St Thomas, Danish West Indies, stepped out of his fine residence on Denmark Hill, he looked, as one local wit had unkindly remarked, 'like an entire procession'! It could not be denied that handsome Mr Palgrave, diplomat, famed author of travel articles in the leading British magazines, made at all times a vastly imposing appearance, and that of this appearance he was entirely conscious.

One blazing afternoon in May, in the year of Grace, 1873, he came in stately fashion down the steps before his house toward his open carriage, waiting in the roadway below. On the box Claude, his Negro coachman, sagged down now under the broiling sun, conversed languidly with one La Touche Penn, a street loafer whose swart skin showed through various rents in a faded, many-times-washed blue dungaree shirt. Seeing the consul-general descending, Claude straightened himself abruptly while La Touche Penn slouched away, the white of an observant, rolled eye on Mr Palgrave.

As this ne'er-do-well strolled nonchalantly down the hill – the hard soles of a pair of feet which had never known the constriction of shoes making sandpaper-like sounds on the steep roadway – he whistled, softly, a nearly soundless little tune. Claude tightened his reins and the small, grass-fed, somnolent carriage-horses plucked up weary heads, ending their nap in the drowsy air. That was how Mr Palgrave liked to find his appointments – in order; ready for their functions. Mr Palgrave – so another St Thomas wit – was not unlike the late General Braddock whose fame is in the American histories; in short, a bureaucratic martinet whose wide travels, soon to bring him greater fame as the distinguished author of *Ulysses*, had failed signally to modify a native phlegmatic bluntness.

He came down the steps, a resplendent figure of a fine gentleman, dressed with a precise meticulousness in the exact mode of the London fashion, and, glancing after the furtive wastrel now well down the hill road, he caught the whistled tune. As he recognized it he frowned heavily, pursing his lips into a kind of pout which went ill with his appearance of portly, well-nourished grandeur. This accomplished diplomat was fastidious, easily annoyed. Not to put too fine a point upon it, he did not like St Thomas.

For one thing he disliked feminine names for places, and the capital town in those days was called Charlotte Amalia, after one of Denmark's queens. It was a coquette of a town, a slender brunette of black eyes and very red lips and cheeks; a Latin brunette of the smoldering, garish type; a brunette who ran to mantillas and *coquetteries* and very high heels on her glistening slippers.

Various times had Mr Palgrave in his blunt manner compared to Charlotte's disadvantage her alleged beauties with the sedate solidity of his last post, Trebizond in Armenia, whence he had come here to the Caribbean. At first these animadversions of his had been lightly received. Charlotte Amalia was a tolerant lass. This was, perhaps, only a strange variety of British banter! Society had let it go at that; would probably have forgotten all about it. But then the consul-general had made it plain, several times, that he had meant quite literally exactly what he had said. At that Charlotte, though still tolerantly, had been annoyed.

Finally he had been – unconsciously (Charlotte granted that quite definitely) – offensive. He had said certain things, used certain terms, which were – inadvisable. The way he used the word 'native', society agreed, was bad diplomacy, to put it mildly. Society continued, because he was a Caucasian and because of his official position, to invite him to its dinners, its routs, its afternoon teas, its swizzel parties. Government House took no notice of his ineptitudes, his comparisons.

The British families, and there were many of these permanently resident in St Thomas – Chatfields, Talbots, Robertsons, MacDesmonds – were, of course, the backbone of his social relationships. Some of them tried to give him hints when they saw how the wind was veering against him and wishing their own diplomatic representative to be clear of criticism, but these well-intentioned efforts slipped off Mr Palgrave's uncompromising broad back like water from a duck's!

Then he had really put his foot in it. The leading English magazine to which he was a valued contributor brought out an article by him – on Charlotte Amalia. Here the already famous author of travel articles had commented, in cold print, and disparagingly, upon the society of which he was, for the time being, an integral part. He had, too, been so injudicious as to compare Charlotte Amalia with Trebizond, vastly to the advantage of the Armenian capital. Trebizond, if the man had any sentiment in him, must, at that period, have seemed very attractive in retrospect.

It was chiefly the British West Indians who took in the magazine, but there were a few others. The news of the article spread like wildfire. Extra copies, at Lightbourn's store, were quickly exhausted. Other copies were ordered. Extant copies were worn dog-eared from frequent readings of that *faux pas*. It finished Mr Palgrave in Charlotte Amalia.

A consul-general, and of Great Britain, can hardly be ignored in a comparatively small community. Nevertheless Charlotte Amalia now drew in her perfumed skirts in no unmistakable gesture. There was, of course, nothing overt about this gesture. Charlotte was far too subtle, far too polite and sophisticated after the Continental manner, for anything crude; anything, that is, smacking of the consul-general's own methods! But there was an immediate difference, a delicate, subtle difference, which, as the weeks progressed, was to make its impact upon the consciousness of William Palgrave, through his thick mental epidermis, in a very strange manner indeed.

For it had penetrated elsewhere than to the very outer edges of St Thomas society. It had got down to Black Quashee himself, down through the various intervening social strata – minor officials, a few professional persons, shopkeepers, artisans – down to Quashee in his tattered shirt; shoeless, carefree Quashee, at the very bottom of Charlotte Amalia's social scheme.

Early that spring, at the time when house servants become mysteriously ill and have to be relieved of their duties for a few days, and the Rata drums, Fad'er, Mama, and Boula de Babee, may be heard to roll and boom nightly from the wooded hills in the island's interior, and the Trade Winds' changing direction leaves an almost palpable curtain of sultriness hanging over the hot, dry town on its three hillsides; in those days when the burros' tongues hang out of dry mouths along dusty roads and the centipedes come into the houses out of the dust and street dogs slink along blazing sidewalks in the narrow slits of house-shade under the broiling sun of late May-time – then, as the Black People came trickling back into the town from their three- or four-day sojourn in the hills when they make the spring songs – then it was that the Honorable William Palgrave began to be conscious of a vague, partly realized annoyance, an annoyance which seemed to hang in the air all about him.

As he lay on his handsome carved mahogany bedstead during an early-afternoon *siesta*; as he sat in his cool shaded office before his great desk with its dispatch-boxes in orderly rows, as he dressed for dinner after his late-afternoon bath – taken in the tin tub which he had lugged about the diplomatic world for the past eighteen years – at such times the new annoyance would drift to him in whispers, on the dull wings of the sultry air so hard to breathe for one of his portly habit.

It was a sound-annoyance, a vague, thin, almost imperceptible thing. It was a tune, with certain elusive words; words of which he heard recurrent bits, snatches, snippets, incidental mere light touches of a delicate, withering sarcasm – directed toward him as a child might blow thistle-down with faint derisive intent in the direction of somebody who has managed to incur its dislike.

The St Thomas Negroes, so it became borne in upon Mr Palgrave's understanding, had 'made a song on' him.

It was a characteristic, quickstep kind of song; something in the nature of a folksong. Of these there are various examples, like the one wherein the more urban St Thomian makes fun of his Santa Crucian neighbor by alleging that: 'De Crucian gyurl don' wish dey skin', and which ends on the rollicking chorus: 'Wash yo'self in a sardine-tin!'

In the course of the weeks in which he was obliged to listen to it, Mr Palgrave came to recognize the tune, and even a few of the words, which, because of almost incessant repetition, had been forced, though with a delicacy that was almost eery, upon his attention. The tune went to the lilt of the small drum – Boula, de babee – somewhat as follows.

The words, of which there were many, resolved themselves, so far as his appreciation of them was concerned, into two first lines, and a refrain, thus:

> Weelum Palgrave is a Cha-Cha, b'la-hoo!
> Him are a koind of a half-a-Jew

Then the refrain:

> Him go back to Trebizond.

There were, in these apparently Mother Goose words, various hidden meanings. 'B'la-hoo', a contraction from 'bally-hoo', is the name of a small, hard-fleshed, surface-water fish, not unlike the flying-fish in consistency, and living, like its winged neighbor, on the surface of deeps. As used in the verses it intensified 'Cha-Cha'. A Cha-Cha – so-called, it is currently believed in St Thomas, because of the peculiar sneezing nasality with which these French poor-whites enunciate their Norman French – is one of a peculiarly St Thomian community, originally emigrés from St Bartholomew's, now so thoroughly inbred as to look all alike – brave and hardy fishermen who cannot swim, West Indian poor-whites of the lowest class, like the Barbadian 'red-legs'. A Cha-Cha B'la-hoo means a particularly Cha-Charish Cha-Cha; an indubitable Cha-Cha. The application of such a term to the consul-general meant that he was of the lowest sort of humanity the St Thomian Negro could name.

Being 'half-a-Jew' did not at all mean that Mr Palgrave partook, as the hearer might easily imagine, of any characteristics believed to inhere in the co-religionists of Moses and Aaron. The phrase had a far deeper – and lower – significance than that. The significant portion of it was that word 'half'. That, stated plainly, meant an aspersion upon the legitimacy of Mr Palgrave's birth. It was, that epithet, essentially a *'tu quoque'* type of insult – *you're another*! It referred directly to one of Mr Palgrave's mordant aspersions upon the quality of the St Thomians, or, rather, upon the class, the Negroes, which was now retaliating. It was not the usual custom of these Negroes to marry. It had not been their custom in Africa. Their Danish overlords did not compel it here. Why should this foreigner, this *Bukra* of the double-chin, cast his aspersions upon them? How was he concerned? Not at all, was Black Quashee's obvious reply, according to the logic of the situation. His equally obvious retort, to drum-beats, was:

> Him are a koind of a half-a-Jew!

But – the real gist of the retort, compared to which these glancing blows at his self-esteem were mere thrusts of the *banderillo*, goads – was the refrain:

> Him go back to Trebizond.

It was not, precisely, a command. It was still less a statement of accomplished fact. Mr Palgrave had not gone back to his esteemed Armenian post, Mr Palgrave had no intention whatever of applying to Downing Street for a transfer back there. It was – a suggestion.

It was that refrain which La Touche Penn had been whistling as he walked demurely away down the glaring white road under the blazing sunlight. Mr Palgrave stared angrily after the slouching figure; stared after it, an uncompromising scowl upon his handsome, florid features, until it disappeared abruptly around a sudden turn halfway down the hill. Then he mounted the step of his barouche and settled himself in the exact center of the sun-heated leather cushion, a linen dust-cloth over his knees.

It was a Tuesday afternoon, and later, at five o'clock, it was Mr Palgrave's intention to call at Government House. Governor Arendrup was receiving that afternoon, as he did once a month, but between now and then there was an interval of an hour and a half which the consul-general meant to spend in making duty calls.

Claude, very erect, drove carefully down the hill, turned the sharp corner around which La Touche Penn had disappeared, and thence, by a devious route, descended the slight slope leading to the chief thoroughfare along the sea's edge. Here he turned to the left, passed that massive structure, the Grand Hotel, driving between it and Emancipation Park, turned once more to the left, and soon the wiry little carriage-horses were sweating up one of Charlotte Amalia's steepest hills. They moved carefully around hair-breadth turns guarded by huge clumps of cacti, and at last emerged near the summit of Government Hill. Claude stopped before the entrance to a massive residence perched atop a still higher rise in the land.

Mr Palgrave climbed steps to the stone and cement terrace of this house and gave to the expressionless black butler his card for Mrs Talbot. The servant took his stick and hat and led the way up a flight of stairs to Mrs Talbot's drawingroom. As the consul-general mounted behind his ebony guide he became aware of a tap-tapping, a light sound as though made by the fingers of a supple hand on a kitchen pan. The tapping went: 'oóm-bom, bom; oóm-bom, bom; oóm-bom, bom', over and over, monotonously. Accompanying this beat was a light, almost childish, voice; one of the black maids, probably, in some distant portion of the great house. The tune was the tune La Touche Penn had been whistling as he slouched down the hill. Mr Palgrave mentally supplied the words.

Weelum Palgrave is a Cha-Cha, b'la-hoo!
Him are a koind of a half-a-Jew –
Him go back to Trebizond!

It was maddening, this sort of thing. It should not be allowed.
Here, in Mrs Talbot's house! A choleric red disfigured Mr Palgrave's
handsome face as he walked into the drawing-room. It took him
several minutes to reassume his accustomed urbanity.

Something Mrs Talbot said, too, was annoying.

'I am sure I cannot say where I acquired the idea, Mr Palgrave,
but – somehow – it came to me that you were not remaining with
us; that you were expecting to go back; to Armenia, was it not?'

'I have no such intention – I assure you.' Mr Palgrave felt himself
suddenly pink in the face. He used his handkerchief. May, in this
climate, is very warm, Mrs Talbot hoped he would not mind the
summer heat.

'We find the sea bathing refreshing,' she had vouchsafed.

Mr Palgrave did not outstay the twenty-minute minimum for a
duty call. As he descended the broad stairway he heard the tap-
tapping once more, but now the words accompanying it were muted.
There was no song. He found himself repeating the doggerel words
to the tapping of that damnable pan.

Him go back to Trebizond.

Absurd! He should do nothing of the sort. Only fancy – blackamoors! To suggest such a thing – to him! He descended the steps to
the roadway, a picture of complacent dignity.

A tiny barefooted black child strolled past, an empty kerosene-tin
balanced on her kinky, kerchiefed head. The child, preoccupied
with a wilted bougainvillea blossom which she held between her
hands, hummed softly, a mere tuneless little murmur, barely audible on the freshening Trade Wind of mid-afternoon. Mr Palgrave,
his perceptions singularly sensitive this afternoon, caught it, however. His directions for the next call were given to black Claude
almost savagely.

Precisely at five he mounted the steps of Government House. He
was saluted in form by the pair of Danish *gendarmes*, in their stiff
Frederick the Great uniforms, from each side of the doorway. He
subscribed his name and titles in the visitors' book. He gave up his
hat and stick to another saluting *gendarme*, and mounted the interior
stairway to the great drawing-room above.

Here all St Thomas society congregated monthly at the governor's reception, and with those who had arrived on time this afternoon the drawing-room was half filled. The Governor's Band, outside on the east end of the iron gallery which runs along the front of Government House, started up an air. Officers, officials, the clergy, the town's gentry, the other resident consuls, and the ladyfolk of all these, passed solemnly in review before the governor, stiff in his black clothes, shaking hands formally in his box-like frock coat, his spotless white kid gloves.

Mr Palgrave, still ruffled from his afternoon's experiences, greeted His Danish Majesty's representative in this loyal colony with a stiffness quite equal to the governor's, and passed within. Ladies seated at both ends of a vast mahogany table in the dining-room dispensed coffee and tea. Mounded along the table's sides stood great silver trays of 'spread', half-sandwiches of white and brown bread covered with cheese, with preserves, with ground meats, with *liver-pastei*. At the sideboard Santa Cruz rum, made in the colony, French brandy imported from Martinique, and Danish beer in small bottles and served with fine pieces of ice in the glasses, were being rapidly dispensed by liveried Negro servants to a crowd which stood eight deep.

From this group a burly figure, that of Captain the Honorable William McMillin, detached itself and accosted Mr Palgrave. The captain, administrator of Great Fountain Estate over on Santa Cruz, here for the day on some estate business for his kinsmen the Comyns family who all lived in Scotland and for whom he managed their Santa Crucian sugar interests, had been as a freshly commissioned Cornet of Horse, one of Wellington's officers more than fifty years before, at Waterloo. The old gentleman invited Mr Palgrave to a bottle of the Carlsburg beer, and the two Britons, provided with this refreshing beverage, sat down to talk together.

In their armchairs the two made a notable appearance, both being large-bodied, florid men, and the aged captain wearing, as was his custom on state occasions, his ancient scarlet military coat. Outside the great open French windows, the band members on the gallery, between pieces, made themselves heard as they arranged their music. Save for the bandmaster, Erasmus Petersen, a Dane, all were Negroes. Through the windows came minor musical sounds as a slide was shifted in an alto horn or as little runs and flutings tested the precision of a new tuning. In the midst of this, delicately, almost incidentally, the oboist ran his swart fingers over his silver keys, breathed into his instrument. A rippling, muted little quick-step came through the windows.

Weelum Palgrave is a Cha-Cha, b'la-hoo!'

Mr Palgrave suddenly shifted in his armchair. Then he remem-bered that he could not appear to notice this deliberate slap in the face, and, though suddenly empurpled, he sat quiet. He collected his wits, invited the captain to dinner that evening, and excused himself.

Claude, attentive for once, noted his emergence below, extricated his barouche, reached the steps where the two wooden-soldierlike *gendarmes* were saluting his master.

'Home!' said Mr Palgrave, acidly, stepping into the carriage.

That evening Mr Palgrave opened his grief to his fellow Briton, as to a person of assured position and integrity, the consul-general's face quite purple between his vexation and the bottle of sound bur-gundy he had consumed at dinner.

The captain took his consul-general's annoyance lightly.

'Man, man!' he expostulated. 'Ye're no so clearly accustomed to "Quashee" and his ways as mysel', I do assure you. Why – there's a song about *me*! My field-hands made it up, years ago. It runs:

> Mars' McMillin la' fo' me,
> Loike him la' to Waterloo!

'And it means that I command them – that is to "la", Mr Palgrave – the same as I gave commands at Waterloo – there were a precious few, I do assure you, sir. I was no more than a cornet at the time, my commission not two weeks old.' The captain proceeded to pooh-pooh the Quashee songs as reason for serious annoyance.

But his explanations left Mr Palgrave cold.

'Your Negroes do not – er – *insist* upon your returning to the Low Countries to fight Waterloo all over again!' was his bitter comment. That suggestion that he return to Trebizond had bitten deep.

He had Trebizond on his mind when he was retiring that night and it is not strange that he went back there where he had spend two profitable years before being assigned to Charlotte Amalia, in his dreams. Somehow, as the strange distortion of the dream-state provides, he was identified with the sage Firdûsi, a great hero of Armenian legend, that same Firdûsi who had defied a Shah of Persia and refused to compose a history of his life at the imperial command.

Identified with Firdûsi, of whom he had heard many tales, Mr Palgrave suffered imprisonment in his dreams; was, like Firdûsi, summoned again and again into the Presence, always with refusal on his lips; always to be sent back to a place of confinement of increasing comfortlessness.

At last Palgrave-Firdûsi returned to an empty cell where for days he sat on the earthen floor, refusing to yield, to stultify himself. Then, on a gray morning, his jailer entered leading a blind slobbering Negro who sat on the floor opposite him. For an interminable period he suffered this disagreeable companionship. The Black was dumb as well as blind. He sat there, day after day, night after night, cross-legged on the hard floor.

At last Palgrave-Firdûsi could stand it no longer. He howled for his jailer, demanded audience. He was led to the throne room, his resolution dissipated, his one overwhelming desire to acquiesce – yes, yes; he would write – only let him be free of that slobbering horror which mewed to itself with its blank slab of a mouth. He threw himself face down before the throne.

The impact of his prostration awakened him, shivering, in his great mahogany bed. The moonlight of the Caribbees poured through the opened jalousies of the airy bedroom high on the hillsides of Charlotte Amalia: and through the open windows came eerily – it was three o'clock in the morning – the very ghost of a little lilting refrain in the cracked voice of some aged man:

>   Him go back – to Trebizond.

Mr Palgrave groaned, rolled over in bed so that his better ear was undermost, sought to woo sleep again.

But now it was impossible to sleep. That tune – that devilish, that damnable tune – was running through his head again, tumultuously, to the small-drum throbbing of his heart. He groaned and tossed impatiently, miserably. Would morning never come?

In a gray dawn Mr Palgrave rose from an unrefreshing bed, tubbed himself half-heartedly. His face, as he looked at it in his shaving-mirror, wielding his Wednesday Wade & Butcher, seemed gray and drawn; there was no color in his usually choleric cheeks. The servants, at this hour, would not have arrived. There would be no morning tea ready.

At a little before seven, fully dressed, Mr Palgrave descended the staircase to his office below. He sat down at his orderly desk, listening to the shuffle of early-morning bare feet outside there on the earthen hillside roadway before his fine house; to the clipped, grave snatches of the Creole speech of the Blacks; to the occasional guffaws of the Negroes about their early-morning occasions; gravely erect; carrying trays, fruits, great tins of cistern-water, atop kerchiefed heads.

Mechanically he reached for his writing-materials, dipped a pen in an inkwell, commenced to write. He wrote on and on, composing carefully, the edge of his mind engaged in listening for the song out there on the roadway. He discovered that he was tapping out its cadence with his foot on the scrubbed pitch-pine flooring underneath his desk: oóm – bom, bom; oóm – bom, bom; oóm – bom, bom; oóm – bom, bom!

He finished his letter, signed it meticulously, blotted it, folded it twice, then heard the latch of the remote kitchen door snap. He rose, walked into the dining-room, and spoke through the inner kitchen door to Melissa his cook who had just arrived.

'Make me some tea at once, if you please.'

'Yes, sar.' It was the dutiful, monotonous, unhurried voice of old Black Melissa as she motivated herself ponderously in the direction of the charcoal barrel in the kitchen's corner.

Mr Palgrave reflectively mounted the stairs to his bed-room. He was putting a keen edge on his Wednesday razor – he used a set of seven – before it dawned upon him that he had already shaved! He returned the razor to its case. What could be the matter with him? He looked musingly into his shaving-mirror, passed a well-kept hand reflectively over the smooth cheeks into which the exercise of moving about and up and down the stairs had driven a little of his accustomed high color. He shook his head at his reflection in the glass, walked out into the upper hallway, redescended the stairs, once more entered his office.

What was this?

He frowned, stared, picked up from the desk the letter he had finished ten minutes before, examined it carefully. It was, unquestionably, in his own handwriting. The ink was barely dry. He laid it back in its place on the desk and began to pace the room, slowly, listening to Melissa's slow movings-about in the kitchen, to the arrival of other servants. He could hear their clipped greetings to the old cook.

Wondering at himself, at this strange mental world where he found himself, he seated himself firmly, judicially, in his ample desk chair, picked up the letter, read it through again with an

ever-increasing wonderment. He laid it down, his thoughts turning, strangely to Trebizond.

And Mr Palgrave could not, for the life of him, recall writing this
letter.

He was still sitting there, staring blankly at nothing, his brows
drawn together in a deep frown, when Claude came in to announce
tea prepared in the dining-room. 'Tea', in St Thomas, Continental
fashion, is the name of the morning meal. 'Breakfast' comes at one
o'clock. Mr Palgrave's cook had prepared amply that morning, but
not bacon and eggs, nor even Scotch marmalade, availed to arouse
him from his strange preoccupation.

After 'tea' he sat again at his desk alone until ten o'clock, when his
privacy was invaded by two sailors from a British vessel in the
harbor, with consular business to transact. He gave these men his
careful attention; later, his advice. He walked out with them an
hour later, turned up the hill and strolled about the steep hillside
streets for an hour.

It was nearly high noon when he returned. He passed the office,
going upstairs to refresh his appearance after his walk. It was blistering hot outdoors under the May noon sunlight drenching the
dusty roadways.

When he went into his office half an hour later he saw the letter
once more. It was enclosed now, in an official envelope, addressed,
too, in his own unmistakable hand-writing, duly stamped for post-
ing. Again, he had no slightest recollection of having done any
of these things. He picked up the letter intending now to tear
it across and then across again and fling the bits of paper into
the waste-basket. Instead he sat with it in his hands, curiously
placid, in an apathetic state in which he seemed not even to think.
He ended by placing it in his coat pocket and was immediately afterward summoned to the one o'clock 'breakfast' in the
dining-room.

When he awakened from his *siesta* that afternoon it was near four
o'clock. He remembered the letter at once. He rose, and before his
afternoon bath examined the coat pocket. The letter was not in the
pocket. He decided to look for it on the desk later.

In half an hour, fresh and cool now after his bath, he descended the
stairway and went straight into his office. The letter was on his mind,
and, frowning slightly, he stepped toward the immaculately neat
desk. He drew down his lip under his teeth in a puzzled expression.
The letter was not on the desk.

The arrival of callers summoned him into the drawing-room. He did not give any thought to the letter again until dinner-time and then he was at the top of Government Hill at one of the British houses and could only postpone his desire to find and destroy it.

The letter failed to turn up, and the next day came and passed, and the next after it, and the days stretched into weeks. He had almost forgotten the letter. It cropped up mentally now and then as a vague, half-remembered annoyance. Things were going better these days. The song and its varied accompaniments of drum-tapping, whistling, humming of the nearly soundless tune, the encompassing annoyance it had caused him – all these things seemed to have dropped out of the hearing, and consequently out of the mind of the consul-general. He felt, as he half realized, somewhat more at home now in Charlotte Amalia. Everybody, it appeared, was perfectly courteous to him. The atmosphere of vague hostility which had vaguely adumbrated his surroundings was gone, utterly dissipated. The charm of the town had begun to appeal to this sophisticated traveler of the earth's surfaces.

Then one morning among the letters which the Royal Mail steamer *Hyperion* had brought into the harbor the night before he discerned an official communication from his superiors in London.

He opened it before any of his other letters, as was natural.

The Under-Secretary had written granting his urgent request to be sent back to Trebizond. He was requested to take immediate passage to any convenient Mediterranean port and to proceed thence direct to the Armenian capital. It was, at the moment, agreeable to the consular service that he should be there. Suggestions followed in the letter's text, designating various policies to be pursued.

He finished the many sheets of thin onion-skin paper, folded the letter and laid it on the desk, and sat, staring dully at his inkwell. He did not want to go back to Trebizond. He wanted to remain here. But – he had no choice in the matter. He cudgeled his brains warily. He recalled his singular apathy at the time when his letter – written, it seemed, as though subconsciously – had disappeared. He had not *wanted* to write that letter. He recalled that there had been confusion in his mind at the time – he could not, he recalled, remember the actual writing, nor sending it after it was written. There was something very strange here, something – unusual! Indubitably he had applied for transfer to Trebizond. To Trebizond he was ordered to go!

Charlotte Amalia, that coy Latin-brunette of a town with her *coquetteries* and her too-garish coloring, and her delicate beauties – Charlotte Amalia had schemed for his departure, forced his hand, driven him out. He sat there, at his desk, thinking, ruefully, of many things. Then his pride came to his rescue. He remembered the slights which had been put upon him, those intangible slights – the almost formless little tune with its absurd, gibberish words; the tapping of pans; the rattle and boom of the hill drums, those detestable night drums on which these stupid-looking, subtle blackamoors were always and forever, and compellingly, tapping, tapping, tapping.

And before very long Mr Palgrave, who did not believe in magic and who pooh-poohed anything labeled 'eery' or 'occult' as absurd; who believed only in unmistakable matters like sound beef and County Families and exercise and the integrity of the British Empire and the invariable inferiority of foreigners – Mr Palgrave came to see that in some fashion not accounted for in his philosophy Charlotte Amalia had played him a very scurvy trick – somehow.

Bestirring himself he began to examine the inventory which he kept of his household gear; many belongings without which no British gentleman could be expected to exist. He indited to the harbor-master a cold, polite note, requesting notice of the arrival of vessels clearing for Mediterranean ports or ports on the Black Sea – Odessa for choice – and he began to formulate, in his small, precise hand-writing, the list of duty-calls which must be made before his departure. In the pauses between these labors he wrote various polite, stiff notes, and in the very midst of such activities Claude summoned him to midday breakfast.

Leading the way to the dining-room after this announcement, Claude paused at the office doorway, turned a deprecating face to his employer.

'Yes?' said Mr Palgrave, perceiving that Claude wished to address him.

'Yo' is leave us, sar,' said Claude, with courteous absence of any inflection or emphasis on his words which would indicate that he was asking a question.

'Yes – I am leaving very shortly,' replied Mr Palgrave unemotionally. He added nothing to this statement. He was a stiff master to his servants, just but distant. Servants had their place and must be kept in it, according to Mr Palgrave's scheme of life.

That night, his sleep being rather fitful, Mr Palgrave noted that the drums were reiterating some message, insistently, up in the hills.

Neither Claude, who as coachman-butler had the closest contact with his employer of any of the house servants, nor, indeed, old Melissa nor any of the others, made any further remark to their employer concerning his departure. This took place three days later, on a Netherlands vessel clearing for Genoa; and Mr Palgrave was probably the very last person in St Thomas who would have asked any personal question of a servant.

Yet he wondered, when it occurred to him – and that was often – just how Claude had known he was leaving.

THE BLACK BEAST

and other Voodoo Tales

The Black Beast

Diagonally across the Sunday Market in Christiansted, on the island of Santa Cruz, from the house known as Old Moore's, which I occupied one season – that is to say, along the southern side of the ancient marketplace of the old city, built upon the abandoned site of the yet older French town of Bassin – there stands, in faded, austere grandeur, another and much larger old house known as Gannett's. For close to half a century Gannett House stood vacant and idle, its solid masonry front along the marketplace presenting a forlorn and aloof appearance, with its rows of closely shuttered windows, its stones darkened and discolored, its whole appearance stern and forbidding.

During that fifty years or so in which it had stood shut up and frowning blankly at the mass of humanity which passed its massive bulk and its forbidding closed doors, there had been made, by various persons, efforts enough to have it opened. Such a house, one of the largest private dwellings in the West Indies, and one of the handsomest, closed up like this, and out of use, as it transpired upon serious inquiry, merely because such was the will of its arbitrary and rather mysterious absentee proprietor whom the island had not seen for a middle-aged man's lifetime, could hardly fail to appeal to prospective renters.

I know, because he has told me so, that the Rev. Fr Richardson, of the English Church, tried to engage it as a convent for his sisters in 1926. I tried to get a season's lease on it myself, in the year when, failing to do so, I took Old Moore's instead – a house of strange shadows and generous rooms and enormous, high doorways through which, times innumerable, Old Moore himself, bearing, if report were believable, a strange burden of mental apprehension, had slunk in bygone years, in shuddering, dreadful anticipation . . .

Inquiry at the Government offices had elicited the fact that old Lawyer Malling, a survival of the Danish reégime, who lived in Christiansted and was invaluable to our Government officials when it came to disentangling antique Danish records, was in charge of

Gannett's. Herr Malling, interviewed in turn, was courteous but firm. The house could not be rented under any considerations; such were his instructions – permanent instructions, filed among his records. No, it was impossible, out of the question. I recalled some dim hints I had received of an old scandal.

Over a glass of excellent sherry which hospitable Herr Malling provided, I asked various questions. The answers to these indicated that the surviving Gannetts were utterly obdurate in the matter. They had no intention of returning. Repairs – the house was built like a fortress – had not, so far, been required. They had assigned no reason for their determination to keep their Christiansted property closed? No – and Herr Malling had no option in the matter. No, he had written before, twice; once in behalf of the rector of the English Church, just recently; also, ten, eleven years ago when a professor from Berlin, sojourning in the islands, had conceived the idea of a tropical school for tutoring purposes and had cast a thickly bespectacled eye on the old mansion. No, it was impossible.

'Well, *skaal*, Herr Canevin! Come now – another, of course! A man can not travel on one leg, you know; that is one of our sayings.'

But three years after this interview with Herr Malling, the old house was opened at last. The very last remaining Gannett, it appeared, had gone to his reward, from Edinburgh, and the title had passed to younger heirs who had had no personal connection, no previous residence in the West Indies.

Herr Malling's new instructions, transmitted through an Aberdeen solicitor, were to rent the property to the best advantage, to entertain offers for its disposal in fee simple, and to estimate possible repairs and submit this estimate to Aberdeen. I learned this some time after the instructions had been transmitted. Herr Malling was not one to broadcast the private and confidential business of his clients. I learned thereof from Mrs Ashton Garde, over tea and small cakes in the vast, magnificent drawing room of Gannett's, a swept and garnished Gannett's which she had taken for the season and whose eighteenth-century mahogany she had augmented and lightened with various furniture of her own in the process which had transformed the old fortress-like abode into one of the most attractive residences I have ever been privileged to visit.

Mrs Garde, an American, and a widow, was in the late forties, a very charming and delightful woman of the world, an accomplished hostess, incidentally a person of substantial means, and the mother of three children. Of these, a married daughter lived in Florida and did not visit the Gardes during their winter in Santa Cruz. The other children, Edward, just out of Harvard, and Lucretia, twenty-four, were with their mother. Both of them, though diversely – Edward, an athlete, had no particular conversation – had inherited the maternal charm as well as the very striking good looks of their late father whose portrait – a splendid Sargent – hung over one of the two massive marble mantelpieces which stood at either end of the great drawing room.

It was quite near the end where the portrait hung, low because the mantelshelf, lacking a fireplace under it, stood two feet higher than an ordinary mantelshelf, balancing a ceiling fifteen feet in height, that we sat upon my first visit to the Gardes, and I noticed that Mrs Garde, whose tea table was centered on the mantelpiece, as it were, and who sat facing me across the room's width, glanced up, presumably at the portrait, several times.

I am of an analytical mentality, even in small matters. I guessed that she was trying out the recent hanging of this very magnificent portrait 'with her eye', as people do until they have become accustomed to new placements and the environmental aspects of a new or temporary home and, my attention thus drawn to it, I made some comment upon the portrait, and rose to examine it more closely. It repaid scrutiny.

But Mrs Garde, as though with a slight note of deprecation, turned the conversation away from the portrait, a fact which I noticed in passing, and which was emphasized, as I thought of it later, by her sidelong glances, upward and to her right, in the intervals of pouring tea for a considerable group of company, which kept going up there again and again. I gave to these facts no particular interpretation. There was no reason for analysis. But I noted them nevertheless.

I saw considerable of the Gardes, for the next few weeks, and then, because I had planned some time before to go down the islands as far as Martinique when the *Margaret* of the Bull-Insular Line which plies among the upper islands should go there for several days' sojourn in dry dock, I did not see them at all for more than two weeks during which I was renewing my acquaintance with Martinique French in the interesting capital town of Fort de France.

I ran in to call on the Gardes shortly after my arrival on Santa Cruz at the conclusion of this trip, and found Mrs Garde alone. Edward and Lucretia were playing tennis and later dining with the Covingtons at Hermon Hill Estate House.

I was immediately struck with the change which had taken place in Mrs Garde. It was as though some process of infinite weariness had laid its hold upon her. She looked shrunken, almost fragile. Her eyes, of that dark, brilliant type which accompanies a bistre complexion, appeared enormous, and as she looked at me, her glances alternating with the many which she kept casting up there in the direction of her husband's portrait, I could not escape the conviction that her expression bore now that aspect which I can only describe by the somewhat trite term 'haunted'.

I was, sharply, immediately, surprised; greatly intrigued by this phenomenon. It was one of those obvious things which strike one directly without palliation, like a blow in the face unexpectedly delivered; an unmistakable change, hinting, somehow, of tragedy. It made me instantaneously uneasy, moved me profoundly, for I had liked Mrs Garde very much indeed, and had anticipated a very delightful acquaintance with this family which centered about its head. I noticed her hand quite definitely trembling as she handed me my cup of tea, and she took one of those sidelong glances, up and to the right, in the very midst of that hospitable motion.

I drank half my tea in a mutual silence, and then, looking at Mrs Garde, I surprised her in the middle of another glance. She was just withdrawing her eyes. She caught my eyes, and, perhaps, something of the solicitude which I was feeling strongly at the moment, and her somberly pallid face flushed slightly. She looked down, busied herself with the paraphernalia of her circular tea tray. I spoke then.

'Haven't you been entirely well, Mrs Garde? It seemed to me that, perhaps, you were not looking altogether robust, if you don't mind my mentioning it.' I tried to make my tone sufficiently jocular to carry off my really solicitous inquiry lightly; to leave room for some rejoinder in somewhat the same vein.

She turned tragic eyes upon me. There was no smile on her drawn face. The unexpected quality of her reply brought me up standing.

'Mr Canevin – help me!' she said simply, looking straight into my eyes.

I was around the tea table in two seconds, held her shaking hands, which were as cold as lumps of ice, in mine. I held them and looked down at Mrs Garde. 'With all my heart,' I said. 'Tell me, please, when you can, now or later, Mrs Garde, what it is.'

She expressed her thanks for this reassurance with a nod, withdrew her hands, sat back in her rattan chair and closed her eyes. I thought she was going to faint and, sensing this, perhaps, she opened her eyes and said: 'I'm quite all right, Mr Canevin – that is, so far as the immediate present is concerned. Will you not sit down, finish your tea? Let me freshen your cup.'

Somewhat relieved, I resumed my own chair and, over a second cup of tea, looked at my hostess. She had made a distinct effort to pull herself together. We sat for some minutes in silence. Then, I refusing more tea, she rang, and the butler came in and removed the tray and placed cigarets on the table between us. It was only after the servant had gone and closed the drawing room door behind himself that she leaned forward impulsively, and began to tell me what had occurred.

Despite her obvious agitation and the state of her nerves which I have attempted to indicate, Mrs Garde went straight to the point without any beating about the bush. Even as she spoke it occurred to me from the form of her phraseology that she had been planning how, precisely, to express herself. She did so now very concisely and clearly.

'Mr Canevin,' she began, 'I have no doubt that you have noticed my glancing up at the wall space above this mantel. It has grown, one would say, to be a nervous habit with me. You have observed it, have you not?'

I said that I had and had supposed that the glances had been directed toward her husband's portrait.

'No,' resumed Mrs Garde, looking at me fixedly as though to keep her eyes off the place over the mantelshelf, 'it is not at the picture, Mr Canevin. It is at a place directly above it – about three feet above its top edge to be precise.'

She paused at this point, and I could not help looking toward the point she had indicated. As I did so, I caught sight of her long and rather beautiful hands. They were clamped against the edge of the low table, as though she was holding on to that as if to something solid and material – an anchor for her nerves – and I observed that the knuckles were white with the pressure she was exerting.

I saw nothing but a wide space of empty, gray sanded wall which ran up cleanly to the high ceiling and out on both sides of the portrait, a clear space, artistically left vacant, one would surmise, by whoever had possessed the good sense to leave the Sargent alone with its wide blank background of gray wall space.

I looked back at Mrs Garde and found her gaze fixed determinedly on my face. It was as though she held it there, by a sheer effort of the will, forcing herself not to look up at the wall.

I nodded at her reassuringly.

'Please continue, if you will, Mrs Garde,' I said, and leaned back in my chair and lighted a cigaret from the silver box on the table between us.

Mrs Garde relaxed and leaned back in her lounge chair, but continued looking straight at me. When she resumed what she was saying she spoke slowly, with a certain conscious effort at deliberation. My instinct apprised me that she was forcing herself to this course; that if she did not concentrate in some such fashion she would let go and scream aloud.

'Perhaps you are familiar with Du Maurier's book, *The Martian*, Mr Canevin,' and, as I nodded assent, she continued, 'You will remember when Josselin's eye began to fail him, he was puzzled and dreadfully worried by discovering a blind spot in his sound eye – it was emphasized by the failure of the other one, and he was vastly distressed – thought he was going stone blind, until the little Continental oculist reassured him, explained the *punctum caecum* – the blind spot which is in the direct line of vision with the optic nerve itself. Do you recall the incident?'

'Perfectly,' said I, and nodded again reassuringly.

'Well, I remember testing my own blind spots after reading that when I was quite a young girl,' resumed Mrs Garde. 'I dare say a great many people tried the experiment. There is, of course, a line of vision *outside* each blind spot, to the left of the left eye's ordinary focus and, correspondingly, to the right of that of the other eye. In addition to this variation of ordinary vision, as I have ascertained, there is another condition, especially evident in the sight of the middle-aged. That is that the direct line of ordinary vision becomes, as it were, "worn", and the vision itself, in the case of a person especially who has used his or her eyes a great deal – over embroidery, or reading, or some professional work which requires concentrated looking, I mean – is somewhat less acute than when the eyes are used at an unaccustomed angle.'

She paused, looked at me as though to ascertain whether or not I had been following the speech. Once more I nodded. I had listened carefully to every word. Mrs Garde, resuming, now became acutely specific.

'As soon as we had arrived here, Mr Canevin, the very first thing that I had to attend to was the suitable hanging of this portrait of Mr Garde.' She did not look toward it, but indicated the portrait with a gesture of her hand in its direction.

'I looked over that section of the wall space to ascertain the most advantageous point from which to hang it. I found the place that seemed to me suitable and had the butler drive in a nail in the place I indicated. The picture was then hung and is still in the place I selected.

'This process had required considerable looking, on my part, at the blank wall. It was not, really, until the portrait was actually hung that I realized – that it occurred to me – that something – something, Mr Canevin, which had gradually become clearer, better defined I mean, was there – above the picture – something which, within that outside angle of vision, outside the blind spot of my right eye as I sat there and looked up and to the right, became more evident every time I looked up at the wall. Of course, I looked at the picture many times, to make quite sure I had it in the right spot on the wall. In doing so the outside vision, the portion of the eye which was not worn and more or less dimmed from general usage, took in the place I have indicated. It is, as I have mentioned, about three feet above the top of Mr Garde's portrait.

'Mr Canevin, the thing has grown – *grown*!'

Suddenly Mrs Garde broke down, buried her face in trembling hands, leaning forward upon the table like a child hiding its eyes in a game, and her slim body shook with uncontrollable, dry sobs.

This time, I perceived, the best thing for me to do was to sit quietly and wait until the poor, overwrought lady had exhausted her hysterical seizure. I waited, therefore, in perfect silence, trying, mentally, to give my hostess, as well as I could, the assurance of my complete sympathy and my desire and willingness to help her in all possible ways.

Gradually, as I had anticipated, the spasm of weeping worked itself out, minimized itself and finally passed. Mrs Garde raised her head, composed herself, again looked at me, this time with a markedly greater degree of calmness and self-possession. The gust of hysteria, although it had shaken her, had, in its ordinary effect, done her good. She even smiled at me a little wanly.

'I fear that you will think me very weak, Mr Canevin,' she said finally.

I smiled quietly.

'When it is possible, it would be of assistance if I could know of this matter as exactly as possible,' I said. 'Try, please, to tell me just what it is that you see on the wall, Mrs Garde.'

Mrs Garde nodded, spent a little while composing herself. She even used her vanity box, a trifling gold affair with the inevitable mirror. After this she was able to smile herself. Then, suddenly quite

serious again, she said simply: 'It is the head and part of the body –
the upper, forward part, to be precise, Mr Canevin – of what seems
to be a young bull. At first only the head; then, gradually, the
shoulders and neck. It seems quite utterly grotesque, absurd, does
it not?

'But, Mr Canevin, extraordinary as that must seem to you, it is – '
she looked down at her twitching hands, then, with a visible effort,
back at me, her face now suddenly ghastly under the fresh make-up
which she had so recently applied to it. 'Mr Canevin, that is not
the terrifying part of it. That, indeed, might, perhaps, be construed
as some kind of optical illusion, or something of the sort. It is – '
again she hesitated, looked down; then, with a greater effort than
before back at me – 'it is the – expression – of the face, Mr Canevin!
It is, I assure you, quite *human*, terrifying, reproachful! And, Mr
Canevin, there is blood, a thick single stream of blood, which runs
down from the center of the forehead, over the creature's poor
nose! It is – somehow, pathetic, Mr Canevin. It is a very frightful
experience to have. It has utterly ruined my peace of mind. That is
all there is to it, Mr Canevin – the head and neck and shoulders of a
young bull, with that blood running down from its forehead, and
that expression . . . '

At once, upon hearing this salient particularization of Mrs Garde's
extraordinary optical experience, that analytical faculty of mine began
forthwith to run riot. There were points of contact with previous
knowledge of the spectral beliefs of the blacks and similar phenomena
of our West Indies in that picture, affairs wherein I am not wholly
without experience. The bull, as at once it occurred to me, is the
principal sacrificial animal of the main voodoo cults, up and down the
islands, where the old African gods of 'Guinea' prevail.

But a bull, with such an expression on its face as my hostess had
briefly described, with blood running down its nose, up there on
the wall space above the high mantelshelf in Gannett House – this
was, truly, a puzzler! I shifted, I remember, forward in my chair,
raised a hand to command Mrs Garde's attention. I had thought of
something.

'Tell me, if you please, Mrs Garde,' said I. 'Is the appearance
which you have described close against the wall, or – otherwise?'

'It is well out from the wall itself,' replied Mrs Garde, striving to
express herself with precision. 'It seems, I should say, to be several
feet away from the wall proper, toward us, of course – not as though
behind the wall, I mean – and, I omitted to say, Mr Canevin, that

when I look at it for any considerable length of time, the head and shoulders seem to sag forward and downward. It is, I should say, as though the animal were just freshly hurt, were beginning to sink down to its death.'

'Thank you,' said I. 'It must have been a considerable ordeal to tell me about it so clearly and exactly. However, it is very simple psychology to understand that the process has done you good. You have shared your strange experience with someone else. That, of course, is a step in the right direction. Now, Mrs Garde, will you permit me to "prescribe" for you?'

'Most assuredly, Mr Canevin,' returned Mrs Garde. 'I am, frankly, in such a state over this dreadful thing, that I am prepared to do anything to secure some relief from it. I have not, of course, mentioned it to my children. I have not said a word to anybody but you. It is not the sort of thing one can discuss – with anybody and everybody.'

I bowed across the table at this implied compliment, this expression of confidence in me, after all, the most casual of Mrs Garde's acquaintances.

'I suggest,' said I, 'that the entire Garde family take an excursion down the islands, like the one from which I have just returned. The *Samaria*, of the Cunard Line, will be at St Thomas on Thursday. Today is Monday. It would be quite a simple matter to make your reservations by wireless, or even by cable to St Thomas. Go away for two or three weeks; come back when you are ready. And leave me the key of Gannett House, Mrs Garde.'

My hostess nodded. She had listened avidly to this suggestion.

'I will do so, Mr Canevin. I think there will be no argument from Edward and Lucretia. They were, as a matter of fact, envying you your visit to Martinique.'

'Good,' said I encouragingly. 'We may call that settled then. I might add that the *Grebe* is going back to St Thomas tomorrow morning. It would be an excellent idea for you to go along. I will telephone the dispatching secretary at once for the permission, and consult Dr Pelletier who is chief municipal physician there. He has a broad mind and a large experience of affairs such as this.'

Again Mrs Garde nodded acquiescently. She had reached, it was obvious, the place where she would carry out any intelligent suggestion to the end of terminating that optical horror of hers.

The Garde family left on board the little Government transport, which runs between our Virgin Islands and from them to and from

Porto Rico, at eight o'clock the following morning. I saw them off at the Christiansted wharf, and the following afternoon a wireless from St Thomas apprised me that Dr Pelletier had proved very helpful, and that reservations for a three weeks' cruise about the islands had been secured for all three of them on board the Cunarder.

I breathed easily, for the first time. I had assumed a fairly considerable responsibility in my advice. I was now, for some three weeks, lord of the manor at Gannett House. I arranged, through Mrs Garde's butler, a white man whom she had brought with her, to give the house servants a day's vacation for a picnic – a common form of pleasure seeking among West Indian blacks – and requested him, quoting Mrs Garde's desire – she had given me *carte blanche* in the entire affair – to take the same day off himself, or even two days. He could, I pointed out, go over to St Thomas on the next trip of the *Grebe* and come back the following day. There would be much to see in St Thomas with its fine shops.

The butler made this arrangement without any demur, and I called on Fr Richardson, rector of the English Church. Fr Richardson, to whom I told the whole story, did no more than nod his wise West Indian head. He had spent a priestly lifetime combating the 'stupidness' of the blacks. He knew precisely what to do, without any further suggestions from me.

On the day when the servants were all away from Gannett House, Fr Richardson came with his black bag and exorcized the house from top to bottom, repeating his formulas and casting his holy water in room after room of the great old mansion. Then, gravely accepting the twenty-franc note which I handed him for his poor, and blessing me, the good and austere priest departed, his services just rendered being to him, I dare say, the nearest routine of a day's work.

I breathed easier now. God, as even the inveterate voodooists of Snake-ridden Haiti admit in their holy week practises – when every altar of the Snake is stripped of its vile symbols, these laid face downward on the floors, covered with rushes, and the crucifix placed on the altars – God is infinitely more powerful than even the mighty Snake of Guinea with his attendant demigods! I believe in being on the safe side.

After this, I merely waited until Mrs Garde's return. Every few days I ran in and spoke with Robertson the butler. Otherwise I left the healing air of the sea to do its work of restoration on Mrs Garde, confident that after her return, refreshed by the change, there would be no recurrence of her horror.

The thing was a problem, and a knotty one, from my viewpoint. I should not rest, I was fully aware, until, by hook or crook, I had satisfied myself about the background for the strange appearance which that lady had recounted to me across her tea table. In the course of the cogitations, wherein I exhausted my own fund of West Indian occult lore, I remembered old Lawyer Malling. There was a possible holder of clues! I have briefly alluded to what I might call a vague penumbra of some ancient scandal hanging about Gannett's. If there existed any real background for this, and anybody now alive knew the facts, it would be Herr Malling. He had passed his eightieth birthday. He had been personally acquainted, in his young manhood, with Angus Gannett, the last of that family to reside here. He had had charge of the property for a lifetime.

To old Malling's, therefore, after due cogitation as to how I should present such a matter to the conservative ancient, I betook myself.

Herr Malling received me with that Old World courtesy which makes a formal occasion out of the most commonplace visit. He produced his excellent sherry. He even used the formula –

'To what, Mr Canevin, am I indebted for the honor of this most welcome visit?' Only he said 'dis' for 'this', being a Danish West Indian.

After chatting of various local matters which were engaging the attention of the island at the moment, I delicately broached the subject upon which I had come.

I will attempt no full account of the fencing which led up to the main aspect of that conversation. Likewise the rather long impasse which promptly built itself up between this conservative old solicitor and myself. I could see, clearly enough, his viewpoint. This cautious questioning of mine had to do with the sacred affairs of an old client. Policy dictated silence; courteous silence; silence surrounded and softened by various politic remarks of a palliative nature; silence, nevertheless, as definite as the solitudes of Quintana Roo in the midst of the Yucatan jungles.

But there was a key word. I had saved it up, probably subconsciously, possibly by design; a design based on instinct. I had mentioned no particulars of Mrs Garde's actual account; that is, I had said nothing of the nature and quality of that which had been distressing her. At last, baffled at all points by the old gentleman's crusted conservatism, I sprung my possible bombshell. It worked!

It was that word 'bull' which formed the key. When I had reached that far in my account of what Mrs Garde had seen over the mantel-shelf in Gannett House, and brought out that word, I thought, for an instant, that the old gentleman who had gone quite white, with blue about his ancient lips, was going to faint.

He did not faint, however. With something almost like haste he poured himself out a glass of his good sherry, drank it with an almost steady hand, set down the glass, turned to me and remarked – 'Wait!'

I waited while the old fellow pottered out of his own hall, and listened to the *pat-pat-pat* of his carpet slippers as he went in search of something. He came back, looking quite as I had always seen him, his cheeks their usual apple red, the benign smile of a blameless old age again triumphant on his old lips. He set down an old fashioned cardboard filing case on the mahogany table beside the sherry decanter, looked over to me, nodded wisely and proceeded to open the filing case.

From this he took a thing somewhat like a large, old fashioned gentleman's wallet, which proved to be the binding placed by old-school lawyers about particular documents, and unfolding this, and glancing at the heading of its contents, and once again nodding, this time to himself, Herr Malling handed the document, with a courteous bow, to me.

I took it, and listened to what the old gentleman was saying, while I examined it superficially. It consisted of many sheets of old-fashioned, ruled foolscap, the kind of paper I have seen used for very old plantation accounts. I held it in my hand expectantly while Herr Malling talked.

'Mr Canevin,' he was saying, 'I giff you dis, my friend, because it contain de explanation of what haff puzzled you – naturally. It iss de account off precisely what hov happen in Gannett's, de Autumn of de year 1876, when Herr Angus Gannett, de late owner, haff jus' retorn from de United States where he haff been wisiting his relatives an' attending de Centennial Exposition at Philadelphia.

'I t'ink you foind, sir, dis document, dis personal account, explain all t'ings now impossible to – er – grasp! I feel free to giff it to you to – er – peruse, because de writer iss dead. I am bound, as you will observe – er – upon perusal, solely by the tenure off life in de testator – er – de narrator, I should say. Dis iss not a will; it iss merely a statement. You will, I imagine, sir, find dis of some interest. I did!'

With a bow to Herr Malling for his great courtesy, I proceeded to read.

2

Gannett House, Christiansted, D. W. I.
October 25th, 1876

My very good friend and brother, Rudolf Malling

This will serve as instructions for you in the affair of the conduct of my property, the town residence on the south side of the Sunday Market which I herewith, for purposes of custodial administration, place in your care. It is my purpose, on the twenty-ninth of this month, to take ship for England, thence direct to the City of Edinburgh; where my permanent address is to be No. 19, MacKinstrie's Lane, off Clarges Street, Edinburgh, Scotland. To this address all communications of every kind and sort whatsoever are to be addressed, both personal and concerning the property if need therefor should arise.

I direct and instruct that the house shall be closed permanently upon my departure, and so maintained permanently, the same being in your charge, and the statement of your outlay for this purpose of closing the house fast remitted to me at Edinburgh.

An explanation is due you, as I clearly perceive, for this apparently abrupt decision. I will proceed to make it herewith.

To do so I bind you to complete secrecy during the term of my natural life on the basis as of *****s'p – which, as a Bro. Freemason you will recognize, of course, even though thus informally given you, and keep my confidence as hereinafter follows strict and close as of the Craft.

I will begin, then, by reminding you of what you already know, to wit, that after the death of my mother, Jane Alicia MacMurtrie Gannett, my father, the late Fergus Gannett, Esq., caused me as well as his kinfolk in Scotland a vast and deep grief by resorting to that which has been the curse of numerous Caucasian gentlefolk as well as of many of the baser sort throughout the length and breadth of the West India Islands. In short, my father entered upon a liaison with one Angelica Kofoed, a mulattress attached to our household and who had been the personal attendant of my late mother. This occurred in the year 1857.

As is also well known to you, a son was born of this union; and also my father, who, according to the law of the Danish West Indies, could have discharged his legal obligation by the payment of the sum of four hundred dollars to the mother, chose, instead, in the infatuation of which he appeared possessed, to acknowledge this son and, by due process of our legal code, to legitimize him.

I was a little past my tenth birthday when the child later known as Otto Andreas Gannett was born, here in our old home where I write this. Thereafter my father ceased all relationship with the woman Angelica Kofoed, pensioned her and, shortly after her child was weaned, caused her, the pension being continued and assured her for the term of her natural life, to emigrate to the Island of St Vincent, of which place she was a native.

My legal half-brother, Otto Andreas Gannett, was retained, with a nurse, in our residence, and grew to young manhood under our roof as a member of the family. I may say here that it is more possible that I should have been able to overcome my loathing and repugnance toward my half-brother had it not been that his character, as he developed from childhood into boyhood and from boyhood into youth, was such as definitely to preclude such an attitude.

I will be explicit to the extent of saying plainly that Otto Andreas 'took after' the Negro side of his blood heritage, although his mother was but an octoroon, no more than slightly 'scorched of the blood', and appearing, like my half-brother, to be a Caucasian. I would not be misunderstood in this. I am very well aware that many of our worthiest citizens here in the West India Islands are of this mixed blood. It is a vexed and somewhat delicate question at best, at least here in our islands. Suffice it to say that the worst Negro characteristics came out as Otto Andreas grew into young manhood. He bears today and doubtless will continue long to bear, an evil reputation, even among the blacks of this island; a reputation for wicked and lecherous inclination, a bad choice of low companions, a self-centered and egotistical demeanor and, worst of all, an incurable inclination toward the wicked and stupid practises of the blacks, with whom, to the shame of our house, he had consorted much before his death in the Autumn of this year, 1876. I refer to what is known as *obeah*.

It is especially in this last mentioned particular that I found it impossible to countenance him. Fortunately my father departed this life five years ago, before this dreadful inclination toward the powers of the Evil One had sufficiently made themselves manifest in Otto Andreas to draw thereto my father's failing attention. I thank my God for that He was pleased to take my father away before he had that cross to bear.

I will not particularize further than to say that the cumulation of these bad attributes in my half-brother formed the determining cause for my departure for the United States, May second, in this year, 1876. As you are aware, I left Otto Andreas here, with strict adjurations as to his conduct and, thinking to escape from continuous contact with him, which had grown unbearably hateful to me, went to New York, thence to the city of Philadelphia where I attended the Centennial Exposition in the hope of somewhat distracting my mind and, later, before returning toward the beginning of October, visited various of our kinfolk in the States of Maryland and Virginia.

I arrived on this island, sailing from New York via Porto Rico, on the nineteenth of October, landing at West-End and remaining overnight at the residence of our friend, Herr Mulgrav, the Judge of the Frederiksted Reconciling Court, and, through the courtesy of the Reverend Dr Dubois of the West-End English Church, who very considerately loaned me his carriage and horses, drove the seventeen miles to Christiansted the following morning.

I arrived just before breakfast time, about a quarter before one o'clock P.M.

I will be explicit to inform you, my good friend and brother, that I had not been so futile minded as to anticipate that my long absence in America would have anything like a corrective effect upon my half-brother. Indeed I was not far from anticipating that I should have to face new rascalities, new stupidnesses upon his part, perpetrated in my absence from home. I anticipated, indeed, that my homecoming would be anything but a pleasant experience, for of such presage I had, in truth, ample background on which to base such an opinion. I arrived at my house, therefore, in anything but a cheerful frame of mind. I had gone away to secure some respite. I came home to meet I knew not what.

No man in his senses – I say it deliberately, for the purpose of warning you, my friend, as you proceed to read what I am about to write – however, could have anticipated what I did meet! I had, indeed, something like a warning of untowardness at home, on my way across the island from Frederiksted. You know how our island blacks show plainly on their faces what their inmost thoughts are, in some instances; how inscrutable they can be in other affairs. As I passed black people on the road, or in the estate fields, I observed nothing on the faces of those who recognized me save a certain commiseration. Murmurs came to my ears, indeed, from their mouths, as one or another murmured – 'Poor young marster!' Or such remarks as 'Ooh, Gahd, him comin' to trouble an' calamity!'

This, of course, was the opposite of reassuring; yet I was not surprised. I had, you will remember, anticipated trouble, with Otto Andreas as its cause and root.

I will not dissemble that I expected something, as I have remarked, untoward.

I entered a strangely silent house – the first thing that came to me was a most outrageous smell! You are surprised, doubtless, at such a statement. I record the facts. My nostrils were instantly assailed, so soon as I had myself opened the door and stepped within, leaving Dr Dubois's coachman, Jens, to bring in my hand luggage, with a foul odor comparable to nothing less wretched than a cattle pen!

I say to you that it fairly took me by the throat. I called to the servants as soon as I was within, leaving the door open behind me to facilitate Jens with my bags, and to let out some of that vile stench. I called Herman, the butler, and Josephine and Marianna, maids in the household. I even called out to Amaranth Niles, the cook. At the sound of my voice – the servants had not known of my arrival the night before – Herman and Marianna came running, their faces blank and stupid, in the fashion well known to you when our blacks have something to conceal.

I ordered them to take my bags to my bedroom, turned to give Jens the coachman a gratuity for his trouble, and turned back again to find Josephine staring at me through a doorway. The other two had disappeared by this time with my hand luggage. The rest, the trunks and so forth, heavier articles, were to be sent over from Frederiksted that afternoon by a carter.

'What is this frightful smell, Josephine?' I inquired. 'The whole house is like a cattle pen, my girl. What has happened? Come now, tell me!'

The black girl stood in the doorway, her face quite inscrutable, and wrung her two hands together.

'Ooh, Gahd, sar, me cahn't say,' she replied with that peculiarly irritating false stupidity which they can assume at will.

I said nothing, I did not wish to inaugurate my homecoming with any fault finding. Besides, the horrible smell might very well not be this girl's fault. I stepped to the left along the inner gallery and into the hall[*] through the entrance door, which was shut. I opened it, and stepped in, I say.

---

[*] A West Indian drawing room is commonly called the hall.

My dear friend Malling, prepare yourself. You will be – well – surprised, to put the matter conservatively.

There, in the center of the hall, its neck turned about so as to look toward whoever had just opened the door from the inner gallery, in this case, myself – stood a young, coal-black bullock!

Beside it, on the floor in the middle of the Bokhara rug which my grandfather had brought with him from his voyage to Turkestan in the year 1837, there was a crate, half filled with fresh grass and carrots; and nearby, and also on the rug, stood a large bucket of water. Wisps of the grass hung from the bullock's mouth as it stared at me for all the world as though to remark, 'Who is this who intrudes, forsooth, upon my privacy here!'

Malling, I let myself go then. This – a bullock in my hall, in my town house! – this was too much! I rushed back into the gallery crying out for the servants, for Herman and Josephine and Marianna. They came, looking down at me, fearfully, over the balusters of the stairway, their faces gray with fear. I cursed them roundly, as you may well imagine. I conceive that even the godly Dr Dubois himself would at least feel the desire so to express himself were he to return to his rectory and find a bullock stabled in his choicest room!

But all my words elicited nothing save that look of blank stupidity to which I have already referred; and when, in the midst of my diatribe, old Amaranth Niles, the cook, came hastening upon the scene from her kitchen, a long spoon in her fat old hand, she, who had been with us since my birth twenty-eight years before, likewise went stupid.

Suddenly I ceased reviling them for ingrates, for fools, for rapscallions, for gallows birds. It occurred to me, very shortly, that this rascality was none, could be none, of theirs, poor creatures. It was the latest devilment of my half-brother Otto Andreas. I saw it clearly. I collected myself. I addressed poor Herman in a milder tone.

'Come Herman, get this beast out of the house immediately!' I pointed toward the now open door into the hall.

But Herman, despite this definite command of mine, never stirred. His face became an ashen hue and he looked at me imploringly. Then, slowly, his hands raised up above his head as he stood there on the stairway looking fearfully over the baluster, he cried out, tremblingly: 'I cyan't, sar, 'fore the good God an' help me de Lord – I cyan't dislodge de animal!'

I looked back at Herman with a certain degree of calmness. I addressed the man.

'Where is Mr Otto Andreas?' I inquired.

At this simple query both maids on the stairs began to weep aloud, and old Amaranth Niles, the cook, who had been staring, pop-eyed and silent through the doorway, turned with an unexpected agility and fled back to her kitchen. Herman, if possible, became a full shade paler. Unsteadily the man forced himself to come down the stairs, holding rigidly to the baluster. He turned and stepped toward me, his face gray and working and the beads of sweat standing thickly and heavily on his forehead. He dropped upon his knees before me there on the gallery floor and, his hands held up above his head, cried out: 'Him dead, sar, from day before yestiddy, sar – it de troof, me marster!'

I will confess to you, Malling, that the gallery reeled about me at this wholly unexpected news. Nobody had told me the night before. Just possibly my hosts had not been aware of it. Another question presented itself to my tottering mind, a question the answer to which would clear up that matter of not being told.

'What time did he die, Herman?' I managed to articulate. I was holding on to the baluster myself now.

'Late, sar,' returned Herman, still on his knees, and swaying backward and forward. 'P'rops two hour after midnight, sar. Him bury de nex' day, sar, dat am to say 'twas yestiddy afternoon, two o'clock, me marster. De body ain' keep good, sar, an' 'sides, all we ain' made sensible of your arrival, sar.'

So that was why the Mulgravs had not told me. They simply had not known of my half-brother's death, would not know until today in the ordinary course of events, at that distance from Christiansted.

My first reaction, I will admit, was one of profound relief.

Otto Andreas would never – I confess to have thought – trouble me again; would not, indeed, again trouble anyone with his shortcomings, his arrogance, his manifold evil habits, his villainies. I was premature . . .

Then, almost mechanically, I suppose, my mind turned to that shambles in my hall, that barnyard beast stabled there, the priceless rug sodden with its filth. I turned to Herman and spoke.

'Get up, Herman! Stand up, man! There is no occasion for you to act in this fashion. I was, naturally, very much annoyed at the animal being in the hall. I am, in fact, still vexed about it. Tell me – ' as the man rose to his feet and stood trembling before me – 'who placed it there, and why has it not been removed?'

At this Herman visibly shook from head to foot, and again his dark visage, which had been somewhat restored to its wonted coloration, turned gray with fright. I sensed somehow that he was less frightened at me than at something else. I am, of course, accustomed to the peculiarities of our Negroes. I spoke to him again, very gently, voicing my previous idea which had stayed my first great anger.

'Did Mr Otto Andreas place the animal there?'

Herman, apparently not trusting himself to speak, nodded his head at me.

'Come now, man, get it out quickly!' I commanded.

Again, to my profound annoyance, Herman fell on his knees before me, mumbled abjectly his statement of inability to carry out my orders.

I struggled with myself to be patient. I had been, I conceived, rather sorely tried. I took Herman by the shoulder, drew him to his feet, walked him, unresisting, along the gallery and into my office. I closed the door behind us and sat down at my work table where I do my accounts and write – where I am now writing this to you. Herman, I perceived, was still trembling. There was something in this which I was – so far – unable to fathom.

'Go and bring me some rum and two tumblers, Herman,' I ordered, still forcing myself to speak gently, calmly. Herman left the room in silence. I sat there waiting for him to come back, intensely puzzled. The bullock, it seemed to me, could wait. By the indications it had been there for a full day or more. The odor was, even here with the door closed, almost unbearable.

Herman returned and set down the rum and the tumblers. I poured out a stiff tot and a smaller one for myself. I drank off my rum and then handed the other tumbler to Herman.

'Drink this, Herman,' I ordered him, 'and then sit down there. I wish to speak with you very seriously.'

Herman gulped the rum, his eyes rolling and, when I had repeated my command, seated himself uneasily on the extreme edge of the chair I had indicated. I looked at him. Fetching and drinking the rum had somewhat helped his agitation. He was no longer visibly trembling.

'Listen to me, now, man,' said I. 'I beg you to tell me, plainly and without equivocation, why is it that you have not taken that bullock out of the hall. That I must know. Come now, tell me, man!'

Once again Herman literally threw himself at my feet and groveled there. He murmured – 'I is beg yo' to believe, me marster, dat I can not do, sar.'

This was too much. I threw my restraint to the winds, caught the black rascal by the neck, hauled him to his feet, shook him soundly, slapped him on both sides of the face. He was unresistant, quite limp in my grasp, poor old fellow.

'You will tell me,' I threatened him, 'or, by Caesar, I'll break every bone in your damned worthless black body! Come now, at once and no more of this intolerable stupidness!'

Herman stiffened. He leaned forward, whispered, tremblingly, in my ear. He did not dare, it seemed, to mention the name he had on his tongue aloud. He told me that Pap' Joseph, their devilish black *papaloi*, as they name him, their witch-doctor, had been the cause of the bullock's remaining in the hall. Furthermore, now that he was started on his confession, he told me that my half-brother had had that filthy wretch staying in the house – can you imagine it, Malling? – for several days before his sudden death; that the two had made elaborate arrangements, there in the hall, for some filthy *obeah* which they were planning between them; that the bullock had been introduced three days ago; other detail which would be here superfluous, and, finally, that, as nearly as he – not a witness of whatever necromancy or sorcery they were working among them – there had been various other blacks on the scene in my hall besides those two – could estimate the matter, Otto Andreas had died, very suddenly and unexpectedly, *in the midst of their incantations*, and that Pap' Joseph himself had given him, Herman, the strictest orders not to remove the bullock from the hall upon any pretext whatsoever until he, Pap' Joseph, should come to take the animal away in person. It was to be watered, fed – hence the bucket and the trough of green food – but not otherwise to be interfered with in any manner whatsoever.

That, of course, explained much; but knowing why poor old Herman had balked at answering my previous questions did not help the affair very greatly. The disgusting creature was still, as it were, pastured in my hall. It was inexplicable – why the witch-doctor had issued such ridiculous orders, I mean to say, because to understand that, one would have to be familiar with the inner workings of their incantations and similar stupidness. However, I saw clearly that Herman could not, being under such pressure of fear – they all dread this Joseph like pestilence or the Evil Fiend himself – do anything by way of removing the animal. I sent him out, and stepped along the gallery and again into the hall.

Here, for the first time, I perceived what my complete stultification upon seeing that bullock calmly occupying my hall on my first visit had prevented my noticing before. At the east end of the hall, a large, strong platform of boards, approached from the side by a ramp or inclined plane, had been solidly built against the wall, at the same height as the marble mantelshelf. Indeed, the platform, which was about twelve feet square, was an extension into the room of the mantelshelf itself. I knew, and you know, of course, what that had involved. The platform was a 'high' altar of voodoo. Some very elaborate rites of the higher manifestations of their horrible practises had been planned here. I was dry-mouthed with pure indignation. The son of my father, Fergus Gannett, even by a person of color, lending himself to that, taking willing part in such atrocious villainy!

I saw that I should have to secure a rope to remove the bullock, which was entirely free, and now standing looking out of one of the windows without so much as a halter on its head. I walked out of the room, closing the door behind me, and as I was about to call Herman to fetch me a rope it occurred to me that I would do well to procure some help. I could not, you see, lead such an animal out of my house on to the public road. It would be a most ridiculous sight and would mark me for years as a subject for derisive conversation among the blacks of the town, indeed of the entire island. I called to Herman, therefore, but when he came in answer to this summons I demanded, not a rope, but the carriage and, when that appeared ten minutes later, I ordered Herman to drive me out to Macartney House.

Yes, I had made up my mind, even to the extent of taking Macartney some way into my confidence, that I would do wisely to have him along. For one thing, he has many cattle. Macartney handing over a bullock – it could be led out through a back passage and into the house yard – to one of his farm laborers would not excite any comment at all in the town.

I thought better and better of this decision during the ten-minute drive to Macartney's, and when I arrived I found him at home and Cornelis Hansen, his son-in-law, who married Honoria, with him.

I explained no more to these gentlemen than that my eccentric late half-brother had seen fit to leave an animal in the hall shortly before his death, and that I begged their aid and countenance in getting rid of the beast, and they both came back with me.

It was close upon three o'clock in the afternoon when we arrived, Macartney having brought one of his cattlemen who sat beside Herman on the box, and taking this fellow with us, equipped with a rope and bull halter, we entered the house and walked along the inner gallery and into the hall.

Here, then, my dear Malling, I am constrained to set down the oddest happening! The bullock, which was a young one, only half grown, was not, as it turned out, the docile, placid creature one might very well have expected.

To put the matter briefly, so soon as the creature saw us enter, and had, apparently, observed the cattleman with his halter and rope, it began to act as though it were positively possessed! It raged about the room, upsetting what furniture was there, breaking some articles, overturning others, the cattleman in hot pursuit; Macartney, Mr Hansen and I doing our best to hem it in and head it off. Finally it took refuge, of all imaginable places, upon the board platform! Yes, it ran up the ramp and stood, at bay, its muzzle positively frothing, its nostrils distended, and a look of the most extraordinary emotion upon its heavy animal face that anyone could – or could not – possibly imagine.

As it stood there, and the three of us and the cattleman stood looking up at it, Macartney burst out with – 'Faith, Mr Gannett, sir, it has every appearance of humanity in its confounded eyes – the beast!'

I looked at it and felt that Macartney might almost be right! The animal had most pronouncedly upon its facial expression every indication of unwillingness to be removed from my hall! The thing was entirely ridiculous, save only that its rushing about was going to cost me a pretty penny for the joiner's work which must be done upon my broken furniture.

Macartney ordered his Negro to mount the ramp and place the halter upon the now apparently cornered beast, and he attempted to do so. He had got nearly to the top when the beast unexpectedly lowered its head and hurled the unfortunate man to the floor, breaking one of his arms between the shoulder and elbow.

At this, once more that day, I lost patience entirely. This stupidness, it seemed to me, had gone far enough. Was my half-brother and his witless knavery to follow and distress and annoy me even from beyond his grave? I decided that I would end the affair there and then.

'Attend to your poor fellow, here, Macartney,' said I, 'and I will return directly. You might take him out and Herman will drive him to the municipal hospital.'

I left the room, walked along the inner gallery to my office, and took my pistol from the drawer of the table where I always keep it.

I came back to the hall, passing Macartney and Hansen as they carried the poor devil with his broken arm, moaning quite piteously, out to the carriage in the roadway below.

The pistol in my hand, I approached the platform. On it the bullock was still standing. It had made no effort to descend. I walked straight down the room and stood before the platform, raised the pistol, and took careful aim at the middle of the animal's forehead. It was only just as I pressed my index finger firmly around the trigger that I caught the expression in its eyes. Then I understood fully what Macartney had meant by his remark that it looked almost 'human'! If I had had time, I confess to you, Malling, I would, even then, and after all that provocation and vexatiousness, have stayed my hand. But it was too late.

The bullet struck squarely in the middle of the beast's forehead and, as it swayed on its stricken legs, a great gout of red blood ran down its soft nose and dripped upon the boards of the platform. Then, quite suddenly, its four legs gave out from under it, and it fell with a round thud on the boards, shaking the solid platform with its considerable weight, and lay still, its head projecting over the edge of the platform.

I left it lying there, the blood running over the edge and dripping on the mahogany flooring of the hall underneath and, as I left the room in the definite certainty that I was finished with this annoyance, all but having the furniture repaired and the stinking shambles cleaned and aired, I carried with me the most extraordinary impression which suddenly grew up in my mind – the most distressful matter imaginable – a feeling which, however illogical the affair may appear to you, I feel certain I shall carry with me to the grave – *the feeling that I had gravely interfered, in some truly mysterious and inexplicable fashion, with my half-brother Otto Andreas's last wishes*!

Macartney and his son-in-law were returning along the inner gallery from depositing the man in my carriage, and I took them into the dining room for some refreshment, laying the pistol on the table.

'So you shot the beast, eh?' remarked Macartney.

'Aye,' I returned, 'and that ends that phase of the trouble, Macartney. The wine and rum are here on the sideboard; be pleased to take your glasses, gentlemen – only, there is another side to all this on which I wish to consult you both.'

We drank a tot of rum and then, the decanter and glasses on the table beside the pistol, we drew up our chairs and I opened to these gentlemen the affair, in confidence – both, as you know, are, like ourselves, members of the Harmonic Lodge in St Thomas, first placing them formally on the *****s'p – of my late half-brother and his bringing the witch-doctor into my house for their infernal deviltry, whatever it may have been.

Both, as soon as I had made this affair clear, were of one mind with me. This, in truth, was a matter for swift and very definite action. We must take into our joint confidence the Policemaster – our brother Freemason, fortunately – Knudsen.

We wasted no time, once we had come to that conclusion. I excused myself, leaving these gentlemen to their glasses and the decanter and, taking the pistol, which I returned to its drawer, entered my office and wrote a brief note to Policemaster Knudsen and dispatched Marianna with it to the Christiansfort.

Knudsen arrived in response to this summons just at four, and we sat down to a dish of tea in the dining room to discuss the matter. Knudsen agreed with us fully. He would send out a pair of his *gendarmes* at once, apprehend Pap' Joseph, lodge him in the fort safely, and bring him here to the scene of this last crime of his at nine o'clock that evening. Macartney and Hansen promised to be here at that hour, and Herman, who had returned from the hospital, drove them back to Macartney House.

Knudsen and his prisoner – handcuffed fast between two *gendarmes* who sat with him in the lower gallery on three adjacent chairs from eight forty-five until the punctual arrival of Macartney and Hansen on the stroke of nine – were the first to arrive. Knudsen and I sat together in my office waiting for the other two men in the interim. Knudsen had a glass or two of rum, but I excused myself from joining him in this refreshment.

Upon the arrival of Macartney and his son-in-law Cornelis Hansen, we dismissed the *gendarmes*, Knudsen instructing them to wait at the farther end of the inner gallery, and took the prisoner into the office where he was provided with a chair. We sat around and looked at him.

This man, rather small and very black, was decently clothed and, except for an extremely villainous expression about the eyes, looked commonplace enough. Yet a mere word of direction from him into the ear of my butler had caused that faithful old servitor of our family for more than thirty years utterly to refuse to obey my orders and dispose of the filthy beast stabled in my hall!

I had sent all the servants home, not even retaining Herman. We had thus the entire house to ourselves. Knudsen nodded to me as soon as we had bestowed ourselves, and I addressed the witch-doctor.

'Joseph,' said I, 'we know that you were here in this house with Mr Otto Andreas, and that you used my hall for some of your incantations. This, of course, places you outside the law on several counts. The code forbids the practice of *obeah* in the Danish West Indies, and you were, plainly, breaking that law. Also, since you have been doing so here in my house, I am concerned in the matter. I have talked the affair over with these gentlemen and, I will be frank with you, there is some of it which we fail to understand; in particular why I discovered a beast stabled in my residence which, as I understand it, is some of your doings. We have brought you here, therefore, to hear your story. If you will reply clearly and fully to what we desire to ask you, Herr Knudsen assures me that you will not be thrown into gaol in the fort, nor prosecuted. If you refuse, then the law shall take its course in this case.

'I ask you, therefore, to explain to us, fully, what this animal was doing in my hall; also what part Mr Otto Andreas had in the affair. Those are the two matters on which we desire to have the fullest information.'

Malling, this black fellow simply refused to speak. Nothing, not a word, not a syllable, could we get out of him. Macartney tried him, Mr Hansen spoke to him; finally Knudsen, who had waited without saying anything, put in his word.

'If you refuse to reply to the two questions,' said he, 'I shall take steps to make you speak.'

That was all. It occupied, in all, more than half an hour. At any rate, my watch showed it nearly a quarter before ten when we paused, and Macartney and Hansen and I looked at each other, baffled; apparently we could get no satisfaction out of this wretch. Then, in the pause which had ensued, Knudsen, the policemaster, addressed me.

'Have I your permission to send my men into your kitchen?' he asked in his curt manner. I bowed. 'Anything you desire, Herr Knudsen,' I replied, and Knudsen rose and walked out into the inner gallery, and through the half open door of the office we could hear him saying something to his *gendarmes*. Then he returned and sat, silently, looking at the black fellow who now, for the first time, appeared somewhat moved. He showed this only by a slight and characteristic rolling of his eyeballs. Otherwise he gave no more sign of communicativeness than he had vouchsafed previously.

We sat thus, waiting, until a few minutes after ten o'clock, Knudsen and the black fellow quite silent, the others of us conversing slightly among ourselves. Then, at eight minutes past ten, one of the *gendarmes* knocked at the door and handed in to Knudsen, who had arisen to open to this summons, a burning charcoal pot and the bayonets from the two men's rifles which had been detached, doubtless by their officer's command. I sensed, at this, something extremely unpleasant. I knew Knudsen's well earned reputation for downrightness. He is, as you are aware, one of those ex-non-commissioned officers of the Danish army who, as a professional handler of men, takes no stupidness from criminals or others with whom his profession causes him to deal.

He set the charcoal pot on the middle of the floor of my office, thrust the two bayonets, points inward, directly within the bed of glowing coals and, turning to the man who had waited at the door, commanded: 'Bring Larsen here, Krafft, and bind this fellow with his hands behind him and his feet trussed together.'

The policemaster spoke in Danish which, I suppose, the black fellow did not understand. Yet I could perceive him wince at the words, which plainly had to do with his subsequent treatment, and his dark face took on that grayish shade which is a Negro's paling.

Almost at once the two *gendarmes* were at the door again. The fellow addressed as Krafft saluted and said – 'We have no rope, Herr Commandant.'

I remembered at that the bull handler's rope which Macartney's man, when carried out for his trip to the hospital, had left behind him. I recalled it as it lay on the floor near that horried platform, as I had myself left the room after the destruction of the animal. No one had been in the hall since that time, some seven hours ago.

'Pardon, Herr Knudsen,' said I, rising. 'If you will send one of these men with me, I will provide him with a rope.'

Knudsen spoke to Krafft, who saluted once more and, stepping aside for me to pass out into the inner gallery, followed me a pace behind while I walked along it toward the doorway leading into the hall.

Malling, my friend, I hesitate to go on; yet, go on I must if I am to make it clear to you, after this long rigmarole which I have already, by nearly a whole day's steady composition, succeeded in setting out for your perusal and understanding. I will try to set it down, the dreadful thing, the incredible horror which blasted my sight and will invade my suffering mind until death closes my eyes for the last time on this earth; my real and sufficient reason for leaving this island where I have lived all my life, which I love as my native land, where all my friends live.

Attend, then, friend Malling, to what I must, perforce, set out on this paper, if you are to understand.

I reached the door, throwing it open, which let out upon us more of that wretched odor which was, of course, all through the house despite opened windows. Lighting a match, I set alight the nearest lamp, a standing, brass mounted affair, which stands quite near the doorway beside my mother's Broadwood pianoforte.

By this light we proceeded, the *gendarme* Krafft and I, along the room toward the other end where the platform still stood, where the carcass of the animal hung, its head over the edge, awaiting the very early morning when old Herman, according to my orders, was, with the assistance of two laborers he was to secure, to remove it and set about the cleaning of the room immediately afterward.

Two-thirds of the way along the room I paused and, pointing in the general direction to where it lay, on the mahogany floor, told Krafft that he would find the rope somewhere near the place I indicated. I caught his silent salute with the corner of my eye as I paused to light another standing lamp, since the light from the first, dimmed by its large ornamental shade, left us, at this point, in semi-darkness and the mantelpiece and platform above it in thick darkness. I had just turned down the circular wick of this second lamp when I heard Krafft's scream and, dropping the box of matches I held upon the floor, wheeled just in time to see him, his hands above his head in a gesture of abandoned horror, sink limply to the floor not five paces from the front of that platform.

I peered toward him, my eyes for the instant slightly dazzled from having been close to the flame of the newly lighted lamp, and then, Malling – then, my friend, I saw *what he had seen;* what had set this tough-grained manhandler of a policeman to screaming like a frightened woman, and himself hurtling to the floor in an uncontrollable spasm of stark, unmitigated terror. And as I saw, and felt the room go around, and envisaged the conviction that this was the end of life – as I myself sank, helpless with the fearsome horror of that eldritch uncanniness, toward the floor, the light fading from my consciousness in the onset of a merciful oblivion, I heard behind me, the agitated voices of Knudsen and Macartney and young Mr Hansen as they, summoned by Krafft's scream, crowded into the hall through the doorway. I had seen, dimly in that not too good illumination from the two standing oil lamps, not the head of the bullock I had destroyed, but – *the head and shoulders of my half-brother Otto Andreas:*

a great blackened hole in his forehead; and the blood dried on his inverted face; as he hung, stark now, and ghastly lifeless from over the edge of the voodoo platform . . .

I awakened in my office surrounded by my acquaintances, a drizzle of cold water upon my face and neck, and the taste of brandy in my mouth puckering my lips. I was on my back on the floor and, looking up, I perceived that the *gendarme*, Larsen, stood over the still seated black fellow, his pistol held near the back of the man's head. As I sat up, assisted by young Mr Hansen, Knudsen turned away from the group and, taking a now glowing bayonet out of the charcoal pot with his gloved hand, curtly ordered Larsen to turn the Negro out of his chair and stretch him, bound as I perceived, according to orders, upon the floor.

The anticipation sickened me slightly, and I closed my eyes; but I had determined not to interfere with Knudsen, who knew his own methods and was, after all, here upon my own request to force from this villain the confession which should clear up the mysteries we had vainly propounded to him.

I was soon in my chair, pretty well restored by the vigorous measures which had been taken with me, and able to hear what Knudsen was saying to the supine prisoner. I saw, too, the pale and stricken face of Krafft, just outside the doorway. He too, it appeared, had recovered.

I will abbreviate a very ugly matter, an affair which sickened me to the heart; which was, nevertheless, necessary as procedure if we were to secure the information we desired.

In short, the black fellow, even in his present distressful condition, refused, point blank, to reveal what we had inquired of him, and Knudsen, with his own hand, tore open his shirt and applied the cherry-red bayonet to his skin. A horrid smell of scorched flesh made itself apparent at once, and I closed my eyes, sick at the dreadful sight. The Negro screamed with the unbearable pain, but thereafter clamped his thick lips and shook his head against Knudsen's repeated orders to answer the questions.

Then Knudsen put the bayonet back, thrusting it well into the glowing charcoal, and took out the other one. He stood with it in his hand above the Negro. He addressed him, in his usual curt, cold and hard tones.

'My man, I warn you seriously. I make you sensible that you will not leave this house alive. I shall go over your entire body, with these, unless you reply to the questions you have been asked.'

With the conclusion of this warning speech, he abruptly pressed the flat of the bayonet across the Negro's abdomen, and after an anguished howl of pain, Pap' Joseph capitulated. He nodded his head and writhed out of twisted lips his consent.

He was at once lifted back into the chair by the two *gendarmes*, and then, gasping, his eyes rolling in a mental anguish plainly greater than that of his grievous bodily hurts, he told us . . .

It appears that there are two 'supreme offerings' in the dreadful worship of these voodooists; one the affair of a human sacrifice which they name 'the goat without horns', and which, according to our informant, was never put into practice in these islands; and the second, their ceremony which they call the 'baptism'. This last, it was, which had been perpetrated in my house! And – one could hardly guess it, even at this stage of this narrative of mine for your private eye, friend Malling – *it was Otto Andreas who was the candidate*!

I should, perhaps, have mentioned that his body, supposedly buried a day and a half before, and which had, to my distraction and that of the man Krafft, been seen hanging over the edge of the sacrificial platform, had been taken down and now lay, decently disposed by Knudsen and Larsen along four chairs in the hall during the short period when Macartney and Hansen had been engaged in reviving me and bringing me back to my office. Earth and splinters of pitch pine were upon the body.

The culmination of that foul rite which they impiously call the baptism is the sacrifice of an animal; sometimes a goat, sometimes a young bull. In this case the bull had been selected.

Before the knife is drawn across the throat of the animal, however, the candidate for the baptism, on hands and knees, and stripped naked as the hour he was born, must 'confront' the goat or the bull. Yes, Malling, as I gathered it from those twisted, pain-galled lips of that black fiend, the two, the candidate and the sacrificial animal, gaze for a long period into each other's eyes; the belief being that in this way the two, for the time being, exchange, as it were, their personalities! It seems incredible that it should be believed, yet such is what he assured us of.

In the ordinary course, the officiating priest having determined that this alleged exchange of personalities had indeed taken place, the animal is abruptly killed, its throat being cut across with a sharpened machete or canebill. At this, the personality of the human being retransfers itself to its proper abode; yet some modicum of it is supposed to remain in the animal, and this on the animal's death, passes out of it and into the custody of the thing they name the Guinea Snake, which is the ultimate object of their nefarious devotions, as a sacrifice, given up by the candidate thereto.

Such, as it was explained to us, is the underlying principle of a voodooist's baptism.

That is how it would have occurred in the case of Otto Andreas, if there had not been a kind of unexpected hitch. Naturally, one would gather, the nervous and mental strain upon such a candidate would be an extremely severe one. In the case of my half-brother it proved too severe.

Otto Andreas had dropped dead, doubtless from heart failure induced by the strain of it all, there on the platform, just at the very moment before Pap' Joseph himself, as he assured us, who was officiating at the baptism, was to slaughter the bull.

The personalities, as the voodooists believed, were at that moment entirely interchanged. In other words, lacking the release and relocation of these, which would have come at the knife stroke across the bullock's throat, the 'soul' of the sacrificial animal died at the moment of Otto Andreas' unexpected death, and – *the soul of Otto Andreas remained in the bullock.*

'An' so, sar,' finished Pap' Joseph, with a devilish leer in his eyes, and addressing me, 'yo' is destroy the life of yo' bruddah, sar, when yo' is so hasty as to shoot de bull!'

The witch-doctor, it transpired from a portion of this account, had given old Herman the orders – not knowing of my imminent return home – to keep the bullock in the hall, because he was 'making magic' to get the 'souls' exchanged back again! It had, of course, been necessary to bury Otto Andreas' body. But we were assured, if the bullock had been left alone, it would, by now, have been changed back into Otto Andreas, a process which, the witch-doctor gravely assured us, required not only a great skill in magicking like his own, but considerable time!

There was only one thing to be done that night. Pap' Joseph was sent back to the Christiansfort, with instructions that he was to be liberated the following morning at six o'clock. Then the four of us, having placed a blanket about the body of Otto Andreas, carried it among us to the cemetery. Arrived there, with the two spades we had fetched along, Hansen and Knudsen set to work to dig up the coffin. It was moonlight and, of course, at that hour of the night no one was in or even near the cemetery.

The earth, even for a newly made grave, was unusually loose, it seemed to all of us. A spade struck wood, about four feet down. Macartney spelled his son-in-law. I offered to do the same for Knudsen, but he refused. Within a minute he said in a puzzled tone – 'What is this!'

He squatted down in the grave and with his gloved hands threw up a mass of soft earth about something he had discovered.

Malling, they had disinterred a smashed coffin, a coffin burst out of semblance to the narrow box which is designed to be the last housing place of a human form. And no wonder it had been burst asunder, from the monstrous thing which came partially to light. We did not wholly uncover what he had discovered down there under the surface of the holy ground. There was no need, Malling.

It had been the stiff, unyielding, bony limb of a four-legged horned animal, from which Knudsen had thrown up the loose earth. A bullock was buried there, where some thirty-six hours previously men had interred the body of my late half-brother Otto Andreas Gannett. Pap' Joseph, it appeared, under that direful compulsion to which he had so reluctantly yielded, had told us the truth.

We hastily enlarged the grave sufficiently to receive the body we had brought with us and, leaving a higher mound than had met us on our arrival, though beaten down with the flats of the spades, we came back swiftly and in silence to my house and there, as brother Freemasons, swore that, save for this information to you, our fellow brother Freemason, which I specified as an exception, we would none of us – and the others during the term of my life – reveal anything of what we had heard to any man. Knudsen answered for his *gendarmes* and from the reputation he bears as a disciplinarian, I have little fear that either of them will ever mention what part of it all they were privileged to witness.

This will serve, then, my friend, to account to you for why I am leaving Santa Cruz and going to Scotland whence our family came here four generations ago, when these islands were for the first time opened to the settlement of planters other than natives of Denmark through the generosity of the Danish government. I can not stay in this cursed house where such things as confound man's understanding have taken place; and so I place my property in your kind and efficient hands, my friend Malling, in the belief that I have made my reasons for such a decision clear.

I am taking with me to Scotland my faithful old servant Herman. I would not leave him here to endure the tender mercies of that pestiferous scoundrel Pap' Joseph, whose orders, out of faithfulness to me, he broke. One cannot tell what would happen to the poor old fellow if I were so inconsiderate.

I remain, yours most faithfully and to command,

ANGUS GANNETT

P.S. Knudsen, of course, insists that some blacks, followers of Pap' Joseph, merely exchanged the bodies of the bullock and my half-brother, during the interval, after my shooting of the beast, in which my hall remained unvisited by any of my household.

A. G.

3

I finished the account and handed it back to Herr Malling. I thanked him for his extraordinary courtesy in allowing me to read it. And then I walked straight to Gannett House to look once more at that hall where all this mysterious succession of strange affairs had taken place. I sat down, after Robertson had let me in, in the place usually occupied by Mrs Garde, and Robertson brought me a solitary tea on the great circular tray.

I could not forbear glancing up toward the place once occupied by that board platform where a voodoo baptism had all but taken place; a strange rite interrupted just before its culmination by the collapse of long dead and gone Otto Andreas, with his unquenchable desire for the fellowship of the Snake! There are strange matters in our West Indies. Well, God was, always had been, always will be, stronger than the Snake. There would be, I felt well assured, no recurrence of that strange vision which had projected itself after all these years, of that bullock's 'almost human' eyes, reproachful, pathetic, as Mrs Garde had said, looking down at the grim Scot with his steady hand leveling his great horse pistol at the point between those eyes.

Mrs Garde returned to her hired house infinitely refreshed by her sea voyage, her mind occupied with other affairs than the horror of the wall near the portrait of her late husband.

There was, as I had anticipated, no recurrence of the phenomenon.

Naturally, Mrs Garde was solicitous to inquire what I had done to remove the appearance which had done so much to destroy her comfort and happiness, but I was loath to explain the matter to her, and managed never to do so. Perhaps her splendid gentility sensed that I did not wish to offer her explanations. Mrs Garde was a Boston Unitarian, and Boston Unitarians are apt to take things on an intellectual basis. Such are not likely to be sympathetically familiar with such other-worldly affairs as the exorcism of a house, routine affair as it had been to good Fr Richardson.

Besides, I have no doubt, Mrs Garde was so pleased at the non-recurrence of the old annoyance, that she probably attributed it to something popularly called 'eye strain'. There was nothing to remind her of that bloody-faced, pathetic-eyed bullock, drooping to its final fall. Otto Andreas Gannett was not even a memory in Christiansted. We had many delightful tea parties, and several evening dances, in that magnificent hall of Gannett House that winter in Christiansted.

Seven Turns in a Hangman's Rope

I first became acutely aware of the dreadful tragedy of Saul Macartney one sunny morning early in the month of November of the year 1927. On that occasion, instead of walking across the hall from my bathroom after shaving and the early morning shower, I turned to the left upon emerging and, in my bathrobe and slippers, went along the upstairs hallway to my workroom on the northwest corner of the house into which I had just moved, in the west coast town of Frederiksted on the island of Santa Cruz.

This pleasant room gave a view through its several windows directly down from the hill on which the house was located, across the pretty town with its red roofs and varicolored houses, directly upon the indigo Caribbean. This workroom of mine had a north light from its two windows on that side and, as I used it only during the mornings, I thus escaped the terrific sun drenching to which, in the absence of any shade without, the room was subjected during the long West Indian afternoon.

The occasion for going in there was my desire to see, in the clear morning light, what that ancient oil painting looked like; the canvas which, without its frame, I had tacked up on the south wall the evening before.

This trophy, along with various other items of household flotsam and jetsam, had been taken the previous afternoon, which was a day after my arrival on the island, out of a kind of lumber room wherein the owners of the house had plainly been storing for the best part of a century the kinds of things which accumulate in a family. Of the considerable amount of material which my houseman, Stephen Penn, had taken out and stacked and piled in the upper hallway, there happened to be nothing of interest except this good-sized painting – which was about three feet by five in size. Stephen had paused to examine it curiously and it was this which drew my attention to it.

Under my first cursory examination, which was little more than a glance, I had supposed the thing to be one of those ubiquitous

Victorian horrors of reproduction which fifty years ago might have been observed on the walls of most middle-class front parlors, and which were known as chromos. But later that evening, on picking it up and looking at it under the electric light, I found that it was honest paint, and I examined it more closely and with a constantly increasing interest.

The painting was obviously the work of a fairly clever amateur. The frame of very old and dry wood had been riddled through and through by wood-worms; it literally fell apart in my hands. I left it there on the floor for Stephen to brush up the next morning and took the canvas into my bedroom where there was a better light. The accumulations of many years' dust and grime had served to obscure its once crudely bright coloration. I carried it into my bathroom, made a lather of soap and warm water, and gave it a careful and much needed cleansing, after which the scene delineated before me assumed a surprising freshness and clarity.

After I had dried it off with a hand towel, using great care lest I crack the ancient pigment, I went over it with an oiled cloth. This process really brought it out, and although the canvas was something more than a century old, the long-obscured and numerous figures with which it had been almost completely covered seemed once more as bright and clear – and quite as crude – as upon the long distant day when that rather clever amateur artist had laid down his (or perhaps her) brush after putting on the very last dab of vermilion paint.

The subject of the old painting, as I recognized quite soon, was an almost forgotten incident in the history of the old Danish West Indies. It had, quite obviously, been done from the viewpoint of a person on board a ship. Before me, as the setting of the scene, was the well known harbor of St Thomas with its dull red fort at my right – looking exactly as it does today. At the left-hand margin were the edges of various public buildings which have long since been replaced. In the midst, and occupying nearly the entire spread of the canvas, with Government Hill and its fine houses sketched in for background, was shown the execution of Fawcett, the pirate, with his two lieutenants; an occasion which had constituted a general holiday for the citizens of St Thomas, and which had taken place, as I happened to be aware, on the eleventh of September, 1825. If the picture had been painted at that time, and it seemed apparent that such was the case, the canvas would be just one hundred and two years old.

My interest now thoroughly aroused, I bent over it and examined it with close attention. Then I went into my work-room and brought back my large magnifying glass.

My somewhat clever amateur artist had left nothing to the imagination. The picture contained no less than two hundred and three human figures. Of these only those in the remoter backgrounds were sketched in roughly in the modern manner. The actual majority were very carefully depicted with a laborious infinitude of detail; and I suspected then, and since have found every reason to believe, that many, if not most of them, were portraits! There before my eyes were portly Danish worthies of a century ago, with their ladyfolk, all of whom had come out to see Captain Fawcett die. There were the officers of the garrison. There were the *gendarmes* of the period, in their stiff looking uniforms after the manner of Frederick the Great.

There were Negroes, some with large gold rings hanging from one ear; Negresses in their bebustled gingham dresses and bare feet, their foulards or varicolored head handkerchiefs topped by the broad-brimmed plaited straw hats which are still to be seen along modern St Thomas's concrete drives and sidewalks. There was the executioner, a huge, burly, fierce-looking black man; with the police-master standing beside and a little behind him, gorgeous in his glistening white drill uniform with its gilt-decorations. The two stood on the central and largest of the three scaffolds.

The executioner was naked to the waist and had his woolly head bound up in a tight-fitting scarlet kerchief. He had only that moment sprung the drop, and there at the end of the manila rope (upon which the artist had carefully painted in the seven turns of the traditional hangman's knot placed precisely under the left ear of the miscreant now receiving the just reward of his innumerable villainies) hung Captain Fawcett himself, the gruesome central figure of this holiday pageant – wearing top boots and a fine plum-colored laced coat.

On either side, and from the ropes of the two smaller gibbets, dangled those two lesser miscreants, Fawcett's mates. Obviously their several executions, like the preliminary bouts of a modern boxing program, had preceded the main event of the day.

The three gibbets had been erected well to the left of the central space which I have described. The main bulk of the spectators was consequently to the right as one looked at the picture, on the fort side.

After more than a fascinating hour with my magnifying glass, it being then eleven o'clock and time to turn in, I carried the brittle old canvas into my workroom and by the rather dim light of a shaded reading lamp fastened it carefully at a convenient height against the south wall with thumbtacks. The last tack went through the arm of the hanging man nearest the picture's extreme left-hand margin. After accomplishing this I went to bed.

The next morning, as I have mentioned, being curious to see how the thing looked in a suitable light, I walked into the workroom and looked at it.

I received a devastating shock.

My eye settled after a moment or two upon that dangling mate whose body hung from its rope near the extreme left-hand margin of the picture. I found it difficult to believe my eyes. In this clear morning light the expression of the fellow's face had changed startlingly from what I remembered after looking at it closely through my magnifying glass. Last night it had been merely the face of a man just hanged; I had noted it particularly because, of all the more prominent figures, that face had been most obviously an attempt at exact portraiture.

Now it wore a new and unmistakable expression of acute agony.

And down the dangling arm, from the point which that last thumbtack had incontinently transfixed, there ran, and dripped off the fellow's fingers, a stream of bright, fresh red blood . . .

2

Between the time when the clipper schooner, which had easily overhauled the Macartney trading vessel *Hope* – coming north across the Caribbean and heavily laden with sacked coffee from Barranquilla – had sent a challenging shot from its swivel-gun across the *Hope*'s bows, and his accomplishing the maneuver of coming about in obedience to that unmistakable summons, Captain Saul Macartney had definitely decided what policy he should follow.

He had made numerous voyages in the *Hope* among the bustling trade ports of the Caribbean and to and from his own home port of St Thomas, and never before, by the Grace of God and the Macartney luck, had any freetrader called up on him to stand and deliver on the high seas. But, like all seafaring men of Captain Macartney's generation, plying their trade in those latitudes in the early 1820's, he was well aware of what was now in store for him, his father's ship and the members of his crew. The *Hope* would be looted; then probably scuttled, in accordance with the freetraders' well-nigh universal policy of destroying every scrap of evidence against them. As for himself and his men, they would be confronted with the formula – 'Join, or go over the side!'

A pirate's recruit was a pirate, at once involved in a status which was without the law. His evidence, even if he were attempting the dangerous double game of merely pretending to join his captor, was worthless.

There was no possible ray of hope, direct resistance being plainly out of the question. This might be one of the better established freebooters, a piratical captain and following whose notoriety was already so widespread, who was already so well known, that he would not take the trouble to destroy the *Hope*; or, beyond the usual offer made to all volunteers for a piratical crew – constantly in need of such replacements – to put the captured vessel, officers and crew through the mill; once they were satisfied that there was nothing aboard this latest prize to repay them for the trouble and risk of capture and destruction.

The *Hope*, laden almost to her gunwales with sacked coffee, would provide lean pickings for a freetrader, despite the value of her bulk cargo in a legitimate port of trade like Savannah or Norfolk. There were cases, known to Captain Macartney, where a piratical outfit under the command of some notable such as Edward Thatch – often called Teach, or Blackbeard – or England, or Fawcett, or Jacob Brenner, had merely sheered off and sailed away in search of more desirable game as soon as it was plain that the loot was neither easily portable nor of the type of value represented by bullion, silks, or the strong box of some inter-island trading supercargo.

It was plain enough to Captain Saul Macartney, whose vessel had been stopped here about a day's sail south-south-west of his home port of St Thomas, capital of the Danish West Indies, and whose cargo was intended for delivery to several ship's brokerage houses in that clearing house port for the vast West Indian shipping trade, that this marauder of the high seas could do nothing with his coffee. These ideas were prominent in his mind in the interval between his shouted orders and the subsequent period during which the *Hope*, her way slacking rapidly, hung in the wind, her jibs, booms and loose rigging slapping angrily while the many boats from the freetrading vessel were slung outboard in a very brisk and workmanlike manner and dropped one after the other into the water alongside until every one – seven in all – had been launched.

These boats were so heavily manned as to leave them very low in the water. Now the oars moved with an almost delicate precision as though the rowers feared some mis-chance even in that placid sea. The *Hope*'s officers and crew – all of the latter Negroes – crowded along their vessel's starboard rail, the mates quiet and collected as men taking their cue from their superior officer; the crew goggle-eyed, chattering in low tones among themselves in groups and knots, motivated by the sudden looming terror which showed in a gray tinge upon their black skins.

Then, in a strident whisper from the first mate, a shrewd and experienced bucko, hailing originally from Portsmouth, New Hampshire, wise in the ways of these tropical latitudes from twenty years' continuous seafaring: 'God! It's Fawcett himself!'

Slowly, deliberately, as though entirely disdainful of any possible resistance, the seven boats drew toward the doomed *Hope*. The two foremost edged in close alongside her star-board quarter and threw small grapples handily from bow and stern and so hung in under the *Hope*'s lee.

Captain Saul Macartney, cupping his hands, addressed over the heads of the intervening six boatloads the man seated in the stern-sheets of the outermost boat.

'Cargo of sacked Brazil coffee, Captain, and nothing else to make it worth your while to come aboard me – if you'll take my word for it. That's the facts, sir, so help me God!'

In silence from all hands in the boats and without any immediate reply from Fawcett, this piece of information was received. Captain Fawcett sat there at the sternsheets of his longboat, erect, silent, presumably pondering what Captain Saul Macartney had told him. He sat there calm and unruffled, a fine gold laced tricorn hat on his head, which, together with the elegance of his wine-colored English broadcloth coat, threw into sharp relief his brutal, unshaven face with its sinister, shining white scar – the result of an old cutlass wound – which ran diagonally from the upper corner of his left ear forward down the cheek, across both lips, clear to the edge of his prominent chin.

Fawcett, the pirate, ended his reflective interval. He raised his head, rubbed a soiled hand through his beard's stubble and spat outboard.

'Any ship's biscuit left aboard ye?' he inquired, turning his eye along the *Hope*'s freeboard and thence contemplatively about her masts and rigging. 'We're short.'

'I have plenty, Captain. Will it answer if I have it passed over the side to ye?'

The two vessels and the seven heavily laden boats lay tossing silently in the gentle swell. Not a sound broke the tension while Captain Fawcett appeared to deliberate.

Then a second time he spat over the side of his longboat and rubbed his black stubbly chin with his hand, reflectively. Then he looked across his boats directly at Captain Saul Macartney. The ghost of a sour grin broke momentarily the grim straight line of his maimed and cruel mouth.

'I'll be comin' aboard ye, Captain,' he said very slowly, 'if ye have no objection to make.'

A bellow of laughter at this sally of their captain's rose from the huddled pirate crew in the boats and broke the mounting tension. A Negro at the *Hope*'s rail cackled hysterically, and a chorus of gibes at this arose from the motley crews of the boats grappled alongside.

In the silence which followed Captain Fawcett muttered a curt, monosyllabic order. The other five boats closed in with haste, two of them passing around the *Hope*'s stern and another around her bow. It was only a matter of a few seconds before the entire seven hung along the *Hope*'s sides like feasting wolves upon the flanks of a stricken deer. Then at a second brief order their crews came over the rails quietly and in good order, Fawcett himself arriving last upon the *Hope*'s deck. No resistance of any kind was offered. Captain Macartney had had the word passed quietly on that score while the pirates' boats were being slung into the water.

After the bustling scramble involved in nearly a hundred men climbing over the *Hope*'s rail from the seven boats and which was, despite the excellent order maintained, a maneuver involving considerable noisy activity, another and even a more ominous silence settled down upon the beleaguered *Hope*.

Supported by his two mates, one of whom was a small, neat, carefully dressed fellow, and the other an enormous German who sported a cavalry-man's moustache and walked truculently, Captain Fawcett proceeded directly aft, where he turned and faced forward, a mate on either side of him, and leaned against the superstructure of Captain Macartney's cabin.

Macartney's mates, taking pattern from this procedure, walked over from the rail and flanked him where he stood just aft of the *Hope*'s foremast. The rest of the freebooters, having apparently been left free by their officers to do as they pleased for the time being, strolled about the deck looking over the vessel's superficial equipment, and then gathered in little knots and groups about the eleven Negro members of the *Hope*'s crew.

Through this intermingling the comparative silence which had followed their coming aboard began to be dissipated with raillery, various low-voiced sallies of crude wit at the Negroes' expense, and an occasional burst of nervous or raucous laughter. All this, however, was carried on, as Captain Macartney took it in, in what was to him an unexpectedly restrained and quiet manner, utterly at variance with the reputed conduct of such a group of abandoned villains at sea, and to him, at least, convincing evidence that something sinister was in the wind.

This expectation had its fulfilment at a harsh blast from the whistle which, at Fawcett's nod, the huge German mate had taken from his pocket and blown.

Instantly the pirates closed in and seized those members of the *Hope*'s Negro crew who stood nearest them; several, sometimes five or six, men crowding in to overpower each individual. Five or six of the pirates who had been as though without purpose near the forward hatchway which led below decks began forthwith to knock out the wedges. The *Hope*'s Negroes, with a unanimity which bespoke the excellent discipline and strategy which Fawcett was generally understood to maintain, were hustled forward and thrust into the forecastle; the hatch of which, as soon as they were all inside, was forthwith closed tight and at once nailed fast by the undersized little Englishman who was Fawcett's ship's carpenter.

None of the *Hope*'s crew had been armed. None seemed to Captain Macartney to have been even slightly injured in the course of this rough and effective handling. Captain Macartney surmised, and rightly, that the pirates' intention was to preserve them alive either for ultimate sale into slavery, which was of course then extant throughout the West India Islands, or, perhaps, to convey them as shore servants to Fawcett's settlement which, it was generally believed, was well in the interior of the island of Andros in the Bahama group, where a network of interlacing creeks, rendering anything like pursuit and capture well-nigh out of the question, had made this private fastness a stronghold.

But Captain Macartney had little time to waste thinking over the fate of his crew. With perhaps a shade less of the roughness with which the Negroes had been seized he and his mates were almost simultaneously surrounded and marched aft to face their captors. It seemed plain that the usual choice was to be given only to the three of them.

Fawcett did not hesitate this time. He looked at the three men standing before him, lowered his head, relaxed his burly figure and barked out –

'Ye'll join me or go over the side.'

He pointed a dirty finger almost directly into the face of the older mate, who stood at his captain's right hand.

'You first,' he barked again. 'Name yer ch'ice, and name it now.'

The hard-bitten New Hampshire Yankee stood true to the traditions of an honest sailorman.

'To hell with ye, ye damned scalawag,' he drawled, and spat on the deck between Captain Fawcett's feet.

There could be but one reply on the part of a man of Fawcett's heady character to such an insult as this. With a speed that baffled the eye the great pistol which hung from the right side of his belt beneath the flap of his fine broad-cloth coat was snatched free, and to the accompaniment of its tearing roar, its huge ounce ball smote through the luckless Yankee's forehead. As the acrid cloud of smoke from this detonation blew away Captain Macartney observed the huge German mate lifting the limp body which, as though it had been that of a child, he carried in great strides to the nearer rail and heaved overboard.

Fawcett pointed with his smoking weapon at Macartney's other mate, a small-built fellow, originally a British subject from the Island of Antigua. The mate merely nodded comprehendingly. Then – 'The same as Elias Perkins told ye, ye blasted swab, and may ye rot deep in hell.'

But Fawcett's surly humor appeared to have evaporated, to have discharged itself in the pistoling of the other man whose scattered brains had left an ugly smear on the *Hope*'s clean deck. He merely laughed and, with a comprehensive motion of his left hand, addressed the larger of his mates, who had resumed his position at his left.

'Take him, Franz,' he ordered.

The huge mate launched himself upon the Antiguan like a ravening beast. With lightning-like rapidity his enormous left arm coiled crushingly about the doomed man's neck. Simultaneously, his open right hand against his victim's forehead, he pushed mightily. The little Antiguan's spine yielded with an audible crack and his limp body slithered loosely to the deck. Then with a sweeping, contemptuous motion the huge mate grasped the limp form in one hand, lifting it by the front of the waistcoat and, whirling about, hurled it with a mighty pitch far outboard.

The German mate had not yet resumed his place beside Fawcett when Captain Saul Macartney addressed the pirate leader.

'I'm joining you, Captain,' he said quietly.

And while the surprised Fawcett stared at him the newly enlisted freebooter, who had been Captain Saul Macartney of the schooner *Hope*, with a motion which did not suffer by comparison with Fawcett's for its swiftness, had produced a long dirk, taken the two lightning strides necessary for an effective stroke, and had plunged his weapon with a mighty upward thrust from under the ribs through the German mate's heart.

Withdrawing it instantly, he stooped over the sprawled body and wiped the dirk's blade in a nonchalant and leisurely manner on the dead ruffian's fine cambric shirt frill. As he proceeded to this task he turned his head upward and slightly to the left and looked squarely in the eye the stultified pirate captain who stood motionless and staring in his surprise at this totally unexpected feat of his newest recruit. From his crouching position Saul Macartney spoke, quietly and without emphasis –

'Ye see, sir, I disliked this larrikin from the minute I clapped eyes on him and I'll call your attention to the fact that I'm a sound navigator, and – ' Saul Macartney smiled and showed his handsome teeth – 'I'll ask your notice preliminary to my acting with you aft that it might equally well have been yourself that I scragged, and perhaps that'll serve to teach ye the manner of man that you're now taking on as an active lieutenant!'

Then Saul Macartney, his bantering smile gone now, his Macartney mouth set in a grim line, his cleansed dirk held ready in his sound right hand, stood menacingly before Captain Fawcett, their breasts almost touching, and in a quarter-deck voice inquired: 'And will ye be taking it or leaving it, Captain Fawcett?'

3

It was more than two months later when the *Hope*, her hull now painted a shining black, her topmasts lengthened all round by six feet, her spread of canvas vastly increased, eight carronade ports newly cut along her sides, and renamed the *Swallow*, entered the harbor of St Thomas, dropped her anchor and sent over her side a narrow long-boat.

Into this boat, immediately after its crew of six oarsmen had settled down upon their thwarts and laid their six long sweeps out upon the harbor water, interested onlookers observed two officers descend over the *Swallow*'s side, where they occupied the sternsheets together. As the boat, rowed man-o'-war style, rapidly approached the wharves it was observed by those on shore that the two men seated astern were rather more than handsomely dressed.

The shorter and heavier man wore a fine sprigged long coat of English broadcloth with lapels, and a laced tricorn hat. His companion, whose appearance had about it something vaguely familiar, was arrayed in an equally rich and very well tailored, though somewhat plainer, coat of a medium blue which set off his handsome figure admirably. This person wore no hat at all, nor any shade for his head against the glare of the eleven o'clock sun save a heavy crop of carefully arranged and naturally curly hair as black as a crow's wing.

So interesting, indeed, to the loungers along the wharves had been the entrance of this previously unknown vessel into the harbor and the subsequent coming ashore of these two fine gentlemen, that a considerable knot of sightseers was already assembled on the particular jetty toward which the longboat, smartly rowed, came steadily closer and closer. The hatless gentleman, who was by far the taller and handsomer of the two, appeared to be steering, the taut tiller ropes held firmly in his large and very shapely hands.

It was the Herr Rudolph Bernn, who had observed the crowd collecting on the jetty through the open windows of his airy shipping office close at hand, and who had clapped on his pith sun helmet and hastened to join the group, who was the first to recognize this taller officer.

'Gude Gott! If id iss nod der Herr Captain Saul Macartney. Gude Gott, how dey will be rejoiced – Oldt Macartney andt de Miss Camilla!'

Within five minutes the rapidly approaching longboat had been laid aside the pier head in navy style. Without any delay the two gentlemen, whose advent had so greatly interested the St Thomas harbor watchers, stepped ashore with an air and mounted the jetty steps side by side. At once Saul Macartney, whose fine clothes so well became him, forged ahead of his well dressed, shaved and curled companion. He wore the dazzling smile which revealed his magnificent teeth and which had served to disarm every woman upon whom it had been consciously turned since his eighth year or thereabouts.

Like a conquering hero this handsome young man – who had taken clearance from the South American port of Barranquilla nearly three months before and subsequently disappeared into thin air along with his vessel and all hands off the face of the waters – now stepped jauntily across the jetty toward the welcoming group whose numbers were, now that the news of his homecoming was beginning to trickle through the town, constantly increasing. He was instantaneously surrounded by these welcoming acquaintances who sought each to outdo his neighbor in the enthusiastic fervency of his congratulatory greetings.

During this demonstration the redoubtable and notorious Captain Fawcett stood quietly looking on through its milling course, a sardonic smile faintly relieving the crass repulsiveness of his maimed countenance. The pirate had been 'shaved to the blood' that morning; dressed for the occasion with the greatest care. His carefully arranged locks were redolent of the oil of Bergamot, filched a week before out of the accessories of a lady passenger taken from the luckless vessel on which she had been coming out to the West Indies to join her planter husband. This lady had, after certain passing attentions from Saul Macartney, gone over the *Swallow*'s side in plain sight of the volcanic cone of Nevis, the island of her destination.

That Macartney had brought Captain Fawcett ashore with him here in St Thomas was a piece of judgement so lamentably bad as to need no comment of any kind. His doing so initiated that swift course of events which brought down upon his handsome head that ruinous doom which stands, probably, as unique among the annals of retribution; that devasting doom which, for its horror and its strangeness, transcends and surpasses, in all human probability, even the direst fate, which, in this old world's long history, may have overtaken any other of the sons of men.

But the sheer effrontery of that act was utterly characteristic of Saul Macartney.

In the course of the long, painstaking, and probably exhaustive research which I, Gerald Canevin, set in motion in order to secure the whole range of facts forming the basis of this narrative – an investigation which has extended through more than three years and has taken me down some very curious by-paths of antique West Indian history as well as into contact with various strange characters and around a few very alluring corners of research – one aspect of the whole affair stands out in my mind most prominently. This is the fact that – as those many who nowadays increasingly rely for guidance upon the once discredited but now reviving science of astrology would phrase it – Saul Macartney was in all ways 'a typical Sagittarian'!

One of the more readily accessible facts which I looked up out of ancient, musty records in the course of this strange affair was the date of his birth. He had been born in the city of St Thomas on the twenty-eighth of November, in the year 1795. He was thus twenty-nine – in his thirtieth year and the full vigor of his manhood – at the time when Captain Fawcett had captured the *Hope* and, having lightened that vessel by emptying her hold of her cargo which he consigned to the sea, and having scuttled his own disabled vessel, had sailed for his home base among the Andros creeks.

From there a month later the transformed *Swallow* had emerged to maraud upon the Spanish Main. He was not yet out of his twenties when he had chosen to tempt fate by coming ashore with Fawcett in St Thomas. He was still short of thirty when a certain fateful day dawned in the month of September, 1825.

True to this hypothetical horoscope of his and to every sidereal circumstance accompanying it, Saul Macartney was an entirely self-centered person. With him the 'main chance' had always been paramount. It was this addiction to the main chance which had caused him to join Fawcett. A similar motive had actuated him in the notable coup which had at once, because of its sheer directness and the courage involved in it, established him in the high esteem of the pirate captain. There had been no sentiment in his killing of the gigantic mate, Franz. He was not thinking of avenging his own faithful lieutenant whom that hulking beast had slain with his bare hands before his eyes a moment before he had knifed the murderer.

His calculating sense of self-interest had been the sole motive behind that act. He could quite as easily have destroyed Fawcett himself, as he characteristically pointed out to that ruffian. He would have done so with equal ruthlessness save for his knowledge of the fact that he would have been overwhelmed immediately thereafter by Fawcett's underlings.

There is very little question but what he would have before very long succeeded to the command of the *Swallow* and the control of the considerable commerce in the slave trade and other similar illegitimate sources of revenue which went with the command of this piratical enterprise. He had already inaugurated the replacement of Captain Fawcett by himself in the esteem of that freebooter's numerous following well before the refurbished *Swallow* had sailed proudly out upon her current voyage. His unquestionable courage and enormous gift of personality had already been for some time combining actively to impress the pirate crew. Among them he was already a dominating figure.

Since well before he had attained manly maturity he had been irresistible to women. He was a natural fighter who loved conflict for its own sake. His skill with weapons was well-nigh phenomenal. In the prosecution of every affair which concerned his own benefit, he had always habituated himself to going straight to the mark. He was, in short, as it might be expressed, both with respect to women and the securing of his own advantage in general affairs, thoroughly spoiled by an unbroken course of getting precisely what he wanted.

This steady impact of continuous success and the sustained parallel effect of unceasing feminine adulation had entrenched in his character the fatal conviction that he could do as he pleased in every imaginable set of conditions.

The first reversal suffered in this unbroken course of selfish domination inaugurated itself not very long after he had stepped ashore with Captain Fawcett beside him. After ten minutes or so, Macartney gradually got himself free from the crowd of friends congratulating him there on the jetty.

Stimulated as he always was by such adulation, highly animated, his Irish blue eyes flashing, his smile unabated, his selfish heart full to repletion of his accustomed self-confidence, he disentangled himself from the still increasing crowd and, with several bows and various wavings of his left hand as he backed away from them, he rejoined Fawcett, linked his right arm through the crook of the pirate captain's left elbow and proceeded to conduct him into the town. Those fellows on the wharf were small fry! He would, as he smilingly mentioned in Fawcett's ear, prefer to introduce the captain at once into a gathering place where he would meet a group of gentlemen of greater importance.

They walked up into the town and turned to the left through the bustling traffic of its chief thoroughfare and, proceeding to the westward for a couple of hundred feet or so, turned in through a wide arched doorway above which, on its bracket, perched guardian-like a small gilded rooster. This was Le Coq d'Or, rendezvous of the more prosperous merchants of the flourishing city of St Thomas.

A considerable number of these prosperous worthies were already assembled at the time of their arrival in Le Coq d'Or. Several Negroes under the direction of the steward of this club-like clearing house were already bringing in and placing on the huge polished mahogany table the planter's punch, swizzles of brandy or rum, and sangaree such as always accompanied this late-morning assembly. It lacked only a minute or two of eleven, and the stroke of that hour was sacred at Le Coq d'Or and similar foregathering places as the swizzle hour. No less a personage than M. Daniell, some years before a refugee from the Haitian revolution and now a merchant prince here in the Danish colonial capital, was already twirling a carved swizzle stick in the fragrant iced interior of an enormous silver jug.

But this hospitable activity, as well as the innumerable conversations current about that board, ceased abruptly when these city burghers had recognized the tall, handsome gentleman in blue broadcloth who had just stepped in among them. It was, indeed, practically a repetition of what had occurred on the jetty, save that here the corporate and individual greetings were, if anything, more intimate and more vociferous.

Here were the natural associates, the intimates, the social equals of the Macartneys themselves – a well-to-do clan of proud, self-respecting personages deriving from the class of Irish Protestant high gentry which had come into these islands three generations before upon the invitation of the Danish Colonial Government.

Among those who rose out of their chairs to surround Saul Macartney with hilarious greetings was Denis Macartney, his father. He had suspected that the Old Man would be there. The two clasped each other in a long and affectionate embrace, Denis Macartney agitated and tearful, his son smiling with an unforced whimsicality throughout the intensive contact of this reunion. At last the Old Man, his tears of happiness still flowing, held off and gazed fondly at his handsome, strapping son, a pair of still trembling hands upon the shoulders of the beautiful new broadcloth coat.

'An' where, in God's own name, have ye been hidin' yourself away, me boy?' he asked solicitously.

The others grouped about, and now fallen silent, hovered about the edge of this demonstration, the universal West Indian courtesy only restraining their common enthusiasm to clasp the Macartney prodigal by his bronzed and shapely hands, to thump his back, to place kindly arms about his broad shoulders, later to thrust brimming goblets of cut crystal upon him that they might drink his health and generously toast his safe and unexpected return.

'I'll tell ye all about that later, sir,' said Saul Macartney, his dazzling smile lighting up his bronzed face. 'Ye'll understand, sir, my anxiety to see Camilla; though, of course, I looked in upon ye first off.'

And thereupon, in his sustained bravado, in the buoyancy of his fatal conviction that he, Saul Macartney, could get away with anything whatever he might choose to do, and taking full advantage of the disconcerting effect of his announcement that he must run off, he turned to Captain Fawcett, who had been standing close behind him and, an arm about the captain's shoulders, presented him formally to his father, to M. Daniell and, with a comprehensive wave of his disengaged arm, to the company at large; and, forthwith, well before the inevitable effect of this act could record itself upon the corporate mind of such a group, Saul Macartney had whirled about, reached the arched doorway almost at a run, and disappeared in the blinding glare, on his way to call upon his cousin Camilla.

The group of gentlemen assembled in Le Coq d'Or that morning, intensely preoccupied as they had been with the unexpected restoration to their midst of the missing mariner, Macartney, had barely observed the person who had accompanied him. They were now rather abruptly left facing their new guest, and their immediate reaction after Macartney's hasty departure was to stage a greeting for this very evil-looking but highly dandified fellow whom they found in their midst. To this they proceeded forthwith, actuated primarily by the unfailing and highly developed courtesy which has always been the outstanding characteristic of the Lesser Antilles.

There was not a man present who had not winced at the name which Saul Macartney had so clearly pronounced in the course of his threefold introduction of Captain Fawcett. For this name, as that of one of the principal maritime scourges of the day, was indeed very familiar to these men, attuned as they were to seafaring matters. Several of them, in fact, vessel owners, had actually been sufferers at the hands of this man who now sat among them.

Courtesy, however – and to a guest in this central sanctum – came first. Despite their initial suspicion, by no single overt act, nor by so much as a single glance, did any member of that polished company allow it to be suspected that he had at least given harborage to the idea that Saul Macartney had brought Fawcett the pirate here to Le Coq d'Or and left him among them as a guest.

Besides, doubtless, it occurred to each and every one of these excellent gentlemen, apart from the impossibility of such a situation being precipitated by anyone named Macartney – which was an additional loophole for them – the name of Fawcett was by no means an uncommon one; there might well be half a dozen Fawcetts on Lloyd's List who were or had been commanders of ships. It was, of course, possible that this over-dressed, tough-looking sea hawk had fooled the usually astute Saul.

As for Fawcett himself, the wolf among these domestic cattle, he was enjoying the situation vastly. The man was intelligent and shrewd, still capable of drawing about him the remnants of a genteel deportment; and, as the details of his projected coming ashore here had been quite fully discussed with Saul Macartney, he had anticipated and was quite well prepared to meet the reaction released at the first mention of that hated and dreaded name of his, and which he now plainly sensed all about him. There was probably even a touch of pride over what his nefarious reputation could evoke in a group like this to nerve him for the curious ordeal which had now begun for him.

It was, of course, his policy to play quietly a conservative – an almost negative – role. He busied now his always alert mind with this, returning courtesy for courtesy as his hosts toasted him formally, assured him of their welcome, exchanged with him those general remarks which precede any real breaking of the ice between an established group and some unknown and untried newcomer.

It was Old Macartney who gave him his chief stimulation by inquiring: 'An' what of me dear son, Captain? Ye will have been in his company for some time, it may be. It would be more than gracious of ye to relate to us – if so be ye're aware of it, perchance – what occurred to him on that last voyage of his from Sout' America.'

At this really unexpected query the entire room fell silent. Every gentleman present restrained his own speech as though a signal had been given. Only the Negro servants, intent upon their duties, continued to speak to each other under their breaths and to move softfootedly about the room.

Captain Fawcett recognized at once that Mr Denis Macartney's question contained no challenge. He had even anticipated it, with a thin yarn of shipwreck, which he and Saul had concocted together. In a sudden access of whimsical bravado he abandoned this cooked-up tale. He would give them a story . . .

He turned with an elaborate show of courtesy to Old Macartney. He set down his half emptied goblet, paused, wiped his maimed mouth with a fine cambric handkerchief and set himself, in the breathless silence all about him, to reply.

'The freetraders took him, sir,' said Captain Fawcett. Then he nodded twice, deprecatingly; next he waved a hand, took up his goblet again, drank off its remaining contents in the sustained, pregnant silence, and again turned to Saul's father.

Settling himself somewhat more comfortably in his chair, he then proceeded to relate, with precise circumstantial detail, exactly what had actually taken place, only substituting for himself as the captor the name of the dreaded Jacob Brenner, who, like himself, had a place of refuge among the Andros creeks, and whom Captain Fawcett regarded with profound and bitter detestation as his principal rival.

He told his story through in the atmosphere of intense interest all about him. He made Captain Saul Macartney pretend to join the cutthroat Brenner and, the wish greatly father to the thought, brought his long yarn to a successful conclusion with the doughty Saul staging a desperate hand-to-hand encounter with his captor after going ashore with him on Andros Island, together with a really artistic sketching-in of his escape from the pirate settlement in a dinghy through the intricacies of the mosquito-infested creeks; and his ultimate harborage – 'well-nigh by chance, or a trace of what he names "the Macartney luck", sir' – with himself.

'I've a very pleasant little spot there on Andros,' added Captain Fawcett.

Then, satisfying another accession of his whimsicality: 'I'm certain any of you would be pleased with it, gentlemen. It's been good – very good and pleasurable, I do assure you – to have had Captain Macartney with me.'

And Fawcett, the pirate, whose own longboat had fetched him ashore here from that very vessel whose capture by freetraders on the high seas he had just been so graphically recounting, with a concluding short bow and a flourish of the left hand, took up his recently replenished crystal goblet and, again facing the senior Macartney, toasted him roundly on this, the glad occasion of his seafaring son's prosperous return.

Saul Macartney walked rapidly across the crowded main thoroughfare so as to avoid being recognized and stopped. He turned up a precipitous, winding and abruptly cornered street of varying width, and, following it between the many closely walled residences among which it wound, mounted at a rapid stride to a point two-thirds of the way up the hill. Here he paused to readjust his clothes and finally to wipe the sweat induced by his pace from his bronzed face with another fine cambric handkerchief like that being used by his colleague about this time down there at Le Coq d'Or. The two of them had divided evenly four dozen of these handkerchiefs not long before from the effects of a dandified French supercargo now feeding the fishes.

It was a very sultry day in the middle of the month of May, in that Spring period when the *rata* drums of the Negroes may be heard booming nightly from the wooded hills in the interior of the islands; when the annual shift in the direction of the trade wind between the points east and west of north seems to hang a curtain of sultriness over St Thomas on its three hillsides. It was one of those days when the burros' tongues hang out of dry mouths as they proceed along dusty roads; when centipedes leave their native dust and boldly cross the floors of houses; when ownerless dogs slink along the inner edges of the baking, narrow sidewalks in the slits of house shade away from the sun.

Saul Macartney had paused near the entrance to the spacious mansion of his uncle, Thomas Lanigan Macartney, which stood behind a stately grille of wrought iron eleven feet high, in its own grounds, and was approached through a wide gateway above which the cut stone arch supported a plaque on which had been carved the Macartney arms. Through this imposing entrance, his face now comfortably dry and his fine broadcloth coat readjusted to his entire satisfaction, Saul Macartney now entered and proceeded along the broad, shell-strewn path with its two borders of cemented pink conch shells toward the mansion.

Through the accident of being his father's first-born son and the rigid application of the principle of primogeniture which had always prevailed among the Macartney clan in the matter of inheritances, old T. L. Macartney possessed the bulk of the solid Macartney family fortune. He had married the only daughter of a retired Danish general who had been governor of the colony. Dying in office, the general had left behind him the memory of a sound administration and another substantial fortune which found its way through that connection into the Macartney coffers.

The only reason why Saul Macartney had not led his heavenly endowed cousin, Camilla, to the altar long before, was merely because he knew he could marry her any time. Camilla's lips had parted and her blue eyes become mysterious, soft and melting, at every sight of him since about the time she was eight and he ten. As for Saul Macartney, he could not remember the time when it had not been his settled intention to marry his cousin Camilla when he got ready. He was as sure of her as of the rising and setting of the sun; as that failure was a word without meaning to him; as that the Santa Cruz rum was and always would be the natural drink of gentlemen and sailors.

Jens Sorensen, the black butler, who had witnessed his arrival, had the door open with a flourish when Saul was halfway between the gate and the gallery. His bow as this favored guest entered the house was profound enough to strain the seams of his green broadcloth livery coat.

But black Jens received no reward for his assiduousness from the returned prodigal, beyond a nod. This was not like Saul in the least, but black Jens understood perfectly why Captain Macartney had not quizzed him, paused to slap mightily his broad back under his green coat, or to tweak the lobe of his right ear ornamented with its heavy ring of virgin gold, all of which attentions black Jens could ordinarily expect from this fine gentleman of his family's close kinfolk. There had been no time for such persiflage.

For, hardly had black Jens's huge, soft right hand begun the motion of closing the great door, when Camilla Macartney, apprised by some subtlety of 'the grapevine route' of her cousin's arrival, appeared on the threshold of the mansion's great drawing room, her lips parted, her eyes suffused with an inescapable emotion. Only momentarily she paused there. Then she was running toward him across the polished mahogany flooring of the wide hallway, and had melted into the firm clasp of Saul Macartney's brawny arms. Raising her head, she looked up into his face adoringly and Saul, responding, bent and kissed her long and tenderly. No sound save that occasioned by the soft-footed retirement of black Jens to his pantry broke the cool silence of the dignified hall. Then at last in a voice from Camilla Macartney that was little above a whisper: 'Saul – Saul, my darling! I am so glad, so glad! You will tell me all that transpired – later, Saul, my dear. Oh, it has been a dreadful time for me.'

Withdrawing herself very gently from his embrace, she turned and, before the great Copenhagen mirror against the hallway's south wall, made a small readjustment in her coiffure – her hair was of the purest, clearest Scandinavian gold, of a spun silk fineness. Beckoning her lover to follow, she then led the way into the mansion's drawing room.

As they entered, Camilla a step in advance of Macartney, there arose from a mahogany and rose-satin davenport the thickset figure of a handsome young man of about twenty-four, arrayed in the scarlet coat of His Britannic Majesty's line regiments of infantry. This was Captain the Honorable William McMillin, who, as a freshly commissioned coronet-of-horse, had actually fought under

Wellington at Waterloo ten years before. Recently he had attained his captaincy, and sold out to undertake here in the Danish West Indies the resident management of a group of Santa Cruzian sugar estates, the property of his Scottish kinsfolk, the Comyns.

These two personable captains, one so-called because of his courtesy title, and the other with that honorable seafaring title really forfeited, were duly presented to each other by Camilla Macartney; and thereby was consummated another long stride forward in the rapid march of Saul Macartney's hovering doom.

The Scottish officer, sensing Saul's claim upon that household, retired ere long with precisely the correct degree of formality.

As soon as he was safely out of earshot Camilla Macartney rose and, seizing a small hassock, placed it near her cousin's feet. Seating herself on this, she looked up adoringly into his face and, her whole soul in her eyes, begged him to tell her what had happened since the day when he had cleared the *Hope* from Barranquilla.

Again Saul Macartney rushed forward upon his fate.

He told her, with circumstantial detail, the cooked-up story of shipwreck, including a touching piece of invention about three days and nights in the *Hope*'s boats and his timely rescue by his new friend, Fawcett, master of the *Swallow* – a very charitable gentleman, proprietor of a kind of trading station on Andros in the Bahamas. Captain Fawcett, who had considerately brought the prodigal back to St Thomas, was at the moment being entertained in Le Coq d'Or.

Camilla Macartney's eyes grew wide at the name of Saul's rescuer. The first intimation of her subsequent change of attitude began with her exclamation: 'Saul! Not – not Captain Fawcett, the pirate! Not that dreadful man! I had always understood that *his* lying-up place was on the Island of Andros, among the creeks!'

Saul Macartney lied easily, reassuringly. He turned upon his cousin – anxious, now, as he could see, and troubled – the full battery of his engaging personality. He showed those beautiful teeth of his in a smile that would have melted the heart of a Galatea.

Camilla dropped the subject, entered upon a long explication of her happiness, her delight at having him back. He must remain for breakfast. Was his friend and benefactor, Captain Fawcett, suitably housed? He might, of course, stay here – her father would be so delighted at having him . . .

It was as though she were attempting, subconsciously, to annihilate her first faint doubt of her cousin Saul, in this enthusiasm for his rescuer. She rose and ran across the room, and jerked violently upon the ornamental bell rope. In almost immediate response to her ring black Jens entered the room softly, bowed before his mistress with a suggestion of prostrating himself.

'A place for Captain Macartney at the breakfast table. Champagne; two bottles – no, four – of the 1801 Chablis – is Miranda well along with the shell-crustadas?'

Again Camilla Macartney was reassured. All these commands would be precisely carried out.

Thereafter for a space, indeed, until the noon breakfast was announced, conversation languished between the cousins. For the first time in his life, had Saul Macartney been to the slightest degree critically observant, he would have detected in Camilla's bearing a vague hint that her mind toward him was not wholly at rest; but of this he noticed nothing. As always, and especially now under the stimulation of this curious game of bravado he and Fawcett were playing here in St Thomas, no warning, no sort of premonition, had penetrated the thick veneer of his selfishness, his fatuous conviction that any undertaking of his must necessarily proceed to a successful outcome.

He sat there thinking of how well he had managed things; of the chances of the *Swallow*'s next venture on the Main; of the ripe physical beauty of Camilla; of various women here in the town.

And Camilla Macartney, beautiful, strangely composed, exquisitely dressed, as always, sat straight upright across from him, and looked steadily at her cousin, Saul Macartney. It was as though she envisaged vaguely how he was to transform her love into black hatred. A thin shadow of pain lay across her own Irish-blue eyes.

Captain the Honorable William McMillin, like many other personable young gentlemen before him, had been very deeply impressed with the quality of Camilla Macartney. But it was not only that West Indian gentlewoman's social graces and cool blond beauty that were responsible for this favorable impression. The young captain, a thoroughly hard-headed Scot with very much more behind his handsome forehead than the necessary knowledge of military tactics possessed by the ordinary line regiment officer, had been even more deeply impressed by other qualities obviously possessed by his West Indian hostess. Among these was her intellect; unusual, he thought, in a colonial lady not yet quite twenty-eight. Nothing like Miss Macartney's control of the many servants of the household had ever seemed possible to the captain.

From black Jens, the butler, to the third scullery maid, all of them, as they came severally under the notice of this guest, appeared to accord her a reverence hardly distinguishable from acts of worship. In going about the town with her, either walking for early evening exercise or in her father's barouche to make or return formal calls, the trained and observant eye of the young Scotsman had not failed to notice her effect upon the swarming Negro population of the town.

Obeisances from these marked her passage among them. The gay stridency of their street conversations lulled itself and was still at her passing.

Doffed hats, bows, veritable obeisances in rows and by companies swayed these street loiterers as her moving about among them left them hushed and worshipful in her wake.

Captain McMillin noted the very general respectful attitude of these blacks toward their white overlords, but, his eyes told him plainly, they appeared to regard Camilla Macartney as a kind of divinity.

In the reasonable desire to satisfy his mounting curiosity Captain McMillin had broached the matter to his hostess. A canny Scot, he had approached this matter indirectly. His initial questions had had to do with native manners and customs, always a safe general topic in a colony.

Camilla's direct answers had at once surprised him with their clarity and the exactitude of their information. It was unusual and – as the subject broadened out between them and Camilla told him more and more about the Negroes, their beliefs, their manner of life, their customs and practises – it began to be plain to Captain McMillin that it was more than unusual; if someone entitled to do so had asked him his opinion on Camilla Macartney's grasp of this rather esoteric subject, and the captain had answered freely and frankly, he would have been obliged to admit that it seemed to him uncanny.

For behind those social graces of hers which made Camilla Macartney a notable figure in the polite society of this Danish Colonial capital, apart from the distinction of her family connection, her commanding position as the richest heiress in the colony, her acknowledged intellectual attainments, and the distinguished beauty of face and form which lent a pervading graciousness to her every act, Camilla Macartney was almost wholly occupied by two consuming interests.

Of these, the first, generally known by every man, woman and child in St Thomas, was her preoccupation with her cousin, Saul Macartney. The other, unsuspected by any white person in or out of Camilla Macartney's wide acquaintance, was her knowledge of the magic of the Negroes.

The subject had been virtually an obsession with her since childhood. Upon it she had centered her attention, concentrated her fine mind and using every possible opportunity which her independent position and the enormous amount of material at hand afforded, had mastered it in theory and practise throughout its almost innumerable ramifications.

There was, first, the *obeah*. This, deriving originally from the Ashantee slaves, had come into the West Indies through the gate of Jamaica. It was a combined system of magical formulas and the use of drugs. Through it a skillful practitioner could obtain extraordinary results. It involved a very complete *materia medica*, and a background setting for the usage and practise thereof, which reached back through uncounted centuries into rituals that were the very heart of primitive savagery.

The much more greatly extended affair called Voodoo, an extraordinarily complex fabric of 'black', 'white', and revelatory occultism, had made its way through the islands chiefly through the Haitian doorway from its proximate source, Dahomey, whence the early French colonists of Hispaniola had brought their original quotas of black slaves.

Voodoo, an infinitely broader and more stratified system than the medicinal *obeah*, involved much that appeared to the average white person mere superficial Negro 'stupidness'. But in its deeper and more basic aspects it included many very terrible things, which Camilla Macartney had encountered, succeeded in understanding, and appropriated into this terrific fund of black learning which was hers as this fell subject took her through the dim backgrounds of its origin to the unspeakable snake worship of Africa's blackest and deadliest interior.

The considerable Negro population of the island, from the most fanatical *Hougan* presiding in the high hills over the dire periodic rites of the 'baptism' and the slaughter of goats and bullocks and willingly offered human victims whose blood, mingled with red rum, made that unholy communion out of which grew the unnameable orgies of the deep interior heights, down to the lowliest piccaninny gathering fruits or stealing yams for the sustenance of his emaciated body – every one of these blacks was aware of this singular preoccupation; acknowledged the supremacy of this extraordinarily gifted white lady; paid her reverence; feared her acknowledged powers; would as soon have lopped off a foot as to cross her lightest wish.

Captain the Honorable William McMillin made up his mind that her grasp of these matters was extraordinary. His questionings and Camilla's informative replies had barely touched upon the edge of what she knew.

And the former captain, her cousin, Saul Macartney, did not know that his heiress cousin cherished any interest except that which she had always demonstrated so plainly in his own direction.

Going in to breakfast, Saul Macartney was nearly knocked off his feet by the physical impact of his uncle's greeting. Camilla's father had been spending the morning overlooking a property of his east of the town, in the direction of Smith's Bay. He had thus missed meeting Saul at Le Coq d'Or, but had learned of his nephew's arrival on his way home. The town, indeed, was agog with it.

So sustained was his enthusiasm, the more especially after imbibing his share of the unusually large provision of wine for a midday meal which his daughter's desire to honor the occasion had provided, that he monopolized most of his nephew's attention throughout breakfast and later in the drawing room after the conclusion of that meal. It was perhaps because of this joviality on his uncle's part that Saul Macartney failed to observe the totally new expression which had rested like a very small cloud on Camilla Macartney's face ever since a short time before going into the dining room.

His uncle even insisted upon sending the prodigal home in the English barouche, and in this elegant equipage – with its sleek, Danish coach horses and the liveried Negroes on its box with cockades at the sides of their glistening silk toppers – he made the brief journey down one hill, a short distance through the town, and up another one to his father's house.

Here, it being well after two o'clock in the afternoon, and siesta hour, he found Fawcett, whom the Old Man had taken under his hospitable wing. The two had no private conversation together. Both were in high spirits and these Old Macartney fostered with his cordials, his French brandy and a carafe of very ancient rum. The three men sat together over their liquor during the siesta hour, and during the session Old Macartney did most of the talking. He did not once refer to his son's capture by Brenner, the freebooter.

He confined himself in his desire to be entertaining to his son's benefactor, Captain Fawcett, to a joyous succession of merry tales and ripe, antique quips. Saul Macartney had therefore no reason to suspect, nor did it happen to occur to Fawcett to inform him, that the latter's account of Macartney's adventures since the time he had last been heard from until the present was in any wise different from the tale of shipwreck upon which they had agreed and which Macartney had told out in full to his cousin, Camilla.

The three had not finished their jovial session before various strange matters affecting them very nearly, odd rumors, now being discussed avidly in various offices, residences, and gathering places about St Thomas, were gathering headway, taking on various characteristic exaggerations and, indeed, running like wildfire through the town.

In a place like St Thomas, crossroads and clearing house of the vast West Indian trade which came and went through that port and whose prosperity was dependent almost wholly upon shipping, even the town's riff-raff was accustomed to think and express itself in terms of ships.

It was an unimportant, loquacious Negro youth who started the ball a-rolling. This fellow, a professional diver, came up to one of the wharves in his slab-sided, home-made rowboat where he lounged aft, submitting to the propulsion of his coal-black younger brother, a scrawny lad of twelve. This wharf rat had had himself rowed out to the vessel from which the two notables he had observed had come ashore that morning. It was from the lips of this black ne'er-do-well that various other wharfside loiterers learned that the beautiful clipper vessel lying out there at anchor was provided with eight carronade ports.

Out of the idle curiosity thus initially aroused there proceeded various other harbor excursions in small boats. The black diver had somehow managed to miss the stanchion of the 'long tom' which Fawcett, in an interval of prudence, had had dismounted the night before. The fact that the *Swallow* carried such an armament, however, very soon trickled ashore.

This nucleus of interesting information was soon followed up and almost eclipsed in interest by the various discussions and arguments which were soon running rife among the shipping interests of the town over the extra-ordinary numbers of the *Swallow*'s crew.

A round dozen, together with the usual pair of mates to supplement the captain, as all these experts on ships were well aware, would ordinarily suffice for a vessel of this tonnage. Accounts and the terms of the various arguments varied between estimates ranging from seventy-five to a hundred men on board the *Swallow*.

A side issue within this category was also warmly discussed. Crews of vessels with home ports in the islands were commonly Negro crews. This unprecedented gathering of men was a white group. Only two – certain of the debaters held out firmly that they had observed three – Negroes were to be perceived aboard the *Swallow*, and one of these, a gigantic brown man who wore nothing but earrings and a pair of faded dungaree trousers, was plainly the cook in charge of the *Swallow*'s galley, and the other, or others, were this fellow's assistants.

But the town got its real fillip from the quite definite statement of a small-fry worthy, one Jeems Pelman, who really gave them something to wrangle about when he came ashore after a visit of scrutiny and stated flatly that this rakish, shining, black hulled clipper was none other vessel than the Macartneys' *Hope*, upon both hull and rigging of which he had worked steadily for three months in his own shipyard when the *Hope* was built during the winter of 1819.

All these items of easily authenticated information bulked together and indicated to the comparitively unsophisticated, as well as to the wiseacres, only one possible conclusion. This was that the Macartney vessel, in command of which Captain Saul Macartney was known to have cleared from a South American port three months earlier, had in some as yet unexplained fashion been changed over into a free-trading ship and that the harsh-featured seadog in his fine clothes who had accompanied Captain Macartney ashore that morning could very well be none other than its commander.

A certain lapse of time is ordinarily requisite for the loquacious stage of drunkenness to overtake the average hard-headed seafaring man. The crew of Fawcett's longboat, after three weeks' continuous duty at sea, had bestowed the boat safely, engaged the services of an elderly Negro to watch it in their absence, and drifted into the low rum shop nearest their landing place; and there not long after their arrival Fawcett's boatswain, a Dutch island bruiser, had been recognized by several former acquaintances as a sailorman who had gone out of the harbor of St Eustasia in a small trading schooner which had disappeared off the face of the wide Caribbean three years previously.

The rum-induced garrulity of this gentleman, as the report of it went forth and flared through the town, corroborated the as yet tentative conclusion that a fully manned pirate ship lay for the time being at anchor in the peaceful harbor of St Thomas; and that its master, whose identity as a certain Captain Fawcett had spread downward through the social strata from Le Coq d'Or itself, was here ashore, hobnobbing with the town's high gentry, and actually a guest of the Macartneys.

By three o'clock in the afternoon the town was seething with the news. There had been no such choice morsel to roll on the tongue since Henry Morgan had sacked the city of Panama.

The first corroboration of that vague, distressing, but as yet unformed suspicion which had lodged itself in Camilla Macartney's mind came to her through Jens Sorensen, the butler. The 'grape-vine route', so-called – that curious door-to-door and mouth-to-ear method of communication among the Negroes of the community – is very rapid as well as very mysterious. Black Jens had heard this devastating story relayed up to him from the lowest black riff-raff of the town's waterfront a matter of minutes after the name of their guest, seeping downward from Le Coq d'Or, had met, mingled with, and crowned the damnatory group of successive details from the wharves.

To anyone familiar with the effect of Voodoo upon the Negro mentality there would be nothing surprising in the fact that black Jens proceeded straight to his mistress to whisper the story without any delay. For fear is the dominant note of the Voodooist. The St Thomas Negroes were actuated in their attitude toward Camilla Macartney by something infinitely deeper than that superficial respect which Captain McMillin had noted. They feared her and her proven powers as they feared the dread demigod Damballa, tutelary manifestation of the unnamed Guinea-Snake himself.

For it was not as one who only inquires and studies that Camilla Macartney commanded awe and reverence from the St Thomas Negroes. She had *practised* this extraordinary art and it was her results as something quite tangible, definite and unmistakable which formed the background of that vast respect, and which had brought black Jens cringing and trembling into her presence on this particular occasion.

And black Jens had not failed to include in his report the drunken sailorman's leering account of that captive lady's treatment by Saul Macartney – how an innocent young wife, off Nevis, had been outrageously forced into Saul's cabin, and when he had tired of her, how he had sent her back to the deck to go across the plank of death.

What desolation penetrated deep and lodged itself there in Camilla Macartney's soul can hardly be guessed at. From that moment she was convinced of the deep infamy of that entrancing lover-cousin of hers whom she had adored with her whole heart since the remoteness of her early childhood.

But, however poignantly indescribable, however extremely devastating, may have been her private feelings, it is certain that she did not retire as the typical gentlewoman of the period would have done to eat out her heart in solitary desolation.

Within ten minutes, on the contrary, in response to her immediately issued orders, the English barouche with its sleek Danish horses, its cockaded servants on the box, was carrying her down the hill, rapidly along through the town, and then the heavy coach horses were sweating up the other hill toward her uncle's house. If the seed of hatred, planted by Saul's duplicity, were already sprouting, nevertheless she would warn him. She dreaded meeting him.

Saul Macartney, summoned away from the somewhat drowsy end of that afternoon's convivial session with Fawcett and the Old Man, found his cousin awaiting him near the drawing room door. She was standing, and her appearance was calm and collected. She addressed him directly, without preamble.

'Saul, it is known in the town. I came to warn you. It is running about the streets that this Captain Fawcett of yours is the pirate. One of his men has been recognized. He talked in one of the rum shops. They say that this ship is the *Hope*, altered into a different appearance. I advise you to go, Saul – go at once, while it is safe!'

Saul Macartney turned his old disarming smile upon his cousin. He could feel the liquor he had drunk warming him, but his hard Irish head was reasonably clear. He was not befuddled. He stepped toward her as though impulsively, his bronzed face flushed from his recent potations, his arms extended and spread in a carefree gesture as though he were about to take her in his embrace.

'Camilla, *allana*, ye should not sadden your sweet face over the likes of me. I know well what I'm about, me darling. And as for Fawcett – well, as ye're aware of his identity, ye'll know that he can care for himself. Very suitably, very suitably indeed.'

He had advanced very close upon her now, but she stood unmoving, the serious expression of her face not changed. She only held up a hand in a slight gesture against him, as though to warn him to pause and think. Again Saul Macartney stepped lightly toward his doom.

'And may I not be having a kiss, Camilla?' His smiling face was unperturbed, his self-confidence unimpaired even now. Then, fatally, he added, 'And now that ye're here, *acushla*, why should ye not have me present my friend, the captain? 'Twas he, ye'll remember, that brought me back to ye. I could be fetching him within the moment.'

But Camilla Macartney merely looked at him with a level gaze.

'I am going now,' she said, ignoring his suggestion and the crass insult to her gentility involved in it, and which beneath her calm exterior had outraged her and seared her very soul. The seed was growing apace. 'I have warned you, Saul.'

She turned and walked out of the room and out of the house; then across the tiled gallery and down the black marble steps, and out to her carriage.

Saul Macartney hastened back to his father and Fawcett. Despite his incurable bravado, motivated as always by his deep seated selfishness, he had simply accepted the warning just given him at its face value. He addressed his drowsing father after a swift, meaningful glance at Fawcett: 'We shall be needing the carriage, sir, if so be it's agreeable to ye. We must be getting back on board, it appears, and I'll be hoping to look in on ye again in the morning, sir.'

And without waiting for any permission, and ignoring his father's liquor-muffled protests against this abrupt departure, Saul Macartney rang the bell, ordered the family carriage to be waiting in the shortest possible time, and pressed a rix-dollar into the Negro butler's hand as an incentive to hasten the process.

Within a quarter of an hour, after hasty farewells to the tearful and now well befuddled Old Man, these two precious scoundrels were well on their way through the town toward the jetty where they had landed, and where, upon arrival, they collected their boat's crew out of the rum shop with vigorous revilings and not a few hearty clouts, and were shortly speeding across the turquoise and indigo waters of St Thomas harbor toward the anchored *Swallow*.

Inside half an hour from their going up over her side and the hoisting of the longboat, the *Swallow*, without reference to the harbormaster, clearance, or any other formality, was picking her lordly way daintily out past Colwell's Battery at the harbor mouth, and was soon lost to the sight of all curious watchers in the welcoming swell of the Caribbean.

This extraordinary visit of the supposedly long-drowned Captain Macartney to his native town, and the circumstances accompanying it, was a nine-days' wonder in St Thomas. The widespread discussion it provoked died down after a while, it being supplanted in current interest by the many occurrences in so busy a port-of-call. It was not, of course, forgotten, although it dropped out of mind as a subject for acute debate.

Such opinion as remained after the arguments had been abandoned was divided opinion. Could the vessel possibly have been the Macartneys' *Hope*? Was this Captain Fawcett who had brought Saul Macartney ashore Captain Fawcett, the pirate? Had Captain Saul Macartney really thrown in his lot with freetraders, or was such a course unthinkable on his part?

The yarn which Captain Fawcett had spun in Le Coq d'Or seemed the reasonable explanation – if it were true. In the face of the fact that no other counter-explanation had been definitely put forward by anybody, this version was tacitly accepted by St Thomas society; but with the proviso, very generally made and very widely held, that this fellow must have been *the* Captain Fawcett after all. Saul Macartney had either been fooled by him, or else Saul's natural gratitude had served to cover, in his estimation of the fellow, any observed shortcomings on the part of this rescuer and friend-in-need.

Camilla Macartney made no allusion whatever, even within the family circle, to the story Saul had told *her*. She was not, of course, called upon to express any opinion outside. She was quite well aware that both versions were falsehoods.

She faced bravely, though with a sorely empty and broken heart, all her manifold social obligations in the town. Indeed, somewhat to distract her tortured mind, wherein that seed of hate was by now growing into a lusty plant, the heiress of the Macartney fortune engaged herself rather more fully than usual that summer season in the various current activities. She forced herself to a greater preoccupation than ever in her attention to her occult pursuits. She even took up afresh the oil painting, long ago abandoned by her, which had been one of her early 'accomplishments'.

It was during this period – a very dreadful one for her, succeeding as it did, abruptly upon her momentary happiness at her cousin Saul's restoration to the land of the living which had dissipated her acute and sustained grief over his presumptive loss at sea in the *Hope* – that she undertook, with what obscure premonitory motive derived from curious skill in the strange and terrible arts of the black people can only be darkly surmised – another and very definite task.

This was the painting of a panoramic view of the town as seen from the harbor. At this she toiled day after day from the awninged afterdeck of one of the smaller Macartney packet vessels. This boat had been anchored to serve her purpose at the point of vantage she had selected. She worked at her panorama in the clear, pure light of many early summer mornings. Before her on the rather large canvas she had chosen for this purpose there gradually grew into objectivity the wharves, the public buildings, the fort, the three hills with their red-roofed mansions, set amid decorative trees. Her almost incredible industry was, really, a symptom of the strange obsession now beginning to invade her reason. Camilla Macartney had suffered a definite mental lesion.

The scrupulous courtesy of the St Thomians, that graceful mantle of manners which has never been allowed to wear thin, was unobtrusively interposed between the respected Macartneys and the dreadful scandal which had reached out and touched their impeccable family garment of respectability. By no word spoken, by no overt act, by not so much as a breath were they reminded of Captain Macartney's recent visit ashore or his hasty and irregular departure. Captain McMillin, therefore, as a guest of Camilla's father, heard nothing of it. He sensed, however, a certain indefinite undercurrent of family trouble and, yielding to this sure instinct, ended his visit with all the niceties of high breeding and departed for Santa Cruz.

Just before he left, on the morning after the farewell dinner which had been given as a final gesture in his honor, the captain managed to convey to Camilla the measure of his appreciation. He placed, as it were, his sword at her disposal! It was very nicely made – that gesture of gallantry. It was not to be mistaken for the preliminary to a possible later offer of marriage. It was anything but braggadoccio. And it was somehow entirely appropriate to the situation. The handsome, upstanding captain left with his hostess precisely the impression he intended; that is, he left her the feeling that he was an adequate person to depend upon in a pinch, and that she had been invited to depend upon him should the pinch come.

A third of the way up one of the low mountains north-ward and behind the three gentle hills on the southern slopes of which the ancient city of St Thomas is built, there stood – and still stands – a small stone gentry residence originally built in the middle of the eighteenth century by an exiled French family which had taken refuge in this kindly Danish colony and played at raising vanilla up there on their airy little estate overlooking the town and the sea.

This place was still known by its original name of Ma Folie – a title early bestowed upon it by Mme la Marquise, who had looked up at it through a window in her temporary apartment in the Hotel du Commerce, in the town, while the roofing was being placed upon her new house, there and then assuring herself that only perched upon the back of one of those diminutive burros which cluttered up the town streets could anyone like herself possibly manage the ascent to such a site.

Ma Folie was now one of the many Macartney properties. It belonged to Camilla, having come to her as a portion of her maternal inheritance, and upon it she had re-established the vanilla planting, helped out by several freshly cleared acres in cocoa. No donkey was required nowadays to convey a lady up the tortuous, steep, little trail from the town to Ma Folie. A carriage road led past its unpretentious square entrance posts of whitewashed, cemented stone, and when Camilla Macartney visited her hillside estate the English barouche carried her there, the long climb causing the heavy coach horses to sweat mightily and helping, as the coal-black coachman said, to keep them in condition.

It was up here that she had long ago established what might be called her laboratory. It was at Ma Folie, whose village housed only Negroes selected by herself as her tenant-laborers, that she had, in the course of years, brought the practice of the 'strange art' to its perfection. She had for some time now confined her practise to meeting what might be called charitable demands upon her.

Talismans to protect; amulets to attract or repel; potent ouangas – only such modest products of the fine art of Voodoo as these went out from that occult workshop of hers at Ma Folie – went out into the eager, outstretched hands of the afflicted whose manifold plights had engaged Camilla Macartney's sympathy; to the relief of those abject ones who called upon her, in fear and trembling, as their last resort against who knows what obscure devilish attacks, what outrageous charmings, wrought by that inimical ruthlessness of one Negro to another which Caucasians hardly suspect.

No vanilla pod, no single cocoa bean, had been stolen from Ma Folie estate since Camilla Macartney had planted it afresh nine years before . . .

It was at about ten o'clock in the morning of a day near the middle of August that a kind of tremor of emotion ran through the town of St Thomas, a matter of minutes after a report of the official watcher and the many other persons in the town and along the wharves whose sustained interest in shipping matters caused their eyes to turn ever and anon toward the wide harbor mouth. The *Swallow*, which three months before had literally run away, ignoring all the niceties of a ship's departure from any port and even the official leavetaking, was coming in brazenly, lilting daintily along under the stiff trade, her decks visibly swarming with the many members of her efficient and numerous crew.

She came up into the wind like a little man-o'-war, jauntily, her sails coming down simultaneously with a precision to warm the hearts of those ship-wise watchers, her rigging slatting with reports like musket shots, the furling and stowing of canvas a truly marvelous demonstration of the efficiency which now reigned aft.

These details of rapid-fire seamanship, swiftly as they were being handled, were as yet incomplete when the long-boat went straight down from its davits into the water and Saul Macartney followed his boat's crew over the side and picked up his tiller ropes.

The *Swallow's* anchorage this time was closer in, and it seemed no time at all to the thronging, gaping watchers on the jetty before he sprang ashore and was up the steps. There was no rum shop for the boat's crew this time. Without their officer's even looking back at them over his shoulder the oarsmen pushed off, turned about and rowed back to the *Swallow*.

Saul Macartney was, if possible, even more debonair than ever. His self-confident smile adorned his even more heavily bronzed face. He was hatless, as usual, and his handsome figure was mightily set off by a gaily sprigged waistcoat and a ruffled shirt of fine cambric which showed between the silver braided lapels of the maroon-colored coat of French cloth with a deep velvet collar, the pantaloons of which, matching the coat's cloth, were strapped under a pair of low boots of very shining black leather.

The throng on the jetty was plainly in a different mood as compared to the vociferous, welcoming mob of three months before. They stayed close together in a little phalanx this time and from them came fewer welcoming smiles.

Plainly sensing this, Saul Macartney bestowed on this riffraff of the wharves no more than a passing glance of smiling raillery. He passed them and entered the town with rapid, purposeful strides as though intent on some very definite business and, utterly ignoring the hum of released though muted conversation which rose behind him as though from an aroused swarm of bees, entered the main thoroughfare, turned sharply to his left along it, proceeded in this direction some forty feet, and turned into the small office of one Axel Petersen, a purveyor of ships' stores.

Blond, stout, genial Axel Petersen stared from his broad, comfortable desk at this entrance and allowed his lower jaw to sag. Then he rose uncertainly to his feet and his four neatly garbed mulatto clerks rose from their four respective high stools with him and, in precise conformity with their employer's facial reaction, their four pairs of mottled-iris eyes rounded out altogether like saucers, and their four lower jaws sagged in unison.

Saul Macartney threw back his head and laughed aloud. Then, addressing Petersen: 'Axel, Axel! I couldn't've thought it of ye! 'Tis but stores I'm after, man – vast stores, the likes of which ye might be selling in the course of a week to five vessels, if so be ye had the fortune to get that many all in one week!' Then, a shade more seriously, ' 'Tis pork I want; beans, coffee in sacks, limes by the gunny sack – a hundred and one things, all of them written down to save ye trouble, ye great, feckless porker! And here – beside the list which I'm handing ye now – is the reassurance – '

And Saul Macartney, thrusting his list of ship's supplies neatly printed on a long slip of paper under the nose of the stultified Petersen, slapped down upon the desk top beside it the bulging purse which he had hauled out of the tail pocket of his beautiful, maroon colored French coat.

'There's two hundred and fifty English sovereigns there forninst ye, Axel. Ye can have it counted out or do it yourself, and if that does not suffice to cover the list, why, there's another shot in the locker behind it, ye *omadhoun* – ye fat robber of pettifogging ships' stewards!'

And before the protruding, bemused blue eyes of portly Axel Petersen Saul Macartney shook banteringly a thick sheaf of Bank of England ten pound notes. By the time he had returned these to the same capacious pocket, he was at the door, had paused, turned and, leaning for an instant nonchalantly against its jamb, remarked – 'Ye're to have the stores piled on your wharf not an instant later than two o'clock this day.' Then, the bantering smile again to the fore, and shaking a long, shapely forefinger toward the goggling dealer in ships' stores, he added, 'Ye'll observe, Axel, I'm not taking your stores by force and arms. I'm not sacking the town – this time!'

Then Saul Macartney was gone, and Axel Petersen, muttering unintelligibly as he assembled his scattered wits and those of his four clerks, the heavy purse clutched tightly by its middle in one pudgy hand, and the long list of the *Swallow*'s required stores held a little unsteadily before his nearsighted blue-eyes, methodically began the process of getting this enormous order assembled.

It was with a perfectly calm exterior that Camilla Macartney received her cousin Saul a quarter of an hour later. The turmoil beneath this prideful reserve might, perhaps, be guessed at; but as the art of guessing had never formed any part of Saul Macartney's mental equipment, he made no effort in that direction.

He began at once with his usual self-confident directness upon what he had come to say.

'Camilla, *acushla*, I've come to ye in haste, 'tis true, and I'm asking your indulgence for that. 'Twas gracious of ye, as always, to be here at home when I chanced to arrive.

'I'll go straight to the point, if so be ye have no objections to make, and say in plain words what I well know to have been in the hearts of the two of us this many a year. I'm askin' ye now, Camilla – I'm begging ye with my whole soul to say that ye'll drive down with me now, Camilla, to the English Church, and the two of us be married, and then sail with me for the truly magnificent home I've been establishing for ye over on Andros.'

Camilla Macartney continued to sit, outwardly unmoved, where she had received him when black Jens had shown him into the drawing room. She had not been looking at her cousin during this character-istically confident and even impulsive declaration of his. Her eyes were upon her hands which lay, lightly clasped, in her lap, and she did not raise them to reply. She did not, however, keep him waiting. She said in a perfectly level voice in which there was apparently no single trace or indication of the tearing, internal emotion which surged through her outraged heart at this last and unforgivable insult – 'I shall not become your wife, Saul – now or ever.'

Then, as he stood before her, his buoyant self-confidence for once checked, his face suddenly configured into something like the momentary grotesqueness of Axel Petersen's, she added, in that same level tone, which had about it now, however, the smallest suggestion of a rising inflection: 'Do not come to me again. Go now – at once.'

This final interview with her cousin Saul was unquestionably the element which served to crystallize into an active and sustained hatred the successive emotional crises and their consequent abnormal states of mind which the events here recorded had stirred up within this woman so terribly equipped for vengeance. The seed of hatred was now a full-grown plant.

Upon a woman of Camilla Macartney's depth and emotional capacity the felonious behavior of Saul Macartney had had a very terrible, and a very deep-reaching, mental effect. She had adored and worshipped him for as long as she could remember. He had torn down and riven apart and left lying about her in brutally shattered fragments the whole structure of her life. He had smashed the solid pride of her family into shreds. He had disgraced himself blatantly, deliberately, with a ruthless abandon. He had piled insult to her upon insult. He had taken her pure love for him, crushed and defiled it.

And now these irresistible blows had had the terrible effect of breaking down the serene composure of this gentlewoman. All her love for her cousin and all her pride in him were transformed into one definite, flaming and consuming purpose: she must wipe out those dreadful stains!

Arrived in the empty library, Camilla Macartney went straight to the great rosewood desk, and without any delay wrote a letter. The black footman who hurried with this missive down the hill actually passed Saul Macartney, likewise descending it. Within a very short time after its reception the captain of the little packet-vessel – upon which, anchored quite close to shore, Camilla Macartney had been painting her nearly finished panorama of the town – had gone ashore to round up his full crew. The packet itself, with Camilla Macartney on board, sailed out of St Thomas harbor that afternoon in plain sight of the restocked *Swallow*, whose great spread of gleaming white canvas showed gloriously under the afternoon's sun as she laid her course due southwest. The packet, laying hers to the southward, rolled and tossed at a steady eight-knot clip under the spanking trade, straight for the Island of Santa Cruz.

Captain the Honorable William McMillin was summoned from his seven o'clock dinner in his estate house up in the gentle hills of the island's north side, and only his phlegmatic Scottish temperament, working together with his aristocratic self-control, prevented his shapely jaw from sagging and his blue eyes from becoming saucer-like when they had recorded for him the identity of this wholly unexpected visitor. Camilla Macartney wasted none of the captain's time, nor was her arrival cause for any cooling of the excellent repast from which he had arisen to receive her.

'I have not,' said she downrightly in response to the astonished captain's initial inquiry as to whether she had dined. 'And,' she added, 'I should be glad to sit down with you at once, if that meets your convenience, sir. It is, as you may very well have surmised, a very deep and pressing matter upon which I have ventured to come to you. That, I should imagine, would best be discussed while we sit at table, and so without delay.'

Again the captain demonstrated his admirable manners. He merely bowed and led the way to the door of his dining room.

Once seated opposite Captain McMillin, Camilla Macartney again went straight to her point. The captain quite definitely forgot to eat in the amazing and immediate interest of what she proceeded to say.

'I am offering the reward of a thousand English sovereigns for the apprehension at sea and the bringing to St Thomas for their trials of the freetrader, Fawcett, and his mates. It may very well be no secret to you, sir, that a member of our family is one of these men. I think that any comment between us upon that subject will be a superfluity. You will take note, if you please, that it is I, a member of our family, who offer the reward I have named for his apprehension. You will understand – everything that is involved.

'Earlier this day it was proposed to me that I should sail away upon a ship without very much notice. I have come here to you, sir, on one of my father's vessels – Captain Stewart, her commander, a trusted man in our employ, has accompanied me all the way to your door. He is here now, waiting in the hired *calèche* which I secured in Frederiksted for the drive here to your house. Perhaps you will be good enough to have some food taken to him.

'I have come, Captain McMillin, in all this haste, actually to request you to do the same thing that I mentioned – you made me see, when you were our guest, that I could wholly rely upon you, sir. I am here to ask you, as a military man, to command the expedition which I am sending out. I am asking you to sail back with Captain Stewart and me for St Thomas – tonight.'

Captain McMillin looked at Camilla Macartney across the length of his glistening mahogany dining table. He had been listening very carefully to her speech. He rang his table bell now that he was sure she was finished, and when his serving man answered this summons, ordered him to prepare a repast for the waiting ship's captain, and to send in to him his groom. Then, with a bow to his guest, and pushing back his chair and rising, he said: 'You will excuse me, Miss Macartney, I trust, for the little time I shall require to pack. It will not occupy me very long.'

4

The story of how the *Hyperion*, newest and swiftest of all the Macartney vessels, was outfitted and armed for the pursuit and capture of Captain Fawcett is a little epic in itself. It would include among many details extant the intensive search among the shipping resources of St Thomas, for the swivelgun which, two days after Captain McMillin's arrival on the scene, was being securely bolted through the oak timbers of the *Hyperion*'s afterdeck.

A surprisingly complete record of this extraordinary piece of activity survives among the ancient colonial archives. Perhaps the recording clerk of the period, in his Government House office, was, like everyone else in St Thomas, fascinated by the ruthless swiftness with which that job, under the impact of Camilla Macartney's eye, was pushed through to a successful conclusion in precisely forty-eight hours. Nothing like this rate of speed had ever been heard of, even in St Thomas. The many men engaged in this herculean task at Pelman's Shipyard worked day and night continuously in three eight-hour shifts.

It is significant that these shipwrights and other skilled artisans were all Negroes. They had assembled in their scores and dozens from every quarter of the widespread town, irrespective of age or the exactions of their current employment, from the instant that the grapevine route spread through the black population of the town the summons to this task which Camilla Macartney had quietly uttered in the ear of her butler, Jens Sorensen.

The *Hyperion*, under the command of her own officers but with the understanding that Captain McMillin was in sole charge of the expedition, came up with the *Swallow* a little under four days from the hour of her sailing out of St Thomas harbor.

Captain McMillin caught Fawcett at a vast disadvantage. The *Swallow*, very lightly manned at the moment, hung in stays, her riding sails flapping with reports like pistol shots as her graceful head was held into the wind. She lay some ten ship-lengths away to the leeward of an American merchant vessel about which the *Swallow*'s boats – now nine in number – were grouped, a single member of the crew in each. Fawcett and his two lieutenants, and nine-tenths of his crew of cut-throats, were ransacking their prize, whose officers, crew and passengers had been disposed of under nailed hatches. They appeared, indeed, to be so thoroughly occupied in this nefarious work as to have ignored entirely any preparations for meeting the *Hyperion*'s attack – a circumstance sufficiently strange to have impressed Captain McMillin profoundly.

The *Hyperion*'s officers, unable to account for this singular quiescence on the part of the pirates, attributed it to their probably failing to suspect that the *Hyperion* was anything but another trading vessel which had happened to blunder along on her course into this proximity. With a strange, quick gripping at the heart, quite new in his experience, Captain McMillin permitted himself to suspect, though for a brief instant only, that something of the strange power which he had glimpsed in his contacts with Camilla Macartney, might in some extraordinary fashion be somehow responsible for this phenomenon.

But this thought, as too utterly ridiculous for harborage in a normal man's mind, he put away from him *instanter*.

The strategy of the situation appeared to be simple. And Captain McMillin formulated his plan of attack accordingly, after a brief consultation with his officers.

Realizing that there could be no effective gunnery from the handful of men in charge of the *Swallow*, Captain McMillin ordered a dozen men in charge of the *Hyperion*'s second mate over the side in the largest of the boats. The maneuver of dropping an already manned boat from the davits – a risky undertaking in any event – was handled successfully, an exceptionally quiet sea contributing to the management of this piece of seamanship.

This boat's crew, all Negroes and all armed with the pistols and cutlasses which had been hastily served out to them, had no difficulty whatever in getting over the *Swallow*'s side and making themselves masters of the pirate vessel. The dozen Negroes had butchered the seven members of the pirate crew left on board the *Swallow* within forty seconds of their landing upon her deck, and Mr Matthews, the officer in charge of them, hauled down with his own hand the Jolly Roger which, true to the freetrading traditions of the Main, flaunted at the *Swallow*'s main peak.

The magnificent cooperation of the fifteen Negroes constituting the *Hyperion*'s deck crew made possible the next daring piece of seamanship which the *Hyperion*'s captain had agreed to attempt. This was Captain McMillin's plan.

The *Hyperion* should lay alongside the American vessel, grapple to her and board – with all hands – from deck to deck. This idea, almost unheard of in modern sea warfare, had suggested itself as practicable in this instance to Captain McMillin, from his reading. Such had been the tactics of the antique Mediterranean galleys.

For the purpose of retaining the outward appearance of a simple trader, Captain McMillin had concealed the thirty-three additional members of his heavily armed crew, and these had not been brought on deck until he was almost ready to have the grapples thrown. These reserves now swarmed upon the *Hyperion*'s deck in the midst of a bedlam of shouts, yells and curses, punctuated by pistol shots, from the pirate crew on board their prize.

These were taken at a vast disadvantage. Their prize vessel was immobile. They had, for what appeared to Captain McMillin some inexplicable reason, apparently failed until the very last moment to realize the *Hyperion*'s intentions. Most of them were busily engaged in looting their prize. Under this process five of the *Swallow*'s nine boats had already been laden gunwale deep with the miscellaneous plunder already taken out of the American ship. Two of these laden small boats and two others of the *Swallow*'s nine were crushed like eggshells as the *Hyperion* closed in and threw her grappling hooks.

Then, in a silence new and strange in Captain McMillin's previous experience in hand-to-hand fighting, his forty-eight black fighting men followed him over the rails and fell upon the pirates.

Within three minutes the American vessel's deck was a shambles. Camilla Macartney's black myrmidons, like militant fiends from some strange hell of their own, their eyeballs rolling, their white teeth flashing as they bared their lips in the ecstasy of this mission of wholesale slaughter, spread irresistibly with grunts and low mutterings and strange cries about that deck.

Not a member of the pirate crew escaped their ruthless onslaught. Hard skulls were split asunder and lopped arms strewed the deck, and tough bodies were transfixed, and the gasping wounded were trampled lifeless in the terrible energy of these black fighting men.

Then abruptly, save for a harsh sobbing sound from laboring panting lungs after their terrific exertion, a strange silence fell, and toward Captain McMillin, who stood well-nigh aghast over the utter strangeness of this unprecedented carnage which had just taken place under his eye and under his command, there came a huge, black, diffidently smiling Negro, his feet scarlet as he slouched along that moist and slippery deck, a crimson cutlass dangling loosely now from the red hand at the end of a red arm. This one, addressing the captain in a low, humble and deprecating voice, said – 'Come, now, please, me Marster – come, please sar, see de t'ree gentlemahn you is tell us to sabe alive!'

And Captain McMillin, bemused, followed this guide along that deck slushed and scarlet with the life blood of those pulped heaps which had been Captain Fawcett's pirate crew, stepped aft to where, behind the main deckhouse, three trussed and helpless white men lay upon a cleaner section of that vessel's deck, under the baleful eye of another strapping black man with red feet and a naked red cutlass brandished in a red hand.

The *Swallow*, her own somewhat blood-soiled deck now shining spotless under the mighty holystonings it had received at the hands of its prize crew of twelve under command of the *Hyperion*'s second mate, the Danish flag now flying gaily from her masthead, followed the *Hyperion* into St Thomas harbor on the second day of September, 1825. The two vessels came up to their designated anchorages smartly, and shortly thereafter, and for the last time, Saul Macartney, accompanied by his crony, Captain Fawcett, and his colleague, the other pirate mate, was rowed ashore in the familiar longboat.

But during this short and rapid trip these three gentlemen did not, for once, occupy the sternsheets. They sat forward, their hands and feet in irons, the six oarsmen between them and Mr Matthews, the *Hyperion*'s mate, who held the tiller rope, and Captain the Honorable William McMillin, who sat erect beside him.

5

I have already recorded my first horrified reaction to the appearance of the handsome black-haired piratical mate whose painted arm my innocent thumbtack had penetrated. My next reaction, rather curiously, was the pressing, insistent, sudden impulse to withdraw that tack. I did so forthwith – with trembling fingers, I here openly confess.

My third and final reaction which came to me not long afterward and when I had somewhat succeeded in pulling myself together, was once more to get out my magnifying glass and take another good look through it. After all, I told myself, I was here confronted with nothing more in the way of material facts than a large-sized, somewhat crudely done and very old oil painting.

I got the glass and reassured myself. The 'blood' was, of course – as now critically examined, magnified by sixteen diameters – merely a few spattered drops of the very same vermilion pigment which my somewhat clever amateur artist had used for the red roofs of the houses, the foulards of the Negresses and those many gloriously flaming flower blossoms.

Quite obviously these particular spatters of red paint had not been in the liquid state for more than a century. Having ascertained these facts beyond the shadow of any lingering doubt in the field of every-day material fact, my one remaining bit of surviving wonderment settled itself about the minor puzzle of just why I had failed to observe these spots of ancient, dry, and brittle paint during the long and careful scrutiny to which I had subjected the picture the evening before. A curious coincidence, this – that the tiny red spots should happen to be precisely in the place where blood would be showing if it *had* flowed from my tack wound in that dangled painted arm.

I looked next, curiously, through my glass at the fellow's face. I could perceive now none of that acutely agonized expression which had accentuated my first startled horror at the sight of the blood.

And so, pretty well reassured, I went back to my bedroom and finished dressing. And thereafter, as the course of affairs proceeded, I could not get the thing out of my mind. I will pass over any attempt at describing the psychological processes involved and say here merely that by the end of a couple of weeks or so I was in that state of obsession which made it impossible for me to do my regular work, or, indeed, to think of anything else. And then, chiefly to relieve my mind of this vastly annoying preoccupation, I began upon that course of investigatory research to which I have already alluded.

When I had finished this, had gone down to the end of the last bypath which it involved, it was well on in the year 1930. It had taken three years, and – it was worth it.

I was in St Thomas that season and St Thomas was still operating under the régime which had prevailed since the spring of 1917, at which time the United States had purchased the old Danish West Indies from Denmark as a war measure, during the presidency of Woodrow Wilson.

In 1930 our naval forces had not yet withdrawn from our Virgin Island Colony. The administration was still actively under the direction of his Excellency Captain Waldo Evans, U.S.N. Retired, and the heads of the major departments were still the efficient and personable gentlemen assigned to those duties by the Secretary of the Navy.

My intimate friend, Dr Pelletier, the pride of the U.S.N. Medical Corps, was still in active charge of the Naval Hospital, and I could rely upon Dr Pelletier, whose interest in and knowledge of the strange and *outré* beliefs, customs and practises of numerous strange corners of this partly civilized world of ours were both deep and, as it seemed to me, virtually exhaustive.

To this good friend of mine, this walking encyclopedia of strange knowledge, I took, naturally, my findings in this very strange and utterly fascinating story of old St Thomas. We spent several long evenings together over it, and when I had imparted all the facts while my surgeon friend listened, as is his custom, for hours on end without a single interruption, we proceeded to spend many more evenings discussing it, sometimes at the hospitable doctor's bachelor dinner table and afterward far into those tropic nights of spice and balm, and sometimes at my house which is quite near the old T. L. Macartney mansion on Denmark Hill.

In the course of these many evenings I added to the account of the affair which had emerged out of my long investigation two additional phases of this matter which I have not included in my account as written out here because, in the form which these took in my mind, they were almost wholly conjectural.

Of these, the first took its point of departure from the depiction of the rope, as shown in the painting, with which Saul Macartney had been hanged. I have mentioned the painstaking particularity with which the artist had put in the minor details of the composition. I have illustrated this by stating that the seven traditional turns of the hangman's knot were to be seen showing plainly under Captain Fawcett's left ear. The same type of knot, I may add here, was also painted in laboriously upon the noose which had done to death Fawcett's other mate.

But Saul Macartney's rope did not show such a knot. In fact, it showed virtually no knot at all. Even under the magnifying glass a knot expert would have been unable to name in any category of knots the inconspicuous slight enlargement at the place where Saul Macartney's noose was joined. Another point about this rope which might or might not have any significance, was the fact that it was of a color slightly but yet distinctly different from the hemp color of the other two. Saul Macartney's rope was of a faint greenish-blue color.

Upon this rather slight basis for conjecture I hazarded the following enlargement.

That Camilla Macartney, just after the verdict of the Danish Colonial High Court had become known to her – and I ventured to express the belief that she had known it before any other white person – had said in her quiet voice to her black butler, Jens

Sorensen: 'I am going to Ma Folie. Tonight, at nine o'clock precisely, Ajax Mendoza is to come to me there.'

And – this is merely my imaginative supplement, it will be remembered, based on my own knowledge of the dark ways of Vodoo – burly black Ajax Mendoza, capital executioner in the honorable employ of the Danish Colonial Administration, whose father, Jupiter Mendoza, had held that office before him, and whose grandfather, Achilles Mendoza (whose most notable performance had been the racking of the insurrectionist leader, Black Tancrède, who had been brought back to the capital in chains after the perpetration of his many atrocities in the St Jan Uprising of the slaves in 1733), had been the first of the line; that Ajax Mendoza, not fierce and truculent as he looked standing there beside the policemaster on Captain Fawcett's gallow platform, but trembling, and cringing, had kept that appointment to which he had been summoned.

Having received his orders, he had then hastened to bring to Camilla Macartney the particular length of thin manila rope which was later to be strung from the arm of Saul Macartney's gallows and had left it with her until she returned it to him before the hour of the execution; and that he had received it back and reeved it though its pulley with even more fear and trembling and cringings at being obliged to handle this transmuted thing whose very color was a terror and a distress to him, now that it had passed through that fearsome laboratory of 'white missy who knew the Snake . . . '

And my second conjectural hypothesis I based upon the fact which my research had revealed to me that all the members of the honorable clan of Macartney resident in St Thomas had, with obvious propriety, kept to their closely shuttered several residences during the entire day of that public execution. That is, all of the Macartneys except the heiress of the great Macartney fortune, Camilla.

Half an hour before high noon on that public holiday the English barouche had deposited Camilla Macartney at one of the wharves a little away from the center of the town where that great throng had gathered to see the pirates hanged, and from there she had been rowed out to the small vessel which had that morning gone back to its old anchorage near the shore.

There, in her old place under the awning of the afterdeck, she had very calmly and deliberately set up her easel and placed before her the all but finished panorama upon which she had been working, and had thereupon begun to paint, and so had continued quietly painting until the three bodies of those pirates which had been left dangling 'for the space of a whole hour', according to the sentence, 'as a salutary example', and had then ended her work and gone back to the wharf carrying carefully the now finished panorama to where the English barouche awaited her.

By conjecture, on the basis of these facts, I managed somehow to convey to Dr Pelletier, a man whose mind is attuned to such matters, the tentative, uncertain idea – I should not dare to name it a conviction – that Camilla Macartney, by some application of that uncanny skill of hers in the arts of darkness, had, as it were, caught the life principle of her cousin, Saul Macartney, as it escaped from his splendid body there at the end of that slightly discolored and curiously knotted rope, *and fastened it down upon her canvas within the simulacrum of that little painted figure through the arm of which I had thrust a thumb tack*!

These two queer ideas of mine, which had been knocking about inside my head, strangely enough did not provoke the retort, 'Outrageous!' from Dr Pelletier, a man of the highest scientific attainments. I had hesitated to put such thoughts into words, and I confess that I was surprised that his response in the form of a series of nods of the head did not seem to indicate the indulgence of a normal mind toward the drivelings of some imbecile.

Dr Pelletier deferred any verbal reply to this imaginative climax of mine, placed as it was at the very end of our discussion. When he did shift his mighty bulk where it reclined in my Chinese rattan lounge chair on my airy west gallery – a sure preliminary to any remarks from him – his first words surprised me a little.

'Is there any doubt, Canevin, in your mind about the identity of this painted portrait figure of the mate with Saul Macartney himself?'

'No,' said I. 'I was able to secure two faded old ambrotypes of Saul Macartney – at least, I was given a good look at them. There can, I think, be no question on that score.'

For the space of several minutes Pelletier remained silent. Then he slightly shifted his leonine head to look at me.

'Canevin,' said he, 'people like you and me who have *seen* this kind of thing working under our very eyes, all around us, among people like these West Indian blacks, well – we *know*.'

Then, more animatedly, and sitting up a little in his chair, the doctor said: 'On that basis, Canevin – on the pragmatic basis, if you will, and that, God knows, is scientific, based on observation – the only thing that we can do is to give this queer, devilish thing the benefit of the doubt. Our doubt, to say nothing of what the general public would think of such ideas!'

'Should you say that there is anything that can be done about it?' I inquired. 'I have the picture, you know, and you have heard the – well, the *facts* as they have come under my observation. Is there any – what shall I say? – any *responsibility* involved on the basis of those facts and any conjectural additions that you and I may choose to make?'

'That,' said Pelletier, 'is what I meant by the benefit of the doubt. Thinking about this for the moment in terms of the limitations, the incompleteness, of human knowledge and the short distance we have managed to travel along the road to civilization, I should say that there is – a responsibility.'

'What shall I do – if anything?' said I, a little taken aback at this downrightness.

Again Dr Pelletier looked at me for a long moment, and nodded his head several times. Then: 'Burn the thing, Canevin. Fire – the solvent. Do you comprehend me? Have I said enough?'

I thought over this through the space of several silent minutes. Then, a trifle hesitantly because I was not at all sure that I had grasped the implications which lay below this very simple suggestion –

'You mean – ?'

'That if there is anything in it, Canevin – that benefit of the doubt again, you see – if, to put such an outrageous hypothesis into a sane phrase, the life, the soul, the personality remains unreleased, and that because of Camilla Macartney's use of a pragmatic "magical" skill such as is operative today over there in the hills of Haiti; to name only one focus of this particular *cultus* – well, then . . . '

This time it was I who nodded; slowly, several times. After that I sat quietly in my chair for long minutes in the little silence which lay between us. We had said, it seemed to me, everything that was to be said. I – we – had gone as far as human limitations permitted in the long investigation of this strange affair. Then I summoned my houseman, Stephen Penn.

'Stephen,' said I, 'go and find out if the charcoal pots in the kitchen have burned out since breakfast. I imagine that about this time there would be a little charcoal left to burn out in each of them. If so, put all the charcoal into one pot and bring it out here on the gallery. If not, fix me a new charcoal fire in the largest pot. Fill it about half full.'

'Yes, sar,' said Stephen, and departed on this errand.

Within three minutes the excellent Stephen was back. He set down on the tile floor beside my chair the largest of my four kitchen charcoal pots. It was half full of brightly glowing embers. I sent him away before I went into the house to fetch the painting. It is a curious fact that this faithful servitor of mine, a *zambo* or medium-brown Negro, and a native of St Thomas, had manifested an increasing aversion to anything like contact with or even sight of the old picture, an aversion dating from that afternoon when he had discovered it, three years before, in the lumber room of my Santa Cruzian hired residence.

Then I brought it out and laid it flat, after clearing a place for it, on the large plain table which stands against the wall of the house on my gallery. Pelletier came over and stood beside me, and in silence we looked long and searchingly at Camilla Macartney's panorama for the last time.

Then, with the sharp, small blade of my pocketknife, I cut it cleanly through again and again until it was in seven or eight strips. A little of the brittle old paint cracked and flaked off in this process. Having piled the strips one on top of another, I picked up the topmost of the three or four spread newspapers which I had placed under the canvas to save the table top from my knife point, and these flakes and chips I poured first off the newspaper's edge upon the glowing embers. These bits of dry, ancient pigment hissed, flared up, and then quickly melted away. Then I burned the strips very carefully until all but one were consumed.

This, perhaps because of some latent dramatic instinct whose existence until that moment I had never really suspected, was the one containing the figure of Saul Macartney. I paused, the strip in my hand, and looked at Pelletier. His face was inscrutable. He nodded his head at me, however, as though to encourage me to proceed and finish my task.

With perhaps a trifle of extra care I inserted the end of this last strip into the charcoal pot.

It caught fire and began to burn through precisely as its predecessors had caught and burned, and finally disintegrated into a light grayish ash. Then a very strange thing happened –

There was no slightest breath of air moving in that sheltered corner of the gallery. The entire solid bulk of the house sheltered it from the steady northeast trade – now at three in the afternoon at its lowest daily ebb, a mere wavering, tenuous pulsing.

And yet, at the precise instant when the solid material of that last strip had been transmuted by the power of the fire into the whitish, wavering ghost of material objects which we name ash – from the very center of the still brightly glowing charcoal embers there arose a thin, delicate wisp of greenish blue smoke which spiraled before our eyes under the impact of some obscure pulsation in the quiet air about us, then stiffened, as yet unbroken, into a taut vertical line, the upper end of which abruptly turned, curving down upon itself, completing the representation of the hangman's noose; and then, instantly, this contour wavered and broke and ceased to be, and all that remained there before our fascinated eyes was a kitchen charcoal pot containing a now rapidly dulling mass of rose-colored embers.

Mrs Lorriquer

The late Ronald Firbank, British author, apostle of the light touch in literary treatment, put grass skirts upon the three lady heroines of his West Indian book, *Prancing Nigger*, as all persons who have perused that delicate romance of an unnamed West Indian island will doubtless remember. In so dressing Mrs Mouth, and her two attractive daughters, Mr Firbank was only twelve thousand miles out of the way, although that is not bad for anybody who writes about the West Indies – almost conservative, in fact. I, Gerald Canevin, have more than once reassured timid female inquirers, who had heard of our climate, but who were apprehensive of living among 'those savages and cannibals!'

I have always suspected that Mr Firbank, to go back for a moment to that gentleman before dismissing him and his book, got his light-touch information about the West Indies from a winter tour aboard one of the great trans-Atlantic liners which, winters, are used for such purposes in the Mediterranean and Caribbean, and which, in St Thomas, discharge their hundreds of 'personally conducted' tourists in swarms upon our innocent, narrow sidewalks, transforming the quiet, Old World town into a seething, hectic marketplace for several hours every two weeks or so during a winter's season there.

For, truth being stranger by far than any fiction, there *are* grass skirts – on such occasions – on St Thomas's streets; piles and stacks of them, for sale to tourists who buy them avidly. I know of no more engaging sight in this world than a two hundred and fifty pound tourist-lady, her husband in the offing, his hand in his money-pocket, chaffering with one of our Cha-Cha women with her drab, flat face and tight-pulled. pulled, straight hair knotted at the back, for a grass skirt!

It appears that, some years back, a certain iron-visaged spinster, in the employ of a social service agency, 'took up' the Cha-Cha women, seeking to brighten their lot, and, realizing that a certain native raffia grass had commercial possibilities, taught them to make Polynesian grass skirts of it. Thereafter and ever since there has been a vast plague of these things about the streets of St Thomas whenever a tourist vessel comes into our harbor under the skilled pilotage of Captain Simmons or Captain Caroc, our pilots.

I open this strange tale of Mrs Lorriquer in this offhand fashion because my first sight of that compact, gray-haired little American gentlewoman was when I passed her, in the very heart and midst of one of these tourist invasions, rather indignantly trying to get rid of an insistent vendor who seemed possessed to drape her five feet two, and one hundred and sixty pounds, in a five-colored grass skirt, and who would not be appeased and desist. As I was about to pass I overheard Mrs Lorriquer say, with both indignation and finality: 'But, I'm not a tourist – I live here!'

That effectually settled the grass-skirt seller, who turned her attention to the tourists forthwith.

I had paused, almost unconsciously, and found myself face to face with Mrs Lorriquer, whom I had not seen before. She smiled at me and I smiled back.

'Will you allow another permanent resident to rescue you from this mêlée?' I inquired, removing my hat.

'It is rather like a Continental *mardi gras*, isn't it?' said Mrs Lorriquer, taking my arm.

'Where are you staying?' I inquired. 'Are you at the Grand Hotel?'

'No,' said Mrs Lorriquer. 'We have a house, the Criqué place, half-way up Denmark Hill. We came down the day before yesterday, on the *Nova Scotia*, and we expect to be here all winter.'

'I am Gerald Canevin,' said I, 'and I happen to be your very near neighbor. Probably we shall see a good deal of each other. If I can be of any assistance – '

'You have, already, Mr Canevin,' said Mrs Lorriquer, whimsically.

I supposed at once she referred to my 'rescue' of her from the tourist mob, but, it seemed, she had something quite different in her mind.

'It was because of some things of yours we had read,' she went on, 'that Colonel Lorriquer and I – and my widowed daughter, Mrs Preston – decided to spend the winter here,' she finished.

'Indeed!' said I. 'Then, perhaps you will allow me to continue the responsibility. When would it meet your convenience for me to call and meet the Colonel and Mrs Preston?'

'Come any time,' said Mrs Lorriquer, 'come to dinner, of course. We are living very informally.'

We had reached the post-office, opposite the Grand Hotel, and here, doubtless according to instructions, stood Mrs Lorriquer's car. I handed her in, and the kindly-faced, short, stout, little sixty-year-old lady was whirled away around the corner of the hotel toward one of the side roads which mount the precipitous sides of St Thomas's best residential district.

I called the following afternoon, and thus inaugurated what proved to be a very pleasant aquaintanceship.

Colonel Lorriquer, a retired army engineer, was a man of seventy, extraordinarily well preserved, genial, a ripened citizen of the world. He had, it transpired on acquaintance, had a hand in many pieces of engineering, in various parts of the known world, and had spent several years on that vast American enterprise, the construction of the Panama Canal. Mrs Preston, whose aviator husband had met his death a few months previously in the exercise of his hazardous profession, turned out to be a very charming person, still stunned and over-burdened with the grief of her bereavement, and with two tiny children. I gathered that it was largely upon her account that the Colonel and Mrs Lorriquer had come to St Thomas that winter. Being a West Indian enthusiast, it seemed to me that the family had used excellent judgment. There could be no better place for them under those circumstances. There is that in the charm and perfect climate of the Northern Lesser Antilles which heals the wounds of the heart, even though, as they say, when one stays too long there is Lethe.

We settled down in short order to a more or less intimate acquaint-anceship. The Lorriquers, and Mrs Preston, were so to speak, 'my sort of people'. Many mutual acquaintances developed as we became better acquainted. We found much in common.

I have set down all this preliminary portion of this story thus in detail, because I have wished to emphasize, if possible, the fact that never, in all my experience with the bizarre which this human scene offers to the openminded observer, has it occurred to me to find any greater contrast than that which existed between Mrs Lorriquer, short, stout, matter-of-fact, kindly little lady that she was, and the quite utterly incredible thing which – but I must not, I simply must not, in this case, allow myself to get ahead of my story. God knows it is strange enough not to need any 'literary devices' to make it seem stranger.

The Lorriquers spent a good deal of the time which, under the circumstances, hung upon their hands, in card-playing. All three members of the family were expert Auction and Contract players.

Naturally, being quite close at hand, I became a fourth and many evenings not otherwise occupied were spent, sometimes at my house, sometimes at theirs, about the card-table.

The Colonel and I played together, against the two ladies, and this arrangement was very rarely varied. Occasionally Mrs Squire, a middle-aged woman who had known the Lorriquers at home in the States, and who had an apartment at the Grand Hotel for the winter, joined us, and then, usually, Mrs Preston gave up her place and Mrs Squire and I paired against the Colonel and his wife.

Even after the lapse of several years, I confess that I find myself as I write, hesitant, reluctant somehow, to set down the beginning of the strange discrepancy which first indicated what was to come to light in our innocent social relationship that winter. I think I can best do so, best open up this incredible thing, by recording a conversation between me and Mrs Squire as we walked, one moonlit midnight, slowly down the hill toward the Grand Hotel.

We had finished an evening at the Lorriquers', and Mrs Lorriquer had been especially, a little more than ordinarily, rude over the cards. Somehow, I can not say how it occurred, we discussed this strange anomaly in our hostess, usually the most kindly, simple, hospitable soul imaginable.

'She only does it when she plays cards,' remarked Mrs Squire. 'Otherwise, as you have said, Mr Canevin, she is the very soul of kindliness, of generosity. I have never been able to understand, and I have known the Lorriquers for more than ten years – how a woman of her character and knowledge of the world can act as she does over the card-table. It would be quite unbearable, quite utterly absurd – would it not – if one didn't know how very sweet and dear she really is.'

It was, truly, a puzzle. It had developed very soon after we had started in at our Bridge games together. The plain fact, to set it down straight, was that Mrs Lorriquer, *at the card-table*, was a most pernicious old termagant! A more complete diversity between her as she sat, frowning over her cards; exacting every last penalty; enforcing abstruse rules against her opponents while taking advantage of breaking them all herself *ad libitum*; arguing, most inanely and even offensively, over scores and value of points and penalties – all her actions and conduct at the card-table; with her general placidity, kindliness, and effusive good-nature under all other circumstances – a more complete diversity, I say, could never be imagined.

It has always been one of my negative principles that annoyance over the details or over the outcome of any game of chance or skill should never be expressed. That sort of thing has always seemed to me absurd; indeed, inexcusable. Yet, I testify, I have, and increasingly as our acquaintance progressed, been so worked up over the cards when playing with the Lorriquer family, as to have to put the brakes down tight upon some expression of annoyance which I should later have regretted. Indeed, I will go farther, and own up to the fact that I have been badgered into entering into arguments with Mrs Lorriquer at the table, when she would make some utterly outrageous claim, and then argue – the only word for it is *offensively* – against the massed testimony of her opponents and her partner for the evening. More than once, Mrs Preston, under the stress of such an exhibition of temper and unreasonableness on her mother's part, has risen from the table, making some excuse, only to return a few minutes later. I believe that on all such occasions, Mrs Preston took this means of allowing her annoyance to evaporate rather than express herself to her mother in the presence of a guest.

To say that it was annoyance is to put it very mildly indeed. It was embarrassing, too, to the very last degree. The subjects upon which Mrs Lorriquer would 'go up in the air', as Mrs Squire once modernly expressed it, were always trivial; always unreasonable. Mrs Lorriquer, although a finished player in all respects, was, I think, always, as a matter of fact, in the wrong. She would question the amount of a score, for example, and, upon being shown the printed penalties for such score on the cover-page of the score pad, or from one of the standard books on the game, would shift over to a questioning of the score itself. The tricks, left on the table, would be counted out to her, before her eyes, by Colonel Lorriquer. Half-way through such an ocular demonstration, Mrs Lorriquer would interrupt her husband with some kind of diatribe, worthy of the mind of a person quite utterly ignorant of the game of Contract and of decent manners. She insisted upon keeping all scores herself, but unless this process were very carefully watched and checked, she would, perhaps half the time, cheat in favor of her own side.

It was, really, outrageous. Time and time again, I have gone home from the Lorriquers', after such an evening as I have indicated, utterly resolved never to play there again, or to refuse, as courteously as might be possible, to meet Mrs Lorriquer over a card-table. Then, the next day, perhaps, the other Mrs Lorriquer, charming, kindly, sweet-natured, gentle and hospitable, would be in such overwhelming, disarming evidence, that my overnight resolution would be dissipated into thin air, and I would accuse myself of becoming middle-aged, querulous!

But this unaccountable diversity between the Mrs Lorriquer of ordinary affairs and the Mrs Lorriquer of the cardtable, outstanding, conspicuous, absurd indeed, as it was, was really as nothing when compared to Mrs Lorriquer's luck at the cards.

I have never seen anything like it; never heard, save in old-fashioned fictional tales of the person who sold his soul to Satan for invincibility at cards, of anything which could compare to it. It is true that Mrs Lorriquer sometimes lost – a single game, or perhaps even a rubber. But in the long run, Mrs Lorriquer, even on the lowest possible basis for expressing what I mean, did not need to cheat, still less to argue over points or scores. She won, steadily, inevitably, monotonously, like the steady propulsive motions of some soulless machine at its mechanical work. It was virtually impossible to beat her.

We did not play for stakes. If we had, a goodly portion of my income would have diverted that winter to the Lorriquer coffers. Save for the fact that as it was the Colonel who played partners with me, it would have been Mrs Lorriquer, rather than the Lorriquer family, who would have netted all the proceeds!

In bidding, and, indeed, in the actual playing of a hand, she seemed to follow no system beyond abject reliance on her 'luck'. I have, not once, but many, many times, known her, for example, to bid two no-trump originally, on a hand perhaps containing two 'singletons', only to have her partner 'go to three' with a hand containing every card which she needed for the dummy. I will not specify, beyond this, any technical illustrations of how her extraordinary 'luck' manifested itself. Suffice it to say that Bridge is, largely, a mathematical matter, varied, in the case of four thoroughly trained players, by what is known as the 'distribution' of the cards. It is this unknown element of 'distribution' which keeps the game, in the hands of a table of experts, a 'game of chance' and not merely a mathematical certainty gaged by skillful, back-and-forth, informative bidding. To put the whole matter of Mrs Lorriquer's 'luck' into a nutshell, it was this element of 'distribution' of the cards which favored her, in and out of season; caused her to win with a continuous regularity; never seeming to cause her to be pleased at her success and so lend to an evening at cards with her at the table that rather unsatisfactory geniality which even a child shows when it 'gets the breaks' at a game.

No; Mrs Lorriquer was, while engaged in playing Bridge, a harridan, a disagreeable old vixen; a 'pill' as, I believe, I once heard the outraged Mrs Squire mutter desperately, under her breath!

Perhaps it would be an exaggeration to allege that as against the Colonel and me, playing as partners for many evenings, the 'distribution' of the cards was adverse with absolute uniformity. I should hesitate to say that, positively, although my recollection is that such was the case. But, in the ordinary run of affairs, once in a while one of us would get a commanding hand, and, immune from the possibility of the 'distribution' affecting success, would play it out to a winning score for the time being. It was after one such hand – I played it, the Colonel's hand as dummy – that I succeeded in making my bid: four hearts, to a game. I remember that I had nine hearts in my hand, together with the ace, king of clubs, and the 'stoppers' on one other suit, and finishing with something 'above the line' besides 'making game' in one hand, that my first intimation of a strange element in Mrs Lorriquer's attitude to the game made itself apparent. Hitherto – it was, perhaps, a matter of a month or six weeks of the acquaintance between us – it had been a combination of luck and what I can only call bad manners; the variety of luck which I have attempted to indicate and the 'bad manners' strictly limited to such times as we sat around the square table in the center of the Lorriquers' breezy hall.

The indication to which I have referred was merely an exclamation from my right, where Mrs Lorriquer sat, as usual, in her accustomed place.

'*Sapristi*!' boomed Mrs Lorriquer, in a deep, resonant, man-like voice.

I looked up from my successful hand and smiled at her. I had, of course, imagined that she was joking – to use an antique, rather meaningless, old-French oath, in that voice. Her own voice, even when scolding over the card-table, was a light, essentially feminine voice. If she had been a singer, she would have been a thin, high soprano.

To my surprise, Mrs Lorriquer was not wearing her whimsical expression. At once, too, she entered into an acrimonious dispute with the Colonel over the scoring of our game-going hand, as usual, insisting on something quite ridiculous, the old Colonel arguing with her patiently.

I glanced at Mrs Preston to see what she might have made of her mother's exclamation in that strange, unaccustomed, incongruous voice. She was looking down at the table, on which her hands rested, a pensive and somewhat puzzled expression puckering her white forehead. So far as I could guess from her expression she, too, had been surprised at what she had heard. Apparently, I imagined, such a peculiar manifestation of annoyance on Mrs Lorriquer's part was as new to her daughter as it was to me, still a comparative stranger in that family's acquaintance.

We resumed play, and, perhaps an hour or more later, it happened that we won another rather notable hand, a little slam, carefully bid up, in no-trump, the Colonel playing the hand. About half-way through, when it was apparent that we were practically sure of our six over-tricks, I noticed, being, of course, unoccupied, that Mrs Lorriquer, at my right, was muttering to herself, in a peculiarly ill-natured, querulous way she had under such circumstances, and, my mind stimulated by the remembrance of her use of the old-French oath, I listened very carefully and discovered that she was muttering in French. The most of it I lost, but the gist of it was, directed toward her husband, a running diatribe of the most personal and even venomous kind imaginable.

Spanish, as I was aware, Mrs Lorriquer knew. She had lived in the Canal Zone for a number of years, and elsewhere where the Colonel's professional engagements as an engineer had taken them, but, to my knowledge, my hostess was unacquainted with colloquial French. The mutterings were distinctively colloquial. She had, among other things, called her husband in those mutterings 'the accursed child of a misbegotten frog', which is, however inelegant on the lips of a cultivated elderly gentlewoman, at least indicative of an intimate knowledge of the language of the Frankish peoples! No one else sensed it – the foreign tongue, I mean – doubtless because both other players were fully occupied, the Colonel in making our little slam, Mrs Preston in doing what she could to prevent him, and besides, such mutterings were common on Mrs Lorriquer's part; were usual, indeed, on rare occasions when a hand at Bridge was going against her and her partner. It was the use of the French that intrigued me.

A few days later, meeting her coming down the hill, a sunny smile on her kindly, good-humored face, I addressed her, whimsically, in French. Smilingly, she disclaimed all knowledge of what I was talking about.

'I supposed you were a French scholar, somehow,' said I.

'I really don't know a word of it,' replied Mrs Lorriquer, 'unless, perhaps, what "R.S.V.P." means, and – oh, yes! – "*honi soit qui mal y pense*!" That's on the great seal of England, isn't it, Mr Canevin?'

It set me to wondering, as, I imagine, it would have set anyone under just those circumstances, and I had something to puzzle over. I could not, you see, readily reconcile Mrs Lorriquer's direct statement that she knew no French, a statement made with the utmost frankness, and to no possible end if it were untrue, with the fact that she had objurgated the Colonel under her breath and with a surprising degree of fluency, as 'the accursed child of a misbegotten frog!'

It seemed, this little puzzle, insoluble! There could, it seemed to me, be no possible question as to Mrs Lorriquer's veracity. If she said she knew no French besides the trite phrases which everybody knows, then the conclusion was inevitable; she knew no French! But – beyond question she had spoken, under her breath to be sure, but in my plain hearing, in that language and in the most familiar and colloquial manner imaginable.

There was, logically, only one possible explanation. *Mrs Lorriquer had been speaking French without her own knowledge*!

I had to let it go at that, absurd as such a conclusion seemed to me.

But, pondering over this apparent absurdity, another point, which might have been illuminating if foresight were as satisfactory as 'hindsight', emerged in my mind. I recalled that what I have called 'the other Mrs Lorriquer' was an especially gentle, kindly person, greatly averse to the spoiling of anybody's good time! The normal Mrs Lorriquer was, really, almost softly apologetic. The least little matter wherein anything which could possibly be attributed to her had gone wrong would always be the subject of an explanation, an apology. If the palm salad at one of her luncheons or dinners did not seem to her to be quite perfect, there would be deprecatory remarks. If the limes from which a little juice was to be squeezed out upon the halved papayas at her table happened not to be of the highest quality, the very greenest of green limes that is, Mrs Lorriquer would lament the absence of absolutely perfect limes that morning when she had gone in person to procure them from the market-place. In other words, Mrs Lorriquer carried almost to the last extreme her veritable passion for making her guests enjoy themselves, for seeing to it that everybody about her was happy and comfortable and provided with the best of everything.

But – it occurred to me that she never apologized afterward for any of her exhibitions at the card-table.

By an easy analogy, the conclusion – if correct – was inevitable. Mrs Lorriquer, apparently, did not at all realize that she was a virtually different person when she played cards.

I pondered this, too. I came to the conclusion that, queer as it seemed, this was the correct explanation of her extraordinary conduct.

But – such an 'explanation' did not carry one very far, that was certain. For at once it occurred to me as it would have occurred to anybody else, her husband and daughter for choice, that there must be something behind this 'explanation'. If Mrs Lorriquer 'was not herself' at such times as she was engaged in playing cards, what made her that way? I recalled, whimsically, the remark of a small child of my acquaintance whose mother had been suffering from a devastating sick-headache. Lillian's father had remarked: 'Don't trouble Mother, my dear. Mother's not herself this afternoon, you see.'

'Well,' countered the puzzled Lillian, 'who is she, then, Daddy?'

It was, indeed, in this present case, quite as though Mrs Lorriquer were somebody else, somebody quite different from 'herself' whenever she sat at the card-table. That was as far as I could get with my attempt at any 'explanation'.

The 'somebody else', as I thought the matter through, had three known characteristics. First, an incredibly ugly disposition. Second, the ability to speak fluently a language unknown to Mrs Lorriquer. Third, at least as manifested on one occasion, and evidenced by no more than the booming utterance of a single word, a deep, man-like, bass voice!

I stopped there in my process of reasoning. The whole thing was too absurdly bizarre for me to waste any more time over it along that line of reasoning. As to the obvious process of consulting Colonel Lorriquer or Mrs Preston, their daughter, on such a subject, that was, sheerly, out of the question. Interesting as the problem was to me, one simply does not do such things.

Then, quite without any warning, there came another piece of evidence. I have mentioned our St Thomas Cha-Chas, and also that Mrs Lorriquer was accustomed to visit the market-place in person in the interest of her table. The St Thomas Cha-Chas form a self-sustaining, self-contained community as distinct from the rest of the life which surrounds them in their own 'village' set on the seashore to the west of the main portion of the town as oil from water. They have been there from time immemorial, the local 'poor whites', hardy fishermen, faithful workers, the women great sellers of small hand-made articles (like the famous grass skirts) and garden produce. They are inbred, from a long living in a very small community of their own, look mostly all alike, and, coming as they did many years ago from the French island of St Bartholomew, most of them when together speak a kind of modified Norman French, a peasant dialect of their own, although all of them know and use a simplified variety of our English tongue for general purposes.

Along the streets, as well as in the public market-place, the Cha-Cha women may be seen, always separate from the Negress market-vendors, offering their needlework, their woven grass baskets and similar articles, and the varying seasonal fruits and vegetables which they cultivate in their tiny garden patches or gather from the more inaccessible distant groves and ravines of the island – mangoes, palmets, sugar-apples, the strange-appearing cashew fruits, every variety of local eatable including trays of the most villainous-appearing peppermint candy, which, upon trial, is a truly delicious confection.

Passing the market one morning I saw Mrs Lorriquer standing in a group of five or six Cha-Cha market women who were outvying one another in presenting the respective claims of various trays loaded with the small, red, round tomatoes in which certain Cha-Cha families specialize. One of the women, in her eagerness to attract the attention of the customer, jostled another, who retaliated upon her in her own familiar tongue. An argument among the women broke out at this, several taking sides, and in an instant Mrs Lorriquer was the center of a tornado of vocables in Cha-Cha French.

Fearing that this would be annoying to her, I hastened across the street to the market-place, toward the group, but my interference proved not to be required. I was, perhaps, half-way across when Mrs Lorriquer took charge of the situation herself and with an effectiveness which no one could have anticipated. In that same booming voice with which she had ejaculated '*Sapristi!*' and in fluent, positively *Apache* French, Mrs Lorriquer suddenly put a benumbing silence upon the bickering market women, who fell back from her in an astounded silence, so sudden a silence that clear and shrill came the comment from a near-by Black woman balancing a tray loaded to the brim with avocado pears upon her kerchiefed head, listening, pop-eyed, to the altercation: 'Ooh, me Gahd!' remarked the Negress to the air about her. 'Whoite missy tahlk to they in Cha-Cha!'

It was only a matter of seconds before I was at Mrs Lorriquer's side.

'Can I be of any assistance?' I inquired.

Mrs Lorriquer glared at me, looking precisely as she did when engaged in one of her querulous, acrimonious arguments at the card-table. Then her countenance changed with a startling abruptness, and she looked quite as usual.

'I was just buying some of these lovely little tomatoes,' she said.

The Cha-Cha women, stultified, huddled into a cowering knot, looked at her speechlessly, their red faces several shades paler than their accustomed brick-color. The one whose tray Mrs Lorriquer now approached shrank back from her. I do not wonder, after the blast which this gentle-looking little American lady had but now let loose upon them all. The market seemed unusually quiet. I glanced about. Every eye was upon us. Fortunately, the marketplace was almost empty of customers.

'I'll take two dozen of these,' said Mrs Lorriquer. 'How much are they, please?'

The woman counted out the tomatoes with hands trembling, placed them carefully in a paper bag, handed them to Mrs Lorriquer, who paid her. We stepped down to the ground from the elevated concrete floor of the market.

'They seem so subdued – the poor souls!' remarked Mrs Lorriquer, whose goggle-eyed chauffeur, a boy as black as ebony, glanced at her out of the corner of a fearfully rolled eye as he opened the door of her car.

'Come to luncheon,' said Mrs Lorriquer, sweetly, beaming at me, 'and help us eat these nice little tomatoes. They are delicious with mayonnaise after they are blanched and chilled.' It seemed rather an abrupt contrast, these homely words of invitation, after what I had heard her call those Cha-Cha women.

'I'll come, with pleasure,' I replied.

'One o'clock, then,' said Mrs Lorriquer, nodding and smiling, as her Black Hans turned the car skillfully and started along the Queen's Road toward the center of town.

We did not play cards that afternoon after luncheon, because Mrs Lorriquer and Mrs Preston were going to an afternoon party at the residence of the Government Secretary's wife, and Colonel Lorriquer and I sat, over our coffee, on the west gallery of the house out of reach of the blazing early-afternoon sun, and chatted.

We got upon the subject of the possibility of another isthmian canal, the one tentatively proposed across Nicaragua.

'That, as you know, Mr Canevin, was one of the old French Company's proposals, before they settled down to approximately the present site – the one we followed out – back in the late Seventies.'

'De Lesseps,' I murmured.

'Yes,' said the Colonel, musingly, 'yes – a very complex matter it was, that French proposal. They never could, it seems, have gone through with it, as a matter of fact – the opposition at home in France, the underestimate of the gross cost of excavation, the suspicion of "crookedness" which arose – they impeached the Count de Lesseps finally, you know, degraded him, ruined the poor fellow. And then, the sanitation question, you know. If it had not been for our Gorgas and his marvelous work in that direction – '

'Tell me,' I interrupted, 'just how long were the French at work on their canal, Colonel?'

'Approximately from 1881 to 1889,' replied the Colonel, 'although the actual work of excavation, the bulk of the work, was between '85 and '89. By the way, Canevin, we lived in a rather unusual house there. Have I ever mentioned that to you?'

'Never,' said I. 'What was the unusual element about your house?'

'Only that it was believed to be haunted,' replied the Colonel; 'although, I must admit, I never – we never – met with the least evidence outside the superstitions of the people. Our neighbors all believed it to be haunted in some way. We got it for a song for that reason and it was a very pleasant place. You see, it had been fitted up, quite regardless of the cost, as a kind of public casino or gambling-house, about 1885, and it had been a resort for de Lesseps's crowd for the four years before the French Company abandoned their work. It was a huge place, with delightful galleries. The furniture, too, was excellent. We took it as it stood, you see, and, beyond a terrific job to get it clean and habitable, it was a very excellent investment. We were there for more than three years altogether.'

An idea, vague, tenuous, grotesque enough in all truth, and, indeed, somewhat less than half formed, had leaped into my mind at the combination of a 'haunted' residence and the French work on the ill-fated de Lesseps canal project.

'Indeed!' said I. 'It certainly sounds interesting. And do you know, Colonel, who ran the old casino; who, so to speak, was the proprietor – unless it was a part of the Company's scheme for keeping their men interested?'

'It was privately managed,' returned the Colonel, 'and, queerly enough, as it happens, I can show you a photograph of the former proprietor. He was a picturesque villain!' The Colonel rose and started to go inside the house from where we sat on the cool gallery. He paused at the wide doorway, his hand on the jamb.

'It was the proprietor who was supposed to haunt the house,' said he, and went inside.

My mind reeled under the stress of these clues and the attempts, almost subconscious – for, indeed, I had thought much of the possible problem presented by Mrs Lorriquer's case; a 'case' only in my own imagination, so far; and I had constructed tentatively three or four connected theories by the time the Colonel returned, a large, stiff, cabinet photograph in his hand. He laid this on the table between us and resumed his Chinese rattan lounge-chair. I picked up the photograph.

It was the portrait, stiffly posed, the hand, senatorially, in the fold of the long, black *surtout* coat, of the sort anciently known as a Prince Albert, of a rather small, emaciated man, whose face was disfigured by the pittings of smallpox; a man with a heavy head of jet-black hair, carefully combed after a fashion named, in our United States, for General McClellan of Civil War fame, the locks brushed forward over the tops of the ears, and the parting, although this could not be seen in the front-face photograph, extending all the way down the back to the neck. A 'croupier's' mustache, curled and waxed ferociously, ornamented the sallow, sinister features of a face notable only for its one outstanding feature, a jaw as solid and square as that of Julius Caesar. Otherwise, as far as character was concerned, the photograph showed a very unattractive person, the type of man, quite obviously, who in these modern times would inevitably have followed one of our numerous and varied 'rackets' and probably, one imagined, with that jaw to help, successfully!

'And how, if one may ask,' said I, laying the photograph down on the table again, 'did you manage to get hold of this jewel, Colonel Lorriquer?'

The old gentleman laughed. 'We found it in the back end of a bureau drawer,' said he. 'I have mentioned that we took the house over just as it was. Did you notice the cameo?'

'Yes,' I replied, picking the photograph up once more to look at the huge breast-pin which seemed too large in the picture even for the enormous 'de Joinville' scarf which wholly obliterated the shirt-front underneath.

'It is certainly a whopper!' I commented. 'It reminds me of that delightful moving picture *Cameo Kirby*, if you happened to see it some time ago, on the silent screen.'

'Quite,' agreed Colonel Lorriquer. 'That, too, turned up, and in the same ancient bureau, when we were cleaning it. It was wedged in behind the edge of the bottom-board of the middle drawer. Of course you have observed that Mrs Lorriquer wears it?'

I had, and said so. The enormous breast-pin was the same which I had many times observed upon Mrs Lorriquer. It seemed a favorite ornament of hers. I picked up the photograph once more.

Down in the lower right-hand corner, in now faded gilt letters of ornamental scrollwork, appeared the name of the photographer. I read: 'La Palma, Quezaltenango'.

' "Quezaltenango," ' I read aloud. 'That is in Guatemala. Was the "Gentleman of the house", perhaps, a Central American? It would be hard to guess at his nationality from this. He looks a citizen of the world!'

'No,' replied the Colonel, 'he was a Frenchman, and he had been, as it appears, living by his wits all over Central America. When the work of construction actually began under the French Company – that was in 1885 – there was a rush of persons like him toward the pickings from so large a group of men who would be looking for amusement, and this fellow came early and stayed almost throughout the four years. His name was Simon Legrand, and, from what I gathered about him, he was a very ugly customer.'

'You remarked that he was connected with the alleged haunting,' I ventured. 'Is there, perhaps, a story in that?'

'Hardly a story, Mr Canevin. No. It was merely that toward the end of the French Company's activities, in 1889, Legrand, who had apparently antagonized all his patrons at his casino, got into a dispute with one of them, over a game of *piquet* or *écarté* – one of those French games of some kind, perhaps even *vingt-et-un*, for all I know, or even *chemin-de-fer* – and Simon went up to his bedroom, according to the story, to secure a pistol, being, for the time, rather carelessly in that company, unarmed. His "guest" followed him upstairs and shot him as he stood in front of the bureau where he kept his weapon, from the bedroom doorway, thus ending the career of what must have been a very precious rascal. Thereafter, the French Company's affairs and that of the casino being abruptly dissolved at about the same time, the rumor arose that Legrand was haunting his old quarters. Beyond the rumor, there never seemed anything to suggest its basis in anything but the imagination of the native Panamanians. As I have mentioned, we lived in the house three years, and it was precisely like any other house, only rather cheap, which satisfied us very well!'

That, as a few cautious questions, put diplomatically, clearly showed, was all the Colonel knew about Simon Legrand and his casino. I used up all the questions I had in mind, one after another, and, it being past three in the afternoon, and over time for the day's *siesta*, I was about to take my leave in search of forty winks and the afternoon's shower-bath, when the Colonel volunteered a singular piece of information. He had been sitting rather quietly, as though brooding, and it was this, which I attributed to the after-luncheon drowsiness germane to these latitudes, which had prompted me to go. I was, indeed, rising from my chair at the moment, when the Colonel remarked: 'One element of the old casino seemed to remain – perhaps that was the haunting!' He stopped, and I hung, poised, as it were, to catch what he might be about to say. He paused, however, and I prompted him.

'And what might that be, sir?' I asked, very quietly. The Colonel seemed to come out of his revery.

'Eh?' he said, 'eh, what?' He looked at me rather blankly.

'You were remarking that one element of the old casino's influence seemed to remain in your Canal Zone residence,' said I.

'Ah – yes. Why, it was strange, Mr Canevin, distinctly strange. I have often thought about it; although, of course, it was the merest coincidence, unless – perhaps – well, the idea of *suggestion* might come into play. Er – ah – er, what I had in mind was that – er – Mrs Lorriquer you know – she began to take up card-playing there. She had never, to my knowledge, played before; had never cared for cards in the least; been brought up, in early life, to regard them as not quite the thing for a lady and all that, you see. Her mother, by the way, was Sarah Langhorne – perhaps you had not heard this, Mr Canevin – the very well-known medium of Bellows Falls, Vermont. The old lady had quite a reputation in her day. Strictly honest, of course! Old New England stock – of the very best, sir. Strait-laced! Lord – a card in the house would have been imposs-ible! Cards, in that family! "The Devil's Bible," Mr Canevin. That was the moral atmosphere which surrounded my wife's formative days. But – no sooner had we begun to live in that house down there, than she developed "card sense", somehow, and she has found it – er – her chief interest, I should say, ever since.' The old Colonel heaved a kind of mild sigh, and that was as near as I had heard to any comment on his wife's outrageous conduct at cards, which must, of course, have been a major annoyance in the old gentleman's otherwise placid existence.

I went home with much material to ponder. I had enough to work out a more or less complete 'case' now, if, indeed, there was an occult background for Mrs Lorriquer's diverse conduct, her apparently subconscious use of colloquial French, and – that amazing deep bass voice!

Yes, all the elements seemed to be present now. The haunted house, with that scar-faced croupier as the haunter; the sudden predilection for cards emanating there; the initial probability of Mrs Lorriquer's susceptibility to discarnate influences, to a 'control', as the spiritualists name this phenomenon – the cameo – all the rest of it; it all pointed straight to one conclusion, which, to put it conservatively, might be described as the 'influence' of the late Simon Legrand's personality upon kindly Mrs Lorriquer who had 'absorbed' it in three years' residence in a house thoroughly impregnated by his ugly and unpleasant personality.

I let it go at that, and – it must be understood – I was only half-way in earnest at the time, in even attempting to attribute to this 'case' anything like an occult background. One gets to look for such explanations when one lives in the West Indies where the very atmosphere is charged with Magic!

But – my inferences, and whereunto these led, were, at their most extreme, mild, compared with what was, within two days, to be revealed to us all. However, I have resolved to set this tale down in order, as it happened, and again I remind myself that I must not allow myself to run ahead of the normal sequence of events. The *dénouement*, however, did not take very long to occur.

It was, indeed, no more than two days later, at the unpropitious hour of two-fifteen in the morning – I looked at my watch on my bureau as I was throwing on a few necessary clothes – that I was aroused by a confused kind of tumult outside, and, coming into complete wakefulness, observed an ominous glow through my windows and realized that a house, quite near by, was on fire.

I leaped at once out of bed, and took a better look, with my head out the window. Yes, it was a fire, and, from appearances, the makings of a fine – and very dangerous – blaze here in the heart of the residence district where the houses, on the sharp side-hill, are built very close together.

It was a matter of moments before I was dressed, after a fashion, and outside, and running down the path to my gateway and thence around the corner to the left. The fire itself, as I now saw at a glance, was in a wooden building now used as a garage, directly on the roadway before one of the Denmark Hill's ancient and stately mansions. Already a thin crowd, of Negroes entirely, had gathered, and I saw that I was 'elected' to take charge in the absence of any other white man, when I heard, with relief, the engine approaching. Our Fire Department, while not hampered with obsolete apparatus, is somewhat primitive. The engine rounded the corner, and just behind it, a Government Ford, the 'transportation' apportioned to Lieutenant Farnum of Uncle Sam's efficient Marines. The Lieutenant, serving as the Governor's Legal Aide, had, among his fixed duties, the charge of the Fire Department. This highly efficient young gentleman, whom I knew very well, was at once in the very heart of the situation, had the crowd back away to a reasonable distance, the fire engine strategically placed, and a double stream of chemicals playing directly upon the blazing shack.

The fire, however, had had a long start, and the little building was in a full blaze. It seemed, just then, doubtful whether or not the two streams would prove adequate to put it out. The real danger, however, under the night trade wind, which was blowing lustily, was in the spread of the fire, through flying sparks, of which there were many, and I approached Lieutenant Farnum offering cooperation.

'I'd suggest waking up the people – in that house, and that, and that one,' directed Lieutenant Farnum, denoting which houses he had in mind.

'Right!' said I, 'I'm shoving right off!' And I started down the hill to the first of the houses. On the way I was fortunate enough to meet my house-boy, Stephen Penn, an intelligent young Negro, and him I dispatched to two of the houses which stood together, to awaken the inmates if, indeed, the noise of the conflagration had not already performed that office. Then I hastened at a run to the Criqué place, occupied by the Lorriquer family, the house farthest from the blaze, yet in the direct line of the sparks and blazing silvers which the trade wind carried in a thin aerial stream straight toward it.

Our servants in West Indian communities never remain for the night on the premises. The Lorriquers would be, like all other Caucasians, alone in their house. I had, as it happened, never been upstairs in the house; did not, therefore, have any idea of its layout, nor knew which of the bedrooms were occupied by the several members of the family.

Without stopping to knock at the front entrance door, I slipped the latch of a pair of jalousies leading into the 'hall' or drawing room, an easy matter to negotiate, stepped inside across the window-sill, and, switching on the electric light in the lower entrance-way, ran up the broad stone staircase to the floor above. I hoped that chance would favor me in finding the Colonel's room first, but as there was no way of telling, I rapped on the first door I came to, and, turning the handle – this was an emergency – stepped inside, leaving the door open behind me to secure such light as came from the single bulb burning in the upper hallway.

I stepped inside.

Again, pausing for an instant to record my own sensations as an integral portion of this narrative, I hesitate, but this time only because of the choices which lie before me in telling, now long afterward, with the full knowledge of what was involved in this strange case, precisely what I saw; precisely what seemed to blast my eyesight for its very incredibleness – its 'impossibility'.

I had, it transpired, hit upon Mrs Lorriquer's bedroom, and there plain before me – it was a light, clear night, and all the eight windows stood open to the starlight and what was left of a waning moon – lay Mrs Lorriquer on the stubposted mahogany four-poster with its tester and valance. The mosquito-net was not let down, and Mrs Lorriquer, like most people in our climate, was covered, as she lay in her bed, only with a sheet. I could, therefore, see her quite plainly, in an excellent light.

But – that was not all that I saw.

For, beside the bed, quite close in fact, stood – Simon Legrand – facing me, the clothes, the closely buttoned *surtout*, the spreading, flaring *de joinville* scarf, fastened with the amazing brooch, the pockmarked, ill-natured face, the thick, black hair, the typical *croupier* mustache, the truculent expression, Simon Legrand, to the last detail, precisely as he appeared in the cabinet photograph of La Palma of Quezaltenango – Simon Legrand to the life.

And, between him as he stood there, glaring truculently at me, intruding upon his abominable manifestation, and the body of Mrs Lorriquer, as I glared back at this incredible configuration, there stretched, and wavered, and seemed to flow, *toward* him and *from* the body of Mrs Lorriquer, a whitish, tenuous stream of some milky-looking material – like a waved sheet, like a great mass of opaque soap-bubbles, like those pouring grains of attenuated *plasma* described in *Dracula*, when in the dreadful castle in Transylvania, John Harker stood confronted with the materialization of that archfiend's myrmidons.

All these comparisons rushed through my mind, and, finally, the well-remembered descriptions of what takes place in the 'materialization' of a 'control' at a mediumistic *séance* when material from the medium floats toward and *into* the growing incorporation of the manifestation, building up the non-fictitious body through which the control expresses itself.

All this, I say, rushed through my mind with the speed of thought, and recorded itself so that I can easily remember the sequence of these ideas. But, confronted with this utterly unexpected affair, what I did, in actuality, was to pause, transfixed with the strangeness, and to mutter, 'My God!'

Then, shaking internally, pulling myself together by a mighty effort while the shade or manifestation or whatever it might prove to be, of the French gambler glowered at me murderously, in silence, I made a great effort, one of those efforts which a man makes under the stress of utter necessity. I addressed the figure – in French!

'Good-morning, Monsieur Legrand,' said I, trying to keep the quaver out of my voice. 'Is it too early, think you, for a little game of *écarté*?'

Just how, or why, this sentence formed itself in my mind, or, indeed, managed to get itself uttered, is to this day, a puzzle to me. It seemed just then the one appropriate, the inevitable way, to deal with the situation. Then –

In the same booming bass which had voiced Mrs Lorriquer's '*Sapristi*', a voice startlingly in contrast with his rather diminutive figure, Simon Legrand replied: '*Oui*, *Monsieur*, at your service on all occasions, day or night – you to select the game!'

'*Eh bien, donc* – ' I began when there came an interruption in the form of a determined masculine voice just behind me.

'Put your hands straight up and keep them there!'

I turned, and looked straight into the mouth of Colonel Lorriquer's service revolver; behind it the old Colonel, his face stern, his steady grip on the pistol professional, uncompromising.

At once he lowered the weapon.

'What – Mr Canevin!' he cried. 'What – '

'Look!' I cried back at him, 'look, while it lasts, Colonel!' and, grasping the old man's arm, I directed his attention to the now rapidly fading form or simulacrum of Simon Legrand. The Colonel stared fixedly at this amazing sight.

'My God!' He repeated my own exclamation. Then – 'It's Legrand, Simon Legrand, the gambler!'

I explained, hastily, disjointedly, about the fire. I wanted the Colonel to understand, first, what I was doing in his house at half-past two in the morning. That, at the moment, seemed pressingly

important to me. I had hardly begun upon this fragmentary explanation when Mrs Preston appeared at the doorway of her mother's
room.

'Why, it's Mr Canevin!' she exclaimed. Then, proceeding, 'There's
a house on fire quite near by, Father – I thought I'd best awaken
you and Mother.' Then, seeing that, apart from my mumbling of
explanations about the fire, both her father and I were standing, our
eyes riveted to a point near her mother's bed, she fell silent, and not
unnaturally, looked in the same direction. We heard her, behind us,
her voice now infiltrated with a sudden alarm: 'What is it? – *what is it*?
Oh, Father, I thought I saw – '

The voice trailed out into a whisper. We turned, simultaneously,
thus missing the very last thin waning appearance of Simon Legrand
as the stream of tenuous, wavering substance poured back from him
to the silent, immobile body of Mrs Lorriquer motionless on its
great bed, and the Colonel was just in time to support his daughter as
she collapsed in a dead faint.

All this happened so rapidly that it is out of the question to set it
down so as to give a mental picture of the swift sequence of events.

The Colonel, despite his character and firmness, was an old man,
and not physically strong. I therefore lifted Mrs Preston and carried
her to a day-bed which stood along the wall of the room and there
laid her down. The Colonel rubbed her hands. I fetched water from
the mahogany washstand such as is part of the furnishing of all these
old West Indian residence bedrooms, and sprinkled a little of the
cool water on her face. Within a minute or two her eyelids fluttered,
and she awakened. This secondary emergency had naturally diverted
our attention from what was toward at Mrs Lorriquer's beside. But
now, leaving Mrs Preston who was nearly herself again, we hastened
over to the bed.

Mrs Lorriquer, apparently in a very deep sleep, and breathing
heavily, lay there, inert. The Colonel shook her by the shoulder;
shook her again. Her head moved to one side, her eyes opened, a
baleful glare in her eyes.

'*Va t'en, sâle bête!*' said a deep man-like voice from between her
clenched teeth. Then, a look of recognition replacing the glare, she
sat up abruptly, and, in her natural voice, addressing the Colonel
whom she had but now objurgated as a 'foul beast', she asked
anxiously: 'Is anything the matter, dearest? Why – Mr Canevin – I
hope nothing's wrong!'

I told her about the fire.

In the meantime Mrs Preston, somewhat shaky, but brave though puzzled over the strange happenings which she had witnessed, came to her mother's bedside. The Colonel placed an arm about his daughter, steadying her.

'Then we'd better all get dressed,' said Mrs Lorriquer, when I had finished my brief account of the fire, and the Colonel and I and Mrs Preston walked out of the bedroom. Mrs Preston slipped into her own room and closed the door behind her.

'Get yourself dressed, sir,' I suggested to the old Colonel, 'and I will wait for you on the front gallery below.' He nodded, retired to his room, and I slipped downstairs and out to the gallery, where I sank into a cane chair and lit a cigarette with shaking fingers.

The Colonel joined me before the cigarette was smoked through. He went straight to the point.

'For God's sake, what is it, Canevin?' he inquired, helplessly.

I had had time to think during the consumption of that cigarette on the gallery. I had expected some such direct inquiry as this, and had my answer ready.

'There is no danger – nothing whatever to worry yourself about just now, at any rate,' said I, with a positive finality which I was far from feeling internally. I was still shaken by what I had seen in that airy bedroom. 'The ladies will be down shortly. We can not talk before them. Besides, the fire may, possibly, be dangerous. I will tell you everything I know tomorrow morning. Come to my house at nine, if you please, sir.'

The old Colonel showed his army training at this.

'Very well, Mr Canevin,' said he, 'at nine tomorrow, at your house.'

Lieutenant Farnum and his efficient direction proved too much for the fire. Within a half-hour or so, as we sat on the gallery, the ladies wearing shawls because of the cool breeze, my house-boy, Stephen, came to report to me that the fire was totally extinguished. We had seen none of its original glare for the past quarter of an hour. I said goodnight, and the Lorriquer family retired to make up its interrupted sleep, while I walked up the hill and around the corner to my own house and turned in. The only persons among us all who had not been disturbed that eventful night were Mrs Preston's two small children. As it would be a simple matter to take them to safety in case the fire menaced the house, we had agreed to leave them as they were, and they had slept quietly throughout all our alarms and excursions!

The old Colonel looked his full seventy years the next morning when he arrived at my house and was shown out upon the gallery by Stephen, where I awaited him. His face was strained, lined, and ghastly.

'I did not sleep at all the rest of the night, Mr Canevin,' he confessed, 'and four or five times I went to my wife's room and looked in, but every time she was sleeping naturally. What do you make of this dreadful happening, sir? I really do not know which way to turn, I admit to you, sir.' The poor old man was in a truly pathetic state. I did what I could to reassure him.

I set out before him the whole case, as I have already set it out, as the details came before me, throughout the course of this narrative. I went into all the details, sparing nothing, even the delicate matter of Mrs Lorriquer's conduct over the card-table. Summing up the matter I said: 'It seems plain, from all this testimony, that Simon Legrand's haunting of his old house which you occupied for three years was more of an actuality than your residence there indicated to you. His sudden death at the hands of one of his "guests" may very well have left his personality, perhaps fortified by some unfulfilled wish, about the premises which had been his for a number of years previously. There are many recorded cases of similar nature in the annals of scientific occult investigation. Such a "shade", animated by some compelling motive to persist in its earthly existence, would "pervade" such premises already *en rapport* with his ways and customs.

'Then, for the first time, the old house was refurbished and occupied when you moved into it. Mrs Lorriquer may be, doubtless is, I should suppose from the evidence we already have, one of those persons who is open to what seems to have happened to her. You mentioned her mother, a well-known medium of years ago. Such qualifications may well be more or less hereditary you see.

'That Legrand laid hold upon the opportunity to manifest himself *through her*, we already know. Both of us have seen him "manifested", and in a manner typical of mediumistic productions, in material form, of their "controls". In this case, the degree of "control" must be very strong, and, besides that, it has, plainly, been growing. The use of French, unconsciously, the very tone of his deep bass voice, also unconscious on her part, and – I will go farther, Colonel; there is another, and a very salient clue for us to use. You spoke of the fact that previous to your occupancy of the Legrand house in the "zone" Mrs Lorriquer never played cards. Obviously, if the rest of my inferences are correct, this desire to play cards came direct from

Legrand, who was using her for his own self-expression, having, in some way, got himself *en rapport* with her as her "control". I would go on, then, and hazard the guess that just as her use of French is plainly subconscious, as is the use of Legrand's voice, on occasion – you will remember, I spoke to him before you came into the room last night, *and he answered me in that same deep voice* – so her actual playing of cards is an act totally unconscious on her part, or nearly so. It is a wide sweep of the imagination, but, I think, it will be substantiated after we have released her from this obsession, occupation by another personality, or whatever it proves to be.'

The word 'release' seemed to electrify the old gentleman. He jumped out of his chair, came toward me, his lined face alight with hope.

'Is there any remedy, Mr Canevin? Can it be possible? Tell me, for God's sake, you can not understand how I am suffering – my poor wife! You have had much experience with this sort of thing; I, none whatever. It has always seemed – well, to put it bluntly, a lot of "fake" to me.'

'Yes,' said I, slowly, 'there is a remedy, Colonel – two remedies, in fact. The phenomenon with which we are confronted seems a kind of combination of mediumistic projection of the "control", and plain, old-fashioned "possession". The Bible, as you will recall, is full of such cases – the Gadarene Demoniac, for example. So, indeed, is the ecclesiastical history through the Middle Ages. Indeed, as you may be aware, the "order" of exorcist still persists in at least one of the great historic churches. One remedy, then, is exorcism. It is unusual, these days, but I am myself familiar with two cases where it has been successfully performed, in Boston, Massachusetts, within the last decade. A salient point, if we should resort to that, however, is Mrs Lorriquer's own religion. Exorcism can not, according to the rules, be accorded to everybody. The bare minimum is that the subject should be validly baptized. Otherwise exorcism is inoperative; it does not work as we understand its mystical or spiritual processes.'

'Mrs Lorriquer's family were all Friends – Quakers,' said the Colonel. 'She is not, to my knowledge, baptized. Her kind of Quakers do not, I believe, practise baptism.'

'Well, then,' said I, 'there is another way, and that, with your permission, Colonel, I will outline to you.'

'I am prepared to do anything, anything whatever, Mr Canevin, to cure this horrible thing for my poor wife. The matter I leave entirely in your hands, and I will cooperate in every way, precisely as you say.'

'Well said sir!' I exclaimed, and forthwith proceeded to outline my plan to the Colonel . . .

Perhaps there are some who would accuse me of being super-stitious. As to that I do not know, and, quite frankly, I care little. However, I record that that afternoon I called on the rector of my own church in St Thomas, the English Church, as the native people still call it, although it is no longer, now that St Thomas is American territory, under the control of the Archbishop of the British West Indies as it was before our purchase from Denmark in 1917. I found the rector at home and proffered my request. It was for a vial of holy water. The rector and I walked across the street to the church and there in the sacristy, without comment, the good gentleman, an other-worldly soul much beloved by his congreg-ation, provided my need. I handed him a twenty-franc note, for his poor, and took my departure, the bottle in the pocket of my white drill coat.

That evening, by arrangement with the Colonel, we gathered for an evening of cards at the Lorriquers'. I have never seen Mrs Lorriquer more typically the termagant. She performed all her bag of tricks, such as I have recorded, and, shortly after eleven, when we had finished, Mrs Preston's face wore a dull flush of annoyance and, when she retired, which she did immediately after we had calculated the final score, she hardly bade the rest of us goodnight.

Toward the end of the play, once more I happened to hold a commanding hand, and played it out to a successful five no-trump, bid and made. All through the process of playing that hand, adverse to Mrs Lorriquer and her partner, I listened carefully to a monotonous, ill-natured kind of undertone chant with which she punctuated her obvious annoyance. What she was saying was: '*Nom de nom, de nom, de nom, de nom* – ' precisely as a testy, old-fashioned, grumbling Frenchman will repeat those nearly meaningless syllables.

Mrs Lorriquer retired not long after her daughter's departure upstairs, leaving the Colonel and me over a pair of Havana cigars.

We waited, according to our prearranged plan, downstairs there, until one o'clock in the morning.

Then the Colonel, at my request, brought from the small room which he used as an office or den, the longer of a very beautiful pair of Samurai swords, a magnificent weapon, with a blade as keen and smooth as any razor. Upon this, with a clean handkerchief, I rubbed half the contents of my holy water, not only upon the shimmering, inlaid, beautiful blade, but over the hand-grip as well.

Shortly after one, we proceeded, very softly, upstairs, and straight to the door of Mrs Lorriquer's room, where we took up our stand outside. We listened, and within there was no sound of any kind whatever.

From time to time the Colonel, stooping, would peer in through the large keyhole, designed for an enormous, old-fashioned, complicated key. After quite a long wait, at precisely twenty minutes before two a.m. the Colonel, straightening up again after such an inspection, nodded to me. His face, which had regained some of its wonted color during the day, was a ghastly white, quite suddenly, and his hands shook as he softly turned the handle of the door, opened it, and stood aside for me to enter, which I did, he following me, and closing the door behind him. Behind us, in the upper hallway, and just beside the door-jamb, we had left a large, strong wicker basket, the kind designed to hold a family washing.

Precisely as she had lain the night before, was Mrs Lorriquer, on the huge four-poster. And, beside her, the stream of *plasma* flowing from her to him, stood Simon Legrand, glowering at us evilly.

I advanced straight upon him, the beautiful knightly sword of Old Japan firmly held in my right hand, and as he shrank back, stretching the *plasma* stream to an extreme tenuity – like pulled dough it seemed – I abruptly cut though this softly-flowing material directly above the body of Mrs Lorriquer with a transverse stroke. The sword met no apparent resistance as I did so, and then, without any delay, I turned directly upon Legrand, now muttering in a deep bass snarl, and with an accurately timed swing of the weapon, sheared off his head. At this stroke, the sword met resistance, comparable, perhaps, as nearly as I can express it, to the resistance which might be offered by the neck of a snowman built by children.

The head, bloodlessly, as I had anticipated, fell to the floor, landing with only a slight, *soft* sound, rolled a few feet, and came to a pause against the baseboard of the room. The decapitated body swayed and buckled toward my right, and before it gave way completely and fell prone upon the bedroom floor, I had managed two more strokes, the first through the middle of the body, and the second a little above the knees.

Then, as these large fragments lay upon the floor, I chopped them, lightly, into smaller sections.

As I made the first stroke, that just above Mrs Lorriquer, severing the *plasma* stream, I heard from her a long, deep sound, like a sigh. Thereafter she lay quiet. There was no motion whatever from the sundered sections of 'Simon Legrand' as these lay, quite inert, upon the floor, and, as I have indicated, no flow of blood from them. I turned to the Colonel, who stood just at my shoulder witnessing this extraordinary spectacle.

'It worked out precisely as we anticipated,' I said. 'The horrible thing is over and done with, now. It is time for the next step.'

The old Colonel nodded, and went to the door, which he opened, and through which he peered before stepping out into the hallway. Plainly we had made no noise. Mrs Preston and her babies were asleep. The Colonel brought the clothes-basket into the room, and rather gingerly at first, we picked up the sections of what had been 'Simon Legrand'. They were surprisingly light, and, to the touch, felt somewhat like soft and pliant dough. Into the basket they went, all of them, and, carrying it between us – it seemed to weigh altogether no more than perhaps twenty pounds at the outside – we stepped softly out of the room, closing the door behind us, down the stairs, and out, through the dining room and kitchen into the walled backyard.

Here, in the corner, stood the wire apparatus wherein papers and light trash were burned daily. Into this, already half filled with various papers, the Colonel poured several quarts of kerosene from a large five-gallon container fetched from the kitchen, and upon this kindling we placed carefully the strange fragments from our clothes-basket. Then I set a match to it, and within ten minutes there remained nothing except small particles of unidentifiable trash, of the simulacrum of Simon Legrand.

We returned, softly, after putting back the kerosene and the clothes-basket where they belonged, into the house, closing the kitchen door after us. Again we mounted the stairs, and went into Mrs Lorriquer's room. We walked over to the bed and looked at her. She seemed, somehow, shrunken, thinner than usual, less bulky, but, although there were deep unaccustomed lines showing in her relaxed face, there was, too, upon that face, the very ghost of a kindly smile.

'It is just as you said it would be, Mr Canevin,' whispered the Colonel as we tiptoed down the stone stairway. I nodded.

'We will need an oiled rag for the sword,' said I. 'I wet it very thoroughly, you know.'

'I will attend to that,' said the Colonel, as he gripped my hand in a grasp of surprising vigor.

'Good-night, sir,' said I, and he accompanied me to the door.

The Colonel came in to see me about ten the next morning. I had only just finished a late 'tea', as the early morning meal, after the

Continental fashion, is still named in the Virgin Islands. The Colonel joined me at the table and took a late cup of coffee.

'I was sitting beside her when she awakened, a little before nine,' he said, 'and as she complained of an "all-gone" feeling, I persuaded her to remain in bed, "for a couple of days". She was sleeping just now, very quietly and naturally, when I ran over to report.'

I called the following morning to inquire for Mrs Lorriquer. She was still in bed, and I left a polite message of good-will.

It was a full week before she felt well enough to get up, and it was two days after that that the Lorriquers invited me to dinner once more. The bulletins, surreptitiously reported to me by the Colonel, indicated that, as we had anticipated, she was slowly gaining strength. One of the Navy physicians, called in, had prescribed a mild tonic, which she had been taking.

The shrunken appearance persisted, I observed, but this, considering Mrs Lorriquer's characteristic stoutness, was, actually, an improvement at least in her general appearance. The lines of her face appeared somewhat accentuated as compared to how she had looked before the last 'manifestation' of the 'control'. Mrs Preston seemed worried about her mother, but said little. She was rather unusually silent during dinner, I noticed.

I had one final test which I was anxious to apply. I waited for a complete pause in our conversation toward the end of a delightful dinner, served in Mrs Lorriquer's best manner.

'And shall we have some Contract after dinner this evening?' I inquired, addressing Mrs Lorriquer.

She almost blushed, looked at me deprecatingly.

'But, Mr Canevin, you know – I know nothing of cards,' she replied.

'Why, Mother!' exclaimed Mrs Preston from across the table, and Mrs Lorriquer looked at her in what seemed to be evident puzzlement. Mrs Preston did not proceed, I suspect because her father touched her foot for silence under the table. Indeed, questioned, he admitted as much to me later that evening.

The old gentleman walked out with me, and half-way up the hall when I took my departure a little before eleven, after an evening of conversation punctuated by one statement of Mrs Lorriquer's, made with a pleasant smile through a somewhat rueful face.

'Do you know, I've actually lost eighteen pounds, Mr Canevin, and that being laid up in bed only eight or nine days. It seems incredible, does it not? The climate, perhaps – '

'Those scales *must* have been quite off,' vouchsafed Mrs Preston.

Going up the hill with the Colonel, I remarked: 'You still have one job on your hands, Colonel.'

'Wh – what is that, Mr Canevin?' inquired the old gentleman, apprehensively.

'Explaining the whole thing to your daughter,' said I.

'I dare say it can be managed,' returned Colonel Lorriquer. 'I'll have a hack at that later!'

The Projection of Armand Dubois

Some time before my marriage, when I was living in Marlborough House, the old mansion on the hill back of the town of Frederiksted, on the West Indian island of St Croix – that is to say, before I became a landed-proprietor, as I did later, and was still making a veritable living by the production and sale of my tales – I had a next-door neighbor by the name of Mrs Minerva Du Chaillu. I do not know whether the late Monsieur Du Chaillu, of whom this good lady was the relict, was related or not to the famous Paul of that name, that slaughterer of wild animals in the far corners of the earth, who was, and may still be, for all I know, the greatest figure of all the big game hunters, but her husband, Monsieur Placide Du Chaillu, had been for many years a clergyman of the English Church on that strange island of St Martin, with its two flat towns, Phillipsbourg, capital of the Dutch Side, and Maragot, capital of the French Side.

The English Church was, and still is, existent only among the Dutch residents, Maragot being without an English Church. Therefore, Mrs Du Chaillu's acquaintance, even after many years' residence on St Martin, was almost entirely confined to the Dutch Side, where, curiously enough, English and French, rather than Dutch, are spoken, and which, although only eight miles from the French capital, has only slight communication therewith, because of the execrable quality of the connecting roads.

This old lady, well past seventy at the time, used to sit on her gallery late afternoons, when the fervor of the afternoon sun had somewhat abated, and rock herself steadily to and fro, and fan in the same indefatigable fashion as ancient Mistress Desmond, my landlady. Occasionally I would step across and exchange the time of day with her. I had known her for several years before she got her courage up to the point of asking me if some day I would not allow her to see some things I had written.

Such a request is always a compliment, and this I told her, to relieve her obvious embarrassment. A day or so later I took over to Mrs Du Chaillu a selection of three or four manuscript-carbons, and a couple of magazines containing my stories, and I could see her from time to time, afternoons, reading them. I could even guess which ones she had finished and which she was currently engaged in perusing, by the expression of her kindly face as she read.

Four or five days later she sent for me, and when I had gone across to her gallery, she thanked me, very formally as a finely-bred gentle-woman of several generations of West Indian background might be expected to do, handed back the stories, and, with much hesitation, and almost blushingly, intimated that she could tell me a story her-self, if I cared to use it!

'Of course,' added Mrs Du Chaillu, 'you'd have to change it about and embellish it a great deal, Mr Canevin.'

To this I said nothing, except to urge my old friend to proceed, and this she did forthwith, hesitating at first, then, becoming intrigued by the memories of the tale, with the flair of a quite unexpected narrative gift. During the first few minutes of the then halting recital, I inter-rupted occasionally, for the purpose of getting this or that point clear, but as the story progressed I quieted down, and before it was finished, I was sitting, listening as though to catch pearls, for here was my simon-pure West Indian 'Jumbee' story, a gem, a perfect example, and told – you may believe me or not, sir or madam – with every possible indication of authenticity. Unless there is something hitherto unsuspected (even by his best friends, those keenest of critics) with the understanding apparatus of Gerald Canevin, that story as Mrs Du Chaillu told it to him, had happened, just as she said it had – to her.

I will add only that I have not, to my knowledge, changed a word of it. It is not only not embellished (or 'glorified', as the Black People would say) but it is as nearly verbatim as I can manage it; and I believe it implicitly. It fits in with much that is known scientifically and verified by occult investigators and suchlike personages; it is typically, utterly, West Indian; and Mrs Du Chaillu would as soon vary one jot or tittle from the strict truth in this or any other matter, as to attempt to stand on her head – and that, if you knew the dear old soul as I do, with her rheumatism, and her seventy-six years, and her impeccable, lifelong respectability, is as much as to say, impossible! For the convenience of any possible readers, I will tell her story for her, as nearly as possible in her own words, without quotation marks . . .

I had been living in Phillipsbourg about two years; perhaps slightly longer (said Mrs Du Chaillu) when one morning I had occasion to go into my husband's study, or office. Monsieur Du Chaillu – as he was

generally called, of course, even though he was a clergyman of the
Church of England – was, at the moment of my arrival, opening one
of the two 'strong-boxes', or old-fashioned iron safes which he had
standing side by side, and in which he kept his own money and the
various parish funds of which he had charge.

The occasion of my going into his office, where he received the
parishioners – you know in these West Indian parishes the Black
People come in streams to consult 'Gahd's An'inted' about every
conceivable matter from a family row to a stolen papaya – was on
account of Julie. Julie was a very good and reliable servant, a young
woman whose health was not very good, and whom I was keeping
in one of the spare-rooms of our house. The rectory was a large
residence, just next-door to the Government House, and poor Julie
did better, we thought, inside than in one of the servants' rooms in
the yard. Every day I would give Julie a little brandy. She had come
for her brandy a few minutes before – it was about four-thirty in the
afternoon – and I discovered that I would have to get a fresh bottle.
Monsieur Du Chaillu was in the office and had the key of the big
sideboard, and I had stepped in to get the key from him.

As I say, he was just opening one of the safes.

I said: 'Placide, what are you doing?' It was one of those meaningless questions. I could see clearly what he was doing. He was opening
his safe, the one in which he kept his own private belongings, and I
need not have asked so obvious a question.

My husband straightened up, however, not annoyed, you understand, but somewhat surprised, because I never entered his office as a
rule, and remarked that he was getting some money out because he
had a bill to pay that afternoon.

I asked him for the key to the sideboard and came and stood beside
him as he reached down into the safe, which was the kind that
opened with a great heavy lid on the top, like a cigar-box, or the
cover for a cistern. He reached into his pocket with his left hand
after the sideboard key, his right hand full of currency, and I looked
into the safe. There on top lay a paper which I took to be a kind
of promissory note. I read it, hastily. I was his wife. There was, I
conceived, nothing secret about it.

'What is this, Placide?' I inquired.

My husband handed me the key to the sideboard.

'What is what, my dear Minerva?' he asked.

'This note, or whatever it is. It seems as though you had loaned
three hundred dollars a good while ago, and never got it back.'

'That is correct,' said my husband. 'I have never felt that I wished to push the matter.' He picked up the note with his now free left hand, in a ruminating kind of manner, and I saw there was another note underneath. I picked that one up myself, my husband making no objection to my doing so, and glanced through it. That, too, was for three hundred dollars. Both were dated between seventeen and eighteen years previously, that is, in the year 1863, although they were of different months and days, and both were signed by men at that time living in Phillipsbourg, both prosperous men; one a white gentleman-planter in a small way; the other a colored man with a not very good reputation, but one who had prospered and was accounted well-to-do.

Well, my husband stood there with one note in his hand, and I stood beside him, holding the other. I did a rough sum in mental arithmetic. The notes were 'demand' notes, at eight per cent, simple interest, representing, the two together, six hundred dollars. Eighteen years of interest, at eight per cent added on, it seemed to me, would cause these notes to amount to a great deal more than twice six hundred dollars, something around fifteen hundred, in fact. We were far from rich!

'But, my dear Placide, you should collect these,' I cried.

'I have never wished to press them,' replied my husband.

'Allow me, if you please, to take them,' I begged him.

'Do as you wish, Minerva my dear,' replied Monsieur Du Chaillu. 'But, I beg of you, no lawsuits!'

'Very well,' said I, and, carrying the two notes, walked out of the office to get Julie her brandy, out of the sideboard in the dining room.

I will admit to you, Mr Canevin, that I was a little put out about my dear husband's carelessness in connection with those notes. At the same time, I could not avoid seeing very clearly that the notes, if still collectible, constituted a kind of windfall, as you say in the United States – it has to do with a variety of apple, does it not? – and I decided at once to set about a kind of investigation.

As soon as I had supplied Julie with a brandy which Dr Duchesne had prescribed for her, I sent our house-boy after Monsieur Henkes, the notary of our town of Phillipsbourg. Monsieur Henkes came within the hour – he stayed for tea, I remember – and he assured me that the notes, not yet being twenty years old, were still collectible. I placed them in his hands, and paid him, in advance, as the custom is on St Martin, and, I dare say, in Curaçao, and the other Dutch possessions, his fee of fifty dollars for collection, instructing him that it was my husband's desire that there should be no actual lawsuit.

I will shorten my story as much as possible, by telling you that the note which had been given by the gentleman-planter was paid, in six months, in two equal installments, and, with my husband's permission, I invested the money in some shares in one of our St Martin Salt-Ponds – salt, you know, is the chief export from St Martin.

The other note, the one which had been given by the colored man, Armand Dubois, did not go through so easily. Here in the West Indies, as you have surely observed, our 'colored' people, as distinct from the Black laboring class, are, commonly, estimable persons, who conduct themselves like us Caucasians. Dubois, however, was exceptional. He was only about one-quarter African – a quadroon, or there-abouts. But his leanings, as sometimes happens, were to the Black side of his heredity. Many persons in Phillipsbourg regarded him as a rascal, a person of no character at all. It seems he had heard, far back, in the days when my husband accommodated his friend, the planter, of that transaction, and had come almost at once to ask for a similar accommodation. That is why the two notes were so nearly of the same date, and perhaps it accounts for the fact that the two notes were both for three hundred dollars. Negroes, and those persons of mixed blood whose Black side predominates, are not very inventive. It would be quite characteristic for such a person to ask for the same sum as had been given to the former applicant.

Dubois made a great pother about paying. Of this I heard only rumors, of course. Monsieur Henkes did not trouble us in the matter, once the collection of the notes had been placed in his hands. It was, of course, a perfectly clear case. The note had been signed by Dubois, and it had more than two years to run before it would be outlawed – 'limited' is, I believe, the legal term. So Armand Dubois paid, as he was well able to do, but, as I say, with a very bad grace. Presumably he expected never to pay. The impudence of the man!

Shortly after I had placed the notes in the hands of Monsieur Henkes for collection, Julie came to me one afternoon, quite gray in the face, as Negroes look when they are badly frightened. On St Martin, perhaps you know, Mr Canevin, servants have a custom similar to what I have read about in your South. That is to say, they invariably address their mistresses as 'Miss', with the Christian name. Why, I can not say. It is their custom. Julie came to me, as I say, very frightened, very much upset – quite terrified, in fact.

She said to me: 'Miss Minerva, on no account, ma'am, mus' yo' go to de door, if yo' please, ma'am. One Armand Dubois come, ma'am, an' is even now cloimbing de step of de gol'ry. Hoide yo'self, ma'am, I beg of yo', in de name of Gahd!'

Julie's distress and state of fright, which the girl could not conceal, impressed me more than her words. I said: 'Julie, go to the door yourself. Say, please, to this Dubois, that I have nothing to say to him. For anything whatever, he must address himself to Monsieur Henkes.'

'Yes, ma'am,' replied Julie, and almost pushed me into my bedroom and shut the door smartly behind me. I stood there, and listened, as Dubois, who had now mounted the gallery steps, knocked, very truculently, it seemed to me – the creature had no manners – on the door. I could hear him ask for me, and the murmur of Julie's voice as she delivered my message. Dubois was reluctant to leave, it seemed. He stood and parleyed, but forcing his way into a house like the rectory of the English Church was beyond him, and at last he went. Several other persons, black fellows, Julie told me, had accompanied him, for what purpose I can not imagine – it was most unusual that he should come to trouble me at all – and these all walked down the street, as I could see through the slanted jalousies of my bedroom window, Dubois gesticulating and orating to his followers.

Julie told me something else, too – something which quite made my blood run cold. Armand Dubois, said Julie, had, half-concealed in his hand, as he stood talking to her, a small vial. Julie was sure it contained vitriol. I was almost afraid to venture out to the street after that, and it was a long time before I recovered from the shock of it. Vitriol – think of it, Mr Canevin! – if indeed that were what he had in the vial; and what else could he have had?

Of course, I did not dare tell my husband. It would have distressed that dear, kind man most atrociously; and besides, the collection of the notes was, so to speak, a venture of mine, carried out, if not exactly against his will, at least without any enthusiasm on his part. So I kept quiet, and commanded Julie to say nothing whatever about it. I was sure, too, that even a person like Armand Dubois would, in a short time, get over the condition of rage in which Monsieur Henkes's visit to him must have left him to induce him to come to me at all. That, or something similar, actually proved to be the case. I had no further annoyance from Dubois, and in the course of a few weeks, probably pressed by Monsieur Henkes, he settled the note, paying seven hundred and twenty-four dollars, to be exact, with seventeen years and eight months' interest at eight per cent.

Of course, Mr Canevin, all that portion of the story, except, perhaps, for Armand Dubois's unpleasant visit, is merely commonplace – the mere narrative of the collection of two demand-notes. Note, though, what followed!

It was, perhaps, two months after the day when I had gone into my husband's office and discovered those notes, and about a month after Dubois had paid what he owed Monsieur Du Chaillu, that I had gone to bed, a trifle earlier, perhaps, than usual – about half-past nine, to be exact. My aunt was staying with us in the rectory at the time, and she was far from well, and I had been reading to her and fanning her, and I was somewhat tired. I fell asleep, I suppose, immediately after retiring.

I awakened, and found myself sitting bolt-upright in my bed, and the clock in the town was striking twelve. I counted the strokes. As I finished, and the bell ceased its striking, I *felt*, rather than saw – for I was looking, in an abstracted kind of fashion, straight before me, my elbows on my knees, in a sitting posture, as I have said – something at the left, just outside the mosquito-netting. There was a dim night-light, such as I always kept, in the far corner of the room, on the edge of my bureau, and by its light the objects in the room were faintly visible through the white net.

I turned, suddenly, under the impulse of that feeling, and there, Mr Canevin, just beside the bed, and almost pressing against the net though not quite touching it, was a face. The face was that of a mulatto, and as I looked at it, frozen, speechless, I observed that it was Armand Dubois, and that he was glaring at me, with an expression of the most horrible malignancy that could be imagined. The lips were drawn back – like an animal's, Mr Canevin – but the most curious, and perhaps the most terrifying, aspect of the situation, was the fact that the face was on a level with the bed, that is, the chin seemed to rest against the edge of the mattress, so that, as it occurred to me, the man must be sitting on the floor, his legs placed under the bed, so as to bring his horrible leering face in that position I have described.

I tried to scream, and my voice was utterly dried up. Then, moved by what impulse I can not describe, I plunged toward the face, tore loose the netting on that side, and looked directly at it.

Mr Canevin, there was nothing there, but, as I moved abruptly toward it, I saw a vague, dim hand and arm swing up from below, and there was the strangest sensation! It was as though, over my face and shoulders and breast, hot and stinging drops had been cast. There was, for just a passing instant, the most dreadful burning, searing sensation, and then it was gone. I half sat, half lay, a handful of the netting in my hands, where I had torn it loose from where it had been tucked under the edge of the mattress, and there was nothing there – nothing whatever; I passed my hand over my face and neck, but there was nothing; no burns – nothing.

I do not know how I managed to do it, but I climbed out of bed, and looked underneath. Mr Canevin, there was nothing, no man, nor anything, there. I walked over and turned up the night-light, and looked all about the room. Nothing. The jalousies were all fastened, as usual. The door was locked. There were no other means of ingress or egress.

I went back to bed, convinced that I must have been dreaming or sleepwalking, or something of the sort, although I had never walked in my sleep, and almost never dreamed or remembered any dream. I could not sleep, and it occurred to me that I would do well to get up again, put on my bathrobe, and go out to the dining room for a drink of water. The water stood, in earthenware 'gugglets', just beside a doorway that led out to a small gallery at the side of the house – which stood on the corner – in the wind, so as to keep cool. You've seen that, a good many times, even here, of course. On St Martin we had no ice-plant in those days, nor yet, so far as I know, and everybody kept the drinking-water in gugglets and set the gugglets where the wind would blow on them and cool the water.

I took a glass from the sideboard, filled it, and drank the water. Then I opened the door just beside me, and stood looking out for a few minutes. The town was absolutely silent at that hour. There was no moon, and the streets were lighted just as they were here in Frederiksted before we had electricity, with occasional hurricane lanterns at the corners. The one on our corner was burning steadily, and except for the howling of a dog somewhere in the town, everything was absolutely quiet and peaceful, Mr Canevin.

I went back to bed, and fell asleep immediately. At any rate I have no recollection of lying there hoping for sleep.

Then, immediately afterward, it seemed, I was awakened a second time. This time I was not sitting up when I came to my waking senses, but it did not take me very long to sit up, I can assure you! For the most extraordinary thing was happening in my bedroom.

In the exact center of the room there stood a round, mahogany table. Around and around that table, a small goat was running, from right to left – that is, as I looked toward the table, the goat was running away from me around to the right, and coming back at the left. I could hear the clatter of its little, hard hoofs on the pitch-pine floor, occasionally muffled in the queerest way – it sounds like nothing in the telling, of course – when the goat would step on the small rug on which the table stood. I could see its great, shining eyes, like green moons, every time it came around to the left.

I watched the thing, fascinated, and a slow horror began to grow upon me. I think I swooned, for the last thing I remember is my senses leaving me, but it must have been a very light fainting fit, Mr Canevin, for I aroused myself, and the room was absolutely silent.

I was shaking all over as though I had been having an attack of the quartan ague, but I managed once more to slip under the netting, reach for my bathrobe, and go over and turn up the night-light. I observed that the door of my bed-room was standing open, and I went through it and back to the dining room, as I had done the first time. I felt very uncomfortable, shaken and nervous, as you may well imagine, but there in the next room I knew my husband was sleeping, and my poor old aunt on the other side of the hall, and I plucked up my courage. I knew that *he* would never be afraid, of anything, man or – anything else, Mr Canevin!

I found that I must have been more upset than I had supposed, for the door out onto the small gallery from the dining room, where I had stood the other time, was unfastened, and half open, and I realized that I had left it in that condition, and I saw clearly that the young goat had simply wandered in. Goats and dogs and other animals roamed the streets there, even pigs, much as they do here, although all the islands have police regulations, and on St Martin these were not enforced nearly as well as they are here on St Croix. So I laughed at myself and my fears, although I think I had a right at least to be startled by that goat dancing about my bedroom table, and I fastened the door leading outside, and came back into my bedroom, and fastened that door too, and went back to bed once more. My last waking sensation was of that dog, or some other, howling, somewhere in the town.

Well, that was destined to be a bad night, Mr Canevin. I remember one of my husband's sermons, Mr Canevin, on the text: 'A Good Day'. I do not remember what portion of the Scriptures it comes from, but I remember the text, and the sermon too. Afterward, it occurred to me that that night, that 'bad night', was the direct opposite; a mere whimsy of mine, but I always think of that night as 'the bad night', somehow.

For, Mr Canevin, that was not all. No. I had noticed the time before I returned to bed on that occasion, and it was a little past one o'clock. I had slept for an hour, you see, after the first interruption.

When I was awakened again it was five o'clock in the morning. Remember, I had, deliberately, and in a state of full wakefulness, closed and fastened both the door from that side gallery into the dining room, and the bedroom door. The jalousies had not been touched at any time, and all of them were fastened.

I awoke with the most terrible impression of evil and horror: it was as though I stood alone in the midst of a hostile world, bent upon my destruction. It was the most dreadful feeling – a feeling of complete, of unrecoverable, depression.

And there, coming through my bedroom door – *through* the door, Mr Canevin, which remained shut and locked – was Armand Dubois. He was a tall, slim man, and he stalked in, looking taller and slimmer than ever, because he was wearing one of those old-fashioned, long, white night-shirts, which fell to his ankles. He walked, as I say, through the closed door, and straight toward me, and, Mr Canevin, the expression on his face was the expression of one of the demons from hell.

I half sat up, utterly horrified, incapable of speech, or even of thought beyond that numbing horror, and as I sat up, Armand Dubois seemed to pause. His advance slowed abruptly, the expression of malignant hatred seemed to become intensified, and then he slowly turned to his left, and, keeping his face turned toward me, walked, very slowly now straight through the side wall of my bedroom, and was gone, Mr Canevin.

Then I screamed, again and again, and Placide, my husband, bursting the door, rushed in, and over his shoulder and through the broken door I could see Julie's terrified face, and my poor old aunt, a Shetland shawl huddled about her poor shoulders, coming gropingly out of her bedroom.

That was the last I remembered then. When I came to, it was broad daylight and past seven, and Dr Duchesne was there, holding his fingers against my wrist, counting the pulse, I suppose, and there was a strong taste of brandy in my mouth.

They made me stay in bed all through the morning, and Dr Duchesne would not allow me to talk. I had wanted to tell Placide and him all that had happened to me through the night, but at two o'clock in the afternoon, when I was allowed to get up at last, after having eaten some broth, I had had time to think, and I never mentioned what I had heard and seen that night.

No, Mr Canevin, my dear husband never heard it, never knew what had cast me into that condition of 'nerves'. After he died I told Dr Duchesne, and Dr Duchesne made no particular comment. Like all doctors, and the clergy here in the West Indies, such matters were an old story to him!

It was fortunate for us that he happened to be passing the house and came in because he saw the lights, and could hear Julie weeping hysterically. He realized that something extraordinary had happened, or was happening, in the rectory, and that he might be needed.

He was on his way home from the residence of Armand Dubois, there in the town. Dubois had been attacked by some obscure tropical fever, just before midnight, and had died at five o'clock that morning, Mr Canevin.

Dr Duchesne told me, later, about Dubois's case, which interested him very much from his professional viewpoint. Dr Duchesne said that there were still strange fevers, not only in obscure places in the world, but right here in our civilized islands – think of it! He said that he could not tell so much as the name of the fever that had taken Dubois away. But he said the most puzzling of the symptoms was, that just at midnight Dubois had fallen into a state of coma – unconsciousness, you know – which had lasted only a minute or two; quite extraordinary, the doctor said, and that a little later, soon after one o'clock, he had shut his eyes, and quieted down – he had been raving, muttering and tossing about, as fever patients do, you know, and that there had come over his face the most wicked and dreadful grimace, and that he had drummed with his fingers against his own forehead, an irregular kind of drumming, a beat, the doctor said, not unlike the scampering footfalls of some small, four-footed animal . . .

He died, as I told you, at five, quite suddenly, and Dr Duchesne said that just as he was going there came over his face the most horrible, the most malignant expression that he had ever seen. He said it caused him to shudder, although he knew, of course, that it was only the muscles of the man's face contracting – *rigor mortis*, it is called, I think, Mr Canevin.

Dr Duchesne said, too, that there was a scientific word which described the situation – that is, the possible connection between

Dubois as he lay dying with that queer fever, and the appearances to me. It was not 'telepathy', Mr Canevin, of that I am certain. I wish I could remember the word, but I fear it has escaped my poor old memory!

'Was it "projection"?' I asked Mrs Du Chaillu.

'I think that was it, Mr Canevin,' said Mrs Du Chaillu, and nodded her head at me, wisely.

The Lips

The *Saul Taverner*, blackbirder, Luke Martin, master, up from Cartagena, came to her anchor in the harbor of St Thomas, capital and chief town of the Danish West Indies, A Martinique barkentine berthed to leeward of her, sent a fully manned boat ashore after the harbormaster with a request for permission to change anchorage. Luke Martin's shore boat was only a few lengths behind the Frenchman's. Martin shouted after the officer whom it landed: 'Tell Lollik I'll change places with ye, an' welcome! What ye carryin' – brandy? I'll take six cases off'n ye.'

The barkentine's mate, a French-Island mulatto, nodded over his shoulder, and noted down the order in a leather pocketbook without slackening his pace. It was no joyful experience to lie in a semi-enclosed harbor directly to leeward of a slaver, and haste was indicated despite propitiatory orders for brandy. 'Very well, Captain,' said the mate, stiffly.

Martin landed as the Martinique mate rounded a corner to the left and disappeared from view in the direction of the harbor-master's. Martin scowled after him, muttering to himself.

'Airs! Talkin' English – language of the islands; thinkin' in French, you an' your airs! An' yer gran'father came outta a blackbird ship like's not! You an' your airs!'

Reaching the corner the mate had turned, Martin glanced after him momentarily, then turned to the right, mounting a slight rise. His business ashore took him to the fort. He intended to land his cargo, or a portion of it, that night. The colony was short of field hands. With the help of troops from Martinique, French troops, and Spaniards from its nearer neighbor, Porto Rico, it had just put down a bloody uprising on its subsidiary island of St Jan. Many of the slaves had been killed in the joint armed reprisal of the year 1833.

Luke Martin got his permission to land his cargo, therefore, without difficulty, and, being a Yankee bucko who let no grass grow under his feet, four bells in the afternoon watch saw the hatches off and the decks of the *Saul Taverner* swarming with manacled Blacks for the ceremony of washing-down.

Huddled together, blinking in the glaring sun of a July afternoon under parallel 18, north latitude, the mass of swart humanity were soaped, with handfuls of waste out of soft-soap buckets, scrubbed with brushes on the ends of short handles, and rinsed off with other buckets. Boatloads of Negroes surrounded the ship to see the washing-down, and these were kept at a distance by a swearing third mate told off for the purpose.

By seven bells the washing-down was completed, and before sun-down a row of lighters, each guarded by a pair of Danish *gendarmes* with muskets and fixed bayonets, had ranged alongside for the taking off of the hundred and seventeen Blacks who were to be landed, most of whom would be sent to replenish the laborers on the plantations of St Jan off the other side of the island of St Thomas.

The disembarking process began just after dark, to the light of lanterns. Great care was exercised by all concerned lest any escape by plunging overboard. A tally-clerk from shore checked off the Blacks as they went over the side into the lighters, and these, as they became filled, were rowed to the landing-stage by other slaves, bending over six great sweeps in each of the stub-bowed, heavy wooden boats.

Among the huddled black bodies of the very last batch stood a woman, very tall and thin, with a new-born child, black as a coal, at her breasts. The woman stood a little aloof from the others, farther from the low rail of the *Saul Taverner*'s forward deck, crooning to her infant. Behind her approached Luke Martin, impatient of his unloading, and cut at her thin ankles with his rhinoceros leather whip. The woman did not wince. Instead, she turned her head and muttered a few syllables in a low tone, in the Eboe dialect. Martin shoved her into the mass of Blacks, cursing roundly as he cut a second time at the spindling shins.

The woman turned, very quietly and softly, as he was passing behind her, let her head fall softly on Martin's shoulder and whis-pered into his ear. The motion was so delicate as to simulate a caress, but Martin's curse died in his throat. He howled in pain as the woman raised her head, and his whip clattered on the deck boarding while the hand which had held it went to the shoulder. The woman, deftly holding her infant, had moved in among the huddling Blacks, a dozen or more of whom intervened between her and Martin, who hopped on one foot and cursed, a vicious, continuous stream of foul epithets; then, still cursing, made his way in haste to his cabin after an antiseptic, any idea of revenge swallowed up in his superstitious dread of what might happen to him if he did not, forthwith, dress the ghastly wound just under his left ear, where the black woman had caused her firm, white and shining teeth to meet the great muscle of his neck between shoulder and jaw.

When he emerged, ten minutes later, the wound now soaked in permanganate of potash, and roughly clotted with a clean cloth, the last lighter, under the impetus of its six sweeps, was half-way ashore, and the clerk of the government, from the fort, was awaiting him, with a bag of coin and a pair of *gendarmes* to guard it. He accompanied the government clerk below, where, the *gendarmes* at the cabin door, they figured and added and counted money for the next hour, a bottle of sound rum and a pair of glasses between them.

At two bells, under a shining moon, the *Saul Taverner*, taking advantage of the evening trade wind, was running for the harbor's mouth to stand away for Norfolk, Virginia, whence, empty, she would run up the coast for her home port of Boston, Massachusetts.

It was midnight, what with the care of his ship coming out of even the plain and safe harbor of St Thomas, before Martin the skipper, Culebra lighthouse off the port quarter, turned in. The wound in the top of his shoulder ached dully, and he sent for Matthew Pound, his first mate, to wash it out with more permanganate and dress it suitably. It was in an awkward place – curse the black slut! – for him to manage it for himself.

Pound went white and muttered under his breath at the ugly sight of it when Martin had removed his shirt, painfully, and eased off the cloth he had roughly laid over it, a cloth now stiff and clotted with the exuding blood drying on its inner surface, from the savage wound.

Thereafter, not liking the look on his mate's face, nor that whitening which the sight of the place in his neck had brought about, Martin dispensed with assistance, and dressed the wound himself.

He slept little that first night, but this was partly for thinking of the bargain he had driven with those short-handed Danes. They had been hard up for black meat to sweat on those hillside canefields over on St Jan. He could have disposed easily of his entire cargo, but that, unfortunately, was out of the question. He had, what with an exceptionally slow and hot voyage across the Caribbean from Cartagena, barely enough of his said cargo left to fulfill his engagement to deliver a certain number of head in Norfolk. But he would have been glad enough to rid his hold of them all – curse them! – and set his course straight for Boston. He was expecting to be married the day after his arrival. He was eager to get home, and even now the *Saul Taverner* was carrying as much sail as she could stand up under, heeling now to the unfailing trade wind of this latitude.

The wound ached and pained, none the less, and he found it well-nigh impossible to settle himself in a comparatively comfortable position on its account. He tossed and cursed far into the warm night. Toward morning he fell into a fitful doze.

The entire side of his neck and shoulder was one huge, searing ache when he awakened and pushed himself carefully upright with both hands. He could not bend his head nor, at first, move it from side to side. Dressing was a very painful process, but he managed it. He wanted to see what the bite looked like, but, as he never shaved during a voyage, there was no glass in his cabin. He bathed the sore place gingerly with bay rum, which hurt abominably and caused him to curse afresh. Dressed at last, he made his way up on deck, past the steward who was laying breakfast in his cabin. The steward, he thought, glanced at him curiously, but he could not be sure. No wonder. He had to walk sidewise, with the pain of his neck, like a crab. He ordered more sail, stuns'ls, and, these set and sheeted home, he returned to the cabin for breakfast.

Mid-afternoon saw him, despite the vessel's more than satisfactory speed and the progress of a long leg toward Boston and Lydia Farnham, in such a devilish temper that everyone on board the ship kept as far as possible out of his way. He took no night watches, these being divided among the three mates, and after his solitary supper, punctuated with numerous curses at a more than usually awkward steward, he went into his stateroom, removed his shirt and singlet, and thoroughly rubbed the entire aching area with coconut oil. The pain now ran down his left arm to the elbow, and penetrated to all the cords of his neck, the muscles of which throbbed and burned atrociously.

The embrocation gave him a certain amount of relief. He remembered that the woman had muttered something. It was *not* Eboe, that jargon of *lingua franca* which served as a medium for the few remarks necessary between slavers and their human cattle. It was some out-landish coastal or tribal dialect. He had not caught it, sensed its meaning; though there had resided in those few syllables some germ of deadly meaning. He remembered, vaguely, the cadence of the syllables, even though their meaning had been unknown to him. Wearing, aching, depressed, he turned in, and this time, almost immediately, he fell asleep.

And in his sleep, those syllables were repeated to him, into his left ear, endlessly, over and over again, and in his sleep he knew their meaning; and when he awoke, a swaying beam of pouring moonlight coming through his porthole, at four bells after midnight, the cold sweat had made his pillow clammy wet and stood dankly in the hollows of his eyes and soaked his tangled beard.

Burning from head to foot, he rose and lit the candle in his binnacle-light, and cursed himself again for a fool for not acquiring a mirror through the day. Young Sumner, the third mate, shaved. One or two of the fo'castle hands, too. There would be mirrors on board. He must obtain one tomorrow. What was it the woman had said – those syllables? He shuddered. He could not remember. Why should he remember? Gibberish – nigger-talk! It was nothing. Merely the act of a bestial Black. They were all alike. He should have taken the living hide off the wench. To bite him! Well, painful as it was, it should be well healed before he got back to Boston, and Lydia.

Laboriously, for he was very stiff and sore all along the left side, he climbed back into his bed, after blowing out the binnacle-light. That candlewick! It was very foul. He should have wet his thumb and finger and pinched it out. It was still smoking.

Then the syllables again, endlessly – over and over, and, now that he slept, and, somehow, knew that he slept and could not carry their meaning into the next waking state, *he knew what they meant*. Asleep, drowned in sleep, he tossed from side to side of his berth-bed, and the cold sweat ran in oily trickles down into his thick beard.

He awakened in the early light of morning in a state of horrified half-realization. He could not get up, it seemed. The ache now ran all through his body, which felt as though it had been beaten until flayed. One of the brandy bottles from the Martinique barkentine, opened the night of departure from St Thomas, was within reach. He got it, painfully, drew the cork with his teeth, holding the bottle in his right hand, and took a long, gasping drink of the neat spirit. He could feel it run through him like liquid, golden fire. Ah! that was better. He raised the bottle again, set it back where it had been, half empty. He made a great effort to roll out of the berth, failed, sank back well-nigh helpless, his head humming and singing like a hive of angry bees.

He lay there, semi-stupefied now, vague and dreadful things working within his head, his mind, his body; things brewing, seething, there inside him, as though something had entered into him and was growing there where the focus of pain throbbed, in the great muscles of his neck on the left side.

There, an hour later, a timid steward found him, after repeated and unanswered knocks on the stateroom door. The steward had at last ventured to open the door a mere peeping-slit, and then, softly closing it behind him, and white-faced, hastened to find Pound, the first mate.

Pound, after consultation with the second mate, Sumner, accompanied the steward to the stateroom door, opening off the captain's cabin. Even there, hard bucko that he was, he hesitated. No one aboard the *Saul Taverner* approached Captain Luke Martin with a sense of ease or anything like self-assurance. Pound repeated the steward's door-opening, peeped within, and thereafter entered the cabin, shutting the door.

Martin lay on his right side, the bed-clothes pushed down to near his waist. He slept in his singlet, and the left side of his neck was uppermost. Pound looked long at the wound, his face like chalk, his hands and lips trembling. Then he softly departed, shutting the door behind him a second time, and went thoughtfully up on deck again. He sought out young Sumner and the two spoke together for several minutes. Then Sumner went below to his cabin, and, emerging on the deck, looked furtively all around him. Observing the coast clear, he drew from beneath his drill jacket something twice the size of his hand, and, again glancing about to make sure he was not observed, dropped the article overboard. It flashed in the bright morning sun as it turned about in the air before the waters received it forever. It was his small cabin shaving-mirror.

At four bells in the forenoon, Pound again descended to the captain's cabin. This time Martin's voice, a weak voice, answered his discreet knock and at its invitation he entered the stateroom. Martin now lay on his back, his left side away from the door.

'How are you feeling, sir?' asked Pound.

'Better,' murmured Martin; 'this damned thing!' He indicated the left side of his neck with a motion of his right thumb. 'I got some sleep this morning. Just woke up, just now. It's better – the worst of it over, I reckon.'

A pause fell between the men. There seemed nothing more to say. Finally, after several twitches and fidgeting, Pound mentioned several details about the ship, the surest way to enlist Martin's interest at any time. Martin replied, and Pound took his departure.

Martin had spoken the truth when he alleged he was better. He had awakened with a sense that the worst was over. The wound ached abominably still, but the unpleasantness was distinctly lessened. He got up, rather languidly, slowly pulled on his deck clothes, called for coffee through the stateroom door.

Yet, when he emerged on his deck ten minutes later, his face was drawn and haggard, and there was a look in his eyes that kept the men silent. He looked over the ship professionally, the regular six bells morning inspection, but he was preoccupied and his usual intense interest in anything concerned with his ship was this day merely perfunctory. For, nearly constantly now that the savage pain was somewhat allayed and tending to grow less as the deck exercise cleared his mind and body of their poisons, those last syllables, the muttered syllables in his left ear when the Black woman's head had lain for an instant on his shoulder, those syllables which were not in Eboe, kept repeating themselves to him. It was as though they were constantly reiterated in his physical ear rather than merely mentally; vague syllables, with one word, 'l'kundu', standing out and pounding itself deeper and deeper into his consciousness.

'Hearin' things!' he muttered to himself as he descended to his cabin on the conclusion of the routine morning inspection a half-hour before noon. He did not go up on deck again for the noon observations. He remained, sitting very quietly there in his cabin, listening to what was being whispered over and over again in his left ear, the ear above the wound in his neck muscle.

It was highly unusual for this full-blooded bucko skipper to be quiet as his cabin steward roundly noted. The explanation was, however, very far from the steward's mind. He imagined that the wound had had a devastating effect upon the captain's nerves, and so far his intuition was a right one. But beyond that the steward's crude psychology did not penetrate. He would have been skeptical, amused, scornful, had anyone suggested to him the true reason for this unaccustomed silence and quietude on the part of his employer. Captain Luke Martin, for the first time in his heady and truculent career, was frightened.

He ate little for his midday dinner, and immediately afterward retired to his stateroom. He came out again, almost at once, however, and mounted the cabin ladder to the after deck. The *Saul Taverner*, carrying a heavy load of canvas, was spanking along at a good twelve knots. Martin looked aloft, like a sound sailorman, when he emerged on deck, but his preoccupied gaze came down and seemed to young Sumner, who touched his hat to him, to look inward. Martin was addressing him.

'I want the lend of your lookin'-glass,' said he in quiet tones.

Young Sumner started, felt the blood leave his face. This was what Pound had warned him about; why he had thrown his glass over the side.

'Sorry, sir. It ain't along with me this v'yage, sir. I had it till we lay in St Thomas. But now it's gone. I couldn't shave this mornin', sir.' The young mate made an evidential gesture, rubbing a sun-burned hand across his day's growth of beard on a weak but not unhandsome face.

He expected a bull-like roar of annoyance from the captain. Instead Martin merely nodded absently, and walked forward. Sumner watched him interestedly, until he reached the hatch leading to the crew's quarters below decks forward. Then: 'Cripes! He'll get one from Dave Sloan!' And young Sumner ran to find Pound and tell him that the captain would probably have a looking-glass within a minute. He was very curious to know the whys and wherefores of his senior mate's unusual request about his own looking-glass. He had obeyed, but he wanted to know; for here, indeed, was something very strange. Pound had merely told him the captain mustn't see that wound in his neck, which was high enough up so that without a glass he could not manage to look at it.

'What's it like, Mr Pound?' he ventured to inquire.

'It's wot you'd name kinder livid-like,' returned Pound, slowly. 'It's a kind of purplish. Looks like – nigger lips!'

Back in his stateroom, Martin, after closing the door leading to the cabin, started to take off his shirt. He was halfway through this operation when he was summoned on deck. He hastily readjusted the shirt, almost shame-facedly, as though discovered in some shameful act, and mounted the ladder. Pound engaged him for twenty minutes, ship matters. He gave his decisions in the same half-hearted voice which was so new to those about him, and descended again.

The bit of mirror-glass which he had borrowed from Sloan in the fo'castle was gone from his washstand. He looked, painfully, all over the cabin for it, but it was not there. Ordinarily such a thing happening would have elicited a very tempest of raging curses. Now he sat down, almost helplessly, and stared about the stateroom with unseeing eyes. But not with unheeding ears! The voice was speaking English now, no longer gibberish syllables grouped about the one clear word, 'l'kundu'. The voice in his left ear was compelling, tense, repetitive. 'Over the side,' it was repeating to him, and again, and yet again, 'Over the side!'

He sat there a long time. Then, at last, perhaps an hour later, his face, which there was no one by to see, now pinched, drawn and gray in the bold challenging afternoon light in the white-painted state-room, he rose, slowly, and with almost furtive motions began to pull off his shirt.

He got it off, laid it on his berth, drew off the light singlet which he wore under it, and slowly, tentatively, with his right hand, reached for the wound in his neck. As his hand approached it, he felt cold and weak. At last his hand, fingers groping, touched the sore and tender area of the wound, felt about, found the wound itself . . .

It was Pound who found him, two hours later, huddled in a heap on the cramped floor of the stateroom, naked to the waist, unconscious.

It was Pound, hard old Pound, who laboriously propped the captain's great bulk – for he was a heavy-set man, standing six feet in height – into his chair, pulled the singlet and then the discarded shirt over his head and then poured brandy between his bluish lips. It required half an hour of the mate's rough restoratives, brandy, chafing of the hands, slapping the limp, huge wrists, before Captain Luke Martin's eyelids fluttered and the big man gradually came awake.

But Pound found the monosyllabic answers to his few, brief questions cryptic, inappropriate. It was as though Martin were answering someone else, some other voice.

'I will,' he said, wearily, and again, 'Yes, I will!'

It was then, looking him up and down in considerable puzzlement, that the mate saw the blood on the fingers of his right hand, picked up the great, heavy hand now lying limply on the arm of the stateroom chair.

The three middle fingers had been bleeding for some time. The blood from them was now dry and clotted. Pound, picking up the hand, examining it in the light of the lowering afternoon sun, saw that these fingers had been savagely cut, or, it looked like, *sawed*. It was as though the saw-teeth that had ground and torn them had grated along their bones. It was a ghastly wound.

Pound, trembling from head to foot, fumbling about the medicine case, mixed a bowl of permanganate solution, soaked the unresisting hand, bound it up. He spoke to Martin several times, but Martin's eyes were looking at something far away, his ears deaf to his mate's words. Now and again he nodded his head acquiescently, and once more, before old Pound left him, sitting there, limply, he muttered, 'Yes, yes! – I will, I will!'

Pound visited him again just before four bells in the early evening, supper time. He was still seated, looking, somehow, shrunken, apathetic.

616 THE BLACK BEAST AND OTHER VOODOO TALES

'Supper, Captain?' inquired Pound tentatively. Martin did not raise his eyes. His lips moved, however, and Pound bent to catch what was being said.

'Yes, yes, yes,' said Martin, 'I will, I will – yes, I will!'

'It's laid in the cabin, sir,' ventured Pound, but he got no reply, and he slipped out, closing the door behind him.

'The captain's sick, Maguire,' said Pound to the little steward. 'You might as well take down the table and all that, and then go forward as soon as you're finished.'

'Ay, ay, sir,' replied the wondering steward, and proceeded to unset the cabin table according to these orders. Pound saw him through with these duties, followed him out on deck, saw that he went forward as directed. Then he returned, softly.

He paused outside the stateroom door, listened. There was some-one talking in there, someone besides the skipper – a thick voice, like one of the Negroes, but very faint; thick, guttural, but light; a voice like a young boy's or – a woman's. Pound, stupefied, listened, his ear now directly against the door. He could not catch, through that thickness, what was being said, but it was in form, by the re-peated sounds, the captain's voice alternating with the light, guttural voice, clearly a conversation, like question and answer, question and answer. The ship had no boy. Of women there were a couple of dozen, but all of them were battened below, under hatches, Black women, down in the stinking manhold. Besides, the captain – there could not be a woman in there with him. No woman, no one at all, could have got in. The stateroom had been occupied only by the captain when he had left it fifteen minutes before. He had not been out of sight of the closed door all that time. Yet – he listened the more intently, his mind now wholly intrigued by this strange riddle.

He caught the cadence of Martin's words, now, the same cadence, he knew instinctively, as that of the broken sentence he had been repeating to him in his half-dazed state while he was binding up those gashed fingers. Those fingers! He shuddered. The *Saul Taverner* was a hell-ship. None was better aware of that than he, who had largely contributed, through many voyages in her, to that sinister reputation she bore, but – this! This was something like real hell.

'Yes, yes – I will, I will, I will – ' that was the swing, the tonal cadence of what Martin was saying at more or less regular intervals in there; then the guttural, light voice – the two going on alternately, one after the other, no pauses in that outlandish conversation.

Abruptly the conversation ceased. It was as though a sound-proof door had been pulled down over it. Pound straightened himself up, waited a minute, then knocked on the door.

The door was abruptly thrown open from inside, and Captain Luke Martin, his eyes glassy, unseeing, stepped out, Pound giving way before him. The captain paused in the middle of his cabin, looking about him, his eyes still bearing that 'unseeing' look. Then he made his way straight toward the companion ladder. He was going up on deck, it seemed. His clothes hung on him now, his shirt awry, his trousers crumpled and seamed where he had lain on the floor, sat, huddled up, in the small chair where Pound had placed him.

Pound followed him up the ladder.

Once on deck, he made his way straight to the port rail, and stood, looking, still as though 'unseeingly', out over the billowing waves. It was dark now; the sub-tropic dusk had lately fallen. The ship was quiet save for the noise of her sharp bows as they cut through the middle North Atlantic swell on her twelve-knot way to Virginia.

Suddenly old Pound sprang forward, grappled with Martin. The captain had started to climb the rail – suicide, that was it, then – those voices!

The thwarting of what seemed to be his purpose aroused Martin at last. Behind him lay a middle-aged man's lifetime of command, of following his own will in all things. He was not accustomed to being thwarted, to any resistance which, aboard his own ship, always went down, died still-born, before his bull-like bellow, his truculent fists.

He grappled in turn with his mate, and a long, desperate, and withal a silent struggle began there on the deck, lighted only by the light from the captain's cabin below, the light of the great binnacle lamp of whale oil, through the sky-lights set above-decks for daytime illumination below.

In the course of that silent, deadly struggle, Pound seeking to drag the captain back from the vicinity of the rail, the captain laying about him with vicious blows, the man became rapidly disheveled. Martin had been coatless, and a great swath of his white shirt came away in the clutching grip of Pound, baring his neck and left shoulder.

Pound slackened, let go, shrank and reeled away, covering his eyes lest they be blasted from their sockets by the horror which he had seen.

For there, where the shirt had been torn away and exposed the side of Martin's neck, stood a pair of blackish-purple, perfectly formed, blubbery lips; and as he gazed, appalled, horrified, the lips had opened in a wide yawn, exposing great shining African teeth, from between which, before he could bury his face in his hands away from this horror, a long, pink tongue had protruded and licked the lips . . .

And when old Pound, shaking now to his very marrow, cold with the horror of this dreadful portent there on the deck warm with the pulsing breath of the trade wind, had recovered himself sufficiently to look again toward the place where the master of the *Saul Taverner* had struggled with him there against the railing, that place stood empty and no trace of Luke Martin so much as ruffled the phosphorescent surface of the *Saul Taverner's* creaming wake.

The Fireplace

When the Planter's Hotel in Jackson, Mississippi, burned to the ground in the notable fire of 1922, the loss to that section of the South could not be measured in terms of that ancient hostelry's former grandeur. The days had indeed long passed when a Virginia ham was therein stewed in no medium meaner than good white wine, and as the rambling old building was heavily insured, the owners suffered no great material loss. The real loss was the community's, in the deaths by fire of two of its prominent citizens, Lieutenant-Governor Frank Stacpoole and Mayor Cassius L. Turner. These gentlemen, just turning elderly, had been having a reunion in the hotel with two of their old associates, Judge Varney J. Baker of Memphis, Tennessee, and the Honorable Valdemar Peale, a prominent Georgian, from Atlanta. Thus, two other Southern cities had a share in the mourning, for Judge Baker and Mr Peale both likewise perished in the flames. The fire took place just before Christmas on the twenty-third of December, and among the many sympathetic and regretful comments which ensued upon this holocaust was the many-times repeated conjecture that these gentlemen had been keeping a kind of Christmas anniversary, a fact which added no little to the general feeling of regret and horror.

On the request of these prominent gentlemen, the hotel management had cleared out and furnished a second floor room with a great fireplace, a room for long used only for storage, but for which, the late mayor and lieutenant-governor had assured them, the four old cronies cherished a certain sentiment. The fire, which gained headway despite the truly desperate efforts of the occupants of the room, had its origin in the fireplace, and it was believed that the four, who were literally burned to cinders, had been trapped. The fire had started, it appeared, about half an hour before midnight, when everybody else in the hotel had retired. No other occupant of the house suffered from its effects, beyond a few incidental injuries sustained in the hurried departure at dead of night from the blazing old firetrap.

Some ten years before this regrettable incident ended the long and honorable career of this one-time famous hostelry, a certain Mr James Callender, breaking a wearisome journey north at Jackson, turned into the hospitable vestibule of the Planter's, with a sigh of relief. He had been shut up for nine hours in the mephitic atmosphere of a soft-coal train. He was tired, hungry, thirsty, and begrimed with soot.

Two grinning Negro porters deposited his ample luggage, toted from the railway station in the reasonable hope of a large emolument, promised by their patron's prosperous appearance and the imminence of the festival season of Christmas. They received their reward and left Mr Callender in the act of signing the hotel register.

'Can you let me have number twenty-eight?' he inquired of the clerk. 'That, I believe, is the room with the large fireplace, is it not? My friend, Mr Tom Culbertson of Sweetbriar, recommended it to me in case I should be stopping here.'

Number twenty-eight was fortunately vacant, and the new guest was shortly in occupation, a great fire, at his orders, roaring up the chimney, and he himself engaged in preparing for the luxury of a hot bath.

After a leisurely dinner of the sort for which the old hotel was famous, Mr Callender first sauntered slowly through the lobby, enjoying the first fragrant whiffs of a good cigar. Then, seeing no familiar face which gave promise of a conversation, he ascended to his room, replenished the fire, and got himself ready for a solitary evening. Soon, in pyjamas, bathrobe, and comfortable slippers, he settled himself in a comfortable chair at just the right distance from the fire and began to read a new book which he had brought with him. His dinner had been a late one, and it was about half past nine when he really settled to his book. It was Arthur Machen's *House of Souls*, and Mr Callender soon found himself absorbed in the eery ecstasy of reading for the first time a remarkable work which transcended all his previous secondhand experiences of the occult. It had, he found, anything but a soporific effect upon him. He was reading carefully, well into the book, with all his faculties alert, when he was interrupted by a knock on the door of his room.

Mr Callender stopped reading, marked his place, and rose to open the door. He was wondering who should summon him at such an hour. He glanced at his watch on the bureau in passing and was surprised to note that it was eleven-twenty. He had been reading for nearly two hours, steadily. He opened the door, and was surprised to find no one in the corridor. He stepped through the doorway and glanced right and then left. There were, he observed, turns in both directions at short distances from his door, and Mr Callender, whose mind was trained in the sifting of evidence, worked out an instantaneous explanation in his mind. The occupant of a double room (so he guessed) had returned late, and, mistaking the room, had knocked to apprise his fellow occupant of his return. Seeing at once that he had knocked prematurely, on the wrong door, the person had bolted around one of the corners to avoid an awkward explanation!

Mr Callender, smiling at this whimsical idea of his, turned back into his room and shut the door behind him.

A gentleman was sitting in the place he had vacated. Mr Callender stopped short and stared at this intruder. The man who had appropriated his comfortable chair was a few years older than himself, it appeared – say about thirty-five. He was tall, well-proportioned, and very well dressed, although there seemed to Mr Callender's hasty scrutiny something indefinably odd about his clothes.

The two men looked at each other appraisingly for the space of a few seconds, in silence, and then abruptly Mr Callender saw what was wrong with the other's appearance. He was dressed in the fashion of about fifteen years back, in the style of the late nineties. No one was wearing such a decisive-looking piccadilly collar, nor such a huge puff tie which concealed every vestige of the linen except the edges of the cuffs. These, on Mr Callender's uninvited guest, were immaculate and round, and held in place by a pair of large, round, cut-cameo black buttons.

The strange gentleman, without rising, broke the silence in a well-modulated voice with a deprecatory wave of a very well kept hand.

'I owe you an apology, sir. I trust that you will accept what amends I can make. This room has for me a peculiar interest which you will understand if you will allow me to speak further, but for the present I confine myself to asking your pardon.'

This speech was delivered in so frank and pleasing a fashion that Mr Callender could take no offense at the intrusion of the speaker.

'You are quite welcome, sir, but perhaps you will be good enough to continue, as you suggest. I confess to being mightily puzzled as to the precise manner in which you came to be here. The only way of approach is through the door, and I'll take my oath no one came through it. I heard a knock, went to the door, and there was no one there.'

'I imagine I would do well to begin at the beginning,' said the stranger, gravely. 'The facts are somewhat unusual, as you will see when I have related them; otherwise I should hardly be here, at this time of night, and trespassing upon your good nature. That this is no mere prank I beg that you will believe.'

'Proceed, sir, by all means,' returned Mr Callender, his curiosity aroused and keen. He drew up another chair and seated himself on the side of the fireplace opposite the stranger, who at once began his explanation.

'My name is Charles Bellinger, a fact which I will ask you kindly to note and keep well in mind. I come from Biloxi, down on the Gulf, and, unlike yourself, I am a Southerner, a native of Mississippi. You see, sir, I know something about you, or at least who you are.'

Mr Callender inclined his head, and the stranger waved his hand again, this time as if to express acknowledgment of an introduction.

'I may as well add to this, since it explains several matters, though in itself sounding somewhat odd, that actually I am dead.'

Mr Bellinger, at this astounding statement, met Mr Callender's facial expression of amazement with a smile clearly meant to be reassuring, and again, with a kind of unspoken eloquence, waved his expressive hand.

'Yes, sir, what I tell you is the plain truth. I passed out of this life in this room where we are sitting almost exactly sixteen years ago. My death occurred on the twenty-third of December. That will be precisely sixteen years ago the day after tomorrow. I came here tonight for the express purpose of telling you the facts, if you will bear with me and suspend your judgment as to my sanity. It was I who knocked at your door, and I passed through it, and, so to speak, through you, my dear sir!

'On the late afternoon of the day I have mentioned I arrived in this hotel in company with Mr Frank Stacpoole, an acquaintance, who still lives here in Jackson. I met him as I got off the train, and invited him to come here with me for dinner. Being a bachelor, he made no difficulty, and just after dinner we met in the lobby another man named Turner – Cassius L. Turner, also a Jacksonian – who proposed a game of cards and offered to secure two more gentlemen to complete the party. I invited him to bring them here to my room, and Stacpoole and I came up in advance to get things ready for an evening of poker.

'Shortly afterwards Mr Turner and the two other gentlemen arrived. One of them was named Baker, the other was Mr Valdemar

Peale, of Atlanta, Georgia. You recognize his name, I perceive, as I had expected you would. Mr Peale is now a very prominent man. He has gone far since that time. If you happened to be better acquainted here you would know that Stacpoole and Turner are also men of very considerable prominence. Baker, who lives in Memphis, Tennessee, is likewise a well-known man in his community and state.

'Peale, it appeared, was Stacpoole's brother-in-law, a fact which I had not previously known, and all four were well acquainted with each other. I was introduced to the two newcomers and we commenced to play poker.

'Somewhat to my embarrassment, since I was both the host and the "stranger" of the party, I won steadily from the very beginning. Mr Peale was the heaviest loser, and although as the evening wore on he sat with compressed lips and made no comment, it was plain that he was taking his considerable losses rather hardly.

'Not long after eleven o'clock a most unfortunate incident took place. I had in no way suspected that I was not among gentlemen. I had begun, you see, by knowing only Stacpoole, and even with him my acquaintance was only casual.

'At the time I mention there began a round of jack-pots, and the second of these I opened with a pair of kings and a pair of fours. Hoping to better my hand I discarded the fours, with the odd card, and drew to the pair of kings, hoping for a third. I was fortunate. I obtained not only the third king but with it a pair of eights. Thus, equipped with a full house, I considered my hand likely to be the best, and when, within two rounds of betting, the rest had laid down their hands, the pot lay between Peale and me. Peale, I noticed, had also thrown down three cards, and every chance indicated that I had him beaten. I forced him to call me after a long series of raises back and forth; and when he laid down his hand he was holding four fours!

'You see? He had picked up my discard.

'Wishing to give Peale the benefit of any possible doubt, I declared the matter at once, for one does not lightly accuse a gentleman of cheating at cards, especially here in the South. It was possible, though far from likely, that there had been a mistake. The dealer might for once have laid down his draw on the table, although he had consistently handed out the cards as we dealt in turn all the evening. To imply further that I regarded the matter as nothing worse than a mistake, I offered at once to allow the considerable pot, which I had really won, to lie over to the next hand.

'I had risen slightly out of my chair as I spoke, and before anyone could add a word, Peale leaned over the table and stabbed me with a bowie knife which I had not even seen him draw, so rapid was his action. He struck upwards, slantingly, and the blade, entering my body just below the ribs, cut my right lung nearly in two. I sank down limp across the table, and within a few seconds had coughed myself almost noiselessly to death.

'The actual moment of dissolution was painful to a degree. It was as if the permanent part of me, "myself" – my soul, if you will – snapped abruptly away from that distorted thing which sprawled prone across the disordered table and which no longer moved.

'Dispassionately, then, the something which continued to be myself (though now, of course, dissociated from what had been my vehicle of expression, my body) looked on and apprehended all that followed.

'For a few moments there was utter silence. Then Turner, in a hoarse, constrained voice, whispered to Peale: "You've done for yourself now, you unmentionable fool!"

'Peale sat in silence, the knife, which he had automatically withdrawn from the wound, still grasped in his hand, and what had been my life's blood slowly dripping from it and gradually congealing as it fell upon a disarranged pile of cards.

'Then, quite without warning, Baker took charge of the situation. He had kept very quiet and played a very conservative game throughout the evening.

' "This affair calls for careful handling," he drawled, "and if you will take my advice I think it can be made into a simple case of disappearance. Bellinger comes from Biloxi. He is not well known here." Then, rising and gathering the attention of the others, he continued: "I am going down to the hotel kitchen for a short time. While I am gone, keep the door shut, keep quiet, and clear up the room, leaving *this* (he indicated my body) where it lies. You, Stacpoole, arrange the furniture in the room as nearly as you can remember how it looked when you first came in. You, Turner, make up a big fire. You needn't begin that just yet," he threw at Peale, who had begun nervously to cleanse the blade of his knife on a piece of newspaper; and with this cryptic remark he disappeared through the door and was gone.

'The others, who all appeared somewhat dazed, set about their appointed tasks silently. Peale, who seemed unable to leave the vicinity of the table, at which he kept throwing glances, straightened up the chairs, replaced them where they had been, and then gathered up the cards and other debris from the table, and threw these into the now blazing fire which Turner was rapidly feeding with fresh wood.

'Within a few minutes Baker returned as unobtrusively as he had left, and after carefully fastening the door and approaching the table, gathered the three others about him and produced from under his coat an awkward and hastily-wrapped package of newspapers. Unfastening this he produced three heavy kitchen knives.

'I saw that Turner went white as Baker's idea dawned upon his consciousness. I now understood what Baker had meant when he told Peale to defer the cleansing of his bowie knife! It was, as plans go, a very practical scheme which he evolved. The body – the *corpus delicti*, as I believe you gentlemen of the law call it – was an extremely awkward fact. It was a fact which had to be accounted for, unless – well, Baker had clearly perceived that *there must be no corpus delicti*!

'He held a hurried, low-voiced conversation with the others, from the immediate effect of which all, even Peale, at first drew back. I need not detail it to you. You will have already apprehended what Baker had in mind. There was the roaring fire in the fireplace. That was his means of making certain that there would remain no *corpus delicti* in that room when the others left. Without such evidence, that is, the actual body of the murdered man, there could be, as you are of course well aware, no prosecution, because there would be no proof that the murder had ever been committed. I should simply have "disappeared". He had seen all that, and the opportunity which the fireplace afforded for carrying out his plan, all at once. But the fireplace, while large, was not large enough to accommodate the body of a man intact. Hence his hurried and stealthy visit to the hotel kitchen.

'The men looked up from their conference. Peale was trembling palpably. The sweat streamed from Turner's face. Stacpoole seemed unaffected, but I did not fail to observe that the hand which he reached out for one of the great meat knives shook violently, and that he was first to turn his head aside when Baker, himself pale and with set face, gingerly picked up from the table one of the stiffening hands . . .

'Within an hour and a quarter (for the fireplace drew as well then as it does tonight) there was not a vestige left of the *corpus delicti*, except the teeth.

'Baker appeared to think of everything. When the fire had pretty well burned itself out, and consumed what had been placed within it piecemeal, he remade it, and within its heart placed such charred remnants of the bones as had not been completely incinerated the first time. Eventually all the incriminating evidence had been consumed. It was as if I had never existed!

'My clothes, of course, had been burned. When the four, now haggard with their ordeal, had completed the burning process, another clearing-up and final rearrangement of the room was undertaken. Various newspapers which they had been carrying in their coat pockets were used to cleanse the table. The knives, including Peale's, were washed and scrubbed, the water poured out and the wash-basin thoroughly scoured. No blood had got upon the carpet.

'My not inconsiderable winnings, as well as the coin and currency which had been in my possession, were then cold-bloodedly divided among these four rascals, for such I had for some time now recognized them as being. There arose then the problem of the disposal of my other belongings. There was my watch, pocket-knife, and several old seals which had belonged to my grandfather and which I had been accustomed to wear on the end of the chain in the pocket opposite that in which I carried my watch. There were my studs, scarf-pin, cuff-buttons, two rings, and lastly, my teeth. These had been laid aside at the time when Baker had carefully raked the charred but indestructible teeth out of the embers of the first fire.'

At this point in his narrative, Mr Bellinger paused and passed one of his eloquent hands through the hair on top of his head in a reflective gesture. Mr Callender observed what he had not before clearly noted, that his guest possessed a pair of extraordinarily long, thin hands, very muscular, the hands of an artist and also of a man of determination and action. He particularly observed that the index fingers were almost if not quite as long as the middle fingers. The listener, who had been unable to make up his mind upon the question of the sanity of him who had presented this extraordinary narrative in so calm and convincing a fashion, viewed these hands indicative of so strong a character with the greatest interest. Mr Bellinger resumed his narrative.

'There was some discussion about the disposal of all these things. The consensus was that they must be concealed, since they could not easily be destroyed. If I had been one of those men I should have insisted upon throwing them into the river at the earliest opportunity. They could have been carried out of the room by any one of the group with the greatest ease and with no chance of detection, since all together they took up very little room, but this simple plan seemed not to occur to them. Perhaps they had exhausted their ingenuity in the horrible task just finished and were over-anxious to depart. They decided only upon the necessity of disposal of these trinkets, and the actual disposition was haphazard. This was by a method which I need not describe because I think it desirable to show them to you.'

Mr Bellinger rose and led the way to a corner of the room, closely followed by the amazed Callender. Bellinger pointed to the precise corner.

'Although I am for the present materialized,' he remarked, 'you will probably understand that this whole proceeding is in the nature of a severe psychic strain upon me and my resources. It is quite out of the question for me to do certain things. Managing to knock at the door took it out of me, rather, but I wished to give you as much warning of my presence as I could. Will you kindly oblige me by lifting the carpet at this point?'

Mr Callender worked his fingers nervously under the corner of the carpet and pulled. The tacks yielded after several hard pulls, and the corner of the carpet came up, revealing a large piece of heavy tin which had been tacked down over an ancient rat-hole.

'Pull up the tin, too, if you please,' requested Mr Bellinger. The tin presented a more difficult task than had the carpet, but Mr Callender, now thoroughly intrigued, made short work of it, though at the expense of two broken blades of his pocket-knife. At Mr Bellinger's further direction, inserting his hand, he found and drew out a packet of cloth, which proved on examination to have been fabricated out of a trousers pocket lining. The cloth was rotted and brittle, and Mr Callender carried it carefully over to the table and laid it down, and, emptying it out between them, checked off the various articles which Mr Bellinger had named. The round cuff-buttons came last, and as he held these in his hand, he looked at Mr Bellinger's wrists. Mr Bellinger smiled and pulled down his cuffs, holding out his hands in the process, and Mr Callender again noted carefully their peculiarities, the long, muscular fingers being especially conspicuous, thus seen under the direct light of the electric lamp. The cuff-buttons, he noted, were absolutely identical.

'Perhaps you will oblige me by putting the whole collection in your pocket,' suggested Mr Bellinger. Then, smiling, as Mr Callender, not unnaturally, hesitated: 'Take them, my dear man, take them freely. They're really mine to give, you know!'

Mr Callender stepped over to the wardrobe where his clothes hung, and placed the packet in his coat pocket. When he returned to the vicinity of the fireplace, his guest had already resumed his seat.

'I trust,' he said, 'that despite the very singular – I may say, *bizarre* – character of my narrative and especially the statement with which I thought best to begin it, you will have given me your credence. It is uncommon to be confronted with the recital of such an experience as I have related to you, and it is not everybody who is – may I say privileged? – to carry on an extended conversation with a man who has been dead sixteen years!

'My object may possibly have suggested itself to you. These men have escaped all consequences of their act. They are, as I think you will not deny, four thorough rascals. They are at large and even in positions of responsibility, trust and prominence in their several communities. You are a lawyer, a man held in high esteem for your professional skill and personal integrity. I ask you, then, will you undertake to bring these men to justice? You should be able to reproduce the salient points of my story. You have even proofs in the shape of the articles now in your coat pocket. There is the fact of my disappearance. That made a furor at the time, and has never been explained or cleared up. You have the evidence of the hotel register for my being here on that date and it would not be hard to prove that these men were in my company. But above all else, I would pin my faith for a conviction upon the mere recounting in the presence of these four, duly subpoenaed, of my story as I have told it to you. That would fasten their guilt upon them to the satisfaction of any judge and jury. They would be crying aloud for mercy and groveling in abject superstitious fear long before you had finished the account of precisely what they had done. Or, three of them could be confronted with an alleged confession made by the other. Will you undertake to right this festering wrong. Mr Callender, and give me peace? Your professional obligation to promote justice and set wrong right should conspire with your character to cause you to agree.'

'I will do so, with all my heart,' replied Mr Callender, holding out his hand.

But before the other could take it, there came another knocking on the door of the hotel room. Slightly startled, Mr Callender went to the door and threw it open. One of the hotel servants reminded him that he had asked to be called, and that it was the hour specified. Mr Callender thanked and feed the man, and turning back into the room found himself alone.

He went to the fireplace and sat down. He looked fixedly at the smoldering fire in the grate. He went over to the wardrobe and felt in his coat pocket in search of negative evidence that he had been dreaming, but his hand encountered the bag which had been the lining of a trousers pocket. He drew it out and spread a second time that morning on the table the various articles which it contained.

After an early breakfast Mr Callender asked for permission to examine the register for the year 1896. He found that Charles Bellinger of Biloxi had registered on the afternoon of the twenty-third of December and had been assigned room twenty-eight. He had no time for further inquiries, and, thanking the obliging clerk, he hastened to the railway station and resumed his journey north.

During the journey his mind refused to occupy itself with anything except his strange experience. He reached his destination in a state of profound preoccupation.

As soon as his professional engagements allowed him the leisure to do so, he began his inquiries by having looked up the owners of those names which were deeply imprinted in his memory. He was obliged to stop there because an unprecedented quantity of new legal business claimed his more immediate attention. He was aware that this particular period in his professional career was one vital to his future, and he slaved painstakingly at the affairs of his clients. His diligence was rewarded by a series of conspicuous legal successes, and his reputation became greatly enhanced. This heavy preoccupation could not fail to dull somewhat the sharp impression which the adventure in the hotel bedroom had made upon his mind, and the contents of the trousers pocket remained locked in his safe-deposit box undisturbed while he settled the affairs of the Rockland Oil Corporation and fought through the Appellate Division the conspicuous case of Burnet vs. De Castro, et al.

It was in the pursuit of a vital piece of evidence in this last-named case that his duties called him South again. Having obtained the evidence, he started home, and again found it expedient to break the long journey northward, at Jackson. It was not, though, until he was actually signing the register that he noted that it was the twenty-third of December, the actual date with which Mr Bellinger's singular narrative had been concerned.

He did not ask for any particular room this time. He felt a chill of vague apprehension, as if there awaited him an accounting for some laxity, a feeling which recalled the occasional lapses of his remote childhood. He smiled, but this whimsical idea was quickly replaced by a somber apprehension which he could not shake off, and which emanated from the realization that the clerk by some strange fatality had again assigned him room twenty-eight – the room with the fireplace. He thought of asking for another room, but could not think of any reasonable excuse. He sighed and felt a positive sinking at the heart when he saw the figures written down at the edge of the page; but he said nothing. If he shrank from this room's occupancy, this room with its frightful secret shared by him alone of this world's company with the four guilty men who were still at large because of his failure to keep his promise, he was human enough and modern enough in his ideas to shrink still more from the imputation of oddity which his refusal of the room on no sensible grounds would inevitably suggest.

He went up to his room, and, as it was a cold night outside, ordered the fire to be made up . . .

When the hotel servant rapped on his door in the morning there was no answer, and after several attempts to arouse the occupant the man reported his failure at the office. Later another attempt was made, and, this proving equally ineffectual, the door was forced with the assistance of a locksmith.

Mr Callender's body was found lying with the head in the grate. He had been, it appeared, strangled, for the marks of a pair of hands were deeply imprinted on his throat. The fingers had sunk deeply into the bluish, discolored flesh, and the coroner's jury noted the unusual circumstance when they sent out a description of the murderer confined to this peculiarity, that these marks indicated that the murderer (who was never discovered) possessed very long thin fingers, the index fingers being almost or quite as long as the middle fingers.

OTHER STORIES

The Moon Dial

Said Yussuf, the young son of the Maharajah of Kangalore, a hill-state in the north of India, looked down through the white moon-light one stifling night in July upon the moon-dial where it stood clear of the encompassing cypresses in that portion of the palace gardens which lay immediately under his window. Said Yussuf never retired without looking down at the spot where its shimmering paleness caused it to stand out clearly even on nights when only the starlight illuminated that space in the closely-shrubbed gardens.

During the day the moon-dial was only a queer, somewhat battered antique, brought from nobody knew where in the reign of the old Maharajah, Said's grandfather, who had remodeled the gardens. But it was Said himself who had named it the moon-dial. He had got that phrase from one of the works of the English writer, George Du Maurier, which his father, who had been educated at Oxford and married an English wife, had placed in the palace library. Said's tutor did not always approve of his private reading, but then Mr Hampton did not know just what that included. During summers, the tutor always went home to England on his three months' vacation, and then Said took refuge in the great library and read to his heart's content of Kipling, Dumas, Gustave Flaubert, and the English Bible. Said, instructed for reasons of state twice a week in the Koran by the Chief Mullah of Kangalore, found the heroic tales of the Old Testament and the incidents in the life of Jesus-ben-Yssuf singularly attractive by comparison with the dry works of Mohammed, the Prophet.

Said had gone up to his quarters this evening, a very hot night, as usual, at about nine-thirty. Now, an hour later, he was lying on his stomach along the broad window seat of his turreted apartment, arrayed only in a pair of European boy's shorts, which were cooler than the orthodox pajamas these stifling nights. It was, despite the heavy heat, a really glorious night, gorgeous with the full moon, though no breath of air stirred the leaf of a single shrub or tree.

The face of the moon-dial, like very old silver, or nickel, was over-scored with curious, cryptic markings which, in daylight, Said was

never weary of examining. This face – for the thing was movable –
he had turned very slightly, late that afternoon, towards the west; he
could not have said why he had done that. It was instinct, a vague
affair like that other instinct which told him surely, because of many
generations of ancestors who had believed in reincarnation, that he
had lived before, many, many times!

Now, there in the window, he looked down at the moon-dial, with
no thought of sleep in his mind.

A French clock, somewhere, chimed eleven. A delicate, refreshing
breeze, hardly more than a breath, shifted the light silk curtains. Said
closed his eyes with the comfort of it, and the little breeze fanned his
back, pleasurably, like the touch of soft fingers.

When he opened his eyes and looked back again at his moon-dial,
he suddenly roused himself to full wakefulness and abruptly pushed
his chin higher on his cupped hands. He gazed now with all his
interest concentrated.

The dial seemed to be glowing, in a fashion he had never previously
observed. A thin lambent, eerie flicker of light played over its ancient
surface, moving oddly. Watching closely he saw the light take on
something like form; a definite movement. Slanting rays seemed to
flow down from some point above; and now, as he watched them
gravely, they came down with greater and greater rapidity. The rays
glowed like roses; they fell like a thin rain striking silently and
appearing to rebound from the dial's surface.

Fascinated, Said rose to his knees and leaned far out of the window
in the pure, warm night air, drinking in this strange spectacle. He
was not in the least disturbed by its unusualness. All this seemed to
him a recurrence of something – the fulfilment of one of those vague,
gossamer-like yearnings of his, which were wholly natural to him,
but which so seldom met their realization in this life! It seemed not
unnatural that rose-colored rays should pour down – they seemed
literally to pour now – and break into veritable cascades there at the
moon-dial . . .

He had always, somehow, felt within himself some strange, subtle
affinity with the moon. He had said nothing of this. It was not the
sort of thing one could discuss with Mr Hampton or even with his
parents. Others than himself, he realized, would consider such an
idea highly absurd.

Moonlight, and more especially the moon at her full, had always
attracted his attention since his earliest recollection. Innumerable

times he had watched it, cold and frosty on winter nights, pale and straw-colored in the spring, huge, orange, warmly luminous in late summer and autumn. It was orange-colored now, enormous, bafflingly exotic.

Great sheets of light seemed now to fall and shatter themselves upon the dial; light, orange and tenuous like the great rolling orb itself; light, alluring, somehow welcoming . . .

A great longing suddenly invaded Said's mind. He wanted to go down there and stand in that light; reach his arms up into it and let it bathe him. He stirred uneasily. He had, many times, dreamed of floating, down to the lawns from his window, levitated, supported by mysterious, invisible arms! Now the longing became an almost unbearable nostalgia, a veritable yearning. The light, where it had broken and splashed off the face of the dial, was dancing luminously, softly, through the shadows of the great encircling cypress trees. It seemed to gather itself together; to roll along the ground. He shut his eyes again and buried his face in his hands.

When he looked back, for he could not for very long keep his eyes away from this spectacle, the light was hurling itself down in shafts and blocks and streams upon the dial-face, with a certain rhythm. The stream was more solid now, more continuous. It broke into whorls and sparkling, dim roulades, and swept earthward, as though redistilled from the magical alchemy of the mysterious ancient dial-face; it seemed to Said that it was circling, tenuously, and yet with a promise of continuity, of increasing power, about the dial's stone standard.

The light stream was interrupted now and again by blank spaces, blocks of black darkness; and looking for these and watching them descend like lacunae in the orange stream, he imagined them to be living creatures and half expected to see them take firmer form and dance there, weaving through and through the flickering maze of whorls.

He wanted to float down there, and the longing made a lump in his throat.

He rose, silently opened his bedroom door, and listened. He could hear his father's quiet breathing, through the open door of a bedroom across the hallway. His mother slept farther down the hall away from the great winding, pillared stairway which led below.

Silently he walked to the stairhead, turned, and went down

He emerged on the lawn a few seconds later. He had only to unfasten a summer screen-door and cross a broad veranda. Then he was across the gravel of the drive and on the velvety lawn, and running towards the moon-dial, a little white figure in white drill shorts, his dark hair glowing in the pouring moonlight.

He paused before pressing through the coppice of cypresses. There was no sound in the open space about the dial, but his instinct for the affairs of the moon warned him that something altogether new and strange was going on out there. He felt no fear, but knew that all this was a repetition of something, some vast and consuming happiness which somewhere, somehow, he had known before; though certainly not in his conscious recollection. It was this feeling about something very, very old, and very lovely – no more than a recurrence or a repetition of something strange and wild and sweet which had gone before; something mellowed and beautiful because of a vast, incomprehensible antiquity.

He walked forward now, very quietly; and, for a reason which he could not explain even to himself but which he knew to be a right instinct, he proceeded, holding himself very erect, through the cypresses and out into the orange stream.

He knew even before he glanced down at them that a great black panther lay crouched, immobile, on either side of him; crystallized in the magic of the moon out of two of those black void-like things, transmuted by the power of the dial into actuality. Lightly he placed a palm on the head of each of the great ebony beasts, and the velvety touch of their fur reassured him.

About the dial softly-moving figures, erect and graceful, moved statelily, with a vast gravity. Within the circle about the dial the flat moonlight lay like a pool of oil. Tall white lilies stood about its perimeter, their calices open to the moon. Their fragrance came to him in recurrent waves, and dimly he heard the music of lutes and the delicate rattle of systra, the soft, musical clanging of cymbals, and a chorus of faint singing, a chant in rhythm to the beat of clanging salsalim. He heard the word *Tanit* repeated again and again, and he found himself saying it.

A cloud sailed majestically across the moon. A delicate sadness tinged the warm night. The lily scent grew faint. The cymbals slowed and dulled.

He felt the great beasts rise beside him. Their fur caressed his hands as they moved forward, gravely, majestically. A hand on each, he walked forward with them, towards his moon-dial. He looked down upon its face and at the faint outlines of mystical figures.

Then he knew a great happiness. It seemed to him that these ancient symbols, which had always concealed their inner meaning from him, were now plain. He was sure now that he had lived before, many times . . .

The cloud passed, and now the figures on the dial-face were once more merely dim old markings. The statuesque black panthers were gone; there were no longer any dancing figures. A little breeze moved the leaves of the deodars.

He looked up, straight into the face of the moon, instinctively opening his arms wide towards that vast, far serenity. He passed a hand gently over the smooth, worn surface of the ancient dial. Then he walked back to the palace and up to his sleeping-quarters. He felt sleepy now. He got into his bed, drew in his breath in a long sigh of contentment, and fell into a deep, dreamless sleep.

His beautiful mother was standing beside his bed when he awakened. It was broad day. She bent over him, and he smiled up into her face as she kissed him.

The Maharanee of Kangalore was a fanciful person. 'Your hair smells of lilies,' she said.

Said could hardly wait for the next night of the full moon. His sure instinct for lunar affairs told him plainly that only at the full would the moon come into conjunction with the dial.

But the experience – if it had been a real experience; sometimes, as he thought of it, he could hardly tell – lay, clear-cut, like one of the cameos in the palace treasure-room, in his alert mind. He thought over, meantime, every occurrence, all the sequences of his adventure in the gardens. He put together all its arabesque details. They crystallized into the certainty that he had been living over again something which he had known before; something very important, very dear to him. He counted off the days and nights until the next possible time . . .

It came on an August night of balm and spice following light rains; a night on which the tuberose and jasmine of the gardens were pouring out an ecstasy of fragrance.

Said had been in the palace treasury that afternoon, with old Mohammed Ali the Guardian, and his mind was full of the beauty of that priceless collection which had come down through countless generations: precious and semi-precious jewels; ornaments – armlets, elephant-ankuses, sword-hilts, jeweled post-tops for palanquins; innumerable affairs, including a vast number of ancient and comparatively modern weapons, weapons of every conceivable variety, which had served for many, many generations the fighting men of his house. He had poured rubies, the ransom of an empire, through his two hands that day; worn Saracenic helmets of light steel, swept through the air with a whistling sound the curved, jewel-encrusted scimitars of his ancestors. Now, from the window-seat, the moon-dial shimmered vaguely among the cypresses. His mind was full of vague, alluring expectations; his body trembled with the anticipation of something dimly recalled, tantalizingly envisaged, now apparently imminent . . .

He went down the stairs and out upon the lawn towards the moon-dial. He wanted to be there, this time, as soon as the lightstream should begin its strange downpouring. He was sure that it would come. He touched lovingly the ancient, scarred face of the dial runed with its cryptic markings. He had, for one brief, exulting moment, he remembered clearly, thought that he understood those markings twenty-eight evenings ago. But, the next day, when he had gone to the dial after eight hours' healthful sleep in between his extraordinary experience and the fresh light of a glorious summer morning, he had discovered that they were once more merely strange marks. The disillusion had saddened him. Things, in life, so often seemed like that! One imagined that success was in hand, and in the morning the gold had turned to ashes.

His mood tonight was one of quivering anticipation. Thrills of an expected gladness shook him, standing there beside his dial, his face turned to the sky where the August moon proudly dominated the heavens.

Abruptly the downpouring enveloped him as he waited there in an ecstasy of wild, unearthly glory.

He felt himself drowned, engulfed, in this utter gorgeousness of feeling which seemed to melt him, body and soul; to carry him willingly, his arms outspread to receive it, up into itself. He felt himself suffused, as he yielded to it; something like a potent fluid invaded him, drenched his utter inner consciousness, satisfied his happy heart . . .

He opened his eyes, closed automatically at the sudden access of the moon's pouring power. He beheld a vast, glorious configuration, splendid, gorgeous, illuminated; growing clearer, more detailed, more utterly satisfying, like the center of all places, the consummation of all desires, the goal of all vague and beautiful thoughts. He felt, somehow, safe, with a wellbeing transcending all experiences; a feeling that at long last he was arriving where he had always belonged; coming swiftly, inerrantly, to the very center and source where he had, fleetingly, in occasional happy glimpses of the mind, always wanted to be; always known that he must and should be.

He stood upon a soft meadow of pale, bright grass, in the midst of a light scent of lilies, outside the slowly opening doors of a lofty temple, which towered up into the heavens and seemed to mingle its pinnacles with the nearby, friendly stars.

Now the great doors stood wide open. He walked towards them. The sense of old knowledge, of what he must do once he came within the temple, was in his mind. He slowed his pace to a formal dignified tread. He passed through the doors of the temple and stood within.

And, before he could turn his head to look about in this vastness, into his very soul penetrated the message: 'Sleep! Tanit commands.'

Beside him he observed a porphyry couch, its finials glowing with complicated whorls and insets of some faintly shining metal like platinum. Upon this, without question, his mind and heart at peace, he reclined, and closed his eyes.

A sweeping, distant, heavenly-sweet breath of music, the music of viols and systra, swept his mind. He slept . . .

* * *

He strode, a tall, commanding figurs, through the narrow streets of the great city where he had lived and worked for many years, the city of London. Above, a waxing moon poured down her gracious light through a black and drifting mass of storm-clouds.

It was chilly and damp, and he had drawn about himself his heavy black outdoor cloak of rich dark cloth. He picked his steps through the filth and mud of the street, while just ahead of him a man-servant bore aloft a flaming cresset-torch to light the uneven way.

He proceeded onward, moved by a strong purpose. This, towards which on this uninviting night he hastened, was no ordinary appointment. What few wayfarers were abroad seemed animated by a great and consuming dread. These glanced furtively at him and at each other as they slunk along, giving each other wide berths. And, in the hand of each, a small, sponge-like object, saturated with reeking vinegar, was held before the face.

At last the two stood before the portals of a magnificent building. The servant knocked. Two men-at-arms, gorgeous in the royal livery, recognizing him, had saluted and allowed him to pass.

The doors, in answer to the servant's knock, now swung open.

A gentleman, splendid in embroidered silks, came forward and bowed. He returned this salutation.

'A dismal night to be thus abroad, My Lord Burlinghame,' he remarked, and the gentleman smiled and nodded.

'The King awaits you – anxiously,' said the gentleman, and turned and led the way.

He stood now, before the King, in a small, richly-furnished apartment, its walls thick with Spanish arras.

'Come,' said the King eagerly, 'sit, most worthy Doctor Campalunis, and relate to me the result of your labors.'

He delayed seating himself until the King himself had resumed his seat. He spoke directly, pointedly.

'I know now the cause, Sire, beyond any doubt or peradventure. A surprising conclusion, upon which the astrological art and actual experiment converge to show its actuality! To state the matter pithily it cometh down to this: it is the superabundance of rats in this your realm of England that causeth the plague!'

The King started, half smiled; grew suddenly serious again, looked mystified, swore roundly a rolling oath.

'By the twenty-four nostrils of the Twelve Apostles! Good Doctor Campalunis, were it not thyself 'twould sound like a scurvy jest!'

He nodded, and smiling slowly, answered the King.

'It was in sooth a sorry task; one which, I doubt me, few physicians would have descended to! Yet did I demonstrate its accuracy; the "calculation" was based upon the conjunction of our lady, the moon, with the planet Venus. And – it pointed to the rats!

'Then did I take three rats, and from them – oh, sorry task! did remove, with these hands, their parasites. These did I transfer to three small beasts of various kinds, a hare, a stoat, and a mewing cat! Proof, Sire! Within twelve hours, upon all three – as the rat-fleas penetrated to their blood – did there appear tumors like to those upon the folk in this calamity we name "The Plague" and which now devastates the realm. Soon thereafter all were dead, each after his nature: the hare without resistance: the stoat fighting; the cat, as though she would never pass – nine lives she hath, according to the ancient saying!

'Experiment thus doth prove the wisdom of our lady, the moon. I counsel thee, then, that all rats be hunted and destroyed, that the plague stay itself and England be not thrice-decimated.'

He was driving back in a great rumbling coach. Beside him, on the silken-cushioned seat, lay the great red silk purse of gold presented to him by the King – the King who, trusting him, had, before his departure, summoned Giles Talbot, his scrivener, and was even now preparing a royal proclamation directing, upon pain of the King's displeasure, all burgesses, shrieves, coroners and mayors to cause the folk to find and destroy the swarming rats and so end the plague . . .

He glanced out through the coach window upon the hastening figures of occasional wayfarers; and, ever and again, cressets lighting the gloomy scene disclosed bearers carrying the victims of the plague, hastily and furtively through the muddy streets to the charnelhouse . . .

Above, the moon, now clear of clouds, looked serenely down upon this theater of death and destruction, where ruthless King Plague had well-nigh replaced the reign of kindly King Charles.

*   *   *

Carrying a small, heavy package, he stepped briskly along a sunny roadway towards a goldsmith's shop. He stepped within and the apprentices raised their heads. Welcoming smiles, murmurs of pleased greeting met him; and then rapid questions in the soft Italian argot.

'What, the masterpiece? Finished at last!'

'*Ecco*, Ascanio, *fratello*. It is done, eh?'

'The Master will be pleased.'

'*Per Baccho*! A purse that it is magnificent!'

He placed his burden upon the central table. The others were all crowding about him now eager to see.

'Touch it not, colt of a jackass!'

'Room for our Ascanio, the new Cellini!'

'Run – fly, Beppo! Fetch the Master.'

He left the inmost wrapping, of silk, where it was, closely draped about the figurine. It stood, shapeless under the unrevealing drapery, about nine inches in height. The apprentices hopped in their anxiety to see it.

Beppo dashed back into the workroom, the Master following. All stood aside as the tall figure, dressed in plum-colored silk like a nobleman, came hurriedly into the room. The bearded face lighted.

'Ascanio! The Virgin – not finished – tell me not – '

'Finished, I believe, to the limit of my poor skill, Messer Benvenuto,' he said, and gravely removed the silk wrapping.

There arose a chorus of shouts, squeals, hand-clappings, murmurs, small mutterings and sighs from the apprentices; then, this dying down, he looked at the Master. The others, too, were looking at him.

His was the ultimate decision, the last opinion of the workroom, of the city of Florence, of the great world. The master goldsmith stood, motionless, silent, frowning slightly, before the figurine.

It was of red gold, the Virgin Mother of God, chaste, beautiful, cunningly wrought; glowing now in the freshness of the new metal; gleaming, exquisite.

The Master took it into his hands. He held it off, squinted at it; held it close, gazing intently, silently. He laid it down, reached into a pouch, brought out a magnifying glass, sat down on the stool Beppo had placed for him. The apprentices dared barely to breathe.

Messer Benvenuto laid it down at last. He returned, without a word, the glass to his pouch. He turned about and looked at his visitor.

Then abruptly, suddenly, he held out both sensitive hands. 'A masterpiece!' he pronounced, and rose from the stool.

'And this – ' he indicated the base of the statue, 'no goldsmith hath so done before. Ascanio. Inspiration! Thou hast gone far – to the end of our art. The moon – as a pedestal for the Mother of God! It smacks of the perfection of art. I hail thee. Ascanio – Master!'

* * *

It was very early dawn, a fresh, cool, sea-dampened dawn, just breaking to a delightful smell of dew-wet heather. He paced up and down on the rough stone flagging. He paused, looked about.

Over towards the east the sun, glorious, burst over the horizon. He had been watching for it from the wall's top, over the gate, and now in its new illumination he gazed out frowningly, beneath the pressure of the great bronze helmet; over the gray and brown gorse hummocks and undulating prairie of rough furze, into the north. There, always concealed, always ready to strike, signaling with their fires to each other, chieftain to chieftain, lay the Picts. Against these this ultimate fortification had been built.

Behind him, to the south, under the wall a great din arose, a noise compounded of the disassembling of *ballistae*, much hammering and wrenching as the heavy timbers were taken apart; metallic clangings as the breastplates and *scuta* were stacked, in tens, a mule-load each; shouts, commands; the ringing, brief blast of a bugle.

The relief, marching briskly, the never-changing quick step of Rome's invincible legions, came now to a last routine duty. He raised to his lips a small golden whistle, fastened about his neck with a leathern thong. His men came in from east and west. He saluted the approaching centurion. The guard above the gate was changed mechanically, the two officers exchanged brief greetings. His own veteran century behind him, he marched off duty; descended towards the gate at the south side.

A vast bustle greeted him. The troops were preparing for their final evacuation of the wall. All about him this clang of weapons being packed rose to heaven.

He was being saluted. He stopped, listened to the message. He was to go to the Emperor, at once. He acknowledged the orders, dismissed the messenger, turned to the west.

'As thou knowest, O Gaius, the barbarian hordes press back our legions. By sheer force of their incredible numbers, they have worn down the defences of the north. They slip through. Rome herself calls, at long last. For Rome's defence we must go.

'But, O valiant one, these legions must go safely. It were to serve Rome ill to lose a single quaternion against these Picts. Take thou of thy men, and stay behind, then, here upon the wall. If, at the expiry of two days, thou are yet alive, then follow the legions. Yet, by all the guile and all the skill and all the love of Rome thou dost possess, hold the gate against the north until we are away. I leave thee to the bravest task of all, O Gaius!' . . .

With his six legionaries, he strode up and down above the gate, watching the north. For a day and a half the three legions had been marching, ever southward, towards their embarkation-points, through the fair and glorious country of Brittania which the wall had made possible; fifteen thousand seasoned veterans, returning to hold off, if might be, for another decade perhaps, the swarming barbarians who were pressing down upon the Mediterranean world.

For the first six hours nothing had taken place upon the Picts' side of the wall; only the increase of signal fires. Then had come the slow gathering of this barbarian horde. Now, on the evening of the second day, as he looked down, despite the threatenings of his sweating legionaries, with their rocks, their small catapults, and now – as a last resort the dreaded firepots, he saw the Picts gathered in their thousands. A dank smell rose from these barbarians; a smell compounded of the sweat of laboring naked bodies, of furze smoke, of the skins of wolves from which they fashioned their scant garments.

Already the gate was down; already, in their hundreds, the Picts swarmed down below there on the south side of the wall, the Roman side. Convinced now that the garrison had departed, that these on the wall's top were merely a scant guard remaining for the purpose of fooling them, of holding off their own inevitable attack, the leaders of the Picts were haranguing them to the massed attack up the ramps to the wall's top.

Abruptly the moon rose over the western horizon. And with its rising a message, authoritative, definite, filled his mind.

'Well done, and bravely, valiant one, friend of Tanit! And now I take thee unto myself, ere thou perish in the body.'

He struggled mentally to reply, as he looked at his hard-bitten, middle-aged men, old legionaries who had remained; who were giving all for *Roma Mater*. They stood now, massed together, just within the barrier which blocked off the ramp's top, their shields interlaced, their spears in a precise row behind them, their short blunt swords in their right hands; silent, ready for their last stand. As he looked at these faithful men his heart went out to them. Their devotion, their iron discipline had never once wavered.

'*Nay*,' he answered. '*Nay*, Lady Diana, grace of all the *Di Romae*, I go not willingly, but purpose rather to stand here with these!'

He stepped towards them, his own, somewhat heavier, sword ready in his hand, his shield affixed to his left arm. The roar of the mounting Picts came bellowingly through to them now as the horde swarmed up the ramp. Now the barrier was down, crumpled before the irresistible urge of numbers. Now the short swords were in play, taking terrible toll, like flails, like machines.

Then all that space was abruptly illuminated, as a huge ball of what seemed to the stricken Picts pure incandescent fire smote the stone flooring of the great wall's top, burst into a myriad fragments of light, gathered itself together, then went out into a sudden blackness; and through this blackness the figure of their centurion showed itself to his legionaries like Mars Invictus; head up, sword raised on high, and then, as abruptly, vanished.

The Picts had disappeared. The legionaries looked at each other blankly. One, Tertullius, looked over the edge.

'All run through the gateways into their territory,' he reported to his companions.

'And Gaius?' one asked. 'What of our centurion?'

'It is the high Gods! He hath gone to Odin!'

'The light swallowed him up. Hail, O mighty Mithras!'

'He is gone from among us, O invincible gods of Rome!'

'He was godlike. His was the kindness of Chrestus!'

'Olympus receives him, doubtless, O Venus Victrix! A great marvel, this!'

Within a few minutes six hardbitten veteran legionaries were at the double on the trail of the main army, going straight south, pausing not over the various and sundry abandoned arms and supplies, jetsam left strewed along that way of retreat.

And upon the unanimity of their report and the surprise which their arrival, without their officer, had caused in the ranks of Maxentius' legions, within the year a shrine to Gaius, who had been taken up by the old gods of *Roma Mater*, was rising in the little hills above Callericum, which had been the centurion Gaius's native village.

* * *

He rose to his feet, stiff from that long reclining, and stretched himself. It was night, a night of warm and mellow airs playing about the olive trees under the full moon of the early Palestinian spring. He gazed, grave-eyed, towards that sinister hilltop where three Roman crosses stood athwart the moon's light, dark and sinister shadows of death and desolation. He looked long at them, stooped, and adjusted a loose sandal-thong; rose again, and turning, began to walk towards the city, beautiful upon its own hill of Zion, the temple pinnacles white and glorious in the pouring moonlight.

But on an olive-bordered slope he paused and looked steadfastedly up into the calm moon's face. There seemed to him to be, struggling towards clear understanding, some message for him in what he had seen that day, the marvels he had witnessed, he, a Greek of Corinth, sojourning in Jerusalem with the caravan of his uncle Themistocles the merchant. The moon had always been his friend, since earliest infancy. Now, aged twenty, he left always an inspiration, a kind of renewed vigor, when she was at full.

She was at full now, and he remembered that these Palestinians based one of their religious observances upon the lunar cycle. It was now begun. The middle-aged man next to him had explained the ritual to him just before sunset, when those bodies had been taken down from the crosses.

It had been a harrowing experience. These Romans were a ruthless lot, 'conquerors of the world', indeed. Greece lay beneath their heel. This Palestinian country, too, was a mere procuratorship, however, not a province like his own Hellas. This execution – he had heard of that method, though he had never witnessed it before – had, however, seemed to meet the approval of the Palestinians.

The 'message' troubled him. Something was pressing through to his consciousness. A duty was being thrust upon him. That, of course, had happened before, in much the same way – warnings, admonitions, growing in his mind. He had always followed them, for, indeed, they had been unmistakable things, matters germane to his inmost thoughts, parts of his own consciousness. What would it be this time? He opened his mind, looking up at that bright, mysterious disk, which, as Aristotle, or was it old Zeno? – he could not remember precisely; he was a merchant, not a philosopher – had taught, regulated the waters of the universe; the tides. An odd conception that! True, doubtless. Something caused the ceaseless ebbings and flowings of his own blue Aegean, of the *Mare Internum* as the Romans named the great sea about which their vast empire now centered itself.

The 'message' had to do with finding someone. He lay down upon the warm grass as yet unaffected by any distillation of morning dew.

'Search – search – here in this city of Jerusalem, for one named – '

The name eluded him. He moved his feet, impatiently. There were ants here. One had crawled upon the side of his right foot. He moved the foot, and it encountered a small obstacle. He sat up, rolled over, reached down. It was a stone, a small, round pebble – *petros*.

Then the 'message' came clear like the emergence of Pallas Athene full-armed and cinctured from the mighty head of Zeus!

'Search! Find – Petros!'

It burned in his brain. He sat there, cogitating it. One named Peter he was to find, here in this city of Jerusalem. He nodded his head in acquiescence. A rich energy suffused him as he looked up once more into the moon's quiet face.

He rose, lightly, drew in a deep, refreshing breath laden with the sweet dry scent of myrtle, then he walked down the hill towards Jerusalem, in search of someone named Peter.

* * *

The faint memory of an evil dream contended with a fetid odor which drifted in through the methodical row of star-shaped windows opposite his polished wooden couch with the henna-stained horsetails at its curved foot. The dream, an unpleasant, vague memory now, faded from his waking consciousness, encompassed by that smell. That would be from the *ergastulum*, the slave-compound of the suffete, Hanno, whose somewhat more pretentious palace towered over his own on the upper slope of the hill. Hanno, now in the field against the revolting mercenaries, was badly served at home. He must send a peremptory message to the keeper of the *ergastulum*! This was intolerable. He rose to a sitting posture, throwing off the linen coverlet with its embroidered horses and stars thickly sewn upon it, and looked down his long body.

There were unmistakable evidences of emaciation, loss of weight. No wonder, with the scarcity of food now prevalent in Carthage. He rose and clapped his hands together.

Through a curtain entered instantly a huge Nubian, Conno, the bath-slave. Conno's soot-black arms were full of the materials for the bath; a red box of polished enamel containing the fuller's powder, large squares of soft linen, several strigils, a cruse of rose-colored oil.

He followed the slave to a far corner of the lofty room, five stories above the roadway below, sweating now, like Conno himself. The early morning heat poured in dryly through the many windows. He cast himself down on a narrow couch of polished marble, and Conno poured a thin stream of the hot water from a small amphora along his back, spreading it about with the palms of his muscular, yet soft hands. Conno was a very skillful bath-slave. He was dumb, too, which, despite the deprecated savagery of a former owner who had had his tongue removed to gain this desirable end, was, somehow, an advantage on a hot and blistering morning like this!

Conno sifted reddish-brown powder onto his back, working it with the water into a paste.

When the paste was set he rolled over and Conno repeated his ministrations. Then he stood up, and the slave rubbed the thin paste into his muscular arms, down his thighs, about his neck, delicately on the smooth portions of his face where his beard did not grow.

After this preliminary kneading, Conno thinned the paste with more hot water, and began to use the strigils. Then Conno skilfully rinsed him from head to foot, the red-stained water running down into an opening in the floor whence a pipe led it away.

Conno kneaded his muscles with oil, and, at last, gathered his paraphernalia together and walked out of the room.

He returned to the part of the room where his bed stood. Here, awaiting him, stood a slender, dark Numidian, a young girl, who deftly dressed his hair, pomading it with great skill.

Two more slaves entered with the garments of the day. They were green, a cool color which he liked to wear. Dressed, he continued to sit, frowning thoughtfully. That dream! Thoughtfully he attempted to reconstruct it, to bring it back to his conscious mind.

In the process his eye lighted on an ornament on the stand beside him, a serpent carved cunningly in ebony, and polished to brilliance, a coiled serpent, its tail in its mouth – emblem of the endlessness of the universe, a symbol of Tanit, goddess of the moon, one of the city's ancient, traditional, tutelary divinities. She was somewhat neglected now in the stress of this famine, result of the mercenary-troops' revolt which had been going on now for five months. Yes, there were even certain rumors that the college of priests which had served from time immemorial the temple of Tanit, was breaking up; these men, or half-men as he contemptuously thought of the white-robed hierophants, were slowly deserting the gentle Tanit for one or another of the severer deities, representing the male principles; *Baalim*, violent gods, requiring a more sanguinary ministry.

Tanit – the dream! A message, it had been: 'Go to the northeast, to where the main aqueduct runs underneath the wall's top. Drive out from there – '

He rose and clapped his hands violently. He strode towards the doorway with its silk curtains wrought in flowers and stars and horses, emblems of the Carthaginian timocracy, and met the hurrying slave. 'Swiftly, Bothon, my litter and a light spear!'

The slave ran. He stood, awaiting his return, gazing pensively out of a window, open to the scorching African sunlight drenching the world of Carthage, up to that magnificent location, the finest in the city, where, near the hill's summit, towered the vast palace of Hamilcar Barca, sea-suffete of the republic. If Barca would only return! No man knew where he was, save that with a few galleys he was at sea. Barca's return, if indeed he should return, must mean a turning-point in this campaign, so far ineffective, against the revolted troops, now compassing the city from the scorching, desert plain below; the campaign of the evil old suffete, Hanno, whose lifetime of debauchery had left him treacherous, ineffective, and leprous.

The slave announced the litter and handed him a light spear. He balanced it in his hand, thoughtfully, then descended to the entrance-way. Here, again, the fetor of that slave-compound assaulted his nostrils. He laid the spear carefully lengthwise of the litter's edge and stepped within. He could feel its hardwood joints creak, even though they were oiled daily; even oil dried quickly in this drenching heat. He heard the muffled grunts of his four burly Nubians as they shouldered the litter. Then he was swaying lightly in the direction of the aqueduct . . .

He stepped out, looked about him. He was not sure what it was he was to search for, even though the 'message' had been peremptory. In the scorching sunlight, that here atop these smoothed stones the squaring and piling of which had consumed the lives of countless war-taken slaves a generation past, seemed almost unbearable, he walked along, slowly, contemplatively, now and again sounding with his spear's polished butt the hollow-sounding stones. Down below there lay the encampment of the mercenaries, their numbers augmented now by revolting desert tribesmen, arriving daily, a vast configuration, menacing, spreading, down there on the sand which danced in the heat-waves . . .

He slowed his pace, stepped softly, now, more slowly. Now he paused, a tall, slender figure, atop the aqueduct. He listened. Ahead there – a chipping rending sound. Someone was concealed below, tearing out stones! The precious water, the city's very life! One of the mercenaries, undoubtedly, who had worked his way in from the broad-mouthed vents, was doing it. As he stood there, listening, he remembered that he had himself warned the Council of that danger. If the water supply were diverted, destroyed, the city would perish! He lay down flat on his side, his ear against the smooth masonry, listening. Ah, yes – it was plain enough now, that chipping, grinding noise of breaking stonework . . .

He rose, ran lightly forward, on his toes, the spear poised delicately. He paused above a large square block of the hewn stone. He laid the spear down, placed both hands under the stone's outer edge, then, violently, skilfully, pulled it straight up. He let it fall against another flat stone, and reaching for the spear, thrust once, straight down through the aperture he had made.

A groan, a gasping sigh, then the soft impacts, growing rapidly fainter, as a body was borne down, knocking against the remoter stone angles and corners down inside the great aqueduct there under the wall's top; a body bobbing and bumping its way on a last brief journey, to the vents below.

Then turning to the west, where a faint moon rolled palely in the blue, scorching African sky, he raised both arms straight towards it, a gesture of salutation, of adoration.

'To thee the praise, O Lady Tanit, tutelary of Carthage; to thee the praise, for this warning! Again, O effulgent one, hast thou saved the city; to thee all praise and thanks, adulation and attribution of power; to thee the adoration of the faithful; O perpetual bride, O glorious one, O effulgence, O precious one, O fountain of bounty . . . '

* * *

He leaned heavily against the rounded edge of the wide war-chariot, three spears in his left hand, long and slender, fresh-ground from the day before by a cunning armorer of Gilgal. He had been wounded twice, both times by hurled darts, tearing his right thigh above the greave which encompassed the lower leg, and again in the top of the left shoulder; flesh-wounds both, yet throbbing, burning, painful.

The slaughter by those confederate Amorites had been heavy, and here on the plain of Beth-Horon, the fighting still progressed, even though the rapidly descending sun had, with its decline, brought no coolness. Great clouds of dust filled the hot, palpitating air. He raised his head, and gazed down towards Ajalon. Above the fringe of distant tall cedars which marked the valley's nearer edge, the moon sailed, pale and faint. To the west the sun was now sunken half-way over the horizon, blood-red, disappearing so rapidly now that he could follow it with his bloodshot, dust-smeared eyes.

The charioteer turned, his reins lying loosely over the sweat-caked backs of the horses and addressed him: 'If but Jahveh would prolong the light, O my Lord Joshua!'

He raised his weary eyes to the west once more. The sun was now merely a rapidly descending tinge of brilliant carmine in the sullen sky. He spoke to his God: 'Let the light as of day continue, O Thou of Sabaoth Who rulest the up-rising and the down-setting of Thy people. Stay, light of sun, that Jahveh's host may see; and thou, too, O luminary of night, do thou, too, aid our host!'

A pink afterglow rose slowly from the west, spread far through the heavens, then, as though reluctantly, faded. The night fell rapidly, the manifold noises of the hand-to-hand conflicts grew fainter; the chariot-horses stirred as a faint breath blew up out of the tree-sheltered Valley of Ajalon. He turned to feel it on his face, and as he turned, a vast portent appeared to him.

For, from the moon, orange now, glowing enormously, there came first one single penetrating ray which seemed to reach down here to the plain of the House of Horon, and spread its radiance along the ground; and then others and others, until the great level plain was illuminated as brightly as though by the sun himself. A breeze swept up from the valley. The horses plucked up nervous heads, their cut manes bristling. The charioteer looked about at him inquiringly. He shifted the three spears into his other hand.

'On,' he cried, 'on, on – where the Sons of Amor press thickest! Drive, drive, like Nimrud of the Great Valley, like the Lion of The House of Judah roaring after his prey! Drive, that we may smite afresh the enemies of the Lord, God of Hosts . . . '

* * *

It was with these mighty words in his mouth and the sense of battle in his brain that he stirred into consciousness on the porphyry couch. A roseate atmosphere filled the temple, as of approaching dawn, or some mellifluous afterglow; and to his nostrils, scorched with the smoke and dust of battle, was wafted the refreshing scent of lilies.

And into his mind drifted the gentle command: 'Up, beloved of the Moon, up; arise, for Tanit comes.'

He stood upright, waiting.

Then he heard a gentle voice, like a silver bell, and yet a voice of power; a voice before which he bent his head and covered his eyes.

'Hail, beloved of Tanit, giver of kindness, fountain of power, hail, and welcome here! Thou hast been permitted to see again thy existences; yet are these but a few, for thy encouragement, O well-beloved. In those past lives thou hast never wavered in thy steadfastness. Carry then through all of this thy present life the certainty of power, and of my love and aid.

'Go now, beloved, and take with thee – this!'

The voice ceased, and he felt, upon his left arm, a gentle touch.

He opened his eyes, lowered his folded arms.

He stood upon the lawn, beside the moon-dial, under the moon. He gazed up at that gleaming serenity with a great, deep love in his heart. It seemed to him that he had just passed through some wondrous, now nearly-erased, experience; an experience of wonder and power. He felt tremendously happy, content, safe. He raised his arms impulsively. Something caught his eye; something that gleamed.

He completed his gesture, but his eyes were, despite themselves, drawn around to the wondrous thing sparkling upon his left arm, just above the elbow! It shimmered like the very diadem of Tanit. He brought his arm up close to his eyes, looked at the glimmering jeweled thing, an inch and a half wide, which encircled his upper arm. It was a bracelet encrusted with shining jewels; a bracelet of some metal that he had seen before, inset, somewhere; pale, beautiful metal, like platinum. He moved it, slightly, up and down his arm, with his other hand. It moved, freely, and when he tried to draw it past his elbow – for there seemed to be no clasp to it – it came freely, and off over his hand and into his other hand. He held it close to his face and peered at it lost in a maze of wonderment mingled with faint recollections of brave happenings; not quite clear, yet somehow sure and certain in his mind.

Then, carrying it, and looking lovingly up again at the moon, he turned, for he felt, suddenly, quite tired and sleepy; and walked back to the house through the cypresses, to the murmur of countless tiny whirrings and pipings of insects in the hedges.

He carried it into his bedroom and lighted the electric lamp on his bureau, and looked at it in the artificial light, closely, admiringly. It reflected this strong light in millions of coruscations; green, yellow, burning red, pale blue, every shade of mauve and lavender and deeper purple, all the manifold shades and variations of the gamut of colors.

He sighed, instinctively, and placed it in one of the smaller bureau drawers.

Then, strangely happy, contented, he went over and climbed into his bed. He stretched himself out and rolled over on his left side, for he felt very tired, although very happy and contented, and almost instantly fell asleep; but into his dreams of heroic deeds and great daring, and faithful vigils, and honorable trial, he carried the strange conviction which had come to him when he had turned the magnificent armlet about under the light.

The markings on the smooth inside of that clear, pale, heavy metal, were the same as the ancient marred runes, on his moon-dial, down in the garden; those runes which he had studied until he knew them by heart, could draw on paper, with a pencil, unerringly.

And now that he knew in his deep inner consciousness what the runes meant he was ready, with a heart unafraid, to live his life, free and full, and clear, and honorable, and beautiful; a life in union with the moon, his beloved . . . He would know how to rule, when The Destroyer of Delights and the Sunderer of Companies came and took his father away – might it be a long day, in the mercy of Allah! – and he, Said Yussuf should reign in his father's room over the great hillstate of Kangalore.

No Eye-Witnesses

There were blood stains on Everard Simon's shoes . . . Simon's father had given up his country house in Rye when his wife died, and moved into an apartment in Flatbush among the rising apartment houses which were steadily replacing the original rural atmosphere of that residential section of swelling Brooklyn.

Blood stains – and forest mold – on his shoes!

The younger Simon – he was thirty-seven, his father getting on toward seventy – always spent his winters in the West Indies, returning in the spring, going back again in October. He was a popular writer of informative magazine articles. As soon as his various visits for week-ends and odd days were concluded, he would move his trunks into the Flatbush apartment and spend a week or two, sometimes longer, with his father. There was a room for him in the apartment, and this he would occupy until it was time for him to leave for his summer camp in the Adirondacks. Early in September he would repeat the process, always ending his autumn stay in the United States with his father until it was time to sail back to St Thomas or Martinique or wherever he imagined he could write best for that particular winter.

There was only one drawback in this arrangement. This was the long ride in the subway necessitated by his dropping in to his New York club every day. The club was his real American headquarters. There he received his mail. There he usually lunched and often dined as well. It was at the club that he received his visitors and his telephone calls. The club was on Forty-Fourth Street, and to get there from the apartment he walked to the Church Avenue subway station, changed at De Kalb Avenue, and then took a Times Square express train over the Manhattan Bridge. The time consumed between the door of the apartment and the door of the club was exactly three-quarters of an hour, barring delays. For the older man the arrangement was ideal. He could be in his office, he boasted, in twenty minutes.

To avoid the annoyances of rush hours in the subway, Mr Simon senior commonly left home quite early in the morning, about seven o'clock. He was a methodical person, always leaving before seven in the morning, and getting his breakfast in a downtown restaurant near the office. Everard Simon rarely left the apartment until after nine, thus avoiding the morning rush-hour at its other end. During the five or six weeks every year that they lived together the two men really saw little of each other, although strong bonds of understanding, affection, and respect bound them together. Sometimes the older man would awaken his son early in the morning for a brief conversation. Occasionally the two would have a meal together, evenings, or on Sundays; now and then an evening would be spent in each other's company. They had little to converse about. During the day they would sometimes call each other up and speak together briefly on the telephone from club to office or office to club. On the day when Everard Simon sailed south, his father and he always took a farewell luncheon together somewhere downtown. On the day of his return seven months later, his father always made it a point to meet him at the dock. These arrangements had prevailed for eleven years. He must get that blood wiped off. Blood! How – ?

During that period, the neighborhood of the apartment had changed out of all recognition. Open lots, community tennis-courts, and many of the older one-family houses had disappeared, to be replaced by the ubiquitous apartment houses. In 1928 the neighborhood which had been almost rural when the older Simon had taken up his abode 'twenty minutes from his Wall Street office' was solidly built up except for an occasional, and now incongruous, frame house standing lonely and dwarfed in its own grounds among the towering apartment houses, like a lost child in a preoccupied crowd of adults whose business caused them to look over the child's head.

*   *   *

One evening, not long before the end of his autumn sojourn in Flatbush, Everard Simon, having dined alone in his club, started for the Times Square subway station about a quarter before nine. Doubled together lengthwise, and pressing the pocket of his coat out of shape, was a magazine, out that day, which contained one of his articles. He stepped on board a waiting Sea Beach express train, in the rearmost car, sat down, and opened the magazine, looking down the table of contents to find his article. The train started after the ringing of the warning bell and the automatic closing of the side doors, while he was putting on his reading-spectacles. He began on the article.

He was dimly conscious of the slight bustle of incoming passengers at Broadway and Canal Street, and again when the train ran out on the Manhattan Bridge because of the change in the light, but his closing of the magazine with a page-corner turned down, and the replacing of the spectacles in his inside pocket when the train drew in to De Kalb Avenue, were almost entirely mechanical. He could make that change almost without thought. He had to cross the platform here at De Kalb Avenue, get into a Brighton Beach local train. The Brighton Beach expresses ran only in rush hours and he almost never travelled during those periods.

He got into his train, found a seat, and resumed his reading. He paid no attention to the stations – Atlantic and Seventh Avenues. The next stop after that, Prospect Park, would give him one of his mechanical signals, like coming out on the bridge. The train emerged from its tunnel at Prospect Park, only to re-enter it again at Parkside Avenue, the next following station. After that came Church Avenue, where he got out every evening.

As the train drew in to that station, he repeated the mechanics of turning down a page in the magazine, replacing his spectacles in their case, and putting the case in his inside pocket. His mind entirely on the article, he got up, left the train, walked back toward the Caton Avenue exit, started to mount the stairs.

A few moments later he was walking, his mind still entirely occupied with his article, in the long-familiar direction of his father's apartment.

The first matter which reminded him of his surroundings was the contrast in his breathing after the somewhat stuffy air of the subway train. Consciously he drew in a deep breath of the fresh, sweet outdoor air. There was a spicy odor of wet leaves about it somehow. It seemed, as he noticed his environment with the edge of his mind, darker than usual. The crossing of Church and Caton Avenues was a brightly lighted corner. Possibly something was temporarily wrong with the lighting system. He looked up. Great trees nodded above his head. He could see the stars twinkling above their lofty tops. The sickle edge of a moon cut sharply against black branches moving gently in a fresh wind from the sea.

He walked on several steps before he paused, slackened his gait, then stopped dead, his mind responding in a note of quiet wonderment.

Great trees stood all about him. From some distance ahead a joyous song in a manly bass, slightly muffled by the wood of the thick trees, came to his ears. It was a song new to him. He found himself listening to it eagerly. The song was entirely strange to him, the

words unfamiliar. He listened intently. The singer came nearer. He
caught various words, English words. He distinguished 'merry', and
'heart', and 'repine'.

It seemed entirely natural to be here, and yet, as he glanced down
at his brown clothes, his highly polished shoes, felt the magazine
bulging his pocket, the edge of his mind caught a note of incongruity. He remembered with a smile that strange drawing of Aubrey
Beardsley's, of a lady playing an upright cottage pianoforte in the
midst of a field of daisies! He stood, he perceived, in a kind of rough
path worn by long usage. The ground was damp underfoot. Already
his polished shoes were soiled with mold.

The singer came nearer and nearer. Obviously, as the fresh voice
indicated, it was a young man. Just as the voice presaged that before
many seconds the singer must come out of the screening array of
tree boles, Everard Simon was startled by a crashing, quite near by,
at his right. The singer paused in the middle of a note, and for an
instant there was a primeval silence undisturbed by the rustle of a
single leaf.

Then a huge timber wolf burst through the underbrush to the
right, paused, crouched, and sprang, in a direction diagonal to that in
which Everard Simon was facing, toward the singer.

Startled into a frigid immobility, Simon stood as though petrified.
He heard an exclamation, in the singer's voice, a quick 'heh'; then
the sound of a struggle. The great wolf, apparently, had failed to
knock down his quarry. Then without warning, the two figures, man
and wolf, came into plain sight; the singer, for so Simon thought of
him, a tall, robust fellow, in fringed deerskin, slashing desperately
with a hunting-knife, the beast crouching now, snapping with a
tearing motion of a great punishing jaw. Short-breathed 'heh's' came
from the man, as he parried dexterously the lashing snaps of the
wicked jaws.

The two, revolving about each other, came very close. Everard
Simon watched the struggle, fascinated, motionless. Suddenly the
animal shifted its tactics. It backed away stealthily, preparing for
another spring. The young woodsman abruptly dropped his knife,
reached for the great pistol which depended from his belt in a rough
leather holster. There was a blinding flash, and the wolf slithered
down, its legs giving under it. A great cloud of acrid smoke drifted
about Everard Simon, cutting off his vision; choking smoke which
made him cough.

But through it, he saw the look of horrified wonderment on the face of the young woodsman; saw the pistol drop on the damp ground as the knife had dropped; followed with his eyes, through the dimming medium of the hanging smoke, the fascinated, round-eyed stare of the man who had fired the pistol.

There, a few feet away from him, he saw an eldritch change passing over the beast, shivering now in its death-struggle. He saw the hair of the great paws dissolve, the jaws shorten and shrink, the lithe body buckle and heave strangely. He closed his eyes, and when he opened them, he saw the figure in deerskins standing mutely over the body of a man, lying prone across tree-roots, a pool of blood spreading, spreading, from the concealed face, mingling with the damp earth under the tree-roots.

Then the strange spell of quiescence which had held him in its weird thrall was dissolved, and, moved by a nameless terror, he ran, wildly, straight down the narrow path between the trees . . .

It seemed to him that he had been running only a short distance when something, the moon above the trees, perhaps, began to increase in size, to give a more brilliant light. He slackened his pace. The ground now felt firm underfoot, no longer damp, slippery. Other lights joined that of the moon. Things became brighter all about him, and as this brilliance increased, the great trees all about him turned dim and pale. The ground was now quite hard underfoot. He looked up. A brick wall faced him. It was pierced with windows. He looked down. He stood on pavement. Overhead a streetlight swung lightly in the late September breeze. A faint smell of wet leaves was in the air, mingled now with the fresh wind from the sea. The magazine was clutched tightly in his left hand. He had, it appeared, drawn it from his pocket. He looked at it curiously, put it back into the pocket.

He stepped along over familiar pavement, past well-known façades. The entrance to his father's apartment loomed before him. Mechanically he thrust his left hand into his trousers pocket. He took out his key, opened the door, traversed the familiar hallway with its rugs and marble walls and bracket side-wall light-clusters. He mounted the stairs, one flight, turned the corner, reached the door of the apartment, let himself in with his key.

It was half-past nine and his father had already retired. They talked through the old man's bedroom door, monosyllabically. The conversation ended with the request from his father that he close the bedroom door. He did so, after wishing the old man good-night.

658 OTHER STORIES

He sat down in an armchair in the living-room, passed a hand over his forehead, bemused. He sat for fifteen minutes. Then he reached into his pocket for a cigarette. They were all gone. Then he remembered that he had meant to buy a fresh supply on his way to the apartment. He had meant to get the cigarettes from the drugstore between the Church Avenue subway station and the apartment! He looked about the room for one. His father's supply, too, seemed depleted.

He rose, walked into the entry, put on his hat, stepped out again into the hallway, descended the one flight, went out into the street. He walked into an unwonted atmosphere of excitement. People were conversing as they passed, in excited tones; about the drugstore entrance a crowd was gathered. Slightly puzzled, he walked toward it, paused, blocked, on the outer edge.

'What's happened?' he inquired of a young man whom he found standing just beside him, a little to the fore.

'It's a shooting of some kind,' the young man explained. 'I only just got here myself. The fellow that got bumped off is inside the drugstore, – what's left of him. Some gang-war stuff, I guess.'

He walked away, skirting the rounded edge of the clustering crowd of curiosity-mongers, proceeded down the street, procured the cigarettes elsewhere. He passed the now enlarged crowd on the other side of the street on his way back, returned to the apartment, where he sat, smoking and thinking, until eleven, when he retired. Curious – a man shot; just at the time, or about the time, he had let that imagination of his get the better of him – those trees!

His father awakened him about five minutes before seven. The old man held a newspaper in his hand. He pointed to a scare-head on the front page.

'This must have happened about the time you came in,' remarked Mr Simon.

'Yes – the crowd was around the drugstore when I went out to get some cigarettes,' replied Everard Simon, stretching and yawning.

When his father was gone and he had finished with his bath, he sat down, in a bathrobe, to glance over the newspaper account. A phrase arrested him: ' . . . the body was identified as that of "Jerry the Wolf", a notorious gangster with a long prison record.'

Then, lower down, when he had resumed his reading: ' . . . a large-caliber bullet which, entering the lower jaw, penetrated the base of the brain . . . no eye-witnesses . . . '

Everard Simon sat for a long time after he had finished the account, the newspaper on the floor by his chair. 'No eye-witnesses!' He must, really, keep that imagination of his within bounds, within his control.

Slowly and reflectively, this good resolution uppermost, he went back to the bathroom and prepared for his morning shave.

Putting on his shoes, in his room, he observed something amiss. He picked up a shoe, examined it carefully. The soles of the shoes were caked with black mold, precisely like the mold from the wood-paths about his Adirondack camp. Little withered leaves and dried pine-needles clung to the mold. And on the side of the right shoe were brownish stains, exactly like freshly dried bloodstains. He shuddered as he carried the shoes into the bathroom, wiped them clean with a damp towel, then rinsed out the towel. He put them on, and shortly afterward, before he entered the subway to go over to the club for the day, he had them polished.

The bootblack spoke of the killing on that corner the night before. The boot-black noticed nothing amiss with the shoes, and when he had finished, there was no trace of any stains.

Simon did not change at De Kalb Avenue that morning. An idea had occurred to him between Church Avenue and De Kalb, and he stayed on the Brighton local, secured a seat after the emptying process which took place at De Kalb, and went on through the East River tunnel.

He sent in his name to Forrest, a college acquaintance, now in the district attorney's office, and Forrest received him after a brief delay.

'I wanted to ask a detail about this gangster who was killed in Flatbush last night,' said Simon. 'I suppose you have his record, haven't you?'

'Yes, we know pretty well all about him. What particular thing did you want to know?'

'About his name,' replied Simon. 'Why was he called "Jerry the Wolf" – that is, why "The Wolf" particularly?'

'That's a very queer thing, Simon. Such a name is not, really, uncommon. There was that fellow, Goddard, you remember. They called him "The Wolf of Wall Street". There was the fiction criminal known as "The Lone Wolf". There have been plenty of "wolves" among criminal "monikers". But this fellow, Jerry Goraffsky, was a Hungarian, really. He was called "The Wolf", queerly enough, because there were those in his gang who believed he was one of those birds who could change himself into a wolf! It's a queer combination, isn't it? – for a New York gangster?'

'Yes,' said Everard Simon, 'it is, very queer, when you come to think of it. I'm much obliged to you for telling me. I was curious about it somehow.'

'That isn't the only queer aspect of this case, however,' resumed Forrest, a light frown suddenly showing on his keen face. 'In fact that wolf-thing isn't a part of the case – doesn't concern us, of course, here in the district attorney's office. That's nothing but blah. Gangsters are as superstitious as sailors; more so, in fact!

'No. The real mystery in this affair is – the bullet, Simon. Want to see it?'

'Why – yes; of course – if you like, Forrest. What's wrong with the bullet?'

Forrest stepped out of the room, returned at once, laid a large, round ball on his desk. Both men bent over it curiously.

'Notice that diameter, Simon,' said Forrest. 'It's a hand-molded round ball – belongs in a collection of curios, not in any gangster's gat! Why, man, it's like the slugs they used to hunt the bison before the old Sharps rifle was invented. It's the kind of a ball Fenimore Cooper's people used – "Deerslayer"! It would take a young cannon to throw that thing. Smashed in the whole front of Jerry's ugly mug. The inside works of his head were spilled all over the sidewalk! It's what the newspapers always call a "clue". Who do you suppose resurrected the horse-pistol – or the ship's blunderbuss – to do that job on Jerry? Clever, in a way. Hooked it out of some dime museum, perhaps. There are still a few of those old "pitches" still operating, you know, at the old stand – along East Fourteenth Street.'

'A flintlock, single-shot horse-pistol, I'd imagine,' said Everard Simon, laying the ounce lead ball back on the mahogany desk. He knew something of weapons, new and old. As a writer of informational articles that was part of his permanent equipment.

'Very likely,' mused the assistant district attorney. 'Glad you came in, old man.'

And Everard Simon went on uptown to his club.

Across the Gulf

For the first year, or thereabouts, after his Scotch mother's death the successful lawyer Alan Carrington was conscious, among his other feelings, of a kind of vague dread that she might appear as a character in one of his dreams, as, she had often assured him, her mother had come to her. Being the man he was, he resented this feeling as an incongruity. Yet, there was a certain background for the feeling of dread. It had been one of his practical mother's convictions that such an appearance of her long-dead mother always preceded a disaster in the family.

Such aversions as he might possess against the maternal side of his ancestry were all included in his dislike for belief in this kind of thing. When he agreed that 'the Scotch are a dour race', he always had reference, at least mentally, to this superstitious strain, associated with that race from time immemorial, concrete to his experience because of this belief of his mother's, against which he had always fought.

He carried out dutifully, and with a high degree of professional skill, all her various expressed desires, and continued, after her death, to live in their large, comfortable house. Perhaps because his mother never did appear in such dreams as he happened to remember, his dread became less and less poignant. At the end of two years or so, occupied with the thronging interests of a public man in the full power of his early maturity, it had almost ceased to be so much as a memory.

In the spring of his forty-fourth year, Carrington, who had long worked at high pressure and virtually without vacations, was apprized by certain mental and physical indications which his physician interpreted vigorously, that he must take at least the whole summer off and devote himself to recuperation. Rest, said the doctor, for his over-worked mind and under-exercised body, was imperatively indicated.

Carrington was able to set his nearly innumerable interests and affairs in order in something like three weeks by means of highly concentrated efforts to that end. Then, exceedingly nervous, and not a little debilitated physically from this extra strain upon his depleted resources, he had to meet the problem of where he was to go and what he was to do. He was, of course, too deeply set in the rut of his routines to find such a decision easy. Fortunately, this problem was solved for him by a letter which he received unexpectedly from one of his cousins on his mother's side, the Reverend Fergus MacDonald, a gentleman with whom he had had only slight contacts.

Dr MacDonald was a middle-aged, retired clergyman, whom an imminent decline had removed eight or ten years before from a brilliant, if underpaid, career in his own profession. After a few years sojourn in the Adirondacks he had emerged cured, and with an already growing reputation as a writer of that somewhat inelastic literary product emphasized by certain American magazines which seem to embalm a spinsterish austerity of the literary form under the label of distinction.

Dr MacDonald had retained a developed pastoral instinct which he could no longer satisfy in the management of a parish. He was, besides, too little robust to risk assuming, at least for some time to come, the wearing burden of teaching. He compromised the matter by establishing a summer camp for boys in his still-desirable Adirondacks. Being devoid of experience in business matters he associated with himself a certain Thomas Starkey, a young man whom the ravages of the White Plague had snatched away from a sales-managership and driven into the quasi-exile of Saranac, where Dr MacDonald had met him.

This association proved highly successful for the half-dozen years that it had lasted. Then Starkey, after a brave battle for his health, had succumbed, just at a period when his trained business intelligence would have been most helpful to the affairs of the camp.

Dazed at this blow, Dr MacDonald had desisted from his labors after literary distinction long enough to write to his cousin Carrington, beseeching his legal and financial counsel. When Carrington had read the last of his cousin's finished periods, he decided at once, and dispatched a telegram announcing his immediate setting out for the camp, his intention to remain through the summer, and the promise to assume full charge of the business management. He started for the Adirondacks the next afternoon.

His presence brought immediate order out of confusion. Dr Mac-Donald, on the evening of the second day of his cousin's administration of affairs, got down on his knees and returned thanks to his Maker for the undeserved beneficence which had sent this financial angel of light into the midst of his affairs, in this, his hour of dire need! Thereafter the reverend doctor immersed himself more and more deeply in his wonted task of producing the solid literature dear to the hearts of his editors.

But if Carrington's coming had improved matters at the camp, the balance of indebtedness was far from being one-sided. For the first week or so the reaction from his accustomed way of life had caused him to feel, if anything, even staler and more nerve-racked than before. But that first unpleasantness past, the invigorating air of the balsam-laden pine woods began to show its restorative effects rapidly. He found that he was sleeping like the dead. He could not get enough sleep, it appeared. His appetite increased, and he found that he was putting on needed weight. The business management of a boys' camp, absurdly simple after the complex matters of Big Business with which he had long been occupied, was only a spice to this new existence among the deep shadows and sunny spaces of the Adirondack country. At the end of a month of this, he confidently declared himself a new man. By the first of August, instead of the nervous wreck who had arrived, sharp-visaged and cadaverous, two months before, Carrington presented the appearance of a robust, hard-muscled athlete of thirty, twenty-two pounds heavier and 'without a nerve in his body'.

On the evening of the fourth day of August, healthily weary after a long day's hike, Carrington retired soon after 9 o'clock, and fell immediately into a deep and restful sleep. Toward morning he dreamed of his mother for the first time since her death more than six years before. His dream took the form that he was lying here, in his own bed, awake – a not altogether uncommon form of dream – and that he was very chilly in the region of the left shoulder. As is well-known to those skilled in the scientific phenomena of the dream-state, now a very prominent portion of the material used in psychological study, this kind of sensation in a dream virtually always is the result of an actual physical condition, and is reproduced in the dream because of that actual background as a stimulus. Carrington's cold shoulder was toward the left-hand, or outside of the bed, which stood against the wall of his large, airy room.

In his dream he thought that he reached out his hand to replace the bed clothes, and as he did so his hand was softly, though firmly, taken, and his mother's well-remembered voice said: 'Lie still, laddie; I'll tuck you in.' Then he thought his mother replaced the loosened covers and tucked them in about his shoulder with her competent touch. He wanted to thank her, and as he could not see her because of the position in which he was lying, he endeavored to open his eyes and turn over, being in that state commonly thought of as between sleep and waking. With some considerable effort he succeeded in forcing open his reluctant eyes; but turning over was a much more difficult matter, it appeared. He had to fight against an overpowering inclination to sink back comfortably into the deep sleep, from which, in his dream, he had awakened to find his shoulder disagreeably uncomfortable. The warmth of the replaced covers was an additional inducement to sleep.

At last, with a determined wrench he overcame his desire to go to sleep again and rolled over to his left side by dint of a strong effort of his will, smiling gratefully and about to express his thanks. But at the instant of accomplishing this victory of the will, he actually awakened, in precisely the position recorded in his mind in the dream-state.

Where he had expected to meet his mother's eyes, he saw nothing, but there remained with him a persistent impression that he had felt the withdrawal of her hand from where, on his shoulder, it had rested caressingly. The grateful warmth of the bedclothes in that cool morning remained, however, and he observed that they were well tucked in about that shoulder.

His dream had clearly been of the type which George Du Maurier speaks of in *Peter Ibbetson*. He had 'dreamed true', and it required several minutes before he could rid himself of the impression that his mother, moved by some strange whimsicality, had stepped out of his sight, perhaps hidden herself behind the bed! He was actually about to look back of the bed before the utter absurdity of the idea became fully apparent to him. The back of the bed stood close against the wall of the room. His mother had been dead more than six years.

He jumped out of bed at the sound of reveillé, blown by the camp bugler, and this abrupt action dissipated his impressions. Their memory remained, however, very clear-cut in his mind for the next two days. The impression of his mother's nearness in the course of that vivid dream had recalled her to his mind with the greatest clarity. With this revived impression of her, too, there marched, almost of necessity he supposed, in his mind the old idea which he had dreaded – the idea that she would come to him to warn him of some impending danger.

Curiously enough, as he analyzed his sensations, he found that there remained none of the old resentment connected with this speculation,

such as had characterized it during the period immediately after his
mother's death. His maturity, the preoccupations of an exceptionally
full and active life, and the tenderness which marked all his memories
of his mother had served to remove from his mind all traces of that
idea. The possibility of a 'warning' in his dream of his dear mother
only caused him to smile during those days after the dream during
which the revived impression of his mother slowly faded thin, but it
was the indulgent, slightly melancholy smile of a revived nostalgia, a
gentle, faint sense of 'homesickness' for her, such as might affect any
middle-aged man recently reminded of a beloved mother in some
rather intense fashion.

On the evening of the second day after his dream he was walking
toward the camp garage with some visitors, a man and woman,
parents of one of the boys at the camp, intending to drive with them
to the village to guide them in some minor purchases. Just beside the
well-worn trail through the great pine trees, half-way up the hill to
the garage, the woman noticed a clump of large, brownish mushrooms, and enquired if they were of an edible variety. Carrington
picked one and examined it. To his limited knowledge it seemed to
have several of the marks of an edible mushroom. While they were
standing beside the place where the mushrooms grew, one of the
younger boys passed them.

'Crocker,' called Mr Carrington.

'Yes, Mr Carrington,' replied young Crocker, pausing.

'Crocker, your cabin is the one farthest south, isn't it?'

'Yes, sir.'

'Were you going there just now?'

'Yes, Mr Carrington; can I do anything for you?'

'Well, if it isn't too much trouble, you might take this mushroom
over to Professor Benjamin's – you know where his camp is, just the
other side of the wire fence beyond your cabin, – and ask him to let
us know whether or not this is an edible mushroom. I'm not quite
sure myself.'

'Certainly,' replied the boy, pleased to be allowed 'out of bounds'
even to the extent of the few rods separating the camp property from
that of the gentleman named by Carrington, a university teacher
regarded locally as a great expert on mushrooms, fungi, and suchlike
things.

Carrington called after the disappearing boy.

'Oh, Crocker!'

'Yes, Mr Carrington?'

'Throw it away if Dr Benjamin says it's no good; but if he says it's all right, bring it back, please, and leave it on the mantel-shelf in the big living room. Do you mind?'

'All right, sir,' shouted Crocker over his shoulder, and trotted on.

* * *

Returning from the village an hour later, Carrington found the mushroom on the mantel-shelf in the living room.

He placed it in a large paper bag, left it in the kitchen in a safe place, and, the next morning before breakfast, walked up the trail toward the garage and filled his paper bag with mushrooms.

He liked mushrooms, and so, doubtless, did the people who had noticed these. He decided he would prepare the mushrooms himself. There would be just about enough for three generous portions. Mushrooms were not commonly eaten as a breakfast dish, but – this was camp!

Exchanging a pleasant 'good morning' with the young colored man who served as assistant cook, and who was engaged in getting breakfast ready, and smilingly declining his offer to prepare the mushrooms, he peeled them, warmed a generous lump of fresh, country butter in a large frying pan, and began cooking them.

A delightfully appetizing odor arising from the pan provoked respectful banter from the young cook, amused at the camp-director's efforts along the lines of his own profession, and the two chatted while Carrington turned his mushrooms over and over in the butter with a long fork. When they were done exactly to a turn, and duly peppered and salted, Carrington left them in the pan, which he took off the stove, and set about the preparation of three *canapés* of fried toast. He was going to serve his mushrooms in style, as the grinning young cook slyly remarked. He grinned back, and divided the mushrooms into three equal portions, each on its *canapé*, which he asked the under-cook to keep hot in the oven during the brief interval until mess call should bring everybody at camp in to breakfast.

Then with his long fork he speared several small pieces of mushroom which had got broken in the pan. After blowing these cool on the fork, Carrington, grinning like a boy, put them into his mouth and began to eat them.

'Good, suh?' enquired the assistant cook.

'Delicious,' mumbled Carrington enthusiastically, his mouth full of the succulent bits. After he had swallowed his mouthful, he remarked: 'But I must have left a bit of the hide on one of 'em. There's a little trace of bitter.'

'Look out for 'em, suh,' enjoined the under-cook, suddenly grave. 'They're plumb wicked when they ain't jus' right, suh.'

'These are all right,' returned Carrington, reassuringly. 'I had Professor Benjamin look them over.'

He sauntered out on the veranda, waiting for the bugle call. From many directions the boys and a few visitors were straggling in toward the mess hall after a morning dip in the lake and cabin inspection. From their room in the guest house the people with whom he had been the evening before came across the broad veranda toward him. He was just turning toward them with a smile of pleasant greeting when the very hand of death fell on him.

Without warning, a sudden terrible griping, accompanied by a deadly coldness, and this immediately followed by a pungent, burning heat, ran through his body. Great beads of sweat sprang out on his forehead. His knees began to give under him. Everything, all this pleasant world about him, of brilliant morning sunshine and deep, sharply-defined shadow, turned greenish and dim. His senses started to slip away from him in the numbness which closed down like a relentless hand, crushing out his consciousness.

With an effort which seemed to wrench his soul and tear him with unimagined pain, he gathered all his waning forces, and, sustained only by a mighty effort of his powerful will, he staggered through the open doorway of the mess hall into the kitchen. He nearly collapsed as he leaned against the nearest table, articulating between fast-paralyzing lips:

'Water – and mustard! Quick. The mushrooms!'

The head-cook, that moment arrived in the kitchen, happened to be quick-minded. The under-cook, too, had had, of course, some preparation for this possibility.

One of the men seized a bowl just used for beating eggs and with shaking hands poured it half-full of warm water from a heating kettle on the stove. Into this the other emptied nearly half a tin of dry mustard which he stirred about frantically with his floury hand. This, his eyes rolling with terror, he held to Carrington's lips, and Carrington, concentrating afresh all his remaining faculties, forced the nauseous fluid through his blue lips, and swallowed, painfully, great saving gulps of the powerful emetic.

Again and yet again the two negroes renewed the dose.

One of the counselors, on dining room duty, coming into the kitchen sensed something terribly amiss, and ran to support Carrington.

Ten minutes later, vastly nauseated, trembling with weakness, but safe, Carrington, leaning heavily on the young counselor, walked up and down behind the mess hall. His first words, after he could speak coherently, were to order the assistant cook to burn the contents of the three hot plates in the oven ...

He had eaten a large mouthful of one of the most deadly varieties of poisonous mushroom, one containing the swiftly-acting vegetable alkaloids which spell certain death. His few moments' respite, as he reasoned the matter out afterward, had been undoubtedly due to his having cooked the mushrooms in butter, of which he had been lavish. This, thoroughly soaked up by the mushrooms, had, for a brief period, resisted digestion.

Very gradually, as he walked up and down, taking in deep breaths of the sweet, pine-scented air, his strength returned to him. After he had thoroughly walked off the faintness which had followed the violent treatment to which he had subjected himself, he went up to his room, and, still terribly shaken by his experience and narrow escape from death, went to bed to rest.

Crocker, it appeared, had duly carried out his instructions. Dr Benjamin had looked at the specimen and told the boy that there were several varieties of this mushroom, not easily to be distinguished from one another, of which some were wholesome, and one contained a deadly alkaloid. Being otherwise occupied at the time, he would have to defer his opinion until he had had an opportunity for a more thorough examination. He had handed back the mushroom submitted to him and the lad had given it to a counselor, who had put it on the mantel-shelf intending to report to Mr Carrington the following morning.

Weak still, and very drowsy, Carrington lay on his bed and silently thanked the Powers above for having preserved his life.

Abruptly he thought of his mother. The warning!

At once it was as though she stood in the room beside his bed; as though their long, close companionship had not been interrupted by death.

A wave of affectionate gratitude suffused him. Under its influence he rose, wearily, and sank to his knees beside the bed, his head on his arms, in the very spot where his mother had seemed to stand in his dream.

Tears welled into his eyes, and fell, unnoticed, as he communed silently with her who had brought him into the world, whose watchful love and care not even death could interrupt or vitiate.

Silently, fervently, he spoke across the gulf to his mother . . .

He choked with silent sobs as understanding of her invincible love came to him and overwhelmed him. Then, to the accompaniment of a tremulous calmness which seemed to fall upon him abruptly, he had the sense of her, standing close beside him, as she had stood in his dream. He dared not raise his eyes, because now he knew that he was awake. It seemed to him as though she spoke, though there came to him no sensation of anything that could be compared to sound.

'Ye must be getting back into your bed, laddie.'

And keeping his eyes tightly shut, lest he disturb this visitation, he awkwardly fumbled his way back into bed. He settled himself on his back, and an overpowering drowsiness, perhaps begotten of his recent shock and its attendant bodily weakness, ran through him like a benediction and a refreshing wind.

As he drifted down over the threshold of consciousness into the deep and prolonged sleep of physical exhaustion which completely restored him, his last remembrance was of the lingering caress of his mother's firm hand resting on his shoulder.

The Tabernacle

AUTHOR'S NOTE: *This is a very ancient tale, running back far into the early history of religion in Europe. It has cropped up, traditionally, in many lands and in various periods. Members of the older religions will understand its implications without explanations. To those unversed in the traditional belief concerning the Sanctissimum (the consecrated bread of Holy Communion among the older, Catholic, religions), it may be mentioned that this bread, known as the Host, is, after consecration at the hands of a validly ordained priest, understood to be 'really' the Body of the Lord. The type of this 'reality' varies among different theologians, but the belief in the essential identity of the consecrated Host with the True Body, with all the implications that follow this belief, is general. As the Lord (Jesus) is Lord of the Universe according to ancient Christian belief, His Body should be sacred to all His creatures. Hence this very ancient tradition that is here told in a modern setting.*

Kazmir Strod knelt very low in his seat in the pine pew of St Stanislas' Church just after he had come back from the altar rail, so low, by purpose, that no one up there at the altar, not Father Gregoreff nor any of the acolytes, could possibly see him. The clean handkerchief he had taken to church, unfolded, was still in his left hand where he had put it, somewhat damp because of his emotion and the fact that it was a warm April day. It was, indeed, so warm that his bees had swarmed the evening before and he had got them, successfully, into the new hive.

The Holy Host remained intact, between his teeth, held lightly. He felt sure that It was not even damp, because he had carefully wiped his lips and teeth, in that same low-kneeling posture, with the clean handkerchief just before rising, genuflecting, proceeding to the altar.

He placed the handkerchief over his mouth now and to the accompaniment of several brief prayers took the Host from his mouth. He held It, very gently, the Sanctissimum, in the clean handkerchief. He felt very strange. He had never done such a thing before.

Bending now, very low, he felt for the small, thin wafer inside the clean handkerchief's folds, broke off a tiny piece, and placed It in his mouth. He must receive Holy Communion or it would be further sacrilege. He swallowed It, with difficulty, for his mouth, under this stress, had remained very dry. He said the prayers of Reception with his mind on them, but as rapidly as he could. He did not leave out a word of those prayers.

Then, and only then, he slipped the handkerchief into his pocket. He was kneeling upright, like the rest of the congregation, the men with shining newly-shaved faces, the women, on the other side of the central alleyway, with multicolored shawls over their sleek heads, when Father Gregoreff was turning toward the congregation at the end of the Mass.

'*Ite, missa est*,' boomed Father Gregoreff, and turned to the altar's end for the Last Gospel.

Kazmir spoke to nobody on the way home. That, too, he imagined, would be sacrilegious, for, like a priest, he was carrying the Sanctissimum upon him.

He went straight to the new hive. There were almost no flowers out at this time of year. On the broad landing board, several dozen bees were lined up in rows, like little soldiers, finishing the sugar-and-water honey he had placed for them to keep them in the hive where he had placed them last night. He was sure the new queen was within. She would be, of course, in the center of the swarm, and he had lifted them, very carefully, off the bush where they had swarmed, into the new hive. It had been an unusually large swarm. He had worn his high rubber boots, his bricklayer's gloves, and a folded net about his head over his cap. Even so, he had had a few stings.

He was going to make this hive the greatest hive there was! He was going to use old, old 'magic', the way it had been done in the Old Country, for luck and for the success of a vegetable garden, and for many other good purposes, even though it was, good purpose and all, sacrilege. God didn't mind such things. It was only the priests who objected. A little bit of the Host placed inside the hive. That was all. That would make the bees prosper, bring luck to the new hive. Over here, in America, you didn't hear so much about doing things like that. But Kazmir knew what to do for bees. Those old-time ways were good ways. They worked. The Holy Host had many virtues. Along with garlic-flowers it was a sure safeguard from vampires. Placed in a coffin, he had heard, It kept the body from decay. With even a tiny crumb of It, wrapped tightly in a piece of clean linen, sewed into your clothes, It was sure proof against the Bad-Eye.

There was practically no sound inside the hive. The bees on the landing board moved slowly, lethargically. If this heat held, there would be flowers soon, and he could discontinue the sugar-and-water honey. Too much of that and the bees laid off working! Bees were like humans, very much like humans, only dumber! They never took a rest, had no relaxations.

He raised the hive's top, carefully, leaned it against the side of the packing box on which the hive itself stood. There were the frames, just as he had placed them yesterday, a little old comb, for the bees to build onto, near the middle. That was all right. He removed the crushed bodies of several bees that had got caught when he had placed the top on the hive in yesterday's dusk of evening. The new queen would be down inside there, somewhere, surrounded by her eager, devoted workers, the swarm that had accompanied her out of the older hive yesterday.

Kazmir crossed himself, furtively, and glanced around. Nobody was looking; indeed nobody was, at the moment, in sight. He took the handkerchief out of his pocket, touched his right thumb and the index finger to his lips reverently, extracted the Sanctissimum and dropped It into the open hive between the frames. Then he replaced the top and went into the house. The bees should prosper now, according to all the old rules. Kazmir had never heard of putting such a charm on bees before. That was his own idea. But – if it worked as the old tales said it worked, for horses and cows and the increase of a flock of goats, why not for bees?

It was a quarter past six by the kitchen clock. Time for the woman and kids to be getting up for seven o'clock Mass. He went up the rough stairs to awaken his wife and their two children. This done, he returned to the kitchen to boil four eggs for his breakfast.

It turned out to be a very quiet hive, the new one. Its bees, too, seemed to be stingers. He received many stings during the summer, more stings than usual, it seemed to him. He had to warn Anna and the children to keep away from it. 'They got a lotta pep, them bees,' he said, and smiled to himself. It was he, applying an old idea with true American progressiveness, who had 'pepped them up'. He gave the process this phrase, mentally, without the least thought of incongruity, of irreverence. The efficacy of the Sanctissimum was the last,

the very last thing that Kazmir Strod would have doubted, in the
entire scheme of the world's regulations and principles.

It was only occasionally nowadays that Kazmir worked at bricklaying. Ten years before, in the Old Country, he had learned that
trade. Always a willful, strong-headed youth, independent of mind,
he had flown in the face of his family custom to learn a trade like that.
All his family, near Kovno, had been market-gardeners. That strong-
headedness had been responsible for his emigration, too. There had
been many disputes between him and his father and older brothers.
The strong-headedness and the trade! There were great openings
for a good bricklayer in America.

But, since he had married – rather late in life, to this Americanized
Anna of his, at twenty-two; he was twenty-seven now – with enough
money to buy this place, earned at the bricklaying, he had reverted to
his gardening. There wasn't as much in gardening, even with good
land like this, and sometimes Anna would nag him to take a job when
a contractor offered one, but there were all the deep-rooted satis-
factions of the soil; the love of it was bred deep in his blood and
bones, and he had a way with tomatoes and early peas and even
humdrum potatoes.

This devotion to the soil, he felt, triumphantly, had been amply
justified that August. He had an offer to go and be gardener on a
great estate, a millionaire's, eighteen miles away. The offer included
a house, and the use of what vegetables he needed for his family. He
accepted it, and told Anna afterward.

Anna was delighted. He had not been sure of how she would take
it, and her delight pleased him enormously. For several days it was
like a new honeymoon. He spread it all over the community that he
wanted to sell his place.

He got six hundred dollars, cash, more than he had paid for it.
There was a couple of thousand dollars worth of improvement he
had dug into its earth, but six hundred dollars was six hundred
dollars! The title passed, after a day and a night's wrangling with the
purchaser, Tony Dvorcznik, a compatriot. Kazmir and Anna and the
children moved their possessions in a borrowed motor-truck.

It was in October that Tony Dvorcznik killed off the bees. Tony did
not understand bees, and his wife was afraid of them. He hired
Stanislas Bodinski, who was one of Father Gregoreff's acolytes, to
do the job for him, for a quarter-share of what honey might be
discovered within the four hives. Stanislas Bodinski arrived, with

sulfur and netting. Tony and his wife stood at a little distance, watching interestedly; telling each other to watch out for stings; marveling at Stanislas Bodinski's nonchalance, deftly placing his sulfur-candles, rapidly stuffing the horizontal opening above the landing boards, the edges all around the hive tops.

Stanislas joined them, removing his head-net, and stood with them while the sulfur fumes did their deadly work inside the hives. Later, they all walked over to the hives, Stanislas reassuring Tony's wife. 'They ain't no danger now. They're all dead by now. Anyhow, they die after they sting you, but you needn't worry none. Jus' the same, you better keep away a little. They's some bees was out the hives when I stopped up them cracks. They'll be flyin' around, kinda puzzled, now.'

The comb was lifted out, to exclamations on the part of Tony's wife, into a row of borrowed milk pans. It piled up, enormously, honey covering the bottoms of the pans viscidly.

'You'd wonder where it all come from,' said Tony's wife, again and again, 'outa them little hives! You wouldn't think they'd hold that much stuff, would ya?'

Stanislas Bodinski arrived at the last hive, with two remaining milk pans, and proceeded to lift the top away from the hive. They saw him look in. Then he stopped and looked close. Then he stepped back, raised his arms in an amazing gesture of wonderment, sank to his knees beside the hive, and made the sign of the cross on his breast many times.

Wonderingly, they approached, Tony's wife murmuring:

'What's *bitin'* him? Is he gone loony, huh?' Then: 'Hey, Tony, they mus' be somethin' awful strange in that-there hive, huh – for Stan to ac' that way!'

There was indeed something strange in the hive, although there was very little honey in it. They did not dare touch it, and, after Stanislas had somewhat recovered himself, and put back the top with hands shaking, the three of them, just as they stood, Tony's wife not even taking off her apron, started for the rectory, to get Father Gregoreff.

The priest came, rather grumblingly, Stanislas following half a block behind the other three. He had run into the sacristy to get the priest's cope and a stole, and something that he had to hold onto, in his pocket, to keep it quiet! He hoped Father Gregoreff would not look behind him and see what he was carrying. He was a bit of a mystic, this Stanislas; otherwise he would not, perhaps, have continued to be an acolyte after he was nineteen. He, too, had come from near Kovno, like Kazmir Strod. Stanislas had listened to strange tales in his earlier boyhood, back there in the Old Country.

He came in through Tony Dvorcznik's gate well behind the rest, furtively. They were all standing, looking at the hive, when he came around the corner of the house. He walked around them, knelt before his priest, seized and kissed his hand. He handed the amazed Father Gregoreff his stole, and the priest put it on mechanically, murmuring, 'What's this? What's all this?' Stanislas rose, hastily invested his pastor with the white cope, and stepped over to the hive. He knelt, and turning to the others, motioned them, authoritatively, to kneel also. They did so, all three, the priest's cope trailing on the ground, a few feet behind Stanislas.

Stanislas, making the sign of the cross, reached his arms into the hive. Carefully, the sweat running down his face, he lifted out a shining yellow, new-wax structure, intact, with infinite care. He turned, still on his knees, and placed what he had lifted in the priest's hands. It was a little church, made of wax, made by the bees whose dead bodies, suffocated by sulfur fumes, now littered the dead hive.

Then Stanislas took the sacring bell from his left-hand pocket, and, his head on the ground, rang it to indicate to all who might be within earshot that they should prostrate themselves before the Sanctissimum.

The Door

Those in the motor car hardly felt the slight, though sickening impact. It was rather, indeed, because of the instinct for something-gone-wrong, than because of conviction that he had struck anything more important than a roll of tangled burlap from some passing moving van, that the driver brought his heavy car to a stop with a grinding of brakes strenuously applied, and went back to see what he had struck.

He had turned the corner almost incidentally; but when he alighted and went back, when the thin gleam of his flashlight revealed to him the heap of huddled pulp which lay there, the driver realized in the throes of a hideous nausea what it was his heavy machine had spurned and crushed . . .

Roger Phillips, intent upon the first really decent act of his whole life, hardly noticed what was forward. He had been crossing the street. He continued to be intent on his own concerns. Interrupted only by a kind of cold shudder to which he gave only passing thought as if with the very outer edge of his mind, he did not stop, but crossed the sidewalk, looking up as he had done many times before to reassure himself that the lights were out in the living-room of the apartment up there on the third floor of the apartment house.

They were out, as he had confidently anticipated, and, reassured, he quickly mounted the steps to the front entrance. Someone came out, hurriedly, and passed him as he entered, the rush taking him by surprize. He turned his head as quickly as he could, to avoid recognition. It was old Mr Osler, his father's neighbor, who had rushed out. The elderly man was in his shirt sleeves, and appeared greatly agitated, so much so that young Phillips was certain he had not been recognized, hardly even noticed, indeed. He breathed an audible sigh of relief. He did not want old Osler to mention this chance meeting to his father the next time he should see him, and he knew Osler to be garrulous.

The young man mounted lightly and hurriedly the two flights of steps that led to the door of his father's apartment. He thrust his key into the patent lock of the apartment door confidently, almost without thought – a mechanical motion. As mechanically, he turned the key to the right. It was an old key, and it fitted the keyhole easily. He knew that his father and mother were at the symphony concert. They had not missed one for years during the season for symphony concerts, and this was their regular night. He had chosen this night for that reason. He knew the colored maid was out, too. He had seen her, not five minutes earlier, getting on a car for Boston. 'The coast,' as he phrased the thought to himself, somewhat melodramatically, 'was clear!' He was certain of security from interruption. Only let him get safely into the apartment, do what he had to do, and as quietly and unobtrusively depart, and he would be satisfied, quite satisfied.

But the lock offered unexpected resistance. It was inexplicable, irritating. His overtensed nerves revolted abruptly at this check. The key had slipped into the slot, as always, without difficulty – but it would not turn! Furiously he twisted it this way and that. At last he removed it and stared at it curiously. There was nothing amiss with the key. Could his father have had the lock changed?

Anger and quick shame smote him, suddenly. He looked closely at the lock. No, it was unchanged. There were the numberless tiny scratchmarks of innumerable insertions. It was the same.

Gingerly, carefully, he inserted the key again. He turned it to the right. Of course it turned to the right; he remembered that clearly. He had so turned it countless times.

It would not move. He put out all his puny strength, and still it would not turn. Hot exasperation shook him.

As he swore under his breath in his irritation at this bar to the fulfillment of his purpose, he became for the first time conscious of a rising commotion in the street below, and he paused, irresolutely, and listened, his nerves suddenly strung taut. Many voices seemed to be mingled in the excited hum that came to his ears. Bits of phrases, even, could be distinguished. Something had happened down there, it seemed. As he listened, the commotion of spoken sound resolved itself into a tone which, upon his subconscious effort to analyze it, seemed to him to express horror and commiseration, with an overtone of fear. The fear communicated itself to him. He shook, as the voice of the growing throng, a blended, corporate voice, came up to him in sickening waves of apprehension.

What if this should mean an interruption? Impatiently wrenching himself away from his preoccupation and back to his more immediate concern with the door, he thrust the key into the lock a third time, this time aggressively, violently. Again he tried to snap the lock. Again it resisted him, unaccountably, devilishly, as it seemed to him.

Then, in his pause of desperation, he thought he heard his own name spoken. He could feel his face go white, the roots of his hair prickle. He listened, intently, crouching catlike there on the empty landing before the door of his father's apartment, and as he listened, every nerve intent, he heard the entrance-door below flung open, and the corporate voice of the throng outside, hitherto muffled and faint, came to him suddenly in a wave of sound, jumbled and obscure as a whole, but with certain strident voices strangely clear and distinct.

A shuffle of heavy feet came to his ears, as if several persons were entering the lower hallway, their footsteps falling heavily on the tiled flooring. They would be coming upstairs!

He shrank back against the door – that devilish door! If only he could get it open!

Something like this, he told himself, in a wave of self-pity that swept him – something like this, unexpected, unforeseen, unreasonable – something like this was always happening to him!

That door! It was an epitome of his futile, worthless life! That had happened to him, just the same kind of thing, a month ago when he had been turned out of his home. The events of the intervening weeks rushed, galloping, through his overtensed mind. And now, as ever since that debacle, there was present with him a kind of unforgettable vision of his mother – his poor mother, her face covered with the tears which she made no effort to wipe away – his poor mother, looking at him, stricken, through those tears which blurred her face: and there was his father, the kindly face set now in a stern mask, pale and with deep lines – his father telling him that this was the end. There would be no public prosecution. Was he not their son? But he must go now! His home would be no longer his home . . .

He recalled the dazed days that followed: the mechanical activities of his daily employment; his search, half-hearted, for a furnished room. He recalled, shuddering, the several times when, moved by the mechanism of long-established usage, he had nearly taken an Allston car for 'home', which was to be no longer his home . . .

He had not sent back the key. He could not tell why he had kept it. He had forgotten to hand it back to his father when he had left, and his father, doubtless unthinkingly, had not suggested its return. That was why he still had it, and here he stood, now, on the very threshold of that place which had been 'home' to him for so many

years, about to make the restitution that would do something to
remove the saddest of all the blots on his conscience – and he could
not get in!

The men, talking with hushed voices, had reached the first landing.
Young Phillips, caught by a sudden gust of abject terror, shrank
against the stubborn door, the door which, unaccountably, he could
not open. Then, his mind readjusting itself, he remembered that he
had no reason for concealment, for fear. Even though he might be
seen here, even though these people should be coming all the way up
the stairs, it could not matter. Let him be seen: what of it? He was
supposed to live here, of course. It was only a short time since he had
actually ceased to live here, and his father had said nothing. No public
charge had been made against him. How one's conscience could make
one a coward!

Under the invigorating stress of this reaction, he straightened
himself, stood up boldly. Realizing that it might appear odd for him
to be discovered standing here aimlessly on the landing, he started to
go downstairs. But by now the narrow staircase was completely
blocked by the ascending group. He stopped, halfway from that
flight. The men were carrying something, something heavy, and of
considerable bulk, it would seem. He could not see clearly in that
dim light just what it was. He stopped, half-way down, but none
of the men carrying the awkward bundle, covered with what looked
like an automobile curtain, looked up, nor appeared to notice him.
Neither did the straggling group of men, and a woman or two, who
were following them.

Fascinated, he gazed at what they were carrying. As they approached
and took the turn in the stairs, so that the electric light on the upper
landing shone more directly upon it, he looked closer. It was the body
of a man! It hung, limp and ungainly in their somewhat awkward grasp
as they shouldered up toward him.

Something about it seemed vaguely familiar, the details presenting
themselves to his fascinated gaze in rapid succession: the trouser-
ends, the shoes . . .

* * *

The men turned the last corner in the winding stairway and came
into full view. As they turned the corner, the leather curtain slipped
and the face of the dead man was for a moment exposed to view.
Roger Phillips looked at it, fascinated, horrified. Then one of the
men, halting for an instant, drew the corner of the curtain over the

face again, and he could no longer see it. The head rolled. The broken body had been grievously crushed.

Roger Phillips, utterly distraught, cowered, a limp heap, against the unyielding door of his father's apartment. He had looked for one horrific instant into his own distorted, dead face!

The men, breathing hard, reached the landing. One of them, gingerly shifting his portion of the burden upon the shoulder of another, stepped forward to ring the bell of the Phillips apartment. No one answered the ring, and the man rang again, impatiently, insistently. The bell trilled inside the empty apartment. The men stood, silently, shifting uneasily from one foot to another. Behind them, a thin mutter came from the waiting stragglers who had followed them, moved by an inordinate curiosity.

'Here's a key sticking in the door,' said the man who had rung the bell. 'Guess we'd be all right if we opened the door and took the young fellow in. There doesn't seem to be anyone home.'

A murmur of assent came from the other men.

He turned the key to the left, then to the right, and the door opened. They carried the broken body inside and carefully laid it out on the sofa in the living-room.

Sea-Tiger

Arthur Hewitt's first intimation of the terrific storm which struck the *Barbadian* off Hatteras, *en route* for the West Indies, was a crash which awakened him out of uneasy sleep in the narrow berth of his cabin. When he staggered up to the saloon-deck the next morning after an extremely uncomfortable, sleepless night, he looked out of the ports upon a sea which transcended anything he had ever seen. The *Barbadian*, heeling and hanging, wallowed in the trough of cross seas which wrenched her lofty bridge-deck.

A steward, who was having a rather difficult time keeping his feet, fetched him a sandwich and a cup of coffee. In a little while two other passengers appeared for breakfast: one a British salesman, and the other an American ship's officer, out of a professional berth and going to Antigua to help take off a sugar crop. The three men, warmed now by the coffee and the comfortable security of the lounge, snored and chattered intimately.

Nevertheless, a sinister foreboding seemed to hang over them. At last Matthews, the American, voiced it plainly:

'I hope she'll make St Thomas! Well – I've always heard that Captain Baird knows his business; a good sailorman, they say.'

'Do you think there'll be any let-up when we get into the Gulf Stream?' This was the Englishman, breaking a long, dreary silence.

'More likely a let-*down*, I'd say,' replied the pessimistic Matthews. 'She'll be worse, if anything, in my judgment.'

This gloomy prediction justified itself the following morning. The *Barbadian* had entered the Gulf Stream, and the malevolent fury of the sea increased with daylight. Hewitt came on deck, and, leaning against the jamb of a partly opened hatch on the protected leeside, looked out upon a world of heaving gray-green water with that feeling of awe which the sea in all its many moods invariably awakened in him. A gust of wind caught his unbuttoned coat, and out of a pocket and onto the wet, heaving deck slid the morocco-bound Testament which his mother had given him years before.

He stepped out through the hatchway, cautiously, making his way precariously across the deck to where it lay caught in the metal scupper. He arrived safely against the rail, which he gripped firmly with one hand, while he stooped to recover the book with the other. As he bent forward the tail-end of an enormous overtopping wave which had caught the vessel under her weather-quarter, caught him and raised his body like a feather over the rail's top.

But Hewitt was not cast into the sea. With a frantic, instinctive movement, he clung to the rail as his body struck violently against the ship's side.

With the *Barbadian*'s righting herself he found himself hanging on like grim death, his body dangling perilously over the angry waters, the Testament clutched firmly in his other hand.

He attempted to set his feet against one of the lower railings, to hook his legs about a stanchion. He almost succeeded, and would doubtless have been back upon the deck in safety had not the crest of the following wave dislodged his one-hand hold on the rail. The angry sea took him to itself, while the laboring ship, bounding into the teeth of the gale, bore on, all unconcerned over his sudden, unceremonious departure.

The incidents of Hewitt's life marched through his consciousness with an incredible rapidity. He remembered his mother poignantly – his mother dead these eight years – and a salt tear mingled with the vast saltiness of this cold, inhospitable ocean which had taken him to its disastrous embrace.

Down and down into the watery inferno he sank, weighted down with his winter boots and heavy overcoat. Strangely enough, he was not afraid, but he responded to the major mechanical impulses of a drowning man – the rigid holding of his breath, the desperate attempts to keep his head toward the surface so as to stay the sinking process, the well-nigh mechanical prayer to God.

His lungs were bursting, it seemed! Hot pain seared him, the red pain of unendurable pressures. He must resist as long as he had consciousness. He clamped his jaws desperately together.

It was calm down here, and dark! Here was no trace of the raging tempest on the surface, that tumultuous surface of lashed fury. The water seemed constantly heavier, more opaque, a vast, pervading indigo.

The pain and the burning pressure were gone now. He seemed no longer to sink. Nor did he rise, apparently. Probably he could not exhale his breath now if he wanted to. Well, he did not want to. It was no longer cold. Here was a world of calm, of perfect peace. Drowning is an easy death, after all . . .

He hoped the *Barbadian* would make St Thomas . . .

His last conscious sensation was of a gentle sinking through a vast, imponderable blueness, which seemed pervading the universe, a restful blueness to which one could yield readily. He relaxed, let himself go, with no desire to struggle. He sank and sank, it seemed . . .

He lay now upon a beach, his chin propped in his cupped hands, his elbows deep in the warm sand. It was from this warmth that he derived his first conscious sensation. A soft sea-wind, invigorating from its long contact with illimitable expanses of tropic seas, blew freshly. He felt very weary, and, it seemed, he had newly awakened out of a very protracted sleep. He turned his head at some slight sound and looked into the face of a girl who lay on the sand beside him.

He realized, as the march of events passed through his mind, that he must have gone through the gate of death. This, then, was that next world of which he had heard vaguely, all his life long. It was puzzling, somewhat. He was dead. He knew he must be dead. Do the dead lie on tropical beaches, under faint moonlight, and think, and feel this fresh wind from the sea? The dead, surely, do not dream. Perhaps they do dream. He had no knowledge, no experience, of course. He had read tales of after-death. Most of them, he remembered, revealed the surprise of the hero at the unexpectedness of his surroundings.

The girl touched him gently on the shoulder, and her hand was unbelievably cool and soothing. As he turned and looked at her in a kind of terror, the faint moonlight abruptly faded. Then the rim of the sun broke, red and sharp, like a blazing scimitar blade, across the horizon. The leaves of many trees stirred, welcoming the tropic day. Little monkeys swung and chattered overhead. A great flaming macaw sped, arrow-like, across the scope of his vision. The girl spoke to him: 'We must be gone to the sea.'

The girl moved delicately towards the place where, near at hand, the turquoise sea lapped softly against weed-strewn boulders and freshly gleaming white sand. As he, too, induced by some compelling impulse beyond the scope of his understanding, moved instinctively to seek the refuge of the sea, he saw his companion clearly for the first time. Stupefied, incredulous, he glanced down at his own body, and saw, glistening, iridescent in the new light of fresh dawn, a great flashing, gleaming tail like that of some fabled, stupendous denizen of enchanted deeps. Then, his wonderment losing itself in a great exultation, he followed his mermaid into the shining, welcoming waters . . .

*   *   *

On an early afternoon – for the sun was high in the heavens – he emerged from the sea into the shallows of that sandy beach where he had awakened to amphibian existence seemingly ages ago. Slowly, painfully, he dragged himself up on the warm sand. He was very weary, for he had finished an enormous swim, away from the scene of a fearful combat which he had waged with a now dimly remembered monster of the great deeps of the warm sea. His companion, who, during these long, dimly remembered eras, had been dear to him, was gone. She had succumbed in the direful struggle with the sea-beast. His heartache transcended the immediate painfulness and fatigue of his bruised and weary body.

He had had his vengeance, though. Beside her body lay that of the seabeast, crustaceous, horrible, slain by him after a titanic struggle, mangled in the imponderable ooze . . .

He rested at last, prone upon the yielding, sun-soaked sand. The insistent light of the glaring sun troubled him, and he moved impatiently. A vague murmur, too, was disturbingly apparent. He decided, wearily, to shift his position to the nearby shade of a palm grove. He turned over, slowly, painfully.

Then the light from the sun smote his eyes, attuned to the cool dimness of the sea-deeps, and as he moved towards the palms he raised a hand to his brow. That disquieting murmur took form abruptly, became intelligible. It seemed, somehow, to take on the familiarity of a remembered human voice. He lowered his hand, puzzled, disturbed, and found himself looking at an electric-light bulb. In its light he saw three men sitting on a leather sofa. He rose on his elbow, still painfully, for he was very weary after that dire combat, and peered at them. He now fixed his dazed stare on Matthews, who was in the middle of the row, and mumbled some incoherent words. The man seated at the end of the sofa rose hastily, and came towards him. He saw that it was Hegeman, the *Barbadian*'s doctor.

'Back awake, eh?' It was Hegeman's cheerful voice. The doctor placed a hand on Hewitt's pulse. 'You'll do,' he announced confidently.

Matthews was standing beside the doctor. Over Matthews's shoulder Hewitt could see, peering, the spectacled face of the salesman. Matthews was speaking.

'We were through the Gulf Stream a day ago, and the sun's out. It was a narrow squeak! Old Baird should have the Board of Trade medal for getting you. Thought you'd never come up!'

'A bit battered but right as rain, what!' The Englishman had added his word of cheer.

'You'll be on your pins in a day or two,' said the doctor. 'Keep still for the present.' Hewitt nodded. He did not want to talk. He had too much to get settled in his mind. Those experiences! Or what seemed to be experiences, the chimeras of the unconscious mind.

'One of the stewards saw you go,' added Hegeman. 'Two of your teeth are chipped, where you clamped your jaws to hold your breath. Plucky thing to do. It saved your life.

Hewitt held out a heavy hand. The doctor took it and placed it gently by his side. 'Go back to sleep,' he ordered, and the three filed out.

During the remainder of the voyage Hewitt slowly recovered from the severe shock of his long immersion in wintry seawater. He was chiefly occupied though, with the strange history of his experience, which continued to stand out quite sharply in his mind. He could not shake off the notion that it had been, somehow, a *real* experience. Why – he could remember the details of day after day of it. He seemed to have acquired some unique knowledge of the ways of the sea's great deeps: the barely luminous darkness of animal phosphorescence; the strange monsters; the incredible cold of that world of pressure and dead ooze; the effortless motion through the water; the strange grottoes; above all, the eery austere companionship of the mer-woman and the final dreadful battle. . . . His mind was filled to overflowing with intimate details of what seemed a long, definite, regulated, amphibian life, actually lived!

There remained, permanently, even after the process of time had done its work in rendering most of the details indistinct in his mind, the desire for the sea: the overwhelming urge to go into, under, the water; to swim for incalculable distances; to lie on dim, sandy depths, the light, blue and faint, from above, among the swarming, glowing, harmless parrot-fish. And, deeper than all, in this persistent urge of consciousness, was the half-buried, basic desire to rive and tear and rend – a curious, almost inexplicable, persistent set of wholly new instincts, which disturbed his mind when he allowed himself to dwell on them. He looked forward to the first swim in the Carribean, after landing at his port, St Croix, in the Virgin Islands.

Fully restored to his ordinary physical vigor, he joined a swimming party on the afternoon following his arrival in Frederiksted. There had been rumors of sharks, but his hosts hastened to reassure their guests. No! Sharks were virtually negligible, anyhow. Sharks were cowardly creatures, easily frightened away from any group of swimmers. If it were a barracuda, now – that would be quite another matter. Over in Porto Rico, so report had it, there had been a case of a barracuda attacking an American school-teacher. Terribly injured – permanently, it was said. Months in the hospital, poor fellow.

But, barracuda rarely troubled the bathing beaches. Occasionally, yes, one would take the bait of one of the Negro fishermen, far out in their little boats, and then the fisherman, if he were agile, would cut his line and row, gray-faced, inshore, perhaps not to venture out again for days. They were the sea-tigers, the barracudas.

Their attack was a fiendish thing. With its eighteen-inch jaw, and its rows of rip-saw teeth, it would charge, and charge again, tearing its helpless victim to ribbons, stripping flesh from bones with relentless avidity. There was no escape, it seemed, once those lightning rushes had begun. They came in such rapid succession that unless the victim were almost on shore there was no escape. Yes, a kind Providence save us from a barracuda!

The party, a gay one, entered the water under the declining afternoon sun. The beach here shelved steeply, four or five steps being quite enough to reach swimming depth. The water was so clear, over its white, sandy bottom, that a swimmer, floating face downward, could see bottom clearly, and count the little parrot-fish, like flashing sunbeams, as they sported about, apparently near enough to be gathered up by extending the hand; a curious, amusing delusion.

Hewitt swam easily, lazily, revelling with satisfaction in the stimulating clear water which in these latitudes is like a sustained caress to the body.

He had never felt so much at ease in the water before. It seemed, however, quite natural to him now. It fitted, precisely, into what had grown to be his expectations during the past few days on the ship. It was as though latent, untried powers deep within him had been stimulated and released by the strange, mental experience he had undergone during those few hours of his unconsciousness. He dived deeply, and all the processes involved – the holding of the breath, the adjustment of muscular actions and reactions, the motions of under-water swimming – were as natural and effortless as though he had been, he told himself musingly, really amphibious.

Unnoticed by him, the remainder of the swimming party, only about half of whom he had met, retired to the beach and spread themselves in little sociable groups along the sandy edge. A few lingered in the shallows.

He was floating on his back, the little waves of that calm sea lapping against his cheeks, when he heard faintly the terrified, cutting scream of a girl. He treaded water, and looked towards the beach, where he saw the various members of the large party rushing towards a young girl whom he had not especially noticed before. The girl was one of those who had remained in the shallows, and as he looked he saw many hands extended towards her, and drawing her upon the sand, and he saw, too, a pinkish froth of fresh blood about the place from which she had emerged.

Something seemed to snap inside his brain. That terrible, atavistic, inexplicable sense of combat, the desire to rend and tear suffused him. In the grip of this strange, primitive, savage urge, he turned abruptly and dived straight down to where a flickering gray shadow passed; to where an enormous barracuda slowed to turn for its light-ning rush at its second victim. Hewitt sped down like a plummet, exulting . . .

A moment later the attention of the group on the beach was distracted from the young girl whose foot had been cruelly gashed by the sea-tiger's teeth, to a seething, foaming, writhing thing that rose from the calm surface of the sea a hundred feet out from the beach, struggled furiously on the lashed surface for a few seconds, and then as abruptly disappeared in a tortured mass of foam. A sunburned young Navy doctor went on binding up the girl's foot, but the rest, wonder-stricken, silent, scanned the surface eagerly for another glimpse of this strange, titanic combat. 'What is it?' 'What can it be?' The questions ran from mouth to mouth.

The barracuda rose again, this time within twenty feet of the beach, and Hewitt lay locked along the steel-gray back, his hands closed in a vise-like grip about the terrible jaws, his tensed muscles corded with the fearful strain. Over and over, sidewise, backwards, forward, moved fish and man as one, locked together in dives and turns and dashes so swift as to baffle the gaping eyes of the amazed onlookers, standing now in a wondering, intrigued row upon the edge of the sand. And always, with great, powerful lunges of feet and sweeps of elbows and hands and knees, now above, now beneath, but ever unrelaxed in that deadly grip, on the frothing surface or in the quiet depths, Hewitt forced his demon antagonist towards the beach.

In the course of their fourth emergence, the two, rolling over and over upon the bottom sand of the shore shallows, shot out upon the beach, and Hewitt, finding his feet, with a great wrench, raised the sea-tiger in his hands and with a great sweeping motion which bent the iron-like head and its cruel jaws towards the rigid, mackerel-like tail, cracked the giant killer's backbone, and flung the barracuda down on the sand where it lay, crushed and broken, writhing out its life in convulsive leaps.

Hewitt took several deep, restoring breaths, and the killing-lust passed from him, the strange urge satisfied by his successful struggle. The members of the swimming party slowly gathered about him. There was, it appeared, nothing much to say. One of the men cautiously rolled over the crushed barracuda with a tentative foot. Hewitt raised his eyes and looked towards the young girl, who was now standing lightly on the bandaged foot, supported by the Navy doctor.

She looked back at Hewitt, and there was a great wonder in her sea-blue eyes. The fresh wind moved her coppery hair, now released from the rubber bathing-cap.

Oblivious of the chorus of admiration and bewilderment of the rest of the swimming party, Hewitt gazed at her, awed, overcome, feeling suddenly weak. For – wonder of wonders! – leaning on the arm of the solicitous young doctor, there stood before him the perfect embodiment of his sea-companion, that strange, alluring product of his recent subconscious experience, his extraordinary dream.

He drew several long breaths, to steady himself. Now the remarks of the swimmers began to break through his dazed consciousness, and he came to himself. He stepped towards the injured girl, fumbling in his rapidly clearing mind for some suitable expression of sympathy . . .

Abruptly the members of the swimming party fell silent, realizing that they stood here in the presence of some inexplicable drama; of something subtle and vague, but something unmistakably finished, appropriate.

'I hope you were not hurt very badly,' was all that Hewitt could manage.

The girl answered him not a word but looked steadily into his face, and Hewitt knew that here was the beginning of his real life.